49. Fáilbhe

50. Rónán

51. Rotheachtaigh

52. Feidhlimidh

53. Cart Imleach

54. Breisrigh

55. Seadna Ionnarraidh

56. Duach Fionn

57. Canna Dearg

58. Lughaidh Iardhonn

59. Eochaidh Uaircheas

60. Lughaidh Laimhdhearg

61. Cárt

62. Oibll

63. Eochaidh

64. Lughaidh Laighdhe

65. Reachtaidh Righdhearg

66. Colhchach Caomh

67. Mogh Corb

68. Fear Corb

69. Adhamair Foltchaoin

---

70. Niadh Seaghamain

71. Ionnadmhar

72. Lughaidh Luaidhne

73. Cairbre Lusc

74. Duach Dallta Deaghaidh

75. Eochaidh Fear Cáine

76. Mureadhach Muchna

77. Mo Feibhis

78. Loch Mór

79. Canna Monchaoin

80. Deirgthine

81. Dearg

82. Mogh Neid

83. Mogh Nuadhat

84. Oibll Olum

85. Eóghan Mór

86. Fiacha Muilleathan

87. Oibll Flann Beag

88. Lughaidh

89. Conall Córc

---

90. Nat Fraoch

91. Aonghus

92. Feidhlimidh

93. Crionhchann

94. Aodh Dubh

95. Fínghein

96. Seaghnusagh

97. Fiacha

98. Flann Rola

99. Dubhshionreacht

100. Murrough

101. Eochaidh

102. Maoleghra

103. Eochaidh Suldubhan

104. Lorcan

105. Buadhaigh

106. Aodh

107. Cathaill

108. Buadhaigh

109. MacCrath

110. Dónal Mór

O'Sullivan's
ODYSSEY

O'Sullivan's
ODYSSEY

RICK SPIER

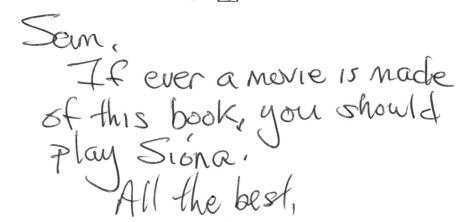

Sam,
  If ever a movie is made
of this book, you should
play Siona.
      All the best,

Moon Donkey Press

While some of the characters and events in this book
are based upon historical people and occurrences, it is important to stress
that the story is a work of fiction and that the portraits of the characters presented
are fictional and products solely of the author's imagination.

Published by MOON DONKEY PRESS, LLC, Clyde Hill, WA USA

First Edition.

Library of Congress Control Number: 2004105408

ISBN 0-9754398-0-4

Jacket and text by Anú Design, Collierstown, Tara, County Meath, Ireland
Printed and bound by Phoenix Color Corporation, Hagerstown, MD
Author photograph ©2004 by Michael Good Photography, Costa Mesa, CA
Rear cover photograph ©2004 by Rick Spier

Moon Donkey Press
3015 92nd Place NE
Clyde Hill, WA 98004

For my daughters, Anna and Molly,
and my wife, Patricia,
who helped me find my way home.

Acknowledgments and Bibliography

First, I want to thank my friend, the artist Tim Goulding (www.tim goulding.com), who was so instrumental in helping me start this project. It was a visit to Tim's house at Eskinanaun and attendant outing to Dunboy that provided the spark of inspiration, and then his aid in initial research that spurred development of the plot. For your art, Tim, for your music, for your heart and for the man you are, *go raibh míle maith agaibh.*

I also want to thank my editor, Marti Kanna (www.newleafediting.com), for her wisdom, insight, and professionalism, and for the loving care she bestowed upon my manuscript. Thanks, also, to Trina Burke (aathema@ wildmail.com) for her consummate skill as a proofreader.

Thank you Karen Carty and Terry Foley of Anú Design (www.anu-design.ie) for doing such a brilliant job with the cover art and text layout.

Thank you Dr. Christopher O'Mahony of Limerick for your invaluable research into the Irish origins of the Fitzgeralds of Lagganstown and Rural Home, and for your persistence in deciphering the garbled clues found within their family legends. Thank you Jennifer Daniel for your insight into the lives and history of the Fitzgeralds of Rural Home and their friends and neighbors. Thank you Keith Bohannon for your assistance in researching the Lochrane Guards and the Battle of Fredericksburg. Thank you Connie Murphy for your assistance with the history of Béara, and for enduring a long evening of questioning when you would rather have been watching soccer. Thanks also to The Honorable Desmond Fitzgerald, The Knight of Glin, for taking me seriously and pointing me in the right direction.

Last being the place of honor, I have reserved it for my wife, Patricia Rovzar, who looked at me one day, and said, "I think you should be a writer, because you'd be really good at it." Without her love, encouragement and support, I would never have written this or any other book.

I am also particularly indebted to the following books and authors:

From Bantry Bay to Leitrim: A Journey in Search of O'Sullivan Béare by Peter Somerville Large; *Beare: A Journey Through History* by Daniel M. O'Brien; *The Berehaven Copper Mines* by R. Alan Williams; *Cracker Culture: Celtic Ways in the Old South* by Dr. Grady McWhiney; *The Irish Roots of Margaret Mitchell's Gone With the Wind* by David O'Connell; *The Fenian Chief: A Biography of James Stephens* by Desmond Ryan; *The Secret Service of the Confederate States in Europe* by James Dunwoody Bulloch; *The Workhouses of Ireland: The Fate of Ireland's Poor* by John O'Connor; *Margaret Mitchell of Atlanta* by Finis Farr; *Southern Daughter: The Life of Margaret Mitchell* by Darden Asbury Pyron; *Beara in Irish History* by Liam O'Dwyer; the doctoral thesis of Edward Mathew Shoemaker, entitled *Strangers and Citizens: The Irish Immigrant Community of Savannah, 1837-1861*; and, from the *Journal of the Cork Historical and Archaeological Society* Volume 83, Number 237, an article entitled *Dunboy Castle, County Cork*, Excavated by Dr. E. M. Fahy, Report compiled by Margaret Gowen under the direction of M. J. O'Kelly, all of University College Cork.

A Note on Language and Usage

In the mid-1800's, the Irish language was still spoken by most of the people living in the west of Ireland. English, although the language of the towns and upper classes, was spoken by relatively few among the peasants, laborers and itinerants who represented the vast majority of the population.

In that regard, most of the dialogue through Chapter Twenty, though written in more or less standard American English, actually occurs in Irish. Where characters switch from Irish to English is either noted or written in obviously dialectic Irish-English. After Chapter Twenty, the Irish language dialogue is either denoted or written in Irish.

Since many of the names of characters and places appear in their Irish forms, for the reader's convenience, a Glossary of the main characters' names with English pronunciations is included below.

Dónal (DOE-nall): Man's name; anglicized as Donnell or Donald

Dónalín (DOE-nul-EEN): 'Little Dónal'

Dónal Cam (kawm): 'Dónal of the crooked legs'

Eibhlín (eye-LEEN): Woman's name; Irish for Helen

Eóghan (OWN): Man's name; usually anglicized as Owen

Liam (LEE-ahm): Man's name; Irish for William

Níall (NEAL): Man's name

Órla (OAR-lah): Woman's name

Riobárd (ri-BAWRD): Man's name; Irish for Robert

Riocard MagEochagáin (RICK-erd Mag-YO-huh-goin): Anglicized as
  Richard MacGeoghegan

Paidín (pah-JEEN): Man's name; 'Little Patrick' (Padge)

Seán (Shawn): Man's name; Irish for John

Sióna (SHOA-nah): Woman's name

Tadhg (TIEG): Man's name; sometimes anglicized as Timothy

contents

book one

• The Iliad •

part one

• Helen •

chapter 1

Dunboy Castle
Béara Peninsula, Ireland
17 June, 1602

As it had when he was a boy, the night sky seemed as big as the mind of God and just as fathomless to the lonely man in the tiny fortress, a blanket of starlit peace in which to wrap himself and shut out the base reality of earthly life. He remembered those nights spent by his father's fire and how safe he'd felt huddled in his arms, as their bard pointed out the stars and told their stories. *And that one is Orion, the great huntsman of the sky,* he could hear the man saying, even as his eyes fell upon it now. His father was a great huntsman, too, a big man with a big sword who'd kept them safe and put food on their table. And so Orion had always been his favorite, because it reminded him of his father and the simpler time in life when a warm fire and a full belly and the comfort of kith and kin were all he needed.

"Why did I ever want for more?" he asked the stars.

But Heaven gave him no answer.

He sighed and closed his aching eyes. He'd not had a decent sleep in days and was weary as he'd seldom been before, weary in body and spirit, world-weary and sad. Yet it would be over soon enough, he knew, for all things passed in their time, even life itself, and then he could sleep for all eternity. So why be in a hurry?

It was a warrior's wisdom, of course, gained from a lifetime of living by the sword, a destiny preordained for the son of the chieftain of a great warrior clan. It showed in the steel of his eyes and the set of his jaw, in the scars that marked his body and the hardness of heart that let him kill and maim without remorse. In one way or another, everything good in his life had been won by the sword, and by the sword he'd kept them, too.

Yet Riocard MagEochagáin was tired of war just then, or rather tired of *losing* the war, especially since victory had slipped through their grasp even as they'd closed their hands upon it. He'd seen it happen, too, at Kinsale on that bitter Christmas Eve when the tide turned. They had the English trapped like rats in a cage, pinned between themselves and their Spanish allies, and had only to wait for disease and desertion to decimate their ranks before mopping up the remnant. But Red Hugh wanted to attack and end it all in one fell swoop. "Let's drive them into the sea and have done with it!" he'd said, his blue eyes blazing. But then Red Hugh O'Donnell hated the English with a particular passion for all those years they'd kept him a prisoner in Dublin Castle. O'Neill knew better, of course, but in the heel of the hunt, he'd yielded to the impulse and emotion of his young kinsman, and that had been that.

MagEochagáin pictured them as they'd been on that evening before the debacle, the chieftains and captains gathered in council around the fire, O'Neill facing them while his two generals, Red Hugh and Dónal Cam O'Sullivan, flanked him right and left. As the night darkened, O'Neill's shadow had loomed large over the tent behind him, just as it had over all of Ireland for the last decade. Yet as O'Neill stood among them, isolated by the loneliness of command, MagEochagáin had seen the doubt in his eyes, and shivered with foreboding. For Hugh O'Neill was their last best hope, the linchpin between the old ways and the new, the one man among them capable of throwing off the English yoke and molding them into an independent and unified nation. In his hands he held their very destiny as a people, and if he wavered the consequences would be catastrophic.

Long into the evening they'd debated, till finally it had come down to Red Hugh and Dónal Cam, the former urging attack and the latter patience, while O'Neill stood by, listening quietly as lesser men decided his fate. For there was no patience to be had from a gaggle of Gaelic chieftains, any more than from a famished wolf among fatted calves. They were all hungry for the fight and a share of the glory, the better to trumpet their own petty triumphs over a jug of whiskey and a shank of beef. They'd no understanding of what would happen to them if they lost, had never even given it a thought. And in the end, O'Neill let himself be swayed by popular sentiment, finding the burden of destiny too heavy to bear alone.

Of course they'd been routed from the field the following morning and hadn't stopped running till reaching Inishannon, fully eight miles away. And though O'Neill tried to rally them there, seeing that they'd lost but few men and were still a sizable army, it was too late, for having once yielded to lesser men, he'd never convince them to follow him again. Sure, Red Hugh had sailed for Spain vowing to return with an army, but no one paid him any heed. They were done with him and his blather and quit the field, leaving O'Neill to slog his way back to Ulster alone.

Only Dónal Cam had kept his head about him, managing to withdraw his men in orderly fashion and keep them together, and being convinced that the Spanish would indeed return with Red Hugh, he'd decided to fight on, using his wild fastness of Béara as a base and refuge. And MagEochagáin had decided to join him, too, being impressed with the way he'd handled himself, both in the council and the field, and having nothing to lose anyway, since his own greedy uncles had snatched all his possessions. In the months that followed, he'd even come to like Dónal Cam and to trust him as a friend, though his heart warned against it. For despite his obvious talents, Dónal Cam was also something of a scoundrel, being self-centered and devious, not to mention a legendary profligate. Indeed, he liked to boast that he'd sired a hundred children by as many different women, while dangling a dozen men from his hanging tree for refusing to yield up their wives or daughters. Yet for all that, he inspired men to follow him, and so MagEochagáin ignored the warning signs.

For a while they'd had some success, raiding into Bantry and the lands beyond, till eventually the Crown wearied of their antics and sent an army to crush them. But before battle could be joined, news came that the Spanish had landed at Ardea on the north side of Béara, and Dónal Cam went to meet them, promising to return as quickly as possible. "I want you to hold Dunboy for me while I'm gone, Riocard," he'd said, laying a friendly hand on his shoulder and looking him hard in the eyes. "It's my home, the seat of my royal and ancient House, and you are the only man I can trust to keep it safe." Then he'd mounted his horse and ridden away, taking with him all his wealth and cattle and relations. And still MagEochagáin had trusted him, staying with his charge as the days turned into a fortnight and Dunboy became hopelessly surrounded, never thinking to pull the garrison and make a run for it, at least not until it was too late. And now here he was, out on the far end of the world, trapped between the English and the deep blue sea.

"God in Heaven," he muttered, "how could I have been so naïve?"

But God was as reticent as the stars.

He sighed and shook his head. How he wished he could just go to sleep and forget about things for a while. But duty wouldn't let him. He was in command and his seven score men were depending on him to keep them alive, even though he knew there was nothing he could do about it. For there were four *thousand* men outside the castle now, and sooner or later they'd breach the wall and come pouring in like the tide, washing the defenders away so completely that no one would remember they'd even been there. Only Dónal Cam could save them from it. But would he come in time, MagEochagáin wondered? Indeed, would he come at all?

Thinking to check for him one more time, he climbed to the parapet, but found his way blocked at the top by a young man, slumped against the wall and sleeping away his watch. It was young Dónal Máire, he saw, one of Dónal Cam's bastard sons, called by his mother's name also to differentiate him from the many others his father had named for himself. As a soldier long inured to military regimen, MagEochagáin's first impulse was to slap the boy so hard that he'd never fall asleep on watch again. But even in the motion, he stopped himself, realizing that his being here at all was punishment enough, his father having forgotten him in his haste to leave. Yet perhaps his bad luck might turn to the good, after all, as Dónal Cam would surely come back for him. Surely he would.

But then MagEochagáin grunted at himself in black humor. 'They say hope springs eternal for the desperate and the damned,' he thought, 'and surely greater truth was never spoken.'

Raising his eyes to the horizon, he turned from east to west and back again, looking hopefully for any sign of relief. But he found nothing but darkness, and after a moment his eyes strayed back to the enemy camp, falling upon the ring of bonfires within which the cannoneers were assembling their pieces. What a brilliant target they'd make, he thought, if only his small guns had the range for it. Yet even more enticing was the tent in the shadows beyond, where their commander was closeted with his generals, probably putting the finishing touches on their plans. He could even picture them at it, knowing them all personally as he did: Sir George Carew, the diminutive, yet ambitious Lord President of Munster; Donogh O'Brien, Earl of Thomond and a pompous ass of the first order; and Eóghan Óg O'Sullivan, Dónal Cam's own greedy cousin, who stood to succeed to his estate and titles. And though they represented the English Crown, they were all just as Irish as he, as indeed were most of their men. It was even so at Kinsale, where Carew and Thomond were also present, and where Irishmen under the Earl of Clanricard turned the tide against O'Neill. Divide and conquer, that was the English game, and they'd played it skillfully, too, setting the clans against each other and letting them hack away till nothing was left. But then, it was a self-fulfilling prophesy in Ireland, where internecine warfare had always been the order of the day, even before the English came.

And now the game was up, it seemed, unless Dónal Cam returned, and soon. For Death was at the door, knocking impatiently, and MagEochagáin knew he couldn't put It off much longer. And God, how he hated this feeling of being trapped, with nothing to do but wait for

Death to come and take him. It made him fear It, and the more he waited, the more he feared It, and the more he feared It, the more impotent he felt to do anything to save himself. It was a new feeling to him, this fear, for always before Death had seemed so far away. Yet now It was his constant companion, standing ever at his elbow, Its cold breath on the back of his neck as It waited impatiently to take him.

What would it be like, he wondered, to die and cross to the Otherworld? Would he find eternal peace and an end of suffering, or damnation and eternal suffering? Indeed, would he find anything at all? Or was the end really just the end, and the other side nothing but a great emptiness devoid even of emptiness, an infinity of *nothing*? He tried to imagine it then, *nothing*, and finding it beyond him, suddenly wondered if that was why men clung so tenaciously to their gods and religions, and even to life itself, because the prospect of *nothing* was simply too horrifying to face. And even worse, now that it was too late for him to do anything about it, did it mean that life itself was truly meaningless beyond the simple pleasure of living?

'What a fool I've been!' he thought bitterly. 'What a tragedy that youth is wasted on the young and wisdom on the old, and the beauty of life on a human race too self-absorbed to appreciate it! Oh, God, if you'll just give me another chance, I swear I'll be a better man! If you'll just let me go back and change it . . .'

But even as he pleaded with his God, his eyes strayed to the cross at the near edge of the camp and, finding the girl still hanging there, he shivered at the thought of what they'd done to her. It was on the afternoon of two days previous that an uproar brought him to the wall, arriving just in time to see Eóghan Óg ride into camp at the head of a column of men and a herd of cattle. Carew and Thomond had come out to greet him, walking beside him as he approached the fortress, while men pulled three covered carts closely behind. They'd stopped just out of cannon shot and, at a signal from Carew, dumped the contents of two carts onto the ground.

For a moment, there was silence on the wall as men craned their necks to see what it was. But then Eóghan Óg pulled something from a bag and stuck it on a stake, which he then thrust upright into the ground. "Oh, good Christ, it's Fionnín O'Driscoll!" someone exclaimed, and then MagEochagáin understood.

At Dursey Island off the western tip of Béara, Dónal Cam had established a refuge for noncombatants, sending many women and children there, along with a portion of his cattle. And thinking the island's treacherous currents and difficult landings would keep them safe, he'd sent only a small garrison under O'Driscoll to guard them. Yet Eóghan Óg was born and raised at Dunboy and, knowing Béara at least as well as Dónal Cam himself, had obviously put his knowledge to nefarious use, taking the island and slaughtering everyone he could find. So it was their heads that lay on the ground, brought back to show the men of Dunboy what lay in store for them. Yet MagEochagáin was unmoved, for though it was a sad thing and horrible, he'd seen it many times before. Indeed, slaughter was a fact of life in Ireland and had been for as long as anyone could remember, and it was even a practical concern for Eóghan Óg if he meant to consolidate his power after getting rid of his rival. Of more pressing concern from a military perspective was the loss of the cattle, since it would weaken Dónal Cam's ability to sustain the fight. But having other things to deal with just then, MagEochagáin shrugged indifferently, and made to turn away.

But then Carew called out to him and, with a sudden sense of foreboding, he'd turned to watch as the third cart was rolled forward and a young girl dumped from it to the ground. She was alive and unhurt, though bound hand and foot and, though he couldn't see her face, from her luxuriant red hair he had an idea of who she was.

And his suspicion was confirmed by Dónal Máire. "That's Eibhlín!" he wailed, recognizing her immediately. "Ah, Jesus, they've got Eibhlín!"

Indeed, she was his sister, the only one of Dónal Cam's bastard daughters of whom he'd ever taken any notice, and for whom it was even rumored he had a less than fatherly eye. But whatever the truth of it, he'd gone to the trouble of sending her to Dursey, thinking she'd be safe there no matter the outcome of the war. Yet now that she was a prisoner, what would Carew do with her? Would he hold her hostage, hoping to use her as a negotiating tool? But MagEochagáin's speculation came to an abrupt end when they ripped off her clothes and bent her over the end of the cart, holding her there while Eóghan Óg had his way with her, her pleas for mercy drowned out by the coarse cheering of his men.

Hearing Dónal Máire scream with rage, MagEochagáin grabbed him just before he leapt from the wall. "Let me go, let me go!" the boy shouted, struggling to free himself. "I've got to help her!"

"No, boy!" MagEochagáin said, turning him away. "There's nothing you can do for her, and if you go out there, they'll just kill you, too. Indeed, that's just what they want, for us to come out in the open so they can cut us to pieces."

"Then let them kill me and have done with it! We're all going to die anyway, and it's better to do it out there like a man!"

"No, Dónal, it isn't certain yet that we're going to die, and I'll not let you throw your life away in anger. Better to live and fight another day, and have your chance at vengeance later. So stay alive as long as you can, boy, for every moment you do brings you that much closer to cutting off that bastard's balls and shoving them down his throat!"

The boy sobbed then and went limp. "I'm sorry, Eibhlín. I'm sorry."

"It's not your fault, Dónal. There's nothing you can do but die with her, and we need you alive." Then MagEochagáin passed him to one of his men. "Take him to the cellar and keep him there till it's over."

Hearing another cheer then, he turned to find Eóghan Óg facing the throng, shaking his hands over his head like a champion at a tournament. But even as he exulted, the host parted and went silent, as three men came forward carrying a large wooden cross. The girl begged for mercy as they dragged her to it, and MagEochagáin wanted to stop his ears against her shrieks as they drove home the nails. But when they raised the cross and planted it in the ground, she went suddenly silent and still, her head drooping on her chest as though she were sleeping. Those gathered round her were silent, too, wondering if she'd died and cheated them of their sport.

MagEochagáin sought out Carew then and, finding his eyes upon him, understood what it was really about. It wasn't for herself that the girl was being crucified, or even that she was Dónal Cam's daughter. Rather it was for what she symbolized, the future of Ireland and, here in a microcosm, Carew was showing what that future held.

But then the silence was broken by a clear and fearless voice speaking in Irish: *"Hail Mary, full of grace, The Lord is with Thee. Blessed art Thou amongst women, and blessed is the fruit of Thy womb, Jesus. Holy Mary, Mother of God, pray for us sinners, now and at the hour of our death. Amen."* Then the girl died indeed and left earthly suffering to the living.

The silence that followed was complete, with even the wind calming as though in mourning. But as he gazed upon her, MagEochagáin took heart from her courage, and his spirit rose within him. For though Carew might kill them and erase their very names from memory, as long as one Irishman remained alive, he would never kill their spirit.

Drawing his father's great sword, he leapt to the top of the wall and swung it in an arc over his head while shrieking at the top of his lungs. Behind him, his men took up the cry, hurling taunts and insults at the besieging army, calling them slaves and traitors to their own people. And seeing the effect it had on Carew's men, MagEochagáin smiled at him viciously, knowing that sooner or later the Irish would be avenged.

And now as he gazed upon the cross, his anger rose again, not at his enemy this time, but at the friend who'd left him to this miserable fate. Leaning down, he grabbed the boy and shook him awake.

"Where is your father?" he demanded, though the boy was too startled to answer. "Where is he? Where is Dónal Cam?"

But even as MagEochagáin spoke, his words were drowned under the high-pitched squeal of incoming shot, followed closely by the crunch of timber and shrieks of fright and pain. "You wanted to die fighting!" he shouted at the boy, pushing him down behind the wall as more shot hurtled their way. "Well here's your chance, and mine, too!"

He knew Dónal Cam wouldn't come now, that he'd left him here to die in this godforsaken place, so far from his green and fertile home.

But it no longer mattered. He was himself again, all fear and weariness vanquished by his lust for battle. And turning to his enemy, he drew his father's sword and shook it at them defiantly, screaming the ancient battlecry of his clan, "*MagEochagáin abú!*" (MagEochagáin to victory!)

Then he leapt from the wall and disappeared into the Darkness of the new day dawning over Ireland.

PART TWO

• Summer of The '48 •

chapter 2

Béara Peninsula, Ireland
17 June, 1848

THOUGH THE DIM LIGHT OF DAWN was just beginning to brighten the windows of the little thatched cottage, following the custom of generations, the inhabitants were already up and busy with their morning routine. For they were people of The Land and lived close to Her, matching their rhythms to Hers and following Her dictates, becoming in time as much a part of Her as the green grass and gray stones, blending as seamlessly as a river with the sea. They lived *on* The Land and *in* The Land and *from* The Land. They lived better when She was good to them and worse when She was not, though never did they blame Her for the troubles visited upon them. For She was everything to them, their beginning and their end, their goddess and their idol, their life and death and mortal salvation. Yet of this Land that so defined them they didn't own even a single acre, though they'd called Her their own for time out of mind. They were merely the tenants of fate, clinging desperately to a fickle lifeline that even the notion of a whim could sever. For this sacred and woebegone Land was Ireland, and these poor people who worshipped Her were the Irish, the misbegotten, redheaded stepchildren of the British Empire, unloved by Mother England and, in their silent passing, unlamented.

And the troubles that were now in this Irish Land weighed heavily upon the tiny cottage, squatting on it like a vulture waiting to pick it clean. Indeed, it might've been carrion already from the look of it, with its whitewash peeling, its door and shutters askew on rusted hinges, its rotting thatch sporting a growth of parasitic green. Nor was it any better inside, where the mood reflected that of the man of the house, which on this morning was blacker than his coal-black hair. In a dark corner he skulked, his eyes gleaming like those of a jungle predator, his two sons, a young man and a small boy, carefully avoiding him, as they knew too well the consequence of freeing his anger.

But then the teakettle whistled shrilly and, springing from the stool to hover over the little boy, the man thundered at him in his native Irish, "Have a hand to that thing, you little thick!"

Flinching reflexively, the boy cowered down as if expecting a blow, too frightened even to do his father's bidding. And indeed, the man raised his hand to strike, though before he could, his elder son stepped between them. Turning his back purposefully on his father, he laid his hand on the boy's head and smiled gently.

"Go on, Dónal," he said. "See to it."

"All right, Eóghan," Dónal replied, choking back his tears, knowing they would only make his father angrier.

As he moved to the hearth, Eóghan turned back to their father. "You shouldn't frighten him like that, Da," he said, looking him hard in the eyes. "He's just a young boy, and anyway, it's me you're angry with!"

"That's right, Eóghan." The man's eyes narrowed dangerously as he stood toe-to-toe with his son. "It's you that I'm angry with, though *furious* would be a better word for it."

From the hearth, Dónal looked up at them, towering above him like trees as they squared off in a titanic contest of wills, the one so much like the other that they could've been twins, but for their different ages. For they had the same piercing blue eyes and thick black hair, the same savage Celtic mustaches and anvil-hard jaws anchoring their rugged faces, the same commanding height and solid build. Handsome they were in the Irish fashion, men of stature and presence, lordly men in whom the heroic blood of old ran true.

And in his elder son and namesake, big Eóghan O'Sullivan indeed saw himself as he'd been at nineteen, before sorrow furrowed his brow and the hard life hardened his heart. For the only mark of his late mother on young Eóghan was the narrow streak of white at the peak of his forehead, a feature that he shared with little Dónal, who otherwise looked nothing at all like his father and brother. His looks were all from his mother, having her same flaming red hair and eyes the color of the new green of Spring, the delicate features of her face translating beautifully into little boy form. And he was a beautiful child, just as she'd been a beautiful woman, with a sensitive manner and introspective nature, which, of course, pleased his father not at all.

But Dónal may as well not have been there for all the notice his father gave him now, his mind being given over to Eóghan, the son in whom he saw himself, the son onto whom he'd projected all his own youthful hopes and ambitions, and for whom he'd suffered and sacrificed to bring them to fruition. For while he'd accepted his own lot in life, that his son would be no better off after him he could not accept. So he'd dedicated all his considerable will and energy toward getting him educated in the best possible fashion, working in the fathomless pits of the Berehaven Copper Mines from dawn to dusk six days a week, walking to Allihies and back in darkness both ways. Then after the artificial darkness of the mines, he would work well into the night, tending the family plot or saving turf on the cold slopes of Guala, so that his mine wages could all go to Eóghan's education. Even on Sundays or the rare holiday he would labor, usually on the Puxley estate at Dunboy, loading copper ore onto ships to earn a few extra pence. When other men gathered in pubs or at the shebeen to take their leisure with a jar and a smoke, he would forswear, again to save his money for his son's education. And through all of it, he'd remained hale and hardy, already outliving the average miner by ten years, as much by the sheer force of his will as anything else. For his son's education was everything to him, his life's work and ambition, and it had taken on a life and substance of its own, coming to control him as surely as opium does an addict.

And like an addict, he'd paid dearly for it, becoming known as a humorless man with neither charity in his heart nor hospitality in his hand, both mortal sins in the communal ethos of rural Ireland. Indeed, the joke went round that the difference between Eóghan O'Sullivan and a nanny goat was that one could get a drink out of the goat. It even was said that he thought himself better than his fellows, that he wanted to be like the English and lord it over his Irish brethren. And from this had come the name they called him behind his back, *Eóghan an Sasanach,* "Eóghan the Englishman." But though their mockery scourged his soul, it only reinforced his myopia. At the mines, so ostracized did he become that no other Irishmen would work with him, though because of his intelligence, productive energy and consummate skill, he'd been retained by the Cornish mine captains and paid at a higher wage scale, thus sealing his reputation as *an Sasanach* while paradoxically furthering his ability to realize his dream.

For his part, young Eóghan proved a natural scholar, excelling at all levels and pursuing his studies with single-mindedness and determination, so much so that his father assumed that he shared his dream, never bothering to ask what Eóghan wanted for himself in life, never thinking his ambitions could be any different from his own. And when young Eóghan was accepted at Trinity College in Dublin, he'd worked even harder so his son could concentrate on his studies without having to support himself, persevering even in the depths of the hunger that gripped the land, denying not only himself but his wife and younger son so Eóghan could rise up, and so, he thought, raise them all.

But then, just the previous evening, the man had gotten the shock of his life, learning that young Eóghan was about to throw it all back in his face, just to follow a cabal of middle-class intellectuals into an ill-considered scheme of rebellion that had about as much chance of succeeding as a stone had of floating. Late into the night he'd argued with the boy, trying to explain in every way he could think of that the time wasn't right, that the leaders didn't know what they were doing, and that he shouldn't risk his life, liberty and seat at Trinity in a fight that couldn't be won, no matter how noble the cause. Still it hadn't sunk in, and finally he'd given it up, hoping his son would see it differently in the light of morning. But then he'd awakened to the sight of him packing his bag and known that he meant to go on with it regardless.

And gazing now upon his elder son, his mirror image and object of all his self-absorbed ardor and emotion, big Eóghan prayed to God to give him the words to show him the light. But it was young Eóghan who broke the silence, speaking as though reading his father's thoughts.

"I know you don't approve of what I'm doing, Da," he said, "but we had it all out last night. I'm going to be part of the rising, and nothing you do or say will change my mind."

"All right, Eóghan, all right," the father sighed. "If it's fighting for Ireland's freedom that you're after, then you'd best get on with it. But don't expect to have my blessing on you, because I'll not give it. And I say again that you're throwing your future away needlessly, for there's not a snowflake's chance in Hell that an armed rebellion can succeed now, not with the country in the state it's in, not with the people half-starved and running down to the sea like lemmings to get away from the Hunger. If there was a chance, however remote, fuck me if I wouldn't go with you! But there's no fight in them now, demoralized as they are, and there's no way they'll follow a bunch of Ascendancy aristocrats, I don't care how elegant their arguments or glorious their names. And even if they did, what are you going to arm them with? We've no guns or powder, and no means of producing any, nor even money to buy them. But even more important, Eóghan, what are you going to *feed* them with? An army marches on its belly, and there's no food to be spared in this poor famished land of ours, at least none that we can get our hands on easily. So if by some miracle there *is* a grand rising of the Gael, they'll be a host of wraiths armed with pikes and pitchforks – those that are lucky, that is! And look what they'll be up against – a modern army led by professional soldiers and armed with the finest guns and equipment that all the stolen wealth of the British

Empire can buy. If you can't see that it's a massacre waiting to happen, then you're as blind and thick as a stone."

But even as he spoke, he could see he was wasting his breath, that, if anything, his son was digging his heels in deeper, the petulance of youth twisting his words into a challenge to his manhood.

"Oh, for Christ's suffering sake, Eóghan," he said, "don't look at me like that. All I want is what's best for you!"

"This is what's best for me, Da," Eóghan replied, "and for you and Dónal, and all of us! And you're wrong about the people, Da, dead wrong. They *will* rise and they *will* fight, and we *will* win! For while it's true that the English are mighty and we are low, they'll tire of knocking us down long before we tire of getting up for more, and in the heel of the hunt, we'll be the ones left standing. It's in our blood, Da. It's part of who we are. We can't abide slavery, and we'll fight to the ends of our strength and to the end of time to free ourselves! And besides, we're not rushing into this in quite the mad haste that you seem to think. There'll be no rising till after the harvest. We'll just be planning and organizing till then."

At that, his father threw up his hands in disgust. "Eóghan, have you no common sense? Or have you learned nothing from our history? Do you not understand the siege mentality the English have developed from seven hundred years of living here as strangers? Why, they're as paranoid of an Irish rising as St. Patrick was of snakes, and believe me, they're not going to just sit on their hands while you traipse merrily about the country organizing a rebellion against them. And if you need proof of it, just look at what they did to that John Mitchel fellow you so dearly love to go on about, that sparrow-fart of a writer. Why, they made up a new law and packed a jury to get rid of him, and that was just for talking about rebellion in a goddamned newspaper! So when they get wind of what you and your cronies are up to, they're going to be mighty put out with you, because you're going to scare them, and they don't like being scared! Indeed, they'll be on you like flies on shit, and then you'll have to fight whether you're ready or not. And believe me, Eóghan, you won't be ready!

"And if that's not enough to give you pause, then think about what will happen to you afterward, when it's all over and you find yourself in some hellhole of a prison, or transported to Australia. Of what possible good can you be to anyone then? And when your sentence is up, what kind of life do you think you'll have? I can tell you it won't be a very good one – at least, not if you intend to live in Ireland! So think of what you're risking here, Eóghan! For Christ's sake, boy, you've got to think this through!"

But his son just shook his head. "I'm not a boy anymore, Da! I'm a man now. I'm a man and I have thought it through, and I know I'm doing the right thing. Great things will come of this and I intend to be part of it. Indeed, I will be part of it! And besides, Da, it's the *honorable* thing to do, whether we can win or not!"

At that, his father felt an overpowering urge to strike him, even clenching his fist to do so. But he didn't raise his hand. Indeed, he couldn't, had never been able to, and, looking into his son's eyes, he knew it wouldn't do any good anyway. His mind was made up, and there was nothing to be done except hope for the best. But how had it come to this, he wondered? How could the boy be so out of touch with reality? What had they done to him in that ivory tower he'd worked so hard to send him to? Or was it his own fault and not the boy's at all? Had he sheltered and pampered him so much that he couldn't see the hard life all around him? Whatever the cause, he was an innocent playing a dangerous game, and he'd be lucky to come out of it unscathed.

"Honor isn't much good to a dead man, Eóghan," he said, "and being a man doesn't mean fighting just for the sake of the fight, or for silly notions like pride and glory, or even because the cause is just. Being a man means weighing your opportunities and having the patience to wait until the time is right, because the greater part of courage is often found in discretion, and only if the alternative is death do you join a fight you can't win. Now I agree that the condition of our people is far from just, and I applaud you for wanting to better it, but the alternative to you, Eóghan, is not death, and the time for armed rebellion is not now, because, like it or not, you *cannot* win! So I beg of you, Eóghan, as your father, I beg of you one last time, don't do this! *Please, don't!*"

'*Please!*' he repeated in his mind. '*Oh, please, God, please!*' But he knew it was in vain, could see there was no bend in his son, any more than there'd ever been in himself. He sighed and shook his head, defeated.

"All right, Eóghan, all right. If you mean to do this thing, then at least do it well. You have not my blessing, but you will have my prayers."

Then he drew himself up to his full height and fixed his son with an icy stare. "I am Eóghan O'Sullivan Béara," he declaimed regally, "Lord of Béara and Bantry, and Count of Berehaven by right of my descent from Dónal Cam. You are my son, Eóghan. See that you remember it!"

Then he turned his back on his dream and stormed out the door, leaving it open behind him.

As he stared into the void left by his father, Eóghan heard a noise and looked down to find little Dónal still huddled on the hearth, forgotten by the men in the heat of their private war.

"Don't go, Eóghan, please don't go," Dónal pleaded tearfully. "Da is right. We need you here. *I* need you here."

Seeing the fear in his little brother's eyes, Eóghan was moved to pity, though it didn't deter him from his purpose. "There now, don't you start on me, too!" he said, smiling.

And in spite of everything, Dónal couldn't help but smile back. For just as he was to their father, Eóghan was everything to him, the shining light in his life, his protector, his playmate, his teacher, the one who comforted him in his frequent illnesses, the one who brought joy into his little world, the one who'd given him an affectionate nickname, calling him *Dónalín*, "little Dónal," the one who made him laugh, and first, last and most of all, the one who made him feel loved.

For while he knew that his mother had loved him, too, she'd been more distant about it, being already worn down by the time he was born, his difficult delivery taking much of what little vitality she had left. As for his father, he was always away at work, and even when he wasn't, it seemed that he was always cross with him, that Dónal could do no right in his eyes. And after his mother died and Eóghan went away to Trinity, there'd been no barrier between them, nothing to blunt the hurt of his father's cuffs and scornful words. So he'd turned inward upon himself, becoming even more silent and introspective than his natural bent, never daring to interact with his father for fear of incurring his wrath, spending most of his time alone. But loneliness was easier to bear than the hurt, and he even found a certain solace in his solitude. At least there was no one to torment him but himself.

Still, he lived for the times when Eóghan came home to visit, running to greet him and squealing with delight as his brother scooped him up and tossed him into the air. For a while then, the sun would shine and drive away the black cloud that was his father, and his heart would overflow with laughter and joy. Then when the time came for Eóghan to leave again, he'd walk him out to the boreen that led away from their house, where Eóghan would pick him up and spin him around, giving him one last bear hug before turning his face to the wider world beyond. Dónal would stand by the ancient wall that surrounded their house and watch him go, waiting till Eóghan paused at the bend and waved, always smiling one last time before disappearing around it. Dónal would wave back, of course, and smile, just as he had through the entire ritual of parting, not wanting Eóghan to see the pain he felt, or to burden him with it.

But this time was different, for it seemed that Eóghan was going on a journey from which he might not return, that he might even die and leave him forever alone. And Dónal didn't understand death, though he'd seen plenty of it in his seven brief years, his earliest memory coming from the age of four, at the wake of his mother's uncle, an old man from Eyeries named Séamus Lynch. If he closed his eyes, he could still hear the keeners wailing their eerie lament, *Ochón! Ochón!*, still see the large wooden box resting on the table and feel the dread as his mother led him toward it, the terror as she'd whisked him suddenly from the floor and held him over it. Yet the terror had turned to wonder when he'd seen that it was just old Uncle Séamus lying there, his eyes closed and face peaceful and serene, a rosary in his folded hands and a small cross upon his chest, seemingly no duller in death than he'd been in life.

"Why is he sleeping in the box?" Dónal had blurted in surprise and innocence. But his surprise turned to mortification when the place went deathly still, as even the keeners gave it up for shock, knowing in that terrible silence that every eye in the place was turned critically upon him. Then his father broke it, cuffing him sharply on the back of the head and growling, "He's not sleeping, you little thick, he's *dead!*" Of course, the laughter that followed was more terrible than the silence, as Dónal stood there in its midst, choking back his tears and wishing for the earth to open mercifully beneath him and swallow him up.

And though Dónal had never heard the word "humiliation" before, that experience would define it for him ever after. *Ochón! Ochón!* It haunted him still.

But so it was that his father's disapproval had put an end to his inquiry into death, and what he knew of it thereafter came from observation and surmise. And with the coming of *An Gorta Mór*, the Great Hunger, he'd had plenty of opportunities for it, too. Indeed, his father's relative prosperity had brought the hungry scratching at their door, starving, filthy wraiths begging in hideous voices for a morsel of food, a scrap, anything to stave off hunger for another day, another hour, another minute. Dónal would cower behind his mother and stay there long after his father drove them away, for fear of their horrible eyes and gaunt, tormented faces, surely, though even more so of the man's anger with her afterward.

"Refuse none from your door," she'd sigh sadly, "for one may be the Christ. They're so hungry, Eóghan."

"And just what would you have me do about it, woman?" he'd roar, and Dónal would feel her tremble. "If we feed one there'll be no end to them, and soon we'll be just as hungry as they are. Is that what you want for us? Is that what you want for your children, to see them wither away before your very eyes?"

But she never answered; indeed, there was no answer to give.

And hunger was another thing Dónal didn't understand, especially since it seemed to affect some but not others. He knew what it was to be hungry, certainly, had often felt the gnawing emptiness as he'd waited for the supper to boil and the prayers to be said. But never had he missed a meal or gone to bed hungry, and he couldn't understand why anyone else would have to when there was so much food in the land. Sure the potatoes had all gone bad for three years running, but still he'd seen the ships being loaded with grain and cattle and sheep in the harbor of Castletownbere and knew there was plenty enough for everyone. So if there was food in the land, he reasoned, then the Hunger must have some cause other than simple lack. Then he noticed how people spoke of it in whispers as though afraid it might hear, as if it were alive and stalking the land and that to speak of it too loudly might draw its attention. So he came to picture it as an apocryphal beast, The Hunger, a yellow-eyed shadow prowling catlike in the night, its bite causing its victims to waste away in a hunger that no amount of food would satisfy.

Then The Hunger had come upon Dónal's neighbors, the families who lived in the little cluster of cottages just across the stream from his own. For, unlike his own father who had a steady income, the neighbors were all tenant farmers and day laborers and subsisted only on their tiny plots of potatoes. They were all of one extended family, descended from a common ancestor who'd settled there several generations before, his small plot having been split among male descendants many times over the years, so that it now supported ten large families, each with its own cottage and tiny subsistence farm. But as their crops failed, they spent what little money they had on food and left the rents unpaid, till eventually the landlord's agent came round with his gang of emergency men to evict them. Dónal had watched with his mother as the people were forced from their homes and herded into a pitiful knot, the women sobbing and the children bawling, while the men just stood by in impotent silence, knowing too well the futility of resistance. After the gang threw their meager possessions into the yard, they battered down the cottage walls and torched the roofs to keep the wretches from moving back into them. Only when they'd left did the families dare to shuffle through the pile of furnishings and clothing, picking only such things as they could carry and wrapping them into small bundles. Then they trudged silently away, down the boreen toward Castletownbere, to what end, whether the horrors of the workhouse or the hold of a coffin ship, or simply starving by the roadside, Dónal never heard. But neither had he forgotten them, nor his mother's words as she watched them go. "The Hunger will be upon them now, surely," she'd said with tears streaming down her cheeks, confirming his suspicions of its nature.

Yet as fearsome a beast as The Hunger had proved, The Fever was even worse, for no amount of vigilance could defend against its nefarious ways. Silently it would steal into a home and take its victims, who once bitten would quickly succumb to its deadly poison. So it had crept invisibly into Dónal's own cottage and taken his mother, leaving him puzzled as to why she'd been chosen while he and his father were spared. Beside her yawning grave he'd stood by his father, the two of them as silent and gray as the old headstones around them, the man neither comforting his son nor expressing any emotion himself, only the stoop in his shoulders suggesting he felt any. They'd listened as the priest mumbled his prayers and watched as the sextons lowered the wooden box and covered it with The Land they so dearly loved, marking her grave like countless others, with just a plain stone brought in from the fields. And still Dónal didn't understand Death, only that his mother was gone and he couldn't follow without embracing It himself.

But of all the troubles that plagued The Land, Dónal knew The English to be the worst, for to hear his father and Eóghan speak of them, it was they who'd unleashed The Hunger and The Fever to do Death's bidding upon the Irish. And while he didn't know any of them personally, he did know that a great English family lived just across the valley at Dunboy, in their Big House that he could see from his front door standing darkly near the water. He'd been aware of them for as long as he could remember, understanding them to be a people apart, though he'd never actually seen any of them. He even knew their name, and that they were hated and feared by their poor neighbors for the devastation they'd brought upon them, though just why they'd done it he couldn't begin to guess. Perhaps it was to punish the Irish for some great sin they'd committed and purge The Land of wrongdoers, just as God had done with His great Flood. But if so, it was a terrible justice they'd wrought, this unholy trinity of The Hunger and The Fever and The English.

Now it seemed that Eóghan intended to challenge The English for mastery of The Land, and that Death would surely strike him down for his audacity and send him to that unknown place where the living could never follow. As he gazed up at his brother, Dónal's heart went cold at the thought and it poured from his mouth in a burst of emotion.

"Don't go, Eóghan, please don't," he begged. "I don't want you to die!"

"I have to, Dónalín," Eóghan replied with a sigh. "I've given my word and there's no going back on it now. But don't worry, everything will be fine. We're going to win this time, and when it's all over you'll be proud of me! You, and Da, too! You'll see."

Dónal didn't say anything else, just pleaded silently with his relentless eyes. Though finding their intensity disconcerting, his brother turned away and busied himself with packing. What could those eyes have possibly seen of the world to give them such depth, he wondered, such perception and awareness? Did he even know how powerful they were, or realize the impact they had on people? But those were questions he couldn't answer just then, and besides, he had problems of his own.

Eóghan closed his small valise, then turned to his brother. "Will you walk me down to the boreen?" he asked, extending his hand in the way he always did when it was time to leave.

Dónal made no move at first, just stared at the hand as if it were something alien to his experience. But then he reached up slowly and grasped it, and let Eóghan lead him outside, holding on as though to an emotional lifeline.

At the gap in the wall, Eóghan stopped and looked across the valley, toward the Big House at Dunboy, rising gray and ominous above the sacred Irish green. Following his gaze, Dónal pictured in his mind the trinity of Terrors that lived there, the Englishman sitting by the fire while The Hunger lay like a hound at his feet and The Fever hovered at his elbow, ever the faithful servant. Somehow he knew them to be central to everything he'd experienced in life, though why, like so many things, he didn't know. Looking up at Eóghan, he thought maybe he would explain it. But his brother said nothing, just sighed and shook his head before kneeling to give him a hug.

"Good-bye, Dónalín," Eóghan said as lightly as he could. "I'll be home again soon."

But at that, Dónal pushed back and fixed him again with his relentless green eyes. "Take me with you, Eóghan. Please?"

"I can't do that, Dónal. Don't you understand? I'm going to war, to fight and kill and maybe even die. I can't take care of you and be a soldier at the same time. You have to stay here with Da where it's safe."

"Da can't take care of me, either. Don't you see that he doesn't love me, and that I'll be safer with you than here alone with him?"

The brutal candor of it struck Eóghan like a blow, for in his heart he knew it to be true. "Even so, Dónal, I still can't take you. I can't and I won't, so please don't ask me again."

"All right, Eóghan, I won't. But don't tell me you're coming back, because I know you aren't."

"And how could you possibly know that?" Eóghan asked, flashing a smile to cover his own sudden uncertainty.

"I don't know. I just do."

Eóghan stood and looked down the road, as though trying to see where it would lead him, thinking for the first time that his father might be right after all. But then he thought of the men who were waiting for him, to whom he'd given his hand and his word. How would he ever explain it to them? And what would they think of him?

"I have to go now, Dónal," he said, still looking at the road. "I've made a promise and I have to keep it. It's the only honorable thing to do."

He knelt and gave his little brother a hug. "I know this is hard for you, but someday you'll understand, and then you'll be proud of me. You'll see. But no matter what happens, Dónal, always remember that I love you. Always!"

Then with nothing more, he set his back to his home and his face to the road, and began the long march toward his destiny.

As always, Dónal watched him go, waiting for him to turn at the bend in the road and wave one last time. But Dónal didn't smile or wave back, and when Eóghan was gone, he knew it was for good. He closed his eyes to burn that last image into memory, then sat down with his back to the stone wall. And as he gazed across the valley at the Big House, he thought of his mother and the parting death had brought from her, that it was final and absolute, and nothing he could do would ever change it. Yet Eóghan was just gone around the bend, and all he had to do was get up and run and they'd be together again. So death was an easier parting to bear, it seemed, because it didn't leave such a hunger in the soul. And Dónal's soul was starving for his brother, a hunger that threatened to devour him from within.

A tear trickled down his cheek, and then the floodgate opened, his little body heaving as he sobbed his brother's name, "Eóghan . . . Eóghan . . . Eóghan . . ."

Finally, when there were no more tears to cry, he got up and went back to his cottage, where he crawled into his father's bed and fell into the empty sleep of emotional exhaustion. It was dark when he awoke, both outside and in, the fire long out and the chill night air stealing in through the open door.

His father hadn't come home. He was alone.

chapter 3

It was dawn when Dónal woke again, the lingering chill in the cottage making him shiver and draw the blanket close around himself as he climbed down from his father's bed. Even as his bare feet touched the cool flagstones of the floor, he knew the man hadn't been home, and for the first time in his little life he was waking up to a cottage with no other people in it. After his mother died in the winter, her maiden aunt, Bríd, had come from Eyeries to watch after him and keep the cottage for his father. But she was a dried-up old shell of a woman, always with her rosary in hand and a scowl on her face, her quick temper leaving him constantly in fear of rousing her ire. His father had bid her good riddance when Eóghan came home, thinking that he'd be staying through the summer. But he hadn't stayed and so Dónal was alone, and nothing was as it had been before, no fire crackling in the hearth, no breakfast boiling in the cauldron, no bright good-mornings or even ill temper to welcome him into the new day, just the four walls around him, cold and silent. Indeed, it reminded him of Uncle Séamus sleeping in his box, and he wondered if this was the silence and emptiness that waited on the other side.

The thought of it made him shiver beneath the blanket, and he ran to the door in a panic, suddenly desperate to get out. But seeing the dawn breaking clear and bright and the land spreading before him in a feast of color, his anxiety evaporated into a sudden urge to relieve himself, and he continued on to the privy.

Coming back inside, he stopped at the threshold to look around the cottage. Everything was in its place just as always, with the big bed set against the left gable end and his father's pine chest beside it, while the hearth was centered in the right gable and flanked by the table and chairs along the front wall and the old pine hutch along the back. That section was always known as "the end of the house," though it was actually the middle of the building, the half beyond being devoted to animals and storage. The walls were of native stone plastered over and whitewashed inside and out, while the roof of thatch was supported by sturdy wooden rafters that pitched steeply from a central beam spanning the gables. Each half had front and back doors set directly opposite each other, but only the "human" half had windows, one flanking either side of the front door.

In sum, it was a cottage typical of "the better class of peasants," as the English called them, though there were few enough in that part of Béara. Indeed, the vast majority of people lived in much poorer circumstances, in cottages that, though walled with stone, had packed earthen floors and roofs of sod, with no windows and few furnishings beyond a pot for cooking and a rickety stool or two. Damp, uncomfortable places they were, dirty and squalid, and the children who lived in them seemed to have constantly dripping noses. Certainly they held no luxuries, for only a man with a steady income could afford the opulence of a pine hutch or a bed of Kerry oak (a wedding present from Dónal's father to his mother, the first and only gift he'd ever given her). Indeed, most people sat and slept and ate and loved and died on their earthen floors, usually huddled around a chimneyless hearth, a poor hole in the roof the only outlet for the smoke.

But then, even Dónal and Eóghan slept on rushes piled by the fire, the extravagance of a second bed beyond their father's capacity or desire. Still, it was no hardship, for Dónal always felt safe and warm curled up next to his big brother, his head pillowed on one of Eóghan's bulging biceps while the other arm wrapped him securely. Often he would lie awake long after Eóghan went to sleep, happily basking in the warmth of his affection. But there was no warmth of affection in the cottage today, and without it the house just didn't feel like home.

Dónal sighed and went to the hearth, where he stirred the ashes with the poker to find an ember with which to relight the fire. But finding them all gray and cold, he took the flint and steel from their place on the mantle and set about making a new fire in the way Eóghan had taught him. As he did, he said a silent prayer of thanks that his father wasn't home, for it was a cardinal sin to let the fire go out, and the man would surely have been furious with him. In a few minutes he had a decent blaze going and smiled with satisfaction as its yellow light stole through the room. At least the place wouldn't be physically cold.

Then Dónal's eyes fell upon yesterday's breakfast floating in the pot, and the sudden gnawing in his stomach reminded him that he hadn't eaten since supper of the day before yesterday. Without bothering to warm them up, he snatched up the potatoes and dropped them into the willow serving basket, then sat down at the table and tore into them like a hawk into a hare. Though they were ice-cold and soggy, in that moment they seemed the sweetest things he'd ever tasted.

Yet in the midst of his meal, a sudden pang of fear struck him. Could it be that the reason for the pain in his belly was that The Hunger had bitten him in the night and now no amount of food would satisfy him, leaving him like all the other poor wretches wandering the land? After all, he had left the door open well into the night, and it was open even now! He jumped up and rushed to close it, not daring to look outside for fear that The Hunger might be lurking there. Upon returning, he slowly started on his meal again, chewing and swallowing each bite carefully as he hoped against hope to feel his belly stretching with familiar fullness. When it began to come midway through his second potato he sighed and finished his meal with relish, relieved that he'd been spared such a dreadful fate.

To wash down his monotonous breakfast, Dónal had only water from the drinking bucket, which he gulped directly from the ladle. As he did, his eyes fell upon the tin milk jugs in the corner, and he thought longingly of the buttermilk they'd had before the Hunger came into the land and his father slaughtered the milk cows to supplement their food supply. He remembered how his mother drove them one by one through the front door for milking and then on through the back when finished, the doors having been placed so as to avoid turning the cows around in the confined space of the cottage. They'd had a rooster and chickens, too, and his mouth watered at the thought of eggs sizzling in butter in the now-unused frying pan. But the chickens went the way of the cows, and since his father sold their little bog pony after the spring planting, there were no more animals to occupy the other end of the house, aside from a few mice. Though he missed the chickens for their eggs and the cows for their milk and butter (and all of them for their meat), he missed the pony for his companionship. He was a genial little fellow named *Spota* for the large white spot on his face, and Dónal would sometimes get to ride on his back when Eóghan took him out to do chores. How he'd cherished those outings with his brother, listening intently to his tales of the old heroes and the people of the *sídhe*, the Otherworld that overlay their own, just a dream away. But Eóghan was gone and Spota, too, as completely as if they'd been dreams themselves.

Finishing his drink, Dónal turned and gave the room a second look, finding it comfortably familiar again now that the fire was lit and his belly full. And though it still lacked the feeling of home, he suddenly realized that with no one else around, he could do whatever he wanted and, with a mischievous grin, he set about exploring the place again, making sure to look into all its nooks and crannies.

After rummaging through the drawers of the hutch and peering up the chimney and under the bed, he came to his father's rickety little chest, a thing that he'd never been allowed to touch, much less open, and gleefully rifled through the squeaky drawers. In the bottom one he made a quite unexpected discovery, finding there an old linen bag tucked beneath a couple of tattered old shirts. Inside were three things he'd never seen before: a white wooden rod, a heavy leather-bound book and, most exciting of all, a long elk-handled dagger in a battered leather sheath. They must be especially precious to his father, he thought, for him to keep them hidden and secret, and he hesitated before going any further, imagining his father's wrath if he should catch him. But then his childish curiosity got the better of him, and he snatched the dagger from its sheath. In contrast to the battered leather, the blade was honed and polished, so that the engraved Irish words, *lamh foisteanach abú*, stood out in sharp contrast. But since he hadn't learned to read his native language yet, the words might as well have been Greek for all he could make of them. Still he grinned broadly as he waved the dagger about, delighting in the *whoosh* of its blade as it sliced through the air. Closing his eyes for a moment, he imagined it to be a great sword and himself a tall and mighty warrior, standing atop the walls of a castle with his red hair waving in the wind.

But suddenly a noise from outside made his heart skip and he looked wildly toward the door, thinking with sudden panic that it was his father. Hastily he returned the dagger to its sheath and the bag to the drawer, slamming it shut without bothering to hide it under the shirts. Hurrying to the door, he jerked it open, fully expecting to see his father striding toward him like a black cloud of peril. But it was only a couple of hooded crows squabbling over some tiny morsel of food under the great yew tree that stood just next to the cottage. Yet just to be sure, he walked to the gap in the circular stone wall that surrounded his cottage and gazed down the path as far as he could see. But still there was no one, just himself and the two crows and the freshening wind.

As he returned to the house, the birds set up a fuss, squawking at him from the branches of the tree as though upset that he'd interrupted their squabbling. But he paid them no heed, the tree itself having caught his eye. It was the biggest tree he knew of, especially this high on the hillside and, according to Eóghan, one of the oldest in that part of Béara, having been planted by the distant ancestor who'd built their cottage. Only across the valley in the forested demesne of Dunboy were there any trees to rival their old yew. But though he could see the Big House from where he stood, he'd never been there, and so his only other experience with trees was the scrubby osiers that grew along stream banks and the odd hollies and cherries. So the great yew was the only real tree he knew of, and he loved to sit under it on summer evenings, listening to the wind whisper through its branches as the sun set over the Broad Atlantic. Yet for as much as he loved it, his father treated it almost like a sacred idol, often standing under it with both hands on its trunk, his head bowed as though in prayer. Indeed, Eóghan had once told him that it was an important symbol of their great family, which like the yew itself was ancient beyond the memory of men. But he'd not told him any more than that, not even the name of the ancestor who'd planted it, and so its importance to his father was a mystery to him, as much so as the newly-discovered treasures that were calling to him from their hiding place in the chest.

Going back inside, Dónal went to the dresser and took them out again, playing with the dagger some more before turning to the book. It was thick and heavy, its tattered leather cover and yellowed pages making it look as ancient as the yew. He liked books, for they were another thing that Eóghan had shared with him, teaching him to read from the lesson books he brought home from school. Opening it gingerly, he flipped through its pages, trying to make out some of the words in the dim light the opaque windows afforded. But he was disappointed, for whereas Eóghan's books had been printed in English in nice uniform block script, this one was hand-written in what he guessed to be Irish.

So setting it aside, he turned to the white rod, which though the least enticing was yet the most mysterious, since he had no idea what its use might be. It didn't appear to be a tool, being just plain and round, and was too small and light to be a shillelagh. Yet it was obviously of some significance to his father, since he'd kept it hidden and secret with his other two treasures. He turned it over in his hands and peered at it closely, looking for any writing or other marks that might yield a clue. But there were none, and so he put it back in the bag with the book and dagger.

What were these things and what did they mean, he wondered as he returned them to their hiding place? Why had his father kept them hidden so, and did Eóghan know about them? He frowned and bit his lip as he pondered, shaking his head when no answers came. How odd it seemed that he'd made such a discovery, only to come away with questions that might remain forever unanswered, since he couldn't confess his mischief by asking his father. He sighed, covered the bag with the old shirts and closed the drawer.

Going back to the door, he looked out upon his new world, the one without Eóghan in it. The sky was clear and blue and the sun shining brightly, illuminating the vivid Irish landscape. But the beauty of it was lost on him amid the feeling of being alone in a great big world.

Turning back to the empty cottage, he wondered what he would do with himself all day.

⟡

Dónal woke with a start and sat upright on the floor, blinking in the dim light of the embers as he tried to orient himself. He'd been having bad dreams again, and at first he thought that was what had wakened him. But then he heard a noise from the door, the sound of someone fumbling with the latch, and knew that his nightmare had blurred into reality. Had The Hunger come to get him, or The Fever or The English? Or was it those bad men that chased him through his dream world, never quite catching him but neither allowing him to get away. He stood and cringed against the hearth, trembling in fear. But then he heard another sound, one that puzzled him at first till he realized it was that of a man urinating against the wall. At that his fear evaporated and he sighed in relief, thinking that any monster that had to pee before coming to get him couldn't be all that bad. But still he stayed by the fire, picking up the poker just in case.

In a moment, the man finished and was back at the latch, making Dónal's heart beat just a bit faster again. But then the door swung open and big Eóghan O'Sullivan lurched inside, though Dónal almost didn't recognize him for the dissolution that was in him. His hair was disheveled and hanging in his eyes, while his chin was dark with two days' growth of beard. His clothes were filthy and his boots caked with mud, and his shoulders sagged as though carrying the weight of Atlas. Yet it was his eyes that held Dónal's attention, being red and swollen, and seeming to stare inward at some dark spectacle rather than outward at the living world. Indeed, Dónal didn't think he even saw him, though he was staring right at him.

Then he noticed the earthenware jug in his father's hand and understood at least part of it, having seen from the neighbors what the drink could do to a man. And even as he watched, his father raised the jug and took a long drink, his gulping audible and somehow disconcerting. Wiping his lips on his sleeve, he belched and, without so much as a word to his son, stumbled to the bed and sprawled across it, the jug still in his hand. Yet in just a moment he was up again, sitting on the edge of the bed with his head in his hands as though weeping. Another belch and his hand was at his mouth, trying to hold back the bile rising within him till, accepting the inevitable, he made to stand and go outside, though his legs turned to jelly and he melted to the floor. But with a last Herculean effort, he managed to push himself to his hands and knees and crawl to the door, just barely getting outside before his guts erupted. After heaving till there was nothing left to throw up but his innards, he turned and tried to crawl back, getting just inside the door before collapsing.

Through it all, Dónal had stayed by the fire, watching in anxious silence as the hard man that was his father dissolved into sloppy drunkenness. It frightened him, for with Eóghan gone and his mother dead, for good or ill, his father was all he had left in the world. Yet at the same time, he felt sorry for him, that he should be in such pain as to cause himself even greater pain in trying to shut it out. And it was that feeling of empathy that moved him from the hearth to his father's side, though he went warily, as if he were a wounded beast that might attack in desperation.

"Da!" he said softly though insistently, shaking his father by the shoulder. "Da, you've got to get up and get in the bed! Da? Can you hear me? You've got to get up!"

Slowly, O'Sullivan's eyes fluttered open and focused on his son, though Dónal had the feeling that he was looking right through him.

"Did you hear me, Da? You've got to get in the bed. Come on, I'll help you."

O'Sullivan didn't answer, just pushed himself slowly onto all fours and crawled painfully toward the bed while Dónal did what little he could to help. Finally, he got himself onto the mattress and lay as he fell, face down and feet dangling over the side.

After hesitating for a moment, Dónal climbed up and lay down beside him. "Don't worry, Da," he said, draping his little arm across the man's broad shoulders. "I'll take care of you."

O'Sullivan's eyes fluttered open at that, and fixed on Dónal's for just a moment, though whether it was appreciation or resentment in them, Dónal couldn't tell. Then they closed again, and he was asleep.

***

When Dónal awoke in the morning, his father was nowhere to be found, and he assumed he'd already gone to work. Taking it in stride, he climbed down from the bed and went through his lonely morning routine, stoking the fire and boiling his breakfast, which he ate alone at the table, finding in it neither the wonder nor the fear of the day before. It was just as though things had always been that way.

After breakfast, he opened the door to see what kind of weather was in it, and finding it fine, ventured out to the wall that surrounded his cottage and climbed to its top. From there, he had a broad view of the south side of Béara, from the high peak of Knockgour on the west to the tall head of Hungry Hill on the east, between which marched the rounded humps of the Slieve Miskish Mountains. From the waters of Bantry Bay directly across from him rose the steep sides of the Big Island (which the English called Bear Island), while across the bay in the distance he could see the Sheep's Head Peninsula. Between the eastern end of Bear Island and the mainland lay the protected anchorage of Berehaven, for which the town of Castletownbere served as port. The haven and the harbor were thick with ships, and he shaded his eyes to gaze at them, wondering as always where they'd come from and where they would go, his fascination with ships and the sea being lifelong.

From there his gaze wandered a bit before settling on the Big House at Dunboy, rising gray and foreboding above the Irish green. It had the look of a fortress about it, especially the tall crenellated tower on the right end, and, indeed, he'd even heard it referred to as Dunboy Castle on occasion, though Eóghan had told him that the *real* castle was the ruin standing on the point beyond. It had once been the home of the O'Sullivans, and he'd even gone there once with their father, though why and for what, he'd never said. Yet though Dónal could see the tall evergreen oaks that marked its location, he'd never been able to make out the ruins, and he sometimes wondered if Eóghan hadn't just made it up.

Tiring of the view, Dónal set about exploring around his home, starting with the ancient circular wall that surrounded it. It had once been tall and mighty, at least to hear Eóghan tell it, an ancient stone ringfort built by the Gael when the world was yet young. *Cathair na Gaoithe* the ancients had called it, "Fortress of the Wind," and as Cahernageeha it was still known, though to Dónal, *Cathair in aghaidh na Gaoithe*, "Fortress *against* the Wind," had always seemed more appropriate, as it had surely been just that to all who'd ever sheltered within its walls. Indeed, the wind was as constant here as the green grass and the gray stones, and how cold it was in winter, whipping the chill off the Broad Atlantic and propelling it up the slopes to freeze the marrow of anyone unlucky enough to be in its path. Yet when the weather was fine and the wind but a gentle breath, how beautifully it sang through the branches of the great yew, Mother Erin's lullaby for her poor children of the mountain and the bog. Indeed, on summer afternoons Dónal liked to sit under the tree and listen to its song as he daydreamed of the time when the fortress was young and strong, and Ireland just for the Irish. But it was centuries now since Cahernageeha was a fortress, and only in a couple of places did the circular wall still rise to its original height. And as Eóghan told it, most of the fallen stone had gone to building the neighboring cottages, for though the people of Béara had a tradition of respecting the monuments of the ancients, should they fall or break on their own, they were fair game for all.

After doing a full circuit of the wall, Dónal hopped down and forded the narrow burbling stream that separated Cahernageeha from the abandoned cottages where his neighbors once lived. They stood no more than a hundred feet to the west, in a cluster too small to properly be called a village. Indeed, the locals called it a *clochán*, the word in its strictest sense connoting a "stone structure," though the agile Irish mind had stretched its fabric to cover a broader frame. And as was typical of the Irish *clochán*, the cottages of this one had been built so close together as to almost touch, as if such huddled proximity would protect the inhabitants from the harshness of the outside world. As such, it was in itself a sort of ringfort, though one more fitting to the peasant farmers the Gael had become, and standing in sharp contrast to old Cahernageeha and the Gael as they'd once been, proud and strong and free. Not that it did them any good, of course. The ejectments happened just the same, the battering ram breaching the walls as a horde of emergency men poured in to sack the *clochán* and rape its pitiful patrimony, setting the people to wander on the long road to oblivion, even leaving it to them to find their own way there. And in a way, the very existence of ringforts had assured that it would be so, for the landscape of Ireland was once as thick with them as it was with clans and petty lordships, all fighting amongst themselves for ascendancy like a pack of jackals over a carcass, the institutionalized disunity of the system leaving the Gael open to conquest and exploitation by a people more cunning and culturally mature.

Eóghan had tried to explain some of these things to him, to teach him some of the history of his people, and though he didn't really understand much of it, he did remember it. But as he stood gazing at the *clochán* just now, he saw only the *present* of his people in the tumbled and broken remains of what had once been their homes. He closed his eyes and pictured them as they'd been before the Hunger, neat and tidy little dwellings with turf-smoke pouring from the chimneys and the sounds of children playing in the yard, the inhabitants as happy and contented as people who lived just beyond the pale of privation could be. When he opened his eyes and looked at the devastation around him, the image seemed absurd, as though the place had never been anything but broken and silent and deserted. It was a sad sight filled with sad memories, and for a moment he hesitated, fearing that The Hunger or The Fever might be lurking there, waiting for him.

But then his curiosity got the better of him. He walked to the nearest cottage, and stood on his tiptoes to peer through the broken window. It looked empty enough and, after a second look to make sure, he clambered over the pile of stones where the door had once been. The earthen floor was overgrown with weeds and grass and littered with stones and charred roof-beams, with even the chimney tumbled down, though the hearth was still intact. But finding nothing of interest, he went on to the next cottage and then the next, finding nothing in any of them to suggest that people had once lived and laughed and loved there.

Stepping from the last one, Dónal's eyes fell upon the rolling waves of ground called "lazy beds," where the people had once grown their potatoes. They'd been left just as they were when the crop failed and the last of them were sent packing. Generations of cultivation were required to make this stony land productive, as season after season the Earth delivered yet more stones from Her belly and the people lugged them from the fields, the stone walls and even the cottages bearing silent testament to that perpetual labor. But then in the blink of an eye, all was brought to naught, for The Land withheld Her grace and the potatoes failed, and the people departed, leaving the overgrown lazy beds as their only memorial.

As he gazed at them, Dónal frowned in puzzlement. "Why will weeds and grass grow here, but not potatoes?" he wondered aloud.

But the ghosts gave him no answer.

In the evening Dónal went out to the lazy beds behind his cottage to dig up a few potatoes for his supper. They weren't really ready to eat yet, and he knew they'd be small and that many plants would be required to make a meal. But his father hadn't come home and so there was nothing to be done about it. Noticing that the little plot was beginning to show the effects of neglect, he took it upon himself to weed and tidy it, before pulling the potatoes in bunches by their greens and going back inside.

The sun was already down beyond the horizon, lighting it with the flame of approaching night by the time supper was ready. But just as Dónal sat down to eat, he heard the sound of approaching footsteps and turned to the door to find his father standing there, looking not at him but at the table, with the potatoes piled high in the basket and two places set.

"I see you've boiled enough for both of us," he said, coming to stand over his son.

"Yes, Da," Dónal replied warily, catching the sharp scent of poteen on his breath. "I was hoping you'd come home for supper."

"Hm," O'Sullivan grunted and, with nothing more, sat down and began to eat.

Sitting opposite his father, his short legs dangling in the air, Dónal nibbled quietly as he watched the big man eat. How he wished he'd say something to him, even if it was bad, just so that he noticed him. But he was too busy packing it in, hunched over with his chin almost on his plate, barely stopping for a breath till he was finished. Then he pushed back his chair, wiped his mouth with his hand and his hands on his trousers, and went to the water bucket for a drink.

"I'm going to bed now, Dónal," he said when finished, "so mind that you don't disturb me."

Then he flopped down on the bed, wrapped himself in the blanket and turned to the wall.

After what seemed only a few moments, his breathing became deep and regular, and Dónal knew he was asleep. Rising from the table himself, he went softly to his place by the fire, feeling as alone as if his father weren't there.

⟨∞⟩

And so things went between them for a time, O'Sullivan rising before dawn and leaving Dónal to spend the day alone, coming home only for supper and his bed, always with the drink on his breath now, though never so far gone with it as that first time. And though they shared a house, they were as separate from each other as two people could be. Indeed, the man hardly seemed to notice that his son was there, his eyes being turned ever inward, though he said nothing of what he saw.

As for the lonely days between, Dónal began to fill them with exploring the countryside, gradually growing bolder and venturing further afield to find things to occupy his time, like the stone circle at Derreenataggert or the twin platform forts at Teernahillane. There were scores upon scores of cottages, too, sometimes single and alone, though more often clustered like the *clochán* adjacent to his home. Always though, they were deserted and half-destroyed, marked with the scars of the battering ram and the torch, the calling cards of The Hunger and The Fever and The English. Indeed, he found that very few people lived on the hillside or in the valley anymore, the population so reduced that most of The Land was turned to pasturage now. Where It had once been filled with people and cottages and cultivated fields, all was now empty and forlorn, as silent as the voices of the dead. All that was left was ruins, and the countless miles of walls built by generations of farmers lugging stones from their fields. They criss-crossed The Land like a Celtic knot, beginning nowhere and ending nowhere, but continuing on forever, it seemed, uniting Ireland in a way Her people never had. And like the standing stones of the ancients, they'd once marked the boundaries between petty domains of human endeavor, but now stood only as mute sentinels marking the silent passing of a people from the planes of history.

Then one afternoon, Dónal set out on the boreen that passed near his home, following it all the way to its junction with the main road just below its steep ascent over Guala. The day was warm and sunny, and he stopped many times to explore things that caught his eye. At the junction, he turned east toward Castletownbere and followed the main road to the stone bridge over the Pulleen River. After taking a drink of the cold clear water, he turned to go back the way he'd come, intending to go home now that it was getting late.

But then a low overgrown mound in the field to his right caught his attention and, seeing a few standing stones protruding through the vegetation, he set off to explore them. Picking his way cautiously through a thick stand of thorny gorse, he waded in among the stones, seeing that they appeared to be arranged in a circle around a central boulder. But with all the overgrowth it was difficult to tell much about them, and he turned his attention to the central boulder, which seemed to be clear of gorse on the north side.

But as he stepped into the small clearing, he stopped and gasped in horror, finding a young family sitting there with their backs to the great stone, the man's arm around his wife and her head on his shoulder, their clasped hands cradling their young daughter between them, frozen for all eternity in a last embrace, a last gesture of love for each other. For they were dead and had been for some time, given their state of decomposition, their flesh turned a ghastly gray-green, their finger-nails long and yellowed, their hair dried to spidery wisps, and their grass-stained teeth a testament to their last desperate bid to delay the inevitable. Where their eyes had been were only black empty sockets showing nothing but the ghosts of their dead memories. But even they were gone now, locked in the Beyond as surely as the secrets of the great stones standing silent guard around them. That they were victims of the troubles was obvious, though whether of The Hunger or The Fever or The English (or all three) was impossible to tell. Most likely, they'd been evicted from their home and set upon the road to wander till, able to go no further, they'd chosen this spot as a final resting place, concealing themselves from the prying eyes of an uncaring world.

And as Dónal gaped at them, transfixed by the waking nightmare, a worm slithered from the man's left eye socket across the bridge of his nose and into the right. Dónal shuddered and took a step backward, only to scream in terror as something touched his back. Whirling around, he fully expected to find The Hunger with its yellow eyes and slavering jaws, but saw instead only a stray branch of gold-speckled gorse. A noise behind him sent him whirling again, and seeing their hair stirred by the wind, he panicked and plunged through the gorse, heedless of the thorns in his desperation to escape, only to trip and fall headlong into one of the stones.

For some time he lay there, dazed and delirious, his ears ringing and stars swirling before his eyes, till finally he could struggle up and totter back toward the road. But after only a few steps his stomach heaved and he vomited as he ran, not daring to stop for fear of what might be following him.

Finally, after what felt like an eternity, Dónal made it back to his home and climbed into his father's bed, in his damaged state not caring whether he incurred his wrath or not. And as he lay there looking at the ceiling, the little family came into his mind again, sitting amid the gorse and standing stones, locked in their eternal embrace. But there was no horror in them now, only sadness that their love couldn't save them. Did they take that love with them to the Otherworld, he wondered? If so, then maybe death wasn't such a bad thing after all.

Then he pictured himself staggering about and vomiting, just as his father had on that night of too much drink, and he wondered why anyone would ever choose to get drunk if that was what it was like. Surely, it could only be that the pain of the world was so great as to make the pain of drinking seem a blessed relief by comparison.

As his eyes closed, he prayed to God that he never have that much pain.

⊙ɷɷɷ⊙

In the dark of night, Dónal awoke to his father shaking him. "What're you doing in my bed, Dónal?" he demanded, the scent of poteen on his breath. "Get over to the hearth where you belong."

But Dónal made no move, just answered in the calm, straightforward manner that Eóghan had always used to blunt his father's anger. "I can't tonight, Da. I'm sick and my head hurts. I bumped it on a standing stone."

O'Sullivan didn't say anything, just sighed with annoyance and went to the hearth to light a candle. "Show me where," he said when he returned. Seeing the bruise on his son's forehead, he gave a low whistle, and said, "Jesus, Mary and all the Saints, Dónal, if that isn't a big one! There must be quite a tale in it, and see that you don't leave anything out!"

Sure that his father would be angry with him, but too injured to care, Dónal closed his eyes and told the story, being sure to be extra hard on himself so that maybe his father wouldn't feel the need. But to Dónal's surprise, he just sighed and nudged him toward the far side of the bed.

"All right then, move over," he said. "I suppose there's room for the both of us here for one night. But don't go making a habit of it now!"

So surprised was he by his father's response that Dónal sat up and gaped. "Are you all right, Da?"

"Am *I* all right?" the man replied, as he blew out the candle and lay down. "Why should anything be wrong with me when you're the one that was after playing billy goat with a standing stone? Go back to sleep, Dónal. We'll talk about it in the morning."

With that, O'Sullivan pulled the blanket over himself and turned his back to his son. But though he settled in, too, Dónal lay awake for some time, wondering where his father's sudden empathy had come from, and whether it would last. Or was he just too tired and drunk to deal with it in that moment, and so was putting it off till morning? But finding no answers, Dónal just decided to enjoy it while it lasted.

"Good night, Da," he said tentatively, moving as close as he dared to the big man's back.

But there was no reply. The moment had passed.

chapter 4

Cahernageeha

Dónal awoke slowly the next morning, struggling up through a fog of troubled dreams and into a painful and muddled awareness. His head ached and his stomach was still queasy and, at the memory of himself staggering about and vomiting like a drunkard, he resolved again never to touch the poteen, especially if this was what the morning after was like. But then the sound of his father clearing his throat brought him upright in surprise, for he'd not expected him to be home. What could be the reason for it, he wondered, for only on rare occasions and for something truly momentous did big Eóghan O'Sullivan take a day or even part of one off from work. Yet there he was at the end of the bed, lurking in the corner like a predator, just as on that morning of Eóghan's departure, his eyes gleaming though the rest of him was shrouded in shadow.

"Are you all right, Da?" Dónal asked timidly, more to reassure himself than anything.

For a long moment his father didn't answer, and when he finally did, his voice sounded faint and far away, as though he were speaking from deep inside himself. "Sure, Dónal, I'm all right. Of course I am. What could possibly be wrong?"

"I don't know, Da. I just thought you'd be at the mines."

"No," O'Sullivan said absently. "Today is Sunday, and the mines are closed for the Sabbath, at least for the men with whom I work. And since I don't wish to load ore today, I'm here at home. Anyway, we have something to attend to later, after the morning Mass."

"We're going to Mass, Da?" Dónal asked in surprise, never having known his father to do so before.

"No, Dónal, there'll be no Mass for us. We just need Father Fitzgerald to help us with our errand. I'll let you know when it's time to fetch him. Now be a good boy, and leave me peace."

Though he doubted that it was in peace, Dónal did leave him then, going outside to relieve himself and gather some potatoes for their breakfast. It was unseasonably cool and foggy and, as he stepped through the lazy beds, he remembered the previous three summers, when cool wet weather brought the blight that killed their crop and those of their neighbors and set loose The Hunger to terrorize them. It was then that his father began bringing food home in a linen bag, much like the one hidden in his dresser, foreign potatoes and Indian corn that he'd bought from the mining company, which imported them to lessen the impact of the blight on its workers. To be sure, The Company didn't do it out of compassion, wanting only to feed its workers so they'd stay on the job (and thereby maintain the flow of profits to the English owners). So only employees were allowed to buy the imported food, and The Company made sure it covered its costs in the undertaking. Not that Dónal knew any of that, only that his father brought home food in the bag and that their neighbors didn't seem to be able to get any.

So while the loss of their crop troubled him in an abstract sort of way, because it so obviously troubled those on whom he depended, it also had the perverse effect of improving the variety and flavor in his diet. For even the potatoes were better than their own varietals, which were known as "lumpers" and tended to be so watery and bland that even cattle turned up their noses at them. Yet a satisfied palate was of no consequence to an empty stomach and, lumpers being hardy and growing abundantly on even the scabbiest land, they'd become the primary source of sustenance for millions of poor peasants, so much so that the Irish had come to be known as the "Potato People" for their dependence upon them.

But like all potatoes, lumpers would keep in storage only for nine months at most, so that even before the coming of the Hunger, the poor Irish who depended on them starved a little bit every summer. Indeed, July and August were known as the "hungry months," that between-time when the new crop wasn't ready and last year's was already exhausted. Then, men who didn't have a steady income (which was most of them) worked as laborers in the fields of the local land-lords and strong farmers, or crossed the Little Water (the Irish Sea) to do seasonal work in England or Scotland, while their women and children went on the road to beg. And if they were lucky and God shed His grace upon them, they could scrape together enough to keep the family alive and intact until the next harvest.

Yet even the lumper's native hardiness was no guarantee of a good crop or a successful harvest, for there were always the vagaries of weather and fate to contend with, not to mention the caprice of man. Indeed, the planting cycle itself seemed to be a prayer for Providential intervention, being governed as it was by a series of holy days: prepare the soil on St. Brigit's Day, plant on St. Patrick's Day, and harvest by All Saints' Day (or Halloween as it was known colloquially). Even the country fairs of spring and autumn were left over from the ancient festivals of *Beltaine* and *Samhain*, when their pagan ancestors gathered to beg fertility of the gods and to thank them for it, respectively.

But all bets were off when the blight appeared in late September of 1845, as even the lumper had no resistance to it. And while much of the bumper crop of that year had already been harvested, it quickly began to rot in storage, and so began the Great Hunger that still gripped the land. For though relatively few people really starved in that first year, the blight returned in July 1846, withering the crops on the vine within a few days and, with the country's meager reserves exhausted by early August, the poor began to starve in earnest. Not that everyone suffered, of course, only the poorest of the poor, though in Ireland that constituted a class of people numbering in the millions. As for those who were a little better off, they got on with their lives as best they could, some even profiting from the misfortune, especially the "grabbers" who snatched up the lands of the departed and formed larger, more productive and efficient farms.

As for those who didn't starve, most were forced to emigrate, which was almost as bad as dying in their reckoning. Indeed, they had no word for it in their Irish language, the closest being *deoraí*, "exile," which was indeed how they regarded it. And from the mass migration arose the custom of the "American Wake," a night of revelry before the departure, so-called because the likelihood of their returning to Ireland was about as remote as that of a corpse returning to life. Many indeed were never heard from again, though others kept in touch, often sending money to aid those left behind, which was itself sometimes used to purchase passages, usually to America, though many went also to Australia, Canada, New Zealand and even England. Not that the destination mattered, of course, for they got an American Wake just the same.

But as bad as things were in 1846, the following year of Black '47 brought even worse, beginning with the winter, which was the worst in living memory, with snow covering the ground for months in many places. Even Béara had snow, a place that rarely experienced so much as a hard frost. And it was then that The Fever came upon them, to prey on those weakened by The Hunger, even taking away many whom it had overlooked, like Dónal's mother. On top of that, food prices soared out of sight; not that it mattered much, since the poor had no money to buy food at any price. Then the blight returned in July, and the smell of putrefied vegetation spread like a black cloud over the land. That was when Dónal's father began to slaughter their animals, the scrawny chickens being good for only one meal each, though the three cows had stretched out nicely, and so the man was still able to send his wages off to Dublin for Eóghan's education.

As for this summer of 1848, the weather had been generally decent thus far, and the potato crop seemed to be holding its own. And since they were well into August now, if St. Brigit and St. Patrick would watch over them just a bit longer, they might have a crop in the shed on All Saint's Day.

Dónal remembered watching as his father prepared the soil, first turning it over to form the characteristic mounded rows, then covering them with a fertilizing mixture of dung and seaweed, before finishing with another layer of soil. The seaweed he'd brought from the coast in osier wand baskets strapped to Spota, while the dung came from the pony himself. When the beds were ready, he and old Aunt Bríd cut seed pieces from a batch of potatoes brought home in his magic bag. "Just the eyes now, woman," O'Sullivan had admonished, "so we can eat what's left." Shooting him a glare that would melt stone, she'd spat back, "I didn't ride over here on a donkey, you know!" After that they'd ignored each other, each having made their points. When the seed pieces were ready, his father used a pointed wooden tool called a *spud* to punch holes in the mounds, planting them at discreet intervals before covering them over.

When at last the work was done, he'd called Dónal and Aunt Bríd into the field, and the three of them stood there for several minutes, staring silently at the lazy beds, pleading for God and Nature and every other force they could think of to be kind to them. And seemingly their prayers had been answered, for a few days later, bright green shoots began to curl up from the rows, growing hale and hardy as though there'd never been such a thing as the blight.

Yet even so, all was not well. For since Eóghan's departure, his father had been too self-absorbed to remember to bring home any food, leaving Dónal with no choice but to dig into their little crop, small and early as they were. And with almost a whole row gone already, it probably wouldn't last even through the following spring, much less through the hungry months. But how was he to broach the subject with his father, he wondered, when he barely had the courage to even speak to him? How he wished his father would awaken from his dark reverie and remember that he had another son, one who needed him desperately now that there was no one else, one who would love him if but given the chance. If only there was something he could do or say to make him realize it. If only . . .

But when he returned to the cottage and found his father still as he'd been, blank staring eyes seeing only the dark panoply within, he knew there was nothing.

As always, they ate in silence, O'Sullivan hunched over his plate and Dónal watching him furtively, hoping for a nod, a word, half a smile, anything to acknowledge his presence, to let him know they were somehow connected. But he hoped in vain.

After clearing the table, Dónal went to the door, meaning to escape the heavy atmosphere of the cottage. But his father stopped him at the threshold. "Don't go far, Dónal," he commanded from his corner. "Remember we have an errand."

"Yes, Da," he replied, hesitating for a moment to see if there'd be more, going on when there wasn't.

Beneath the great yew tree, he sat down and closed his eyes, the warm morning sun and his full belly soon lulling him into a light sleep. Yet when he awoke, he was surprised to find that nothing was as it had been, that he was no longer in his yard under the tree, but in the midst of a stone circle overgrown with gorse. And as he watched in fascination, a worm crawled from inside his head, out through his left eye and back in through the right, though he felt nothing of its movement. How could that be, he wondered, that a bug should be inside his head and he should feel nothing? Then a small boy appeared before him, gasping in horror at what he saw, and suddenly he understood. He was the dead man sitting against the stone, his black empty sockets now windows from the Otherworld through which he gazed upon the ghosts of his dead memory. But no, this wasn't a memory, and that small boy was no ghost, but The Hunger come to take him to that place beyond where no one could follow. Indeed, it was leaning over him now, its catlike eyes yellow slits of evil as it grasped him in its claws, and drew him inexorably toward its gleaming fangs. And though he wanted to run, his dead legs wouldn't respond, and his dead voice made no sound, beyond the scream inside his own head.

But then a curious thing happened, for rather than biting him, The Hunger shook him and spoke to him. "Dónal, what's the matter with you?" it demanded. "It's only me, for Christ's sake!"

With a start, Dónal awoke from his nightmare to find his father bent over him, a frightened look on his face and for the moment definitely focused on the world outside himself.

"I'm sorry, Da. I had a bad dream."

"To be sure!" O'Sullivan exclaimed, the frightened look replaced by a bemused smile. Yet it was gone as quickly as it had come. "It's time now. So get yourself together and let's be off with ourselves."

"All right, Da, I'm ready," Dónal agreed, though his heart was still racing. Noticing the spade in his father's hand, he asked, "Where are we going?"

"We're going to Castletownbere to fetch Father Fitzgerald," O'Sullivan replied, without looking at him. "Then you're going to show us where you found the dead ones yesterday, so we can bury them."

At that, Dónal stopped dead in his tracks, the terror of his nightmare and yesterday's encounter still fresh. "No, Da, *please* don't make me go there!" he exclaimed, more afraid of it than of his father. "I don't want to see the dead people again! I'm afraid of them!"

"That's fine, Dónal. You don't have to look at them. Your job is to show me where they are. Mine is to bury them, and Father Fitzgerald's is to say the prayers. When we get there, you can wait by the road if you want. But you are going. Understand?"

"Yes, Da," Dónal replied, knowing he had no choice.

"Good. Then let's go."

After that, they went along in silence, Dónal fairly running to keep up with his father's swift gait, so that he was red-faced and puffing by the time they neared the western end of Castletownbere. Indeed, he was just wondering how he would make it all the way to where they were going when, to his relief, he saw Father Fitzgerald approaching in his little one-horse trap. He was an old man, bespectacled and bald, though a fat jolly sort with a fondness for the drink, at least judging from his pink face and ever-present jar at weddings and wakes. "I've just the one fault, you know," he'd sigh sheepishly, for though the Church officially frowned on such revelry, he'd always turn a blind eye so long as his glass was kept full.

Yet for all his genial nature, it seemed to Dónal that he didn't like his father very much, though for what reason, he couldn't guess. Perhaps it was because he never went to Mass, or perhaps that was the *reason* he never went to Mass. But whatever the cause, there was no time to ponder it just then.

"Hello, Father!" O'Sullivan called, as the priest reined in his horse. "I was just on my way to fetch you!"

"Well, if that isn't a coincidence!" Father Fitzgerald exclaimed. "I was just on my way out to see you. I have something rather . . . urgent to discuss with you, I'm afraid."

Catching his tone, Dónal wondered what it meant. But if his father noticed, he gave no indication.

"And a pleasure it would be, good Father, to have you in my humble abode," O'Sullivan said, bowing sarcastically. "But I'm afraid my errand takes precedence."

"Don't play the flip with me, Eóghan O'Sullivan!" Father Fitzgerald said, his features collapsing into a withering scowl. "If you have something to tell me, then get on with it!"

"All right, dado, keep your shirt on," O'Sullivan said disrespectfully. "Our young Dónal here has found some dead ones near that overgrown stone circle at Clonglaskan. I'm going to collect them for burial, and thought you might want to give them the benefit of clergy."

For a long moment, Father Fitzgerald said nothing, as the conflict of his emotions played across his face. "All right, Eóghan, I'll come with you," he said finally, though against his better judgment, it seemed to Dónal. "What I have can wait, and I'm in no hurry to tell it anyway. So you and the boy climb aboard and we'll be on our way."

Grunting his agreement, O'Sullivan picked up Dónal and swung into the seat beside the priest, settling his son on his lap with an arm wrapped around him. Father Fitzgerald snapped the reins then and off they went, bouncing along faster than Dónal had ever gone before, the thrill of speed matched only by his delight at sitting in his father's lap, both new experiences for him. A broad grin spread across his face and, when the trap hit a bump and went momentarily airborne, he couldn't help but throw back his head and laugh, thinking that if there were a Heaven, it couldn't be any better than this.

But at the sound of it, his father shook him sharply and shot him a warning glance. "Quiet, you, or there'll be no supper in it."

"Oh, leave the boy alone, Eóghan," Father Fitzgerald scolded. "He's just having a bit of fun."

"This is not your child," O'Sullivan shot back, glaring at the priest, "and I'll thank you to keep your opinions to yourself!"

"We're all children of God, Eóghan, and–"

"Yes, but you are not God, Father Fitzgerald, and this is not your child!"

"Oh, all right, have it your way," the priest said, glaring at O'Sullivan in turn. "You're as stubborn as a stone, Eóghan O'Sullivan, and just as thick! But luckily for you, it's not for me to judge you, else you might find things a bit warm for your liking."

"Yes, well, you let me worry about that! You just keep your eyes on the road . . . and mind that stone there! Or do you think it's going to get up and move itself, just because it's you coming?"

"I see it, I see it! God help me, but if I'd wanted someone to nag me, I'd have gotten married!"

"Sure, that's the reason you're a priest as it is, because no woman of sound mind and two good eyes would have you!"

"You just watch yourself, Eóghan O'Sullivan, or I'll have you excommunicated!"

"Excommunicated, my arse. Why, you couldn't get a whore excommunicated from a nunnery! As I recall, *you* were the one who almost lost your collar for that 'one fault' of yours!"

And there was more like that, the two of them behaving like an old married couple, constantly sniping at each other without ever getting to the point. It made Dónal wonder again at the source of their animosity, considering they so rarely saw each other. Indeed, his mother's funeral and wake were the only such occasions he could remember and, even then, they'd only spoken to each other of necessity, it seemed. Thinking back, he remembered that a great many people had come to pay their respects, as she had a large family in Eyeries and many friends, though unlike the wake of Uncle Séamus, there'd been no merry-making or raucous behavior, since she was considered a great loss to the community and was leaving behind a young son. But he remembered people saying what a shame it was that she'd married a man like *Eóghan an Sasanach* and how, even in death, he was treating her poorly, waking her for only one day rather than the customary three. "Sure, if this is a proper wake, then I'm a Tinker!" one man had complained loudly. "There's little enough food and no drink at all, and not a keener to be heard within miles of the place! And while I'll grant you that the cost of a wake has put many a family in the workhouse, there is such a thing as common decency!" Though Dónal didn't really understand it, he did see that an insult was intended.

Yet if his father had heard, he gave no sign. Indeed, he'd withdrawn so completely that he may as well have been dead himself for all he gave of his feelings, being a mute island in the midst of that sea of humanity and emotion. Nor had anyone spoken to him or tried to console him, then or at the burial, not even Father Fitzgerald and, as soon as all the prayers were said and the coffin lowered into the snow-covered ground, he'd simply turned and walked away, leaving Dónal to run along behind, trying to keep up with his long angry strides.

But if there was a cause for the animosity, there were no clues to be found in Dónal's memories, and when they crossed the little stone bridge over Dunboy Creek and the Big House came into view, he gave it up to crane his neck for a good look. For it seemed so huge and imposing from this close that he marveled that people could live in such a place without constantly losing themselves. But in a moment it was gone from view, and they were passing the twin gate houses standing like threatening shadows to the left of the road, their cold gray walls and crenellation giving them a military cast appropriate to the siege mentality of the people living within, while the iron gate between sent an unmistakable message of unwelcome. Beyond them stood a forest of tall evergreens that looked cool and inviting compared to the dusty road and, despite the forbidding gate, Dónal longed to stop and stroll beneath them, and maybe spy out some of the secrets of the people sequestered beyond. But as quick as the thought, the buggy was past and speeding on toward a place he didn't want to go.

As they crossed the stone bridge over the Pulleen River, Father Fitzgerald slowed the horse to a walk. "Are we near the place?" he asked.

"That's it," Dónal replied, pointing to the stones poking through the gorse. "The dead ones are in the middle." Then to his father he said urgently, "You said I didn't have to look at them again, Da."

"Of course you don't, Dónal," Father Fitzgerald said. "You've done a brave deed as it is in bringing us so far."

"You wouldn't want to give him a big head, now would you?" O'Sullivan said. But before the priest could retort, he turned to Dónal, and said, "All right, then. You've done your part and you can wait here if you want. It's time for the holy Father and myself to do our bit." Hefting the spade then, he said, "Shall we, Father?"

"Good Lord, man, you don't mean to bury them here, do you?" Father Fitzgerald demanded, as though seeing the spade for the first time.

"Of course, I do. What did you think, that I was going to carry them all the way back to Killaconenagh? Anyway, this is as good a place as any. They're *dead* after all, for Christ's sake!"

"Eóghan, what are you thinking, man? We can't bury them in unconsecrated ground, and under a pagan idol, no less! I mean, have you no decency?"

To Dónal's surprise, his father actually laughed. "Whatever else may be said of you, good Father Fitzgerald, surely, no one can fault your devotion to the letter of the law! But see here now. Those people are dead and their souls already with Christ, so what difference does it make? Sure, that's a pagan idol, but it was a holy thing to the ancients who built it, and they did so only out of ignorance of God and not in His despite. And as for it not being consecrated, well, Father, I beg to differ, for indeed, Ireland is nothing but consecrated ground, all made holy by the communion She has taken from the bodies and blood of our martyrs, the uncounted legions who've died defending the true faith! Ireland is the Holy Ground, consecrated by the suffering of our people, and no decree of man can make it better. And anyway, Father, would you dishonor those poor people by denying them their dying wish?"

"Their dying wish, Eóghan? And just how are we to know what that might be?"

"Read the signs. After starving in a land of plenty, they used their dying breaths to crawl into that hole and hide so no one would dump their bones into that abomination of the Famine Grave. So knowing that, in the end, all they wanted was their own bit of the Holy Ground to rest in together, would you do them a final injustice, simply because the Pope has put his seal of approval on one bit of dirt but not another?

"No," O'Sullivan said softly, seeing resignation in the priest's eyes. "I knew you wouldn't. Because whatever else I might think of you, James Fitzgerald, I do know you to be a man of compassion."

"Yes, you're right. Against my better judgment and the law of the Church, I wouldn't have you bury them in the Famine Grave." Then he smiled at O'Sullivan in a curious sort of way, as if he were a puzzle with one piece missing, without which none of it made any sense. "Sometimes, I think there might be hope for you yet, Eóghan O'Sullivan."

"Hope?" O'Sullivan retorted, his eyes suddenly narrow and angry. "Hope for what, that I'll suddenly wake up one day and see the error of my ways?"

"Yes, more or less."

"Yes, and Jesus might come back someday, too, or so they say. But I wouldn't wait up nights, if I were you."

Then O'Sullivan turned his back and walked away, leaving the priest to follow as he could.

Dónal watched them until they reached the gorse, then sat down with his back to the boundary wall, not wishing to see any more. Tilting his head back to look at the sky, he noticed it was becoming overcast, with the freshening wind pushing dark clouds in from the sea, the signs of an imminent summer storm. Soon the land was all in shadow and the wind blowing hard and chill, making him shiver and wrap himself into a tight little ball to keep warm. The horse was getting skittish, too, stamping and blowing, seeming to wish the men would hurry up as much as Dónal did. Seeing a flash of lightning in the distance, he turned to look over the wall, and was relieved to find Father Fitzgerald approaching.

"Up with you, boy," the man called. "We're finished now, and have only to say the prayers before we're off." But when Dónal didn't respond, he held out his hand. "They're all covered over with a cairn and there's nothing to frighten you anymore. So come and pay your respects."

Though not reassured, Dónal took the old man's hand and scrambled over the wall, and together they walked back toward the stones.

"We'd best be getting on with it, if we know what's good for us," O'Sullivan called as they approached. "There's a gale coming or I'm a Tinker!"

"All right, Eóghan, I see it," the priest said, though even so, he hesitated. "Ah me, but what should I say? I don't know anything about them, not even their names."

"How about the Twenty-third Psalm, Father?" Dónal asked. "It's my favorite, and it's short enough, too."

"And a child shall lead them," the priest said, nodding in agreement. Turning back to the grave, he began, "The Lord is my shepherd, I shall not want . . ." shouting now to make himself heard over the wind and thunder.

"It's not much but it'll have to do, if we don't want to end up with them!" he said when finished, turning toward the road without waiting for an answer.

"Come along, Dónal," O'Sullivan said, slinging his spade over his shoulder and following after.

Despite the weather and his fear of the place, Dónal couldn't help but linger a moment, to think of the little family buried under the stones and try to grieve for them as he knew he should. Yet he couldn't, some instinct telling him that they were better off dead than wandering the roads, stalked by The Hunger and The Fever and The English. For indeed, they were together now and happy, sitting warm and dry by the hearth of God, protected for all eternity from the hurts of the world.

A tear did fall from his eye then, though not for them, but for himself and all those left behind to suffer. When would their turn come to be happy?

Long before they reached Cahernageeha, the rain was falling in sheets, pelting them like pebbles and soaking them through, while lightning flashed overhead and thunder rolled through the hills. O'Sullivan was driving them now, having swapped Dónal for the reins when the priest's spectacles became hopelessly smeared, and he pushed the horse as fast as it could go, snapping the whip and shouting encouragement, seemingly oblivious to the trap's fearful bouncing and yawing. But though he could feel the old man's anxiety in the way he gripped him, Dónal felt no fear himself, for he could see that his father was in control, his focused eyes and steady hands guiding them as surely as if out for a Sunday jaunt. And what a strange feeling it was, to be so comforted by his presence, secure in the knowledge that he would keep him safe though all the world collapsed around them. It was almost as good as sitting in his lap and feeling his strong arms around him, and if it would but continue, he didn't care if they ever got home.

Yet Father Fitzgerald didn't share his confidence and let his displeasure be known. "Eóghan, for the love of God, man," he shouted over the thunder, "slow down before you kill us!"

"Better that than scorched by lightning!"

"Well, maybe if you'd come to Mass a little more often, it wouldn't be such a worry to you!"

"Oh, bugger off with you! If I wanted someone to nag me, I'd get married again!"

"Not that any woman of sound mind and two good eyes would have you!" Father Fitzgerald retorted, laughing in spite of himself. "But come now, Eóghan, slow down a bit. Even if you don't kill us, you're going to break an axle, in which case I'll have to stay with you till you fix it, and I know you don't want that!"

"Yes, Father, and my congratulations to you!" O'Sullivan said, reining back slightly. "You finally found something that puts the fear of God into me!"

"Well, it's good to know that something in this world does. I was beginning to believe that you're a man who truly fears nothing, not even the eternal wrath of God."

"Oh, I have my fears all right, as does any man with half a brain," O'Sullivan admitted, with a candor that surprised everyone. "But that isn't one of them."

"Ah, well, I suppose there's no hope for you after all. And a pity it is, too, for a man of your potential."

Though O'Sullivan shot him a questioning glance, Father Fitzgerald said nothing more, and they bounced along in silence after that, until finally the ancient gray walls of Cahernageeha emerged from the gray curtain of rain ahead. O'Sullivan guided the horse through the gap in the wall and pulled him to a stop just by the front door. Grabbing Dónal, he hopped down and hurried into the cottage, leaving Father Fitzgerald to fend for himself.

"What about my horse?" the priest called.

"I'll take care of him in a minute!" O'Sullivan shouted back. "Just get yourself inside!"

After setting Dónal down by the hearth and telling him to get undressed and wrap his blanket around him, O'Sullivan stoked up the fire. "Here, Father, give me your cassock and I'll–" But his words turned into a startling roar of laughter.

Following his eyes, Dónal saw Father Fitzgerald standing in a puddle of water, dripping and steaming like a drowned rat, his shapeless old hat drooping over his ears and onto his spectacles. It was an altogether undignified look for a priest and, despite his wariness of offending him, Dónal couldn't help but join his father, the merriment of one feeding the other like food to their famished souls. And indeed, Dónal wasn't laughing at the old priest, but for the joy of sharing it with his father, a connection they'd never had before. Feeling his son's eyes upon him, O'Sullivan winked, the simple gesture of approval filling Dónal with warmth and happiness. And so he laughed, and his father laughed with him.

For his part, Father Fitzgerald sensed that there was more going on than met the eye, and so he left them to it, even finding a bit of mirth himself in their shared happiness. To be sure, it warmed his heart to see big Eóghan in a good mood for a change. What a different man he was with a smile on his face, barely resembling the *Eóghan an Sasanach* of local repute. Perhaps his heart was lightened by the good deed he'd done, or perhaps he was just tired of frowning. But whatever it was, the priest knew it wouldn't last, that it would be buried forever beneath what he had to tell.

"I must be a comic sight, indeed," he said, gently breaking into their moment, "if you two would risk the wrath of a priest to indulge your humor. But if you're quite finished poking fun at an old man, Eóghan, perhaps you'll see to my poor horse. He's still in the storm, and I'd like to get him out of it."

"Sure, Father, I'll put him in the shed. While I'm at it, why don't you hang your cassock by the fire and wrap yourself in my blanket. I'll be back in two shakes of a lamb's tail."

Upon returning, O'Sullivan found Dónal warming himself by the fire, and Father Fitzgerald gazing through the open window toward the *clochán* of ruined cottages.

"I've seen it so many times in my life," the priest said, sighing and shaking of his head, "but each time it hurts like the first, so that I think I'll never get used to it."

"That's what you get for being compassionate," O'Sullivan said. "As for me, I've outgrown that particular sensibility, because I've seen the trouble it can cause." Then his eyes went far away and his voiced dropped to barely more than a whisper. "If only I could make Eóghan see it so . . ."

"Ah, yes, young Eóghan," Father Fitzgerald sighed. "It's about him that I wanted to see you. I have news, Eóghan, and I'm afraid it's not good."

At those words, Dónal looked up in dread, fearing the worst, though his father just took it in stride.

"Yes, I thought as much," O'Sullivan said. "I heard about the so-called rising in Ballingarry, that it was a farce and a failure before it even began. So Eóghan has been arrested, is that what you've come to tell me? I tried to warn him, of course, but he wouldn't listen. Indeed, he's as stiff-necked as a dead Orangeman, though where he gets it is beyond me!"

"Ah, no, Eóghan," the priest sighed, looking uncomfortable. "I'm afraid it's a bit more complicated than that. But come sit by the fire with me so I can tell it properly."

Noting his demeanor then, O'Sullivan's face went suddenly gray. Slowly, and as though in a dream, he followed the man to the fire and sat facing him, with Dónal between them on the hearth.

"So, Father Fitzgerald," he asked when the priest seemed hesitant, "what news have you, and how did you come by it when I've heard nothing?"

"To answer the last first, I have news because I recently succored a man who was in the rising. Of course, it went against the orders of my bishop, but damn it all, the good Catholics of this country have suffered enough, and it's time that something be done about it! And even though they failed, at least those lads tried, and so to shelter one of them for a few days seemed the least I could do myself. After all, I've been Irish far longer than I've been a priest!"

Pausing then, he looked at O'Sullivan sheepishly, their roles as confessor and supplicant seemingly reversed for the moment. But if he was moved by it, O'Sullivan gave no sign. "Go on," he said simply, as cold and distant as he'd been warm and present a few moments earlier.

But Father Fitzgerald hesitated again, looking at the floor as if gathering his thoughts. "No, Eóghan, your son wasn't arrested. Nor was he anywhere near Ballingarry, in fact. Rather, he was above in the County Limerick with one of the Young Ireland leaders, a Dublin man named

Richard O'Gorman, helping him prepare their so-called Confederate Clubs for a rising after the harvest. But then the government suspended *habeas corpus* and ordered the arrest of all the leaders and, when they heard of it, O'Gorman and his men set out into the countryside to raise the people. Apparently they had some success at it, too, for they gathered a large following and laid siege to the village of Abbeyfeale, and even succeeded in seizing the Limerick and Tralee mail along with the guards' muskets, before their luck ran out. In the meantime, O'Gorman rode off toward Newcastle West with your son and a small group of others, hoping to raise that part of Limerick as well. But upon hearing the news of Ballingarry, O'Gorman returned to Abbeyfeale, leaving young Eóghan and three others at a crossroad tavern as lookouts.

"And from there, Eóghan, I'm afraid the news goes from bad to worse. For apparently the landlord was an ardent loyalist and, while the lads were at their tea, sneaked out to tip off the authorities. And before they knew anything was amiss, a troop of Redcoats came marching up and surrounded them. Of course, they were ordered to drop their arms and come out at once, though being young and foolish, it would seem, they refused, and even made matters worse by wounding one of the soldiers with the one musket they had. After that, they were given no second chance to surrender, and indeed the soldiers kept up such a hail of gunfire that they couldn't even if they'd wanted. And even when a fire started in the tavern, they didn't let up, but kept the boys trapped inside until the roof collapsed and they were all burned beyond recognition."

Father Fitzgerald fell silent then, unable to say the words that were in all their minds.

"Is it known for certain that Eóghan was there?" O'Sullivan asked, in a distant voice that came from the Darkness within him.

"It seems beyond doubt, Eóghan. No one came out after the soldiers arrived, and the landlord stated without equivocation that only the four rebel men were there when he left, and four bodies were indeed found in the wreckage."

"So my son is dead, is that what you're telling me, that my Eóghan is dead?"

"I'm afraid so, Eóghan. And while it may be of little comfort to you just now, I want you to know that I'm as saddened by it as any sadness I've ever known. Your Eóghan was such a fine young man, a bright ray of hope for the future–"

But O'Sullivan was no longer listening to him, as he sat with his eyes closed and his fists clenched, the final loss of hope too much for him to bear.

"Stop," he said softly, though seeming not to hear, the priest rattled on. "Stop!" he said again. And again, louder, "Stop!"

And suddenly he had Father Fitzgerald by the throat, the look in his eyes turning the old man's face white with terror.

"*STOP!*" O'Sullivan screamed. "*STOP! STOP, for the love of God, STOP!*" But then his rage collapsed into a deeper, more primal emotion. "Can't you just stop?" he begged, his voice breaking as the grief poured out.

And then, unable to cope any longer, he bolted from the cottage into the driving rain, leaving Dónal to bear it alone.

chapter 5

Cahernageeha

FROM THE DAY OF EÓGHAN'S DEPARTURE, Dónal had known in his heart that he wouldn't see him again, and so Father Fitzgerald's news came as no surprise to him. Still, there were tears of grief in his eyes, though not so much for the news or even for Eóghan, as for himself and the connection he'd made and lost with his father. For in just that brief moment, as they'd shared a laugh at the comic appearance of an old priest, the man had opened his heart to him, giving him hope that there might be a place for him there after all. But then the terrible news had brought his father's world tumbling down around him and unless he could rise phoenixlike from the ashes, Dónal knew there'd never be a place in his heart for him. So he huddled by the fire and wept in despair for his father's love.

But then a groan from Father Fitzgerald brought him out of it. "Are you all right, Father?" he asked thickly, finding the old man shaken and stunned. "Da didn't mean to hurt you. He's just mad with sadness right now. So please don't do anything to him. He's not a bad man inside himself."

The words were simple really, just those of a child, and yet the priest could only wonder at the depth and subtlety of the boy's perception and empathy. Then he felt the intensity of Dónal's Spring-green eyes boring into him as though trying to see into his very soul, making him distinctly uncomfortable for all the difference in their ages.

"Yes, I'm all right, Dónal," he said softly, averting his gaze, "and no, I won't do anything to your Da. You're right about him being mad with grief, and so I forgive him, though I must say it's been a long time since I've been treated quite so roughly. But he does want looking after, now doesn't he? Lord only knows where he's off to in this devilish storm."

"He's been drinking a lot since Eóghan went away," Dónal said, his eyes clouded with worry. "I don't know where he does it, but I hope that's where he's gone. It might help him forget for a while."

Again the priest's eyes shot to him in wonder, knowing that he'd looked inside his father's soul and felt the torment there. "Just how old are you anyway, Dónal?"

"I'm seven-going-on-eight, Father," Dónal replied, suddenly child-like again.

"Indeed? Then tell me, if you will, just how it is that a child of your tender age understands so much of the feelings of other people?"

"I don't know Father. I just do, I guess."

"Well, you really are a remarkable boy for it, and your father must be very proud of you."

"No, he isn't proud of me, Father," Dónal said, smiling sadly before turning away.

As he watched him tend the fire, Father Fitzgerald knew he was right, seeing then that his father, a prideful, hard-headed man, was stupid as well, and that his son was paying for it. Yet for all that he wished to comfort the boy, he found nothing to say. Sighing then, he shook his head. With so much sorrow in the world, and so little he could do about it, was it any wonder that his calling had driven him to the drink?

But then a flash of lightning jolted him from distraction and, as thunder shook the cottage, he pulled the blanket around his shoulders and went to the door. "The storm hasn't let up at all, and the sky is as black as the Earl of Hell. I hope your Da finds himself a safe place to shelter in."

"I'll go look for him when it stops raining," Dónal said from the hearth.

"That's awfully brave of you, boy," Father Fitzgerald said, as he closed the door and returned to the fire. "But from the looks of the sky, I don't think you'll be going anywhere before nightfall, and boys of seven-going-on-eight shouldn't be wandering around all alone in the darkness."

"No, I'm afraid of the dark, anyway. I wish I wasn't so small and weak! I wish I could just grow up and be a man all at once. Then I wouldn't be afraid of anything."

"You know, Dónal, there's an old saying about that. *Be careful what you wish for,* it says, *for you just might get it.*" Seeing the question in the boy's eyes, he smiled gently and ruffled his hair. "You'll grow up soon enough, and when you do, you'll be surprised that it happened so quickly. So cherish your childhood while it's in you, because it's the time of life when the troubles of the world touch you the least."

"But being a child didn't keep The Hunger from that little girl we buried, Father. And why is the world so full of troubles, anyway? Why are people so mean? If we were just nicer to each other, wouldn't the troubles all go away?"

"Out of the mouths of babes," the old priest muttered, shaking his head in wonder. "There is great wisdom in what you say, Dónal, for isn't that the true message of Christ, after all, to love our fellows as we would love ourselves? And though it may not cure all the ills of the world, surely it would go a long way. But we don't all live that way, sadly enough, and I have to admit that it's hard to live by the Word when you see all your fellows ignoring it. 'What difference does it make?' you might think. 'If I don't do it someone else will!' But don't you see how wrong that kind of thinking is? For the actions of one man can make a difference in the world, if he but has the moral courage to stand up for what's right, even if he's the only one. Does that make any sense to you, Dónal? Do you understand what I mean by 'moral courage'?"

"Does it mean the kind of courage that Eóghan had when he went off to fight the English even though he knew he couldn't win?"

"Yes, that's exactly what it means," Father Fitzgerald said.

Dónal nodded and turned away, and the priest could feel from the hunch of his shoulders that he didn't want to talk anymore, his grief being too raw and present perhaps. And so they sat in silence for a while, staring at the fire, each alone with his thoughts, though taking comfort from the presence of the other.

When suppertime came, the storm was still raging, and they had to make do with the few small potatoes in the house, which was barely enough for Dónal much less the two of them. Afterward they returned to the fire until, hypnotized by the dancing flames and sedative warmth, their eyes became heavy and their heads began to droop.

"I don't think the rain is going to stop soon, Father," Dónal said. "So why don't you sleep here tonight? You can have Da's bed."

"Yes, Dónal, I think that's a good idea," the old man agreed, stifling a yawn. "Why don't we say our prayers, and be off to bed then?"

"All right, Father." Dónal clasped his hands before him and bowed his head.

"Is there anything special you'd like to pray for tonight?"

"Yes, Father. I'd like to pray for Eóghan's soul, and for my father's, too."

"All right, Dónal, I'll do that," the priest agreed, wondering if the child would ever cease to amaze him.

When it was done, they went to their separate beds and, though Dónal went right to sleep, Father Fitzgerald lay awake for a time watching him, thinking that the beauty that was in him made the rest of it almost bearable.

⚬Ɫ𝕸Ɫⵔ

In the morning they woke to find the storm ended but the land blanketed with dense fog and a wet, penetrating chill like the frigid touch of Death.

"Suicide weather," Father Fitzgerald remarked, looking out the door. "It's as thick as pea soup and without a trace of wind in it, which is odd enough in itself, I'd say, *unnatural* even. I just hope it's not a harbinger of worse to come.

"Ah well. The day will bring what it will and worry has never yet stopped it from coming. But fog or not, I think I'll try for home now. My housekeeper will be worried that I didn't come home last night, and I'd not have her send the peelers to look for me. A man could get hurt in weather like this, and I'd not have it on my conscience.

"And perhaps you should come with me, Dónal, at least till your father turns up. We can leave him a note, if you like, to let him know where you are."

"No, Father. I want to stay here and look for Da. But don't worry for me. I spend most of my time alone now, and I can look after myself."

"All right, then, suit yourself. But mind what I said about getting hurt and don't go out till the fog clears. There's no point in it, anyway; you'd never find him in this stuff. But promise me now, or I'll insist that you come with me."

"All right, Father, I promise."

"Good man," Father Fitzgerald said, and smiled. "Then I'll be off with myself. But I'm glad I was able to spend this time with you, Dónal. You're a fine boy and good and thoughtful company. Take care of yourself, and start coming to Mass again!"

"Yes, Father," Dónal said, bowing his head meekly.

The old man turned to go then, though he hesitated at the threshold. "There's a shebeen I know of where you might find your Da, or at least hear news of him. It's hidden in the rocks on the slope of Guala just below the road. Seán Ahern is the man to ask for. But don't try for it till the fog clears. Understand?"

"Yes, Father."

"Good man," Father Fitzgerald repeated. Then he closed the door behind him, leaving Dónal entombed in the fog.

ᏀᎢᎢᏞᎾ

Slowly, the day wore itself away, the time passing with glacial indolence, it seemed, as the fog sat heavily upon the land and Dónal's spirits. Through most of it he huddled by the fire, going out only to retrieve some potatoes for his breakfast and a bit of turf from the shed, the back of his neck tingling and his heart pounding from fear the trinity of Terrors might be lurking about. But there was nothing, just the dead of the fog, the only sounds his own footsteps and the slow drip of dew from the roof and tree branches. After that he had nothing to do other than brood on Eóghan and the madness of his father, and nothing to keep him company but his loneliness. So the day dragged on interminably, till he was exhausted from doing nothing, worn out with boredom's mindless reverie, wishing night would fall so he could drop the pretense of staying awake just because the sun was shining somewhere above the fog.

When suppertime finally came, he left the cottage again to get more potatoes, having eaten all he'd gathered in the morning. But as he turned the corner, the stench of decay hit him with the force of a runaway coach, and his heart pounded as he hurried through the fog to the lazy beds. What he saw there sickened him with fear and loathing, for the plants were all rotten and putrid, their leaves spotted and slimy where they'd been green and healthy just that very morning. Nor were the potatoes themselves any better he found, being brown and corklike inside, unfit even for maggots.

So the blight had returned under the cover of fog, sneaking in like a thief in the night to steal away the entire crop, just as it had done the previous three summers. But Mam and Eóghan were still alive then, and his father had provided for them with his magic bag. Now they were gone and the man consumed with madness and the drink, and Dónal was all alone with nothing to eat, and no idea when or even if his father would come home.

At that, panic took him and he ran back to the cottage door, his empty stomach gnawing at him painfully, his hunger made urgent by fear. But though the cottage seemed safe and warm, he couldn't bear the thought of spending another second in it, the Terrors lurking in the fog paling in the face of loneliness and hunger. He had to find his father *now*, or go mad with fear.

Without a second thought, he ran from the door into the gathering dusk, going as fast as he dared along the boreen toward Guala, making for the shebeen of Seán Ahern. The darkness grew ever deeper as he went, and soon he could see nothing around him, not even the stone walls bordering the boreen, having only its rutted track to guide him. And it was quiet, too, and cool as a crypt, the sound of his footsteps and even his breath ringing like thunder in his ears, so loud that they couldn't help but draw the three Terrors down upon him. But though his fear of them grew with each forward step, his fear of hunger and loneliness was greater, driving him on into the darkness, fear ahead and fear behind, without and within, fear all-consuming.

Then the boreen suddenly ended at a junction and, knowing he'd reached the main road, his spirits lifted a little, for now his objective was not so far away, just up the road to the mountain shoulder. Yet it was further than he thought, having never been up Guala before, and the road was slippery and steep, so that his legs were soon burning with fatigue and he was puffing and sweating despite the chill. Indeed, so absorbed did he become with the effort of the climb that he forgot his hunger for the moment and even his fear. Nor did he notice that the fog was thinning until the road suddenly flattened out and, stopping to catch his breath, he found himself standing above a billowing sea of white that spread as far as he could see in all directions, with only the bare heads of the Slieve Miskish Mountains poking above it. And he was all alone with it, it seemed, the last person alive on Earth, standing on the roof of the world with only the stars above for company.

Still, being free of the fog buoyed his spirits and, turning to the west, he followed the road along the mountain shoulder, looking for any sign of a path leading away to the south. Finding nothing, he soon came to the western edge where the road plunged down again toward the village of Allihies in its seaside vale. It lay shrouded in fog, too, he saw, and with a sinking heart he turned east again, knowing there was nothing to do but go back the way he'd come and hope for a sign to point the way.

Yet even as he neared the eastern edge, something caught his eye away to the right, a thin wisp of smoke trailing up from the fog, the tell-tale sign of a whiskey still. Without pausing to consider, he turned from the road and headed toward it, picking his way slowly among tumbled boulders as the fog engulfed him in milky oblivion, leaving only the downward slope of the land to guide him. And soon he was completely lost, knowing neither the way forward nor the way back, groping along blindly, panic-stricken and hysterical, sure that each step would be his last.

But then he scrambled over a boulder and his bare feet landed on bare earth. Realizing that he was on a path, he followed its narrow track through the gorse and heather, hoping against hope that it would take him where he wanted to go. Suddenly he saw something up ahead, a reddish-gold light approaching in the fog, a candle perhaps, or a lantern.

"Da, is that you?" he called hopefully, stopping the light's advance.

"Who's there?" a voice demanded, though whether it was his father's or not Dónal couldn't tell.

"It's me, Dónal. Is that you, Da?"

But the voice didn't respond, though the light began to move again, coming slowly closer until it outlined the shape of a man, piercing the veil of fog like a ghost from the Otherworld. And when he saw his face, Dónal's hope indeed turned to horror. He turned and fled along the path, oblivious to the danger of rock and root and thorn, certain that one of the Terrors was after him. But then another light ahead brought him to a sudden stop, a narrow slit between two standing stones outlined in red like the doorjambs of Hell. Hazarding a backward glance, he saw the other light still approaching and plunged ahead, bursting through the opening and running headlong into a group of men on the other side.

"Here now," one of them said, scooping him up and holding him eye to eye with himself. "What are you after, you little rat? Don't you know better than to butt in where you're not wanted?"

But Dónal was too startled to answer, having gone from the frying pan into the fire, it seemed. For his captor was a giant of a man, if he was man indeed and not mountain troll, a tall standing shadow more massive even than his father, his broad face and squinty eyes giving him an unsavory look, evil even, that of a man who looked at his fellows as prey upon which to feed.

"I asked you a question, rat," the man persisted, shaking him hard, "and you'd better answer if you know what's good for you!"

"I'm just looking for my father," Dónal managed to squeak. "His name is Eóghan O'Sullivan. Have you seen him?"

"Eóghan the Englishman?" the man demanded, his face contorted with rage. "You're the son of Eóghan the Englishman? Why I ought to—"

But he didn't get to finish his threat, as another voice cut him off. "Leave him alone, Paddy," it boomed with authority. "If it's hate you have for the man, sure, it's no business of mine. But the boy has done you no harm and I'll not see him punished for the sins of the father. So put him down and go back to your drink. If it's mischief he's up to, I'll have the truth of it soon enough."

"Sure, Seán, whatever you say," Paddy said sarcastically, dropping Dónal roughly to the ground.

Spinning around then, Dónal saw that the speaker was the apparition from the fog, though he was no monster, surely, but a man, albeit with a monster's face. For his right cheek and lower forehead were a mass of angry scars, looking as though the skin had been melted and then smeared crudely back into place, especially around his right eye, its empty socket mercifully hidden by a black patch. Yet the rest of his face was completely normal, handsome even, with smooth pale skin and a brilliant blue eye that sparkled even in the firelight. And it was the look in that one eye that set Dónal at ease, his fear and anxiety melting away like snow under a warm spring sun.

"I'm Seán Ahern," the man said gently, kneeling so as to be eye to eye with him. "I'm sorry if I frightened you, coming out of the fog like that. Even after all these years, I forget the effect my face has on those who've not seen it before. But you have nothing to fear from me, young O'Sullivan, nor from these other fine fellows, so long as you're with me. So come sit by the fire and tell me what brings you here on such a night as this."

"I came to find my Da," Dónal said, "because the blight has come back and our potatoes are all rotten, and I'm scared and hungry and all alone."

To the men gathered there, it was the worst answer he could've given, and even at his young age, Dónal knew it. Yet Ahern took the terrible news in stride, his one eye not even blinking, though a buzz of agitation went up among the others, as the one called Paddy snatched Dónal up again and slapped him across the head.

"You watch your mouth, you little rat!" he snarled. "There was no blight in my fields when I came up here, and anyway, you wouldn't know it if it was growing out your arse. Why, I ought to wring your scrawny little neck for spreading such a rumor!"

But before he could make good on his threat, Ahern's shillelagh whistled through the air and landed sharply on his head, knocking him to the ground and Dónal with him. "I told you to leave him alone, Paddy O'Sullivan," he said, dropping his stick and pushing Dónal behind him. "Now get up and get out of here!" But when Paddy didn't move, he kicked him in the ribs. "I said, get up!"

"Jesus, Seán!" one of the others exclaimed, moving between them. "He meant no harm. It's just that we're all so afraid of the blight, we don't even want to hear the word!"

"Yes, well, I'm afraid of it, too!" Ahern retorted angrily. "But that's no reason to be violent to the children! And anyway, the boy is telling the truth and you all know it. So you'd best be getting home to see if there's anything to be saved. In any case, I'm closed for the night."

Turning his back on them then, he took Dónal by the arm and led him to the fire. "Sit down and warm yourself while I get you something to eat," he said gently.

As Ahern got the food, Dónal watched Paddy's friends pick him up and lead him away, relaxing only when they'd slipped between the standing stones. Letting his eyes stray to his surroundings then, he saw that he was in a little dell formed of boulders and the mountainside, the small spring-fed pool at the far end making it the perfect hiding place for an illicit whiskey still, though surely the ancients who'd placed the stones at its entrance had spirits of a different kind in mind. The still itself was balanced over the fire on a triangle of rocks, the raw whiskey dripping into a jug from a coiled metal tube as its unmistakable odor permeated the air.

"Here, you can have these," Ahern said, giving him a couple of potatoes. "But first, we should introduce ourselves properly, don't you think?

"I'm Seán Ahern," he said, extending his right arm.

But finding his sleeve pinned at the wrist, Dónal could only stare.

"Ah, me," Ahern sighed, regarding his nub in the firelight, "even after all these years, I still forget it's gone. You'd think the pain that's still in it would remind me.

"But here then, shake this one," he said, extending his left hand. "And I don't have to ask, because I already know that your name is Dónal, and that you came here looking for your father.

"Well, as you can see, he's not here now," Ahern said in response to Dónal's nod, "though he was earlier. But he said he was going home when he left. Are you sure you didn't pass him on the way? You could easily have missed him in the fog, you know."

"No, I'm sure," Dónal replied, his voice small and meek, his weariness and the fog lending a dreamlike quality.

"Well, maybe he went the other way, down the main road by Dunboy and up the boreen past Killaconenagh, though why he would take the long way in this fog is beyond me. But then he's mad with grief, and was more than a little drunk when he left."

"He's been drinking a lot lately."

"I know, because he's been getting it from me, and I've been giving it to him in the hope that it would dull the pain that's in him. Otherwise, I'm afraid his grief for young Eóghan might be the death of him."

"He's not grieving for Eóghan, but for himself."

Ahern looked at Dónal curiously then, thinking it a perceptive observation for a child. "Yes, Dónal, you're probably right, though in this case, I think perhaps it's one and the same. You see, I know your

Da pretty well; indeed, I'm his only friend in all the world. And I knew young Eóghan, too, and how proud he was of him and the fact that they were so much alike. Or so he thought, anyway, for other than their looks and perhaps their stubbornness, I don't think they were alike at all. But your Da was blind to it, so intent was he on living your brother's life for him. And that's why it came as such a shock when he realized that young Eóghan was his own man and would follow his own path in life, no matter what he thought of it. And now he's suffering for it, tearing himself apart for not realizing it sooner, and so perhaps saving Eóghan's life. But then, we all suffer sooner or later for what we love too much in ourselves."

"It wouldn't have made any difference. Eóghan would've gone anyway."

"Oh? And why would you say that?"

"Because that's just the way he was," Dónal replied, holding Ahern's gaze in his own, the man finding the source of his acuity in its intensity.

But unlike Father Fitzgerald, Seán Ahern was a man of grit, and he neither blinked nor looked away, just opened his soul to the boy's inspection, showing him with his one steady eye that he was trustworthy and true. And Dónal saw it, too, his intensity melting into a smile of friendship, which Ahern readily returned.

"If my Da really has only one friend, at least he picked a good one." Dónal said.

"Yes, he did at that," Ahern chuckled, flattered in spite of himself.

But then the smile was gone and Dónal's eyes were again probing and intent. "I didn't know Da had any friends. No one seems to like him, and people even call him names, like Eóghan the Englishman. Why is that, Mr. Ahern? He's not an Englishman."

"No, he isn't, that's true enough. But they don't mean it that way. They mean it as an insult, the lowest and worst they can think of, though few have ever dared to say it to his face."

"But why, Mr. Ahern? Why do they want to be mean to him?"

"Well, it wasn't always that way, Dónal. There was a time when he was our leader and everyone looked up to him."

"What happened, then? Did he change?"

"No, I don't think it's that he changed so much as that people began to see him for what he really is and didn't like what they saw."

"But why not, Mr. Ahern? I don't understand."

"Well, then let me see if I can explain it so you will. You see, Dónal, what your Da has that sets him apart from his fellows, that makes him different in their eyes, is ambition. Do you know what that word means, 'ambition'? It means that a person wants to *get* something or to *have* something or to *be* something very badly, so badly that he's willing to forsake everything and everyone else, and work himself practically to death in order to get it. And what your Da wanted, what was his ambition, was to be something better in life than a miner and a farmer, a man who toiled his days away for little or no gain just like his father before him and his before him, while leaving nothing to his own children but the same destiny. Now that's not so bad in itself, I'd say, because we'd all like to have a bit more in life, a bit more food, a bit more money, better clothes and a better house maybe, enough so that we don't always have to worry about where our next meal will come from, or whether our roof will leak in the winter and our children get sick from the cold. But your Da wanted even more than that, Dónal. He wanted to be like his ancient forefathers, who were great lords of wealth and power, and ruled over all of Béara till the English came and took it away from them. Indeed, he wanted to get it all back and be a great lord himself and raise his family back to where they once were. Yet after a while, he saw that he couldn't do it, no matter how he worked and sacrificed, not with the way things are for the Irish in Ireland. And it vexed him mightily, too, to know that no matter what he did, his life would be a waste and his family none the better for it.

"But then young Eóghan was born and he came up with a different scheme, which was to give up his ambition for himself and put it all on his son, so that maybe he could achieve what his father could not, or at least start the family on the way. So that became his ambition in life, to help young Eóghan raise himself up, and the first thing to do, he saw, was to get him a proper English education so he'd at least have the tools to get on in life. Indeed, he'd have even sent him to England for it, if he could've afforded it. As it was, and over the objection of Father Fitzgerald, who wanted him to go to a Church school and become a priest, he sent him to the National School in Castletownbere, where the instruction was in English and all about preparing the students for life in the English world, which is, after all, the world of the ruling class.

"And while that was suspect in itself, it was something more basic that got your Da into trouble with his fellows. You see, we Irish have always had a tradition of looking out for each other, of sharing what little we have so that everyone can survive and live as well as possible. 'Clannish' the English call us, though I'm not sure they really understand what they mean by it, since they don't understand us at all. But it's always been that way among us, even when we were free and had great lords of our own, Gaelic lords like your O'Sullivan ancestors. But your Da didn't want to share what was his. He wanted to keep it all so he could spend it on young Eóghan's schooling. So people began to say of him that he was greedy, that he had no concern for his neighbors and those less fortunate, and that he thought himself better than them, indeed, that he wanted to be like the English and lord it over his Irish fellows.

"Then to make matters worse, he got a job that other Irishmen couldn't get, working as an assistant to the mine captains for a high wage, while his fellows barely made anything at all. That was back in 1834, when the owners brought in Cornish miners from England to take over some of the work from the Irish. Your Da was one of those who was supposed to be replaced, but the mine manager, Captain John Reed, told the owners he needed him too badly and wanted him as his assistant. But even though Captain Reed ran the mines, that decision could only be made by John Puxley himself, and he came over from England to do so personally. Indeed, it was his last visit to Béara that anyone knows of. He even called your Da down to the Big House to meet with him, though what happened there, neither I nor anyone else knows, for he's never breathed a word of it. Yet I could see that it had galled him mightily, to have to cool his heels like a serving man in the very place from which his ancestors once ruled over all of Béara. In any case, he was a changed man afterward, and he became distant and aloof, angry and sullen, and it was then that his ambition became the driving force of his life and blinded him to all else.

"But the people didn't know any of that. All they knew was that he had a better job than they did and made more money, and that though he had great influence with the management, he never used it to help his fellows get better wages and working conditions, even when they went on strike for it.

"So that's when they began to call him Eóghan the Englishman, because it seemed that he'd sold his soul to the English so he could rise up and be like them, and leave his fellows stuck where they were. And though he pretends not to care, I know their scorn has been hard on him, because he's a man of vision and knows that his ambition would benefit all the Irish sooner or later, for it would give us a leader, a man of intelligence and ability, a man we desperately need if ever we're to break these chains of bondage that are upon us.

"But now young Eóghan is dead, and your Da thinks all his suffering and sacrifice were in vain, that he's wasted his life on a dream that won't ever come true. So that's why the madness is upon him, Dónal, and why he grieves for himself. His dream is dead, and he thinks he may as well be dead, too, because in the heel of the hunt, his life has been a waste after all. So do you understand him a little better now?"

"No, I don't, Mr. Ahern," Dónal said, tears starting in his eyes, "because he still has me! I would help him with his dream, if he would let me."

Ahern sighed, his heart filled with empathy but knowing the boy spoke of that which he did not know. "I've tried to tell him that, Dónal, that he needs to put his grief behind him and get on with being a father to you. But he's not ready to hear it yet. His loss is still too raw and painful. But he'll come to his senses soon enough. He's a good man in his heart, and a strong one, too, and he'll remember his love for you."

"He doesn't love me, Mr. Ahern," Dónal said, his voice hard and certain. "But I want him to. I'd do anything to get him to love me like he loved Eóghan."

"No, Dónal, you're wrong," Ahern said, though he wasn't so sure himself. "He does love you and, in the heel of the hunt, he'll remember it."

"I hope so."

"Of course he will. Like I said, he's my friend and I know him pretty well."

"But why is that, Mr. Ahern? Why are you his friend when no one else is?"

"Ah, me, but you are the one for questions, aren't you?"

Ahern paused then, as he considered his answer, and whether or not he wanted to give it. Then he sighed and gazed into the fire, his one eye suddenly far away as he took himself back in place and time, the better to see those distant events with the two eyes he'd had then.

"You see, Dónal," he began without preamble, his voice distant and hollow, "I was once a miner, too, before misfortune came upon me. It happened one day in the Mountain Mine, a thousand feet below the surface, when we were blasting out the ore. I set the charge just as always, with enough fuse to give me plenty of time to get away. Yet something went wrong when I lit it, the fuse was bad or some powder had spilled, I still don't know. But in any case, the charge exploded in my face, and the next thing I knew I was lying on my back in darkness, with my ears ringing and a blinding glare in my head, and my . . . my . . ."

Ahern paused and closed his eye, feeling the pain that was in him then, and in him ever since. "And my face was on fire. I haven't the words to describe the pain of flesh burning off your body, melting away like wax from a candle. But it's nothing, a mere trifle, compared to the pain of living with the memory of what you once were, knowing that nothing remains but scarred bits and pieces, the flotsam and jetsam of what was once a man."

Opening his eye, he smiled sadly. "You may not believe it, but I was handsome before it happened. Indeed, I was known far and wide as 'the handsome Ahern,' and I was as vain of my looks as any woman. But it seems almost funny to look back on now, for you never think something like this will happen to you. No, these things are supposed to happen to other people, those less lucky or prudent, or who've somehow made themselves deserving of it. But then one day misfortune strikes, with no rhyme or reason that you can see, and just like that, your life is changed forever. One second you're well and whole and going about your business, and the next you're a mangled pile of flesh, begging God to let you go back just that one second in time so you can change it and make the hurt go away. But He won't, of course, and that's what makes it so tragic. And so goddamned comical. But as I said, we all suffer sooner or later for what we love too much in ourselves.

"Anyway, there I was, with my face on fire and my hand missing, sure that I'd died and gone to Hell. But then your Da was with me, putting out the fire and binding up my arm, telling me everything would be all right and that he'd get me out of there and to a doctor. Then he lifted me up and carried me to the ladders, which at that time was the only way in and out for the miners. A thousand feet up they stretched, many of them with broken or missing rungs, a torturous climb even for a young man, strong and healthy, and with just his own weight to carry. But your Da didn't even hesitate. He just tied me onto his back and started, going all the way without stopping, up and up and up, the ropes cutting into his shoulders as my dead weight pulled against him. Nor did he stop when we got to the top, but carried me all the way to the surgeon's house in Allihies, before going to find my wife.

"And that, Dónal, is why I'm friends with your Da, because he saved my life, and no matter what the rest of the world thinks of him, he's a hero to me. Sure, he is."

There was a silence then, as they regarded each other thoughtfully, Dónal seeing a side of his father he'd not known before, and Ahern watching the emotions play across his face as he digested it. Nor was it easy for Dónal to reconcile, the abusive, sometimes violent father and the selfless hero, *Eóghan an Sasanach* and the good Samaritan who'd buried the hapless family in the stone circle, not to mention the ingenuous man with whom he'd shared a laugh at poor Father Fitzgerald. They all chased each other in circles till his head was spinning with them, and still he was no closer to the answer he sought – why his father didn't love him.

Giving it up, he sighed and looked at Ahern. "I should go now, Mr. Ahern. I need to find my Da and tell him about the blight. Can you show me the way back to the road?"

"There's no point in it, Dónal. Either your Da went home the other way and knows about the blight already, or he's somewhere else and we'll never find him in the fog. So we may as well stay here where it's safe and warm till the fog lifts or morning comes. Why don't you eat your supper while I tend to my still? Then we'll talk some more, if you like."

After finishing their respective tasks, they did talk more and of many things, Dónal being indeed the one for questions and Ahern equally the one for answers, as he sat by the fire like the bards of old and painted pictures with his words. Eventually, of course, they came to the subject of mining, on which Ahern spoke at length, finding in Dónal an apt and interested audience. After explaining the various terms and kinds of work and equipment involved, he came to the miners themselves, telling him that there were basically two kinds: "developers" and "tributers," the former working in teams to open the shafts and levels so the latter could have air to breathe and space to work. As for the developers, the most important aspect of their work was making sure the levels followed the veins; otherwise the tributers wouldn't be able to dig out the ore.

"And that's just what your Da is so good at," he said, "knowing which way the vein will go and opening the levels in the right direction to follow it. Indeed, his skill is so legendary that men say he can smell the copper in the stone. Even Captain Reed asks him for advice, and when in doubt never makes a decision till he's been consulted, which is saying a lot since John Reed has been a miner for almost fifty years."

Then Ahern turned to the tributers, explaining the work they did, and how their pay was based on the amount of ore they dug and how much copper it contained, and that they had to agree to dig in a certain place and to bring up a certain amount of ore with a certain amount of copper in it for a certain price, all before they actually did any of the work and without knowing for sure whether there was any copper at all where they agreed to dig. Such an agreement was called a "bargain," he said, and since the tributers had to buy all their tools and supplies from the Company Shop, they could actually end up owing the Company money if they took a bad bargain, leaving them with none to buy food or clothing or pay the rent. Of course, since even the best miners guessed wrong at times, all the tributers had gone into debt to the Company at one time or another, and once in, most of them never got out.

Then, too, there was the gombeen man to worry about, the money lender who preyed upon the foolish and the desperate. "Nothing to worry about," he'd say with a nod and a wink. "I'll just put you down in the book and we'll make a little loan of it, with just the bit of interest for my trouble, of course. Just make your mark there and it's all taken care of." But he was even worse than the Company Shop, for he often evicted those who couldn't repay him and re-leased their land to those who could, usually grabbers or strong farmers. Though Dónal didn't know much about money, he understood that the gombeen man was to be avoided like the plague, much like the boodyman with whom that old Aunt Bríd had often threatened him, an apparition named "Cromwell" that came in the night to take bad children away in his bag.

But it was a terrible thing altogether, Ahern said, coming back to the subject, that a man could labor from dawn till dusk in the worst conditions imaginable, and in the tail of the day, have nothing to show for it but debt. Yet it worked out well for the owners since, when all the accounts were totted up, it often cost them virtually nothing to bring out the ore. It wasn't fair, he acknowledged, but because there were plenty of people willing to take their places at even a starvation wage, and more so, because only mine employees could buy cheap food from the Company Shop, the people dared not risk their jobs by complaining, and so the English owners grew rich and fat while the Irish starved. So in many respects, the Irish were like slaves without masters, enslaved to their jobs but having no masters to feed and clothe and house them, leaving them free to starve and freeze and sicken on their own.

In some ways, Ahern said, they'd even come full circle back to the ancient times, becoming like the *Fir Bolg*, a people who'd inhabited Ireland before the coming of the Gael. "The Men of the Bags" the name meant, and they were so-called because, before migrating to Ireland, they'd been enslaved in Greece and forced to carry soil in bags to build fertile fields for their masters. And now here were the Irish centuries later, reduced to digging copper from the ground and loading it into linen bags for shipment to England. He even held up one of the bags to illustrate, and Dónal saw that it was identical to his father's.

"My Da has a bag like that," he said. "But he carries food in it, not copper."

"Yes, Dónal, I know, and don't you see that's my very point? Hunger is a powerful weapon for the Berehaven Mining Company, because it keeps the Irish enslaved to their jobs, and these bags are a symbol of it, just as they were to the *Fir Bolg*. But then that's the way of the world, isn't it? The strong rule and the weak suffer, and it's been that way ever since Adam ate the apple.

"But you know, Dónal, what really makes no sense is that the strong who oppress us usually aren't evil men in themselves. Take our John Puxley, for instance. He's no more evil than you or me, I'd say, unless he's changed a great deal since I saw him last. He's just a product of the times we live in, and if he didn't oppress us, someone else surely would."

"Who is he, Mr. Ahern?" Dónal asked. "Is he the Englishman that lives in the Big House?"

"Well, yes and no, Dónal. It's true that he owns the Big House, though he doesn't actually live in it. In fact, it's been fourteen years since he's even set foot in it."

"Then why would he have it if he doesn't want to live in it?"

"That's another long one in the telling, Dónal. But the short of it is that the Big House is really more of a symbol than a home, anyway. It's a symbol of the wealth and power of the British Empire, and its purpose is to remind us of who is weak and who is strong. It's always there doing its job, too, even if its owner is absent. Indeed, that so many of the big landlords are absent these days is one reason things have gotten so bad for us, because it's easier to ignore suffering if you don't have to see it with your own eyes. And it runs to the very heart of our troubles with the English, which is the grievance of the land, and until something is done about it, there'll never be any justice for the poor people of Ireland. But since nothing will ever be done as long as the English rule us from London, it seems to me that Home Rule is the only real answer to the problem.

"And it was Home Rule that your brother's group, the Young Ireland, was after. I know the grievance of the land was near and dear to Eóghan's heart, and that he was much influenced in that by a friend of his named John Mitchel. I've read some of Mitchel's writings myself, and those of James Fintan Lawlor, too, and I think they're right in saying that the land is an issue that could unite us like never before. But then, the road to Home Rule is long and with many turns, and we must walk it in darkness with no one to lead us. Alas for O'Neill and the Flight of the Earls!

"But that's another story entirely, isn't it?" Ahern said, smiling ruefully. "I know I should stick to making whiskey and leave poetry to the bards, but we have no bards anymore, at least not like in the old days. The English took them away when they conquered us, just as they took away our kings and chieftains and heroes. Now all we have to keep the lore alive are men like me, hedge shanachies who pass it on by word of mouth, losing a little here, adding a bit there, till no one can tell anymore if our myths are history or our history myths. But then I've heard it said that history is just a joke anyway, one that the living pull over on the dead. So I suppose it really doesn't matter, does it, because the past is what it was, and today is what it is, and all we can ever hope to change is tomorrow.

"But all that aside, Dónal, I want you to know how sorry I am for the loss of your brother. He was a good man, and I know you miss him."

Sudden tears welled up in Dónal's eyes then and, seeing them, Ahern pulled him into his embrace. But it only made him weep the harder, as it emphasized his father's aloofness.

"I didn't want him to go," Dónal said. "He was my best friend, the only one I've ever had. And now he's gone."

"He's not the only one, Dónal. I'm your friend, too, you know. I don't know if I can be as good a one as Eóghan, but from now on you'll never have a better, I can promise you that."

Lifting his head then, Dónal gazed intently at Ahern, trying to divine the truth of his words. "Thanks, Mr. Ahern."

"Call me Seán, Dónal, like a good friend should."

"Thanks, Seán," Dónal replied, burying his face again.

After a moment, he sighed and pulled away again. "Da didn't want him to go either. He said he was throwing his life away for nothing. Is that true, Seán? Did no good come of it?"

"Ah, me, Dónal. I don't know how to answer that, except to say that you can't always see the good in something right away. And so it will be with Eóghan's rebellion, I'm afraid, that it may be many years before we can see the good in it."

"But that doesn't make it hurt less today."

Finding nothing to say to that, Ahern could only wrap him in his arms again and hope his embrace would say it for him. After a bit, he felt him nodding and laid him down gently by the fire.

"Here, Dónal," he said softly, "you take my blanket."

"But what about you, Seán? Won't you get cold?"

"Oh no, son, not me. Once you've been on fire, you never get cold again."

chapter 6

On the Slopes of Guala

It was almost dawn when Seán Ahern slipped between the stones and emptied his bag of potatoes onto the pile he'd made. He'd worked through the night to harvest them from his little plot on the mountainside, there thankfully being no blight in them yet. Still it would be a close race to get them rendered down into poteen, even with a head start and, tired as he was, he knew he had many hours of work ahead of him.

"Ah, well, no rest for the wicked," he yawned, stretching his arms over his head and twisting at the waist.

Seeing Dónal still sleeping peacefully, a wistful look came into his eye as he thought of his own young son, who'd been born after the misfortune and had never known him as he'd been before, whole and unscarred. Yet Ahern knew he loved him, as unconditionally as if he were Adonis himself, and for that he'd have burned a thousand times and gladly, for it made his life worth living.

"I owe you a debt, Eóghan O'Sullivan," he said softly. "You let me live to see my son and feel the healing warmth of his smile, and I can't think of a better way to repay it than to do the same for you."

Kneeling beside Dónal then, he gently pushed his hair back from his eyes. "Wake up, Dónal. The morning is upon us."

But when Dónal saw Ahern's ravaged face hovering over him, he gasped and flinched, thinking one of his dark dreams had come to life.

"There's nothing to be afraid of, Dónal," Ahern said, smiling reassuringly. "It's just me, your new old friend, Seán Ahern."

"I'm sorry, Seán," Dónal said hastily, fearing that he'd hurt the man's feelings. "I just forgot where I was."

"That's all right. I'm much the same when I sleep in a strange place. But rise up now. There's a new day in it, and we've much living to do before the sun sets again."

By the time they'd had a bit of breakfast, dawn was breaking in earnest, its golden light promising a day of sunshine and warmth. For the fog was gone, stealing away in the night, the blight having no further use for camouflage, it seemed.

After smooring the fire and covering the potatoes with his blanket, Ahern led the way from the dell and along the twisting and uncertain path. All around them, the land was tumbled and broken and strewn with boulders the size of horses, and the wind was stronger even than at Cahernageeha, buffeting Dónal so hard that he had to lean into it to make headway. Yet even in this inhospitable setting, the land was littered with cottages as far as the eye could see, even on the slopes that rose another five hundred feet above the road, enough to house hundreds of people, if not more. But, of course, they were all abandoned and derelict, bearing the scars of ejectment and surrounded with defunct lazy beds, the marginal land having given up its marginal people, gone like a fart in the wind.

As they neared the road, Dónal heard the whinny of a pony and was surprised to find Spota tethered in the field ahead.

"Spota!" he shouted, and rushed past Ahern to embrace the pony, which seemed just as happy to see him. "Where did you come from? I thought I'd never see you again!"

"There's a reunion of old friends in it, I see!" Ahern said.

"He was our pony before Da sold him. Is he yours now, Seán?"

"Yes, he's mine, and pleased I am to have him. He's a fine fellow and a good friend."

"I know. He was my friend, too, and I cried when Da sold him."

"He still is your friend, Dónal. Sure, he'll always be your friend.

Just like me. I'll always be your friend, too."

Dónal didn't reply to that. He didn't have to, for the healing warmth of his smile said it all.

⚬ⷬⷪⷪⷪ⚬

The stench of death hung heavy in the air, as they walked up the path to Cahernageeha, the death not only of the potato and the traditional way of life it supported, but of the future, also, and perhaps even of hope. For once again The Land had withheld Her grace, and once again Her people would go hungry, their hold on Her becoming ever more tenuous as their numbers dwindled, their presence but a fading memory.

"Do you smell it, Dónal?" Ahern asked. "Do you smell the blight?"

But the boy was already inside, peering through the shadows at the body draped across the bed, concerned with his own problems for the moment and not the greater calamity outside.

"Da?" he asked tentatively from the bedside. "Are you all right, Da?"

"Don't bother him, Dónal," Ahern said softly, coming to stand behind him. "Let him sleep it off and we'll talk to him later."

"Are you sure he's just sleeping, Seán? He's not . . . he's not dead, is he?"

"No, he's not dead. He's just drunk, and there's nothing to be done about it just now. So come outside and show me your potatoes. They're in worse shape than he is."

Dónal let Ahern lead him away, through the door and out to the lazy beds, where they stood with heavy hearts, gazing upon the devastation of the blight.

"So the Hunger is upon us again," Ahern sighed, more to himself than Dónal, "and we can only pray to God that we are not among its victims. And yet, if not us then surely someone else, and what kind of Christians are we to pray for God's mercy only that our fellows should starve? How could we wish such a fate on anyone, even our worst enemies, to condemn them to a slow and agonizing death, suffering the

102

worst kind of pain imaginable, worse than fire even, as the body devours itself from the inside, the torture increased tenfold by the knowledge that the land is overflowing with food? But then again, how are we to face it ourselves? Where do we find the moral courage to suffer such a fate that our fellows might live? And even if we do, what of our children, for even if the Hunger is God's will, surely they are innocent in His eyes?

"Where do we even look to find the answers?" he asked plaintively, raising his face skyward. "Will You not show us the way?"

But Providence gave him no answer and, after a moment, he sighed again and shook his head. "I can only do what I can do. I have a wife and a son, and since they depend on me for their sustenance, then I must live so that they might live. Indeed, I *will* live for them, no matter what it takes, and may God forgive me if I'm wrong."

Bowing his head then, he crossed himself, and said a silent prayer for forgiveness, before raising his eyes again to the devastation.

"But so an end has come of the Potato People," he intoned, as though delivering an epitaph, "and whatever comes after, we will be changed and changed utterly, for surely this calamity of the potato famine will haunt us unto the end of time."

With nothing more then, he took Dónal by the hand and led him back to the cottage.

⟨ᕕᕗ⟩

Ahern slumped in a chair by the fire, head back and snoring softly, the warmth and quiet and monotony of the watch having overcome him. And Dónal's eyes were getting heavy, too, as he sat by the bedside, watching his father's chest rise and fall rhythmically. On an impulse and heedless of the consequences, he climbed onto the bed and stretched out next to him, laying his head softly on his broad chest. It was a strange feeling, being so close to him, feeling the strength that was in him and the fire of his life, hearing the rattle of his breathing, and smelling his rich earthy odor, a mixture of sweat and turf smoke, soil and poteen, the scents of Ireland all mingled together.

"Please get better, Da," he whispered. "Please."

᠁

Seán Ahern found them so later, Dónal snuggled close to his father and both of them still asleep. They looked so peaceful together and so natural that it was hard for him to believe it wasn't always that way between them. Not wishing to disturb them, he sat down in the chair and watched for a while, thinking of his wife and son, and their love that warmed the chill places of his heart. Reflecting on his misfortune in the mines, he remembered the days spent on his sickbed, his young pregnant wife sitting at his side, holding his hand and telling him softly that she loved him and that everything would be all right. At first he'd refused to listen, being stuck in the mire of self-pity and grieving for the man he'd never be again, sure that no one could love him as he was, even fearing that she'd take their baby away so he wouldn't frighten it. Yet she'd persisted, staying by his side day after day, night after night, telling him over and over that she loved him, until slowly the walls began to crumble and he'd opened his heart to healing.

Then one day the most amazing thing happened – he'd actually smiled at her. But she'd burst into tears at the sight and, overcoming his fear of the answer, he asked her why.

"I'm crying for happiness, Seán, because now I know you'll be well and whole again."

"No, Órla, I will never be that again. I'll always be half a man, and you deserve better."

"But half of Seán Ahern is better to me than two of any other man!" she'd said, laughing through her tears. "I love you, Seán, and I'll always love you, no matter what. And so will our child."

And as a tear started in his eye, Ahern looked down at his empty sleeve, and touched the eye-patch and the angry scars, and silently thanked God for blessing him with all the riches any man could reasonably desire.

Ahern woke with a start and, looking toward the bed, saw that while Dónal was still asleep, his father was awake and staring at the ceiling, his face gray and his eyes red and swollen.

"God be with you, Seán," O'Sullivan said softly.

"God be with yourself, Eóghan," Ahern replied. "How are you feeling?"

"Oh, I've been better. And yourself?"

"I'm fine."

"And what brings you here today? Did Dónal come for you?"

"Not exactly. It's true that I did come here with him this morning, but it was concern for you that brought him to my shebeen last night."

"Last night, did you say? However did he find it?"

"Father Fitzgerald told him where to look and he used his wits from there. He's a brave little boy, Eóghan, and smart and resourceful, too. Indeed, he's a son worthy of you, as much as young Eóghan ever was, and I think it's time you realized that and started being worthy of him!"

O'Sullivan's eyes narrowed dangerously at that and, aware of his swift and unpredictable temper, Ahern knew he'd best tread lightly.

"You can bristle and glare all you want, Eóghan," he said sternly, leaning forward in his chair, "but it doesn't alter the truth. If anything, your defensiveness tells me that I've hit the mark. Now, I know you're grieving for young Eóghan, but you have another son, one who loves you and needs you desperately. And if you'll only open your heart to him, you'll find healing. Trust me on this, Eóghan, for I know whereof I speak."

O'Sullivan's look softened a bit at that, the edge of his anger blunted by the conviction in Ahern's voice. "Did he really come to you out of concern for me?"

"Yes," Ahern replied simply, looking him hard in the eyes.

O'Sullivan sighed then and shifted his gaze back to the ceiling.

"My heart is filled with emptiness, Seán, and there's a hunger in my soul that no nourishment will satisfy. I had a home and a family, and

I could've had friends and the respect of my neighbors, and put my energies to good advantage for us all. But I was a fool, chasing a fool's dream, a mirage that lay just over the next horizon, and at the tail of the day, all I have to show for it is a great hoard of *nothing*. My life is wasted, and the bitterness is more than I can bear."

Ahern let the silence hang heavy for a moment, before grasping his friend's hand.

"Yes, Eóghan, you've been a fool, for you wanted something no man can have – to turn back time and build your future upon the ghosts of the past. But the past is gone, Eóghan, dead and buried, and it won't come again. You are a copper miner, the son of a copper miner and himself the son of a farmer, and himself and himself and himself as far back as you care to go, and though you're a lordly man in yourself, your patrimony is long bereft of its lordship. So yes, you've been a fool, a fool for not realizing your limitations and appreciating the blessings you were given, and believe me, Eóghan, you were indeed blessed. But it's not true that you have nothing, or that your life is a waste. You have another son, one who's worthy of your respect and who would give you his very life if you asked. The past is gone and you can't alter it, and nothing is all that is to be gained by dwelling upon it. But the future is a clean slate and you can still affect what will be in it.

"So it seems to me, Eóghan, that you've been given an opportunity for redemption, not in the hereafter, but in the here and now, and all you have to do to attain it is to be a father to your son. And as I said, I speak to you whereof I know, for I've stood at this crossroads of life and made this choice myself."

Releasing his hand, Ahern sat back in his chair. "So, my lord O'Sullivan Béara, here's your chance to prove yourself as big a man as me! Be a father to Dónal. Be a father to your son."

O'Sullivan said nothing for a time, just continued to stare at the ceiling as though he'd find all the answers there. But seeing his eyes glistening, Ahern knew that he'd heard him, though it would be a close thing still, for to put his whole life aside and start over was a lot to ask of any man, especially one like big Eóghan O'Sullivan.

But then the man sighed heavily, as though a heavy burden had been lifted and, pulling Dónal into his embrace, kissed the top of his head.

"Da, you're awake!" Dónal exclaimed, jerking his head up to look at his father.

"Yes, I'm awake," O'Sullivan replied softly. "And thank you, my son, for caring about me."

At the words "my son," a happy smile radiated from Dónal's face to warm the chill places in his father's heart. And despite everything, the man couldn't help but smile back.

"Good man, Eóghan," Ahern said, thinking that his debt was paid with interest, and Eóghan O'Sullivan would be the gombeen man of his soul no longer.

"Thanks, Seán," O'Sullivan replied, a queer sort of look coming into his eyes. "Thanks for giving me back my vision."

At that, Ahern's smile faded, being unsure of what was meant. But Dónal gave him no chance to ponder it.

"Da, I have to tell you something about our potatoes," he said tentatively.

"I know, Dónal," O'Sullivan sighed, releasing him as he sat up. "The blight is upon us again. I smelled it when I came home last night, and in the fields I passed along the way. But don't worry, son. I've money put aside and my income is steady. So we'll be all right. The only thing is we have nothing to eat just now."

"Yes, you do," Ahern said. "I've brought you some of my own. There was no blight in them yet and hopefully they'll keep. I put them by the fire to keep them warm and dry."

"Thank you, Seán. It was good of you to think of us."

"Sure, Eóghan, it was the least I could do. But now, if it's all the same to you, I think I'll be going. I've another long night ahead of me and need to get on with it."

Leaning down, he smiled and ruffled Dónal's hair. "You're a lovely fellow, Dónal, and the sooner I see you again, the happier I'll be."

"That might be even sooner than you think," O'Sullivan said. "After

Fionnuala died, you offered to look after him while I'm at work, and now I think I'll take you up on it. He's spent enough time in this cottage alone and could do with some companionship. Of course, I'll pay you for it."

"Not to worry, Eóghan. I've my Tadhg to look after anyway, and one more is no bother, especially with a boy like yours. So I'll see you both tomorrow."

He turned to leave then, and they followed him outside into the warmth and sunshine.

"There's a better day in it than yesterday," Ahern said, shading his eye. "Here we've been in the darkness all this time when we could've been out in it."

"Darkness was more appropriate for the occasion, I think," O'Sullivan countered.

"Perhaps. But like it or not, light always follows, Eóghan."

"Meaning?"

"Meaning there's always hope. Mind my words, Eóghan, and you'll find what you seek."

"Safe home to you, Seán."

"And to you, Eóghan. And to you."

When he was gone, O'Sullivan sighed and closed his eyes, feeling a certain inner peace as the sun bathed his face. The world hadn't changed, he knew, and all its troubles would still be there in the morning. But none of it seemed to matter just then. For Ahern had reminded him that he had another son, and that there was yet hope after all.

Opening his eyes, he looked across the valley toward the Big House rising gray and ominous above the Irish green. No, he thought defiantly, though the son he loved too much was gone, he wasn't beaten yet. Yet even as he did, he felt a small hand grasp his own.

"Do you miss him, Da?" Dónal asked.

Looking down, O'Sullivan thought how much like his mother he was, fragile and sensitive and beautiful. And for the first time, he saw that there was something of himself in him, too, for he was brave and determined and could be as tough as shoe leather.

"Yes, I miss him," he said. "I miss him like I miss the sun when I'm below in the mines. I miss him like the flowers would miss the rain were it never to fall again, or the night the stars should they all go dim. I miss him like Seán misses his right hand, that's how much I miss him."

"I miss him like that, too," Dónal said, reminding his father that it didn't happen just to him. "He was my best friend, and I'll always miss him."

"He was a good brother to you, wasn't he, Dónal?"

"He was my hero. But I think Seán is right, Da. I think you're a hero, too."

"Seán thinks I'm a hero? When did he tell you that?"

"Last night he told me how you saved his life. He said he would've died in the mines if you hadn't carried him up the ladders, and that his family would've been left with no Da. So that's why he thinks you're a hero, and why I think he's right."

"Thank you, Dónal," O'Sullivan said thickly, pulling him close. "That's the nicest thing anyone has ever said to me."

There was a silence between them then as they stood side by side, gazing across the valley, their eyes drawn inexorably to the Big House.

"Will you tell me the story of our family, Da?" Dónal asked after a bit. "Eóghan would only tell me a little, and I want to know the rest."

"Yes, Dónal, I'll tell you someday," O'Sullivan sighed. "Indeed, someday."

chapter 7

Béara Peninsula

THE SUN WAS JUST BEGINNING TO RISE behind them as Dónal and his father made their way across the high shoulder of Guala, the wind as fierce as ever though the sky was clear, heralding a day of fine weather to come.

It had still been dark when his father's coughing awakened him, and by firelight they'd eaten their breakfast, in silence as always though with a different feel to it now, one of solace and connection, as they shared their meal rather than just eating at the same time and table. And for the first time in months, the house felt like home again, a place where a family lived and shared their love and laughter, struggles and suffering, secure in the knowledge that they had each other. Nor was Dónal in any hurry to leave it, wishing he could spend the whole day basking in his father's company, talking to him and getting to know him, and letting him know that he cared about him. But it was not to be, as his father had already missed one day of the work week, a thing unprecedented in itself, and was anxious to get back to it, rising from the table and smooring the fire as soon as they'd finished.

Yet before they left, he surprised Dónal by removing a stone from high on the far side of the chimney and picking him up so he could see what was hidden inside. "See that purse in there?" he asked. "That's where I keep my money, and I wanted you to know in case something happens to me. But don't ever take it out unless I tell you to or something does happen to me, and even then, don't let anyone see you, and don't tell anyone about it other than Seán or his family. Do you understand?"

"Yes, Da," Dónal replied dutifully, thinking rather of the three treasures hidden at the bottom of the dresser, though not daring to admit to his snooping by asking about them.

Anyway, there was no time, as they left immediately, striking out for Allihies in the still gray of dawn, Dónal running along beside his father and wondering how he could possibly keep up. But seeing him struggle, O'Sullivan snatched him up without breaking stride and swung him onto his broad shoulders, shocking him so that he couldn't even express his delight.

"How's the view from up there?" he asked jovially.

"Oh, it's grand, Da!" Dónal exclaimed, meaning his father's gesture rather than the view. And what a feeling of power to be up so high, like a rajah astride his royal elephant, riding in luxury while the powerful legs beneath him ate up the miles. But more powerful still was the simple knowledge that his father cared, for it made him feel safe and secure, a suit of spiritual armor against the troubles of the world.

"My own Da used to carry me like that when I was a boy," O'Sullivan had said, half to himself. "I'd forgotten about it till just now."

"Was he a miner, too, Da?"

"Yes, he was. Indeed, he was among the first to be hired when the mines opened back in 1812, and he worked there till the day he died."

"What happened to him? Did The Hunger get him?"

"No, Dónal, he and my Uncle Phillip were killed in the Dooneen Mine when the timbering gave way and buried them under a load of stone. I was only fifteen at the time, though I was already there myself, working a crew in the Mountain Mine with Seán. It took me two days to get their bodies out and bring them home to Cahernageeha, and then I had to bury them right away, since by that time they were in no condition to wake. It still makes me angry to think about, having to throw them in the ground like that, especially since the Company knew the Dooneen was unsafe and did nothing about it. I vowed then to avenge them someday, and I mean to still."

"I wish you didn't work in the mines, Da," Dónal said, uncomfortable with all the talk of death. "I'm afraid something might happen to you, too."

"No, Dónal, the mines won't get me. I know them too well. Indeed, they're part of me, just as I'm part of them, blood brothers till the bitter end."

"Do you like it then, Da, being a miner?"

"To tell you the truth, I've never even thought about it. It's just what I was meant to do, I think, to labor in the mines so that Eóghan would have a better life after me. And you, too, of course. Perhaps that's even why I'm so good at it. It's not a bad life, all things considered, at least for a man like me, one with no money or education or prospects. Anyway, it's better than being a farmer and always living at the mercy of the weather and the blight and the landlord. But it's not a prospect you'll have to face, Dónal, because I intend to see that you have alternatives, so your life will be better than mine. And since the first step on that road is education, you'll be going to Allihies with me from now on."

"Am I to go to school then, Da?"

"No, Seán will tutor you, and that will be even better," O'Sullivan replied, leaving off that he didn't want to make the same mistake he'd made with Eóghan, and expose him to people and ideas that might lead him astray.

After that, they went in silence, O'Sullivan striding along at a great pace, seemingly unaffected by the additional weight on his shoulders. But though his breathing was even and controlled, Dónal could hear the rattle in it, just as he had the day before when lying next to him, and he seemed to have a tickle in his throat that wouldn't go away, at least judging from his constant hacking and spitting.

"Are you sick, Da?" he asked when the hacking turned into a short but racking fit.

"No, Dónal, I'm always like this in the morning. It's from the dust in the mines. But don't worry; it goes away."

Even so, the coughing returned when they crested the mountain shoulder, so deep and violent this time that his father had to put him down. Finally it passed and they went on, but not before Dónal noticed the tears in his father's eyes and the flecks of red in his spit. And despite his assurances, he couldn't help but worry, even though his breathing now seemed clearer.

But soon they came to the western edge of Guala, and O'Sullivan stopped to give Dónal a good look at the vale below. It was crescent-shaped, he saw, a natural amphitheater defined by the Slieve Miskish wrapping around the blue expanse of Ballydonegan Bay. Bleak and stony were the mountains to the north and those to the south green and lush, while in the crook the village of Allihies nestled amid the meadows from which it took its name, *Na hAill Achaidh*, "the cliff fields."

And though it was a place of many contrasts, between green and gray, barren and lush, land and sea, the one between Man and Nature dominated. For while the morning sun had yet to shine upon them, the meadows were awake and bursting with activity, as people scurried every which way, some walking or riding while others drove wagons or maneuvered handcarts or barrows, all amid the din of machinery and thick gray smoke rising from many stacks. Altogether, it had a grim, forbidding look, so different from the peaceful valley they'd left behind, almost as if the high road across Guala were a bridge between two different worlds, one of light and the other of darkness, bucolic tranquility versus Faustian chaos. And on the stage below, a human drama played itself out, though whether it was tragedy or comedy depended upon one's allotted role in the theater of life. Not that Dónal thought of it in such terms, of course, the impact upon him being visceral rather than cerebral, though no less profound.

Yet then his eyes strayed beyond the bay to the Broad Atlantic spreading majestically to the horizon, and he felt the brevity of industrial Man in both space and time, certain in his perceptive heart that Nature reigned supreme and eternal. Shading his eyes to the golden light hovering above the sea, he smiled to himself, thinking how glorious must be the life of a sailor, to be out there in the midst of all that shimmering peace.

But glancing up at his father to see if he shared the vision, his smile faded, for he found his eyes turned inward upon himself, much as they'd been in the dark days when he was drowning in grief and the drink.

"Are you all right, Da?" he asked, hoping to break the spell.

"Hm? Oh, yes, I'm all right. Why do you keep asking if I'm all right? I was just thinking of when I was a boy and used to come with my Da when he went to work. In those days only the Dooneen Mine was open, just beyond the north end of Allihies, and I'd spend my days there, playing in the old ringforts, or wandering out to the ruins at Pointnadishert, or even all the way to Reentrusk at the north end of the bay. There's a hollow there in the side of Eagle Hill called Eskinanaun, or 'hollow of the ivy' in our language, and indeed, it's filled with wild ivy growing on the rock faces. There was one strand near the top of the hollow that I was particularly fond of, for it grew in the shape of a small tree, with its limbs flung out like a fan from a slender bare trunk.

"And do you know what I liked most about it, Dónal? It was that it grew there in that shape with only it's own nature to guide it and no help from the hand of man. I've often wondered if it's still there, though I've never gotten around to checking on it."

Looking down at his son, O'Sullivan was surprised to find his face split with a smile. "Now what are you grinning like a jackass about?"

"I've never heard you talk like this before, Da, about things you like or that make you happy. I like it. It makes me feel good."

But the smile faded from O'Sullivan's lips, and his eyes strayed back across the valley to the old Dooneen Mine, now long played out and abandoned, its disused engine house hovering above it like a tombstone. After a moment, he sighed and turned to the road.

"Come on, Dónal. It's getting late."

From where they'd stood, the road plunged steeply down along the cliff edge, the drop to their right being sheer in some places, though the land to their left sloped more gently. It was thick with empty cottages, too, although as the road took them lower, there were more and more that were occupied and still sheltering scores of people, who with their noise and activity underscored the dichotomy between the two sides of Guala. Indeed, their proximity made Dónal's heart beat faster, though with anxiety rather than excitement.

At the bottom of the hill near a churning engine house, O'Sullivan turned right at a tee-junction and led the way along a narrow rutted road, holding Dónal's hand now so they wouldn't get separated in the traffic. To the left just across the fields lay the unimpressive little village of Allihies, while on the hillsides ahead and to the right stood more engine houses. Closer at hand along the narrow channel of the Caminches River lay the steam-powered stamping mills where the ore was pounded into bits amid all-pervasive noise and vibration.

Just short of the stream, O'Sullivan opened a gate on the right and led the way toward a cottage sitting alone in the field above. It was pleasant and cheery-looking, despite the incessant noise, with fresh thatch and whitewash, and flowers blooming in boxes under the windows, while the green meadow swirled around it and on to the sheer slopes behind. And seeing Seán Ahern rise from a stool next to the door only made it better.

"God be with you, Eóghan," Ahern greeted them in the traditional Irish manner, "and with you, too, Dónal."

"God and Mary be with you, Seán," O'Sullivan replied. "And with you, too, Tadhg," he added, meaning the boy who appeared in the doorway.

"And with you, Mr. O'Sullivan," the boy said politely, though he had eyes only for Dónal.

And Dónal's eyes were on him, too, for that matter, noting that he was a couple of years older and big for his age, having broad shoulders and a sturdy neck to go with a sprightly smile and posture of aggressive confidence, while his mop of sandy blond hair gave the impression of a halo, a stark contrast to the naked mischief dancing in his blue eyes. Yet there was a friendly gleam in them, too, a spark of congeniality

115

that challenged the world not to like him.

"So you must be Dónal," he said, not waiting for introductions. "Da has talked about nothing but you since he got home last night." Then he paused and smiled mischievously. "But he didn't tell me you were a runt."

The unexpected jibe stung Dónal like a slap in the face, though as quickly as he'd taken him down, the boy built him back up. "Not that it matters, mind you, because if you're half the man Da says you are, then we'll get along famously.

"I'm Tadhg Ahern," he said then, stepping up and extending his hand.

Seeing the acceptance in his eyes, and realizing that his hand was offered not just in greeting, but in friendship, Dónal smiled broadly and took it.

"I'm Dónal O'Sullivan," he replied, feeling his hand engulfed in Tadhg's broad paw.

"That may be your name to the rest of the world, but you'll always be *runt* to me!" Tadhg said, punching him in the chest in punctuation.

Though his first instinct was to shrink from confrontation, Dónal felt his father's eyes upon him, and wanted desperately to live up to his expectations. So he stood his ground, and though cold with fear, squared his little shoulders and clinched his fists.

"I may be a runt, Tadhg Ahern," he said, "but that's the last time you're ever going to hit me!"

"Careful, runt," Tadhg said, stepping in close to accentuate his height advantage. "I can take you down just anytime I feel like it."

"Sure, it's true that you're bigger, stronger and meaner than me," Dónal said, then borrowed a line from his brother, "but you'll get tired of knocking me down long before I get tired of getting up for more, and in the heel of the hunt, I'll be the one left standing!"

Tadhg just laughed delightedly, it being exactly the sort of reaction he wanted.

"All right, runt, calm down," he said, stepping back. "Da said you were brave, and now that I see it's true, I like you even more."

Of course, Dónal couldn't help being pleased by that. "Friends?" he asked on impulse, extending his hand again.

"Friends forever!" Tadhg affirmed, taking it.

And as they stood there, grinning at each other like they'd just seen the Queen's knickers, their fathers exchanged knowing glances.

"Reminds me of our first meeting," O'Sullivan said, swelling with fatherly pride.

"Yes, and like us, they'll be the best of friends, too," Ahern replied, "if they don't kill each other trying, that is. I just hope I can keep them away from serious trouble."

"Oh, they'll be fine," O'Sullivan said, patting him on the back. "All you have to do is watch them every second of every minute of every day, and there'll be no problem. And after all, Seán, what else have you to do with your time?"

"Go to work, Eóghan," Ahern grunted, finding no encouragement in the prospect.

"Yes, the morning is getting on with itself. I have to go now, Dónal. So you and Tadhg be easy on the old one and stay out of trouble. Do you understand?"

"Yes, Da," Dónal replied, "I'll be good."

"Not if I have anything to do with it," Tadhg muttered under his breath.

"Quiet, you," his father scolded.

"All right, then," O'Sullivan said, ignoring them and extending his hand to Dónal. "Walk me down to the road."

When they came to the gate, O'Sullivan stopped and ruffled his son's hair. "I'll see you in the evening. All right?"

"Yes, Da," Dónal nodded, then bit his lip. "And Da? Please be careful."

"I always am."

"Safe home to you, Da," Dónal called, though his father just waved without turning around.

When he was out of sight, Dónal sighed and raised his own hand, before heading back toward the cottage.

"Why did you wave like that?" Tadhg asked, coming down to meet him. "You looked like you were saying good-bye to a dead one! What were you thinking in that red head of yours?"

"I was thinking that I never waved good-bye to my brother when he went away, and I feel bad about it because he's never coming back. So I figured I'd better wave in case something happens to Da and he doesn't come back."

"I see," Tadhg said, gazing at him thoughtfully. "At least I see that Da was right about you again."

"What do you mean?"

"He told me you were old for the age that's in you and that I may not always understand you. But it makes sense, I suppose, now that I think about it. After all, runts do have to be smarter than other people if they want to get on in the world!"

"Well, if I was you, Tadhg Ahern," Dónal retorted, buoyed by his newfound confidence, "I wouldn't be telling people that a runt was braver *and* smarter than myself!"

"And just why not? No one who knows me will believe it anyway, and I don't care about the rest!" Then he wrapped a friendly arm around Dónal's shoulders, and said, "Come on inside and I'll show you my ore collection. They all have copper in them and my Da helped me pick them out. He was a miner, you know, and I'm going to be one, too, when I grow up. Say, maybe we can even have our own crew together, just like our fathers in the old days. We'll even call ourselves 'Ahern and O'Sullivan' like they did."

"No, Tadhg, I don't think so. My Da says he wants me to be something different when I grow up."

"He says *what?*" Tadhg demanded, giving him a look that questioned his sanity. "Well, what *does* he want you to be? A farmer? My Da says farming is just for people who can't do anything else! You don't want to be a farmer, Dónal, trust me!"

"Well, no, I don't. But my Da says the same thing about mining."

"I think I need to have a talk with him! Being a miner is the best job a man can have! I mean, think about it, Dónal. You get to go down in the mines and walk in the tunnels and climb the ladders and blast rocks into smithereens. What could be more fun than that?"

It was Dónal's turn to be aghast then, thinking of Ahern's horrible injuries and how he'd come by them. Had he not told his son? Or did the darkness and danger just sound like a big adventure to him? But he didn't ask the question, for they were at the cottage door and within Ahern's hearing, and he didn't want to stir the man's painful memories.

Anyway, Tadhg was already after his rocks and, left alone for the moment, Dónal took the opportunity to look around. The cottage was more or less like his own, he saw, having the same design, though some of the furnishings weren't as nice, especially the bed. But as his eyes strayed to the front left corner something caught his eye, an odd sort of light, or a hint of silver perhaps, though both and yet neither adequately described it. Turning to it, he saw that it was wood-framed and rectangular, tall and mysterious, and his innate curiosity propelled him toward it like a cat to an open drawer. But as he stepped before it, a young boy suddenly appeared and gaped at him in surprise.

"*Ah, Jesus,*" Dónal yelped in fright, noticing that though the boy yelped, too, no sound came from his lips.

"What?" Tadhg demanded, dropping his box of rocks. "What is it?"

"What's the matter, Dónal?" Ahern asked more calmly, an amused sort of look on his face as he looked up from his book.

But Dónal couldn't answer, only stare at the boy staring back at him with his mouth open and eyes wide with fright. Yet when he noticed the white steak in his red forelocks and his bright eyes the color of the new green of Spring, the light of understanding began to glow in his mind. Could it be himself, he wondered, that ragged-looking boy with the tattered clothing and grimy face, scratched and scabby shins and bare feet stained the color of earth? Was it possible that he really looked like that, a wild thing sprung of the mountain and the bog? He hoped not. But then Tadhg stepped up behind him and, seeing him appear behind the boy, he knew it was true.

"For Christ's sake, Dónal, it's just a mirror," Tadhg said. "You'd think you've never seen one with the way you're carrying on."

"I haven't!" Dónal exclaimed. "What is it?"

"It's a mirror, Dónal," Ahern explained patiently, reaching out to rap it with his knuckles, "just a bit of glass with silver paint behind it, a sort of window that shows back whatever happens to be in front of it. That boy you see there is you. That's what you look like to the rest of us. Go ahead and touch it if you want. It won't bite."

Dónal did as suggested, his hand tentative and shaking. But finding it just as Ahern had said, a piece of glass harmless and mundane, he couldn't help but be a bit disappointed.

"What's it for, Seán?" he asked, noticing that his fingers left grimy smudges.

"Vanity, mostly," Ahern replied, "which is a nice way of saying 'insecurity.' You stand in front of it when you're getting dressed or combing your hair to make sure everything is just the way you want it. Usually only the rich have them, because they're so expensive, and only they have the luxury of making a fuss over themselves. And of course, women are especially fond of them, as you might understand."

Looking at himself and the two Aherns then, at their simple clothes and peasant demeanor, Dónal knew they would never need it for the purpose described.

"Then why do you have one, Seán?" he asked, almost accusingly.

"Ah, well, I should have known you'd ask that, I suppose," Ahern sighed, wincing as though in pain, "and as much as I don't want to answer, I'll do so out of respect for my wife."

But before continuing, he paused to look down at Tadhg and pull him in close, needing his comfort, it seemed.

"After the misfortune came upon me in the mines, I spent a long time in this cottage convalescing, lying on that bed there, staring up at that ceiling, mourning for the hurts that were in me and for the man I'd never be again. Yet when my body had healed as much as it was going to, still I lay there, afraid to go outside, afraid of how people would look at me and what they'd think or say. And though my wife did everything she could to reassure me, to make me see that it didn't matter and that she loved me anyway, still I lay there. But after a while, even she couldn't take any more. 'Seán, my love,' she said, 'you can't live the rest of your life in this cottage! We're going to have a child and I can't mother you both. So tell me, if you will, what it will take to get you out of that bed and back into the world of the living.'

"I don't know why, but the answer was right on the tip of my tongue, like I'd known it all along. 'I have to know what I look like, Órla,' I said. 'I can't face the world and the looks I'll get without knowing what people are seeing. I know I shouldn't care, but I'm just a man, and I have my weaknesses like any other man. So help me to know what I look like and then I'll get on with living. I promise you I will.'

"A tear spilled from her eye then and rolled slowly down her cheek. 'I love you, Seán, my darling,' she said. 'Always know that I love you, no matter what!'

"Then she went out and was gone all day. But when she came home in the evening, she had that mirror with her. She wouldn't tell me where she got it or what she had to pay for it, or even where she got the money. And, of course, I wanted to cry the first time I looked in it. Indeed, I could feel my lost eye burning with the tears of my soul. But Órla put her arms around me and said, 'Look into that one eye that's left to you, Seán. Look through that window into the heart of yourself and tell me if the man inside looks any different.'

"So I did as she said. I looked inside myself into my heart of hearts. And do you know what I saw there? I saw Seán Ahern smiling back at me, Seán Ahern with two blue eyes and two hands and no scars on his face, still the handsome Ahern of old. And so I knew that I was still me on the inside, and that nothing could ever change me unless I let it. And do you know what else I saw, Dónal? I saw how lucky I was."

Releasing Tadhg, Ahern stepped to the mirror. "So that's the story of how poor Seán Ahern came to have a mirror," he said, smoothing his hair and straightening his clothes. "Now I stand in front of it every morning before I go out, and thank God for making me the luckiest man in the world!"

Looking down at Dónal, he smiled slyly. "I told you it was for vanity, didn't I?" Then he said to Tadhg, "Come on, son. Let's leave our man to discover himself in peace."

Needing no encouragement, Dónal eagerly turned back to his reflection, noting how much he looked like his mother and how little like his father and Eóghan. But most striking to him was that he was so very dirty, for not since his mother died had he had a bath or clean clothes to wear. Closing his eyes, he recalled the piping hot water and the rough soap called "spoileen," the pleasant languor of soaking and the warmth of the fire as he dried before it, not to mention the crisp feel of clean clothes, fresh from the line.

"I need a bath," he said. Seeing the critical appraisal in his mirror-twin's eyes, he wondered if that was how other people looked at him, forming their judgments from the sanctuary of their side of the mirror.

"What, are you daft?" Tadhg demanded from the hearth. "You don't really like to take baths, do you?"

"No, of course not! It's just that I haven't had one in so long, and I'm so dirty."

"Even so, you're thick for thinking it, and I'd not say it in front of anyone else if I was you!" Then he abruptly changed the subject, not wanting to dwell on unpleasantness, it seemed. "But if your highness is finished admiring yourself, maybe you'd like to come over here and have a look at something really interesting."

Glancing at himself one last time, Dónal moved away from the mirror and joined Tadhg at the hearth, listening politely as he gave a short lecture on copper ore, while Ahern read a book.

"Do you go to school, Dónal?" Tadhg asked after a bit, setting his rocks aside.

"No. Do you?"

"No, but Da teaches me at home. I can read and write and do sums and speak English. I'll bet you can't do any of those things."

"Oh yes, I can! Eóghan taught me. He was really smart and went to university in Dublin."

"I know. Da told me about him. He said he was really brave, and died fighting the Redcoats. He said you were really sad about it, too. But I don't think you should be sad; I think you should be proud of him. I don't have any brothers or sisters myself, and Da says I'm not going to because of the injuries he got in the mines. I don't see what that has to do with getting a baby, but he wouldn't explain it to me, just said I'd understand when I grow up. He says that about a lot of things."

There was more like that from Tadhg, though Dónal wasn't listening anymore, as he was eyeing Ahern's big leather-bound book.

"What are you reading, Seán?" he asked, when Tadhg paused for a breath.

"It's called *The Iliad and The Odyssey*, Dónal," Ahern replied. "It was written thousands of years ago by a Greek bard named Homer, and tells of the Trojan War and the journey of brave Odysseus, who was a great hero like our own Eóghan Mór. Aside from the Bible, of course, and *The Cattle Raid of Cooley*, I'd have to say it's the greatest story ever told. If my son will hold his tongue for a bit, I'll tell it to you, if you like."

"Oh, yes, Seán, I love stories," Dónal agreed eagerly, even as Tadhg groaned and rolled his eyes.

Setting the book aside, Ahern the shanachie began to speak, his powerful voice casting a spell on the boys and opening a window onto the past. Through it they saw the fatal beauty of Helen and the treachery of Paris, the fury of Menelaus and the dire combat on the plain, Achilles and Ajax, Agamemnon and Odysseus, and Trojan Hector whose valor kept them at bay, his death and debasement at the hands of Achilles who himself met an ignoble end, and finally the wooden horse and sack of Troy, destroyed so utterly that none could now tell where it had stood. Yet all of that was but a prelude for the saga of Odysseus, his wanderings and many adventures, Calypso and Polyphemus, Circe and the Sirens, his descent into Hades and the terrible choice between Scylla and Charybdis, against all of which was set his epic longing for home, which by the time he got there didn't feel like home anymore.

And what was the moral, Ahern asked when all was told? To be like Odysseus rather than Achilles, a complete man who understood the value of life and how to survive by his wits. Seeing their questioning stares, he cited the wooden horse by way of example, a stratagem to which Achilles would never have resorted, since to him honor and virtue were more important than winning, or even life itself. *Let's have a fair fight and may the best man win*, was his credo, which was easy enough for him to live by, since he was the best man and would never lose a fair fight. Yet so strong was his will and so larger-than-life his persona, that others could not help but follow him, even at the cost of their own lives. So it was that the Greeks fought by the code of chivalry, as did Hector and his Trojans, while the war dragged on and countless men died, to the advantage of neither side. Yet to Achilles, who in his naïveté would always choose death before dishonor, that was better than stooping to trickery or treachery, even if it killed them all in the end.

But Odysseus, on the other hand, though noble of spirit and himself a valiant warrior, was also cunning and shrewd, and more intelligent than his friend Achilles, more subtle of perception and deeper of thought. And he understood that *life* is what is important and that it shouldn't be given up lightly, and while he valued honor and virtue, they were of no use to a dead man in his way of thinking. Better to live and fight another day, for who was to say that defeat might not be avenged, and where was it written that he who conquered by wit was not the best man, after all? And in the heel of the hunt, didn't Achilles affirm it himself when Odysseus met him in Hades?

So that was the wisdom to be gleaned from it, Ahern concluded, to understand the conflict between self-interest and doing the right thing, and to know when to sacrifice one for the other, there being circumstances in life where a man just couldn't have both. But as he finished, Dónal's mind wandered to another place and time, and heard another voice say: *Honor isn't much good to a dead man, Eóghan.*

"He was like Achilles, wasn't he?" he said, thinking aloud.

"What, Dónal?" Ahern asked, having fallen into his own reverie. "Who was like Achilles?"

"Eóghan."

"Hm, perhaps, at least in some ways. But then he was young and naïve, so who's to say that he wouldn't have found fuller wisdom in maturity?"

"No, I don't think so," Dónal sighed, his eyes far away. "He was too much like Da, I think."

Ahern could only stare at that, his one eyebrow raised in surprise. Where did that depth of vision come from, he wondered? Was it conscious, or was he just a medium for something transcendent?

But Tadhg gave him no time to ponder it, as he yawned and stretched. "That was a good story, Da," he said, having listened raptly in spite of himself, "and I'm glad you told it so I won't have to read it for myself. I hate reading, especially big long books like that."

"I don't!" Dónal countered, his eyes now focused and intent. "I *love* to read. Can I read your book sometime, Seán?"

"Sure you can, Dónal, though it's not actually mine. It's from the library of the Big House. My friend, Riobárd Puxley, loaned it to me. He's the nephew of the owner and looks after the place for him."

"What's a 'library?'" Dónal asked. "I've never heard that word before."

"It's a place where books are kept. Indeed, there's a whole room full of them there, stacked on shelves that cover the walls from floor to ceiling. Riobárd gets them for me when he goes round to check on the place. I've read scores already, though there's hundreds more to go, at least to hear him tell it. But I'll get to them all someday."

"Not if you keep reading the same one over and over, you won't!" Tadhg interjected. "How many times have you read that one now? Five?"

"Oh, at least, though if I read it that many more, I'll still learn something new. And that's another lesson for you, boys. There's always something new to be learned, even from something old."

"Even something as old as you, Da?" Tadhg jibed, the mischief dancing in his eyes.

"Here, now!" Ahern growled, though with a wink at Dónal. "If you can't show your father the proper respect, then be off to the sty with the other piglets!"

"Come on, Dónal," Tadhg said, taking it as an invitation to play. "Let's leave the old one to his books and go have some real fun!"

"Stay close by!" Ahern called after them. "We'll be leaving soon."

Emerging from the cottage, Dónal was surprised to find it mid-morning already, the time having flown under the enchantment of Ahern's storytelling. And what a difference the sunlight made to the place, driving away the gray and grim, leaving the meadows green and lush and the mountains soft and warm, while the bay sparkled with turquoise and aquamarine and the strand gleamed like a star in the night. Only the smoke and racket of the stamps remained of his earlier impression, though they were soon forgotten as Tadhg led him on a merry romp, turning over rocks and peering down holes, chasing butterflies and visiting Spota in his shed. Indeed, it was a grand morning altogether, and his spirit was high within him, banishing all sorrow and loneliness.

But as Tadhg chased him to the front of the cottage, something caught his eye from the road, a dark horseman flying along like a rider of the Apocalypse, and he stopped to watch as the man jumped the wall and rode menacingly to the door, whistling as though calling a dog. He was dark of eyes and hair and dressed to match, his devilish look amplified by the bloodied spurs at his heels and the smoke and hammering in the background. And as their eyes met for a moment, Dónal shuddered, finding in him The English of his dark imaginings, fully expecting The Hunger and The Fever to appear at his stirrups. Yet the man had no time for him, turning to Ahern as he appeared in the doorway.

"Halloo, Mr. Puxley," Ahern greeted him in English, his smile perfunctory and without warmth, that of a servant perhaps, or an enemy. "I've yeer jug here, and 'tis extra good, so it is, though with the blight that's in it, only Himself knows when there'll be more."

"I'm sure Robert will see to your needs, Ahern," the man replied curtly, taking the jug and flinging a few coins onto the ground. "He always does, though why he wastes his time on the likes of you is beyond me. But then, he always did take being 'more Irish than the Irish' literally. Indeed, what with learning your bloody gibberish of a language and calling himself *Riobárd*, I shouldn't be surprised if he takes up popery next."

"Ah, sure, ye needn't worry for him so. He's a solid Protestant if ever there was a one so born. Perhaps he is a bit less sparin' than some, but 'tis nothin' in yeer teachin's against it, now is there?"

"Don't try that Irish bull on me, Ahern!" Puxley said, leaning over him menacingly. "I know what you're getting at and you'd be well advised to remember your place!"

"Sure, Mr. Puxley, I never forget it so," Ahern said, his smile now definitely that of an enemy.

"See that you don't!" Puxley said, for all his bluster, missing the point entirely.

Without waiting for a reply, he jerked his horse cruelly around and galloped toward the road, jumping the wall again and almost running down a group of women.

"Who was that man, Seán?" Dónal asked, coming to Ahern's side. "And why is he so mean?"

"That, Dónal, was Mr. Richard Puxley, the brother of my friend, Riobárd. He's the bookkeeper at the mines and our local gombeen man. But why he's so mean, I'm afraid I can't tell you. He was just born that way, I suppose."

"He's nasty all right," Tadhg affirmed. "Why I heard he once slashed a boy's face with his whip just for looking at him!"

"Yes, and I've heard worse than that," Ahern said, "though whether it's truth or rumor, I can't say. But in any case, he's gone now and we should be, too. So get our Spota and strap on his baskets. We have a delivery to make."

"Where to, Da?" Tadhg asked.

"Below to Ballydonegan. And then I have to go to the smithy at the Mountain Mine to collect a new coil for my still. And when our errands are done, we'll bring our odyssey full circle by coming home again."

"But will it still be home when we get here?" Tadhg asked puckishly.

"That's never a thing to take for granted."

127

The day was warm indeed by the time they passed the abandoned *clochán* that had once been the village of Ballydonegan, and skirted the strand, making for the stone pier beyond. Though the pony was heavily laden, with both boys on its back and kegs of whiskey in the willow baskets at either side, the load seemed small in comparison to the many wagons bulging with copper ore, all tied up in the ubiquitous linen bags and piled imperfectly onto the beds. They lined the road leading to the pier, waiting to transfer their cargo to two small ships, one tied up and the other waiting in the bay. It was the first stage in shipping the ore to Wales for smelting, Ahern explained, the small ships taking it around to Dunboy where it could be safely loaded onto larger ships or deposited in the storage yard. And it was in that capacity that Dónal's father (and Ahern before his misfortune) labored there on Sundays, loading and unloading ore. Indeed, the two of them had sometimes wagered their whole day's pay that they could transfer more in an hour than any four men combined, and such was their strength of body and will and friendship that they'd never once lost.

But as they threaded their way among the wagons, Dónal had eyes only for the ship at the pier, having seen many from a distance, of course, but never one from this close. How trim and sturdy it looked, how straight and tall its mast, and how inviting the little crow's nest at the top. How grand it would be to scamper up the rigging and stand there with all the world at his feet, bathing in golden sunlight as the ship sliced through pliant waters, urged along by the very breath of God.

"I think I'd like to be a sailor," he thought aloud, blushing when Tadhg groaned and shot him his already-familiar "Are you daft?" look.

"So you like the look of Riobárd's sloops, do you?" Ahern asked. "He got them from old Ned, his father, when he died back in 1840. But Riobárd was a sailor even before that."

"I've never been so close to a ship before. Will we get to go on it?"

"No, Dónal, not this time, I'm afraid. They're trying to get them loaded and we'd just be in the way. I'll send for Riobárd to meet us here."

But even as he turned to do so, he saw his friend approaching.

"Ah, there you are Riobárd," he called in Irish. "God be with you."

"God and Mary be with you, Seán, and also with you, Tadhg," Puxley replied, also in Irish, his accent suggesting it wasn't his native language.

Yet as Tadhg responded, Puxley's eyes slipped to Dónal, who was regarding him curiously, noting that while there was a family resemblance, he didn't look much like his brother. For one thing, he was tall and slender where Richard seemed rather short and pudgy, even on horseback, and though his hair was the same color, his eyes were china blue and his gaze pleasant and direct, rather than quick and furtive. Then, too, he was very handsome, being stylishly dressed in a fine suit of clothes and wearing his hair longer than customary among gentlemen, which gave him something of an exotic look, at least for a place like Béara. But the stamp of approval in Dónal's eyes lay in his genuine smile and casual manner as he greeted Ahern and Tadhg, indicating that he regarded them as friends despite their obvious difference in class, and he found himself drawn to him just as much as he'd been repelled by Richard.

And yet there was something troubling about him, too, in that he seemed awfully familiar, though for the life of him, Dónal couldn't remember seeing him before. It was as if he were someone he knew but was seeing out of context and so couldn't place. But Puxley gave him no time to contemplate, kneeling before him so as to greet him eye to eye.

"And you must be young Dónal," he said, his smile and manner friendly. "I know you from the look of your mother, our lamented Fionnuala. I'm Riobárd Puxley, and it's my pleasure to meet you."

"I'm Dónal," he replied, feeling suddenly awkward, "Dónal O'Sullivan Béara."

At that, the two Aherns' eyes went wide with surprise, and Dónal felt himself blush under their scrutiny, wondering himself why he'd said it. Only once before had he heard his father refer to himself that way, on that morning Eóghan went away, and he understood its meaning no more now than then. It had just come out of his mouth as though

129

preordained for the occasion.

"The old memories die hard, I see," Puxley said, his eyes suddenly cautious, like a shade had been drawn behind them. "But it's my pleasure to meet you nonetheless, Dónal O'Sullivan Béara, and I'd like to get to know you better when time permits. Perhaps you'll call on me sometime. My house isn't far from yours, just across from Dunboy at Oakmount. I'll speak to your father about it, if you like."

"No, sir," Dónal said, without knowing why. "I think you'd better leave that to me."

"All right then. I await your convenience."

With that, he rose and turned to Ahern, nodding toward the whiskey kegs.

"Are those for me?"

"Indeed. Do you want me to take them out for you?"

"No, I'll send a man," Puxley said, adding that he had things to attend to and needed to go. But after cordially taking his leave and walking a few steps away, he turned back to them.

"Oh, I almost forgot," he said, opening his hand to show what looked like two lumps of quartz. "I've a little treat here for the boys, an American confection that I picked up on my last trip to Liverpool."

"What is it, Mr. Puxley?" Tadhg asked, eyeing it dubiously.

"It's called 'rock candy,'" he replied, his eyes only on Dónal. "But don't let the name fool you. It's pure cane sugar."

Tadhg took a lump then and Dónal after him, the two of them eyeing each other tentatively as they put it into their mouths. But as soon as it hit their taste buds, their eyes lit up and they giggled like gossiping girls, drunk on sweetness, delirious with delight, for while it might have been made of sugar, it tasted like pure heaven.

"Don't chew it, now, boys," Puxley warned, grinning with satisfaction. "Just suck on it. The pleasure will last longer that way."

"Thanks, Mr. Puxley," Tadhg managed to say. "This is the best thing I've ever tasted!"

"You're welcome, Tadhg. And you, too, Dónal. Now, if you'll excuse me."

When Puxley's men had unloaded the kegs, Ahern led the way back toward Ballydonegan, the boys walking now, being tired of riding.

"He sure is different from his brother," Tadhg remarked.

"Yes, he is," Ahern agreed, "and Richard is insanely jealous of him, too, as less-gifted brothers tend to be. But then, Riobárd was his father's favorite, and he has the ear and trust of his uncle John. So perhaps Richard's feelings are understandable, at least from a certain point of view."

"Do you like him?" Dónal asked.

"Indeed, I do, and more than that, I trust him! He's been a great help to me over the years, especially with keeping the peelers away from my shebeen. Then, too, he thinks of himself as Irish and treats us as countrymen, whereas Richard lives among us as a stranger, even though he was born and raised here. But Riobárd is unique in that, I'd say, which is a pity, because if more of the English were like him things might be better between us. But then again, sometimes I think we'll never understand each other, we're just that different as people."

"Oh. Then I like him, too, I guess."

"You sound as if you aren't sure."

"No, I'm not."

"And why not?"

"Because of the way he looked at me when I told him my name."

"Well, I wouldn't read too much into it if I was you. I think he was just surprised."

'Me, too,' Dónal thought, though he kept it to himself.

Still, he wasn't sure of Puxley, and it troubled him mightily that he seemed so familiar. And even the candy seemed suspect, as if he were trying to win his favor with it.

Then they came to the lower end of Allihies, and Ahern pointed out the church on the right, saying that it was for the few Protestant families in the area, while in the field behind it stood the ancient ruins and burial ground of the old church of Kilnamanagh, for which the local parish was named. Ahead in the center of the village stood the new parish church, St. Michael's and, looking toward it, Dónal saw that it

131

bifurcated a row of attached two-story houses, which with a shorter row opposite constituted the village, a sort of elongated *clochán* bordering the street between.

For its size, Allihies was surprisingly busy, with lots of people going to and fro, stepping into the shops and public house, or simply hovering about the street. Many of them, men, women and children alike, were seriously maimed or disfigured from injuries suffered in the mines or at the stamps or on the dressing floors. And seeing them, it was then that Dónal decided he wanted nothing to do with being a miner, Tadhg's enthusiasm notwithstanding.

At the upper end of the village, they passed the local constabulary and several men in blue uniforms sunning themselves out front.

"Ye wouldn't have a drop on ye, Seán, would ye?" one called in English.

"Not for a useless old bostoon like yeerself, I wouldn't!" Ahern retorted without slowing.

"Sure, 'tis good to hear. I'd hate to have to put ye in the lockup and so deprive meself later."

"Pay no attention to that old hypocrite, boys!" Ahern said, dropping back into Irish. "He's just another traitor taking blood money to keep his own people down."

"Yes, Dónal, those peelers are the worst enemies we have," Tadhg seconded, trying to sound authoritative.

"Along with the landlords and grabbers and shopkeepers and gombeen men, I'd say," Ahern affirmed.

"And The Hunger and The Fever and The English," Dónal added, imagining them at the head of a legion of blue-uniformed peelers and black-suited men with little account books, all arrayed against the ragged and barefoot peasants that were his own.

"Yes, and them, too," Ahern sighed, looking at him thoughtfully. "But don't worry. They won't last forever, and as impossible as it may seem now, our day will come again. Indeed, it will."

Yet in that moment, Dónal found it hard to believe.

As they ascended into the bleak hills and were engulfed in the industrial hubbub of the Mountain Mine, Dónal saw the blue-green of copper everywhere, in the tumbled boulders and among the cliffs and crags, and even in the pebbles of the roadbed. Of course, it was the tell-tale sign that led men to dig here in the first place, and to keep digging year after year, following the veins like the children of Hamelin as they ran deeper and deeper into the earth. Still, he was surprised at its prevalence and, recalling the laden wagons at the pier and the heaps in the storage yard, wondered how much had already been removed, and how much was still locked in the earth. When was it his father said the mines opened – 1812? He didn't know how many years ago that was, but if they'd been digging like that since his grandfather's day, then the amount taken out must be staggering, enough to form another Guala, at least. With that understanding, he began to appreciate how extensive the mines really were, and how far into the earth they went. And thinking of the fathomless darkness and remembering Ahern's story and the maimed and disfigured of Allihies, even as the noise and chaos assaulted his senses, he knew that he really, *really* did not want to be a miner.

But then they were at the smithy and Ahern was tying up the pony, telling the boys that he would be a few minutes and that they were to stay close by and out of trouble.

"Come on," Tadhg said, as soon as his father's back was turned. "Let's go look at the Cornish Village."

"But your Da said to stay here," Dónal protested.

"We're not going far. And Jesus, Dónal, don't be so serious about everything!"

Not wanting to seem like a killjoy, Dónal allowed Tadhg to lead him away, along a path and over the crest of a low ridge, where they stopped to view a small cluster of cottages lying just below them in a sheltered cove of the mountain. They were neat and tidy-looking, all freshly thatched and whitewashed, with sturdy doors and painted shutters bordering windows of good clear glass, some even with second stories and chimneys on both ends. Altogether, they had a look of order and prosperity, of hominess, and confidence even, as suggested by the ample space between them. For this was no *clochán* of peasants huddled fearfully together, but a cheerful oasis where people lived in comparative luxury.

"That's the Cornish Village," Tadhg said. "That's where all the Cornish miners live, except for Captain Reed, whose house is by the dressing floors. They get to live there without paying rent, just because they're Cornish and not Irish."

"Really? How do you know?"

"Because I'm smart!" Tadhg replied, then grinned and shrugged. "And because Da told me, and believe me, Dónal, my Da knows *everything!*"

"Yes, I know."

"It's not fair, that we have to pay rent and they don't. But Da said the Company had to do it to get them to come here."

"What did they want them for?"

"Da doesn't know. He said there were Irish miners who could do the work just as well and for less money. And that's not fair either, he said, to take jobs away from us and give them to them. So that's why no one likes them, except for Captain Reed and his son. But then, they've been here from the beginning and didn't take anyone's jobs."

'And that's why no one likes my Da, too,' Dónal thought, holding his breath while expecting Tadhg to say it. But to his relief, he didn't, though Dónal changed the subject just to be sure.

"What's that building all by itself there, the one with the slate roof?" he asked.

"Let's go find out!" Tadhg replied, pulling him along the path.

"But your Da said to stay out of trouble!"

"What he doesn't know won't hurt him! And besides, what harm could there be in just looking in the windows?"

'A lot!' Dónal thought, though he didn't protest, finding himself caught up in the excitement.

And indeed, Tadhg led him on a merry chase, dodging from boulder to boulder so no one would see them coming, approaching the building from the blind side and then creeping furtively to the window.

"I'll go first," Tadhg whispered, "and you keep a lookout."

But Dónal was having none of it, rising with him to peer over the sill. It was a church, he saw, from the pulpit and double row of pews, though at the moment it was occupied only by children, boys on the left and girls on the right, a dozen or more stretched across the front row. Before them stood a man reading aloud from an open book, while the children chorused along, reading from books of their own. They were having school, he realized, remembering Eóghan's descriptions of his own classroom, and he watched in fascination as they put down their books and took up their slates, writing feverishly as the master posed problems.

Yet it wasn't the passing of knowledge that held him enthralled, but the children themselves. They were all spotless and neatly groomed, with their clothes freshly laundered, and all of them wearing shoes! Indeed, they reminded him of Eóghan and the way he'd looked when going to school, and he could even picture him there among them. But what Dónal could not picture there was the boy he'd seen in Seán Ahern's mirror, the filthy, barefoot urchin with matted hair and tattered clothes, a wild thing sprung of the mountain and the bog. For he was *different* from them, he realized, knowing instinctively that *different* meant *less than*, and all because of who he was and what he looked like. All because he was Irish.

And even as the knowledge struck him, branding his soul with inferiority, one of the children glanced toward the window, a girl about his own age with bright eyes and ribbons in her hair, and he ducked quickly down lest she see him and point him out to the others, and they gather at the window to gaze upon his poverty, cold and silent, aware that their ascendancy required no expression.

Without a word to Tadhg, he sprang from the window and ran, toward the path and away from those terrible eyes, desperate for the safety of his own world. As he crested the rise, Tadhg caught up and pulled him to a stop.

"Why did you run away like that?"

"I didn't want her to see me."

"Who? That girl that looked at the window?"

"Yes."

"Why not? All she did was smile at me and then go back to her lesson. What were you afraid of? That she would call the master on us? So what if she did? We weren't doing anything, just looking in the window."

"No, that's not it. I just didn't want her to see me, that's all."

For a long moment, Tadhg didn't say anything, just regarded him thoughtfully, eyes narrow and appraising. "It's because you're dirty, isn't it? And because you're barefoot and your clothes are old and ragged, and you're ashamed of it. You're ashamed of yourself, aren't you?"

Dónal didn't have to reply, for the look in his eyes said it all.

"Ah, Dónal, don't you see that we're this way because they made us so? Because they came and took the land and the good jobs away from us, and now we barely have enough to eat, let alone money to buy good clothes and shoes. So I think they should have to look at us, every day, all the time, so they can't forget what they've done to us, and how much they've hurt us. And I think we should be proud to stand up in front of them, and let them know that even after all they've done to us, we're still here, and always will be. Anyway, that's what my Da said. And I believe him. Don't you?"

"I guess so," Dónal allowed, wishing for all the world that he could be like Tadhg, so strong and sure of himself and his place in the world. And not just to make a show of it either, like he had for his father, but really be like him.

"Sure you do," Tadhg said, punching him lightly in the arm. "Because like I said, my Da knows everything!"

In spite of himself, Dónal couldn't help but smile, feeling the warmth of Tadhg's friendship wash over him in a wave.

"Come on, I'll race you," Tadhg said, and took off without waiting for a reply.

When they reached the smithy, Dónal bringing up the rear, they found Ahern waiting for them, a look of consternation on his face.

"Here now, why are you running like the Evil Thing is after you?" he exclaimed. "Is there trouble in your wake, after I told you to behave yourselves?"

"No, Da!" Tadhg protested, his look of innocence wanting only for a halo. "Dónal and I were just having a race, that's all!"

"Hm," Ahern grunted, his one eye piercing and dark. "I know you too well, Tadhg Ahern, to be taken in quite so easily!"

"We didn't do anything bad, Da, really. All we did was have a look at the Cornish Village and then race back here."

"All right then," Ahern sighed, thinking that not even one day was gone and already they were in it up to their necks. "Since nothing seems to be following you, I suppose I'll have to take you at your word, or at least assume that you got away with it, whatever it was.

"But come on now, boys. We're on the last leg of our odyssey and home is in sight."

"Will we have to choose between Scylla and Charybdis?" Tadhg asked, as he climbed onto Spota's back and pulled Dónal up behind him.

"Not this time, son. It looks like clear sailing from here."

"Too bad. I was hoping for some fun."

⬥

In the evening while Ahern busied himself with supper, the boys played in the yard, doing a reprise of their morning romp, finding in each other's company endless possibilities for fun. But when the evening whistle blew, Tadhg gave it up and went down to the roadway to await his mother's arrival from her work in the home of Captain Reed. When she appeared, he shouted, "Mam!" and ran into her embrace. And as they walked up the path, Dónal noticed how much alike they were, with the same strong and sturdy form, head of thick sandy blond hair and twinkling eyes, in which the joy of living shone defiantly when they smiled. As they neared and Ahern came out to greet them, his wife fairly danced into his arms and embraced him with such passion that it might've been years since she'd seen him last, rather than just a few hours.

"I love you, Seán my darling," she said, kissing him shamelessly on the lips, not caring that Dónal or even the whole world was watching.

"And I love you, Órla," Ahern replied softly, the two of them squeezing each other tightly before opening their embrace to their son, closing him in with their arms even as he wrapped his around them. "And you, too, Tadhg. And you, too."

Watching them, Dónal couldn't help but feel envious, wishing that his family was still intact and that they could love each other that way. But then the woman turned her smile upon him, warming his heart with its radiance, and he suddenly understood why Ahern thought himself so lucky.

"You must be Dónal," she said, coming to him, the touch of her fingers in his hair making his scalp tingle and his ears burn.

"And you must be Helen of Troy," he replied, the words again coming from his mouth as if preordained, though turning him scarlet nonetheless, sure as he was that Tadhg was rolling his eyes in disgust.

But she just laughed and clapped her hands delightedly. "Ah, Seán, of all the things you told me about him, you never once mentioned his silver tongue!"

Looking at him appraisingly for a moment then, she nodded her head in affirmation. "Yes, you'll break a heart or two in your day, young O'Sullivan of the sweet mouth, what with those lovely green eyes and that fine red hair! But no, Dónal, no Helen am I. Órla is my name, and just plain Órla I am, never mind the size of my head at the moment."

Bending down, she kissed the top of his head, turning his face scarlet again. "It's my pleasure to meet you, and the more I see of you, the happier I'll be."

Not knowing what else to say, Dónal just gazed into her smiling eyes. But then a movement beyond caught his eye, and he turned to find his father coming up the path.

"Da!" he shouted, running to greet him, intending to jump into his embrace just as Tadhg had his mother's, though the man's appearance stopped him in his tracks.

"Are you all right, Da?" he asked, noting his gray skin and glassy red eyes, and the trickle of blood at the corner of his mouth. "Have you been coughing again?"

"I'm fine, Dónal, and please stop asking me," O'Sullivan said, his voice hoarse and his manner irritable. "It's just the dust from the mines. But it goes away. Just ask Seán there."

But Ahern just changed the subject (suspiciously, in Dónal's mind), saying he would walk them up Guala if they would stay for supper, an offer O'Sullivan gladly accepted. And as they gathered around the table, sharing the blessing and then their meal, Dónal felt more at home than he ever had before, as the Aherns reached out to embrace their friends and pull them into the bosom of their family. But more than that, it was the connection he felt with his father, sitting close beside him and listening as he talked about his day in the mines, and then telling him in turn about his day with the Aherns. The only cloud came when he told of Riobárd Puxley's invitation to visit, and his father reacted angrily, telling him to stay well away from the Puxleys, as they were enemies and not to be trusted. But it passed just as quickly, and the rest of the evening was spent in harmony.

Later, when the long day was done and they were back at Cahernageeha, Dónal lay in his blanket by the fire and reflected on his odyssey, thinking it seemed a lifetime since he'd awakened that morning, and wondering if he would feel the same the next night. He hoped so, for the day had been grand and glorious, and if he lived a million such days, he would never tire of them. Still, the best of it was the time spent with his father and, when memory of the rest had faded, he was sure those parts would live on in his heart.

Hearing his father clear his throat, he turned toward the bed, finding him wrapped in his own blanket and facing the wall.

"I love you, Da," he said, speaking softly in case he was already asleep.

"I know you do, Dónal," O'Sullivan replied without turning. "Now go to sleep."

PART THREE

• The Clan Dónal Cam •

chapter 8

Castletownbere
Christmas Morning, 1848

IT WAS SO PEACEFUL AND COMFORTING, sitting among the faithful in the crowded pew, the familiar ritual of the Catholic Mass warming Dónal's soul even as the proximity of his fellows warmed his body. It was something he'd come to look forward to, the one hour of each week he could spend among them without fear, knowing they brought only their goodness with them into the House of the Lord. It buoyed his spirits and gave him hope, and he wished with all his heart that his father would come, too, to share in it and bring the goodness that was in him, so his fellows could see it and perhaps forget their disdain and unkind epithets.

Yet it wasn't the service or his fellows, or even his father that was on Dónal's mind just then. Rather, he was thinking of himself and the many changes in his life, and how much happier he was now than ever before. For the autumn months had been good ones for himself and his father, as they discarded the broken shell of their old relationship and evolved from related strangers into father and son. Of course, it helped that the man had put away his anger and come to a new understanding of his son, allowing him to break out of his emotional shell and begin to blossom. And blossom he had, as the inspired tutelage of Seán Ahern opened and stretched his mind, and the irrepressible Tadhg kept him challenged and stimulated with his boundless energy and limitless appetite for adventure. Even his body made up for lost time, benefiting from the long walks over Guala and the merry romps with Tadhg, not to mention the days spent rambling over the country-side with Ahern, visiting places of historical or mythological import, about which the man seemed to know everything.

And one of those outings stuck out in his mind especially, though not for where they'd gone or what he'd learned. It was that last Saturday in September, when they'd taken the road from the old Dooneen Mine all the way to Reentrusk at the north end of the bay, where the hollow of Eskinanaun slashed through the stony hillside like a green scar. Following the boreen into it, they came upon a lone cot-tage near the top, just below which was the ivy vine that Dónal's father had so lovingly described, the one that grew against the rock face in the shape of a tree. But while it was indeed beautiful and unique, Dónal found it less impressive than the view back toward Allihies, with the mountains and bay spreading out so magnificently before him.

But even as he admired its heartbreaking beauty, he felt strange eyes upon him and turned to find the most heartbreakingly beautiful girl standing in the cottage doorway. She was about Tadhg's age or perhaps a bit older, with luxuriant red hair and eyes the color of afternoon sky. And seeing her, he stood very still, fearing to break the spell and send her back to the enchanted world from which she must surely have come. Even so, she felt his gaze across the void, and for a long moment they knew only each other, the rest of the world falling away and ceasing to exist. But then a voice called her by name and she was gone behind the closed door, though not before blessing him with a smile.

Turning back to his companions, he found Tadhg rolling his eyes in disgust. "Jesus Christ!" he exclaimed. "Not only does he like to take baths, but he likes *girls*, too!" But Dónal didn't care. The girl had smiled at him, and he knew he'd never be the same.

Yet he'd seen no more of her after that, and though he often thought of going back to Eskinanaun, he never had. For he was busy with boys now, with the circle of friends into which Tadhg introduced him, starting with Níall Harrington and Liam Kelly who lived just a few fields above the Aherns. They were a year older than Tadhg, born of twin sisters just a day apart, and looked so much alike that people habitually referred to them as the "Kellington Twins," an epithet enhanced by the fact that they were inseparable and had the maddening habit of finishing each other's sentences. Then there was Pat Donegan, the only son of the last Donegans at Ballydonegan, and Art O'Shea and Dan MacCarthy, both orphaned by the Hunger and now living with relations in Allihies. They were all rough boys, children of the mountain and the bog, fitting as anonymously into the landscape as the gorse and heather, the grass and stone. Yet they were loyal and trustworthy, and readily accepted Dónal, even though he was younger.

Not that Tadhg gave them any choice in the matter, since he was their undisputed leader owing to his size and indomitable spirit, and the fact that he was the best fighter among them. For it was common for young boys to kill their free time by roaming about in familial gangs and picking fights with each other, just as their ancestors had feuded with neighboring clans and fought each other in countless petty wars, as much to alleviate the boredom of their pastoral existence as anything else. Typically the confrontations were decided by single combat, usually with the eldest brothers of the respective "clans" engaging in fisticuffs until one was knocked senseless or beaten bloody or just gave it up. And so, having no brothers of their own, the boys had come together more or less by default and as much for mutual protection as camaraderie, and by unspoken consent Tadhg became their leader and therefore their champion.

Yet the hierarchy had been turned on its head soon after Dónal joined them, on the first Saturday in October when the mines were closed to settle accounts from the previous month and let bargains for the coming one. Knowing that some of the men would be flush and eager to squander it on the drink, Ahern went to his shebeen and took the boys with him, thinking they couldn't get into too much trouble that high on the mountain. Once there, he pointed out the remains of an old ringfort and the boys charged off like hounds after a fox, thinking there'd be lots of fun to be had there. Yet they were disappointed, finding little of interest beyond the crumbling earthen walls. So they sat down with their backs to the inner wall and talked about mining and how they'd be a crew together when they grew up.

But then an angry voice shouted from above them, demanding to know what they were doing there. Of course, they jumped up in surprise, even as four boys jumped down from the wall and stood before them, all brothers and doing their best to look tough and menacing. Their age range appeared to be about the same as Dónal's and his friends', though it was difficult to be sure for the size that was in them. Indeed, the eldest was almost as tall as a man and heavily built, with mean dark eyes and a crown of kinky auburn hair.

"This is our fort, Tadhg Ahern," he said, "and if you don't want the father and mother of a good beating, then you'd better get out!"

So he gave his challenge and waited for Tadhg to meet it. But seeing that even the smallest of these brothers looked like more than a match for him, Dónal fully expected Tadhg to yield. Surely there'd be no shame in it, for how could his friends expect him to step into a certain thrashing? But Tadhg had other ideas.

"Ah, bugger off with you, Padge, you fat ugly gobshite!" Tadhg retorted. "This place is no more yours than are the four winds, and it'll take more than bluff to get us out!"

"Tadhg, what are you doing?" Dónal demanded, grabbing him by the arm. "We don't want this place, and it's surely not worth fighting for. Let's just give it to them and find something better to do!"

"Yes, Tadhg," Padge snickered. "You'd better listen to your little runt of a friend there, if you know what's good for you! He knows when to be afraid!"

"Shut up, Dónal!" Tadhg exclaimed angrily. "It's my place to handle this, not yours! And anyway, if I don't deal with him now, I'll just have to do it later, else we'll never be able to get around him."

But Dónal wasn't listening, just staring coldly at the big boy. "I'm not afraid of you, or anyone else! It's just that we've better things to do than fight over this old place."

"Oh, I see the way of it, now," Padge sneered. "You're going to run out on a fight, but it's not because you're afraid of me. You're going to let me kick your molly arse out of here just because you like having it kicked. Well grab your ankles, runt, and let's get on with it!"

"I said, I'm not afraid of you!" Dónal shouted, his voice shrill with anger, "and if it's a fight you're after, then I'll give you one!"

"If that's the way you want it!" Padge clenched his meaty fists and advanced on Dónal.

But Tadhg jumped between them. "Only cowards pick on the little ones, Padge! You know I'm the one for this and not him! Or are you afraid to fight somebody your own size?"

"It was his idea, not mine! But go on with you, runt, and let the big fellows settle this! You can pick up Tadhg's teeth for him when we're done!"

"Get out of my way, Tadhg! I can take care of myself!"

"Are you daft, man? He's twice the size of you!"

"Fighting was your idea, Tadhg! I was all for leaving and being done with it! So you got me into it, and if you aren't going to help, then get out of the way!"

Tadhg opened his mouth to protest further, but seeing the steel in Dónal's eyes, he knew it to be in vain. "All right, Dónal. If you're set on this, then I won't stop you. But come over here and talk to me first!"

"Running out on me, are you?" Padge taunted.

"Ah, bugger yourself, Padge!" Tadhg said, as he pulled Dónal off to the side, then spoke to him so the other boys couldn't hear. "You've never been in a fight before, have you Dónal?" When Dónal shook his head, he asked, "Has anyone ever taught you how to fight?" When the answer was again negative, he shook his own head. "Oh, good Christ, if you aren't in for it now!"

"I'm not afraid of him!" Dónal hissed through clenched teeth.

"It doesn't matter whether you're afraid of him or not! He's going to beat the shit out of you, and I'm afraid of that, and even more of what Da will do to me for letting him! So listen carefully and maybe, just maybe, he won't kill you. Now, he's twice the size of you, and if he gets his hands on you, you're done for. Your only chance is to stay away from him and dodge in and out when you hit him. If he swings for your head, duck and dodge to the side. If he runs at you, dodge to the side and hit him as he goes by. But whatever you do, don't let him get his hands on you because, to be honest, I don't know if I can get him off, especially with his three mugs there backing him up. But if he does get ahold of you, remember Odysseus and the Cyclops."

Though he had no idea what Tadhg meant, Dónal nodded anyway. Then Tadhg pulled him close so that their foreheads touched.

"What, are you kissing now?" Padge shouted, sharing a laugh with his brothers.

"Any questions, Dónal?" Tadhg asked, ignoring him.

"Just one. Who is he, anyway?"

"He's Paidín O'Sullivan, the son of Big Paddy."

Dónal pulled away then and took a couple of steps toward Padge. "I know your Da, Padge. I met him the night Tadhg's Da gave him a good thrashing. If a one-eyed, one-handed cripple can do that to him, then you can't be much, either."

Rage spread across Padge's face then, his eyes narrowing into mean little slits. Snorting like a bull, he charged so fast that Dónal had no time to think, only to react, dropping to the ground so the big boy stumbled over him and smacked headfirst into the wall.

"Good man, Dónal!" Tadhg shouted. "That's showing him!"

But his smile quickly disappeared when Padge rose shakily to his feet. "I'm not done with you, runt!" he said, approaching more cautiously this time, his anger controlled and deadly.

And though Dónal dodged to the side and tried to back away, Padge was too quick for him, wrapping him in a bear hug before he could do anything about it, squeezing until his lungs burned for air.

"Are you afraid of me now, runt?" Padge grunted.

Seeing the malice in his mean little eyes, Dónal was indeed afraid. He flailed his one free hand, smacking Padge about the head and trying to push away, but to no avail. Then he remembered Tadhg's words and, the meaning becoming suddenly clear, he jabbed a finger into Padge's eye. Though the boy dropped him and wailed in pain, Dónal didn't give him time to recover, just struck him with his fist squarely in the nose, breaking it with an audible pop and splashing blood on both of them.

For a moment, Padge just blinked in surprise, too stunned to move. Then tears welled up in his eyes and washed the meanness away, and suddenly he was just a little boy again, hurt and hurting, his injury running much deeper than his shattered nose.

"Good man, Dónal!" Tadhg said, slapping him on the back while the others cheered.

But Dónal just turned away, running from the ringfort toward the road, oblivious to the calls of his friends, not wanting them to see his own tears.

"What's your hurry, Dónal?" Ahern asked when he ran into the dell. "Have you been into mischief?"

But Tadhg was right behind him and it was he who answered. "No, Da, it's not like that. We won. Or rather Dónal won. Paidín O'Sullivan and his brothers came into the ringfort while we were there, and told us to get out or they'd give us a thrashing. But Dónal challenged Padge to a fight and beat him! Even though Padge is twice his size, he beat him! You should have seen him, Da! He was brilliant!"

"Is that true, Dónal?" Ahern asked, turning his piercing eye on Dónal. "Were you brilliant?"

"No, Seán, I wasn't," Dónal replied, his voice small and quavering. "I think I broke his nose. It was all so stupid, because it wasn't worth fighting over. I hurt him and it wasn't even worth fighting over!"

"Ah, Dónal, there aren't many things in this world that really are worth fighting over, except to defend the weak against those who would take advantage of them. But, ah well. Padge will survive, and surely he had it coming. He's a bully and a coward, just like his father, though maybe now he'll think twice before picking on the small and weak. And as much as I disapprove of fighting, I have to admit that one less bully in the world is a good thing. So don't be too hard on yourself. You did the right thing."

Later, as they walked home in the darkness, Dónal told his father about the fight and what Ahern had to say. "Yes, Seán is right," he said. "Sometimes you have to fight to protect yourself and your rights, or those of your family and countrymen. The world is full of bullies, son, and if we don't stand up to them they'll grind us under, sooner or later. So you did the right thing and I'm proud of you for it."

"Are you proud of Eóghan for fighting against the English, Da?"

"I suppose I should've seen that coming. Yes, Dónal, I'm proud of him for having the courage of his convictions and standing up for what he believed in, for fighting for his countrymen and those too weak to defend themselves against the British Empire. I didn't want him to go because I didn't think he could win, and I didn't want to lose him."

Then he paused and shook his head. "No, that's not it, really. It was for purely selfish reasons that I didn't want him to go. You see, I didn't want him to throw away all I'd sacrificed to get him educated, so that he could be a man of substance in the world and restore us to our former glory. And that's the part that I'm not proud of him for, that he didn't stop to think it through before acting. Now he's wasted not only my sacrifice but his own future, as well, and left me with this bitter dilemma of being both proud and angry at the same time."

O'Sullivan fell silent after that, and Dónal left him alone with it, understanding that his father needed to heal from within, and find a way to forgive his son and himself on his own terms. Yet in later years when he looked back on it, Dónal always regretted not speaking the thought in his mind: 'Eóghan's life wasn't yours to live, Da.'

But he didn't say it, and afterward there was no need, since his father seemed like a new man in so many ways, especially in regard to their relationship. And of all the changes in his life, that was the most significant for Dónal. Of course he reveled in his father's new attentiveness, so much that he no longer noticed the man's abiding introspection, or saw the melancholy that came over him in the dark and empty hours of the night. Only once had he caught a hint of it, on a fine Sunday evening when they'd taken their chairs outside after supper and sat under the great yew tree to watch the sunset. A gentle breeze had whispered through its boughs, while the sun sank in a blaze of glory and the shadows lengthened around them.

"Isn't it grand, Da?" Dónal had asked through a yawn. But when his father didn't answer, he glanced up and saw that he wasn't watching the sunset at all, but staring absently at the Big House, his mind in another place and time entirely.

"Are you all right, Da?" he asked, more to break his father's mood than to get a response. But still the man didn't answer, just plucked him lightly from his chair and cradled him in his arms, holding him till long after night fell and brought the stars to watch over them.

And still O'Sullivan sat there, staring through the darkness toward Dunboy, picturing the Big House as it was on that fateful evening of June 17, 1834, when John Reed took him there at the bidding of his master. The old man was sitting by the fire in a great wing-backed chair, sipping brandy from a snifter, a hound lying at his feet and a servant hovering at his shoulder. Slowly his eyes came up and he smiled in a self-satisfied sort of way, looking his visitor up and down as though he were a slave on the auction block, before staring him coldly in the eyes. It was then that O'Sullivan understood the date to have been chosen deliberately, the anniversary of the fall of Dunboy, just as a reminder of who was who in the grand scheme of things. For though the big Irishman with the regal pedigree might be the world's greatest miner and command the respect of even Captain Reed, John Puxley was the lord of the manor, and that was what really mattered in the world. In the end, the old man said nothing, just gave a little backward wave of his hand like a priest shooing a penitent from the confessional, and that was it.

O'Sullivan closed his eyes against the memory of it, regretting with all his heart that he'd let himself get sucked in, for the rage he brought away had consumed him and sent him spiraling into a bitter destiny, only to realize too late that it was just what the old man intended. But so it was that he'd squandered his prime on an impossible dream, and his family, too, the little boy in his arms being all that was left to him.

"I should've taken you all away from here," he murmured to the sleeping boy. "I should've protected you from our bitter legacy of Dunboy. Indeed, Dónal, I can still take you."

Yet his words were as empty as the night air, and he knew it, too, having gone too far down the road to ever turn back. His mood was as black as the night by the time he heaved a world-weary sigh and lay his son by the fire.

But Dónal didn't see it, feeling only the warmth of his embrace, the faraway look in his eyes forgotten in the light of morning. And anyway, he was preoccupied with a problem of his own, which was how to ask his father for new clothes. For the sight of himself in Seán Ahern's mirror had left him self-conscious and obsessed with his appearance, especially as compared to the Cornish children. And though he began to bathe himself and wash his clothes every Saturday evening, still he looked like a wild thing sprung of the mountain and the bog. So, after days of agonizing, he finally just blurted it out one morning over breakfast. His father listened with a bemused sort of smile, having noticed his sudden obsession with cleanliness, though giving it little thought. But now it all made sense, and seeing his son's anxiety in asking, he understood his feelings to be more than superficial. And though he was sorely tempted to ask why, he also sensed that his son didn't want to tell him.

"All right, Dónal," he said, deciding to treat him as a man and respect his privacy. "I suppose you're about due for it, and though you're a bit young yet to be wearing shoes, I can afford them. So we'll go into town soon and take care of it. How does that sound?"

Dónal was too overjoyed to answer, running into his father's arms and burying his face in his chest.

Making good on his promise, O'Sullivan took him to a shop in Castletownbere the very next Saturday morning, and bought him two sets of clothing and a pair of shoes, insisting only that they be large enough to "grow into." Not that Dónal minded, being happy just to get new clothes, and to share the experience with his father.

But when it came time to pay, the English shopkeeper leaned in close, and spoke in a voice as soft and confidential as a priest in the confessional. "Shall I put you down for it, then?" When O'Sullivan answered with only an icy stare, he sighed. "Ah, well. As you wish."

"Never go into debt with a shopkeeper, Dónal," O'Sullivan said, as he counted out the money. "They're the worst gombeen men of all."

"I know, Da,'" Dónal agreed, smiling brazenly. "And sure, if they don't think they're doin' you a favor for it, too!"

Though the man scowled at Dónal, he didn't dare retort, as much from fear of losing the sale as from his large and intimidating father. He just muttered "Bloody Irish" under his breath as the door closed behind them, as though the two words said it all.

As they walked away, O'Sullivan smiled and patted his son on the back. "Good man, Dónal!" he said, making Dónal's spirit swell with the pride of approval, so much that he forgot to see if the passersby noticed his new clothes.

But then he saw Father Fitzgerald taking note of him at Mass the next morning, giving him a quick once-over and a nod of approval, and he grinned back with unabashed pride, till remembering it was a deadly sin.

Not that the old man cared. He was just happy to see the boy back after such a long absence, indeed, his first Mass since his mother died in the winter. But a few days earlier, a message came to the priest out of the blue inviting him to Cahernageeha for supper. Upon his arrival, O'Sullivan greeted him warmly, which was a surprise in itself, and showed him to a seat by the fire, pouring him a drink and exchanging a few pleasantries before coming to the point, though reluctantly it seemed.

"I've been feeling guilty about keeping Dónal from Mass," he said without preamble, "and I want him to start going again."

"Ah, so the truth will out in the end, will it not, Eóghan," the priest said. "Well, that's simple enough, I'd say, though it begs the question of why you couldn't just bring him to Mass and save me the trip?"

"Well, it's this way, Father. He'll be coming, but not me."

"And why not, Eóghan?"

"You already know and I'll not spell it out for you," O'Sullivan replied irritably. "I've made my choice in the matter, as a man and on the basis of knowledge. But Dónal is still a boy and innocent in the ways of the world, and I'd not have it on my soul to choose for him."

"Your choice might be made, Eóghan, but I don't think it was knowledge so much as anger with me. Would it help to change your mind if I admitted I was wrong in trying to entice young Eóghan to the seminary? I didn't understand things as I do now, and I'm truly sorry for the anguish I caused you. Indeed, I'd not have it on my soul that I was the cause of driving a man from his Church and his God, especially a man such as yourself with such enormous potential for the good. So come back to us, Eóghan, won't you? It's never too late, you know."

O'Sullivan hesitated, touched by the old man's sincerity. But then he shook his head. "No, I think not," he said. "At least . . . not yet."

"Ah, well. You will do as you will do, and nothing I can say will change it. But Eóghan, that still doesn't explain why you called me here, when you could've just sent the boy on his own. I'd have seen him at Mass and come around to him. Indeed, I've a soft spot for him, don't you know? He's really quite remarkable."

"Which is exactly why I wanted to speak to you first. As you know, he's also my only son now, which means he's the only one left to carry on our noble lineage, something he can't do as a celibate. So I need to know that you won't try to entice him into the priesthood, especially if something should happen to me while he's still a child. If he chooses it for himself when he grows up, then so be it and on his own head. But I'd not have him influenced while he's yet a child."

"Have you not been listening to me, Eóghan?" Father Fitzgerald said, becoming irritable himself. "Did you not hear me apologize for trying to influence young Eóghan? Do you really need more than that?"

"As much as you needed for me spell out the reason I asked you here, I need to hear this from you. Without equivocation."

"All right, Eóghan, all right. If swearing an oath is the price for this boy's immortal soul, then I'd be a poor priest indeed not to pay it. I give you my word, Eóghan O'Sullivan, as a man of God and with God as my witness, that I will not in any way try to induce your son to join the priesthood, either while he is a child or when he becomes a man, and whether you are in this world or the next. Will that do?"

"Yes, Father Fitzgerald, it will. And I thank you for it."

But the old priest just shrugged. "You're an arrogant man, Eóghan O'Sullivan," he said, fixing him with an icy stare, "and too stupid to see the ends of your own arguments! God is eternal, and His Holy Church is eternal, and it will get along just fine without your progeny among its stewards. Yet the lineage of Dónal Cam is not eternal, and will not survive without your son to carry it forward, and as a good Irishman, I can see the value in having it continue. But don't insult me by thanking me for being smart enough to figure it out on my own."

"I meant no offense, Father."

"Still, you've given plenty! But as I seem to be getting soft in my old age, I'll forgive your trespass. Now, is there anything else you want, Eóghan, and I'll warn you that now is not a good time to ask!"

"No, Father. That's it."

"Good!" the old man said. "Then if it's all the same to you, I'll not stay for supper, thank you, as I seem to have lost my appetite." Turning to Dónal, he added, "But I'll see you bright and early next Sunday morning, young man. And don't you dare be late!"

As he settled into his trap, the old priest turned to O'Sullivan with a crooked little smile. "Ah, me, Eóghan. In all the excitement I almost forgot some important news of my own. I've been relieved of my duties here in Castletownbere, and reassigned to Ballylongford in the County Kerry. I'll be leaving soon, but my curate, Father Michael Enright, will remain as parish priest. I think you'll find him an empathetic sort. Indeed, you should have a chat with him sometime."

Then Father Fitzgerald snapped the reins and drove away, leaving O'Sullivan gaping after him. "Why you dirty old . . ." he muttered, leaving the curse unspoken in respect of Dónal's youth.

Not that he'd have heard it anyway, being busy with his own thoughts. "Da?" he asked after a moment. "Who was Dónal Cam?"

But O'Sullivan just shook his head. "Not now, Dónal," he said, his eyes on the Big House. "The time hasn't come for it yet."

"When will it come, Da?"

"Someday. It will come someday."

"Is this one of those things I'll understand when I grow up?"

"No, Dónal. You won't have to wait that long."

But the autumn slipped into winter and someday didn't come, and though Dónal hadn't forgotten it, he didn't ask again. And given his father's reluctance, perhaps it was, after all, one of those things that was better not to know.

Nor did Dónal ask him to come to Mass, understanding that it would come with time or not at all. Still, he hoped for it, especially that very morning, when his father uncharacteristically walked him into town. But in the event, he went no further than the church steps.

"You go on and I'll meet you here later," he said, walking away before Dónal could say anything.

As Dónal watched him turn the corner, feeling suddenly empty and alone, he wanted to run after and beg him to come back, in case he was gone forever like Eóghan. But instead he just went into the church and took his habitual seat near the door. 'I got along without Eóghan,' he thought, 'and I can get along without Da if I have to.'

But then his eyes strayed to the Crucifix behind the altar, and it seemed that Christ was looking down at him, his face twisted in agony at his unkind thoughts. 'Oh, Jesus, did you hear me?' he asked silently, feeling suddenly guilty for bringing anything but goodness into the House of the Lord. Shutting out his disappointment then, he tried to think good thoughts, so the god on the Cross would stop staring at him.

And now as Father Enright intoned the closing prayer, Dónal said a silent prayer of his own, for his father and for Eóghan, asking God to grant them peace and thanking Him for all the good things they'd done for him. When the service was over, he hurried outside to meet his father, bringing the peace of the Mass with him, a smile on his face and in his heart, even as the sun peeked through the clouds to shine upon him like rays of hope.

But the sight of his father drove it all away. For he looked as if he'd been beaten with a stick, with his face gaunt and gray as Irish weather, his hair disheveled and eyes bleary and red. Even as he swept him into an embrace that spoke of joy and yet seemed so desperate, Dónal could feel his ribs under his jacket and hear the rattle in his lungs.

"Are you all right, Da?" he asked, knowing what the answer would be, and that he wouldn't believe it.

"I'm fine, Dónal!" O'Sullivan replied, his chuckle seeming contrived. "I'm as strong as a bull and just as mean. So don't worry for me; I'll be here for a long time yet!"

At that, Dónal sighed, and buried his face into his father's chest, knowing there was no point in pressing it.

"I hope so, Da," he said, the words as desperate as his father's hug. "Because I love you."

"I know you do, son. Merry Christmas!"

chapter 9

Cahernageeha
17 June, 1849

THE WIND SIGHED MOURNFULLY through the branches of the great yew, as though singing a lament for the sadness of Erin and all the troubles of her poor hapless people. And sitting with his back to its trunk, Dónal felt the weight of that sadness as his own troubles bore down upon him, sapping his strength and crushing his spirit like snow on spring blossoms. For his father had had a bad night of it, continuing the trend of late, and he'd been up with him, holding his hand and doing his best to care for him, as much from his own fear as any sense of familial duty, and even though Ahern had come to stay with them till he "got better." But Dónal knew he was too far gone to ever get better, the racking cough having worn him down to a ghost of himself, becoming more constant as he grew weaker, and weakening him more as it became constant. How much more could he take, he wondered, with his body consuming itself like a candle and even his indomitable spirit breaking? And as much as he feared losing him, wouldn't death be a welcome relief to his suffering? Yet his father seemed to be holding on purposefully, and he wondered if it had anything to do with the special errand they were going on today, or the fact that it was exactly a year since Eóghan's departure.

"I wish they'd hurry up!" he said, thinking aloud.

"No you don't," Tadhg replied from beside him.

"What do you mean by that?"

"Nothing."

Tadhg shrugged and walked away, leaving Dónal to scowl at his back. It wasn't like him to make oblique statements and not explain himself. But then he'd been uncharacteristically quiet and subdued since arriving with Spota in the early morning, as if he'd been told a dark secret against his will and couldn't relieve his burden by passing it on. Just what was going on, Dónal wondered, and why did everyone seem to know but him?

Then he heard Ahern's deep voice boom out in exasperation. "For Christ's sake, Eóghan," he demanded, *"can't you just let it go?"* But there was no answer, just a silence that yet spoke volumes, and suddenly he knew Tadhg was right.

Sighing, he laid his head back against the rough bark, closed his eyes and tried to remember the happy days of autumn before his father's illness had turned their lives upside down. But it was just a blur to him now, something that had been taken away before he'd even had a chance to enjoy it. For with the wet and cold of winter, his father began to waste away under the onslaught of his illness, so that by St. Patrick's Day, he was too weak to go to work. Seeing his father lying sick in the bed, the very one in which his mother had died, was a frightening and horrible experience, and Dónal did everything in his power to nurse him back to health. And sure, if he didn't get better after a few days, even going back to work briefly, though the effort merely hastened his decline, so that within a couple of weeks he was bedridden again. Then there'd been the night when Dónal was sure he was dying and ran all the way to Castletownbere to fetch the doctor, though his diagnosis made him wish he hadn't.

"You have the 'miner's con,' Eóghan, and there's nothing I can do for you," Dr. Armstrong had said in English, speaking frankly, as he knew O'Sullivan would want.

"To be sure, Phillip," O'Sullivan had rasped weakly, "I could've told you myself, I've seen that much of it in my time." Then he'd glanced at Dónal, and asked pointedly, "How long do I have?"

"Not long I'm afraid, a few weeks at most. So you'd best get your affairs in order. Is there anything I can do to help?"

But O'Sullivan had just shaken his head 'no,' unable to answer through his coughing.

After that, Dónal lived in constant anxiety, scarcely daring to leave his father's side, fearing that he might die while he was away. Then their money began to run low, and he had the added worry that they might go hungry, even though Ahern assured him to the contrary.

But then Captain Reed and his son, John, Jr. (or *Seán Óg*, as he was affectionately known), came to visit and brought a collection they'd taken up among the Cornish miners. Presenting it to O'Sullivan in a leather pouch, Captain Reed said in English, "There's thirty pounds in it, Eóghan. We hope it will see you through your time of need."

"Thirty pounds, did ye say!" Ahern exclaimed. "'Tis indeed a princely sum, and a gift well given so."

"'Tis no gift," Seán Óg protested, "but a token of respect for the best miner with whom we've ever had the privilege of working!"

But O'Sullivan just stared at Captain Reed. "Will my son get a pension, John?"

"No, Eóghan, he won't," Captain Reed replied. "Company policy is that pensions go only to wives and not to children. But then, you knew that already, didn't you."

"Thirty pieces of silver for a life's work," O'Sullivan sighed, taking the pouch, "*traitor's* wages, and even that from the kindness of strangers. But sure, if I'm not forgettin' my manners so. Thank you for your generosity, John, and please pass it along to the others. 'Twill help my son get on in the world, and maybe he won't have to follow his Da into the darkness like I did my own."

After that, the four men talked quietly among themselves, reminiscing in the way that men do when they've spent their lives together, but don't really know each other. When the time came to go, Captain Reed took O'Sullivan's hand, and said, "*Slán abhaile, a Eóghain a chará*" (Safe home, Eóghan, my friend).

But his words made Dónal shudder, understanding that Captain

160

Reed meant something other than the physical home in which they were gathered, that he was saying good-bye to someone he didn't expect to see again.

O'Sullivan didn't reply, just nodded. But as they were leaving, he called out, "I don't want my boy in the mines, John! See to it, will you?"

At that, Captain Reed looked at Dónal as though seeing him for the first time, delving into his eyes like they were veins of ore that would lead him into the trackless depths of his soul, and so reveal his intrinsic worth. Then he nodded at O'Sullivan, before disappearing into the night.

The next evening brought Riobárd Puxley to their door, and Dónal was so surprised to see him that he almost forgot to ask him in. But Ahern came to the rescue, jumping up from the hearth and greeting him warmly before leading him to the bedside. Yet he didn't stay long, as he seemed ill-at-ease and had little to say, especially since O'Sullivan just glared at him. Dónal held the door for him as he left, and passing, Puxley nodded for him to follow into the yard. Obliging, he stood before him uncertainly, wondering what he wanted and still unsure of his feelings for him, especially since his father was as hostile as Ahern was friendly, leaving him in a quandary as to which lead to follow. Nor did it help that Puxley seemed not to trust *him,* at least judging by the shade he kept drawn behind his eyes.

Sensing his unease, Puxley pulled a lump of rock candy from his pocket. "It's all right, Dónal," he said in his English-accented Irish. "It's just a gift between friends. Indeed, you deserve it for the way you've looked after your father. Every man should be so lucky as to have a son like you."

Dónal took the candy then, though he thrust it stubbornly into his pocket. "Thank you, Mr. Puxley," he said in English, just to let him know he wasn't fooling anyone.

"The old memories die hard, indeed, I see, Dónal O'Sullivan Béara," Puxley said, his sad smile making Dónal regret his words. But before he could say anything else, Puxley mounted his black stallion and rode away, leaving him staring into the night.

After that, there were no more visits, and the days dragged slowly by, one merging seamlessly into another till it seemed that time ceased to exist in the face of his father's illness. Yet now that the end was near and there were so few days left, it seemed like no time at all, and Dónal chided himself for not appreciating it, and for his unkind thoughts on that Christmas morning that now felt like a different lifetime. How would he get along, he wondered, all alone in the world and with no family of his own? Sure, Ahern had said he would come to live with them, but he knew it wouldn't be the same. For as bad as his life had been at times, still it was familiar, and how could he give that up? How could he bear not being in his own home by his own hearth among his own kith and kin, not surrounded by the protective walls of old Cahernageeha, not hearing the wind sigh through the great yew, the everyday things that rooted him to the Earth and his life upon it?

With the sudden knowledge that it would all be taken from him in the end, panic seized him and he jumped up, intending to run into the cottage and tell his father that he couldn't die, that he had to go on living and never mind the pain, for he couldn't bear the pain of living without him.

But even as he did, the cottage door opened and there was his father leaning on Ahern, the wasting sickness having left him feeble and shuffling like a man twice his age, as thin as mountain air, his face gaunt and his eyes hollow and bloodshot. Indeed, he looked as if he were dead already, a victim of The Hunger like those Dónal found among the gorse, there being nothing left of the vigorous man who'd once cast his shadow over all before him, holding the world in the sway of his prodigious will. Yet even so, the sight of his son brought a smile to O'Sullivan's lips, though it looked more like a grimace on his haggard face.

"Are you ready, Dónal?" he rasped, his once-commanding voice now just a hoarse whisper.

"I don't know, Da," Dónal replied apprehensively. "Where are we going?"

"Why, we're going to Dunboy, of course," O'Sullivan said, the old fire flashing suddenly in his eyes. "Haven't you figured that out yet?"

"To the Big House, do you mean?"

"No, not there, but to the *real* Dunboy, the ruins of the old castle that was once our ancestral home. Didn't I say I'd tell you the story someday? Well, that day has come, and now I will pass the legacy on to you, just as my father did to me and you will to your son when the time comes."

Then O'Sullivan paused and drew himself up, mustering all his will to put away the wasted and feeble man he'd become and be again the giant of old.

"Today all secrets will be revealed," he said, his voice regaining some of its old strength and power, "and, anointed with the light of knowledge, you will become a man, my son!"

ᚷᚻᚻᚲ

The morning was wearing away by the time they passed through the crenellated gatehouses and into the sylvan calm of Dunboy Wood, leading the pony at a snail's pace to avoid jostling the frail passenger in the cart. Having never been in a forest before, Dónal gazed in wonder at the trees towering overhead, their crowns thrusting so high as to leave his neck stiff. But they were soon in the open air again, as the road passed through a broad dandelion-speckled meadow in which cows grazed amid the buzzing of flies. Bordering it to their left was the small estuary of Dunboy Creek and beyond that Béara Sound and the Big Island, while up ahead, the road climbed a little knoll through an allée of tall rhododendrons still sporting the odd blossom amid their dense green foliage.

Thus far, Dunboy was nothing like he'd thought it would be, the threat of the gates having evaporated in the cool forest and sun-dappled meadow. Yet it returned when they crested the knoll and found the Big House suddenly close at hand, hovering above Dunboy Inlet like storm clouds on the horizon. But it was the size of it more than anything that set Dónal to gaping, and he couldn't imagine that only one family lived there (or *didn't* live there, as Ahern had pointed out).

"See what money will buy, Dónal?" Ahern asked, as if reading his thoughts.

"It isn't the *things* money buys," O'Sullivan interjected, "but the *power*, and the *freedom* that comes with it. The Puxleys are *free* people and we are not, and as long as they hold the power in this country, we never will be!

"Do you feel it, Dónal? Do you feel the weight of the British Empire squatting on your chest and crushing your spirit like ore in the stamps? That house is a symbol of their dominance, built to remind us of our bondage, as if we could ever forget it! Do you feel it, Dónal? Do you?"

And though he did feel it, still he couldn't help but wonder what it would be like to live there, knowing even in the thought that he would never know. For the drapes were drawn and the doors shut against him and his like, the pleasures of the Big House being reserved for that exclusive trinity of The Wealthy and The Powerful and The Free.

But then a noise from the inlet distracted them and, turning, they saw a ship tied up there, and two men scurrying up twin gangplanks with bags of ore on their shoulders, while a crowd of others cheered them on. As they came to the bottom of the knoll, one of the spectators noticed them and pointed them out to the men around him, and in a moment they'd all gone silent and turned to stare.

Then a single voice rang out, from a huge man who stood on the near gangplank hefting a bag of ore on each shoulder. "So, Englishman," he taunted, "have you come to watch the new champion at work?"

But though O'Sullivan bristled at the insult, it was Tadhg who answered it for him. "Ah, go bugger yourself, Paddy, you fat ugly gob-shite! It doesn't take much of a man to bully a sick one, though I might warn you that he doesn't stand alone! Or have you forgotten how my one-handed, one-eyed Da took you down last summer, or how this little runt here broke your big molly-boy's nose?"

Then he jerked Spota's tether and continued along the road, while a roar of laughter drowned out Paddy's retort, leaving him red-faced and shaking his fist, though making no move to follow.

"Good man, Tadhg!" Ahern said quietly, though his son just shrugged and stared sullenly ahead, his mood growing ever darker, it seemed.

In a moment, the ship was out of sight, as the road plunged into a shallow dell by the opening of the inlet before continuing on the other side as a steep rocky path. Gaining the top of the rise, Dónal knew he'd come to the real Dunboy, which Eóghan had pointed out from afar. And what a strange place it was, with its overgrown walls and crumbling stump of a building close at hand, the broad grassy lawn behind it sloping gently down to the wind-tossed waters of the sound, the view foreshortened by the Big Island rising steep and bulbous beyond. Running off diagonally to their right was the far edge of Dunboy Wood, while the left border was marked by a line of evergreen oaks standing atop a low cliff that plunged steeply down to the water. And for all the mystery and intrigue, it seemed quiet and peaceful enough, like the burial ground at Killaconenagh perhaps, the only sound the oak leaves rustling in the ever-present wind.

But then his father's voice broke in upon it. "This is it, Dónal!" he exclaimed, standing by the cart upright and tall, eyes gleaming and voice powerful. "This is the *real* Dunboy, our ancestral home and the seat of our ancient power and majesty. Come with me now, and I will tell you our story."

Intending to help, Ahern moved to his side then, though O'Sullivan just pushed him away. "No, Seán. I will walk into my house on my own two feet."

Taking the bag he'd brought, O'Sullivan led them slowly to the far end of the ruined building, and stopped beside a gap in the wall. There wasn't much left to look at really, just two side walls that still rose a dozen feet or so, though the far end was almost completely gone and not much more remained of the near one. It was a small place, not more than fifty feet on its long side which, even in the days of its majesty, was nothing to compare to the Big House. Yet Dónal could see that it had once been strong and fair, from the sharply mitered stonework on the outer corners, the gracefully arched window wells in the side walls, and the fragments of shaped and molded stone that littered the ground. Indeed, judging from the thickness of the walls, extreme violence must have been required to devastate it so completely.

Feeling his father's feeble hand on his shoulder, Dónal looked up to find tears in his eyes.

"Are you all right, Da?"

"Yes, Dónal, I'm all right. I was just marveling that it's already been seven years since I brought Eóghan here, though it seems like only yesterday. It was the proudest, happiest day of my life, and I never in my wildest dreams imagined that seven years hence, he'd be dead and I'd be here with you. He was always so strong and lordly, even as a child, and I naturally assumed that he would succeed me. Indeed, so extraordinary was he, that it seemed to me that all of us who'd come before had lived only that our line might someday culminate in him. He was our *messiah*, I thought, the anointed one who would restore the sept of O'Sullivan Béara and raise our family back to its rightful place, and so vindicate the generations of suffering that came before. He'd be the greatest leader Ireland had ever known, I thought, and no less was my ambition for him, and my dream. So how could I have guessed that he'd throw it all back in my face? How could I have guessed *that*?"

O'Sullivan's voice had risen in anger as he spoke, and his fury hung heavy in the air. "Yet now I see that it was only my vanity that made him so," he continued more softly, "for I saw *myself* in him, and it blinded me to the reality of him, which I now know to be far less than my vanity made of it.

"So in the heel of the hunt, Dónal, I'm glad that things worked out as they did, for otherwise I'd never have come to see the reality of you, or understand that you are indeed the chosen one, and that it's you that we've all lived to produce. You are the reality that my vanity made of Eóghan, and you are the one who will redeem us. And as I stand here now, I see with the clarity of hindsight that it's been you all along. So now that my time draws near, it comforts me to know that our legacy will be safe in your hands, and that you will build from it a glorious future for yourself and the O'Sullivans, and, indeed, for all of Ireland."

O'Sullivan smiled at Dónal then, though his eyes were as hard as his grip on the boy's shoulder. "And you *will* do that for me, won't you, my son?" he asked, his tone harsh and demanding.

Yet Dónal could only gape, too stunned to reply. Could his father really be happy that Eóghan was dead? And what did he mean that he was the "chosen one?" Indeed, what did any of it mean, and what did it have to do with him?

But O'Sullivan was too wrapped up in himself and his mission to notice. Indeed, his smile broadened, taking his son's silence and wide eyes for affirmation.

"Good man, Dónal!" he said, patting him on the back. "Good man."

But Dónal didn't feel like a good man, and as much as he'd wanted his father's approval in the past, he wasn't interested in it just then.

"Come now," O'Sullivan said. "We've much to cover and I have but little time. So let's get on with it, shall we?"

Without waiting for a reply, he launched into a detailed explanation of what the fortress had once looked like, saying that it had been built as a "tower-house," a type of castle popular in Ireland in the fourteenth and fifteenth centuries, mainly because the English government had paid a ten-pound subsidy to anyone who would build one, which was a small fortune in those days. Originally it had been four stories tall including the ground floor, which was used as a cellar and armory while the upper three housed the chieftain and his family. As to its layout, the gap in the wall before them had been the doorway, while the hollow in the wall to their right was a guard room, and the rough stone steps that climbed inside the wall to the left were the staircase to the upper floors. Then he pointed out the stump of an outer watch tower attached to the far right corner and the remains of the exterior bawn wall that once surrounded the castle on three sides, the cliff side needing no wall due to its height and steepness.

It was a strong place when new, he concluded, built on a site long recognized for its defensive advantages, at least judging from the stone ringfort that had been there when the O'Sullivans first arrived. It had been demolished, of course, and its stone used to construct the new fortress, though its name remained to memorialize it: *Dún Baoi*, "Fortress of Baoi." Baoi was a goddess in the old days before Christianity, he explained, and so important to the people of Béara that they'd even called themselves after her, *Tuatha Baoi*, "the Tribe of Baoi." But she was mostly forgotten now, and the place was just called Dunboy in the English fashion.

"But even as strong as the site was, it's not the reason the chieftains chose it for their seat!" he continued, turning Dónal around and pointing to the sea. "Do you see that ocean out there? *That* is what made our ancestors rich and powerful, not this scabby land of Béara or even the fertile fields of Bantry beyond. Some of the richest fishing grounds in all the world are to be found out there, and for centuries ships have come to fish them, from Europe and even beyond. But the chieftains owned the fishing rights, and a ship could neither fish nor shelter in the haven without first paying them a fee. And that is why they chose this site for their seat, because it commands the waters for miles around and no ship could come near without their knowledge. Indeed, so jealously did they guard the source of their wealth, that the chieftains were known as 'The O'Sullivan of the Slender Ships' after the private navy they maintained to collect the fees. So all things considered, they could hardly have chosen a better site for their stronghold.

"Yet in the heel of the hunt, even Dunboy couldn't protect them, as the advent of gunpowder and cannons made stone castles obsolete. But that story comes later and I don't want to get ahead of myself. So let's go inside and have a seat, and I'll continue in the proper order."

O'Sullivan led them to the window well of the right-hand wall then, sitting Dónal on his right and Ahern on his left, while Tadhg sat sullenly before them on a piece of fallen stonework.

To Dónal's surprise then, his father reached into his bag, pulled out the three treasures he kept hidden in the bottom of his dresser, and laid them carefully on his lap.

"These are the heirlooms of our House, Dónal, come down to us from the wealth and power of old. But while they may not be much to look at, no chests of gold or fertile tracts of land or even fishing rights could be more valuable, for they are the symbols of our ancient claim to this land and proof of our direct lineage from its rightful lords.

"This is the Sword of War," he said grandiosely, pulling the dagger from its ragged sheath. "It comes down to us all the way from Eochaidh Súildubhán, Eochaidh the Dark-Eyed, from whom we take our name of O'Sullivan, meaning the 'Descendants of Súildubhán.' Do you see the words there on the blade, 'the gentle hand advances'? It's the battle cry of the O'Sullivans, which, along with our name and common ancestry, unites us into a family, a clan, a sept, one of the greatest Ireland has ever known!"

O'Sullivan returned the dagger to its sheath and held up the white rod. "This is the White Rod of Peace, the symbol of office that passed to each new chieftain. I have it from my father and he from his in a direct line stretching back into the darkness of history. It's made from a bough of white hazel, which in the old days was thought to protect the bearer from evil spirits, and is said to have come from the staff of a druid."

He lay it aside in turn and picked up the book. "This is *The Book of O'Sullivan Béara*," he said reverently, "the most important heirloom of all, for it tells the story of who we are and from whence we have come. Study it carefully, Dónal, for in the ancient and continuing story of the O'Sullivans you'll find the ancient and continuing story of Ireland. For indeed, we are Ireland and She is us.

"It tells the story of the O'Sullivans," he said, opening the book, "and of our family in particular, the great chieftains of O'Sullivan Béara. It was written for Dónal Cam's grandson, Dónal the Spaniard, by his cousin, Don Phillip the historian. Both men lived in exile in Spain at the time, which is why Dónal was called 'the Spaniard' even though his blood was all Irish. After his father died, Dónal the Spaniard came back to Ireland, and Don Phillip gave him this book as a parting gift. See the dedication? It says:

For my gracious and gallant cousin,
The O'Sullivan Béara,
Dónal son of Diarmuid son of Dónal Cam.

May you find what you seek beyond the waves.

Phillip O'Sullivan Béara.
Anno Domini 1662."

Then O'Sullivan flipped through the pages until he came to a long list of names. "Here is the genealogy of our family, Dónal, and once we've gone through it, you'll begin to understand the full meaning and import of these heirlooms, and of who you are and why they've come to you."

Pointing to the first name on the list, he said dramatically, "Now, look here, Dónal. Look at that first name at the top of our genealogy."

"Adam of Eden," Dónal read aloud, and looked curiously at his father, wondering if it meant what he thought it did.

"Yes, Dónal, Adam of Eden. Adam of the Bible, the First Man of Genesis. You see, the genealogy of the O'Sullivans, as well as those of all the other great and ancient septs of Ireland, has been kept by druids and monks, bards and shanachies since the very beginning of time, since God first brought forth Creation and Adam walked unsullied in the Garden. For genealogies were very important among the Gaelic people in the old days, because whose son you were and to whom you were related determined your position in society. But with the fall of Dunboy, the Gaelic order came to an end, since most of the septs were broken and their ancestral lands confiscated by the English. So as a practical matter, genealogies lost their importance and people stopped keeping them, since being chieftain of a broken sept possessed of no lands didn't mean very much to people who were struggling just to survive from day to day. I suppose it could be argued that it really means nothing to you and me either, since we have no land and no sept to lead. But I disagree. I believe that knowing our heritage, who we are and from whence we've come, only emphasizes the degree to which we've fallen, and feeds our righteous anger at what has been taken from us, the ability to live as free men in our own country, self-suffi-cient and with the dignity that is the birthright of every child of God on His Earth! And we *need* that righteous anger, Dónal, for that's what has sustained us through our generations of struggle against those who oppress us. But also mark what I tell you now and don't take your oppression personally, because the English don't even see you as a person. That was my mistake and my downfall. I let John Puxley make it personal between himself and me. I let the anger blind me, and now here I am at the tail of the day with nothing more to pass on to you than I had at the beginning, just these poor heirlooms and our claim to a dormant lordship. So don't let the anger blind you as it did me, Dónal! Just keep its fire smoored in your gut and its spirit at your elbow, and it will sustain you through your time of struggle!"

As O'Sullivan sat proudly amid the hallowed ruins of his ancestors, the wellspring of all his passion and despair, Dónal had a vision of the man and Dunboy as they'd once been, young and strong and proud, symbols of the might and majesty of the Gael. But when a coughing fit took him, twisting his frail body and staining the hallowed ground with his blood, the mirage vanished, and he saw them as they really were, a broken old man and a crumbling ruin, each a perfect reflection of the other in their fall from Grace. And in that moment, he could but pity them.

Continuing with the genealogy, O'Sullivan read the names that came after Adam, Seth and Enos and Caidhionon, and so on through thirteen generations to Gael Glas, the eponymous ancestor of the Gaelic people. Then came another twenty generations before Éibhear Fionn, son of Míl, brought the Gael to Ireland from Celtic Spain, and from Éibhear and his brothers and uncle all the great Gaelic septs were descended. Briefly he told of how they'd vanquished the *Tuatha Dé Danaan* and *Fir Bolg*, and how Éibhear had taken as his portion the parts that became the provinces of Munster and Leinster. Then he rattled off another forty-seven generations down to Oilill Olom, King of Munster, and his son, Eóghan Mór, progenitor of the *Eóghanacht* dynasty, of which the O'Sullivans were a branch. In speaking of the *Eóghanachta*, he explained that the name, *Eóghan*, meant 'born of the yew,' a tree sacred to the Gael for time out of mind, since it was the longest-lived thing in their experience and so a symbol of immortality. And that was why the ancestor who'd settled at Cahernageeha had chosen the yew for his totem, to signify his descent from the immortal *Eóghanacht* dynasty. "Even if it takes a thousand years," he'd said upon setting the seedling in the ground, "we will take back what is ours."

Then O'Sullivan explained that the ceremonial seat of the Kings of Munster had been at Cashel in the County Tipperary, (*Caiseal an Rí* in Irish, "Fortress of the King"), and that the O'Sullivans were the senior branch of the *Eóghanacht Chaiseal*, "the Descendants of Eóghan of Cashel." Even so, the next King of Munster, Fiacha Muilleathan, son of Eóghan Mór, had made his home at a place called *Cnoc Rafann*, (or, "Knockgraffon," as the English had made it), a few miles south of Cashel and, after him, it was the ancestral seat of the O'Sullivans until they were driven out by the Normans and moved into the west. Then he explained that Fínghein son of Aodh Dubh, tenth in descent from Eóghan Mór, had been the last of the O'Sullivan line to be King of Munster, though his descendants continued to be lords of power and prestige at Knockgraffon.

Around the time of Aodh Dubh and Fínghein, there'd been a Golden Age in Ireland, a time of prosperity and enlightenment when Irish monks had tended the light of civilization and taken it back to Europe, which lay shrouded in the darkness of Germanic conquest. But it had come to an end when the Germanic sea raiders known as "Vikings" plundered the great monasteries and settled along the coasts, establishing their city-states of Dublin, Wexford, Waterford, Cork and Limerick. Of course, Brian Boru had eventually defeated them at Clontarf, though both he and his son, Murrough, died in the battle, leaving no one to continue their work of unifying the Irish. So a time of great turmoil had followed, when the kings of the greatest septs fought each other for supremacy, each seeking to become High King and reign over the others. And so it was that they'd been bitterly divided and easily conquered when the final assault came at the hands of the Viking people known as "Normans," who'd settled in northern France and given their name to its province of Normandy. In 1066, they'd conquered England under their duke, William the Bastard, invading Ireland a hundred years later under his descendant, King Henry II.

Between Fínghein and Eochaidh Súildubhán, there'd been seven Lords of Knockgraffon and, after him, six more before the last, Dónal Mór, was driven out by the Normans in 1192. He'd led his people into West Kerry, settling initially on the Iveragh Peninsula near Valentia Island. Of course, the O'Sullivans had found the land harsh there and a poor trade for the gentle fields of Tipperary, where their lives had been gracious and bountiful and they'd lived in relative peace. To illustrate their feelings, Don Phillip quoted a few stanzas of an ancient poem called *The Old Hag of Béara*, and O'Sullivan read them aloud.

The ebbing that has come on me
is not the ebbing of the sea.
What knows the sea of grief or pain?
For happy tide will flood again.

I am Baoi, the Hag of Béara,
the richest cloth I used to wear.
Now with meanness and with thrift
I even lack a change of shift.

Were it not for Femhin's plain
I'd envy nothing old;
I have a shroud of aged skin,
while Femhin's crop is gold.

And just as Baoi lamented the loss of her youth and beauty, he explained, measuring the extent of her fall by her exile into the desolate country of Béara, so far away from the golden plain of Femhin in her beloved Tipperary, so the O'Sullivans lamented the loss of Knockgraffon. Yet they were resilient people, and made the best of their situation as they found it, becoming warlike and aggressive in order to survive and carve out a homeland for themselves among the hostile native clans.

Going back to the genealogy then, he told of how they'd split into sub-septs in the years following, as they'd multiplied and spread over the western baronies of Kerry and Cork. Of Dónal Mór's ten sons, eight were treacherously murdered along with their father in 1214, in a feud with a branch of the MacCarthys that had begun as a dispute over spoils of war. Yet two sons had escaped to carry on the line of the chieftains, and from the elder, Giolla Mochuda, had come the sept of O'Sullivan Mór (the Great O'Sullivans) and its sub-sept of *Mac Giolla Mochuda na Cruacha* or "MacGillycuddy of the Reeks," as the English made it. The chieftain of O'Sullivan Mór ("The" O'Sullivan Mór) was thereafter regarded as the "high" chieftain, and while certain rights and duties were due unto him, practically speaking, he exercised little authority over the sub-chieftains.

From the younger, Giolla na Flann, had come their own sept of O'Sullivan Béara, and it was his grandson, Annadh of the (prominent) Cheeks who'd led them south into Béara. Under his leadership and that of his heirs, the O'Sullivans subjugated the O'Driscolls and other native septs, spreading over the whole of Béara and even into Bantry. Annadh's son, Amhlaibh, was the one who'd built the tower-house at Dunboy and first taken the title of "The" O'Sullivan Béara, ruling over a territory as great as that of The O'Sullivan Mór. And it was his son, Tadhg the Strong, who'd realized the potential of the sea, and built the fleet of "slender ships" to collect the fishing and harborage fees, while his own son, Diarmuid the Stammerer, built the grand Franciscan monastery in Bantry.

Between Diarmuid and Dónal Cam then, the white rod passed to a new chieftain seven times, and though little enough was written about them, it wasn't because they were obscure or do-nothing types. Rather, it was because they were such strong rulers, intelligent and capable men of wealth and power, and because Béara was so isolated and well-fortified with castles, that they were able to exercise their power in relative peace and with scant interference from outside authority. Indeed, they may as well have been kings themselves for all the King's Writ was worth at Dunboy.

And the reason for it was their cash income from the sea, with which they'd been able to finance their own army and navy to protect themselves and enforce their authority and, even more important, to free themselves of their dependence upon the poor land of Béara and what little it could produce. Without it, they'd have been just another obscure sept of cattle lords, dependent upon the whims of Nature for their livelihood, and upon their neighbor's indulgence for their security. Indeed, it was much the same with John Puxley and his cash income from the mines, O'Sullivan said by way of analogy. Without it he'd have been just another mildly comfortable middleman, dependent upon the rocky soil of Béara for his living, though with it, he'd become the wealthiest commoner in all of Ireland, *and* one of the most powerful.

"So do you see how it works, Dónal?" O'Sullivan asked, gazing at him intently. "Do you see how a cash income frees a man from his dependence upon the land, a thing that ultimately no man can depend upon? It's a very important lesson for you to learn, because dependence upon the land means not surviving when it fails you. And if you need more than my word, just look at the horrors we suffered because so many millions were dependent solely upon the land for their survival, with no cash income to fall back on when the land failed them. Not that it was through any fault of their own, mind you, since that ultimately rests upon the English and the way they've used Ireland as a slaver does his slaves, to produce for themselves and with no thought to the well-being and prosperity of the Irish. Except for the few cases where it means taking away our natural resources, like the copper from John Puxley's mines or the timber from the great forests that once covered the land, they've done almost nothing to develop industry in Ireland so that Irishmen may earn a living. They've made us tenants in our own country and reduced us to serfdom, yet they call us 'drunkards' and 'lay-abouts' in our idleness and poverty, when, in fact, their laws have ensured that we have no opportunity to be otherwise!

"And that is the fault that I find with England and her governance of Ireland, that she has allowed us no means to fend for ourselves and so left us vulnerable to tragedy when the land fails us! And *that*, Dónal, is the reason to be angry at what has been taken from you, the ability to live as a free man in your own country, self-sufficient and with the

175

human dignity that is your birthright! And *that*, Dónal, is why our anger is so important, because it gives us the strength to keep fighting for what is right for ourselves and our people, no matter the obstacles set in our way!

"Do you understand what I'm saying, son? Are you beginning to see how everything is connected, and does it make any sense to you?"

Dónal didn't answer right away, as he was still struggling through all the names and dates and facts to understand the bigger picture of their errand. Sure he understood that the Irish were downtrodden and the English to blame and, in a general sense, he understood the part about making a living separate from the land. Yet he didn't see the connections, or what his father expected him to do about it. But then the man jumped ahead without him.

"From the look on your face," he said, misreading it entirely, "you're probably wondering if the common people were better off when the O'Sullivans ruled them than we are now with the English."

The answer was probably no, he had to admit, saying that little had changed since those days for, as in the present, most of the people were just poor peasants struggling to pay the rent and taxes and have enough left over to feed themselves. And then as now, most of the wealth was held in the tight-fisted hands of the few, who tended to be cruel and arbitrary in their treatment of the peasants, whom they held to be of less account than cattle. Still, the O'Sullivans weren't any more cruel and arbitrary than any other chieftains or lords of their time, for that was just the way things were, and they did unto others lest others do unto them. Yet the same couldn't be said of the present, since the Irish in Ireland were treated differently than the English in England, even though both were supposed to be under one United Kingdom with the same laws and Queen and Parliament. And a prime example of that was to be found in the potato famine, which happened because the effect of English rule in Ireland was to crowd millions of poor people onto marginal land and force them to subsist on a single crop. And though the blight hit potato crops in England just as hard, there'd been no Great Hunger there and, even if there had been, the English government would surely have stepped in and done something about it. So while the country was called The United Kingdom of Great Britain and Ireland, the truth of it was that Ireland was just one of many colonies whose sole purpose was to produce for England, and in order for Ireland to be bled dry and denied a share of the prosperity, Paddy had to be kept in his place. And it was that double standard of treatment that lay at the very heart of English injustice in Ireland, and the reason the Irish would never have justice unless they had their own independent government.

So the *real* question to ask then, he said, was whether the Irish would be better off now if they'd been ruled by their own people for the last three centuries rather than by the English. And the answer to that was a resounding yes, the reason being that there'd been great advances in government during that period, especially since the American and French Revolutions, when the people overthrew their tyrants and set up governments that ensure the rights and freedom of all citizens. And if Ireland had had Her own independent government, at least some of those lofty ideals and principles would surely have been incorporated, to the betterment of the nation and all Her people. Indeed, that was the goal of Wolfe Tone and the men of '98, and even of Eóghan and his men of '48, to establish an Irish Republic based upon the democratic ideals of America and France. So in the final analysis, it seemed, the true effect of English colonialism in Ireland had been to arrest Her development as a nation and keep from the people the enlightenment of the civilized world.

"And finally, Dónal, and maybe more to the point, would an independent Irish government have stood back while millions of Irishmen starved or emigrated?"

But O'Sullivan left the question unanswered, his silence saying more than words ever could.

Pausing only to collect his thoughts then, he plunged back into the genealogy, speaking briefly of the five chieftains between Diarmuid the Stammerer and Dónal Cam's grandfather, Diarmuid of the Powder, so called because he'd accidentally blown himself up with gunpowder right there in the cellar of Dunboy. He'd been succeeded by his brother, Amhlaibh, though his son had murdered him and set himself up in his place. And that was Dónal Cam's father, Dónal Knockatee, whose epithet (and epitaph) derived from the fact that he'd been killed by his cousin, The MacGillycuddy, in a duel atop the mountain of Knockatee. But Diarmuid of the Powder had had four sons, the eldest being another Diarmuid, who was illegitimate and so not eligible to succeed his father, while Dónal Knockatee was his second son, followed in order by Eóghan and Phillip. And though there would later be strife between Eóghan and his nephew, Dónal Cam, these four brothers were especially close and held great affection for each other. For that reason, it became a tradition to name male children after them, which had been followed in their family right down to the present day.

"But now, Dónal," O'Sullivan said, "we come to the time of Dónal Cam, the man from whom we are descended. He was the greatest of all the O'Sullivan Béara chieftains, though he was also the one who brought war and ruin to Dunboy, after which our power was broken and has yet to be restored."

He was born in 1561, O'Sullivan said, and grew to be a tall, handsome man with red hair and piercing blue eyes, though he was also slightly bow-legged, hence the epithet of *Cam,* "crooked." He was only two years old when his father died and, because of his youth, the *derbhfhine,* the leading men of the sept, elected his uncle Eóghan to succeed as The O'Sullivan Béara, and chose his uncle Phillip as *tánaiste,* "heir apparent." So in his youth, it looked as though Dónal Cam would never follow his father as chieftain, and he spent his childhood in Eyeries in the fosterage of his uncle Diarmuid, who instructed him in the use of the sword and other weapons, as well as in military tactics. In his teens, he was sent to Waterford for his higher education, which included instruction in English and Latin.

Dónal Cam grew up during a time of great troubles in Ireland, when the Earl of Desmond, Gerald Fitzgerald, led a rebellion against English rule that raged throughout Munster. His uncle Eóghan threw in his lot with Desmond and the rebels, only to be imprisoned by the

Crown after the rebellion was crushed in 1583, though he was later pardoned and restored to his lordship. Yet Dónal Cam didn't follow his uncle's example, but remained loyal to the Crown. Or maybe *neutral* was a better way to put it, because it seemed that even then he wanted to be chieftain in his uncle's place, and was just watching and waiting to see if Eóghan would make a mistake that would allow him to further his designs. In any case, he took no part in the rebellion, except in 1579, when, at the age of eighteen, he successfully defended Béara against a party of cattle raiders comprised mostly of MacSweeneys and O'Donovans. With only fifty men he slew three hundred of the invaders and drove off the rest, hanging the leader, Diarmuid O'Donovan, from an oak tree that still bore his name, *Dairchín Dhiarmuida*, "Diarmuid's little oak tree." And it was in that action that he established his reputation for bravery, swordsmanship and military expertise.

As for his designs on the lordship, in the old days under the Gaelic system, the chieftains were elected by the leading men of the sept under the law of tanistry, at least theoretically. But in reality, what usually happened was that the strongest man of the ruling family seized the White Rod for himself, then had his followers elect him, just to put the face of lawfulness on it. And that's why Eóghan was able to succeed as chieftain when Dónal Cam was a child. Yet the English followed the law of primogeniture, under which the eldest son always inherited his father's estate in its entirety, no matter what. And since they wanted to promote their laws and customs in Ireland, they came up with a new policy in the 1500's designed to encourage the Irish chieftains to accept English law and hopefully become more loyal to the Crown. Under it, the chieftains were to surrender their lands to the Crown, in exchange for which the Crown would grant them back along with an English title of nobility. "Surrender and re-grant" they called it, and within a few years most of the chieftains had bent the knee, including Eóghan, who surrendered his lordship along with The O'Sullivan Mór and The MacCarthy Mór, in return for which he received a charter from Queen Elizabeth and the title, "Sir Eóghan, Lord of Béara and Bantry."

Yet in this English scheme, Dónal Cam saw an opportunity for himself, for having accepted English law as a condition of re-grant, Sir Eóghan had also subjected himself to primogeniture, making his lordship, unwittingly perhaps, vulnerable to challenge from the son of his elder brother. And that's just what Dónal Cam did, bringing a case before the English courts that advanced himself as the rightful lord under primogeniture. Of course, under the old way of doing things, he should've brought his case before The MacCarthy Mór, his ultimate overlord in the Gaelic system. But since his uncle was lawfully elected under tanistry, and also because he was in disfavor with the Crown owing to his rebellion, he knew he had a better chance of winning in an English court. Of course, he was playing right into English hands in doing so, since it was their intent to further their power in Ireland, an unspoken part of which was to break up the great Irish lordships and reduce the power of the chieftains, which was exactly what happened to the O'Sullivans. For the case dragged on for two years and caused a huge rift among them, with some supporting Dónal Cam while others backed Sir Eóghan. In the end, the court's decision was to split the lordship, and give all the lands east of Adrigole to Sir Eóghan, while the rest went to Dónal Cam, including the title of The O'Sullivan Béara and, more important, the income from the fishing grounds and haven. Of course, Sir Eóghan was not at all pleased with the outcome, even though he got the better farm land and town of Bantry in his portion, and while Dónal Cam got what he wanted, he also weakened his sept and lordship, making bitter enemies of Sir Eóghan and his son, Eóghan Óg.

But, of course, that suited the English purpose, too, which was to divide and conquer, a scheme the Irish were always too willing to play into, disunity being as ever their Achilles heel. Indeed, it was more or less institutionalized under the Gaelic system, where there were 150 kings and God only knew how many petty chieftains, all out for nothing but themselves and the greater nation be damned. Then, at the end of the 1500's, the great Hugh O'Neill used the cause of Catholicism to unite the Irish and rally them around himself, and for a while his prospects looked promising. But O'Neill put the fear of God into the

English, because of the possibility that an independent Ireland might form an alliance with the Catholic powers of Europe, especially Spain and France, and so allow them to invade England from both east and west. More recently, of course, Daniel O'Connell used the cause of Catholic Emancipation, though it deepened the rift along religious lines, especially in the North where there were so many Protestants. For the English put the fear of God into the Orangemen, convincing them that they'd become a persecuted minority if Home Rule should ever come to fruition. But so the game went on, divide and conquer, and the Irish never seemed to learn.

So it was that in 1594 Dónal Cam became chieftain of a divided sept. And that was just at the beginning of the Nine Years War, another time of troubles in Ireland, which began this time in Ulster under the leadership of O'Neill and his kinsman, Red Hugh O'Donnell. It was in the North, too, where most of the early fighting took place, Munster being still too devastated by the Desmond Rebellion to join in it. And again, Dónal Cam chose to stay out of it, being content to watch and wait, to see how things would go before casting his lot. He was an extremely patient man, which was unusual for an Irish chieftain, being in that regard more like an Englishman, who as a people have the patience of Job. It was something he had in common with O'Neill, who'd been raised and educated in England, not returning to Ireland till he was almost eighteen.

Of course, O'Neill knew of Dónal Cam and sought an alliance with him, though he made no move until the autumn of 1601, when King Phillip III of Spain sent a fleet to Ireland. Sensing that O'Neill had the upper hand, Dónal Cam immediately declared for him and raised Béara into rebellion, hoping to expand his lordship by being on the winning side. Perhaps he even saw an opportunity to become King of Munster again and return his people to Knockgraffon. Who could say? In any case, O'Neill was so happy to have him in his camp that he made him commander of all the southern forces, just as O'Donnell was of the northern.

So it was that Dónal Cam marched with O'Neill to Kinsale, where they trapped the Crown forces between themselves and the fortified town, which was held by the Spanish under Don Juan del Aguila. With the weather being particularly nasty and the siege dragging on, fever came into the English camp, killing the soldiers by the score. And since many if not most of them were actually Irish, scores more deserted to O'Neill, as he seemingly had the advantage and would surely win. So with his enemy surrounded, all O'Neill had to do was exercise a little of his characteristic patience and let disease and desertion destroy them for him. But, unfortunately for every Irishman who'd lived since, that was not the way of things. For, growing tired of the siege and being holed up in the town, the Spanish sent a message to O'Neill urging him to attack and, hoping to bring the affair to a quick and glorious end, O'Donnell agreed with them.

Already a living legend among the Gael, Red Hugh O'Donnell was a capable soldier and general, a man who inspired his troops as much with his flaming red hair and dashing good looks as with his zeal and heroism. But he was also vain and impulsive, and had an exaggerated regard for himself and his abilities and of his place in the grand scheme of things. In no way was he the equal of O'Neill, either as general or statesman, and in no way should he have been directing the war. Yet so insistent was he to attack that O'Neill held a council to discuss the matter with his commanders. Of course, Dónal Cam was of like mind with O'Neill and argued against it. But the flare of O'Donnell appealed mightily to the chieftains and captains, most of whom were like Red Hugh himself, men who knew how to fight but had little concept of soldiery or the political issues involved.

So in the heel of the hunt, O'Donnell carried the day and the rebels attacked on the morning of Christmas Eve, 1601. But their plans were betrayed by an informer, ever the scourge of Irish rebellions, and they were soon routed from the field and scattered to the four winds, sending O'Neill reeling home in defeat. Indeed, the English victory was so complete that they held unchallenged sway after Kinsale, and though there'd been many risings since, not one had come as close to succeeding.

O'Sullivan paused then, a distant look coming into his eyes as he gazed at the wind-tossed waters of the sound. "I've often pictured them as they stood in council on that wintry evening," he said, "Dónal Cam and O'Neill and Red Hugh, the trinity of leaders standing before the chieftains like Magi, holding in their hands the gifts of freedom and justice and prosperity for the newborn nation of Ireland. But one of our wise men was a fool, and the new Ireland born that Christmas became a twisted abomination of what its sire intended. Yet I've always considered that to be Dónal Cam's finest hour, when he followed the cool lead of his intellect rather than the fire of his Irish heart. If the others had but followed him . . . *If!*"

The single syllable trailed into the silence that followed and rung in Dónal's ears with the beating of his heart. '*If! If! If!* If only I'd kept Eóghan from leaving, then I wouldn't be here now.' The thought came into his mind unbidden and hung there against his will, tormenting him with might-have-beens.

But then O'Sullivan's eyes focused again as he looked upon his son. "So, Dónal, what happened to O'Neill, do you think? Why didn't he follow his own counsel and conscience when he knew in his heart that he was right? Well, there's no way of knowing for certain, of course, but I think he sensed the historical importance of the moment and understood that either victory or defeat would bring consequences both profound and irreversible. He stood like Atlas at the crossroads bearing the future of Ireland on his shoulders, knowing that if he failed, posterity would point the finger of blame at him. And in the heel of the hunt I think he found the burden just a little too heavy. He was just a man, after all, and all men are subject to weakness on occasion, even the Great O'Neill.

"Yet great men play for high stakes, and the consequences of weakness can be sweeping and enduring. So it was that O'Neill's moment of weakness sealed the fate of Ireland and the Irish for generations to come, and though Red Hugh often gets the blame for it, O'Neill was the leader, and the blame belongs rightfully with him."

O'Sullivan paused, and the distant look came into his eyes again. "I'm sure the pain of it must've torn out his heart, as he lived out his declining years in exile, wondering what might have been if he'd acted differently. And don't I know that feeling myself, that desire to go back in time so that I can live just one moment over again, just that one critical moment where I said or did something that would change my life forever, just to have it back so I could change my destiny for the better. 'Oh, God in Heaven,' I've pleaded, 'if you'll just let me go back and change it.' And O'Neill must have pleaded, too, as he watched his life's work slip away in those moments at Kinsale. But going back is a wish God doesn't grant, and our history is full of things that might have been, and there's nothing to be done about it now but try not to make the same mistakes again. And that's why I'm telling you these things, Dónal, so that you won't make the same mistakes and your life won't turn out to be just so many might-have-beens."

O'Sullivan was silent then, his eyes turned inward as if watching his own life's work slip away in those last few minutes with Eóghan. And Ahern was silent, too, as he stared at the water, his blind side turned purposely toward them, it seemed to Dónal. But then O'Sullivan sighed, remembering that there was hope yet and it sat beside him, waiting for him to continue.

"But so it was that disunity defeated the Irish at Kinsale, because it wasn't an English army that defeated O'Neill, but an *Irish* one fighting for the English cause. As I said before, most of the soldiers were Irish, as were many of the senior commanders, including the Lord President of Munster, Sir George Carew, and the Earls of Thomond and Clanricard, Donogh O'Brien and Ulick mac Riocard Burke. Indeed, it was Clanricard and his men who turned the battle into a rout."

And why did they fight for the English? O'Sullivan asked. In truth they didn't, being as good Irishmen are wont to be, rather just out for themselves and what they could gain by being on the winning side. So it was every man for himself, just as under the old Gaelic system, which was indeed still in place in much of the country. Not even O'Neill was fighting for the *nation* of Ireland, since there wasn't one in the modern sense of the word and never had been, but rather for the time and freedom to give the Irish a chance to *become* a nation. For he was a man of vision, and something of a dreamer, too, and believed that driving out the English would allow him to mold Ireland's disparate elements into a true nation and bring prosperity and peace to her people. Yet even O'Neill was out for himself to a certain extent, for it was his ambition to be the leader of that new Irish nation, which would have been only fair, given that he was the man best qualified. But he lost and, ever since, Ireland had been but a colony, which was why the English conquest had arrested the development of Ireland as a nation.

"But when Dónal Cam joined O'Neill, wasn't he just out for himself, too?" Tadhg demanded, eager, it seemed, to cast aspersions, his surly mood still upon him.

"Yes, he was, Tadhg," O'Sullivan allowed, "at least when he joined. But you shouldn't judge him only on his initial motivation. The important thing is that he joined the side of right, and that he kept fighting even after the disaster at Kinsale."

For after Kinsale, he continued, Dónal Cam had a choice of what to do next. He could lie low at Dunboy and hope for a pardon, or carry on the fight. In making his decision, he was ironically much influenced by Red Hugh and his argument that King Phillip would surely send another fleet to Ireland if the Irish could demonstrate a will to continue. Indeed, Red Hugh sailed off to Spain right after Kinsale in hopes of convincing King Phillip to do just that. So with the prospect of Spanish aid on the horizon, Dónal Cam decided to fight on and brought his army back to the sanctuary of Béara. Of course, part of his motivation may have been that he saw an opportunity in the power vacuum; that is, that he could take over leadership of the rebellion. Indeed, with O'Neill defeated and discredited, and O'Donnell in Spain partly to avoid disgrace, it seemed that he was the only logical choice. Moreover, if he succeeded, perhaps he could be more than just Lord of Béara and Bantry or even King of Munster. Perhaps he could be High King of Ireland.

An eager light came into O'Sullivan's eyes. "Just imagine it for a moment, Dónal: a free and independent Ireland with an O'Sullivan on the high seat of Tara! With such a victory, Dónal Cam would've eclipsed our ancestors, even the greatest of whom were never High Kings."

Then the light of might-have-been faded from his eyes. "But as I said before, when great men play for high stakes, the consequences of losing can be sweeping and enduring, and unfortunately for us, so it was with Dónal Cam."

For after garrisoning Dunboy with a small force of mercenaries under Riocard MagEochagáin, Dónal Cam undertook a number of forays against the English, even going as far afield as Cork City. Of course, the English couldn't ignore such a bold challenge, and turned their full attention to wiping out this last threat. Knowing the English would strike against his stronghold of Dunboy, Dónal Cam ordered MagEochagáin to refortify it for an artillery attack. In so doing, they took down the top two floors of the tower-house to make it a smaller target, and used the stone to build a second bawn wall, which they packed on the outside with earth to cushion against cannonballs. Then they settled in to wait.

Of course, Dónal Cam expected the assault to come by land, with the English marching down the length of Béara, its rough terrain and lack of roads being as much of an impediment as any castle. But the English commander, Sir George Carew, a shrewd military strategist and himself a Munster man, knew that, too. And rather than falling into the trap, he ferried his army of four thousand men across Bantry Bay to the Big Island, landing them just across from Castle Diarmuid (as Castletownbere was known then).

At about the same time, Dónal Cam received a message that a Spanish fleet had landed at Ardea on the north side of Béara, and he set off to meet them on June 5th, leaving MagEochagáin and his mercenaries at Dunboy, while the main force of about a thousand men under Captain Richard Tyrrell took up station across the channel from Carew. Yet upon reaching Ardea, Dónal Cam was disappointed to find only a single Spanish ship with but a handful of soldiers aboard, though its hold held a king's ransom in gold. But what Dónal Cam needed then was soldiers and lots of them, and no amount of money would buy them in Béara, where every able-bodied man was already serving, either for him or against. But there were also two Jesuits aboard, one of whom, Eóghan MacEgan, Bishop of Ross, assured Dónal Cam that more ships were on the way and would arrive within a few days. So with the prospect of an army in the offing, he decided to wait at Ardea.

In the meantime, Carew ferried his army over to Béara, making an uncontested landing and soon outflanking Tyrrell and sending him scurrying to safety at Ardea. Then he moved on Dunboy and quickly surrounded it, trapping MagEochagáin and his seven score men inside. The siege dragged on for eleven days while Carew ferried over his artillery and the gunners assembled it, during which time MagEochagáin sent out an envoy to sue for quarter, and whom Carew promptly hanged. Also, Carew sent a contingent to raid Dursey Island, where Dónal Cam had sent the non-combatants and a large herd of cattle, thinking the treacherous waters of the channel and difficult landings on the steep Dursey coast would ensure their safety. But the raiders were led by his cousin, Eóghan Óg, who'd been born and raised at Dunboy and knew western Béara as well as anyone. So it was that the feud with Sir Eóghan came back to haunt Dónal Cam, for the raiders took Dursey by surprise and slaughtered everyone they could find, whether man, woman, or child, before driving the cattle back to Dunboy.

When the guns were finally assembled in the early hours of June 17th, Carew immediately gave the order to fire, and the assault continued throughout the day. The fighting was extremely vicious and there was great loss of life on both sides, MagEochagáin and his men knowing themselves to be fighting for their lives. By evening, about half of the defenders were dead, and those who weren't took refuge in the cellar. Most were wounded and some died during the night, their blood drenching the floor while the walls reverberated with their agony. Having fought bravely and fiercely, MagEochagáin himself was covered with wounds and dying, so the men elected Thomas Taylor, a renegade Englishman, to lead in his place.

In the morning when Carew called upon them to surrender, Taylor answered that he would blow up the castle with both besieged and besiegers unless Carew promised to spare their lives, and grimly sat himself down with a lighted candle next to the kegs of powder that were stored in the corner. But Carew was having none of it. Instead of attacking, he pulled his soldiers back and resumed the bombardment, intending to collapse the walls and bury the defenders alive rather than waste more soldiers. But when the walls indeed began to collapse, the men inside decided that hanging would be a better way to die, and compelled Taylor to surrender. Yet when Carew's men came into the cellar to march out the survivors, MagEochagáin mustered what little strength he had left and snatched up the lighted candle, intending to blow them all up just as Taylor had threatened. But an English officer grabbed him before he could reach the powder, and held him while others killed him. Most of the survivors were hanged that day, while Taylor and other renegades were executed later. For their chaplain, Father Dominic Collins, Carew reserved an especially cruel fate, taking him to his native Youghall to be martyred. On the evening before his execution, his arms and legs were broken in three places each, and then he was thrown into a cell to suffer through the night. In the morning, he was dragged through the streets by a horse before being hanged, drawn and quartered. As for Dunboy itself, Carew blew up the remnants on June 21, using the same gunpowder MagEochagáin had tried to ignite. So ended the siege of Dunboy, and the ruins around them were all that was left.

O'Sullivan shook his head sadly and lapsed into silence. Beside him, Dónal pictured the ghastly scene of that last night and morning, hearing the sounds of agony and smelling the stench of blood and fear. He saw the survivors herded into a wretched knot, each hoping against hope that the hangman wouldn't take him next, yet each knowing that his turn would come, sooner or later. In his mind then, Dunboy became a tomb holding the spirits of those brave men, and he saw MagEochagáin staggering toward the powder, blood streaming from his wounds as he made one last effort to defy his enemy. It was the bravest thing Dónal ever heard of, apart from his own father carrying Ahern out of the mines, and it seemed so unfair that he should die.

"Why didn't Dónal Cam come back to help them?" he asked, speaking even as the question formed in his mind.

"Isn't it obvious, Dónal?" O'Sullivan replied. "Carew had him outnumbered four to one, and Dónal Cam needed MagEochagáin to delay his advance long enough for the Spanish to come and even the odds. If he'd come back sooner his whole army would've been destroyed and his cause lost for sure. But by sacrificing MagEochagáin, he kept it intact and lived to fight another day. And as hard-hearted as that may sound, Dónal, it was actually a brilliant strategy and Carew bit into it. But generals are often faced with the necessity of sacrificing a few men for the greater good of their army, and the true cowards are the ones who can't bring themselves to do it. Also, you have to remember that Bishop MacEgan had said more Spanish soldiers were on the way, and for Dónal Cam to have attacked without them would've meant throwing away the lives of all his men, which would've been highly irresponsible, since in the heel of the hunt he wouldn't have saved MagEochagáin anyway!

"But if that's not reason enough for you, just think of Odysseus and his choice between Scylla and Charybdis. He was warned by the gods that if he chose Charybdis, he might lose his ship and all his men in the whirlpool, while if he chose Scylla, on the other hand, he would definitely lose six men, though the rest would get through safely. Naturally he chose Scylla, because sacrificing six men to save the rest was the only reasonable thing to do. And Dónal Cam faced the same choice with Dunboy, to lose some of his men in a delaying action or his entire army in a pitched battle against overwhelming odds. And anyway, it's a basic rule of military service that your commander may spend your life in any way he sees fit, and do so with neither your foreknowledge nor your consent, and MagEochagáin and all his men knew that. Is it fair, you might ask? Well, it doesn't really matter, because that's the only way an army can function. So before you decide to join one, Dónal, think about it carefully, because from the moment you do, your life is in your own hands no longer.

"Now as for MagEochagáin, as long as there was hope of Spanish aid, Dónal Cam had nothing to gain by fighting a battle he couldn't win, when there was still hope of winning by living to fight another day. And while it's true that, in the event, the Spanish didn't come, Dónal Cam can't be blamed for waiting, especially since he had the word of a Jesuit bishop to persuade him. So he did the right thing in not coming back, for he couldn't have saved MagEochagáin anyway."

"Then why did he leave him here in the first place?" Dónal demanded, doubting very much that MagEochagáin would've seen it quite the same way.

"Have you not been listening, Dónal, or are you just being stubborn?" O'Sullivan shot back, his tone stinging like a slap in the face. "Dunboy was a diversionary tactic designed to keep Carew away from his main force until the Spanish arrived! Can you not understand that?"

"No, he can't understand it," Tadhg interjected angrily, "not when you speak to him like that! He's just a young boy and yet you're talking to him like he's as old as yourself, using those big words that he's never even heard before! And I don't see what all this has to do with him, anyway! Dunboy is dead and buried and you'll never raise it again no matter how you try! So why don't you just forget about it and let Dónal live his life the way he wants to, or else he's going to end up being just like you, a dried-up, bitter old shell of a man!"

"That's *enough*, Tadhg!" Ahern exclaimed. "You hold your whisht or there'll be hell to pay!"

"No, Da, I'll not do it, not when it's Dónal I'm speaking for, and to hell with you and your hell to pay!"

"Here now, that's enough from both of you!" O'Sullivan interjected. "As much as I admire you standing up for your friend, Tadhg, these things don't concern you and it's not your place to pass judgment, especially since you don't understand them yourself. So give me peace to finish my story."

Seeing that he could do no more, Tadhg got up and walked away, muttering a curse under his breath.

"I'm sorry for my son, Eóghan," Ahern said, watching as Tadhg strode down to the water, "but he takes his friendships rather seriously."

"No matter," O'Sullivan replied with a shrug. "He's just a young boy himself, and anyway, my Dónal is lucky to have such a friend.

"You'll have to forgive me for talking over your head, son," he continued, turning back to Dónal, "but I haven't the strength to go back and explain it all over again. Anyway, most of it is here in the book, and Seán will help you. So let's just go on with the story while there is still time."

But Dónal couldn't answer for fighting back the lump in his throat. His father hadn't spoken sharply to him in months, and he'd thought he never would again. Then, too, he'd just told him that he wouldn't be around to help him, that his time had come and it would be up to Ahern. So between his hurt and his fear, he was an emotional wreck.

But if his father saw it, he gave no sign, just went on with the story as if nothing had happened.

After the fall of Dunboy, he said, Carew figured that Dónal Cam would lose the will to fight and come begging for a pardon. So he left Béara to attend to other matters and took most of his army with him, leaving only a small force to harry the rebels and keep them occupied. But still having had a sizable army, and Spanish gold to pay them and plenty of cattle to feed them, Dónal Cam wasn't ready to give up yet, especially since he still believed the Spanish would come. But as the realization set in that they wouldn't, his allies began to desert him, the final blow coming in December when his herd was captured, leaving him no option but to retreat.

So on the last day of 1602, Dónal Cam and a thousand followers set out from Glengarriff to seek refuge with O'Neill in Ulster. Of them, only four hundred were soldiers, while the rest were mostly women and children. For fourteen days they marched through snow and freezing weather, foraging food from the famished landscape while fighting off attacks from both the English who pursued them and the local chieftains. At the Shannon, they could find no boats to take them across, so they slaughtered the few pack animals that were left to them, and stretched their untanned skins over wooden frames to make flimsy little boats. All day the boats went back and forth, while the rearguard kept the pursuers at bay. And once across, they still had miles of hostile country to fight their way through, their ranks dwindling all the while as war, hunger and the elements took their toll. So by the time they reached safety with The O'Rourke in County Leitrim, only Dónal Cam himself, his uncle Diarmuid, thirty-two soldiers and one woman were left of the thousand who'd set out. Yet that any of them survived at all is a testament to his hardiness and strength of will, and historians have written of his epic march as a high point in Irish military history. Still, it marked the end of his career in Ireland, since the Crown had recognized Eóghan Óg as Lord of Béara and Bantry and saw no reason to remove a man of proven loyalty in favor of a proven rebel.

So realizing that his life was in danger, Dónal Cam sailed away into exile, joining his wife and sons in Spain, where he'd sent them before marching with O'Neill. There King Phillip III rewarded him handsomely for his service to the Catholic cause, giving him a generous pension and making him Count of Berehaven and a Knight of the Order of Santiago. But though he lived comfortably enough in Spain, he also never gave up hope of returning to Ireland, and was even planning an invasion when he was killed in 1618 while interceding in a quarrel on behalf of his cousin, Don Phillip. The man who stabbed him was John Bathe, an Anglo-Irish Catholic and Dónal Cam's erstwhile friend and confidant, whom Don Phillip afterward suspected of being an English spy. Indeed, his account of the incident left no doubt that Bathe started the argument merely as a pretext to kill Dónal Cam and thus keep him from fomenting rebellion in Ireland. In any case, Dónal Cam was succeeded in his possessions and titles by his elder son, Dónal, who himself fell the following year at the Siege of Belgrade, and was succeeded by his brother, Diarmuid.

As for his sons, Dónal Cam was determined to further their interests (and his own) by integrating them into the Spanish nobility. In that regard, he persuaded King Phillip to admit them to the Order of Santiago and to accept them as pages in his court. But at the age of only sixteen, Diarmuid fell in love with one of his mother's handmaidens, a girl named Maighréad O'Driscoll, and married her in secret.

But upon learning who the boy's father was, the country priest who'd performed the ceremony became fearful of incurring Dónal Cam's wrath, and confessed to him what he'd done. And indeed, Dónal Cam flew into a murderous rage and threatened to kill the girl. But he calmed down soon enough and persuaded his friend and fellow exile, Florence Conry, the Archbishop of Tuam, to declare the marriage invalid and commit the girl to a convent in France. Of course it broke young Diarmuid's heart to be deprived of his love, so when Dónal Cam died a few months later, he immediately went to France to retrieve her. Yet she, too, was dead, having given up her life in the birthing of their son. Then, upon returning to Spain, Diarmuid found his brother dead, too, and named his infant son in his memory.

Of course, Diarmuid loved young Dónal dearly and never treated him as anything but his son and rightful heir, even though he was legitimately neither in the eyes of the Church, owing to the annulment of his parents' marriage. After Dónal was grown, Diarmuid married a Spanish noblewoman from a rich and powerful family, and fathered a child by her in 1647, a daughter named Antonia. When Diarmuid died in 1659, Antonia's mother and her family used their influence with the Court and Church to have Antonia declared his sole legitimate heir, even though he'd named Dónal in his will. And so it was that Antonia succeeded to Diarmuid's estate and titles, and Dónal and his wife and son were turned out of his father's house with only the dagger and the white rod and the clothes on their backs and, but for the charity of Don Phillip, would've been reduced to begging in the streets. In the meantime, Antonia's mother arranged for her to marry one of her own relations, and when she died childless in 1718, her entire fortune went to her husband, thus ending the legacy of Dónal Cam in Spain.

"But now, Dónal," O'Sullivan said, "we've come back to where we started, for that Dónal son of Diarmuid was Dónal the Spaniard, for whom Don Phillip wrote this book. And so it is that Don Phillip's story ends there with Diarmuid, while the rest has been written by Dónal the Spaniard and his heirs."

O'Sullivan turned the page then to a new genealogy and, looking at the list of names, Dónal saw that each generation had indeed been recorded in a different hand.

"See, Dónal? There is my name where my father wrote it, and then your name at the bottom of the list where I wrote it next to Eóghan's. The pages that follow record the story of all these men who've come between us and Dónal the Spaniard, though there's been precious little to write about most of them, I'm afraid. Indeed, most have been just poor farmers, with their only distinction in life being that they died fighting the English in one rising or another. But the genealogy has been kept and their lives recorded so as to keep intact the connection to our past, and in preparation for the day when we rise up to reclaim our own. So let's have a look at the genealogy, and then you'll know the full story of our family, the Clan Dónal Cam."

Continuing then, O'Sullivan read of Dónal the Spaniard and the dates of his birth and death, saying that with Don Phillip's help, he returned to Ireland in 1662 with enough money to lease the land around Cahernageeha and build the cottage within it. By that time, the heirs of Eóghan Óg had lost their lordship, fighting with another O'Neill in the war against Cromwell, as rebels *for* the Crown this time, ironically enough. But then, when a spider weaves a tangled web, he's likely to catch nothing but himself. And so it was with the O'Sullivans, for while they'd owned all of Béara prior to the war, they didn't own a single acre afterward.

But though they'd lost their land, they weren't quite a broken clan yet when Dónal the Spaniard came among them and, finding them restive in their sudden poverty, he hoped to rally them around himself and his claim to the lordship. So he revealed his identity and showed them the book and the dagger and the white rod as proof that he was indeed the heir of Dónal Cam. Of course, no one accepted the truth of it at first, partly because they didn't want anyone competing for what little they'd been able to salvage, and also because of the old feud between Dónal Cam and Eóghan Óg, whose grandson they still recognized as chieftain. But then the agent for the new English landlord got wind of it, learning the truth about Dónal through an English spy in Spain. And since he wanted to make sure that Béara remained peaceful, he told the O'Sullivans of the circumstances of Dónal's birth, which, ironically enough, proved his claim to being Dónal Cam's grandson, though it brought him nothing but scorn from his cousins. "The O'Sullivan Bastard," they called him, and "The Count of Bastardhaven," though the epithet that stuck to him was "Dónal the Spaniard," which was even worse because it labeled him as a foreigner, an outsider.

So his life on Béara was harsh and, though he resigned himself to it, he never gave up hope for his son, and he planted the yew tree to symbolize that enduring hope. And before he died, he brought his son, Phillip, here to Dunboy and invested him with the heirlooms and the titles that were rightfully his, and so passed to him the burden of the past and the hope for the future.

Then O'Sullivan's voice dropped to barely more than a whisper. "Then on the night of his death, a banshee was heard at Cahernageeha, which caused quite a stir among the other O'Sullivans, for they knew that banshees only follow the line of the rightful chieftain. Yet for all that, they still refused to accept young Phillip and his claim."

As for Phillip, he died at the Siege of Limerick in 1691, having come no closer to restoring his patrimony than his father. His own son Diarmuid was also at Limerick, and brought his father back and buried him at Killaconenagh, where Dónal the Spaniard and all but one of his descendants were buried, right down to O'Sullivan's own father.

It was during this Diarmuid's time that the Puxleys first settled at Dunboy, two brothers named Henry and John. They came initially as agents for the English landlord, but soon established themselves as middlemen by acquiring some rather substantial leaseholds. Yet the better part of their income came from smuggling, and they recognized the strategic significance of Dunboy and built their stronghold here, just as the O'Sullivans before them. Indeed, they even wanted to build on the site of the old fortress, but the local people wouldn't work there for fear of the ghosts that were said to haunt it. So they'd built a new tower-house above the inlet instead, calling it Dunboy Castle after the old one and even fortifying it, Béara being yet wild and dangerous in those days.

In doing so, of course, they made a great and enduring enemy of Diarmuid, who considered it an insult that Englishmen should settle on the site of his ancestral home and usurp even its very name. He even tried to incite the O'Sullivans to rise and drive them out, but his relations wouldn't hear of it, being the Puxleys' chief partners in the smuggling business. And though a rift did develop between them later on, when Morty Óg O'Sullivan began to smuggle Wild Geese instead of wine and killed that first John Puxley in the feud that ensued, Diarmuid was long dead by then and the Puxleys too entrenched to be easily driven off. So Henry Puxley succeeded his father at Dunboy, and John of the copper mines succeeded him, and here they remained while the O'Sullivans were yet consigned to serfdom and tenantry. But since a good Irishman neither forgives nor forgets, their trespass on Dunboy was still remembered and their Big House seen as the very symbol of dispossession.

"The Puxleys are your mortal enemies, Dónal," O'Sullivan said then, his voice as cold and hard as the old stone walls, "and when it comes time to strike a blow for Ireland, be sure you settle the oldest score first! Do you understand me?"

But while Dónal understood perfectly, he couldn't answer, just stared wide-eyed at his father.

"I asked if you understood me, Dónal," O'Sullivan said, the softness of his words not concealing the threat in his voice.

"Yes, Da," Dónal replied, telling his father what he wanted to hear.

But could he really do it, he wondered, even to a bad person that did bad things to innocent people? His eyes strayed to the dagger on his father's lap, and he tried to imagine himself sticking it into another human being, and then watching as the light faded from his eyes and his life evaporated like mist on a desert wind. It was so horrible that he couldn't even think about it, and shut his eyes against the mental images.

But again his father saw none of it, being too wrapped up in himself and his mission. "Good man!" he said, sounding self-congratulatory. "I know I can count on you to do the right thing when the time comes."

And then he went back to the story, again as if nothing had happened, as if his words had been nothing more than a passing comment on the weather.

Diarmuid died in 1733, he said, and was succeeded by his second son, Dónal, since the eldest, Eóghan, had died in 1715 while fighting for the Old Pretender in Scotland. Diarmuid also had two other sons named Phillip and Diarmuid Óg who, as soon as they grew to manhood, went to France to serve in the Irish Brigade. Phillip became a captain and died at the Battle of Fontenoy in 1745 while leading his men in the charge that broke the English ranks and won the field for France. But Diarmuid Óg survived the battle and eventually went on to Russia, where he became a general in the army of the Tsars, rumor having it that his descendants still lived in Moscow under the name of Sulivanov. As for Dónal the chieftain, he died in 1753 and was succeeded by his son Eóghan, who died of the fever along with his wife just three years later. His young sons, Phillip and Eóghan, survived and were raised by their uncle, another Diarmuid.

It so happened that Diarmuid had a son named Dónal, who grew especially close to Eóghan, the younger of his cousins. And as soon as they were old enough, they went to France to serve in the Irish Brigades, just as their great-uncles before them. There was no word of them again until just before Phillip's death in 1782, when a stranger came in the night asking for The O'Sullivan Béara. He'd served with Dónal and Eóghan in Dillon's Regiment and had come to tell Phillip that they'd been killed at the Siege of Savannah in 1779, while serving with the French Army in the American Revolution. Indeed, Dónal had died in his arms and his last request was to tell his father what had become of them. Of course, his father, Diarmuid, had died himself in 1777, but Phillip thanked the man and offered him a meal and a bed for his trouble. But being anxious for his own home after many years away, he wouldn't stay, so nothing more was known of them than that.

As for Phillip, he died a few months later and was succeeded by his son, Dónal, who lived in total obscurity up until the week of his death. It came as a result of trying to help Wolfe Tone and the United Irish in 1796 in their first attempt at a rising, when the French sent an invasion fleet to Ireland. But it was scattered by a storm and only some of the ships made it through, making landfall right there at Berehaven. Dónal himself was a United man and, upon learning that Wolfe Tone and the French were in the bay, he stole a boat and rowed out to join them, volunteering his services as a guide when they sent a foraging party ashore. But a trap had been laid for them by a band of loyalists led by a certain Daniel O'Sullivan, who'd been a captain in the British Army and was himself a descendant of Eóghan Óg, indeed, the last of that line to style himself The O'Sullivan Béara. And he captured the entire landing party without firing a shot, herding them off to the British Army headquarters at Bantry. But while the Frenchmen were treated honorably as prisoners of war and eventually repatriated to France, poor Dónal was hanged on the spot and without so much as the benefit of clergy. Nor did Captain Daniel speak in his defense, being rather the one who pushed him from the gallows, remembering the old feud between their ancestors. As a final insult, his body was dumped into a pauper's grave, and couldn't be located when his widow came to retrieve it.

"So it was," O'Sullivan said, closing the book, "that he was the only one of Dónal the Spaniard's descendants not to be buried at Killaconenagh. And just as a final bit of irony in our twisted tale, your mother's mother was a niece of Captain Daniel, and so you have united within you both lines of descent of the O'Sullivan Béara chieftains.

"And with Dónal we come down to the present day, for he was my own grandfather, and you already know of my father and me. And so it is, Dónal, that the story of the O'Sullivans comes down to you, from Adam through Éibhear Fionn and Eóghan Mór and Súildubhán and Dónal Cam and me, it has all come down to you. All that has come before lives in you, and what is yet to be will pass through you. You are our future, our salvation and our redeemer. For nine generations we've carried the burden of the Clan Dónal Cam, the sacred quest to reclaim our own, and now you have come to deliver us. So let us do now what we came here to do, that you may begin your epic journey into history."

O'Sullivan pushed himself up from his seat then, and extended his bony hand to Dónal. "Come, my son. It's time for the legacy to pass on."

But Dónal just stared at his father in horror, for with those words, the full meaning of Dunboy had finally come home to him. 'He wants me to be like *Jesus!*' he thought, and a picture of himself dangling from a cross flashed through his mind. But then he looked into his father's sunken eyes and saw in his withered spirit what the quest had done to him, and how heavily the past weighed upon him. '*No,*' he thought with sudden clarity, 'he wants me to be like *him!*' And with the thought his shoulders sagged, as though the unredeemed aspirations of all those dead ancestors had suddenly shifted from his father onto him. In that moment, he felt that all the world was looking at him, just as he had at Uncle Séamus's wake, and he heard the same silence roaring in his ears as his mind screamed out, '*Oh, God, please help me, for I can't help myself!*' But God's only reply was silence, and he knew he had no choice.

"Come, Dónal," O'Sullivan beckoned. "There's nothing to fear."

But staring at his father's outstretched hand, Dónal knew there was *everything* to fear. Yet his destiny lay in that hand now, and slowly, as though in a dream, he reached out to grasp it.

O'Sullivan smiled then, and as he did, the time-worn lines of care vanished from his face, as if he had use for them no more, having laid down the burden of his heart. He'd given his life to the Clan Dónal Cam, and while in the end he'd been no better than his forefathers, neither had he been any worse. For he'd brought a son into the world to carry on, and now that his time was up, it would have to do.

"Good man, Dónal!" O'Sullivan said, his voice cracking with emotion. "Good man!"

Then he led the way back through the ruined doorway to a shallow depression that might once have been a pond. With Ahern's help, he knelt by its side and flipped over a long flat stone. Beneath it was another stone, buried in the ground so that only one face showed, into which was carved the outline of a footprint.

"This is the coronation stone of the chieftains," O'Sullivan said. "Dónal Mór brought it from Knockgraffon, and Amhlaibh borrowed it for his inauguration but never returned it. Dónal Cam assumed it had been lost in the sack of Dunboy, but Dónal the Spaniard found it here in the old pond. It's a sacred relic of our sept, the central piece of a ceremony that's been used by the Gael for time out of mind, before Christianity even, when druids proclaimed the new king and symbolically married him to the land by setting his foot into the stone. And if the king was pure in mind and body and his rule just and good, then Áine, patron goddess of the *Eóghanachta*, would bless the sept with peace and bountiful harvests. But since we have neither goddess nor druid in these latter days, Seán and I will have to perform the ceremony ourselves."

Picking up the book again, O'Sullivan opened it to the genealogy of the Clan Dónal Cam, and handed it to Ahern. "So, shanachie," he said solemnly. "Let us begin."

Taking the book (reluctantly, it seemed to Dónal), Ahern turned to face the afternoon sun, spreading his arms like a priest offering a lamb to Apollo, his one eye closed as the sun's healing fire bathed his charred skin. As he stood there, still as the heartbeat of Death, it seemed that all the world stopped and held its breath in anticipation, waiting for him to speak. (Years later, Dónal would ask him what he'd been thinking, and his answer would be to shrug and say, "I was asking God to forgive your father for laying his burden upon you. *Forgive him, Father*, I said to myself, *for he knows not what he does*.") Then, without lowering his arms or even opening his eye, Ahern began to speak, his deep voice booming over the green lawn and blue waters and through the crystal air to cover all the Earth, it seemed.

"Hear me, O People of the Gael," he intoned, "as I recite the lineage of one who has come to claim his own." Lowering the book then, he began to read from the genealogy, his handless arm still in the air, looking now more like a Christian priest. "He is Dónal, the son of Eóghan, the son of Diarmuid, the son of Dónal . . . " he read, intoning each name slowly and reverently, " . . . the son of Dónal Cam, the son of Dónal, the son of Diarmuid, the son of Dónal . . . " and on through Dónal Mór and Súildubhán, Eóghan Mór and Éibhear Fionn, finally ending with " . . .the son of Jareth, the son of Malalel, the son of Caidhionan, the son of Enos, the son of Seth, the son of Adam who was made by Almighty God and before whom there were no others."

And when he turned and looked solemnly at him, Dónal was sure it was tears that made his one blue eye sparkle. "Who are you who has come to claim the White Rod of The O'Sullivan Béara?" he asked, his deep voice softer now, even sad.

Dónal hesitated for a moment, his eyes having fallen upon Tadhg, who'd appeared from nowhere, it seemed, to stand beside his father. "Don't do it," he saw him mouth.

But it was too late; the words were already tumbling from his mouth. "I am Dónal son of Eóghan son of Diarmuid of the Clan Dónal Cam."

Then his father spoke, saying in the same solemn voice as Ahern, "Dónal son of Eóghan son of Diarmuid, place your right foot into the royal footprint, and kneel before me."

Dónal did as told, and though the sculpted depression in the rock was much too large, his father took no notice. "By your rightful lineage, I proclaim you Chieftain of the great and ancient sept of O'Sullivan Béara, and as tokens of your office I give into your right hand the Sword of War, and into your left the White Rod of Peace. Use them in their proper balance and with the wisdom and prudence that is due your office."

Turning to the old pond, O'Sullivan scooped some rainwater from its bottom, and let it trickle slowly onto Dónal's head. "With the holy waters of our ancestral home I anoint you, and proclaim you The O'Sullivan Béara, Lord of Béara and Bantry, and Count of Berehaven by right of your descent from Dónal Cam O'Sullivan Béara. May God

201

keep you and guide you as you go forth from this sacred place."

Then O'Sullivan stood back from his son and bowed as low as his feeble body would allow. "Arise, my lord O'Sullivan Béara."

But before Dónal could comply, he heard the sound of clapping hands and raucous laughter from behind the ruined wall and, looking toward it, saw Richard Puxley and Paddy O'Sullivan emerge and come toward them, accompanied by a man he'd not seen before, though from the family resemblance he had to be a Puxley. He was young and handsome, strongly built though not especially tall, and dressed in the latest Ascendancy fashion from the finest shops of Dublin. As Dónal watched, the young man strode boldly to within a few feet of his father and stood there, sneering derisively as he eyed him up and down. Then he raised his right hand, and Dónal started as the sun flashed on the object he held, thinking it to be a knife. But then he saw that it was just a silver flask, and that he was merely taking a drink.

"Ah," the young man grunted, and swiped his sleeve across his mouth. "Of all the things that I despise about this miserable country, whiskey is not one of them!" he said in gentrified but drink-slurred English.

Then he let his eyes rove over Ahern and Tadhg, and he smirked as they lingered on Dónal, still kneeling with his foot in the stone, dagger and rod in hand. "That was really quite a show," he said, turning back to O'Sullivan. "Indeed, that was the best exhibition of low comedy I've seen in quite some time. Of course, I have no idea what you were jabbering about in your bloody gibberish of a language, but it must have been quite a serious matter from the sound of it."

The young man snickered then at his own lubricated humor. "Paddy, just who are these clowns, anyway?"

"'Tis Eóghan O'Sullivan, the one in front o' ye, Mr. Puxley," Paddy replied in thick-tongued English, "and his son, Dónal, kneelin' before him. The scar-faced fellah is Seán Ahern, the poteen man, and his own son, Tadhg."

"Ah, yes, Eóghan O'Sullivan," the young man said. "We've heard of you, haven't we, Richard? But what business brings you out today, trespassing on the property of your masters?" But before O'Sullivan could reply, he turned to Paddy and asked, "Do you suppose he has the wit to speak English?"

"Sure, Johnnie," O'Sullivan said, "we speak your language right enough. We've no choice since you squatters haven't the decency to learn ours!"

"That's Mr. Puxley to you, *paddy!*" the young man spat back, his eyes narrowing dangerously. But then he relaxed, and the smirk returned. "But I see that you know me, and I suppose one shouldn't wonder at that, since even the lowest of slaves knows his master by sight, even if he hasn't the wit to recognize his own servility. But aren't you the one who claims descent from Dónal Cam, the one who calls himself The O'Sullivan Béara, though you're better known as The O'Sullivan Bastard? Oh yes, we know all about Dónal the Spaniard and his brood of self-deceived peasants and their bankrupt claims to Dunboy. Indeed, we've watched you watching us from that windswept hillside of yours, gnawing the bitter ends of your resentment, too stupid to realize that your day has passed. So don't you think that if we considered you any real threat we'd have wiped you out years ago? No? Ah, well, I'm sure my logic is as wasted on you as my breath. You people never seem to understand your place, in history or in society, and I'm sure your little monkey of a son there will carry on in your footsteps. But come now, O'Sullivan Bastard. You've not answered my question. What brings you trespassing upon my property?"

"Gettin' a little ahead of yourself, aren't you, boyo?" O'Sullivan replied, smirking in his turn. "Or has your old Midas of a gran'da finally found a way to take his money with him, and so graced the world by takin' his leave of it?

"But sure, I brought my son here to show him the homeplace of his ancestors, and to tell him of how it was stolen by barbarians from across the sea, just so he'd know what kind of people his 'betters' are. We were kings in this country when you people were still lurkin' in the woods. We've been here since time began and we'll be here when it ends. For this is *my* country, Johnnie, not yours, and as long as one Irishman is left alive, it never will be!"

O'Sullivan stepped close to the young man then and glared down at him. "Our day will come again, you know!" he said, repeating it in Irish, " *Tiocfaidh ár lá!* "

But the young man was unmoved, knowing the threat to be empty. "Oh yes, I'm sure it will, though none of us will be here to see it. For today is *my* day, and tomorrow, and all the days of your miserable life and those of your son's, too. So your bravado does you no credit, O'Sullivan Bastard, because it's just a fool's dream and you're a fool for dreaming it.

"Now then, I really should do my civic duty and call the constables on you. But I think not. Your little comedy has left me in good spirits, and I'm feeling rather magnanimous today. So you have my permission to stay. Just don't let the gate hit your arse on the way out.

"Come, cousin," he said, turning his back pointedly on O'Sullivan. "Let us leave these clowns and return to our chess." Then to Paddy, he said, "Thank you for reporting the trespassers. Tell the foreman I said to give you an extra penny. Now back to work with you," he ended, shooing the man away with the back of his hand.

As soon as they were out of sight, O'Sullivan turned to Ahern, and said, "Help me, Seán, before I fall!"

Ahern came to him then and eased him to a seat on the wall. But Dónal stayed where he was, still with his foot in the coronation stone, seething with righteous anger at the way they'd been treated. And in that moment, the unbearable weight was suddenly gone from his shoulders, his fear and doubt forgotten, for he'd seen the truth of his father's words. He looked at the dagger in his right hand, the Sword of War that had rested in the hands of all his ancestors since Súildubhán. Then he looked at his father gasping for breath, withered before his time yet unbent before the arrogance of youth, unbowed before the tyrant who'd relegated him to a mean and desperate estate.

And catching his father's eyes, Dónal grinned at him. "Good man, Da!" he exclaimed. "Good man!"

The torch had been passed.

chapter 10

The Burial Ground of Killaconenagh

THERE WAS NO YEW TREE in the old burial ground, Dónal noticed, no totem of immortality to stand guard and ensure safe passage to the Otherworld. Yet looking at the plain wooden coffin at his feet, he couldn't imagine the spirit within not continuing. For he'd been larger than the life he'd lived, after all, and surely the Fianna would welcome him as one of their own.

For big Eóghan O'Sullivan was dead, having passed away in the misty gray of morning, just four days after paying his last respects to Dunboy. It had been the death of him in the end, sapping what little strength he had left and draining away his last ounce of fight, so that when they reached Cahernageeha, he was too spent to walk inside, leaving Ahern no choice but to carry him. Not that it was much of a chore, there being so little left of him, yet it broke his heart to see his friend so withered and helpless, a whisper of the man he'd once been. But O'Sullivan was too far gone to notice, lying on the bed like he was part of it, eyes closed against the torment of breathing, hating it, and yet loathe to let it go just yet.

And there he stayed until the end, drifting in and out of consciousness, Dónal ever at his side, holding his hand as though to keep him from drifting into mortal dream, not yet ready to let him go. It seemed so unfair, that they'd only just found each other and already the time was up, before he even had a chance to take it for granted.

Ahern saw the way of things, too, and sent Tadhg to fetch Órla, so that she would be there to comfort Dónal when the time came. He was glad for it, too, though she said nothing at all, just stood behind him, her lovely rough hands on his shoulders, comforting him as only a woman could, because only a woman could be a mother.

Then on the evening before his father's passing, something happened that would haunt Dónal for the rest of his days. It was a night of storm, with the wind howling from the sea and rain lashing at the windows, while thunder pounded at the door. And in the midst of it, Órla cocked her head and put a hand to her ear, listening for something she couldn't quite catch. "The wind has a voice tonight," she remarked, innocently enough. "It sounds so mournful and sad, like it's keening for poor Eóghan."

At that, Ahern cocked his head to listen, too. "It sounds more like the yowling of a cat to me, or a vixen in heat."

"It's none of those things," O'Sullivan said, and Dónal jumped at the sound of his voice, coming clear and strong from the bed. Then he heard it, too, and turned to his father, hoping he would explain. But he didn't even look at him, just closed his eyes and sighed.

"Send for the priest, Seán," he said in a voice from beyond the grave. "She's come for me."

But Ahern didn't reply, just nodded gravely, knowing what his friend meant. Going to the door, he braved the storm to scan the darkness, though the noise stopped the moment he opened it.

"Ah, well," he muttered. "I've never heard of a Cork man actually *seeing* her before, though they say it happens in other places."

Then he sent Tadhg into the turbulent night, telling him to fetch Father Enright before it was too late. Closing the door after him, he returned to the bedside, finding O'Sullivan dozing restlessly, but Dónal staring at him, wide-eyed and questioning.

"Who is it, Seán?" he asked, his voice barely a whisper. "Who has come for my Da?"

Not wanting to answer, Ahern hesitated for so long that Dónal indeed thought he wouldn't. Yet he relented, but not before taking Dónal to sit with Órla at the fireside.

"It's the banshee, Dónal," he said softly, his ravaged face red and horrible in the flickering firelight. "It's his time to go now and she's come to lead him across the divide."

"I don't understand, Seán," Dónal said, gaping in horror. "Please tell me what you mean!"

"The banshee is a messenger from the Otherworld, a spirit woman who keens outside the door when Death is near. They only attach themselves to noble Gaelic families and not even to all of them, though it's said that once they do, they follow them through all their generations, never minding that they've long ceased to be noble. As for this one that's come for your Da, it's said that she has followed your family since the fall of Dunboy, lifting her voice in mourning at the passing of each successive chieftain. As for how she came in the first place, there's a story about the siege that was never written in the book, though it's been passed down by word of mouth. Apparently Carew had a young girl crucified outside the walls, hoping to draw the defenders out into open battle, where his superior numbers could overwhelm them and bring a quick end to the siege. But it backfired on him, because the girl showed such courage in her torment that MagEochagáin and his men were inspired to hold on, leaving Carew to reduce the fortress the hard way. And being that he was a Protestant and allowed no priests in camp, the girl died without benefit of clergy, leaving her soul restless in death. And that, Dónal, is the reason that she has haunted your family ever since."

"But why does she haunt us and not Carew? He's the one who killed her!"

Ahern sighed and looked away from him then, knowing he wouldn't like the answer. "Because she was Dónal Cam's daughter," he said softly, before retreating to the bedside.

Dónal's eyes were round and staring as he watched him go. No wonder it was never written in the book, he thought, and no wonder his father hadn't told him. Who could find a hero in a man who'd sacrifice his own daughter to keep himself alive, and who would want to be heir to such a legacy? It made a lie of everything his father had said

207

about MagEochagáin, and he was angry with him for the deception. But then the banshee took up her cry again, and he remembered that his father was dying, and suddenly nothing else mattered.

In a fit of desperation, Dónal opened the door and shouted into the storm, "Go away and leave us alone! Go away!"

The noise ceased at the sound of his voice, of course, and though it might've been the rain playing tricks with the light, he thought he saw something dart through the gap in the wall, a small animal perhaps, a fox or maybe a stoat. Had it been only that after all and not a specter of the Otherworld? He couldn't be sure, but at least there was no more wailing after that, though it's absence didn't improve his father's condition.

Later, when Tadhg returned with Father Enright, the death watch began in earnest as the priest saw that the time was near and administered the last rites. Then, when the murky windows began to brighten with the light of dawn, O'Sullivan opened his eyes, just as a man would on any morning of the world. Turning to Dónal, he smiled, his eyes peaceful and serene, and squeezed his hand lightly, his grip having but the strength of a ghost in it.

Then he turned to Ahern. "Keep him out of the mines," he said to his only friend, softly and yet clear as the new dawning day. "He has a higher destiny before him."

Ahern said nothing, just nodded his assent. Then O'Sullivan looked toward the light in the window before closing his eyes, his breathing becoming so shallow and quiet that Dónal didn't even notice when it stopped.

But Father Enright saw it, as clearly as if he'd seen his spirit rise from his body and begin its Heavenward journey. "He is with God now," he said, laying his hand softly on Dónal's shoulder, "and with us no more."

The words, and the knowledge that he was now alone in the world, made Dónal's heart go cold, and he watched absently as Father Enright sprinkled holy water around the body to keep evil things away, bowing his head as he said a prayer for the resting of his soul, before going to the fireside to huddle in its healing warmth.

Órla pulled him close and wrapped him in her arms. "It's all right if you want to cry, Dónal," she said, her own voice cracking.

But he didn't feel like crying. Indeed, he didn't feel anything really, just a cold numbness, a detachment from the world around him, as if it were all a dream and nothing were real. He knew his father was gone from him, of course, gone to that place where he couldn't follow, no matter how hard he ran to catch up. So he felt no remorse as he had with Eóghan, no blaming himself for not running after. Indeed, there was even a certain comfort in the finality of it. He would miss him, surely, but it would fade with time, just as it had with his mother. So he shed no tears for his father, or for himself. From now on, his heart would bleed only for Eóghan.

"No, Órla, I'm all right," he said calmly, which only made her weep the harder.

After a bit, Father Enright asked Ahern if he needed help in preparing the wake. But Ahern explained that there wouldn't be one, since Eóghan O'Sullivan had no friends or family other than those who were already there, and that they intended to bury him that very day. The priest argued against it initially, saying that to hurry it was indecent and disrespectful, expressing perhaps his own Irish dread of a poor burial. But Ahern replied that since no one would come to a wake anyway, there'd be more disrespect in not tending to him immediately. And in the end, Father Enright relented, proving himself to be just as Father Fitzgerald had said, a man of empathy.

So they came down to Killaconenagh in the afternoon, following slowly after the coffin as it bumped along behind Spota. The two sextons hoisted it over the wall and took it to the same front corner where Dónal's mother was buried, their family plot, he now understood, though there was only a bit of broken grave slab etched with the word, *O'Súileabháin*, to mark it as such. But Killaconenagh being ancient and every bit of it used for burial many times over, his father would soon be joined with his forefathers in a very literal sense, as shown by the bits of bone poking from the dirt thrown up by the sextons.

The ground was cool and damp by the graveside, being shaded by trees, and the feel of it on his bare feet reminded him of the winter of Black '47, when he'd stood in the snow by his mother's grave and his feet had been blue and frozen by the time he'd gotten home. The memory of it made him wince as he pictured his father holding them in a cauldron of water while they "thawed," slapping and cursing him as he'd thrashed and shrieked. But no, he didn't want to remember that, only the good times they'd had, like his father saying, "Good man!" as they'd left the shop or carrying him on his shoulders, or *anything* but that!

But then Father Enright said it was time to begin, and the Aherns gathered around Dónal, Órla behind him with her hands on his shoulders while her husband and son flanked him. But just as the priest was ready to begin, there came the sound of horse's hooves on the road, and Riobárd Puxley coming at a gallop. As he dismounted and came through the gate, Órla stiffened and pulled Dónal closer, as if to shield herself from the man, and he wondered at the reason for it.

But Puxley gave him no time to consider, as he walked to the grave-side and nodded to those gathered round it, his eyes lingering on Dónal. "Please forgive me for being late," he said in Irish.

"As it so happens, Mr. Puxley, you're just in time," Father Enright replied. "And thank you for coming."

"Thank you, Father," Puxley said with a polite nod.

And though Father Enright did begin then, it was several minutes before he had Dónal's attention, as he was busy wondering what Puxley was up to, and why he had come. "The Puxleys are your mortal enemies", his father had told him, and surely he'd seen the truth of it in young Johnnie. Yet here was one of them come to pay his respects, standing silently with his head bowed, as if he truly mourned his father's passing. Feeling his eyes on him, Puxley glanced his way, though Dónal quickly shifted them to Father Enright, forcing himself to listen.

When it was finished and the coffin lowered into the grave, Dónal sprinkled a handful of dirt over it. "Safe home to you, Da. May you find what you seek beyond the waves."

And with nothing more, he turned and walked away, leaving the others to follow after.

They walked silently back toward Cahernageeha, the two boys in front and the adults behind, Puxley leading his horse by the reins. But Dónal was lost in thought and paid them no heed, instinctively knowing that he'd come to a turning in the road of life, and that nothing would be as it had been before. He would live with the Aherns now as had been arranged, and for the first time in almost two hundred years, there'd be no O'Sullivans at Cahernageeha. But perhaps that was just as well; the place had never brought them any luck, and maybe a change would help. And he wouldn't miss it anyway, as too many things had happened there that he didn't want to remember, though somehow he knew that his curse of an excellent memory wouldn't let him forget. Only the great yew gave him pause, and he hoped that whoever moved in would show it the proper respect.

With the tree in mind, Dónal looked up the hill toward Cahernageeha. But what he saw stopped him dead in his tracks, and he shaded his eyes against the sun to make sure they hadn't deceived him. No, he was right! The old tree was indeed lying lopped and broken, having knocked down part of the ring-wall as it fell. Then a movement by the cottage door caught his eye, a group of men raising a tripod, and he understood.

"They've cut it down!" he screamed, and charged up the boreen, driven by his anger and heedless of the Aherns and Puxley, who called for him to wait.

In a moment, he heard the pounding of hooves and Puxley thundered by, storming up the boreen like a dark wind, the long tails of his coat flapping in the wind of his speed. And as he rounded a corner, Dónal could see him with the other Puxleys, Richard and Johnnie, and he pumped his legs even harder, blind now to everything but his *mortal enemies*. On he went through the gap in the wall, lowering his head and making straight for Johnnie, meaning to fling himself upon him. But before he could, Riobárd snatched him lightly into the air and held him tight.

"Let me go!" Dónal screamed, kicking and flailing against him. "Let me go, let me go, let me go!"

"Stop it, Dónal!" Puxley commanded in Irish, squeezing him tighter. "You can hurt no one but yourself!"

Realizing the truth of it, Dónal went suddenly limp, though he turned a look on Johnnie that would boil water. "You cut down our tree," he exclaimed in English, "and I'm goin' to get you for it!"

"Excuse me, young O'Sullivan Bastard," Johnnie said, stifling a stage yawn, "but I believe you're mistaken on that point. I cut down *my* tree. This is Puxley land, after all, and not O'Sullivan, so that tree belongs to us, as does this hovel that you call a house and this pitiful heap of rock that surrounds it. And since your father is dead and you have no estate in his leasehold, I've decided to evict you and put an end to your tenure. Indeed, we've had quite enough of you people sitting up here watching us, gnawing at the ends of old schemes, even as your own hatred defeats you. And as for you, I should wash my hands clean and have you transported to Australia. I don't think you'd find it very pleasant, either, as the passage is long and lonely for the sailors, making them apt to take certain liberties with young boys. And, of course, you'll have the orphanage to look forward to when you get there, *if* you get there, that is. But then, I wouldn't want that to happen to the newly anointed Count of Bastardhaven. So I'll be merciful and let you stay in Ireland a bit longer. But just don't you cause any trouble, else I might have to change my mind."

"Sure, Mr. Puxley, 'tis your land and no denyin'!" Dónal said. "But you didn't have to cut down the tree."

"Yes, well, as for that, I need a new bow for deer hunting, and I hear your Irish yew is excellent for the purpose. As for the rest, I should think it would make excellent firewood."

Dónal stiffened at his words, but Riobárd spoke before he could retort. "For Christ's sake, John, the boy has just come from burying his father! He's all alone in the world now, and but for the charity of friends would have nowhere to go. So can't you have a little sympathy for him? At least give him a few minutes to collect his things."

Then to Dónal, he said in Irish, "There's nothing to be gained by any mischief now. You can't hurt him, only yourself. So if I put you down, will you behave?"

"Yes, Mr. Puxley," Dónal replied in English. "You can put me down now. I can wait."

"All right, then."

"I don't know why you insist on identifying with these people, Robert," Johnnie said. "It causes grandfather no end of grief and gains you nothing but a reputation for eccentricity."

"John, you wouldn't understand even if I explained it to you."

"Yes, I suppose you're right. But in any case, it hardly matters. I'm leaving Ireland shortly, and if I never come back, it will be too soon."

"For us, too!" Dónal muttered in Irish.

But Puxley just sneered at him. "Yes, boyo, you can curse me in that monkey-babble language of yours all you want. But you have exactly five minutes to gather your belongings before we turn this hovel into a memory. So if you don't want it falling down around you, I suggest you get busy."

Dónal said nothing else, just turned to the Aherns, who were huddled together like it was their own eviction. "Tadhg, I need your help," he said in Irish and, without waiting for a reply, turned and walked toward the cottage.

But he paused when he came to the tree lying lopped and broken, its song extinguished by the casual hand of malice. *Eóghan. Born of the yew. The immortal Eóghanachta.* He wondered if Johnnie even knew what he'd done.

"Good-bye, old friend," he said. "I hope he shoots himself with his new bow!"

Then he led Tadhg into the cottage and closed the door. Going first to the dresser, he pulled out the old linen bag with its trinity of treasures, and stuffed his meager possessions inside. From the chimney, he retrieved the little bag of money from its hiding place and handed it to Tadhg.

"Here," he said. "Stuff this down your trousers and make sure it doesn't rattle, else they'll take it."

After a last look around, he picked up the bag and led Tadhg outside.

213

"What do you have there?" Johnnie asked, eyeing the bag suspiciously as he walked past.

"'Tis nothin' but me clothes, yeer worship," Dónal replied over his shoulder, knowing Riobárd would protect him.

"You mind your manners, young clown, or you'll find out what 'pederasty' means on your way to Australia."

"Go dtaga seacht mallacht na mbaintraoi agus a leannaí ort!" Dónal retorted, ("May the curse of the widows and orphans be upon you!")

Ignoring the reply, he took Órla by the hand, and walked away.

part four

• Sióna and Mr. Shooks •

chapter 11

Kealogue Townland, Allihies
17 June, 1856

AS ALWAYS, IT WAS MORE LIKE A MEMORY *than a dream. He knew where he was and what was happening, just as if his conscious mind were looking back on it. Indeed, it* had *happened to him; he was back at Uncle Séamus's wake, a little boy standing by the coffin waiting for his mother to pick him up and show him the man sleeping in the box. He even felt himself rise in the air and hover over the coffin, just as he had on that living day so long ago. But with a start, he saw that it wasn't Uncle Séamus there at all, but a girl robed in white, her long red hair spilling all around her. She was so young and beautiful that it broke his heart, yet so serene in death that God Himself must surely have led her across the divide. She looked like someone he'd seen before, indeed someone that he knew well, though he couldn't remember her name or how he knew her. Then his eyes strayed to her delicate hands where they lay clasped on her chest, and he gasped in sudden horror at the jagged wounds on her wrists and fresh blood that stained her robe. There was blood on her feet, too, he saw, from wounds like those on her wrists, and blood stained the white fabric at her crotch. His eyes darted to her face again, and he saw that it wasn't serene at all, but twisted and ghastly, as though she'd died in fear and torment. Then her eyes opened and she looked at him, and he saw that they were the color of the new green of Spring, and that there was a streak of white in her hair.* Are you my sister? *he wanted to ask her. But she began to wail in a voice so mournful and melancholy that it froze his heart. He wanted to stop his ears against it and close his eyes, to shout,* Put me down! *and run away from the horror. But he couldn't move, couldn't speak, couldn't even breathe. Then another voice spoke above the wailing, his father's, though it came from inside his own head.* What are you going to do about this? *he demanded.* What?

⟨ɯɯɯɔ⟩

Dónal sat on a stool beside the cottage door, his back against the stone wall and arms crossed against the cool of dawn, watching as the dew-spattered meadows of Allihies bloomed with the dawning of a new day. The mine machinery was still quiet, and the only sound he heard was Órla singing as she went about her morning chores. Taking a deep breath of turf-scented air, he stretched himself like a cat waking from a nap, trying to clear the cobwebs that yet clouded his brain.

For he'd been up for hours already, bad dreams having disturbed his sleep again, making him thrash at his blanket and gasp for air as he'd struggled up through the horror and into the dead of night. After lying in the darkness until the fear subsided and his heart stopped pounding, he'd dressed quietly and come outside, hoping the chill night air would chase away his demons. Yet the memory of it lingered, leaving him fatigued and moody.

But then Ahern's voice cut in on his thoughts, calling for Órla to help him from the bed, his speech slurred from the seizure he'd suffered winter before last. It reminded him of how frightened Tadhg had been to see his father so near death, and how happy he'd been when he'd recovered. He'd no experience with death in the way that Dónal did, no way of knowing that time eases the pain and heals the scars. And how Dónal envied him that innocence.

Of course, he'd been glad for Ahern's recovery, too, the man having been a father to him, loving him like his own son and treating him as such. But more than that, he'd been Dónal's friend and mentor, his tutor and touchstone, the one who praised him for his successes and

218

helped him learn from his failures. In some ways, Ahern shared more in common with him than with his own son, Tadhg being more like his mother, practical and solid and concerned with the here and now, though he did share his father's wry sense of humor. But he had little interest in history, which he found dry and lifeless, while it was his father's special love and Dónal's, too. Then there was their common love of music, which Ahern had discovered soon after Dónal came to live with them, giving him his old set of *uilleann* pipes and teaching him to play them. So quickly did he progress that within a couple of years he was playing at wakes and weddings, *céilís* and American Wakes, already acknowledged as the best piper in that part of Béara.

So Ahern was doubly blessed, and took great pride in his two sons' growth and maturity (and in his own ability to nurture their talents and strengthen their weaknesses). Indeed, he would often recall the dark days after his misfortune, thinking that he could never have guessed then how happy he'd be now. Then the second misfortune had come upon him, and in some ways it had been more devastating than the first, since he'd had to give up his shebeen and the income from it, which with Dónal and Tadhg helping had grown to a tidy sum in recent years. But the seizure had left him partially paralyzed on his right side, so that his stride was scattering and little strength remained in his handless arm. "It's a blessing that it wasn't my good side," he'd jested, "else I wouldn't be able to give you boys your daily floggings anymore!"

Dónal and Tadhg had shared his good humor, of course, happy to see that he hadn't lost it with his mobility, though both were long past the size of being manhandled. At seventeen, Tadhg was almost as tall as his father and half again as broad, bull-necked and barrel-chested, and generally acknowledged to be the strongest young man in Allihies, stronger than Padge O'Sullivan even, who, like his father, had grown into a giant of a man. Tadhg was handsome in a man's man sort of way, too, with a head full of wiry blond hair and a full red beard that he sometimes had to shave twice a day, not to mention the mat on his chest and back that earned him the nickname of "goat boy" from his father.

219

But his nature was still jovial and gregarious, and his ire as quick to pass as it was to rouse, especially where his brother was concerned. For in Tadhg's eyes that's just what Dónal was and he always treated him as such, just as Dónal did him.

But while Tadhg had grown right up to the expectations his boyhood size had set for him, Dónal had far exceeded his own. At just over fifteen, he was already taller than both Tadhg and Ahern, and yet to finish growing. And whereas Tadhg was stocky and burly, Dónal was lean and wiry, the delicate features of his childhood having matured into a finely chiseled mask, with a straight and narrow nose, and a beardless chin square enough to anchor his face with manliness, though it was his relentless eyes that yet defined him. They were still the color of the new green of Spring and blazed in bright contrast to his red hair with its streak of white, which, to Ahern's chagrin, he wore longer than was customary among the men of Béara. "Who do you think you are, the Blessed Savior?" the man had asked at him once. "I've an excuse with my monster's face, but if you don't cut your hair soon, the lads are going to start asking you to dance with them!" But long hair suited his image of himself, making him look aristocratic, he thought, and so he steadfastly refused to cut it. Indeed, he did have a certain air of nobility about him, despite his rough clothes and peasant manners, a noble savage perhaps, or a latter-day chieftain of the Gael. He looked nothing at all like his father, and people who didn't know him as his son would never have guessed it. Not that the man's stigma attached to him anyway, as people just considered him one of the Aherns and treated him accordingly.

Yet Dónal was considered something of an oddity in Allihies, a fellow that was "hard to get round," as the saying went. Part of it was his long hair, of course, which people didn't understand and thus found threatening, while a bigger part was the intensity of his gaze, which those who didn't know him well found intimidating. It was a reflex on his part to having been hurt the most in life by people who were close to him, a purely unconscious defense against letting people in till he knew whether he could trust them or not. Living his formative years under the cloud of his father's anger had left that mark on him, and he could no more escape it than he could change it. Only in Órla did he ever confide his feelings, for only she had the knack of unlocking his heart and turning his introspection outward, and so easing his burden. Indeed, she was his *anam chara*, his soul friend, for he could tell her things about himself, while of everyone else he asked questions. Still, he'd grown increasingly introspective as the years passed, spending a lot of time alone just as he had as a child. Indeed, he still found a certain solace in his solitude, and a certain freedom, for it allowed him to stand on the side and observe, and form his own opinions with no pressure to make them conform to anyone else's. Not that he was taciturn or uncivil, being unfailingly cordial to everyone and even friendly in a distant sort of way, but he was decidedly a loner, an individual living outside the *clochán* of communal Irish life.

But perhaps the biggest reason that Dónal was "hard to get round" was his reputation for being the best fighting man in Allihies, having proved himself in countless battles over the years, beginning with the mountainside fight with Padge. After word of it had gotten round, every fighting clan in Allihies had come looking for him, anxious to see if their champion could best him. At first, Tadhg had tried to stand in for him, saying that it was his place since he was the eldest and biggest (and since he wanted to protect his position as leader). But Dónal wouldn't let him, always taking the fight for himself and, somewhat to Tadhg's chagrin, always winning. For having learned the lesson of Odysseus, he'd fought with his wits rather than brawn, and being invariably younger and smaller than those pitted against him, he'd also felt no obligation to fight fair. Indeed, he would often strike while the other boy was still working himself into the mood, or even when his back was turned, and he always made sure that his first shot was his best one, often ending the fight before it had even begun. How many times he'd been accused of not fighting fairly, he couldn't begin to remember. But he had a stock answer for it: *I don't fight to fight fair. I fight to win!* So eventually, his reputation had been made and the boys had left him alone, which was all he'd wanted from them in the first place.

But all the biting and gouging and head-butting had changed Dónal's status within his own clan of friends, elevating him to the leadership in place of Tadhg, a fact that rankled the older boy, though he did his best never to let it show. Yet there were the odd times when he couldn't help himself, like on that Sunday afternoon when they'd trekked all the way out to the old ringfort at Lehanmore to play war. As they'd divided themselves into opposing "armies," Tadhg had had a sudden brainstorm, exclaiming to Dónal, "I know. Let's pretend we're at Kinsale. I'll be Red Hugh and you can be The O'Neill," instinctively ceding pride of place. But Dónal had just sneered and replied smugly, "I don't have to *be* anyone! I *am* The O'Sullivan Béara!" Tadhg had gaped at him then, his expression a curious mixture of hurt and anger. "Well excuse me, your fucking highness!" he'd snapped, "I thought you were just a poor bog rat like the rest of us!" Then he'd turned his back and stomped away.

After that Dónal had been more careful in his treatment of Tadhg, intuitively understanding his friend's predicament and feeling guilty for his own insensitivity. Of the two of them, Tadhg was the natural leader, big, strong, and handsome, full of confidence and charisma, just the kind of man that Irishmen liked to follow. People were drawn to him instantly, and he was universally liked and admired. Yet for as long as they'd known each other, he'd always walked in Dónal's shadow, even in the eyes of his own father, and knew in his heart that he always would. So he couldn't help but be a bit jealous of his "little brother," though he was big enough to keep it buried deep inside so long as Dónal never threw it in his face, which after Lehanmore, he never did again.

Then, too, Dónal had a few things over which to be jealous of Tadhg, like the fact that he was fearless around girls and had them standing in line to be his sweetheart. At *céilís* he would dance with every unmarried girl present (and even some of the married ones if he knew them well enough), seldom bothering to follow the priestly dictate of keeping the Holy Ghost between them. Dónal would watch him from behind the haven of his pipes, spinning and reeling, laughing and flirt-ing, sending the girls into a tizzy like a fox in a henhouse. Where had all that rakishness come from, he would wonder, still remembering him as the boy who didn't like girls, and how could he get some of it for himself? He'd even spoken to Órla about it, hoping for some insight from the female perspective. Yet though she'd been sensitive enough and done her best to help, he'd come away feeling more frustrated than ever. "Just find yourself a girl that you can talk to," she'd said, "and things will fall into place." But didn't she see that that was just the problem? How could he find a girl he could talk to when he was too shy to talk to them? Had he but known it, the girls found him even more attractive than Tadhg, and some were even trying to use his foster brother as a way to get to know him. But they were always frustrated by his perceived aloofness, though it made him even more attractive in their eyes.

So Dónal suffered in silence while Tadhg danced with the girls. And wasn't he just the catch, too, especially since he'd made a success of himself in the haulage business. It had been his father's idea initially (a way to keep him out of the mines, the man had confided to Dónal), and though Dónal had taken a passive hand in it by loaning him the money from his legacy, it was Tadhg's characteristic drive and energy that made it work. From the initial wagon and two horses that he'd bought from an émigré family, he'd expanded to five wagons and twelve horses, while Dan MacCarthy and Art O'Shea now worked for him full time. Some of the horses he hired out to run the horse whims that still powered certain operations in the mines, while the rest were used to transport ore from the storage floors to Ballydonegan. He'd even had to lease the field behind their cottage as a place to corral them, and would soon need even more land since he expected his business to expand again. In that regard, having a Puxley for a friend hadn't hurt him any, as Ríobárd had quietly used his influence at the mines to steer more and more of its business his way.

Tadhg's success had been a real boon to his family, too, since his father could no longer work and depended on his support. And having financed it, Dónal had also profited, though he didn't much care for the image of himself as a gombeen man. So he'd eventually forgiven the loans in exchange for a share of ownership, which Tadhg had insisted on making a full one-half even though he did little of the actual work. For by that time, Dónal had a job himself, having become Richard Puxley's "assistant" bookkeeper the summer before, replacing a man who'd emigrated to America, having finally given up trying to support a family on the pittance Puxley paid him. It was Riobárd's idea, though he'd used Ahern as his proxy in suggesting it to Dónal. After laying out the reasons for accepting the job, Ahern had ended by saying, "Anyway, it'll keep you out of the mines like I promised your Da." But Dónal had needed no encouragement in that regard. He'd ventured into the Kealogue with Pat Donegan and the Kellingtons once, and seen for himself what a hellhole it truly was. So he'd gone with Riobárd to see Richard, who'd been leery of Dónal's youth at first, though he'd relented after seeing a demonstration of his arithmetic skills. But he'd been outraged at the salary his brother demanded, protesting that he'd paid the previous man only half that amount, and he'd been experienced in the job. But Riobárd hadn't given him a choice, and in the end he'd agreed, though insisting that Dónal start then and there.

So Dónal had gone to work for the Berehaven Mining Company, not as a miner but as the keeper of its ledger, which was about as close to holding its purse strings as an Irishman could get. Upon learning of it that evening, Tadhg had remarked, "I wouldn't work for that nasty old gobshite if you paid me!" And indeed, Dónal had to put up with much ill will and ill humor from Puxley initially. But he'd worked hard and learned quickly, and soon was so proficient that even Puxley had had to admit he was worth the extra money, though not to Dónal's face, of course.

So with Dónal's job and Tadhg's business, the family was able to live reasonably well, at least to the extent of not constantly having to worry about where their next meal would come from. They were still dirt poor, of course, and near the bottom of the socio-economic ladder, but they were not at the bottom and, during the Great Hunger, being even one rung up generally had meant the difference between life and death. Yet it irked Dónal that their success was due to the paternalism of Riobárd Puxley, and he'd said as much over supper of a recent evening. But Ahern had brought the discussion to a quick end by snatching Dónal's plate from in front of him and flinging it into the fire. "Well, if your pride prevents you from enjoying the fruits of our friendship with Riobárd," he'd barked, "then you can just go hungry like everyone else! You ought to be thankful we have such a friend and that he's taken an interest in you and your welfare, and all without asking anything in return, I might add!"

Dónal had said nothing else, just stalked from the cottage and didn't come back till after everyone was asleep. Ahern had never so much as raised his voice to him before, and he'd been hurt and deeply puzzled by it. But as he lay by the fire, it occurred to him that perhaps Seán had his own qualms about associating with a Puxley, especially since it had let him survive when so many others of his station had perished. Perhaps he even felt guilty about it, and thus the raw nerve. So Dónal had apologized the next day, though his mind hadn't changed on the subject, and still he was leery of Puxley and wondered when he would reveal his ulterior motive.

As for the majority of Irish workers at the mines, very little had changed over the years. They were still poorly paid and worked in appalling conditions, owing their souls to the Company Shop while the Cornishmen were favored with better wages and free housing. But at least they had a friend at the top now, since Seán Óg Reed had succeeded his late father as Mine Captain in 1852. He'd been born and raised among them in Allihies and, having a certain empathy for their condition, would often bend the rules to help them. But also in 1852, the Caminches Mine had given out and closed, displacing scores of workers and their families. Some had emigrated, of course, but most couldn't afford the passage and went to the new workhouse that had opened in Castletownbere earlier in the year. Few had been admitted, however, though not from want of eligibility. Only rate-paying landowners could sit on the board that administered the workhouse (thereby excluding most native Irish) and, since votes were allotted on the basis

225

of property valuation, John Puxley held effective control over admissions. Thus was he able to exclude "his" miners and thereby keep the supply of labor high and its cost "appropriately" low. Not that they'd have been any better off inside, the workhouse being the refuge of last resort, the place where people went when all hope was gone. *Good-bye, God,* the macabre joke went, *I'm off to the workhouse!* and to Dónal it seemed that truer words were never spoken.

For he'd been unlucky enough to bear witness when it first opened its doors, himself and Tadhg having been attracted by the commotion after delivering a keg to a ship's captain in the harbor. Hundreds of desperate people had camped about the gate hoping for admission, men, women and children of all ages, all soaked and steaming from the soft weather. Only in Black '47, when a horde of famished wraiths descended upon Castletownbere on their way to the workhouse in Bantry, had such a wretched assemblage of misery been witnessed in Béara. Though the workhouse was built to house only six hundred souls (which was about all that was left of them by the time they entered), that number had been far exceeded from the very first day. For when the Master had come to open the gate, a sickening wail went up from the waiting tide of humanity, and they'd surged forward, crushing those in front so that he'd had no choice but to open it and let them all in. Even so, a number of people had been trampled in the rush and lay where they'd fallen, forgotten by friends or loved ones in their desperation to get inside. Only the porters had come to collect them, heaving their pitiful bodies onto a cart destined for the famine grave.

Dónal had been physically sickened by the sight of it, had wanted to stop his ears against their anguish and close his eyes to their despair. Yet he'd forced himself to watch until the last poor unfortunate staggered through, a woman clutching a baby to her barren breast. Then the gates clanged shut behind her, leaving nothing outside but the dead and the ghost of Hunger. Tadhg had turned to him then, his fearless blue eyes bulging with fear. "*Jesus, God and The Spirit!*" he'd exclaimed, almost in tears. "Jesus and God in Heaven, please let me die rather than go into that place!" Dónal had said nothing, too stricken himself to reply. But that last image of desperation burned itself into his consciousness, so that his jaw tightened with the memory ever after.

So even though there'd been fewer outbreaks of blight in recent years, hunger was yet present, making the workhouse and emigration a sad fact of Irish life. Every month or two it seemed that another cottage would be suddenly lifeless and empty, blotting the Irish green like a canker. "Famine houses," Dónal had come to call them, though he hardly noticed them anymore, hunger being a familiar part of the landscape and not a mystery anymore. Still, he found them an apt metaphor for the "Great Silence" that had gripped his country in the wake of the Hunger and the failure of '48. Like an abused child his Erin had become, huddling in a corner and wondering what She'd done to deserve such ill treatment, wanting desperately to be rid of Her tormentor yet deathly afraid of rousing its wrath. She'd become a country of ghosts, and he felt them everywhere, in the fields and on the roads, haunting the scrub and the empty cottages, and especially when he ate, hovering just a mouthful of food away.

To the English it seemed that Ireland had finally been pacified, the harshness of Her experience having brought Her to heel. But Dónal knew such optimism to be unfounded, for the people were just as discontented and disaffected as ever, lacking only an effective means of expressing it. Given organization and leadership, he knew their discontent would roar into flame like dry kindling. But that was the problem – there was no organization and no leadership. O'Connell was dead and buried and all but forgotten, while the Confederate clubs of Young Ireland had folded like houses of cards after their defeat, the leaders scattered to the four winds. True, the Ribbon Men and other secret societies were active, but they were disjointed and haphazard, operating only at the local level. What was needed was a national organization with a centralized command and integrated network of units covering the entire island, all trained, armed and coordinated in secret, for surely the Empire would quickly squash any open attempt at rebellion. Yet the task of building a secret Irish army seemed so daunting that Dónal doubted it would ever be done. For one thing, where would the arms come from, and the money to buy them? How could such a large endeavor be kept secret in a country notorious for informers? Who would train the troops, and who would lead them? How would they know where to strike, and when? How would they overcome the Empire's ability to simply outlast them? But most daunting of all, how and where and when would one even go about starting?

So while he'd grown from boy to adolescent, those were the problems that occupied his mind as he pondered the '48 and his brother's death and wondered what he could do about it. Among the many causes of failure, lack of unity of purpose had clearly been paramount, the history of Desmond and Kinsale and Cromwell and the Boyne and '98 having repeated itself yet again. Only this time, it hadn't been dissension among the leaders so much as a lack of understanding between them and the people. Smith O'Brien and Meagher and O'Gorman and O'Mahony were men who favored legislative independence from Britain certainly, though not necessarily radical social revolution aimed at improving the lot of the impoverished majority. Yet they'd expected the starving masses to rise spontaneously in rebellion solely on the vague premise that it would be better for them to be governed from Dublin than from London. Only Mitchel and Lalor had understood that rectifying economic and social inequities were things the Irish peasantry could better understand than the esoteric ideal of the Republic. A full belly and tenure in their leasehold they would die for, surely, but a bourgeois parliament in Dublin they could live without. So in order to get the people's support in the future, the leaders would have to promise them changes that would make a difference in their lives. And for those leaders to understand that, they'd have to be cut from a different cloth than the comfortable, middle-class tweed of Young Ireland. But of what, exactly?

Yet for that question and all the others, Dónal had no answers, and the more he thought about it, the more he knew he'd find none in Allihies, stuck as it was out on the far end of the world. He was sure that his destiny lay in serving Ireland, but he'd have to seek for it in that wider world that lay beyond Castletownbere. Moreover, he knew that now would be the time to do it, when he had no ties to bind him to Béara other than love of the place and affection for its people. Sure, he'd even thought of leaving today, the anniversary of Dunboy, the significance of the date not being lost on him. The only problem was that he had no idea where to go or whom to see, or even of whom to ask the questions. Indeed, what if he spoke to the wrong person and ended up in jail or transported for his effort? So he'd decided to exercise a little English patience and wait, hoping for a sign to point him in the right direction.

It was hard on him though, with his dreams tormenting him and Eóghan's unavenged death haunting him. And of Eóghan, he'd found himself thinking more and more as the years went by, of all the hurts in his life that being the one that hadn't faded with time. For he felt his brother's life had been stolen from him, just as the land of Ireland had been stolen and by the very same thief. The boodymen he'd feared as a child, The Hunger and The Fever, had diminished as his knowledge of them had grown. Yet in The English he saw the root of all the evil he'd ever witnessed in the world, the impoverishment of Ireland and the marginalization of Her people, the Great Hunger, and especially Eóghan's death. Not that he was quite that chauvinistic in his thinking; he didn't hate The English just for their Englishness, or blame them for the blight that killed the potatoes. But he held their men of Empire accountable for the monumental tragedy that was Ireland in the mid-nineteenth century, just as he held them accountable for Eóghan's death and his hurt that wouldn't heal. So it was his destiny to fight them, to lead his people out of the darkness and into the light of civilization. After all, his father had said that he was the Chosen One, the messiah who would vindicate their generations of sacrifice, the nameless and faceless legions who'd vanished into the dustbin of unrecorded history. It was his *destiny*, by God, and he *would* fulfill it!

But the morning sun shone bright on the ocean and the fields were awash in luxuriant green, while Órla's song mingled on the crystal air with the homey smell of turf. He sighed, and smiled at the heartbreaking beauty surrounding him. Though it might be his destiny to leave it someday, in that moment he was content to be just where he was, at his own cottage door in his own little corner of the Holy Ground.

Just then, Tadhg came whistling around the corner, a broad grin spreading across his face at seeing Dónal leaning back on the stool. With three quick strides and a kick he sent it spinning into the yard and Dónal down hard on his rump. But before he'd even had a chance to laugh at his mischief, Dónal had spun around with catlike agility and kicked his own feet from under him. In a moment the two were tangled into a scuffling ball, rolling over and over on the grass as first one and then the other had the upper hand. But Tadhg being stronger and the better wrestler, he soon had Dónal pinned beneath him.

"Give up?" he asked, pulling Dónal's arm painfully behind his back. But in the next moment he was on his own back and yowling, having neglected to account for Dónal's other arm, which he'd thrust hard into his crotch.

"Ah, Jesus, you little runt!" Tadhg moaned. "I always knew you for a molly!"

"Who are you calling a runt, *shorty*?" Dónal shot back.

The commotion in the yard brought Órla to the door, and her voice startled the young men, as they crouched on the ground eyeing each other like wolves.

"Here, now! What are you barbarians up to?" she demanded. "And don't just sit there gaping at me like I've three heads on my shoulders. Answer me!"

"Nothing, Mam," Tadhg said with a smile that was all innocence and no sincerity. "Dónal just slipped off his stool, and I was helping him up." He stood then and helped Dónal to his feet. "See, Mam?"

"Oh, sure, and I was just born yesterday!" Órla glared at them each in turn. "But if you two piglets are finished rolling in the mud, then bring yourselves inside to the table. The breakfast is boiled and it'll not get any warmer!" Then she turned her back on them and disappeared into the cottage.

"After you, little brother," Tadhg said, nodding toward the door.

But Dónal wasn't listening. A horseman on the road had caught his eye and he turned to watch him approach.

"Now I wonder what he wants at this hour," Tadhg said, following his gaze. "Hopefully, he has some business for me. I've two wagons idle and salaries to pay."

"Or maybe his uncle died and left you the mines!"

"Ah, that's for you, *runt*!" Tadhg said, making an obscene gesture.

But Dónal held his reply, watching as the man rode up the path.

"God be with you, Riobárd!" Tadhg called in Irish.

"God and Mary be with you, Tadhg," Puxley replied, "and you, too, Dónal."

"It's been a while since we've seen you," Tadhg said. "How have you been keeping?"

"Well enough. How is your father getting on?"

"Oh, he's as mean as ever, though that's what seems to keep him going these days. Shall I fetch him for you?"

"No, that's all right. I don't want to disturb his breakfast. Anyway, it's Dónal I've come for, if you can spare him for a moment."

"Sure, Riobárd, you can have him all day for all the good he is to me. But you might want to check with that brother of yours first. He's the Devil's own, from what Dónal tells me!"

"Yes, Richard is a caution, isn't he? But as a matter of fact, I have spoken to him, because I do need Dónal for the whole day."

Turning to Dónal then, he continued. "It seems that I've made a mess of my books, and I need you to come to Oakmount and straighten them out for me. I'll be sailing from Ballydonegan as soon as my ship is loaded, so why don't you come with Tadhg on his delivery and go with me?"

"Your wish is my command, Mr. Puxley," Dónal said in English, adding a bow for effect. Still, the prospect intrigued him, as he'd always wanted to sail on a ship.

"Right, then. I'll see you at Ballydonegan," Puxley said, ignoring Dónal's insolence and English. "Good day to you, Tadhg, and give my regards to your old ones." With that, he turned his horse and rode away.

"You know, you might find it in your heart to be a little nicer to him," Tadhg said, watching him go. "He's never done anything but right by us."

"He's a *Puxley*," Dónal retorted, as though that said it all.

⧉

Dónal stood next to Puxley and watched as he steered his little ship skillfully through the choppy waters off Dursey Island, handling the wheel with the casual confidence of an expert sailor. It was a glorious day for sailing, with the sun shining bright and warm, and the wind high enough to push them along at a good clip. They seemed to be making good time, too, having already rounded Dursey Head and turned east toward Bantry Bay, the steeply-rising cliffs and meadows of Béara sliding swiftly by.

Off the starboard bow lay Crow Head and Crow Island, and further ahead the old ringfort at Lehanmore in its sloping green pasture. Dónal was surprised at how small and vulnerable it looked, perched precariously between the immensities of sea and sky, when it had seemed so large and imposing from the land. He remembered the day he'd gone there to play war, and how terrified he'd been as a defender when the other boys had come shrieking down the hill with blood in their eyes and the savage howl of the Gael on their lips. He'd had to remind himself that it was just a game and his friends weren't really going to skin him alive and roast him for their supper. Still, it was then that he'd understood how MagEochagáin must have felt at Dunboy, trapped in a little fortress with Death staring him in the face, and nothing to do but wait for it to come and get him. And as Lehanmore slid into the distance, he sighed, finding it easier to picture the place filled with cattle than with warriors.

But then Puxley was asking him a question, speaking for the first time since they'd set sail. "So, Dónal," he asked in English, the language of the sea, "how do you like sailing, now that you've found your sea legs?"

"Oh, 'tis grand so!" Dónal allowed. "'Tis somethin' I've always wanted to do, though never till now have I had the chance. We'd a fine view

232

of the haven from Cahernageeha, and sometimes I'd sit on the wall for hours and watch for ships sailin' in or out. Sure, if there weren't times when I even thought of runnin' away to sea myself! I still think about it now and again, even though I know I'll never do it because . . ." But Dónal left his thought unfinished, having suddenly remembered to whom he was speaking.

"Because of what?" Puxley prodded, his interest seeming a little too keen.

"Because there's other things that I have to do. You know, Mr. Puxley, I didn't catch the name of your ship."

"That's *Captain* Puxley while we're at sea, and I call her *The Copper John* after my uncle, though I'm sure that if he knew, he'd find it a dubious distinction at best."

Dónal glanced curiously at Puxley then, surprised at hearing that sort of disrespect for his family chieftain. Yet he was even more surprised at the mischievous grin on his face, and that it showed even in his eyes, the man having let down his guard for once, it seemed.

"'Tis a funny thing, you know," Dónal said softly, as though thinking aloud, "but I've never seen your eyes light up like that before. Sure, 'tis almost as if I've seen the real you for very the first time."

"You don't trust me, do you, Dónal?" Puxley asked, his grin fading.

"No."

"Even though I've never done you any harm."

"Even though."

"Well then, tell me, young O'Sullivan Béara, just what would I have to do to prove myself to you?"

"You'd have to be someone else."

"Ah, I see. The old memories again."

"The past weighs heavily in Ireland, Captain."

"It does indeed, and that's fair enough, I suppose. Personally, I've always felt a little mistrust of one's fellows to be a healthy thing, since we are, after all, the most dangerous, blood-thirsty predators on the face of the planet, and seem inclined to prey mostly upon each other. So I don't begrudge it of you. Just be sure you're equally mistrustful of those who do mean you harm."

"Oh, but you mistake me, Captain Puxley. I trust *everyone* – to act in their own selfish interest, that is."

"I see," Puxley said, eyeing him sharply. "Indeed, I see that I've underestimated you, and that I'll have to be more careful, since I must assume that I can only trust you as far as you trust me."

"Aye, Captain, 'twould be statin' it fairly so."

"Aye, indeed, Mr. O'Sullivan."

After that they didn't speak again till they rounded Fair Head and passed into the sound.

"There's Dunboy," Puxley said, pointing toward the ruins, "the source of all those memories that lie between us."

"Not all of them," Dónal replied, though his mind wasn't on Puxley. Rather, he was trying to picture the place as it had been in its glory, a mighty fortress commanding the waters for miles around, seat of The O'Sullivan of the Slender Ships.

But then he noticed a man watching them from atop the wall, gazing intently at the ship and coming to the sea cliff as they passed nearby. And seeing him that close, Dónal detected an air of nervousness about him, of expectancy even, and he wondered who he was and why he seemed so interested in the ship. Certainly he wasn't a Puxley by the look of him, nor from his dress did he appear to be a servant or laborer. Then he felt the man's eyes upon him and understood that it wasn't the ship he was interested in at all.

"When we land, Mr. O'Sullivan," Puxley said, as if hearing his thoughts, "please go see who that man is and what he wants. We can't have people trespassing on the Holy Ground, now can we?"

"Aye, Captain," Dónal answered distractedly, still holding the man's gaze.

And as soon as the ship landed at the quay, he hurried to the old fortress, remembering the way like he'd walked it a thousand times, though it was only his second visit to Dunboy. Upon cresting the rise, he saw that the man had come away from the cliff and now stood just a few feet away, obviously expecting him. And though he felt the hair on the back of his neck rise in warning, he didn't pause, just walked right up to him, looking him in the eyes while at the same time taking the measure of him.

He was fortyish, unremarkable in height and build, with a bald top-knot and unimpressive beard, and his clothing, while clean and neat, fell rather short of making the man. Still, there was an air of physical strength about him, though he didn't seem the laboring type, and a broad intelligent forehead capped his hawklike face. But like Dónal himself, it was his eyes that defined him, being fanatical in their dark intensity, an impression accentuated by the profound and restless energy that pulsed from him like a thrumming engine. And as those relentless eyes bored into him, Dónal had no doubt that he himself was under considerable scrutiny, though for what reason, he couldn't imagine.

"I suppose you want to know who I am and what I'm doing here," the man said without preamble, his voice of moderate tone, the lilt of his English suggesting that he'd once had an Irish accent, though some other influence now obscured its nativity. But he wasn't a Cork man, in any case, of that Dónal was sure.

"Sure, if that isn't just what Mr. Puxley sent me round to ask," he replied, trying to mask his own curiosity.

"Ah, Mr. Puxley sent you. And would that be Mr. *John* Puxley?"

"No sir, 'twould be his nephew, Mr. *Robert* Puxley, the man on whose ship you saw me just now. 'Tis true that Mr. John owns this fine estate, but he abides in Wales now and has done for many years."

"Ah, so Mr. Puxley is an *absentee* landlord," the man said thoughtfully, an odd sort of look coming into his zealot's eyes. "Then I'll not be finding him at home, will I? Ah well, no matter. My business with him can wait. Indeed, it's been waiting for almost seven centuries now, so a bit longer won't hurt."

Dónal started at those words, hearing sedition lurking in them. But if the man noticed, he gave no sign of it.

"For the time being," he continued, "I'm just happy to be here, walking this hallowed ground made sacred by the blood of MagEochagáin and his men. Did you know, lad, that this was once the seat of the O'Sullivans of Béara, and that they were the lords of Béara and Bantry in the days before the Flight of the Earls?"

Then he began to recite his knowledge of the O'Sullivans and Dunboy, which Dónal found surprisingly complete though mistaken in some particulars. But though he knew all of it and more, he listened politely, until the man said, " . . . and the castle was built by Annadh na Leacan, or 'Annadh of the Cheeks,' it would be in English, and it was he who first styled himself The O'Sullivan Béara—"

"Amhlaibh," Dónal interjected.

"I'm sorry, what was that?" the man asked. "What did you say?"

"'Twas Annadh's son, Amhlaibh, who built it, and himself who first took the title."

"Well, now, that's news to me, and mind you, I have my information from a very reliable source! Yet you seem so sure of yourself. I'd like to know why, if you don't mind."

But Dónal hesitated, realizing that he knew nothing of this man or of his purpose, except that he himself seemed to be part of it. Still, the only way to find out was to answer his question.

"I know because I have a book that tells the whole history of Dunboy and its lords," Dónal said. "'Tis called *The Book of O'Sullivan Béara*, and 'twas written by Dónal Cam's nephew, Don Phillip O'Sullivan. I assume you know who Dónal Cam was."

"But that's incredible! Of course, I've read Don Phillip's account of the siege in his book, *Historiae Catholicae Compendium*, but I didn't know he'd written another book on the subject. I'd dearly love to see it, though I'm even more curious to know how you came by it."

But Dónal didn't answer, just walked to the old pond and uncovered the coronation stone. After removing his right shoe, he placed his foot into the indentation, finding to his surprise that it now fit perfectly.

"I have the book," he said, "because I'm descended from Dónal Cam himself, in a direct line from father to son through eleven generations. I *am* The O'Sullivan Béara, and the rightful lord of Dunboy. Does that answer your question?"

"Why, yes, it does," the man replied thoughtfully, though his manner suggested he'd known all along. "Indeed, it answers a great many questions."

Then he smiled, the warmth of it touching Dónal so that he couldn't help but smile back.

"Well, now," the man said, rubbing his hands together. "I suppose I should give you an accounting of myself since I appear to be trespassing on your land. But what name should I give you, my lord O'Sullivan Béara? I'm known by a few and each has significance to those who call me so. All of which suits my purpose, of course, since I wish to be known well to some but not at all to others. So perhaps I should just tell you all of them, and leave it to you to decide how well you wish to know me."

Then he grasped his lapels and began to speak as though addressing an assembly. "Among the Gael I'm known as *An Seabhac Siúileach*, or 'the Wandering Hawk' as it would be in English, a somewhat romantic sobriquet, I must say, though one that speaks more to my looks and reputation than of me as a man. Yet it was given to me by my countrymen, and so I bear it with pride. As for the English, they've twisted that same *An Seabhac* into the shape of their own tongue and made me into Mr. Shooks, which is how I'm known among the worthy constables and magistrates of our fair island. That name I also bear with pride, since it keeps them from knowing me by my real name, the one that has come down to me from my ancestors. That is 'Stephens,' which I believe to be from *Fitz*Stephens and so Norman in its origins, yet like so many others, now more Irish than Irish itself. My Christian name is 'James,' and as far as I know, my father chose it simply because he liked the sound of it. So 'James Stephens' is my proper name, and though it's not very Irish-sounding, I assure you that no Irishman alive or dead has ever been more dedicated to Erin.

"So now you know my names," he said, extending his hand to Dónal, "and how you choose to call me is up to you. But it's my pleasure to make your acquaintance in any case, my lord O'Sullivan Béara."

"Call me Dónal, Mr. Stephens," he said, finding the man's grip as firm as the look in his eyes.

237

"Call me James, and consider us well met!" Stephens replied with a bow.

"All right, James. Now I know your name. Still, it tells me nothin' of you and your errand, and I've to report to Mr. Puxley."

"Ah well, just tell your man I'm a poor pilgrim come to pay his respects to the martyrs of Dunboy. That's the bald face of the truth, too, though it has little enough to do with why I've come to Béara. That would take a bit more explaining, and I'm not so sure such a man as himself would grasp it."

"Sure, but you never know that he might surprise you. Why don't you try it on me first, and I'll let you know if he's a likely one."

"Well now, Dónal. It does seem a bit early in our friendship to be divulging my personal business to you. Why, I don't even know if I can trust you."

"Sure you do, James, else you'd never have told me your name!"

"I see," Stephens said, regarding Dónal thoughtfully. "Indeed, I see that one has to get up early if one is to pull one over on you. But then I like that in a man. It means that he has his eyes open and his wits about him, and that's just the type of men I'm looking for. So I think I'll take this chance meeting as a good omen and tell you what I'm after."

Stepping in close then, Stephens laid a conspiratorial hand on Dónal's shoulder. "You see, while it's true that I'm on a pilgrimage in this fair country of ours, I'm not wandering about quite as aimlessly as I would have people believe. Indeed, my madness has a method to it, and that is to gauge the mood of the people, to see how they feel about their circumstances and whether they're happy with the way our country is being governed, and if not, whether there's sufficient feeling in favor of the Republic to give an armed revolt a reasonable chance of succeeding."

At that, Dónal's mouth fell open and he gaped at Stephens in shock. For in those few succinct words, the man had laid out the very proposition he'd been pondering and, even more, he was actually doing something about it. He'd found a way to start, and though it didn't seem like much, many great things had begun from less.

"So, perhaps it is a bit much for a Puxley to grasp, wouldn't you say?" Stephens asked.

"Yes," Dónal agreed, shaking his head as though to clear it. "Yes, it is so."

"Yes," Stephens said, his fanatical eyes growing almost gentle. "But you seem to be a bit put out by it yourself. Have I erred in baring my soul to you so soon?"

"No," Dónal replied, his voice thin and uncertain, even in his own ears.

"Are you sure?"

"Yes! Yes, I'm sure. 'Tis just that I've spent the last seven years ponderin' that very thing, and I find myself in a bit of shock hearin' it come back to me so directly."

"Well now, that's more like it! So give me your opinion then, since you've had so much time to think about it. Are the people of Béara ready to fight for their freedom?"

"Sure, they are, though given the state they're in, 'twould be expectin' a bit much of them to rise just now. I mean, sure they're ready and willin' to fight, but at this point they're just not able, at least not with any reasonable expectation of winnin'. They're too demoralized from hunger and emigration, and since The '48, they'll not credit such a scheme, anyway. What they need is organization and trainin' and arms to fight with and, most important, leaders who can put all that in place and sustain it long enough to see it through. On top of which, James, it has to be done in secret, or 'twill be over before 'tis even begun. But if and when all that is accomplished, then I'd say the people will be ready to fight, because then they'd have a reasonable expectation of winnin'.

"My own brother was killed in The '48," he continued, his eyes straying to the ruins. "His name was Eóghan, and he'd everything in life to live for, yet he died for nothin', because no good ever came of it and none ever will.

"And I don't want there to be any more Eóghans," he said, turning a hard look on Stephens. "So whatever it is you're schemin' up, make sure you do a thorough job of it! I'd not have us throw our lives away for nothin'."

Stephens didn't say anything for a moment, seeing that Dónal's grief was still fresh. But when he did speak, his voice was firm with the courage of his convictions.

"You're wrong about The '48, Dónal, for much good has come of it already, though from where you stand, you may not be able to see it."

"And just how do you figure that?"

"Because I'm a man of '48 myself. I stood at the barricades in Ballingarry with Smith O'Brien and O'Mahony and Meagher, and I was at the Widow MacCormack's house, and I commanded the rearguard that covered the retreat, and I got shot in three places for my troubles, I might add. And like you, I've spent the years since contemplating our defeat, and rather than an inglorious end, I see in it an opportunity for a new beginning. Most of that time I spent in exile in Paris, where I learned the art of conspiracy and guerilla warfare while fighting in the resistance to Louis Napoleon, knowledge and experience that will be invaluable to the task at hand.

"Now I've come home again, to walk among the people and gauge their sympathy for insurrection. And if I find it sufficient, then I propose to create just the sort of secret organization you described, with the goal of establishing an Irish Republic by any means necessary.

"And you should know, too, Dónal, that the organization will exist not only in Ireland, but also among the millions of our brethren exiled in America. From them will come the money and arms, and the experienced soldiers to train our recruits. Indeed, many of the leaders of '48 are there and have already begun to organize with just such a goal in mind.

"And finally, Dónal, you should know that my determination in this enterprise was born of my experience in '48, and that I started to work on it immediately thereafter. So if I can bring it to fruition, then your brother will not have died in vain after all, now will he?"

"No," Dónal conceded softly. "No, he won't."

"No, indeed! So now that you know my name and purpose, Dónal

O'Sullivan Béara, tell me where you stand, with the Republic or against it?"

"I stand with Ireland, and with all patriot men who would see Her free."

"Does that mean you'll join with me if I call? Will you fight for Ireland with me?"

Dónal didn't answer immediately, just stared at the man before him, so unprepossessing in appearance and yet so intense of manner and magnetic of charm. His words were just the ones he'd longed to hear, even down to his formula for revolution. But was he indeed the man who could bring it off, the one who would succeed where so many others had failed? He closed his eyes and tried to think for a moment without those fanatical eyes boring into him. But all he could see was the girl in the coffin and all he could hear was his father's voice demanding to know what he was going to do about it. What indeed, and what choice did he have, really?

"Yes, James, I'll join you if you call," he said finally, his voice sounding like someone else's in his ears. Opening his eyes then, he found Stephens smiling at him, and any hesitation he may have felt evaporated in its warmth. "In fact, I'll join you now!"

"Thank you, Dónal!" Stephens said, touched by his confidence. "Thank you. I know you'll be a great asset to our cause, and when Ireland is free, you'll be remembered as the man who avenged Dunboy!"

Dónal felt himself flush at that. For all that he'd thought about his destiny, it had never occurred to him that posterity might remember his deeds. But then he thought of O'Neill and Kinsale, and the terrifying possibility that he might be remembered as a failure. It was just too horrible to contemplate in that moment, and he knew he'd have to let it go or be paralyzed by fear.

"So what do we do now?" he asked, trying to shake off his dread.

"*We* don't do anything yet, Dónal," Stephens replied to his relief. "What I will do is continue my journey, and see if the rest of the country is as disgruntled as Rebel Cork. What you will do is be patient, and trust me to know when the time is right. I'll call for you then, indeed,

I'll even come myself if I can. In the meantime, you're not to say a word to anyone about our meeting or conversation. You're to forget that James Stephens or Mr. Shooks or *an Seabhac Siúileach* was ever here. Tell Puxley what I told you earlier, that I'm a pilgrim come to visit the ruins, that I seemed harmless enough and you didn't bother to get my name. I've a horse tied up in the woods yonder, and I'll leave now by the back way. And you'd better be getting back yourself before Puxley wonders what's become of you.

"May God keep you until we meet again, my lord O'Sullivan Béara," Stephens said reverently.

The words touched a chord in Dónal's memory, and he thought of the last time he'd stood on that spot and heard himself addressed that way. He looked down at his bare foot in the coronation stone and suddenly felt the same sense of helplessness he'd felt then. Yet he'd accepted the White Rod and pledged himself to the Clan Dónal Cam, and there was nothing he could do about it now.

But then Stephens spoke again and brought him back to the present. "Good-bye, Dónal," he said with a wink, and headed toward the trees.

"*Slán abhaile, a Sheabhaic Shiúileach,*" Dónal called after him, (Safe home, O Wandering Hawk).

When Stephens was gone, Dónal put his shoe on and covered the stone before heading back to the inlet. At the top of the rise, he turned and looked at the forlorn ruins of Dunboy. Nothing had changed in the seven years since he'd been there; indeed, it might've been only seven minutes for all the notice the stones had taken.

'Someday, Ireland will be free,' he thought. 'But will it look any different then?'

Back at the ship, Dónal found that Puxley had left him a message saying he'd been called away on urgent business and would have to attend to his books later, and that he should to go back to Allihies. When he reached the high shoulder of Guala, he turned and looked across the valley toward Cahernageeha. Though the old fortress wasn't visible from where he stood, in the old days he'd always known where it was because he could see the top of the great yew. For ten lost generations it had stood there, watching over the hapless chieftains of the Clan Dónal Cam. And though it was now gone, just as they were, it wasn't forgotten. No, never forgotten!

"Dunboy isn't all I'm going to avenge," he said to the ghosts.

chapceR 12

Allihies
18 April, 1858

THE SUN WAS BREAKING THROUGH THE CLOUDS as Dónal skipped down the steps of St. Michael's and ran across the road to the meadow beyond, splashing water from rain-filled puddles along the way. A spring gale had been blowing for more than a week, and the rain had been constant and oppressive, driven by the wind from the sea. All of Allihies was sodden with it, even the spirits of the people, and it hadn't helped that they'd had to walk to Mass in a blinding downpour, bringing their dank smell inside with them.

As usual, he'd sat in the balcony, it being as far away from old Father Nolan as he could get and still be in the building. He'd long ago decided that the man had become a priest simply because he couldn't do anything else in life. Nor did Dónal think him much good even at that, his droning sermons being heavy with evil and the wages of sin, and light on the true message of Christ. Then when there was trouble he was nowhere to be found, though he was quick to the fore when there was drink to be taken. It was enough to drive any thinking man away from the Church. How he missed Father Enright and his insightful, uplifting approach to the ministry. But it was a long way to Castletownbere of a Sunday morning, and it seemed even further coming back, especially when there was work waiting, which was always.

So he'd slouched in the balcony, nodding as the raindrops drummed a sonorous beat on the slates above him. But then the rain stopped and the sun broke through, filling the stained glass with a riot of color and his mind with the possibilities of the day. As soon as the last Amen was said, he raced down the back stairs and into the spreading light, pleased to find blue sky on the horizon and receding clouds above.

And now as he watched from the meadow, a rainbow arced suddenly toward the north side of the bay, and he followed it to its end on the little promontory of Pointnadishert. The light sparked his memory and he smiled at the thought of his father playing there as a child while his own father labored in the Dooneen. But then a voice interrupted his reverie.

"You should see yourself," Tadhg said, "grinning like a jackass in clover! And just what is it that you see out there? Leprechauns dancing down the rainbow to their pot of gold?"

"Yes, leprechauns dancing down the rainbow, tra la, to their pot of gold, la la," Dónal sang, dancing in a demented circle and flailing his arms in the air.

"Fuck me, Dónal, but I think you've been cooped up in the house too long! What you need is a good day's work to clear your head and put your feet on the ground. And that's just what we have waiting for us! So let's get on with it, shall we?"

"You were right to begin with, Tadhg," Dónal retorted, watching the rainbow fade. "Fuck you, and your good day's work, too! I haven't seen the sun in a week and now that it's finally come, I've no intention of wasting it on shoeing horses and rimming wagon wheels."

"Don't start that with me!" Tadhg exclaimed, spinning Dónal around to face him. "We've a big job this week and we need to be ready for it! So whatever foolishness you have in mind will just have to wait! Now get your arse moving and get home with you!"

"No, Tadhg, not today!" Dónal said, grinning defiantly. "I have to practice my pipes."

"What do you mean practice your pipes?" Tadhg demanded, clenching his fists. "We've had no work for days, with the indecent weather, and you with all the time in the world to practice! But did you so much as look at them? No, you just skulked about the house all sullen and surly. Yet now that we have a chance to get some work done, you want to practice!"

"That's right, I do. And I will, and don't even think about trying to stop me."

"As if I could ever stop you from anything once your mind is set! All right, Dónal, go ahead. Have yourself a nice leisurely afternoon while I work for both of us. But tell me, just for the sake of curiosity, what's put this sudden bug up your arse?"

A distant look came into Dónal's eyes then as he gazed toward Pointnadishert. "All right, I owe you that much, I suppose. I've had this tune clattering about in my head that I couldn't get quite right, and practicing didn't help. It had to be done in my head first. And then as I was sitting in Mass, just as the rain stopped and the sun lit the windows, it came to me like a revelation, all finished and ready to play. So I need to go off alone now and play it while it's still fresh in my head. It's a lament for my brother," he ended with a shrug.

At that, the fire went out of Tadhg's eyes, and he nodded in understanding. For if it was true that time heals all wounds, then Dónal had a long life ahead of him.

"Sure, go on with yourself," he said. "Pat and Dan will be there anyway, and if we need help, I'll send for Níall and Liam."

"Thanks, Tadhg."

"For what?"

"For being such a good brother to me!" Dónal replied, and turned away.

"I'm a better brother to you than Eóghan ever thought about being!" Tadhg muttered, though he waited till Dónal was out of hearing.

⚬〰〰〰⚬

Dónal hurried past the old Dooneen works and on toward Cod's Head, his pipes in their case and his new tune spinning through his head. As he walked, his mind wandered to the newspaper article he'd read the day before, reporting that Mr. Shooks had been seen in Cashel in the County Tipperary and was suspected of spreading sedition in the area. He'd seen other snippets, too, mostly oblique references containing little specific information. Then, too, he'd heard the name dropped in gossip, especially when the drink had loosened tongues and men were wont to wag on matters better left unmentioned. But at least he knew that Stephens was still out there, for he'd heard nothing from him since their meeting that had seemed so fateful at the time, though it was almost two years ago now. For months after he'd watched the road for his hawklike face, wishing him to come and induct him into his clandestine army of rebellion. But after a while it had become obvious that Stephens meant what he'd said about being patient, and Dónal had done his best to comply, though he'd found it an easier virtue to preach than to practice, especially since he knew the work to be proceeding without him.

Yet in some ways, those months had been the happiest and most carefree of Dónal's life. He and Tadhg were making good money and so the family never had to worry about food or rent. More important, having committed to Stephens had lightened his burden somewhat, for at least he now saw a clear path toward his destiny, even though he'd yet to take the first step along it. Still, he'd used the time to learn as much as he could about warfare and tactics using the books from Dunboy, such as *Pacata Hibernia*, which told the English version of Dunboy, as well as others that contained accounts of Napoleon at Austerlitz, Wellington at Waterloo, Washington at Trenton and The Bruce at Bannockburn. He'd been fascinated by Caesar's account of his campaign against the Celts, relating how their size and shrieking fury and headlong charge were enough to blanch the stoutest Roman heart, though not enough to overcome the indurate Roman discipline. Indeed, the story was all too familiar to Dónal, the Celts having all the impulse and emotion of a drunken pub brawl or O'Donnell at Kinsale, grand fighters but poor soldiers. It underscored in his mind their need for leaders, for men of ability and patience and vision, men like O'Neill and Dónal Cam. But since the demise of the old Gaelic system after the Flight of the Earls, there'd been no professional officer class among the native Irish. Sure there were tens of thousands serving in the British Army, but only with rare exceptions did they rise above the rank of sergeant, and most who did were of the Anglo-Irish Ascendancy or anglicized Gaelic aristocrats, people whose loyalty was above suspicion. And the English were very careful not to create such a class among the Irish lest they turn around and lead a revolt against them. So the Irish soldier was taught discipline and how to follow orders, that is, how to be effective cannon fodder, but not how to lead or command.

So Dónal did what he could to teach himself, using his business partnership with Tadhg to build on his childhood experience of leading his clan of friends. (He'd lost his job in the mining office when John Puxley died at the end of 1856 and left the mines in trust to young Johnnie, and so had become Tadhg's partner in more than name only.) Indeed, he'd thrown all his energy and native intelligence into it and, somewhat to Tadhg's chagrin, they'd reaped the benefits almost immediately. For the first thing Dónal had done was to paint signs for their wagons, proclaiming them to be the property of "Ahern and O'Sullivan, Haulage Contractors, Allihies" (all in English, of course). Tadhg had laughed at first, saying that everyone who needed to know their names and occupation already did. But then the signs had gotten them a lucrative contract on The Big Island during the expansion of the Bear Island Naval Station, and after that he'd been a bit more respectful of Dónal's ideas.

As for Dónal himself, probably the greatest benefit he reaped from his new activities was that his sleep was no longer troubled by bad dreams, perhaps because he now had at least the beginning of an answer to his father's question, *What are you going to do about this?* True, he'd yet to free Erin or restore the Clan Dónal Cam, but at least he was working in that direction, and apparently that was enough to mollify the ghosts that haunted him. The past was still with him, of course, pushing him inexorably toward his destiny, but it was no longer present and palpable, a dark shadow at his elbow scrutinizing his every move. It let him sleep through the night and left him alone during the day, and he was happier than ever before.

Yet now as he turned off the road and onto the headland of Pointnadishert, Dónal cleared his mind of James Stephens and everything else, to relive that last morning together with Eóghan. Upon reaching the ruins of a tiny church, he sat down on a wall facing the sea and took his pipes from their case, quickly inflating the bag and running through the scales to unlimber his fingers.

Then he closed his eyes against the light of the present, and pictured himself and Eóghan as they'd been on that dark day long ago. And as he began to play, Eóghan turned his back and walked away from him, each slow step seeming an eternity, the pipes an extension of his soul skirling with the misery of that moment, the haunting melody rich with his pain, the tune the beating of his broken heart, as forsaken and forlorn as the scabby land of Béara, yet just as heartbreakingly beautiful. *Ochón, it keened, ochón for Eóghan, and ochón for me!* And at the end, Eóghan turned and waved but didn't smile, letting his hand linger in the air before disappearing around the bend, never to return.

He held the final note as long as he could, letting it die as the vision receded. A darkness came over him then, and he slumped on his pipes, his body limp and numb as if the tune were his mortality and its playing his death knell. The world was gone from him and, as he stood at the veil of the Otherworld, ready to cross into oblivion and reunite with Eóghan, a woman's voice called from the void, the banshee of the Clan Dónal Cam come to lead him across the divide.

But then with a flash like the instant of birth, he realized that it wasn't her speaking to him, but a woman of this world and, bolting from his seat and dropping his pipes, he spun around to face her.

"*Fuck me!*" he shouted, his heart racing. "Where did you come from?"

"Here, now!" she said, hands on hips and blue eyes glaring. "There's no need to curse me like that, when all I did was compliment your piping!"

"I'm sorry! I didn't mean to curse at you. It's just that you scared me, sneaking up like that!"

"Why, I did nothing of the sort! I walked right up to you in the broad light of day, and if you didn't see me coming then it's your fault and none of mine. But if you're going to be rude to me, then I'll just take back my kind words and bid you a good day. I've better things to do with my time than to waste it on you!"

"No, wait!" he exclaimed, grasping her arm. "Don't go away mad! I said I was sorry, and I never say it unless I mean it. And I do mean it, you know."

"Well now, that's better!" she said with a pretty smile. "That was the grandest bit of music I've ever heard, and I'd have been sad indeed to find the musician a boor, especially such a handsome young man as yourself."

At that, Dónal flushed and his eyes dropped to the ground. But she just laughed delightedly.

"Now don't tell me you've never heard it before!" she scolded playfully. "You're as scarlet as your hair!"

"No," he replied, still looking at the ground. "Never."

"Well, I find that hard to believe," she said, and when Dónal looked up he found her still smiling at him, her kindness touching him so that he could only smile back.

Then suddenly he had the strangest feeling they'd met before, there being something very familiar about her, though he couldn't put his finger on it, a memory lying just beyond the pale of recollection. Taking a good look at her then, he saw that she was dressed in layers of rags and that her red hair was bobbed so short it wouldn't lie down, suggesting an essential wildness about her, as if she'd washed up from the sea, perhaps, or blown in on a wind. Yet her face was soft and lovely, its beauty accentuated by the contrast, and in that moment he thought her the most beautiful woman he'd ever seen, and the saddest. For though her eyes were frank and steady, there was a haunted look about them, as if they saw things that were better left unseen, memories that were better unrecalled. It was that combination of beauty and sadness that touched his heart and made him want to wrap her in his arms and protect her from the world, to heal its hurts and smooth away the scars.

"Do you really like it?" he asked, looking at her sideways, as if to deflect a negative reply.

"Yes, I really do. You played as if your heart were broken and could never be mended, like your lover had been taken from you and you'd never get her back. The sound of it drew me to you, and I felt as if I were at the gates of Heaven as I stood here and watched you pour out your inner beauty. Tell me, young piper, how does a man come by such beauty as you, on both the outside and the inside and all at the same time?"

Dónal felt himself go warm again, though he didn't blush, a more primal emotion stirring him this time. "I could ask you the same question."

"Oh, I'm not beautiful," she said, blushing and dropping her eyes in turn. "I'm just me."

"But that's just what's so beautiful about you," he said, and smiled as she looked up at him. "Just you!"

She held his gaze for a long moment then, looking inside him, trying to fathom the depths within. "You're not like other men, are you?" she asked finally.

"No, I'm not."

"No, I don't think you are. Artists are always different, whether they want to be or not. And what do you call that tune that sets your soul to music?"

"I call it 'The Lament for Eóghan O'Sullivan,'" he replied, having given it not a thought before that moment. "He was my brother, and he died in The '48, and if you find beauty in my tune, it's only a reflection of the man he was. For he was the best man I've ever known and his like will not be again."

"Oh, I don't know about that!" the woman said, and though Dónal understood it to be a compliment, he didn't acknowledge it, since to do so meant he would have to accept it as true.

"Why did you come here?" he asked, trying to change the subject.

But at that, the smile vanished from her face and the ghosts behind her eyes came to the fore. She said nothing at first, just walked past Dónal and into the ruins of the little church, to the killeenagh that

251

was there, the burial ground for unbaptized children.

"I came here to keen for someone, too," she said, looking at the small stones that marked the graves, "someone I loved as much as you loved your brother. Eithne was her name and she was my daughter, though her spirit fled before she came into the world."

Dónal's heart went out to her for the sadness in her voice, and he would've done anything in that moment to make it go away. "I'm sorry. I didn't know."

But then another thought occurred to him, one that filled him with sadness for himself. "Is your husband with you, then?" he asked, trying to keep dejection from his voice.

The young woman looked up at Dónal then, her eyes suddenly angry and hard. "What husband?" she hissed through clenched teeth. "I never had a husband! The man *raped* me!"

Then the anger was gone, and she was suddenly soft and vulnerable again, her delicate shoulders sagging under the weight of sadness, a tear falling from her eye. "He raped me. After my Da died in the mines, I was all alone and defenseless, and he waylaid me in the dark. Then the fool went home to his wife with my smell on him, and said that I'd seduced him and made him pay for the service. Of course, she came after me with her friends and relations, and they beat me until I was bruised and bleeding. I screamed and begged and pleaded with them. I told them he raped me. But that only made it worse. When they were done with me, they cut off my hair so the world would know me as a harlot, and left me with not a friend in the world. So I had no one to help me with Eithne, and I fainted from the pain of it and didn't know that the cord was wrapped around her neck until it was too late. That was five years ago now, though I remember it like it was still happening, trying to get her to breathe and to live. But I was barely fifteen years old myself and my own Mam dead since I was two, and so how could I have known what to do? The women of the village should've been there to help me, yet they'd scorned me and made me an outcast, in the end taking even my baby from me! So that's why I've kept my hair cut so short, to flaunt it in their faces and

252

make them worry after the affections of their husbands. And sure, the odd one comes scratching at my door late at night, come to offer me a few shillings for a ride and a tale to tell his friends over a jar. And though I always turn them away, it doesn't keep them from coming back. Still, if it torments their wives, then it's worth the trouble."

She paused and shook her head, her eyes on the stone between her feet. "I should've left this place years ago. It's been nothing but Hell to me. But I just can't bear to leave Eithne all alone. I know how it feels to be alone, and I can't do it to her."

She looked up at Dónal and smiled sadly. "I don't know why I'm telling you this. I didn't mean to burden you with my troubles. I just wanted someone to know the truth, and you seem so kind and gentle."

But the thoughts that were in Dónal's mind then were anything but kind and gentle, as his blood boiled at the injustice done to her, feeling in that moment that he would do anything to avenge her.

"Who did it to you?" he demanded, his voice urgent with fury. "Tell me the name of the man that raped you, and I'll kill him for you, and make the rest of them see their iniquity as well!"

"No, young piper. I'd not have blood on your own hands on my account, no matter the justice that's in it. Anyway, it's too late. He's been dead over three years now and his relations have mostly emigrated. And as for the rest of them, the damage is done. They all believe I'm a harlot, and no amount of argument will ever change their minds. Sure, they believe it because they want to, because it's easier than opening their minds and finding out the truth, because they're afraid of what it might tell them about themselves! Anyway, I don't care what anyone thinks anymore. All I care about right now is what you think. So tell me, young piper, what do you think? Do you think I'm a harlot?"

"No, of course not. I think you're the victim of a terrible injustice, and I admire you for your strength to turn the other cheek. I don't know if I could do it."

"Sure you could. You're a good man inside, and you'd do the right thing. I know you would."

And when she smiled at him then, his memory suddenly opened

and he saw her as she'd been on that afternoon long ago.

"Sióna," he said, the name coming from deep in his memory. "Your name is Sióna, and you live at Eskinanaun, in the cottage above the ivy that grows in the shape of a tree."

"So you do remember me, then!" she exclaimed, her smile growing broader. "I was hoping you would. I remember you standing there in the hollow, smiling at me like I was Gráinne and you my Diarmuid."

"You are, though my name isn't Diarmuid. It's Dónal, Dónal O'Sullivan Béara."

"And I am Sióna MacSweeney."

"Sióna MacSweeney," he repeated slowly, as if savoring it on his tongue. "It fits you. Indeed, it does, like wet on water or sweet on honey, like turf in the hearth or stars in the night sky. It fits you like the green fits Erin, and I can say no better than that!"

"Oh, I like that!" she exclaimed, clapping her hands, "Indeed, I do! You're a bard as well as a piper, I see."

"No, no bard am I. That's the province of my foster father, Seán Ahern the shanachie, the one who taught me the pipes. Indeed, they were his before he lost a hand."

"Well, he's a grand teacher then, for I've never heard the like of it before! And will you play something else for me, Dónal?"

"Sure, anything you like."

"I feel like dancing," she said, moving away from the wall and onto the grass, "so make it something happy that will loosen my feet and free my mind."

"I have just the thing for you," he said, and launched into a jig he'd learned just the week before.

At the sound of it, she let out a whoop and began to dance, at first in the classic mode with her back straight and arms stiff at her sides, her feet a pale blur on the green grass. But when Dónal slowed to a waltz, her dance changed as well, becoming lithe and sinewy as her arms came up and her feet slowed, her body curving into fluid arabesques as she whirled above the green. Then he shifted into a slide, and her movements became a blinding whirl, so broad a grin splitting her face in that moment that she looked like freedom incarnate. And Dónal smiled, too, both at her joy and that he'd brought it to her, that they'd shared this happy moment and that no one could ever take it away. Then he whooped and quickened the tempo, so that the tattered shawl in her hand floated behind like a silken veil, swirling and dancing in rhythmic accompaniment.

And when they came to the end, she flopped to the ground and lay staring at the sky, her breast heaving as she gasped for air. "That was grand and brilliant! You're a grand brilliant piper, Dónal O'Sullivan Béara!"

But he made no reply, just watched her lying in the grass, thinking how nice it would be to lie down beside her, to kiss her lips and hold her against him, to feel the heat of her and know that she felt it from him, that she wanted him as much as he wanted her. And as though feeling his eyes upon her, she turned and smiled, making his desire almost painful. Laying aside his pipes, he rose from the wall, intending to go to her and make his passion known. But even as he did, she sprang up from the grass, and he knew the opportunity was lost.

"It's getting late," she said, shading her eyes to look at the sun. "As much as I hate to say it, I have to go home now and tend to the animals. Will you walk me to the road, Dónal?"

"Sure, I'll walk you all the way to Eskinanaun, if you like. I've nothing to do today that can't wait till tomorrow."

"No, not this time, Dónal. But I'll meet you here again sometime, if you like."

"How about next Sunday after Mass?" he replied, jumping on the offer before she had a chance to change her mind. "I'll bring my pipes."

"Sure, that would be grand. Next Sunday it is then. Now let's be on our way before my sheep start worrying about me."

⚬∞∞⚬

Dónal stood at the door of Ahern's cottage, wishing in vain for the storm to lift so he could keep his date with Sióna. The good weather of the previous Sunday had been but a tease, the rain returning with a vengeance Tuesday night and with few breaks since. Indeed, it was so bad they'd not even gone to Mass that morning, and only rarely in his nine years with the Aherns had Órla let them skip it. "God put the weather in it," she would say, "and if there's rain on Sunday, then he means for us to be wet!" Yet a hail storm had come up that morning just as they were about to leave, and she'd relented at the last minute. "Since God put the hail in it today, I'll take it as a sign that he means for us to stay home!" she'd said, and settled in by the fire. Since then, Dónal had paced the cottage like a caged animal, going to the door every few minutes to check on the weather, hoping each time to see blue sky on the horizon. But it was no good. He couldn't even see the horizon. So he closed the door, sighing heavily as he did.

"That was a mournful sound if ever I've heard one," Órla said, raising an eyebrow. "What's gotten into you, Dónal? You're as nervous as a rebel in the loft when there's Redcoats in the parlor!"

But it was Tadhg who answered her. "I'll bet I know what it is, Mam. I'll bet he's got himself a girl that he's all hot after seeing."

And seeing a look of guilt mixed with anger on Dónal's face, he hooted and clapped his hands.

"That's it, that's it, isn't it, Dónal?" he demanded. "You've finally found yourself a girl that would put up with all your silence and brooding, and now the rain's keeping you from her! I'll bet that's what you were up to last Sunday, too, off to pick flowers and hold hands and whisper sweet nothings in her ear. Is that what you were after, when I was stuck here doing the work of two?"

"Shut up, you!" Dónal shouted, stung by Tadhg's words, surely, but more so that he'd guessed his secret. "That's not what happened! I went to play my pipes just like I told you!"

"Oh, I'm sure!" Tadhg taunted. "After all, a man has to have something to charm them with! But come on, Dónal, you can tell me. What's her name, now? Is it Máire Driscoll or Kate Shinnick, or maybe even one of those Tuohy sisters? Any of them would be perfect for you, since none have a thing by which to recommend themselves!"

"I'm warning you to shut your mouth, Tadhg Ahern!" Dónal shouted, taking a threatening step toward him. "Else I'll shut it for you!"

"You just feel free to try!" Tadhg retorted, standing up.

"Here, now, that's enough!" Ahern barked. "What's gotten into you two? You've not come at each other like that since you were children!"

"Why don't you ask him, Da?" Tadhg replied. "He's the one who can't face the truth."

Yet before Ahern could do so, Órla moved to Dónal and put her hands on his shoulders. "What's the matter with you, son? Is there anything I can help you with?"

But Dónal just shrugged his shoulders and looked at the floor. "No, there's nothing. I just need to get out of here for a while, that's all."

Lifting his face so that she could see his eyes, Órla held his gaze for a long moment. "Go on with you, then. But put on your coat, and Seán's hat, too! It won't keep you dry but at least it'll keep me from worrying."

"Thanks, Órla," he said, stooping to kiss her cheek.

She hugged him then, and whispered so the others wouldn't hear, "If you need to talk when you get back, I'm here to listen."

"Give her a kiss for me, too, while you're at it!" Tadhg shouted as Dónal closed the door.

◯∭◯

It was raining harder than ever when Dónal reached the path to Pointnadishert, and he could barely see two feet in front of him. He knew that Sióna wouldn't be there, of course, though he couldn't help feeling disappointed. But then it wasn't that much further to her cottage, and perhaps she wouldn't mind if he paid her a call. Yet again, what if she did, and told him never to come back? That would be worse than having to wait another week to see her. But a week was seven days and he didn't think he could wait even one. So on he went, muttering to himself, "Oh, what the hell. I can always turn around when I get there."

By the time he got to Eskinanaun, Dónal was so nervous that he found himself wishing her to be out. But no, there was light in the windows and the smell of turf on the sodden air, so she was there. Stopping under the eave to the door, he stared hard at it, wondering if he should screw up his courage and knock, or just slink away in the rain, leaving her none the wiser? Closing his eyes, he did his best to calm himself, to slow the mad galloping of his heart. Was it worth all this fear, he wondered? Was anything? He took a deep breath and slowly let it out.

"None but the brave!" he said, then opened his eyes and knocked.

At first there was no answer but the sound of a barking dog. So after a moment, he knocked again, more insistently this time. "Sióna!" he called, knocking yet again. "Sióna, are you there?"

But just as he was beginning to think she wasn't home after all, the door suddenly flew open and a fist came flying out, catching him on the left cheekbone just under his eye, and knocking him over backward onto the rain-soaked grass.

"How many times do I have to tell you rotten bastards?" he heard her shout through the fog in his brain. "*I'm not a harlot!*" Then the door slammed with such vehemence that an avalanche of water came tumbling from the roof.

Dónal staggered as he rose from the wet grass and shook his head to clear it. "Sióna! Sióna, it's me! Dónal O'Sullivan!" he called, not daring the door. But when it again flew open, he was ready for her. "Sióna, it's Dónal O'Sullivan!"

"Dónal, oh Jesus, Dónal, I didn't know it was you!" she exclaimed, rushing out and flinging her arms around him. "Have I killed you entirely, and will you ever forgive me?"

But he was so surprised by her embrace that he couldn't answer, just wrapped his arms around her and held on tight, delighting in her closeness, her smell, her touch, the beat of her heart. Could she feel his own, he wondered, beating as if it were about to jump out of his chest?

Closing his eyes, he kissed her on top of the head, and heard her sigh at the touch. But then she pushed back, and for a moment he was afraid he'd gone too far.

"Oh, but you're soaked to the bone," she said, taking him by the hand and leading him to the door. "Let's get you inside where it's warm and dry."

As she led him across the threshold, Dónal heard a low growl from the end of the house and saw a large shaggy dog crouched threateningly before the hearth.

"Be still, Con!" Sióna snapped at him. "Don't you know a friend when you see one?"

At that, the dog relaxed and wagged his tail in friendly fashion, coming to Dónal and giving him a good sniff.

"There's a good man!" Dónal said, scratching him behind the ears and then along the spine, the dog craning his neck and pumping his leg in appreciation. When finished, he pointed at the hearth, and said, "Go on with you, now, back to the fire!" and the dog obeyed as if they were old companions, curling up by the fire with his snout on his paws.

"Well, I like that, now!" Sióna said, hands on hips. "You just walk in and order my dog around like you own the place, and what's more, he does what you tell him! Why, the only person he's ever obeyed other than me is Riobárd Puxley, the man who gave him to me!

"How did you do that?" she demanded, turning to Dónal with a searching look. "Are you a wizard that you can enchant all before you, or is your charm reserved for just Con and me?"

"I don't think it's that so much," he replied, searching her eyes, too, "as that you're the only one who finds me enchanting."

"Oh," she sighed, and he knew he'd touched her. "Now that's really too much! Handsome and musical and poetic, and now modest into the bargain. How could any girl deny such a one as you?"

But he had no answer, having never thought of himself in such terms. Sióna didn't give him a chance to consider it either, as she reached up and gently touched his swollen eye.

"That doesn't look good. You're going to have a shiner, surely. But that's what you get for taking a lady at unawares, coming out of the storm like a dark spirit from the sea. Next time give me a warning, and I'll know to put on a better welcome. Why, I've neither tea in the kettle nor a bite to offer you. But I do have some old clothes of my Da's you can wear while yours are drying. They may not fit so well, but at least they're dry. Sit down by the fire while I fetch them for you."

Dónal watched her intently as she walked away, noting how her simple shift clung to her body like a second skin, suggesting her essential femininity hidden beneath the rain-soaked linen. His heart was still pounding from their embrace in the rain, and the sight of her so close to naked did nothing to calm it. When she glanced at him, he turned away quickly, embarrassed that she'd caught him.

"Go on with you now," she said, not seeming to notice. "I'll just be two shakes."

Dónal took a seat by the fire then and distracted himself with the dog.

"He likes you," he heard her say from just behind him, startled at her silent approach. "But then he's always been a smart one, so he has." Then she handed him a bundle of clothes, and said, "I'll turn my back while you change."

When she had, Dónal quickly stripped off his wet clothes and pulled on the trousers. They were cut for a shorter man than himself, the legs dangling several inches above his ankles, though they fit well enough in the waist. Then he pulled on the shirt and began to button it, glancing at her as he did, stopping when he found her watching. How long had she been, he wondered?

Her face was intent and she said nothing, just came to him and reached toward the buttons. But as she did so, he slid his hands gently into hers, caressing them softly, his eyes locked relentlessly onto hers. At his touch her lips parted slightly, and for a heart-wrenching moment he thought she was going to protest, to withdraw her hands and tell him to go. Yet she said nothing, and indeed began to move her hands in concert with his, caressing him in the same motion of being caressed, her eyes on his, her heart beating with his. In that moment nothing else existed beyond themselves, neither earth nor sky nor people, not even the dog by the fire or the cottage around them. Their minds were clear and focused on the moment, alive with anticipation of what the next would bring, knowing without knowing what it would be.

Then he lowered his head slowly and kissed her lightly on the lips, pulling back just enough to gauge her reaction, to give her a chance to tell him to stop. But her eyes were closed and her mouth open and inviting, and when he slid his arms around her, she moaned ever so slightly, the sound of it sending a thrill through his body and galvanizing his senses. Then his mouth was on hers and they were locked in a desperate embrace, their bodies surging together as though melting into one, their senses jolted with lightning bolts of desire, their movements frenzied and urgent. He closed his eyes, too, and gave himself over to the pleasure of it, the sheer, unbelievable pleasure.

But then her hands were on his chest and pushing him away, leaving him suddenly alone and frustrated, gaping at her in disbelief. *'What are you doing?'* he wanted to shout, confused and agitated. *'Why are you stopping me? Why would you want to?'* Yet before he could protest, she dropped her shift to the floor and stood naked before him, stunning him with the abruptness of it. And still he gaped at her, though now in wonder, never in his wildest dreams having imagined that a woman's body could be so beautiful, or so beautifully different from his own. He drank her in with his eyes, committing every part of her to memory as though he'd never see her so again. Then his eyes came up to hers and found them locked on his.

"You're so beautiful, Sióna," he whispered, "so incredibly beautiful!"

She came to him then, the feel of her nakedness against his chest setting his skin afire with pleasure, while the urgency in his loins became almost painful. Deftly she slipped the shirt from his shoulders and the trousers from his waist, leaving him as shamelessly naked as she. For only a moment he hesitated, before sweeping her lightly into his arms and carrying her to the low bed at the far end of the house.

"Don't hurt me, Dónal," she said as he laid her gently down.

"Never!" he promised.

"After what happened to me, I never thought I'd want to do that with a man again," she murmured, as he softly stroked her back. "But then you cast a spell on me with your eyes and your pipes and your poetry, and when you came all the way out here to see me in the worst weather this side of Hell, *well,* I knew I was done for! And done for I am, Dónal O'Sullivan Béara, hopelessly and eternally done for you."

"And I for you, Sióna MacSweeney," Dónal replied, rolling her over so he could look her in the eyes. "And I for you."

ᏫᎢᏚᎭᏉ

It was early evening and the rain having stopped, they'd come out to check on the sheep, holding hands and talking about this and that as they walked, like two people who'd spent a lifetime together rather than just a few hours. Indeed, he'd thought more than once of Órla's sage advice about finding a girl he could talk to, for Sióna was that girl if ever there was a one so born.

Yet even so, she'd done most of the talking, filling the brief interludes in their lovemaking with the details of her life. In that way he'd learned that she held her cottage from Riobárd Puxley and that he let her live rent-free in exchange for tending his sheep, which he rarely took an interest in other than when he wanted a lamb for his table. Yet he'd been the one who'd saved her from having to leave, and he'd given her the dog, saying it was to help her with the sheep, though she was sure he'd done it to give her company and protection. And through it all, he'd been the perfect gentleman, never once making any advances even though he'd surely heard the rumors. All of which surprised Dónal, having never seen that side of Puxley, though he also had to admit he'd never given him a chance to show it.

She'd named the dog for her father, telling him they were blow-ins from the County Limerick, where they'd lived by the Shannon. Her mother had named her for the goddess of the river, which had riled the local priest mightily, himself being of the opinion that children should be named for saints and not pagan idols. But her mother hadn't cared much for priests, and that was something they had in common, though the woman died when Sióna was only two. Her father had brought her to Eskinanaun when she was ten, coming himself for a job in the mines, though he'd had a tough go of it, as the locals resented him for taking away one of "their" jobs when so many were in need. He'd been killed in the Mountain Mine in what had been deemed an "accident," though she still believed he'd been murdered, and by the same man who'd raped her. But then, she'd never know the truth of it, now would she? She'd also revealed his name, though Dónal had guessed it already.

So he had a lot to think about as they crossed the shoulder of Eagle Hill, though with Con whirling around them like a dervish and occasionally nipping at their heels, it was hard to keep his train of thought.

"It's funny how they run around in circles like that," he said, thinking out loud.

"Sure, that one even runs circles round the house when I let him out for his morning constitutional. He can't help himself, the herding instinct is that strong in him."

"I know just how he feels. I've often felt that my life is running circles around me and I can't stop it from happening."

"What do you mean?"

"Ah, well, it's a long one in the telling and I'm sure to bore you with it."

But Sióna just slipped her arms around his waist and laid her head on his shoulder. "How could you bore me when I've got nothing in the world to do but listen to you?" she murmured, and when he sighed, she knew that he'd heard, and understood.

Even so he didn't say anything for a long time, just gazed pensively over the broad estuary of the Kenmare River toward the Iveragh Peninsula, the very place where the Gael first set foot upon Erin and Amhergin spoke his immortal verse: *I am the wind that breathes on the sea . . .* O'Sullivans lived there, too, though he knew nothing of them, having never ventured forth to meet them. 'The world is so big,' he thought, 'and I'm so small. How will I ever change it?'

"Don't you ever get lonely, living out here all by yourself?" he asked finally, giving voice to his sudden melancholy.

"Oh, I don't know," she sighed. "I don't know whether I'm never lonely, or just lonely all the time and can't tell the difference."

He just nodded at that, knowing only too well what she meant.

"When I introduced myself as Dónal O'Sullivan Béara," he began slowly, "I was giving you my title as well as my name. You see, I'm the direct lineal descendant of the old chieftains, and the rightful heir to their lordship."

Then the whole story came tumbling out, from the history of the O'Sullivans and Dunboy to the Clan Dónal Cam and his own family. He spoke of himself and of his place in it, and what he thought it meant for his future, even telling her of James Stephens and the things he'd done to prepare himself for the struggle he knew to be coming. Indeed, he told her everything he could think of to tell her, speaking so long that the sun was sinking by the time he finished. Then at the very end, he told her everything that he could remember of Eóghan, of what he'd meant to him and how he still missed him, even to that very day, that very minute.

When he was finally done, he took a deep breath and sighed as he let it out. "Well, that's my story. What do you think of it?"

"I think it's the saddest thing I've ever heard," she replied, and he realized she was crying, "and I hurt for you that you've suffered so much, but more that you choose to have so much more to suffer."

He was silent again for a long time, trying to come up with an answer that would take the sting from her words. "It's who I am, Sióna," he said finally, almost defensively, "and if I was a different man, we wouldn't be together now."

"No, indeed we wouldn't. But so it is that I hurt for myself, too, because now I know you're going to leave me someday, and having known the fullness of you even for a few hours, how can my life be anything but empty without you?"

At that Dónal pushed her gently away so he could look her in the eyes. "No matter where my destiny leads me, Sióna, I'll always come back to you. I *promise* you that, and you must believe me!"

"I see that you believe it, Dónal," she said, searching his eyes and finding no lie in them. "You're a good man and I know you mean well, and perhaps you will indeed do as you say. But don't expect me to marry you until you're done with everything else, because I'd not have you coming back to me just because you felt you had to! Nor will I go with you, either, for though I may give myself to you, body and soul, I'll always be my own person, too. Do you understand, Dónal?"

"Yes, Sióna, I do," he said slowly, stunned at her mention of marriage, though he knew it to reflect his feelings for her. "But don't send me away, either, for I'd not go back to the emptiness I had before."

"Nor would I, Dónal. So we'll be together for as long you wish, and though I'll wait for you when you leave, I place no bond on you to return.

"But enough of that for now," she said, smiling suddenly and taking him by the hand. "It's cold out here, and the bed is so nice and warm! Take me to it, my scarlet piper, and cast your spell upon me!"

And for his answer to that, she didn't have to wait.

The morning sky was clear and the new day full of promise as Dónal and Sióna watched it dawn. Feeling that the world was smiling upon him, he couldn't help but smile back. It was all so beautiful, so new and exciting, as if his eyes were seeing it for the very first time. And though he knew he'd come to another turning in the road of life, and that nothing would be as it had been before, for the first time he felt complete and happy, light in body and spirit, and full of hope. For he'd eaten from the tree of knowledge, and found it good.

Then he sighed and closed his eyes, knowing that even the most perfect of moments must end.

"I have to go now," he said reluctantly. "They'll be wondering what's become of me, and besides, I have work to do."

"Will I see you again soon?" she asked, snuggling her face into his chest.

"Is tonight soon enough for you?"

"Well, it's not ideal, mind you, but I suppose it'll have to do." Then she frowned. "What are you going to tell them when they ask where you've been?"

"The truth. If I told them anything else, I'd just have to keep on lying and sooner or later they'd figure it out, anyway. So why not just get it over with?"

"They'll hate me for it, you know. It'll just confirm the rumors, and they'll try to keep you from seeing me again."

But he just smiled, shaking his head gently. "They may not understand at first, I'll grant you. But they're not given to prejudice, and once I've explained things, they'll see the sense in it. They're kind and loving people who want what's best for me, and once they've met you and seen us together, they'll know that what's best for me is you, Sióna."

"Sure, they might, but what of everyone else? What are you going to do when your friends turn their backs on you because you've taken up with the village Jezebel?"

"You're not the village Jezebel, Sióna, and my friends will see the truth of it, else they're not my friends. And I don't care what anyone else thinks, only what we think. Anyway, everyone knows me and my reputation as a fighting man, and I assure you no one will dare say a thing to my face."

"But they won't have to, Dónal, not when whispers behind your back will do just as well. They'll make an outcast of you, and I can tell you it's not a very pleasant way to live. Are you really prepared to suffer that for me?"

"I'll suffer anything for you, Sióna, anything at all. Besides, my father was an outcast, and if he could bear it, then so can I."

"But, Dónal, do you really want to be like your father?"

For that, he had no answer.

As Dónal approached Ahern's cottage, he saw Tadhg standing in the doorway and waved to him. But he didn't wave back, just leaned inside for a moment and then came down to meet him.

"Just where have you been?" Tadhg demanded. "Mam's been worried sick, and making Da and me sick with all her nagging. And where did you pick up that shiner? Have you been brawling with the sailors in town?"

"No, Tadhg, I haven't. And as for the rest, it'll be easier if I just tell you all together."

As they walked up the path, Dónal saw Ahern waiting in the doorway with a scowl on his face. "So our prodigal son returns at last. And have you a tale to tell of your wanderings, O brave Odysseus?"

But Dónal didn't reply, just brushed past him into the cottage, where he knew the real inquisition awaited. Indeed, he felt Órla's eyes upon him as soon as he entered, looking him over and apparently not liking what they saw, as they became suddenly hard and angry.

"Seán! Tadhg! Out with you!" she snapped at her men huddling in the doorway.

"What? What did–" Ahern began.

"I said *out*, and close the door behind you!"

"Órla, what the devil–"

"Seán, don't make me say it again!" The look in her eyes left him no doubt that discretion would be the better part of valor.

"All right, I'm going." He herded Tadhg out before him.

"All right, Dónal," Órla said, not waiting for the door to close. "Who is she?"

"Sióna MacSweeney," he replied, his look braver than he felt.

For a long moment, she didn't react at all, and he wondered if she'd even heard him. But then she called to her husband, screaming his name a second time when he didn't answer immediately.

"Seán, get in here!" she commanded when he opened the door. "And close the door behind you!"

"For the love of God, woman," Ahern whined, "would you make up your mind?"

But Órla ignored him, her eyes fixed coldly upon Dónal. "Tell him where you've been, and with whom, and what you've been up to!"

"I've been with Sióna MacSweeney," Dónal said, still holding Órla's gaze.

"Well, now that sets our minds at ease, doesn't it, Órla? Here, we thought you might be in some sort of trouble, when all you were doing was fornicating with a harlot. I feel so silly for fretting!"

"She's not a harlot!" Dónal countered, turning to look the man in the eye.

"Oh, indeed! And just how do you figure that, when what you've been doing is the very proof of it? Or would you have us believe that it was all in innocence, that you were so wrapped up in conversation that you forgot to come home? If that's what you'd have us believe, then go polish your halo! It seems a bit tarnished!"

"No, Seán, I'd not have you believe that. I'd not have you believe anything but the truth."

"You know, Dónal, it wouldn't hurt to at least *feign* a little remorse for yourself. You've committed a cardinal sin here, young man, and it's not a thing to be taken lightly!"

"And I don't take it lightly, Seán, I can assure you. But sin or no sin, I stand by Sióna MacSweeney, and I tell you that she is not a harlot!"

"That's not quite the opinion that's current in the village, or would you have us also believe that you're right while everyone else is wrong?"

"Since when do you care what the village believes? Or do you now wish to take back all the things you've taught me, and have me just follow the herd and not think for myself? Well, even if you do, I'm not going to do it, because I know the truth about Sióna MacSweeney, and she is not what rumor makes of her!"

"Well for the love of God, Dónal," Ahern shouted in exasperation, "would you please explain how you know this when no one else does?"

"I know because I listened to her with an open mind, and didn't judge her merely on vicious gossip like the rest of you narrow-minded busybodies!"

Ahern's one eye narrowed dangerously then, and his face went crimson, for if there was one thing he prided himself upon, it was his liberality.

"You'd better have a good reason for speaking to me so, else I'm apt to forget my fondness of you and give you the mother and father of a good beating!"

"I listened to her, Seán, and I saw the truth in her eyes. And the truth is that Paddy O'Sullivan *raped* her!"

Ahern's expression softened then, and he gazed at Dónal appraisingly. "All right, you've got my attention now. Give me the rest of it."

"He raped her, Seán," Dónal said, then calmly told the rest of the story.

"But the worst of it," he concluded, "is that she's lived alone and scorned now for five years, just because no one bothered to listen to her side of the story. So that's the terrible truth of Sióna MacSweeney, and when you meet her you'll see for yourself."

"All right, then," Ahern said, obviously moved. "I can see that you're convinced, and if it is true, then this poor girl has been horribly mistreated and my heart goes out to her. But though I trust your insight, I will reserve my own judgment until I have indeed met her and seen for myself. Now be assured, Dónal, that my concern is only for you, and that I really don't care what anyone else thinks. But son, if I find the truth to be other than you have, will you listen to me when I tell you so?"

"Sure, Seán, I'll listen to you. Haven't I always?"

"When it suited you. But all right, then. We'll visit with her this Sunday after Mass."

"All right. We'll be expecting you. If that's settled, then Tadhg and I have work to do."

But Órla stopped him. "Just a minute, young man, I'm not finished with you yet. You still have a sin to answer for. Or have you conveniently forgotten your Commandments?"

"No, Órla, I haven't forgotten them. But my conscience is clear, no matter what Father Nolan may say to the contrary. I love Sióna, and I'll marry her as soon as she'll let me!"

"As soon as she'll let you? What do you mean by that?"

"She'll not share me with my destiny."

"And wise she is for it, too! But Dónal, you don't intend to live with her in sin, do you? Why, to do so will make her the very thing you've so eloquently argued she isn't! At least in the eyes of the people it will, and they'll make your lives hell for it!"

"There you go again with what other people think! I don't care what other people think! My life is mine to live as I see fit, and to Hell with anyone who doesn't like it!"

"Brave words they are, Dónal, but those of a child. A real man doesn't throw caution to the wind just to indulge his impulses. I'd give a thought to the consequences if I was you, not only for yourself but for Sióna."

But Dónal just shook his head. "Órla, I love you as my mother, and I respect you above all others. But my life is not yours to live, no matter your good intentions or concern for my welfare. It's *mine*, the only thing I really have in this world at the tail of the day. So as you love me, let me live as I see fit!"

Órla's eyes softened as he spoke, and she sighed when he'd finished. "Our boy is telling us that he's a man now, Seán, and that it's time for us to mind our own business and let him go his own way. All right, Dónal. I've done my best to prepare you for it, and I'll just have to trust that I've done a good job. So you have my blessing to go your own way, and though I may not always agree with you, you will always have my love, unconditional and absolute.

"But, Dónal, don't scorn the wisdom that has come to your elders through living the hard life. And don't turn your back on those who would help you, for accepting it doesn't mean you can't take care of yourself, it means you are taking care of yourself. And one last thing, Dónal. If Sióna MacSweeney has truly suffered all that you say, be very, *very* careful that you don't add to it! Do you understand me?"

Though he didn't answer, she could see by the look in his eyes that he'd heard, and understood. "All right, then. Go on with yourself. I'm done with you now."

But Ahern wasn't finished yet and stepped between Dónal and the door.

"You've never been one to make things easy on yourself, have you? But you're right when you say your life is all you really have in this world, and I would remind you that you only get one chance at it. *So don't fuck it up!*"

chapter 13

Eskinanaun
Béara Peninsula

DÓNAL AWOKE WITH A START, his senses alert and focused on the sound of Con's urgent growling. He knew it to be a warning and his heart pounded as he waited, though he dared not move until he knew more. Then came a soft rapping and a man's voice at the door.

"Are you there, girlie?" he called furtively. Dónal tensed at the sound of him fumbling at the latch, though his next words turned his fear to anger. "I have money and whiskey for you! Are you there?"

"Sióna," Dónal whispered, shaking her lightly. "Sióna, wake up."

"No, Dónal, not now, I'm too tired," she groaned. "Wait till the morning, my love."

"Sióna, listen to me! There's a man at the door!"

"Oh, bloody hell," she hissed, bolting upright. "How many times do I have to tell them?"

"No," he whispered, pulling her back. "I'll take care of it. You stay here." She started to protest, but he put his finger to her lips. "Don't worry. I'll take care of it!"

He got up then, pulled on his trousers and padded to the door. When the man knocked again, he whisked it open and flung him bodily across the room. Springing to exploit his advantage, he saw there was no need, as Con had him pinned with a warning growl and his paws upon his chest.

"Jesus, call him off before he kills me!" the man begged.

"He won't kill you unless I tell him to," Dónal said. "So just be still with yourself and don't give me a reason."

"Yes, sir, whatever you say, sir," the man replied. "Nice dog, there's a good fellow."

Being sure to take his time about it, Dónal lit a candle from the hearth and then stood over the man.

"Dónal O'Sullivan!" the man exclaimed. "What are you doing here? You're a bit young yet for the likes of her, aren't you?"

"Well, now, Tom Donovan," Dónal replied. "It seems that it's me that should be asking the questions, since you've come to my home uninvited in the middle of the night."

"Your home? Do you mean to say that you live here? With *her*? Don't you know what she is?"

"No, Tom, as a matter of fact, I don't," Dónal said through clenched teeth. "So why don't you enlighten me?"

But catching his anger and knowing his reputation, Donovan wisely dissembled. "I . . . I think I'd best be going now, Mr. O'Sullivan. I'm sorry for intruding."

"Yes, Tom, I think you're right," Dónal agreed, as he pushed Con aside and jerked Donovan to his feet. "After all, we'd not want herself and the young ones to worry, would we? Be sure and give them our regards." Then he pushed Donovan through the door and slammed it behind him.

"You know he's going to tell his friends, don't you?" Sióna asked as he got back in bed. "By tomorrow evening the whole village will know."

"It was going to happen sooner or later, so why not get it over with? Anyway, let the fools think what they will! It won't change anything."

"It's not that simple, Dónal, and you know it! There'll be trouble in it, and you can't know how you're going to feel till it happens! So don't make promises you may not be able to keep!"

Dónal was silent for a moment, and when he spoke his voice was cold and hard. "I've already told you, Sióna, there's not a man in West Béara who'll dare face me, and I don't care what they say behind my back!"

She let it go then, knowing she would get nowhere with him in that mood. Anyway, she believed him now, at least the part about no one daring to face him, having seen Donovan cower before him. It was a side of Dónal she'd not seen before, an inner darkness that she found difficult to reconcile with his otherwise kind and sensitive nature. And though she was sure he'd never direct it at her, still it frightened her to think what he might be capable of if the darkness ever got the better of him.

Turning to face him then and seeing his eyes flash green in the candlelight, she was suddenly afraid he'd read her thoughts. But then he touched her face, and she felt it in the depths of her soul, and when he spoke, her fears vanished in the music of his words.

"I love you, Sióna, and nothing will ever change it!"

⟨⟨⟨⟩⟩⟩

Dónal stood by the steps of St. Michael's, glaring across the meadows toward the sea. There had indeed been trouble, just as Sióna had predicted, and it started the very morning after Donovan's visit to Eskinanaun, when a group of men passed Dónal on the road without returning his greeting, though he'd heard them snicker behind his back. And there was more, too, at the Mountain Mine and later at the pier, where Tadhg almost got into a fight over him.

"Don't you care what they're saying about you," Tadhg demanded on the way home, "that you're living in sin with a harlot and committing adultery and fornication and God only knows what other mortal sins?"

"She's not a harlot," Dónal replied, almost wearily.

"Sure, I told them as much! But they're having none of it from me! Anyway, there's not much I can say about the mortal sins, that part of it being true enough! Now before you tell me you don't care, let me just remind you that you're not alone in this. They're already getting after me about it, not that I care, mind you. But sooner or later it'll get back to Mam and Da, and I do care about them! So you've got to put a stop to it, Dónal, now, before it gets out of hand!"

"And just what would you have me do? I love Sióna, and I'll not turn my back on her, not for anyone!"

"Ah, Jesus, Dónal, why did you have to pick her when you could have any girl you want? They all think you're just the cutest little thing, you know."

"Because she's like me."

"If that's true, then God help her!" Tadhg sighed. "Sure, God help us all!"

By the end of the week, no one would speak to Dónal aside from the Aherns and his handful of friends, and he knew they were under siege for standing by him. And though he tried to tell himself that it didn't hurt and he didn't care, in his heart he knew Sióna was right, that it was easy to say when it wasn't actually staring him in the face. Still, it was the idea of it that angered him, that a compact of closed minds had excommunicated him without a hearing, just as they'd done her. So he decided to test the courage of their convictions, standing by the church door and glaring silently at all who passed, daring them to say it to his face. But he may as well have been invisible for all the notice they gave. Only one even glanced his way, Padge O'Sullivan, curiously enough, though he said nothing and quickly averted his gaze.

Now the church was full and the bells finished ringing, though Father Nolan was late as usual, which was just what Dónal was counting on. He took a deep breath and let it out slowly, forcing his anger to a manageable level, lest rage render him impotent. Then he strode through the doors and down the aisle, the low rumble of voices dying around him so that by the time he reached the front, the congregation was as still and silent as a corpse, and just as cold.

Looking into their eyes, Dónal found a mixture of contempt and curiosity, and he smiled inwardly, for the first time getting the joke and knowing it was on him. How innocent he'd been to think that people brought only goodness into the House of the Lord, how naïve to assume he could sit among them without fear. For they'd not abjured sinfulness, that incurable affliction known as human nature, but merely shed it like a serpent's skin at the door, their piety but a clever hypocrisy. And sure, though the room might be full of Catholics, he knew in that moment there wasn't a Christian among them.

"You all know me here," he began, his voice soft but resonant. "You all know what kind of man I am, one who speaks the truth. And on this Sabbath morning, I've come to tell you the truth about Sióna MacSweeney."

He paused to let his words sink in and glanced about the room, making eye contact with as many people as possible. "The truth of Sióna MacSweeney is that she's not the harlot you believe her to be, indeed, that you make her to be with your slander and gossip. The truth is that a man raped her when she was a young girl, and when his wife discovered his infidelity, he lied to her and said that she'd seduced him and made him pay for the service. And the woman chose to believe him, because the lie was easier to accept than the truth, that he betrayed her and assaulted a young girl. But she was a spiteful woman, too, and would have vengeance for her hurt, no matter the innocence of her victim. So she and her friends attacked Sióna MacSweeney and beat her cruelly and mercilessly, and then cut off her hair to mark her as a harlot, the better to convince themselves and the world of the truth of it. And this they did because it was easier to believe a lie than to face a painful truth."

Dónal paused and looked around the room again and, finding fewer of them looking back now, knew he'd touched a few guilty consciences. "But that's not the end of the story, for the man left Sióna with child, and when the baby came there was no one to help her bring it into the world because her neighbors had turned their backs on her, and so it died because people who should've shown her sympathy and charity lacked the moral courage to face the truth!"

Then Dónal gave vent to his rage and his voice thundered through the rafters like fire and brimstone, filling the room with righteous indignation. "*You did that!*" he roared, stabbing his finger at them in accusation. "You who sit here in God's House and call yourselves Christians, *you did that, you and you and you!*"

He paused again and glared around the room, before continuing in a calmer voice. "But Christ told us not to judge lest we ourselves be judged. All right, then. I'll not judge you in the manner in which you judged Sióna MacSweeney, without a hearing or trial. I'll give you a chance now to prove me wrong, to prove that she really is the harlot you would have her be. All it will take is for the men among you who've actually had carnal relations with her to step forward and give their testimony. Or if the men lack the courage to confess their sins, then let their women come forward and tell of their infidelity."

Pausing again, he saw that not even his friends were looking at him now, such was the blanket of guilt he'd spread over the room. "Come, now," he coaxed, spreading his arms in invitation. "This is your chance to redeem yourselves and prove me wrong, to condemn Sióna MacSweeney with fact rather than with gossip and rumor, to pull the lever and let her swing at the end of her rope of sin!"

But no one came forward, no one spoke. Indeed, he wasn't even sure they were breathing. "What's the matter? Are you all cowards? Or can it really be that no one can honestly give such testimony? If that's the case, then the confessional is going to be awfully busy this week!"

He shook his head as he looked around at them. "A young girl's innocence is stolen from her, yet she's treated as if it's somehow her fault. Am I the only one who fails to see the logic in it?"

Just then, Father Nolan entered from the presbytery. "What's going on here?" he demanded, seeing all the downcast eyes and thinking Dónal was leading them in prayer.

"Nothing, Father," Dónal replied. "I was just leaving."

But as he walked toward the door, Padge O'Sullivan stood up and barred his way, and for a moment Dónal's heart raced with apprehension. Would he come at him for maligning his father, even though he'd not mentioned him by name? Or worse yet, did he intend to speak against Sióna?

But then Padge smiled, and Dónal's anxiety melted in its warmth. "Good man, Dónal," he said, then moved aside.

Dónal and Sióna sat on a stone above the hollow, watching the Aherns approach in a wagon. But for them, the old boreen was empty, since no one else lived out this way anymore. It was different before the Great Hunger, of course, for though the land was stony and from a distance looked to be covered in a blanket of rock, there was much green among the nooks and hollows, enough at least to graze a few sheep and sow a few lumpers. But now the cottages were empty and silent, just the bleaching bones of what had once been houses, the ghosts of what had once been homes, with only the wind and the lonely bleating of sheep to disturb their sleep. Yet the isolation suited the two lovers, for it freed them to live their lives as they pleased, far removed from the narrow opinions and disapproving glances of their fellows, and in that freedom they also found peace. Though all the rest of the world might be at war, there was peace at Eskinanaun.

The day was turning cooler as it aged and clouds were rolling in from the sea. Sióna shivered at a sudden gust of wind and Dónal wrapped her in his arms.

"You feel good," she said, snuggling in close, "inside and out."

"You, too," he replied, and kissed her forehead.

"You should have your pipes here. You could sit up here and serenade the sunset, and it would echo through the hollow and sound like a thousand pipers all playing at once."

"Yes, you're right. I'll fetch them tomorrow."

After that they were silent, their embrace saying all that needed to be said.

When finally the Aherns started up the last steep slope toward them, they rose and climbed down to meet them. Sióna stood close by Dónal, and he put his arm around her in reassurance, knowing the apprehension she felt. Indeed, he wasn't sure how it would go himself. For while the Aherns had been in the balcony that morning, he'd come straight home afterward and had no idea of their reaction. But as they neared and he saw them all smiling, his fears melted away.

"Welcome to Eskinanaun!" he shouted as Tadhg brought the team to a halt.

But Tadhg just ignored him as he jumped to the ground and went straight for Sióna, sweeping her up in his massive arms and spinning her around in circles, before setting her down and planting a kiss on her cheek. Though she yelped in surprise when he picked her up, she was laughing with delight by the time he was done.

"I'm Tadhg Ahern," he trumpeted, giving her his most winning smile, "and everything Dónal has said about me is true, only more so!"

"Yes, he said you were bigger than life," she said, "and now I see what he means!"

"I am that, sure, and more so," Tadhg said, puffing out his chest.

"Leave it to you to break the ice," Dónal said, jealous in spite of himself that he'd done it so easily.

"She's lovely, Dónal," Tadhg exclaimed, slapping him on the back, "though a bit thin in the skin for my taste. But a couple of good meals in her and she'll be worth the trouble, I'd say!"

"And what possible trouble could a beautiful woman be to a man in love?" Ahern said. "You may as well say the sun troubles him by warming his face, or the rain by nourishing his crops."

He took Sióna by the hand and kissed her cheek.

"I'm Seán Ahern, and it's my pleasure to meet you."

"Dónal told me you were the shanachie," Sióna replied, returning his smile, "but he didn't tell me of your silver tongue! Now I know he comes by it honestly."

"If only it was true. But all his talents are his own, I'm afraid. The best I can say is that I've helped him along with them. Ah, but here's someone else come to meet you."

The smile faded from Sióna's face then as she turned to Órla. "So you've come to judge me, too, have you?"

"No, dear, I haven't come to judge," Órla replied, "only to meet the woman my son is in love with. Any doubts I might've had about you he laid to rest this morning at Mass. Or did he not tell you of his sermon? It was one the good people of Allihies won't soon forget."

"What did you say, Dónal?" Sióna demanded, turning on him suspiciously.

"Come walk with me and I'll tell you all about it," Órla said, though Sióna just stared at her suspiciously. "Come, dear. You're going to have to learn to trust me if we're to be friends."

Looking into her eyes then, Sióna found empathy and tenderness, and as they grasped hands, an understanding was born between them, a bridge of compassion over her chasm of doubt.

As they walked away, Ahern put his arm around Dónal. "It was a fine thing you did this morning, and we're all proud of you for it. It takes a rare courage to face a room full of closed minds and point out their hypocrisy. But people don't like facing themselves, you know, so don't be surprised if nothing comes of it. Just know that we're with you, come what may."

"And the boys, too, Dónal," Tadhg added. "They were all fighting mad by the time you finished, so I sent them round to the public houses after Mass just to keep an ear on the chat and make sure it went your way. And mark my words, there'll be some broken heads if it didn't. But could you believe Padge, now? Of all of them, he'd have been the last I'd expect to back you up!"

"Yes, I was surprised, too!" Dónal agreed. "There I was all ready for him to come at me, and what does he do but pat me on the back. Maybe it's time I got to know him better. I should call round and thank him at least."

"I wouldn't bother if I was you. He keeps to himself pretty much now that his old ones are gone and his brothers all in Australia."

"I know, and I feel a certain responsibility for it, too. He was never the same after that fight on the mountainside."

"Now, don't go beating yourself up over that! He only got what was coming to him, and besides, you did worse to many that came after!"

"That's true, but I hurt him inside, and then his Da never let him live it down!"

"Ah, well, you'll do as you please, as always, and I'll not waste my time trying to talk sense to you. So come to the wagon now and see what we've brought you."

Peering into the cargo bed, Dónal found his pipes in their case and the bag of O'Sullivan heirlooms, as well as something else that quite surprised him.

"Your mirror, Seán?" he exclaimed. "I can't take that!"

"Oh, yes, you can," Ahern assured him, laying his hand on his shoulder. "I know how lucky I am and I don't need it to remind me anymore. So I give it to you, and if ever you're feeling the weight of the world on your shoulders, just look yourself in the eyes and say, 'It could be worse.'"

"Sage advice, I'm sure, but I'd have to be pretty low indeed for it to make me feel better!"

"You'd be surprised how handy it can be!"

They took the things inside then and settled themselves by the fire, talking of this and that till the women returned. As they came in, Dónal rose to greet them and Sióna went straight into his arms.

"She told me what you did," she said, her voice breaking and tears in her eyes. "I love you, too."

Dónal didn't reply, just kissed her softly on the lips, bringing a groan of mock disgust from Tadhg. "Ah, Jesus! Can't you two wait till we're gone?"

But Dónal just grinned at Sióna. "Don't mind him. He's just jealous!" Then remembering Ahern's gift, he pulled her to the mirror. "Look what they've brought us!"

But Sióna's smile quickly faded when she saw herself.

"What's the matter?" Dónal asked, seeing her distress.

"I . . . I didn't know I looked like that. I'm wild and ragged like something from the bog, my hair is so . . . *short*! I'm sorry, Dónal, but I want to be beautiful for you, just as you are for me!"

Hearing the sadness in her voice, and recalling the trauma of his first look in the mirror, Dónal felt a twinge of guilt for letting her look.

"I think you're the most beautiful woman in the world, Sióna MacSweeney, just as you are," he said, gently raising her eyes to his. "I can buy you new dresses, if they'll make you feel better, and your hair will grow if you let it. But those things are just the surface; it's the beauty within you that I cherish, for it's constant and abiding."

"Oh, my love," Sióna sighed. "How do you always know just the right thing to say?"

"Oh, Christ," Tadhg groaned, "if it isn't getting deep in here!"

"Whisht with yourself, you little piglet!" his mother scolded.

"It seems our guests are getting restless," Dónal said. "Should we boil them a meal to quiet their grumbling?"

"That sounds like a grand idea!" Ahern exclaimed.

"Sure, let's eat!" Tadhg seconded.

"If that isn't just like a man!" Órla chided. "Love is in the air and yet all you can think of is your stomach!"

"Love doesn't fill the belly, woman!" Ahern said.

"No, but it does fill the soul," Órla shot back, "and what good is a full belly on an empty soul?"

When they'd finished eating, Dónal took out his pipes and settled in by the fire. "What should I play?" he asked.

"Something lively, please." Sióna said. "I feel like dancing!"

"Me, too!" Tadhg agreed, leaping to his feet and sweeping Sióna up with him.

Dónal obliged them with a lively set of jigs that went on for so long, they were both out of breath and sweating when he finally stopped. Ahern kept the rhythm by slapping his leg and stomping his feet, while Órla clapped her hands and even Con got into the act, barking and nipping playfully at their heels.

And as he played, Dónal thought of all the times he'd watched Tadhg dance with the girls while he'd hidden behind his pipes, desperate to join the fun but too painfully shy to do so. But this time it was different, for now Tadhg was dancing with *his* girl, and no matter how handsome and charming he might be or how good a dancer, she'd still be his girl when it was over. The thought of it brought a smile to his face and he quickened the tempo, just so his friend would have to work harder to amuse her.

When he finally stopped, they all applauded, and Ahern slapped him on the back, saying, "Good man, Dónal! That was grand!"

"Yes, it was indeed!" a man's voice seconded from the doorway, and they all looked up in surprise, having missed his arrival amid the joyous noise.

"Riobárd!" Ahern exclaimed happily, and rose to greet him. "What brings you all the way out here?"

"God bless all here," Puxley said as he crossed the threshold. "When you told me our Dónal had taken up residence with my shepherd, I thought I'd better come out to check on them. And how are you keeping, Sióna?"

"Grand so, Riobárd," she replied rising to greet him, "and the flock, as well. Come have a seat by the fire. I'll put on some tea and collect a few potatoes from the garden."

"Thank you, Sióna, that sounds grand," Puxley replied. "But first, I think you and Dónal might want to come outside. I've brought you something."

They followed him then, and when Dónal saw Puxley's wagon filled with the furnishings from Cahernageeha, his jaw dropped in surprise. They were all there, the hutch, the table and chairs, the chest, the three-legged stool, even incidentals like the milk can and churn, the cauldron and willow baskets. But best of all, was the great bed of Kerry oak.

"Did you save all this for me?" Dónal asked, addressing Puxley in Irish, his expression a mix of wonder and suspicion.

"I did," Puxley replied. "It seemed the least I could do to make up for the way my relations treated you. It's all a bit dusty from my barn, I'm afraid, but in good condition otherwise. I didn't save the old mattress, of course, so I brought one of my own. Consider it a house-warming gift."

Puxley paused then, obviously expecting to be thanked. But Dónal had no intention of it. It was only his own being returned, after all, and that but a token of all that had been stolen. The old memories died hard, as Puxley himself had said, and no end of good deeds on his part would change it.

"We'd better get it inside before the rain comes," Dónal said, ignoring the reproving glances of the others. Without waiting for a reply, he hefted two chairs and carried them inside.

When it was done, Sióna sent Seán and Tadhg to fetch fresh water while she went for potatoes and Dónal for turf. As he approached the door on his way back, Dónal heard Puxley speaking softly from inside and stopped to listen.

"I see you've given them my mirror," he said, and the words struck Dónal like a stone. Peering furtively inside, he saw Puxley lay his hand on Órla's shoulder and gently turn her to face him.

"Don't!" she said. "They might see us!"

"After all these years, Órla, I still dream about you and our one afternoon together," Puxley said, ignoring her entreaty. "Does it truly mean nothing to you?"

Dónal felt himself go cold then, as Ahern's voice spoke from his memory: *She wouldn't tell me where she got it, or what she had to pay for it.* Now he knew the answer to both.

"Truly, it doesn't," she said coldly. "And why would you care, anyway, you who've had more women than you can even remember?"

Puxley sighed and dropped his hand from her shoulder. "You're right, Órla, I don't remember the others, and since you there haven't been any. You ruined me for other women."

She opened her mouth to reply, but hearing Seán and Tadhg return with the water, Dónal hailed them loudly, so as to warn of their approach. Despite his fury, he knew he'd have to keep this secret forever, lest it destroy three people he loved.

Puxley came outside then and spoke to Dónal. "I'll be taking my leave of you now. I want to get home at a decent hour, and it'll be slow going in the wagon. Do you mind helping me turn it around?"

"Musha, yeer honor, 'tis yeers to command, I am," Dónal said in English, bobbing and tugging at his forelock.

"And what is that supposed to mean?" Puxley asked, obviously taken aback.

"Ah, 'tis nothin', yeer honor, nothin' but the truth of it so," Dónal replied, and turned his back.

Though Puxley wanted to say more, Sióna and the Aherns returned then, and he decided to let it be.

"I thought you were staying for tea," Sióna said, seeing Dónal busy with the horses.

"I'm sorry, but I really must go," Puxley replied. "I'm sailing for Wales in the morning, and I want to get to bed at a decent hour. But I'll see you when I get back. Good luck to you, and see that you take care of each other."

"Thank you for everything, Riobárd," Sióna said. "You've been very kind to me and I want you to know that I appreciate it." Then she stood up on her tiptoes and bussed him quickly on the cheek before retreating to the cottage.

"She's a rare one, Dónal," Puxley said, smiling after her, "and you're lucky she picked you."

But Dónal was having none of it. "If you're ready, Mr. Puxley," he said in English, "I think I'll see you on your way for a bit, at least to the bottom of the hill."

"As you wish, Dónal. And thank you."

Taking his leave of Ahern and Tadhg, Puxley followed Dónal onto the wagon. At the bottom of the hill, he stopped the wagon and turned to Dónal.

"I can tell you have something to say," he said in English. "So. What is it?"

"I know what you did!" Dónal said, glaring at him. "I heard you talking to Órla, and I know what you did!"

Puxley held his gaze only for moment, before sighing and looking toward the bay. "When she came to me for the mirror, I didn't know she was married, and she didn't tell me why she wanted it, only that she'd do anything to get it. She was so young and beautiful, and something about her desperation touched the cold empty place in my heart. It made me want her like I'd never wanted a woman before, not for an afternoon's recreation, but for all eternity. I suppose you could say it was love at first sight, but that only begins to describe what I felt for her. And though she'd come to me offering her body, I was the one ready to do anything for her, and I told her so. But she would hear none of it. 'Just take me,' she said, 'and then give me the mirror.' So I did, because I thought it would be better to have a little bit of her than nothing at all."

He paused then and shook his head sadly. "I suppose I was naïve in that, for that little bit has haunted me through all the years since." He sighed again, before continuing. "When we'd finished, she got up and calmly dressed herself, never minding that I was watching. Then she looked at me with contempt, and said, 'Thank you.' Nothing more, just that. And then she left."

He turned to Dónal then, and his sadness was plain to see. "Of all the things she could've possibly said to me just then, I don't think anything could've been more demeaning. For in that moment I knew how all those women had felt when I'd finished with them, like a bit of rubbish that's been used up and discarded. How ironic it seems that in that moment of complete degradation, I should see for the first time what love really is, and spend the rest of my life loving a woman I can't have. Yet I have to admit that my suffering has made a better man of me, for now at least I have a conscience."

Dónal didn't know what to say then, for as much as he didn't want to believe it, Puxley was obviously telling the truth. And as much as the deed disgusted him, he couldn't really hate him for it. He was just a man after all, neither saint nor Satan, and who was to say he'd have fared any better? But at least now he understood Puxley's paternalism toward the Aherns. Then he frowned as the thought struck him.

"Is Tadhg your son?" he asked, fearing the answer, yet desperate to know.

"No, he isn't. He was born six months later and wasn't early."

Dónal sighed and nodded, relieved that he didn't have another awful secret to keep. He knew there was nothing more to say, so he turned away and climbed down from the wagon. But after taking a few steps, he turned and called for Puxley to stop.

"Thank you for keeping my things all these years," he said, speak-

286

ing in Irish, "and thank you for bringing them to me."

"You're welcome, Dónal. And thank you for proving my theory that no good deed ever goes unpunished! Safe home to you."

They lay by the fire basking in the warmth of afterglow, her head cradled on his arm and her body snuggled into his, covered only by their love and one thin blanket. But for the crackling of the fire and their beating hearts, the room was still and silent.

"Why did you go with Riobárd?" she asked absently, mesmerized by the dancing flames.

"There was something I wanted to ask him."

"Oh, and what was that?"

"What kind of man he is."

"And what did he say?"

"He said he isn't perfect."

chapter 14

Eskinanaun
17 June, 1858

PAUSING IN HIS READING TO GLANCE at Sióna sleeping in her chair, Dónal smiled, thinking how beautiful she looked in the firelight. Should he take her to bed, he wondered? It was late enough, surely, despite the lingering glow of the long summer evening.

But then Con whined softly from the hearth and, seeing the pleading look in his expressive eyes, Dónal lay the book aside and patted his leg. "Come here, boy," he said, and the dog happily obeyed, laying his head in his lap and closing his eyes appreciatively as he scratched behind his ears. "Good man, Con," and the dog looked back as if to say, 'I love you, too.'

Dónal smiled happily. He was with the woman he loved and they in their own home by their own fireside, and how could life get any better than that?

Then suddenly Con growled and padded to the door, where he stood listening attentively. In a moment, Dónal heard what had distracted him, the clop of horses' hooves on the boreen.

"Now who could that be at this hour?" he said, following Con to the door. Opening it, he found three men reining in their horses. The dog growled again and strained against Dónal's grip on the scruff of his neck.

"Who's there?" Dónal called into the darkness, speaking in Irish.

"Excuse me," a voice returned in English, "but is this the home of Dónal O'Sullivan Béara?"

"'Tis indeed," Dónal replied. "And who might be askin'?"

At that two of the men dismounted and handed their reins to the third, before slowly approaching the door. Dónal could make nothing of them in the gloaming, and when they were a few feet away, he held up his hand for them to stop.

"'Tis close enough, gentlemen, till I know your names and errand," he said, Con seconding with a growl.

"You'll have the answer to both when you see me in the light," one of them replied, and Dónal knew he'd heard the voice before.

"All right, then. But just yourself so."

The man stepped into the light of the doorway then, and when Dónal saw his hawk-like face and fanatical eyes, his jaw dropped in surprise.

"James Stephens!" he exclaimed. "Is it yourself indeed?"

"Yes, Dónal," Stephens replied, smiling broadly. "Did I not tell you I'd come when the time was right?"

"Sure, you did so. But I've been so long without a word that I thought you'd forgotten me or given it up!"

"Oh no, my lord O'Sullivan Béara, I've done neither. In fact, I've been quite busy these past two years, and I think you'll be pleased with what I have to report. May I come inside and fill you in?"

"Of course, James, and your friends, as well!" Dónal replied enthusiastically, stepping aside for them and ordering Con back to the fire. But the dog stood his ground, bristling and growling, refusing to yield until Dónal raised his voice.

"Con, back to the fire!" he commanded in Irish, having momentarily forgotten that the dog didn't understand English. Con obeyed then, though grudgingly it seemed, since he didn't lie down and continued to growl.

"All right, James, he'll behave himself now," Dónal said, returning to English.

Stephens nodded and turned to the man still on horseback. "Keep the horses ready, Joseph, and call us immediately if anyone approaches."

Then he and the other man came inside and Dónal closed the door.

Turning to his companion, Stephens laid a hand on his shoulder. "Dónal, let me introduce Thomas Clarke Luby," he said rather formally, "a Dublin man himself and my chief lieutenant in these matters that concern us. Thomas, please allow me to present Dónal, The O'Sullivan Béara."

"*Failte go Eisc an Eidhnein*," Dónal said as he shook Luby's hand, and repeated it in English, "Welcome to Eskinanaun."

"As you can see, Thomas," Stephens said, "Dónal is a native Irish speaker, something we men of the Pale were deprived of by the geography of our birth. But now, gentlemen, to business and quickly, shall we? The peelers are on the lookout for us, and though we gave them the slip at Lauragh, we need to move on before the night is much older."

"Sure, James. But come and warm yourselves by the fire. I keep no drink in the house, but we've tea in the kettle and poreens in the kish.

"Sióna, this is James Stephens, the man I've told you about!" he said, turning to find her eyeing him suspiciously.

"How do you do, Mrs. O'Sullivan," Stephens said, bowing formally. "I wasn't aware that Dónal was married."

"Sure, he ain't so!" Sióna replied haughtily, not bothering to stand. "I'll not take his name till he's done with ye."

"Her name is MacSweeney," Dónal replied to Stephens's questioning glance.

"Ah, a daughter of the Clan of the Battle Axes, are you?" Stephens said smoothly, their living arrangement being of no consequence to the Republic. "It's been many a long year since your people came from Donegal into the service of MacCarthy Reagh, and longer still since O'Donnell brought them as gallowglass from our sister kingdom of Scotland. But, though not native to our Emerald Isle, few among the Gael have given Her greater service and, in this latter day, none have a greater right to call themselves Irish. So, Miss MacSweeney, with such a rich heritage behind you, you should understand that it isn't me who calls your man from you, but She who is the mother of us all, our own beloved Erin."

"Sure, 'tis grand for yourself, Jimeen," Sióna retorted archly. "But I'll not be his wife till he can give all of himself, even though 'tis the Virgin that's after sharin' him!"

Stephens's jaw went slack at that, having seldom received such a comeuppance, and never from a woman.

"But since Dónal is committed to yeer scheme come hell or high water," Sióna continued, "ye'd best be gettin' on with it. The sooner he's done with yeerself, the sooner I can have him to me."

"An excellent point, Miss MacSweeney!" Stephens said, happy to take the bone she'd thrown him. "Time is indeed of the essence and we've much to accomplish, both now and in the future. So if you will kindly excuse us . . ."

"Sure, go on with yeerselves. Ye'll not bother me."

"Ah, well now, Miss MacSweeney. That's not quite what I meant. What we have to discuss here is rather of a confidential nature, you see, and it might be better we did so in private."

"'Tis outside that ye want me to go, is it? Why, I'll do nothin' o' the sort! 'Tis my house that I'm in and divil if I'll be ordered about in it!"

Stephens turned to Dónal for help, his expression a curious mixture of frustration and puzzlement. "You might as well give it up, James," he said with a sheepish grin. "There's no changin' her mind once it's made up. Besides, we've no secrets from each other, so she might as well hear it from you now as from me later."

"Be that as it may, Dónal, it would be better if you made an exception in this case. Our work is highly sensitive in nature, and knowledge of it may be as dangerous to the innocent as to the conspirators. Moreover, if you decide to join us, you'll have to swear an oath of secrecy, the breaking of which will be punished with the utmost severity. While that and your intrinsic patriotism should be enough to ensure your loyalty, how can I be sure of Miss MacSweeney's?"

"I'll swear to it, meself," Sióna interjected, "and if I break it, then ye can kill me and say I told ye so!"

The room was silent as a tomb then as the men gaped at her. "Would that every Irishman had such a woman at his side," Stephens said. Then he actually knelt and kissed her hand, as if she were a queen and he her humble servant.

"Would that every woman had a man like Dónal," she retorted, jerking her hand away.

"You are indeed a lucky man, Dónal," Stephens said. "For such a woman as her, I might be tempted to put aside my duty to God and country myself and live the quiet life. I commend you on your commitment to our cause. But, seeing that we're all in agreement now, let's get on with it, shall we?"

The three men took seats around the fire then, and Stephens gave Dónal a brief summary of what he'd been up to since their last meeting. He'd spent months traveling around the country on what he called his "three thousand mile walk," trying to get his finger on the pulse of the people and determine their level of enthusiasm for the Republic. What he'd found was quite extraordinary, though some of it had left him feeling rather pessimistic.

First of all, it had surprised him that the common people seemed to have no understanding of being part of a greater Irish nation. True, they spoke of Ireland as their country, but only in the vaguest sense of the word. Indeed, to the average Cork man, Antrim seemed as distant and foreign as the islands of Japan. In some places there was even outright hostility toward other regions, as evidenced by the fact that in Connaught, Leinstermen were considered to have so little Irish in them as to be no different from foreigners and disliked as such. Part of it Stephens attributed to the old Gaelic system, under which loyalty was local and clan-based rather than national in character, but more so to the simple fact that most people lived their entire lives without ever venturing more than a few miles from where they were born. Even the very sense of their Irishness they realized only in a negative way and by comparison to the English, and the potato famine had showed them what a great handicap it was to be Irish in an English world. Why, people even blamed their misfortunes on their Irishness, and so were abandoning their language and culture in favor of those of the English. The language was dead in the east already and dying in the midlands, while only in the west could Gaelic-only speakers still be found, though their numbers were dwindling even there. As Cromwell had condemned Irish Catholics to Hell or Connaught, so had the Great Hunger done the same to the Irish language and culture.

Secondly, he'd found that the people whom he'd expected to be most disaffected, the tenant farmers, were actually the least. It seemed that for all the inhuman suffering it had caused, the blight had actually strengthened them by culling the weak and small, thereby reducing competition and increasing the average size of their holdings, leaving them much more prosperous as a class. Though it was a great insult to be called a grabber, the strong farmer had become a fixture on the Irish landscape by doing just that, and was now the force of reckoning among the tenantry. And with their newfound prosperity, they were more interested in bettering their harvests than furthering the nationalist cause.

So the tenantry couldn't be counted on for support, nor for similar reasons could the upper classes and respectable people of the towns, most of whom were downright hostile to the concept of independence. Yet why should they expect any different from them, he argued, given the bent of human nature toward complacency in the face of creature comfort. That had been the fatal illusion of Young Ireland, that the prosperous would wish to replace the *ancien régime* just because the peasants suffered under its yoke, a mistake he intended to correct by centering his movement among the truly disaffected.

And just who were those men, he asked? They were the laborers, both urban and rural, the small tradesmen and the sons of peasants and small farmers, the disenfranchised and disinherited men who yet constituted a majority of the Irish people. From their ranks, he thought it possible to forge a cadre of dedicated, motivated, disciplined men who would be capable of bringing the Republic to fruition. Moreover, there were tens of thousands of their brothers serving in the British Army, many of them stationed at home in Ireland, who for the most part rendered but superficial loyalty to the Crown. Indeed, for most of them the army was the employer of last resort, a lesser evil than starvation, emigration or the workhouse, and they'd gladly turn their guns on the Empire given the right opportunity. It was true, he allowed, that Young Ireland had expected the same from them, yet they'd counted on spontaneous mutinies in conjunction with a spontaneous rising of the people, and Ballingarry gave morbid testimony to the efficacy of spontaneity. But that flaw of Young Ireland he would correct by patiently organizing and training a national fighting force of the type discussed at their first meeting. And the final faction of that force, and possibly its most important, would come from the millions of exiles in America, who would supply not only trained men but money and arms, as well. He himself had friends who were influential in the Irish-American community, many of them men of '48 like himself, and they'd established an American wing of the organization in conjunction with his own in Ireland. He was to be the supreme commander of both in order to ensure unity of purpose on both sides of the Atlantic. The recruiting drive was already underway in both places and, by the end of summer, he hoped to have thirty thousand men under oath and in training in Ireland alone.

"Having said all that," Stephens concluded, "let me sum up by restating the obvious, that our goal is to move with all deliberate speed toward establishing an independent Irish Republic by whatever means necessary."

It was then that Luby spoke for the first time. "And let it be plain from the start, too, that the first order of business of that new Republic will be to institute an equitable distribution of the land of Ireland among the Irish people. It is the paramount issue that faces our society, for only if the land belongs to the people can we be sure that this calamity of the Great Hunger will never repeat itself."

Stephens smiled indulgently at that, like a schoolmaster at a favored student. "You must excuse Thomas for his vehemence. He's a disciple of Mitchel and Lalor, and much influenced by their thoughts. Not that I disagree with him, of course, for I've often said that unless the land of Ireland belongs to the Irish people, independence isn't worth the trouble and sacrifice of obtaining it. But let us ford one river at a time, gentlemen. When we're free of English paternalism, then we as a people can steer our political course as we see fit.

"But now, Dónal, we've reached the point of decision. I've told you of my activities and plans, and I can tell you nothing more without knowing if you are with us. You know what I intend to do and how I intend to do it, and now you know we have a chance to succeed given the overwhelming support we enjoy among the people, both here and in America.

"So, Dónal, are you indeed with us?"

"Sure, James, I'm with you," Dónal replied. "I have been from the start, you know!"

"Then you're ready to take the oath?"

"Yes, I'm ready."

Stephens smiled delightedly then, like a child with a new toy. "Good! Very good! Our movement is strengthened tenfold by your addition, and I thank you sincerely for your confidence in me."

Turning to Luby, he asked, "Do you have your Bible handy, Thomas?"

But before he could answer, Dónal interjected. "If it's all the same to you, James, I'll not swear on the Bible, but on this." He picked up the book he'd been reading earlier. "'Tis the book I told you of before, the one Don Phillip wrote about my family."

He handed it to Stephens and retrieved his other heirlooms. "This is the rod of office held for time out of mind by the chieftains of our line. 'Tis also the token of peace a new chieftain takes into his left hand at his inauguration, and since I've chosen war, I'll lay it aside now and not take it up again till our independence is achieved."

Setting it aside, he held up the dagger. "This comes to me from Eochaidh Súildubhán, the distant ancestor from whom we take our name. 'Tis also the token of war that a new chieftain takes into his right hand. Emblazoned on its blade is our battle-cry, *lamh foisteanach abú*, 'the gentle hand advances.' If you've no objection, I'll hold it in my right hand and place my left on the book."

"As you wish, my lord O'Sullivan Béara," Stephens replied. "Please repeat after me."

I, Dónal, The O'Sullivan Béara, do solemnly swear in the presence of

Almighty God, that I will do my utmost, at every risk, while life lasts, to establish in Ireland an independent democratic Republic; that I will yield implicit obedience, in all things not contrary to the law of God, to the commands of my superior officers; and that I shall preserve inviolable secrecy regarding all the affairs of this secret society that may be confided in me. So help me God. Amen.

"Congratulations!" Stephens said when finished, and Luby echoed it.

"Thanks," Dónal replied with a grin, shaking their hands in turn. "Now that we've the formalities out of the way, what next? I've been waitin' for years and I'm past ready to get on with it."

But before Stephens could reply, Sióna rose and stepped between them. "Forgettin' somethin', now aren't ye, lads? I'm after speakin' it, too, ye know."

"It really isn't necessary, Miss MacSweeney," Stephens replied. "I'll consider you bound by Dónal's oath, just as if you were husband and wife. And besides, we have no provisions for inducting women into the organization."

"Man, woman, what difference does it make? We all bleed the same color o' red. And I might be able to help in ways ye've not considered. What man would suspect a mere woman o' treason, after all, devious though ye think we are. So go on with ye. Take a bite o' the apple and use it to yeer advantage for a change!"

"Yes," Stephens said after a moment, stroking his beard thoughtfully. "Yes, I believe you're right, Miss MacSweeney. You just might be of great assistance in the job I have in mind for Dónal. So if you're indeed set on joining us, I'll give you the oath."

"I am!" Sióna said, holding her head up proudly. "So get on with it so!"

Stephens smiled slightly at her impertinence, though he gave her the oath with the same formality as he had Dónal. But when finished, he shook not her hand but his, saying, "I underestimated your good fortune earlier, my lord O'Sullivan Béara. You're indeed a *very* lucky man to have such a warrior queen at your side!"

"'Tis neither that I am, Jimeen," Sióna said, "just a woman who'll fight to keep her man."

"Which is the same thing, Miss MacSweeney," Stephens said, not to be denied the last word. "But let's all sit down again so I can give Dónal his assignment, and then Thomas and I must away. We've miles to go and the hours are but few."

Then Stephens briefly described the organizational structure of the movement, explaining that he'd chosen to do it that way for security reasons. The informer was ever the bane of Irish nationalism, he said, so he'd devised a scheme under which any one man would know only a handful of other men, so that the informer's chain of information would automatically be broken without exposing much of the organization. He himself was at the top of the pyramid, of course, his official title being "Chief Organizer of the Irish Republic." Beneath him would be one Vice Organizer for each the four provinces, who would be in command of the operational cells, or "circles" as he referred to them, each of which in turn would be headed by a colonel, or "center." Beneath the centers would be captains, sergeants and privates, all organized so that each man would know the identities of only the other eight men in his circle, plus that of his superior officer.

Having explained that, Stephens came to the part that he wanted Dónal to play. "In addition to the circles I've described, the 'regular army' if you will, I'm also organizing a small number of special circles in strategic areas. Their responsibilities will include sabotage, intelligence, reconnaissance and smuggling of men and materiel, and their centers will take orders directly from me and only from me. No other man in the organization will even know of their existence, save Thomas here.

"So what I would like you to do, Dónal, is recruit, train, and command a special circle here in West Béara. The reasons for it are two-fold: Firstly, the importation of men and especially arms into Ireland will have to be done covertly, and Béara, with its many secluded harbors and rich heritage of smuggling, will be a prime place for landing them. Secondly, when the armed struggle actually begins, the military and police establishments in the area will have to be neutralized, including the Naval Station on Bear Island, the Coast Guard Station in Eyeries, and the constabularies in Allihies, Eyeries, and Castletownbere, and it will be up to you to formulate plans of attack and then lead the regular army in the assaults. Initially, your circle will operate independently, but once the rising begins, you will take command of all personnel and operations in West Béara."

Stephens spoke at length on the details and timing of what he wanted done, before giving Dónal a written copy of the oath and telling him to destroy it once he had it committed to memory. Then he turned to the manner of communication between them, saying that Luby would send a contact man with any additional orders he might have. He'd not be anyone Dónal knew, so he gave him the code words by which they were to identify themselves, and explained the system he would use to encode the messages. When finished, he asked if Dónal had any questions.

"Just one," he replied with a grin. "What exactly is our movement to be called anyway?"

"For security reasons, it'll just be 'our movement' for the time being, though I'm leaning toward the *Irish Republican Brotherhood* when the time comes. But don't use it outside your circle. If it was to become common knowledge, the government might realize the national scope of what we're doing and we'd lose our element of surprise. As of now, they only suspect Mr. Shooks of being something of a crackpot, and I'd like to keep it that way as long as possible."

Stephens stood up then and the others followed. "So if you have no further questions for me, Thomas and I will take our leave. I suppose I should warn you to be patient and not to worry if you don't hear from me for some time. This great undertaking won't bear fruit overnight."

"Not to worry, James," Dónal assured him. "'Tis my destiny to fight for Ireland, and all my life till now has been spent in preparation. So I can wait a bit longer."

"Good man, Dónal," Stephens said, patting him on the back. "Erin has need of Her sons, especially those who have a stake in the country like yourself."

Then he and Luby took their leave and Dónal followed them to the door, watching as they disappeared into the night.

"*Slán abhaile, a Sheabhaic Shiúileach,*" he said to the darkness, (Good-bye, O Wandering Hawk).

"It's a big job he's given you," Sióna said from just behind him. "Do you not wonder why he chose you?"

"He chose me because I'm the right man for it," Dónal said defensively, a little irritated at her skeptical tone.

"Sure, you are indeed, Dónal," she agreed, though he thought he heard just a hint of condescension in her voice. "But how would he know that having met you only once before?" Without waiting for him to answer, she turned and went back to her chair.

How indeed, he wondered, staring into the night as if it were a curtain over the stage of his future. Obviously Stephens knew more about him than he'd let on. But how?

But the night gave no answers, and after a bit he sighed and closed the door. His life had changed again and nothing would be as it was before. For he was a soldier of the Irish Republican Brotherhood now, and war had come to Eskinanaun.

◯⚋⚋⚋◯

They were gathered in the cottage at Eskinanaun, Sióna, Tadhg, the Kellingtons, Art O'Shea, Dan MacCarthy and Pat Donegan, sitting in a semi-circle and facing Dónal as he stood by the fire. He'd recruited each of them individually in the days following Stephens's visit, and brought them together for their first meeting as an operational cell. He'd not given them the oath yet, preferring to have them all take it together so as to strengthen the bond of loyalty, nor had he given them the details of their role in the movement. They were anxious to get on with it, of course, but there were some things he had to say first.

"We've all been friends for a long time," he began. "I'd trust any of you with the lives of my children when I have them, and I know you all feel the same about me and each other. That's the reason I've asked you to join me in this, because the penalties for treason are stiff and we have to know we can trust each other. But there are only eight of us, including Sióna, and we need a ninth to complete our circle."

"Sure, I can only think of about a hundred others who'd want to join!" Tadhg said. "Do you want me to put out some feelers?"

"No. I already have someone in mind."

"Well, don't keep us in the dark, for Christ's sake! Who is it?"

"Padge O'Sullivan."

"What?" Tadhg demanded, giving him the old "are you daft?" look. "Why would you want him when there are so many other good men to choose from. Why not Mick Singleton or Chris O'Mahony, for instance, or Éamon Hill? If this is all about trust and secrecy, then why pick someone we hardly know?"

"There are a lot of reasons for it," Dónal replied, trying not to sound defensive in his first decision as their leader, "the obvious one being that other than yourself, he's the biggest, strongest man around and we might just have need of brute force now and again. But then there's what he did for me on that Sunday at St. Michael's to consider. Like everybody else who was there, he knew that I was talking about his Da, but he stood up and spoke for me anyway, just because it was the right thing to do. It took moral courage for him to do that, and that's another thing we'll have need of before all is said and done. Then there's what I did to him when we were boys. He's had it tough since then, and I feel I owe him for it. But the most important reason to choose him is something he said to me when I broached the subject to him yesterday. He said that he'd stayed in Ireland rather than leaving with the rest of his family because he knew there'd be another rising someday and he wanted to be part of it! So that's why I want him with us, and why I'll have him!"

"Well, I can see that your mind is made up, and as usual there'll be no talking sense to you. But tell me, Dónal, what are you going to do if the rest of us don't want him?"

"I'm going to recruit seven more men, and if any one of you ever repeats a word of this, it'll be the last thing you ever do!"

The room was silent then; they'd heard the threat and knew he meant it. "Once you're in, *death* is the only way out of the Brotherhood," he said, looking at each of them in turn. "This isn't a game we're playing anymore. This isn't a bunch of boys breaking each other's heads over bragging rights. This is *war*, and in war, killing and dying are just part of a day's work! So if any of you is having second thoughts, now is the time to leave."

When no one stirred, he smiled slightly, though his eyes remained intent. "Good men! But there's one last thing to consider, and that's the fact that I'll be your commander and, as such, will hold the power of life and death over you. Though you're all my friends and I hold your lives dearer than my own, from now on the Republic comes first, and if sacrificing any or all of you is what best serves the Republic, then I'll not hesitate to do it. My own father told me long ago to consider carefully before deciding to join an army, because from the moment you do, your life is no longer in your own hands. So it will be that your lives are in my hands, and whether you live or die may well hinge on my ability as a commander. So if any of you lacks confidence in me to lead you, now is the time to leave, and indeed, it will be your *last chance!*"

Though he'd spoken to all of them, his eyes had been on Tadhg alone, and it was he who answered for them.

"Sure we'll follow you, Dónal," he said nonchalantly, though his eyes were as hard as Dónal's. "Haven't we always followed you, and isn't it our destiny to go on doing so? And if you should find sacrificing our lives harder in practice than in theory, just remember that Dónal Cam did the right thing!"

For a long moment then, Dónal just stared at Tadhg, stunned by what he'd said. *Our* destiny! In all the years that he'd spent thinking of his own, it had never occurred to him that it was linked to others, that it was but one small piece in a shifting puzzle and his own success or failure might depend more upon others than himself. It made him feel small, like the little boy who'd stood alone on the mountaintop above a world covered in fog. Was this the loneliness of command he'd always heard about?

But then Tadhg spoke again, gently prodding Dónal from his abstraction. "We're ready to take the oath now."

Still Dónal didn't speak, just nodded his head, before going to the door and giving a whistle. In a moment, a shadow blocked out the light as a tall man stooped to enter.

"God bless all here," Padge said as he joined them by the fire.

"Now we're all here," Dónal said, and gestured for them to join hands. He gave them the oath, and they repeated it back to him, even Sióna joining in the solemnity of the moment.

"Now we're complete," he said when finished, "a circle unending, sworn to each other and to the Republic. So let us remain until Ireland is free."

chapter 15

Ballydonegan
29 December, 1860

PEERING THROUGH THE RUINED DOORWAY into the night, Dónal cupped his ear against the skirl of the wind and listened for approaching hoof beats. He and Tadhg and Padge had been holed up in the deserted cottage since about midnight and were waiting for Sióna to come and give them the all-clear before continuing. By way of diversion they'd taken three wagons over Guala that morning on the pretext of having work on Bear Island, and then brought them back through Bealbarnish Gap under the cover of darkness. As it turned out, the ruse was probably unnecessary given the Devil's own weather that was in it. The night was as black as ink from the thick layer of clouds, and it was cold and damp with a biting wind from the sea. Even the boldest wouldn't venture out, especially with the short hours now upon them. Still it was better to be safe than sorry, and he was glad they'd gone to the trouble, even though it made a long day of it.

After a moment, he turned from the doorway and slumped down beside Tadhg. Whatever he'd heard wasn't Sióna, and anyway Dan MacCarthy was on watch and would signal her approach. The others had already taken up their stations and all that remained was for her to make a final sweep of the area and then come for them. It couldn't have been more than fifteen minutes since she'd left, he reflected, and he wanted her to do a thorough job of it. Still, he was anxious to get on with it.

"They say the waiting is the hardest part," Tadhg said softly, feeling his tension. "But don't worry. All things come to those who wait."

Dónal didn't bother to reply. He was lost in thought, going over the plan again in his mind. It was simple enough, really, and he knew his men were well-trained and ready for it. They'd spent the last year and a half drilling for just this sort of assignment and were past the point of boredom with it. For in all the time since Stephens had suddenly appeared in the night, Dónal hadn't heard another word from him, no orders, no instructions, nor even a simple message to let him know the game was still on. It was as if the Irish Republican Brotherhood was just a pleasant dream that evaporated in the light of morning. Of course, there'd been the odd report of a new secret society in the papers, and here and there a mention of Mr. Shooks, especially after the arrests of O'Donovan Rossa and other members of his Phoenix Society. During their trial, an informer had even given direct testimony on the subject, saying that Shooks was preparing the way for an armed invasion of Irish-Americans intent upon overthrowing the British government in Ireland.

Alarmed by this and needing information, Dónal had ordered Tadhg and Padge to spend their evenings in those public houses where men of republican sympathies were known to congregate. In this way he'd learned that the Phoenix Society was indeed part of the Brotherhood, and while the publicity from the trial had been damaging, it had by no means proved fatal to the movement. On the contrary, it demonstrated that the government still didn't know the full extent of the organization or who its leaders were, and seeing that the security arrangements could survive such a breech even buoyed his morale. Still, the waiting was hard on his men, and he'd found it increasingly difficult to keep them motivated and focused. They were Irishmen after all, and for all that he cautioned patience, it just wasn't in their nature.

So he'd felt a certain sense of relief when the stranger had fallen in beside him as he walked through Allihies and handed him a yellowed newspaper. "I think there's an article in there that you'll find interesting," he'd said. "It says that a war is expected between England and France."

"Yes, the Irish Brigade is on the advance!" Dónal had replied, giving the proper coded response. "So the game is on at last, is it?"

But the man had just bid him good day and continued on through the village. Bending down to tie his shoe, Dónal had glanced quickly around to make sure that no one was watching and then hurried home to decipher the message. It was short and direct:

> Large shipment blasting powder arriving mines 27 Dec.
> Appropriate by any means necessary, but cover your tracks.
> Ship for transport will wait at Pulleen Harbor midnight till
> six AM each night 28 Dec through 3 Jan. Good luck. Luby.

"What does 'cover your tracks' mean?" Sióna had asked when he read it to her.

But Dónal had just stared at the message, his mind already racing ahead to what he knew must happen. "It means to steal it in such a way that no one will know it's been stolen," he'd answered finally, still not looking at her.

"But they've a peeler guarding that building twenty-four hours a day! So how do you propose to steal it without leaving him the wiser?"

He'd looked up at her then, and the hardness of his eyes frightened her, though not nearly as much as the plan he outlined. "May God have mercy on our souls!" she'd said in a hushed voice, and then crossed herself.

And now as he thought about what he must do, Dónal gripped the dagger hidden beneath his coat, the ancient blade of Súildubhán in its shabby leather scabbard. He'd spent the evening before honing it to razor sharpness, and then polishing it so that it glowed red in the firelight. How long since it had struck a blow in anger? he'd wondered. Whose hand was the last to wield it in battle, and how many foes had felt its bite? As he'd turned it in the light, the battle cry jumped out in stark relief, *The Gentle Hand Advances*. He'd always thought it so ironic, that an instrument of Death should be wielded by a gentle hand. But seeing it glow with the flicker of hellfire brought understanding, and he'd marveled at the innocence that had kept him from it before.

He gripped the hilt nervously now, knowing that after this night he'd never be innocent again.

But then Tadhg was nudging him in the ribs. "There's the signal. She's back."

Dónal leapt to his feet and bolted through the door. In a moment Sióna appeared over the rise and rode slowly toward him, MacCarthy running along beside. She stopped a few paces shy and stared down at him, loath to speak it seemed.

"Well?" he prompted. "Is it clear or not?"

"Yes, Dónal, it's clear. There's just the one guard, and the boys say no one else has been there for hours."

"Right then," Dónal said, turning to the others. "You three get to the wagons. Sióna will lead, and I'll bring up the rear. You all know what to do after that. Now go on with you!"

"Let's go, boys," Tadhg seconded, and led the other two away.

Dónal turned to his horse, which was tethered beside the cottage. But as he mounted, he saw that Sióna hadn't moved to take up her position.

"What are you waiting for?" he hissed in annoyance. "You need to be well out in front if you're to give us proper warning!"

But still she didn't move, and something about her reticence made him suddenly uneasy. He moved his horse in close to hers and sat looking at her for a moment. Like the rest of them she was disguised as a Wren Boy, with her jacket turned inside out and her hat pulled low over her forehead, while the scarf around her face left only her eyes exposed. Yet even in the darkness, he could see the distress in them.

"What is it, Sióna?" he asked more gently.

Still she said nothing, though she desperately wanted to talk to him, and even more for him to talk to her. For in the fortnight since he'd received his orders, he'd been a different man from the one she'd shared her home and heart with, having withdrawn into himself so completely that he barely seemed to notice her. What was going on inside him? she wondered. What did he feel about this thing he was about to do? Did it pain him, or did he just view it with detachment, like a surgeon removing a boil? She didn't even know which to hope for, a man of conscience who'd be forever scarred or one with a heart of stone that nothing could move. Either way, he'd never again be the man he'd been before, the man she needed more desperately than the air she breathed. But would she still feel that way in the morning? If only he would open his heart and talk to her. If only there was some way she could show him that he had a choice, that he didn't have to bear his father's cross. But she'd watched him honing his Sword of War, and now it stood between them like a wall cutting off her heart from his.

"The guard is Brendan Collins," she said finally, whispering so the others wouldn't hear. Then she turned and rode away.

The wagons rolled by him one by one, but Dónal hesitated before following. Brendan Collins wasn't a name he wanted to hear. But then all the peelers were local men with deep roots in the community. Yet as long as they wore the uniform of oppression and swore allegiance to a foreign crown, they were all his enemies. So in the heel of the hunt, did it really matter who was on duty tonight? He sighed and spurred his horse to follow.

They passed like ghosts through the abandoned *clochán* of Ballydonegan, their movement cloaked in darkness even as the skirling wind obscured the sound. When they neared the Kealogue Mine, the wagons stopped and Dónal rode to the front, where he found Liam standing in the road beside Sióna.

"Is it still clear?" he murmured.

"Yes," Liam replied softly. "But there's a light of some sort over by the magazine. Probably a fire from the looks of it."

"He's probably just keeping himself warm," Dónal said as he dismounted. "It's no bother; we'll just have to be more careful. Go on now and take Padge's place on the wagon, and send him to me."

"Sure, he's already here," Liam replied with a grin, and Dónal actually jumped when he realized that Padge was standing right behind him. For all the size that was in him, the big man was as stealthy as a black cat on a dark night. When Dónal had asked him how he'd come by it, he'd replied that he'd learned to be invisible around his father, since he never knew what might send him into a murderous rage. And Dónal had understood completely.

"*Jesus*, don't do that!" Dónal hissed, perturbed at being startled. "We've got to be quiet, and I can't very well do it with you sneaking up on me like that!"

"Sorry, Dónal," Padge replied with a shrug. "I'll be more careful."

"See that you do!" Turning to Liam and Sióna, Dónal said, "You two take your places and wait for the signal. Padge, you come with me."

Without waiting for replies, Dónal set off toward the powder magazine. Peering around the corner of a building, he saw the guard huddled over a fire that was burning in a small metal tub.

"The idiot has a fire going, all right," he whispered to Padge, "and he's sitting on a stool with his back to the building."

"That'll make it harder to do it quietly," Padge whispered back, drawing a knife from inside his jacket. "But if you lure him away from the fire, I'll take him from behind."

"No, you just wait here," Dónal said, pulling the scarf from his face and turning his jacket right side out. "I'll take him myself."

In the next moment he was striding boldly into the light, hailing the guard jovially. "God be with you, Brendan. It's not a fit night out for man or beast, now is it?"

The guard started at his sudden appearance and leapt from his seat, but relaxed upon seeing who it was. "God and Mary be with you, Dónal," he replied with a welcoming smile. "Indeed, it's a bad one, and sure, if I'm not surprised to find you out in it."

"I was just on my way to Ahern's and saw your fire from the road," Dónal replied as he sidled up next to Collins. "You don't mind if I warm myself a bit, do you?"

"Sure, you're as welcome as a fresh pint! Lord knows I could use the company. I've been here all alone since sundown and will have no relief till morning."

"Do you mean to tell me you have to guard this place all night by yourself? That seems a bit harsh to me!"

"All night and every night! I'm the new man on the force, you see, and the youngest, so that's why I get stuck with the nastiest job. But things could be worse, I suppose. The pay is better than I could get doing anything else, and I've the three young ones to consider. And the uniform's not bad, either, especially with the way Mary smiles at me when I'm wearing it. But hopefully we'll lay on a new man soon, so I can spend the nights with her and the young ones again instead of out here."

"Yes, it's rough duty, all right," Dónal said absently, though speaking of himself now rather than Collins. He'd known this man since coming to live with the Aherns. Indeed, he was only two years older than Tadhg, and was related to all the men in the circle, excepting Dónal himself. Why did it have to be him, he wondered? He was no demon spirit, come from a foreign Empire to grind them underfoot. He didn't even understand that the uniform he was so proud of made him a traitor to his people, wouldn't get it no matter how patiently it was explained to him. He was just a simple man trying to provide for his family, content with a bit of fire to warm his body and a bit of company to warm his heart. But then, there were no innocents in the game of life, Dónal reminded himself. Collins had made his choice and he alone was answerable for it.

"Are you all right, Dónal?" Collins asked, laying a friendly hand on his shoulder. "You've the queerest sort of look on your face!"

"Sure, I'm grand," Dónal lied, smiling to hide the turmoil inside. Then he pulled a flask from inside his coat and offered it to Collins. "Here, Brendan. Maybe a drop will help the night pass quicker."

"Sure, if it wouldn't indeed, and I thank you for it! Of course, I'm not supposed to drink while on duty, but just a drop to warm me won't hurt, now will it?"

Raising the flask to his lips then, he took a long pull, grunting with satisfaction when finished.

Dónal felt himself go numb as he watched, for he'd just executed the man as surely as if he'd swung the ax. Feeling the hairs on his neck rise, he glanced quickly over his shoulder, as though expecting to find the Dark Angel hovering at his elbow. But there was no one there, only the dark of night and the darkness of his deed.

Collins made to return the flask, but Dónal just pushed it back. "No, Brendan, none for me, thanks. I've already had my fill for the night, and a drop more would be too much. But you're welcome to another, if you like."

"You're a good man, Dónal. And it's fine stuff, surely, though it does tend to linger on the tongue."

"That's because it's real parliament Scotch," Dónal said, giving the line he'd rehearsed.

"Ah, that explains it!" Collins took another short swig and swirled it around his mouth before swallowing. "It's my first taste of it and I must say I rather like it. Are you sure you'll not have one with me?"

"No, Brendan, you go ahead and finish it."

"I will, but only because you insist."

As he downed what was left, Dónal watched as though in a dream, hating what he was doing and himself for doing it, the lies, the deceit, and especially this Trojan Horse of a flask. How could something that had seemed so simple in the abstract be so horrible in the deed? He was a soldier, after all, and soldiers were supposed to kill their enemies, and Brendan Collins was his enemy! But in that moment and in that place, it seemed such a futile thing to do. Would this little bit of powder really make a difference in the outcome of the war, he wondered? How many more men would it kill, and at the tail of the day, would it be worth it? He tried to think of the famished woman staggering through the gate of the workhouse, clutching her baby to her barren breast. He was doing it for her, he told himself, and for the untold millions of others like her. But if asked, would she approve? He doubted it.

'Oh God,' he prayed silently, 'if you'll just let me go back . . .' But the deed was done, the Greeks were through the gate, the sack of Troy only a matter of time.

Collins finished the last of it and Dónal returned the flask to his pocket, then settled in to wait. It didn't take long, for the man already had a queer look on his face.

"Oh, Dónal," he said, clutching his gut, "I'm not sure the Scotch agrees with me."

Then the first wave of real pain hit him as the poison began to burn through his stomach. His body convulsed, his eyes bugged out, and he opened his mouth to scream, but it was cut off by a second wave of pain that knocked him to the ground. Over and over he rolled, kicking his feet in agony and tearing at his gut. Then the scream finally came, high-pitched and horrible like a cat being boiled alive, and Dónal's heart leapt into his throat at the sound of it, not in pity for his torment but in fear that someone would hear. He tried to cover his mouth with his hand, but it was no use; the man was bucking like a fresh stallion. Then he remembered the dagger under his coat, and the Gentle Hand of Death drew forth the Sword of War.

For just a moment, Collins went stiff at the shock of cold steel ripping through his heart. But then he relaxed and sighed, even as the light of life faded from his eyes. Yet they remained open and locked on Dónal's, and though his dead mouth could no longer ask it, the question was there to see: *Why?*

But Dónal had no answer. Indeed, he stood up and backed away, suddenly desperate to escape those staring eyes. Yet his legs were as heavy as lead and he could barely move them. It was like all those nightmares where the bad men were chasing him and he couldn't get away, and for a desperate moment he thought it was a dream, and if he could only wake himself it would all go away. But then someone spoke behind him, and he knew with crushing certainty that it was no dream.

"Jesus, Dónal, you've *killed* him!" Liam exclaimed, his voice an astonished whisper.

Dónal blinked his eyes in shock. 'No, I didn't, he's just sleeping!' he wanted to shout. It just didn't seem real, yet the blood spreading around the dagger hilt told him that it was. He looked up and saw that they were all there, gaping in disbelief at Collins's inert body, all of them drawn to the scene by his tortured screams. Only Sióna hadn't abandoned her post, though he knew it wasn't devotion to duty that kept her away.

"Why did you kill him, Dónal?" Liam asked, and the others looked at him expectantly, their eyes round and unblinking.

He'd known that question would come sooner or later, and he had an answer all prepared. Yet with all of them staring at him, his mind was as suddenly blank as the dead man's lying at his feet. Why *had* he killed him? Indeed, why had he *wanted* to? To strike a blow for the Republic, or for the Clan Dónal Cam, or for Eóghan? Or was it simply because he thought it was what his father wanted him to do? Surely, he couldn't tell them *that!*

He looked at the young men gathered round the body, at their fresh innocent faces and horrified eyes. He'd known them for most of his life and they'd been the only friends he'd ever had. Yet in that horrible moment, he knew they'd never look on him with friendship again. For he'd opened a door onto Darkness and dragged them all through it, and he'd never be able to close it.

'Oh God, my God,' he prayed again, 'if you'll just let me go back and change it . . .'

But then Tadhg spoke up. "Liam, you thick, what did you think he was going to do? Politely ask him for the loan of his keys?"

"I thought he was going to do what he *said* he was going to do!" Liam said angrily, his voice now a shout. "I thought he was going to sneak up on him and knock him out so he wouldn't see us, then make it look like we just blew it all up rather than stealing it!"

"Well, it didn't work out that way, and he had to change the plan," Tadhg retorted, "and killing him was the only way to complete our mission in secret!"

"The Devil take our *mission!*" Níall scoffed, taking up the argument for Liam. "That's Brendan Collins there! Sure, if he isn't my own cousin and Liam's, too!"

"And my second cousin," added Pat, "and Art and Dan's!"

"Sure, we're all related to him!" Tadhg said. "And so what? That doesn't change the fact that he was our enemy, that he was an agent of the Empire sworn to uphold the very laws that keep us down! Have you forgotten that we're at *war* here, or did you just think that we were playing at it? We're at war and that man was our enemy, and if Dónal hadn't killed him, he'd have stopped us from doing our duty! You lads had just better remember that you've sworn an oath to the Republic, and that it comes before clan and friendship and even family!"

"I didn't swear to kill my own relations," Níall shouted, "and if that's what the oath means, then I don't want any part of it!"

"Well you *are* part of it, Níall, whether you like it or not!" Tadhg replied. "You swore the oath and *death* is the only way out of it!"

"Oh?" Níall spat back. "And does that mean you'll kill us, too, Dónal, if we don't want to play your little game any more?"

"No, Liam, *he* won't kill you!" a voice said from the shadows. "That's *my* job!"

And though even Tadhg turned to it in surprise, Padge wasn't looking at them, just nonchalantly picking at his nails with his knife.

"So!" Liam said, glaring at Dónal. "Now I see why you wanted to bring in an outsider, to keep the rest of us in line if you didn't have the stomach for it yourself!"

"Wrong again, Liam," Padge said, moving to Dónal's side. "He brought me in to do the work that *you* might not have the stomach for, like getting rid of Irishmen that are traitors to their own people, and like it or not that's part of the oath, too."

"Well, you can say whatever you like, Paidín O'Sullivan," Liam retorted, "but I didn't swear to kill my own relations!"

"Yes, you did, Liam!" Tadhg said, also moving to Dónal's side. "You swore to do your utmost to establish an independent Republic in Ireland, and to do that, we have to rid ourselves of the British Empire. But don't you see that the Empire isn't just a thing unto itself with no heart or mind or soul? It's made up of *people*, of individuals who are dedicated to upholding its laws and systems and traditions, and to perpetuating them into the future. So in order to rid ourselves of the British Empire, we have to rid ourselves of those people who are dedicated to upholding and perpetuating its rule in Ireland. Brendan Collins was one of those people, as is every other Irishman who supports the Empire. So if you think you didn't swear to kill him, Liam, then you're sadly mistaken. And if you think you can get out of your oath because you don't like it, well, you're even *more* mistaken! As I told you before, *death* is the only way out of this circle, and if you try to cross us on it, there won't be anything left for Padge by the time I'm done with you! Do you understand me, Liam Kelly?"

"So that's the way of it, is it?" Liam said. "The three of you lording it over the rest of us and bullying us along whether we will or not!"

"You swore to follow orders, Liam," Tadhg reiterated, "and you did it of your own free will. Dónal warned you that you may not always like them, but you swore anyway. So you've none to blame for your predicament but yourself!"

"Sure, I swore an oath and I'll stand by it, too!" Liam replied. "But if murdering our own is the price of the Republic, then it hardly seems worth it."

"You can decide that once we've got it!" Tadhg said. "Now if you're done with your grousing, I suggest we finish the job and get out of here!"

Tadhg made to go for his wagon then, but Liam stepped in front of him. "Just a minute, Tadhg! I've one more thing to say to you!"

"Well, get on with it, then, before the whole British Empire comes down on us!"

But Liam didn't speak for a long moment, just glared up at Tadhg. "We've known each other all our lives, and except for Níall, I've always considered you my best friend. But I'll not be threatened and bullied, not by you or anyone else. So as of right now, our friendship is at an end! Do you understand me, Tadhg Ahern?"

Tadhg just nodded his head calmly. "Does that go for you, too, Níall?" he asked, his eyes still on Liam.

"Do you really have to ask?" Níall replied.

Tadhg looked at him then, and at the other three beside him. "Sure, if that's the way you want it, then it's fine with me. Soldiers don't need to be friends anyway, just comrades. Now, if there's nothing else, then get to your stations!"

With that he turned his back on them and knelt to close Collins's eyes. The others hesitated for a moment, then silently melted into the darkness, some to retrieve the wagons, while the others joined Sióna on the watch. When he knew they were gone, Tadhg pulled the dagger from the dead man's chest and wiped the blood on his shirt, then stood to give it back to Dónal.

But seeing the round-eyed look of shock on his friend's face, he handed it to Padge instead. "Are you all right, Dónal?" he asked softly, taking him by the shoulders.

At the touch of Tadhg's hands, Dónal blinked as if waking from a dream. He'd watched the drama unfold among his friends as though in a trance, unmoving and unable to speak, locked in the grip of horror at what he had done. He'd thought it would be so easy, no different from the noses he'd broken and testicles he'd squashed during his days of clan warfare. But to hurt a man who'd dared you to do it was one thing; to *kill* a man who'd done *nothing* to you was something else entirely. Nor did Tadhg's argument that Collins was an agent of the Empire bear any weight with him. Sure, in the big picture it was true enough, but all he could think of in that moment was the little picture – Collins's wife and three young daughters. What was to become of them, and what did they care that the Republic would make them better off in the long run when they'd lost their provider? And then there were his own friends to consider, and what he'd done to them. Tadhg and Padge had been right that he should've told them what he meant to do up front. And why hadn't he, he wondered? Had he been afraid they'd see the truth in his eyes, that he wanted to kill the guard whether it was necessary or not, just to prove himself? He didn't know, for he couldn't remember how he'd felt then, in that other lifetime when he'd been innocent. Of only one thing was he certain now, that after this night, they'd never follow him into battle again.

And what would his father think?

"Are you all right?" Tadhg asked again, shaking him slightly. "Don't worry about the lads. It's just their first glimpse of war and what it's about and they need some getting used to it. But give them time and they'll come around. Sure, they'll see that once again you've stood up for them and taken the brunt of it upon yourself rather than ordering one of them to do it, and they'll appreciate you for sparing them."

But Tadhg's words of kindness merely disgusted him, for Dónal knew he'd done nothing worthy of anyone's appreciation.

"Sure, I'm fine," he said, brushing his friend's hands brusquely from his shoulders. Moving to Collins, he took his ring of keys and handed them to Tadhg. "Here. You unlock the door and start opening the kegs. Padge, you go see what's taking them so long with the wagons."

Without waiting for replies, he grasped Collins by the jacket and dragged his body to one side. Then he moved the fire a safe distance away, before going inside to help Tadhg with the kegs. In a few minutes, Níall brought the first wagon to the door, and Padge brought in the bundle of empty ore bags from its hold.

They worked as swiftly as they could in the dim light, transferring the powder from the kegs to the bags so that it would look like a load of copper ore to the casual observer. When the wagon was loaded, Níall drove it away toward Guala, and Pat pulled up with the second, to be soon followed by Art with the third. When they'd finished loading the powder, they stacked the empty kegs around the two they'd left full and dumped Collins' body onto the pile, the idea being to make it look as though he'd triggered an accidental explosion with his fire, and to cover up the evidence of his murder in the process. Then Padge set the fuse and stretched it out the door.

"You go on now," Dónal said when all was ready, "and tell Sióna to go home. I'll catch up with you on the road."

"Be careful!" Tadhg hissed as they rolled away.

"It's a bit late for that," Dónal muttered under his breath. Then he settled in to give them a head start. When he thought he'd waited long enough, he lit the fuse and leapt onto his horse, though he waited, just to be sure it wouldn't go out.

He wasn't far up the Guala road when a blinding flash and thunderous explosion ripped the fabric of the night, making him duck his head reflexively even though he was far enough away to be out of danger. Behind him he knew that doors would be opening and people stumbling into the night, and he spurred his horse to greater speed, wanting to be well away from them. But in his haste to get away, he almost ran into the back of the last wagon, avoiding it in the darkness only from Tadhg's warning.

"Is everything all right?" Dónal asked as he pulled up alongside.

"It couldn't be better if we paid for it!" Tadhg replied and, though he couldn't see him, Dónal knew he was grinning in the darkness. "I suppose they're all awake below and wondering what happened. I wish I could see the look on Seán Óg's face right about now!"

Yet the only faces Dónal could picture in that moment were those of Mary Collins and her three young children. He spurred his horse and rode ahead, stopping only when he came to the far side of Guala where the road plunged steeply down. Somewhere in the valley below lurked the ghosts that had driven him to this ghastly juncture, and he shook his fist in the darkness, cursing them for their callous indifference.

But then the wagons were upon him again and he had to concentrate on getting them safely down, no mean feat on a such pitch-black night. Yet all went smoothly and soon they were turning off the main road at the entrance to Dunboy, rolling on past the gates toward Pulleen Harbor. Though it was so dark that they could barely see ten feet in front of themselves, they hurried along at a quick pace, anxious to get the job done and rid themselves of their cargo. Still, it seemed an eternity before a voice suddenly called in English for them to halt.

As he waited in the darkness, Dónal could hear the lapping of waves on rocks and knew they were near the little harbor, though he could see nothing of it nor any sign of a ship. Then he heard footsteps and saw a faint light approaching, wincing at the sudden brightness as the man uncovered a corner of his lantern.

"I'll lead you in from here," he said in English, re-covering the lantern and taking Dónal's horse by the bridle. "Another hundred yards and you'd have run right into the ship at the pace you were going!"

As the man tugged at his horse and other men appeared from the shadows and surrounded the wagons, an alarm bell went off in Dónal's head. 'We've walked into a trap!' he thought, being sure from the man's accent that he was English rather than Irish. Yet he had no choice but to go along, for in the darkness he couldn't see if the men were armed or even where his own men were.

But then the man released the bridle and uncovered his lantern enough for Dónal to see that a small ship lay just ahead, its gangway leading down from a rock shelf on which a number of empty wine casks stood. "All right, lads," he said. "Let's get this stuff aboard and be quick about it!"

"Let's give them a hand!" Dónal said to his men, relieved that he wasn't being ambushed after all.

The sailors worked quickly and efficiently and in no time at all, it seemed, had the bags of powder in the casks and the casks stowed safely in the little ship's hold. They'd obviously loaded cargo in the dark before, and Dónal remembered the rumors he'd heard of smugglers who still operated from the secluded inlets of Béara. Though they weren't smuggling Wild Geese out to France anymore, if James Stephens had his way they'd soon enough be smuggling them in from America. As he looked to the west, the moon peeped through a hole in the clouds and silhouetted the little ship against the immense ocean beyond.

'I'm glad I'm not sailing out in that little thing tonight,' he thought, and turned for his horse. He was ready for it to be over.

Just then, the man with the lantern stepped to his side. "The captain wants a word with you," he said. "If you'll come with me, please."

But Dónal was having none of it, remembering how young Red Hugh O'Donnell had spent five years imprisoned in Dublin Castle after being kidnapped aboard just such an English ship. "If the captain wants a word with me, then let him come ashore."

"He thought you'd say as much," the man replied, holding out his hand, "so he told me to give you this."

Dónal took the small lump from the man's hand and felt at it curiously. Like a memory that lay just beyond recall, it was vaguely familiar, having the texture of quartz though not heavy enough to actually be stone. Then on an impulse, he licked it, and finding it sweet he understood.

"All right, I'll go aboard with you." Turning to Tadhg, he said, "Wait here. I'll be right back."

The man led him astern to where another man stood by the rail. "He's here, Captain."

"Thank you, Mr. Parker," the man replied. "Leave us, if you please."

"Aye, Captain."

As Dónal gazed at the silhouette by the rail, a thousand questions chased each other through his mind. Yet all that came from his mouth was one simple English word.

"Why?"

"*Why*, you ask?" Riobárd Puxley said, turning to face him. "I was hoping you would already know."

"No, I don't."

"Well, it's really quite simple. You see, I was born and raised in Ireland, and I've lived here all my life. My father's mother was Irish, a servant girl in my grandfather's household, and from her I have the native Gaelic blood in my veins. I also have her blue Irish eyes and black Irish hair, her pale Irish skin and even her quick Irish temper. I speak the Irish language and call myself by an Irish name. In short, Dónal, Ireland is my home and I consider myself an Irishman. Yet, my Irish countrymen don't see me as such. To them I'm an Englishman, or even worse, *Anglo-Irish*, a foreigner with no legitimate roots here, a colonist who lives among them as a stranger. So that's why I'm doing my part to free Ireland, so that my countrymen will accept me as one of their own. Now do you understand?"

Dónal didn't respond immediately, just looked Puxley hard in the eyes. "See that you take good care of that powder, Mr. Puxley," he said finally. "I killed a man to get it, an Irishman, one that I've known all my life. I stuck a dagger in his heart and watched him fade away, and though his voice was gone his eyes still spoke to me, askin', *Why, Dónal, why?* Do you love Ireland that much, Mr. Puxley, enough to kill for Her?"

"Dónal, I love Ireland enough to die for Her!"

Dónal extended his hand in acceptance then; a man couldn't say more than that. "*Slán abhaile, a Riobárd,*" he said, ("Safe home.")

"*Go raibh míle maith agaibh, a Dhónail,*" Puxley replied, his smile

319

flashing in the moonlight, ("A thousand thanks.")

With nothing more then, Dónal turned and left the ship.

"Who were you talking to down there?" Tadhg asked.

"A friend," Dónal replied, and slipped the candy into his mouth.

❦

As always, it was more like a memory than a dream. He was a little boy again, rising over the coffin to view the horror inside. Yet it wasn't the young girl lying there at all, but Brendan Collins, his dead eyes open and screaming the question, Why? *He looked away to escape those horrible, accusing eyes, but there was the girl before him, hanging from a cross.*

"What have you done?" *she asked, making his blood run cold.* "What have you done?"

❦

He woke with a start and sat up in bed.

"Are you all right, Dónal?" he heard Sióna ask from her chair by the fire.

She'd not been home when he'd arrived earlier in the evening, and he'd been too exhausted to go out and look for her, having spent the day standing watch while the others slept in a thicket. And he'd been deeply disappointed by her absence, needing desperately for her to hold him just then, to tell him it would be all right.

He rose from the bed and went naked to the fire, standing close to let the flames cleanse him of sin.

"Sure, I'm grand," he lied, not looking at her. "And yourself?"

"Grand, sure," she replied, and he knew she was lying, too. "I've boiled you a supper if you want it, and there's tea in the kettle."

"No, I don't want anything to eat," he sighed, still not daring to look at her. "All I want just now is to know if you still love me."

"Yes," she replied softly, "I love you still."

He was away from the fire then and kneeling before her, his head in her lap and his arms wrapped tightly about her. She stroked his hair as he sobbed out his grief, tears falling from her own eyes.

"Of course, I love you, Dónal. How could I not love you when you're all that's ever made me happy? I just wish you could learn to love yourself."

chapter 16

Eskinanaun
3 June, 1861

THE GRASS WAS COOL IN FRONT of the cottage, and Dónal draped his
arms lazily across his eyes to shield them from the bright morning sun.
The day was shaping up to be a fine one, with hardly a cloud in the
sky and just the faintest breeze coming in from the sea. The hollow
was flush with the color of wildflowers and alive with the music of
songbirds, even the soft bleating of the sheep blending harmoniously
into the sensual feast set forth by Nature.

Yet for all the beauty surrounding him, Dónal was aware of only the
Darkness within, of the emptiness in his soul and the pounding in his
head from having drunk himself to sleep yet again. But though he was
suffering from it now, still it was better than waking in the middle of
the night, drenched in sweat from the dreams that tormented him, his
heart pounding with fear of the ghosts that haunted him.

He'd slept late this morning, and as usual Sióna was nowhere to be
found when he arose, having learned by bitter experience to give him
a wide berth in the morning. Often now, they didn't speak their first
words of the day till he came home in the evening, and then she usually went to bed early so she wouldn't have to watch him wallow in the
drink and his own self-pity. Indeed, they'd pared their relationship
down to the bare essentials, a word, a nod, a gesture, the kind of reserved
civility that one extends to strangers. And though the separation tore

her heart out, she'd not spoken a word of it to him, stubbornly telling herself that he'd exorcise his demons if she just gave him time and space, and then things would get back to normal. Ignore it and it'll go away, was her watchword. Yet just the opposite had happened, and the walls between them grew higher with each passing day.

Nor had Dónal made any effort to tear them down, being too pre-occupied with introspection to care. He'd failed so miserably in his own estimation of himself, failed in his calling and failed to fulfill his destiny. He was no leader of men, he realized now, and he was certainly no killer, and how could he expect to fight for Ireland's freedom if he couldn't bring himself to smite Her foes? Not that it really mattered anymore, considering he no longer had any men to lead. Within a few weeks after the raid, Art and Dan and Pat had signed on with a merchant ship out of Bantry and sailed for the Orient, while Níall and Liam had emigrated to America. It was just as well, too, Tadhg had reassured him, for he was sure it would only be a matter of time before one of them spoke of their deed in the confessional, and surely old Father Nolan would pass it along to the peelers. Better to be well rid of them if they didn't have the stomach for it, he said. There were other men and better who'd be pleased to take their places. Yet his words rang hollow in Dónal's ears. He knew he'd never lead men into battle again, for he himself didn't have the stomach for it, and without the struggle for freedom, what purpose was there in life?

But Dónal wasn't thinking of any of that as he lay in the bright sunshine. He was thinking of the time when his father had berated him for crying over a skinned knee and Eóghan had cradled him in his arms and told him it would be all right. How he wished Eóghan were here now to hold him, and to tell him everything would be all right. But he wasn't and there was no going back. His life was what it was and he would just have to live with it.

He sighed and sat up, squinting against the bitter brightness of the sun. Maybe a bit of tea and something to eat would make him feel better. At least it would ease the pain in his head. He got up and went into the cottage, intent upon making himself a breakfast. But as he rummaged through the cupboard, his eyes fell on his pipes standing in the corner. The case was dusty he noticed, and a spider web ran between it and the wall. How long it had been since he played them he couldn't remember, months at the least and surely not since that dreadful night of the raid. While he didn't feel like playing them now, either, he couldn't take his eyes off them, as a spark in his memory suddenly took him back to that glorious day when he'd first played the lament for his brother and met Sióna at Pointnadishert. It seemed like another lifetime now, for that day had been the beginning of the best time of his life, the only time in which he'd been truly happy and at peace with himself and the world. But that time was dead and buried, and its like would be no more. Why had he not left well enough alone, he wondered? Why had he wanted more?

He put down the kettle and picked up his pipes, headed back outside and sat down on a stone at the edge of the hollow. He didn't even think about what to play, his fingers just knew. He closed his eyes and let his consciousness flow into the music, feeling his soul float with it through the hollow and echo off the cliffs. It was the lament for his brother, of course, though it wasn't for Eóghan that he played it now. *Ochón*, the pipes keened. *Óchon for Dónal and his life that is no more, ochón.* Over and over he played it, till the melody was lost amid the echoes and the hollow was filled with the music of the Otherworld, ethereal and beautiful and sad. *Óchon, óchon, óchon.*

When he could play no more, he set his pipes aside and dried his eyes on his sleeve. Then he heard Sióna's voice close behind him and it startled him, just as it had on that first day they'd met.

"I heard you playing and came to listen. How could I help myself when it casts such a spell over me?" Gently, tentatively she laid her hand on his shoulder. "Will you not let it go, Dónal, before it destroys you and me with you? Your life isn't over, you know, it's just going to be different than you thought it would be. You can still serve Ireland without being a soldier."

Dónal sighed and shook his head. "I don't know if I can, Sióna, I just don't know," he said, his voice choked and cracking. "It hurts so much that I don't know if I'll ever be free of the pain. Maybe it would be better if you just forgot about me and moved on. I don't want to drag you down with me."

"I can't forget about you, Dónal, nor can I move on without you. You're part of me now and I can't leave you behind any more than I could my arms and legs. But I can move on with you, and I can help you heal yourself, if you'll only let me. Won't you please let me, Dónal? Won't you please?"

"I don't know, Síona. It's so terrible this thing I've done. I don't know if I can just put it behind me and move on."

"But won't you at least try? You have so much to lose if you don't."

"What, Síona, what do I have left to lose?"

"Why, you have yourself to lose, Dónal, and the rest of your life. Yes, you've done something terrible, but there's so much good in you, and as long as you're alive, you can share that goodness with the world. All you have to do is put the past behind you and dedicate yourself to the future. I know you can do it, and I'll help you, if only you'll let me.

"Look at me, Dónal," she said, raising his chin with her fingers. "You are a good man, and I believe in you, and I will always, *always* love you, no matter what."

As he looked at her then, she smiled, and the light of it drove the darkness from his eyes. For the first time in days, he smiled himself. He said nothing, just stood and pulled her to him, and hugged her as though he would never let go.

"Will you make love with me, Síona? I need to feel you close to me."

"Of course I will, my love," she replied, and he could hear the smile in her voice. "I've missed you so. But not just now though. Riobárd is coming up the boreen."

Without putting her down, Dónal turned and looked down the hill, and waved in reply to Puxley. "I'll have to speak to him about his timing," he said, though in his heart he was actually glad of the visit. He'd not seen him since the night of the raid, for Puxley had sailed for America soon thereafter and only recently returned.

But then the smile vanished as the thought of America reminded him of James Stephens and the Brotherhood. 'It's starting!' he thought with sudden anxiety. 'He brought men from America and came to give me my marching orders!' He set Sióna down then and went to meet Puxley.

"God be with you, Dónal!" the man said as he dismounted. "And with you, Sióna."

"God and Mary be with you, Riobárd," Dónal replied. "What brings you out so far of a Sunday morning? It must be important to keep you from your habitual pew."

"It is indeed, Dónal, but not so much so that it can't wait till we're all settled by the fire." Though Puxley smiled, Dónal noticed a guarded look in his eyes.

"Is it about the Brotherhood?" he asked, dreading the answer but desperate to know. And what would Puxley say when he told him he was done with it?

"No, it isn't, though I wish it was. I must say I'm rather discouraged with the way things have gone. I'd expected to be bringing men and arms from America by now, but there's been little progress on that front, and after my visit there I can see why. The *Fenian* Brotherhood, as they call it on that side of the water, is more of a Sunday social club than a revolutionary army. Its leaders all silver-tongued orators and quick with the handshake and a toast to the Ould Sod, but slow to get anything done. What's more, Meagher, O'Gorman, Mitchel and many others of '48 have refused to join, with some of them even campaigning against us. I know it has frustrated James to no end since he was counting on their support, especially as fund-raisers. But that story can wait, Dónal. What I have to tell you now is a different matter, though it touches on your involvement with the Brotherhood. But let's go inside and sit down, shall we? It might take a while."

"Sure, Riobárd," Dónal replied with a sudden smile, relieved that the Brotherhood wasn't calling just yet. "Come inside and make yourself at home. Do you have a hunger on you? We'll boil you a breakfast if you want."

While Sióna busied herself with the kettle, Dónal settled in a chair across from Puxley and waited for him to begin. But the man didn't speak or even return his gaze, just stared at the fire and drummed his fingers nervously on his leg as he waited for Sióna to finish and take her seat. Dónal had never seen him so ill at ease and it made him nervous again.

"What is it, Riobárd?" he asked when he could take the suspense no longer.

At that, Puxley sighed and pulled an envelope from inside his jacket. "I have a letter for you, Dónal. I brought it back from America, from New York City to be exact. It's sealed and I haven't read it, of course, though the author told me what it says."

He paused then and scowled at the envelope as though it concealed something unpleasant, and Dónal held his breath in expectation. "This letter is from your brother, Dónal," he said finally, his voice as heavy as stone. "It's from Eóghan."

At first the words didn't register, so unexpected and out of context were they, and Dónal just stared blankly at Puxley. But then the meaning hit him, and he blinked his eyes in shock. He could feel Sióna beside him, silently imploring him to look at her. But he had eyes for only Puxley.

"Did you just say what I think you did?" he asked finally, "that the letter is from Eóghan?"

"Yes, you heard correctly."

Dónal leaned forward and glared at Puxley. "Is this your idea of a joke, Riobárd? Eóghan's been dead for thirteen years now! Or are you telling me that he wrote that letter before he died and that you're just now giving it to me?"

"The answer to both questions is no, Dónal. Eóghan is alive and living in New York, where he's been since 1849. I know it's true because I've seen him there on more than one occasion, the latest being on my recent trip when he gave me this letter. You see, I know Eóghan quite well, better than you do at this point. He and I spent a great deal of time together before he went away to university. Indeed, he was like a son to me, and I made it my business to further his interests whenever

I could. I'm the one who got him into Trinity, you know, and it was I who introduced him into Dublin society and gave him a monthly stipend so that he could mingle freely. And I'm afraid it was also I who introduced him to liberal politics and progressive thought, thinking as I did that he had the potential to be a dynamic force for change in our country. He was so intelligent and principled, possessed of genuine sincerity and guileless charm, and all of it packaged in the guise of Adonis. But he was also incredibly naïve and believed too strongly in the essential goodness of his fellow man, which, of course, was his Achilles heel. It showed in the single-minded zeal with which he plunged into the Young Ireland rising, even though I warned him that he was courting disaster. 'Be patient,' I told him. 'Ireland doesn't need you to die for Her but to *live* for Her.' But he wouldn't listen to me any more than he would your father. It was his destiny to fight for Ireland's freedom, he told me, and no man could deny his destiny. Of course, I tried to explain to him that a man constructs his own destiny from the choices he makes, but it was no use. His mind was made up and there was no changing it. Later, when I heard he was dead, I felt as though a part of me had died with him, so much did I cherish him. So imagine my joy when I heard he was alive."

"Then why didn't you tell me so that I could share in it?" Dónal interjected angrily. "All these years I've suffered from missing him, and I could've been with him all along! Why didn't you tell me, Riobárd? Why did you pretend to be my friend and yet withhold from me the one thing I wanted more than anything in the world? *Why?*"

"I didn't pretend anything, Dónal. I *am* your friend, and Eóghan's, too. It wasn't *my* choice to keep it from you, but his."

Dónal gaped in disbelief then, choking back the lump in his throat. "But why would he do that?"

"I believe his reasons are explained in here," Puxley replied, dropping the letter into Dónal's lap. "Why don't you read it and let Eóghan tell you in his own words."

But Dónal just stared at the letter, unable to conceive that it had rested in Eóghan's hands, that he'd addressed it and sealed it and sent it to him. How could this be happening? he wondered. How could Eóghan have been alive all this time and yet he was only just learning of it? He picked up the letter and turned it over in his hands, gingerly, as though it would bite him if he weren't careful. He read the address and saw his own name written there, along with Eóghan's as the sender. Slowly he tore it open and pulled out the sheets of paper. Among them was a daguerreotype of a man in military dress, his right hand tucked between the buttons of his jacket while his left rested on the hilt of his sheathed saber. It was Eóghan, of course, and Dónal stared at him as if in a dream, unable to believe it was actually his face looking back at him. Other than the uniform, he looked much the same as the last time he'd seen him, the passing years seeming hardly to have touched him. Turning it over, he found inscribed in English on its back: *First Lieutenant Eóghan O'Sullivan Béara, 69th Regiment, New York State Militia.*

Still in a daze, Dónal began to read the letter:

Dillon, O'Gorman & O'Sullivan
Attorneys at Law
39 William Street
New York, New York   5 May, 1861

My dearest brother Dónal:

Please accept my sincerest apology for the great shock this letter is certain to have caused. From our mutual friend, Riobárd, I know you have thought me dead these past thirteen years, and I ask your forgiveness for letting you believe it. I had good reasons for doing so and will explain them in due course. But to take things in their proper order, let me first tell you of my adventures in '48 and how I came to be in America.

As to my purported demise, suffice it to say that I was not inside the public house when the attack began, but rather in the privy out back. After making good my escape in the smoke and confusion, I joined my friend and commander, Richard O'Gorman, in a perilous trek to refuge in the County Clare. We endured many hardships along the way, walking by night and hiding by day, foraging for food, and even donning women's clothing by way of disguise. And though I must admit these privations pale in comparison with those experienced by Dónal Cam on his epic march to Leitrim, still it was a harrowing experience that I shan't soon forget. After some weeks hiding in Clare, we made good our escape on a ship bound for Istanbul, where we found ourselves unhappily stranded for several months. As a result, we did not finally arrive in New York until mid-1849, and were then still some weeks in getting ourselves situated. So by the time I felt secure enough to correspond with Riobárd, Da had passed away and you were living with the Aherns.

Naturally, Dónal, my first impulse was to send for you immediately to join me in New York. Yet Riobárd assured me you were safe and secure and well cared for, and that he would keep a watchful eye on you. Also, he informed me that before Da died, he took you to Dunboy and made you The O'Sullivan Béara, and it was that more than anything that made me hesitate to disclose my whereabouts. You see, Dónal, I have always felt it imperative that our family line remain unbroken in Béara so that we may reclaim our patrimony when Ireland is again free and independent. Since I knew it would be many years before I could return, if indeed ever, I decided to set aside my own claim and recognize you as the legitimate chieftain. (Indeed, I even reduced it to writing at the time and have enclosed a witnessed copy of the document for your benefit.) For that reason, I felt it best that you grow up in Ireland among the people of Béara and decided to wait until your twenty-first birthday to contact you, fearing that to do so sooner might tempt you to leave Béara and join me in America.

But alas, Dónal, the road to Hell is paved with even the best of intentions, and now events beyond my control have skewed my plans and forced me to accelerate my timetable. For as you now understand, Riobárd has sent me regular reports on your status and progress, and I must say I am most distressed to hear of your recent involvement with that fellow from Kilkenny, especially since he so callously endangered your life. While I concede that Riobárd disagrees with me, I have met the man myself and did not find him in the least bit persuasive. Nor, may I say, did my comrades among the exiles of '48, who include such men as Thomas Francis Meagher and John Mitchel, as well as my own law partners, the said O'Gorman and John Blake Dillon. In my opinion the man is a scoundrel of the first degree and is only using you to further his own vainglorious ends. While I approve of your devotion to your country and your courage to act on your convictions, I strongly disapprove of your association with this man and his cronies and urge you to desist immediately. And Dónal, lest you think I have grown complacent with the status quo in Ireland, let me say that throughout my long years of exile, I have never ceased to support the cause of Her liberation and have done everything in my power to further it.

In that regard, I have a proposition for you now which I think you might find appealing. As you may be aware, eleven of our Southern states have illegally seceded from our Union and moved to form their own nation, which, in their arrogance, they call the Confederate States of America. Naturally, this is not looked upon favorably by those of us in the North, and we intend to bring our wayward brethren back to the fold by any means necessary, including force of arms. Indeed, the United States

Government has raised an army for just that purpose, into which tens of thousands of Irish-Americans have already enrolled. Among them are the Irishmen of the 69th Regiment of the New York State Militia, for which Meagher and I have raised a company of Zouaves in New York City. Meagher himself is our captain, while I have the honor to have been elected first lieutenant. Colonel Michael Corcoran from the County Donegal is our regimental commander, and he hopes to unite the 69th with other Irish regiments and form an Irish Brigade such as those which formerly served in the armies of Catholic Europe. As for our motivations in joining this noble endeavor, they are, first, that we feel it our patriotic duty to our adopted homeland, and second, to gain valuable military experience which we may then employ in liberating our Motherland of Her ancient oppressor.

In that regard, Dónal, and having all things considered, I believe it to be in your best interest to leave Ireland now and join me in America, so that we sons of the Clan Dónal Cam may serve together in these momentous and historic undertakings, both in America and Ireland. I assure you the experience of serving in a real army will be far more meaningful than the amateurish blunderings of your present association. Riobárd will see to the details and expenses of your passage and of your lady friend if she will come. So please do not consider that a hindrance.

In closing, let me say that I eagerly anticipate our long-awaited reunion, and await your reply by return post.

Until then, I am your devoted brother,
Eóghan

When finished, Dónal frowned and cocked his head as if puzzled. It seemed an odd sort of thing for a long-lost brother to write, having neither warmth nor anything of Eóghan personally, being all terse and businesslike, like a letter a solicitor might write to a client. If anything, its tone was paternalistic, as though Eóghan still thought him the little boy he'd left by the roadside all those years ago. He picked up the daguerreotype and stared at it intently, hoping it would show him something of what lay in Eóghan's heart. But the picture painted no words. It was just a memory made visible, an instant frozen in time and space, yielding no more insight into the man's soul than the scribbled words on the sterile page. Indeed, for all the joy he should've felt in finding Eóghan alive, the letter just left him empty.

Dónal glanced at Puxley then, hoping that he might be of some help. But the man was gazing into the fire, though whether just lost in thought or studiously ignoring him, he couldn't tell. Then Sióna stirred and, glancing at her, he was startled to see the fear in her eyes as she stared at the daguerreotype, almost as if she saw the image of a recurring nightmare in it. Silently, she held out her hand and he passed it to her.

"What does the letter say, Dónal?" she asked, still staring intently at the image. "I want to hear his words while I look into his eyes."

Dónal hesitated a moment, as yet unsure of his own emotions. But seeing the look in her eyes, he picked up the letter and began to read aloud. When he'd finished, she didn't say anything or even look at him, just handed back the daguerreotype and turned to the fire. He looked at her questioningly for a moment, then turned back to Puxley.

"What do you think, Riobárd? Should I go?"

"That's for you to decide, I'd say," Puxley replied, still looking into the fire. "But if you'd have the benefit of my insight, I'm certainly willing to give it to you."

"I would."

"All right then. To begin with, it's obvious Eóghan doesn't think James Stephens the right man to lead the Brotherhood, and as your brother, he naturally doesn't want you to make the same mistake he did by following inept leadership. But by the same token, I don't think it's really that so much as Eóghan and his friends just don't like James as a man. Now I know him better than you do and, honestly, he can be hard to get round at times, especially for men like Eóghan and his friends who are accustomed to thinking of themselves as the torch-bearers of Irish republicanism. But the Brotherhood and James's leadership of it are established facts. So in the long run, if things work out as planned, Eóghan and his friends will have to find a way to work with him or be left out of the process, which I happen to know won't suit them either.

"As for myself, Dónal, I have nothing but the highest regard for James Stephens, and I know that without his energy, dedication and extraordinary talent for organizing, no revolutionary movement would exist in Ireland today. Nor do I believe he is just using you for his own ends. If I even suspected as much, I would never have brought you to his attention. And as for Eóghan's claim of valuable military experience to be gained from serving in the American Army, well, that's probably true enough, in and of itself. But you also have to consider that you could get killed in the process, which would be of no benefit to Ireland whatsoever. And even if this war produces a legion of trained soldiers, still our freedom won't be won by a mass invasion from America. Indeed, such an undertaking is patently impracticable, especially in light of what I've seen of the American Fenians. No, our freedom will be won from within by the people who are still here, so the planning and preparation for the rising have to be done in Ireland rather than in America.

"So for that reason, Dónal, I'd say that you'd be of greater service to Ireland by staying here rather than joining Eóghan in America. Indeed, your work here is extremely important to the movement, and because of your particular talents and skills, you can't be easily replaced. Remember that James handpicked you for your assignment and you're one of only a handful of men in the entire country, and by far the youngest, to have been so honored. And if that isn't enough for you, I would also remind you that you're a soldier under orders, and to leave your post without permission would be desertion. You swore an oath to the Republic, Dónal, and *death* is the only way out of it."

When Puxley finished speaking, Dónal nodded to indicate he'd heard, though he was no longer looking at him. He had eyes only for the daguerreotype in his hands, even the pages of the letter having fallen to the floor. Nor was it Puxley's words that echoed in his head, but Sióna's: *You can serve Ireland without being a soldier.*

"Yes, you're right," he thought aloud, and then smiled, his path to redemption suddenly being as clear to him as if God Himself had pointed the way. Sióna turned from the fire then, and though he could feel her eyes on him, he didn't want to look at her lest she see the truth.

"I'm sorry, Dónal, what did you say?" Puxley asked, being lost himself in thought.

"I said you're right, Riobárd," Dónal said, turning his smile on Puxley. "You're right, and that's why I have to go to America, so I can bring Eóghan home with me. The work here is what's important, and he could get himself killed for nothing over there. So I have to go, because only I can convince him of it."

"I'm not sure I understand you, Dónal," Puxley said with a frown. "Why do you think you can change his mind when he's obviously chosen otherwise?"

"Because I'm his brother," Dónal replied, in a tone that suggested it was enough.

"Yes, but why do you think you can convince him to come back? Don't you think he would've come home already if he really wanted to? The men of '48 were pardoned long ago, and even Smith O'Brien has returned from Australia, so the only thing keeping Eóghan in America has been the exercise of his own free will. True, he does feel a strong sense of duty toward the legacy of Dónal Cam and he does want your family to continue in Ireland, but he doesn't want to come back and do it himself, and that, Dónal, is his true reason for wanting you to stay here. It's all so self-serving, don't you see? Even his invitation to join him now is self-serving, because he's afraid Stephens will get you killed and then he'll be obliged to come back himself. So he wants you there with him so that he can watch after you and then send you back here when it's safe again.

"Now before you get angry with me, let me say again that I know him better than you do. He's not the same idealistic young man who set off to change the world thirteen years ago. Indeed, the world has changed him, very much so and not all of it for the better, I might add. He's been very successful in America, you see, and he's found the good life very much to his taste. Somewhere along the way, he lost the warmth and empathy that were the essence of his inherent decency and gave him such potential to better the lot of his fellow man. That potential he squandered in grubbing for the almighty dollar, and what he now calls service to his fellow man is helping his wealthy landlord clients victimize their poor tenants. Indeed, Dónal, I have to admit to being more than a little disappointed in him. But then the leaf doesn't fall far from the tree, as they say, and maybe there was just too much of his father in him, after all."

Under other circumstances, Puxley's criticism of Eóghan might have sent Dónal into a rage. Yet just now, it didn't seem to matter; he'd made up his mind and nothing would change it.

"Which is exactly why I should go, Riobárd, to save Eóghan from himself and America before it's too late!"

"But don't you see, Dónal, it's already too late? For better or for worse, Eóghan's an American now, and has no more intention of returning to Ireland than of flying to the moon."

Dónal's smile faded then, and his eyes went stone hard. "That's your opinion, Riobárd, and though I respect you, I'll reserve my judgment till I see him myself, and the sooner the better. So when can you book us a passage?"

"No, Dónal, I'll not go with you!" Sióna interjected, without turning to face him. "I'll not leave my home. It's the only place I've ever been happy, and I'll not leave it for the sake of any man, not even you. I told you in our beginning that you'd leave me someday, and that I wanted you to be free to do so when the time came. So go to your brother now. I know that's what you want, and for some reason I can't explain, it seems to me your true destiny, anyway. If you want to come home, I'll be here to welcome you. No matter how long you're away or what the world has done to you, I'll always be here to welcome you home."

Dónal's first inclination was to argue with her, but seeing her shoulders square and her chin high, he knew she'd made up her mind.

"There's no *if* about it, Sióna. This is the only place I've ever been happy, too, and it's because of you. So I will come home to you, no matter whether Eóghan comes or not. But I have to try, Sióna, and I think you know why."

She faced him then, looking at him as if he were already a memory. "Sure, I know why, Dónal, maybe better than you do. But don't make promises you may not be able to keep. You can't know what the future will bring. And Dónal, if he'd sent for you sooner, you and I would never have met."

Though he wanted to challenge her, Dónal had nothing to say, and anyway, she'd already turned away.

"All right then," he said, turning back to Puxley. "When can you book me a passage?"

"Your mind is made up, then?" Puxley asked.

"It is."

Puxley took a deep breath and sighed. "Ships sail from Queenstown to New York all the time, so it's more a matter of when you want to go than when I can book it."

"Then I want leave here on the 17th."

Puxley actually smiled at that. "There is a certain symmetry in it, I suppose. All right. Shall I take you to Queenstown on the *Copper John*?"

"No, I want to ride. I've never seen any of the country beyond Castletownbere, and this seems like a good opportunity. I'll take one of our old horses and sell it in Queenstown."

"As you wish. I'm acquainted with a horse trader there and I'll give you a letter of introduction. As for your passage, I'll book you no earlier than Saturday the 23rd, which should give you ample time for sightseeing along the way."

Puxley paused then and leaned forward in his chair. "What should I say to James? He's not going to be very pleased about this, you know."

"Tell him the truth," Dónal replied with a black grin. "Tell him I chose clan over country."

Puxley grunted in amusement and narrowed his eyes. "Sure, 'tis moighty Oirish of ye, Paddy!" he said in his best imitation a country brogue. Then he shook his head and continued quietly in Irish. "You're making a mistake, you know, as big a one as Eóghan made when he left. Your place is here, with the Brotherhood and with Sióna. Is there nothing I can say to make you change your mind?"

"No, Riobárd, there's nothing. But you've been a good friend to me over the years, and though I didn't always appreciate it before, I want you to know I do now."

"It's nice of you to say so," Puxley said, rising from his chair, "but I'd rather you listen to me than appreciate me. Ah, well. Since it appears there's nothing more for me to do here, I'll take my leave of you. Good-bye, Sióna. If you need anything, let me know."

"Thank you, Riobárd, I will," she replied, but didn't rise to see him out or even turn from the fire.

"I'll walk you out." Outside, Dónal said, "Keep an eye on her, will you?"

"Of course. It's my job, don't you know." He mounted his horse and bent down to shake hands. "Good-bye, Dónal. May you find what you seek beyond the waves."

"How did you know about that?" Dónal asked, mildly perplexed that a Puxley should know such an intimate detail of his family history.

"You said it yourself once," Puxley replied, a bit of mischief dancing in his eyes, "at your father's funeral, if you recall. But I first learned of it by reading the book."

"The *book*? But how did you come to have it?"

"Eóghan brought it to me, of course. He said it was my right as a clansman."

"I don't understand, Riobárd. A clansman of whom?"

"Of Eóghan, of course," Puxley replied, smiling broadly. "And of you. I told you my grandmother was an Irish girl serving in my grandfather's household at Dunboy. But what I didn't tell you, Dónal, and apparently no one else has either, is that she was your grandfather's *sister*."

For the second time that day, Dónal felt himself go numb with shock. But before he could recover, Puxley tipped his hat, and said, "Safe home to you, my Chieftain." Then he turned and rode away.

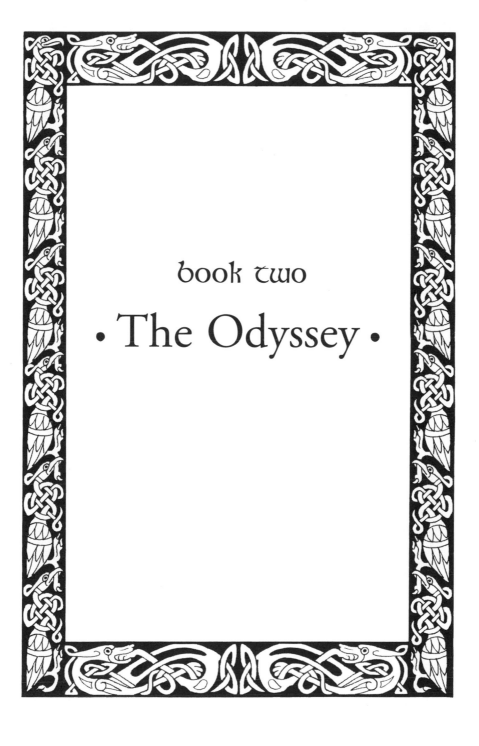

book two

• The Odyssey •

part five

• The Traveler •

chapter 17

Eskinanaun
17 June, 1861

SITTING ON THE EDGE OF THE BED, Dónal blinked his eyes against
the light and struggled to clear his drink-clouded head. The day had
come on him earlier than he would've liked, no surprise considering
he hadn't gone to bed till dawn. Tadhg and Padge were the culprits, of
course, having come at sundown to give him a sendoff, and then kept
him at it till well into the short hours. How many jugs of poteen
they'd gone through, he couldn't remember, though it was at least
three. Indeed, the two of them were already drunk when they rode up
the boreen, passing a jug between them and belting out a bawdy song.

Padge had greeted Dónal loudly when he came out to meet them,
but Tadhg said nothing for a long moment, just looked at him with a
broad grin on his face and the familiar mischief dancing in his eyes.
Then he thrust the jug into Dónal's hands, saying only one word,
"Drink!"

Dónal replied with a grin of his own and took a long drink, the
burn of it making him shiver and grunt. "The stuff just never gets any
better, does it?"

"Sure, but it never gets any worse either," Tadhg replied, and the
evening went downhill from there.

Sióna joined them on the lawn, and they lit a fire and sat around it
laughing and drinking and singing until the night sky was thick with

345

stars and the moon shining bright. After a while Sióna slipped into the cottage, and Tadhg hooted at her, saying, "What are you doing sneaking off to bed? You'll not get any sleep with us here anyway, and I've no intention of leaving!"

But she came back with Dónal's pipes in hand. "That may be true enough for you, Tadhg Ahern! But then we all know that when God passed out boorishness, you grabbed yourself two handfuls."

"Ouch!" Padge said, feigning a pained expression. "That was a good one!"

"Quiet you," Tadhg said, "or you'll find out what a good one feels like!"

But Sióna just ignored them. "Play for me, Dónal. I want to dance."

Dónal obliged and Tadhg danced with her, whirling her about the lawn while Padge capered about them in his own drunken frenzy. And, as always, Con was there, barking and nipping at their heels, as if trying to herd them back into the corral of sanity.

As he watched their shadows dancing over the whitewashed cottage and listened to the echoes in the hollow, Dónal had the eeriest feeling that the music had worked its ancient magic and summoned the Otherworld to join in their revelry. But then it struck him that to the English, they *were* the Otherworld, sharing Ireland with them, surely, yet separated by race, language, religion and culture, a people as mysterious and exotic as the fairies.

'We're not of their world,' he thought. 'We're the Irish, conceived of the stone and born of the green, washed up by the sea and drowned in our love of the land, eternal as the stars and fleeting as the moment, wise and simple, grand and pitiful, majestic and mean, bold and craven, reveling in melancholy, the fiercest tempest in the tiniest teapot. Yet of all the thick Irishmen in the world, I'm surely the thickest, for here I'm off to New York to drag a happy exile back to a place he was willing to go to war to get away from! For surely if God was to ever bugger the Earth, Béara would be on the business end of it!'

Maybe it was the drink tickling his reason then, but the thought struck him as enormously funny, so much that he began to laugh out loud, doubling over in mirth when Tadhg gave him the old "are you daft?" look.

"You little runt," Tadhg demanded, "what's so goddamned funny?"

"You are!" Dónal answered between bouts of laughter. "I am! We all are! We're all just a bunch of clowns that God set here on this suffering little island for no other purpose than His own good humor! And what's so funny is that we don't even get that the joke is on us!"

But Tadhg just shook his head in bewilderment. "God help him, but he's gone round the bend for good this time!" he said, spinning his finger around his ear.

"Yes, and who did I find waiting there for me but yourself, Tadhg Ahern! We're each just as daft as the other, don't you see? All of us! So daft that after seven centuries of trying to dig our way out of the hole, we've only managed to make it deeper! So that's the reason I'm leaving, so I can bring my brother back to lead us out of it. I thought I could do it, and that was the joke on me. I'm not the Messiah, after all."

"Nobody ever thought you were, Dónal, except your father, and that was just his own broken dreams talking. Anyway, it won't be one person who'll deliver us, but all of us pulling together. Only we ourselves can dig us out of this hole, and each person will have to do his part, including you!"

"That's right! And my part is to bring Eóghan back to lead us. *That* is how I can serve Ireland."

"Perhaps, assuming he's everything you think he is, and that he'll come back with you in the first place. But none of that really matters to me, Dónal. Just that he's your brother and you haven't seen him in thirteen years is reason enough for me. I'd do the same if it was my brother. Hell, I'd even do it if it was *you!*"

Then Tadhg pulled Dónal to his feet and embraced him so fiercely that he took his breath away. "But just remember there's people here who love you," he said with a crack in his voice, "so you come back to us, Dónal, just as soon as ever you're able!"

"See?" Dónal murmured into his friend's ear. "I told you you were daft."

The eastern sky was pale with the dawn by the time Tadhg and Padge drove away. Of course, their coming had ruined Dónal's plan of spending the evening alone with Sióna. But then she hadn't seemed to mind, joining in the revelry and holding up her end with the drink. Maybe she'd even preferred it that way, he thought as he sat on the bed, to drown herself in drink and merriment so she could put off the pain of parting for a while. For though she'd put a brave face on it, he sensed her inner torment, hearing it in her silence and feeling it in her distance, and seeing it in her look that seemed to both plead and accuse. Yet while he saw her pain, he couldn't help but be annoyed that she didn't believe in him, that she didn't support him in his quest to redeem himself. Why couldn't she just trust him to return as he said he would, and what made her so sure he wouldn't come back? But then he remembered how it had been when Eóghan left, how he'd known without knowing that he wouldn't come back. But that was different, he told himself. Whereas Eóghan was going off to war, he was only going on a journey, a there-and-back-again that would keep him away for only a matter of months, three or four at the most. But he hadn't tried to explain it to her, nor had she to him, so the walls between them grew higher even as their time together grew shorter.

'Ah, well,' he thought. 'There's nothing to be done about it now except to prove her wrong by coming back!'

Even as he thought it, Sióna spoke to him from the end of the house. "I've your tea and breakfast ready, if you want it," she said and, though he knew she was trying to be casual about it, he could hear the strain in her voice.

"I don't know if I can eat anything just now, but the tea sounds grand," he replied, getting up and going to the hearth. "I'll take the breakfast with me and eat it on the road. It must be at least noon by the sun, and I'd meant to leave early."

She turned to him then with a cup of tea in her hands. "Here, drink this. It'll make you feel better."

But Dónal's anger flashed when he saw the look on her face, the one that both accused and pleaded. "Goddamn it, Sióna, stop looking at me like that! I told you I would come back, and I *will!*"

But her expression didn't change. "You can't know that, Dónal. You can't know what the future will bring till it's right there, staring you in the face. What if you get to America and change your mind? Or what if something happens to you and you can't come back even if you want to? What if you have an accident? What if your ship sinks? What if you get caught in the war and get killed? What then, Dónal?"

"Oh, for Christ's sake, Síona, I can't help things that are beyond my control!"

"Yes, you can, Dónal, you can help them by not going! If you want Eóghan to come back here, then write him a letter just like he did to you. He'll come if he wants. But I think Riobárd is right. Eóghan is happy in America, and happy for you to carry your father's cross so that he doesn't have to. Can't you see that?"

"No, I don't see that and neither do you! You don't even know the man!"

"*Neither do you!*" Síona shouted back, her face within an inch of his.

Dónal was silent then, having to admit the possibility of her being right. He closed his eyes and tried to picture Eóghan as he'd seen him last, but all he could see was the image in the daguerreotype, the man in uniform. Did he indeed know that man? He couldn't be sure. Yet neither could he change his mind about going to him. Something inside just wouldn't let him, and whether it was devotion to clan or country or just stubbornness, he couldn't tell.

"Síona, listen to me, please," he said at last. "A letter won't work, and don't ask me why, I just know it won't. I have to go in person. It's the only way I can convince him that his place is here. And only if I bring him back with me, or at least try my best to, can I forgive myself for killing Brendan Collins."

Síona sighed and stared at him before answering. "You're wrong if you think that, Dónal, as wrong as snow in August. The only way you can forgive yourself is to stay here and make Brendan's death mean something. You started down this road with the Brotherhood, and though I was against it and what you did, you have to stick with it and see it through! You swore an oath to the Republic, as you're so fond of saying, and only by redeeming your oath to bring it about can you redeem yourself!"

Now Dónal was on the horns of a dilemma, for he could see the logic in her argument and that she might be right again. Yet still he couldn't change his mind, or wouldn't. For better or for worse, he was going to answer Eóghan's call.

"I can't not go, Sióna," he said, trying not to plead. "I can't help it. I *have* to see him."

Sióna sighed again, looking at him almost with pity in her eyes. "No, I suppose not, any more than I could help trying to stop you. You love living in the past and its hold is too strong to deny. It's calling you to your brother's side, and you'll deny all else to follow it, your home, your love, your duty, even what you thought to be your destiny. It even seems to me to be your true destiny, to deny everything you have for something that exists only in your mind. And as much as I want to, I can't protect you from it. You are your own man and I'll make no claim on you. So follow your destiny, Dónal my love, but if you find it doesn't lead you where you want to go, then come back to me. I'll be here."

She reached up and kissed him lightly on the lips, then stood back and smiled, though there were tears in her eyes. "If you mean to go, then you'd better get on with yourself. I'll wait for you outside."

Dónal found nothing to say as he watched her walk through the door, his heart breaking at the pain that was in her, and still more that he'd put it there. This was not the way he'd meant to leave things between them, but he still believed in his heart that everything would be all right when he returned. And he *would* return!

So he went about getting himself ready for the road then, packing the things he'd meant to pack the night before. As he did, he came across the tattered linen bag that held his family heirlooms and, remembering that he'd left the book on the table, went to fetch it. It was still open to the page he'd been writing on, the page that recorded his father's place in the roll of the chieftains. Though he'd written his biography years before, he'd never been able to come up with a suitable epitaph, and had sat down to it the day before, not wanting to leave with it undone. After struggling for an hour or more, in the end he'd simply written the truth:

Eóghan son of Diarmuid son of Dónal, Twenty-first O'Sullivan Béara and Tenth Count of Berehaven. He was the greatest of all his race since Dónal Cam. But it wasn't enough.

Dónal closed the book against the tears that suddenly stung his eyes. When would it *ever* be enough? he wondered.

When he was ready to go, he called Con to him and gave him a good scratching behind the ears. "There you go, old son. It'll have to do you for a while, so hang onto it."

Then he rose to leave, but stopped at the doorway for a last look around, taking in the hearth where he and Sióna had shared so much of their inner selves, and the bed where they'd shared the rest.

"Good-bye, house," he said before walking outside. "I'll be home soon."

Sióna was waiting on the lawn with his horse, all bridled and ready. And as he approached, she flung herself into his arms.

"Oh, hold me, Dónal!" she said, clinging desperately. "Hold me like you did the first time, like you don't know if you'll ever get to hold me again. Hold me like you love me."

"I *do* love you, Sióna," he said, squeezing her to himself, "and I'll be back before you know I'm gone. Just trust me, Sióna, and you'll see."

She leaned back from him then, and tried to smile, though her eyes were streaming with tears. "Sure, I've nothing to fear, now do I? My scarlet piper will come home to me, and then all will be right with the world."

Without waiting for him to answer, she pulled his face down and kissed him with all the passion and sorrow within her. "I love you, too, Dónal," she said as she pulled away from him, "and I'll wait for you here always. Always."

Then she could bear it no more and ran for the cottage, closing the door behind her without a backward glance.

Dónal felt a chill steal into his heart as he stared at the door. It seemed to have such finality, as if it were Death Itself standing between them, rather than just so many sticks of wood. He thought of his parting from Eóghan so many years before, of his brother leaving and him staying behind, certain he'd never see him again. Then he pictured Sióna inside the cottage, feeling the same way about him, and thought his heart would surely break for her.

'All I have to do is open the door, and her pain will end,' he thought. But he didn't do it.

"I'm coming back," he said to the door, but it didn't answer.

A moment more and he sighed and mounted his horse. At the bottom of the hollow, he stopped for a last look back. There was a small light in the left-hand window, the one close to the bed, and he knew she'd put a candle there for him.

"I'm coming back!" he shouted at the light. Then he turned away.

⚬ͽͱͱͼ⚬

As he neared Ahern's cottage, Dónal saw a team hitched to one of the wagons and Tadhg lounging by the door. Seeing him, Tadhg called inside and Seán and Órla came out.

After exchanging greetings with the Aherns, Dónal turned to Tadhg. "What's with the wagon? Has the good woman given you dispensation to work on the Sabbath?"

But it was Ahern who answered. "I thought we'd get you started on the road, at least as far as the top of Guala."

"Oh, that's grand of you! Come all the way to Queenstown if you like!"

"No, Guala will do us for now. I wouldn't want my other son to get ideas of going to America, too."

"I'm not going anywhere, Da," Tadhg scoffed. "After all, what would the girls do without me?"

Ahern just shook his head at that, rolling his one eye heavenward.

Then Órla spoke, asking a question that Dónal would rather she hadn't. "How is Sióna bearing up?"

"Not too well," he replied honestly. "She just won't believe I'm coming back. But maybe you could have a talk with her, Órla. Maybe she'll trust you."

"Sure, I'll do that, Dónal, and we'll watch after her while you're gone. But son, you're the one she trusts above all others, and if you weren't able to convince her, then I don't see how I can. She went through a terrible ordeal, you know, yet for the love of you, she put it aside and trusted you with her body and her heart. But as brave as she is, she's still fragile inside. So I hope you were patient with her. You *were* patient with her, weren't you, Dónal?"

"I did the best I could," Dónal replied defensively. "But she didn't make it easy on me."

"I see," Órla said, nodding her head slowly, and he was sure she saw more than he intended. "Well then, I suppose you'll just have to prove her wrong, won't you?"

"I'm coming back, Órla."

"Good!" she said, then stepped up to embrace him. "Take care of yourself and come back to us as soon as ever you're able. You're a fine man, Dónal, and I'm proud of you. And wherever you go, know that my love and prayers will be with you."

"I love you, too, Helen of Troy," he replied, holding her close.

"Safe home to you, my young O'Sullivan of the sweet mouth." She stepped away, then slapped her forehead and said, "But wait, I almost forgot something."

Slipping into the cottage then, she came back with a linen ore bag in her hand, and he knew from its dampness that it was full of potatoes. "Here you go, so you can save your money for later."

"Thanks, Órla. And speaking of money, I need to be going. Riobárd has my ticket and travel money, and I was supposed to pick them up early this morning. Hopefully he won't be out when I get there."

"Oh, I wouldn't worry about Riobárd," Ahern said. "Knowing him, he'll be waiting by the roadside. But get on with you. There's no sense pushing your luck."

Dónal hitched his horse to the wagon then, and climbed onto its seat beside Ahern, waving a final good-bye to Órla as they rolled away. Soon they neared the high shoulder of Guala where the road flattened out, and Dónal turned in the seat for a look at Allihies and Eskinanaun as they slid away behind him. Though the sun was shining brightly, there was a slight haze in the air that softened all the hard edges, making it seem in that moment like Eóghan's daguerreotype, a memory made visible, present and yet remote, a place in the living world whose time was long past.

"Taking a last look?" Ahern asked.

"Until I see it again, I want to remember it just that way."

As they drove along the mountain shoulder, Dónal thought of how it had always been a divide in his life, between his years at Cahernageeha and those at Kealogue and Eskinanaun. But now he was leaving it all behind, and Guala would be just another mountain among many along the way. Soon there would be a new divide in his life, the Atlantic Ocean, dividing him from his home just as it divided the Irish nation between the Old World and the New.

But then they were at the far side of Guala, and Tadhg reined in the team. "You're on your own from here, old son," he said. "I don't like to take my wagons down this side if I can help it."

"You mean *our* wagons, don't you?" Dónal retorted. While Tadhg helped his father down, he unhitched his horse and came to stand before them. "Is there anything you want from New York?"

"How about a rich American girl so I won't have to work so hard?" Tadhg replied with a grin.

"Just one? Sure, it'll take at least two to keep you in clover."

"Ah, that's for you, runt!" Tadhg said, embracing Dónal so hard he grunted. "But take care of yourself. I'll see you when you get back." Then he set him down and turned away, lest he see the mist in his eyes.

Dónal turned to Ahern and gazed at him fondly, thinking how hard and long were the years that were in him. He was over fifty now, a great age in a country where life was so precarious that the average man died before reaching twenty. He was frail and thin, his gait scattering, his hand unsteady and his speech slurry, and though his white hair still grew thick and shiny, it made the angry scars on his face look even more vivid by contrast. Yet his one blue eye still sparkled with wit and intellect, that part of him at least being as young and vital as ever.

"As a father you've been to me, Seán," he said at last. "And a good friend."

"Yes, and you've been a good son to me, Dónal. And I shall miss you in all the days we are parted." Embracing him with as much strength as he had left, he added, "So remember me when you're out in the wide world, so far away from those who love you."

"I will, Seán, I will," Dónal said, looking him hard in the eye. "But just remember that I *will* come home!"

"Sure, Dónal, I know you will. I just hope it'll still be home when you get here. But until then, take my son's advice and take care of yourself!"

Then he turned to the wagon and Tadhg helped him up.

"I'll see you both soon," Dónal said after mounting his horse. He smiled, though there was no mirth in his heart.

"Safe home to you, Dónal," Tadhg said. "And to you, too, Odysseus," he added, meaning the horse. "Since I'm not likely to see you again this side of Heaven, go with my good wishes that you have the best of oats, the finest of mares, and the skinniest of riders with the softest of arses through all the rest of your days."

The horse whinnied and tossed his head, as if he'd understood.

"Sometimes you have to wonder who's smarter," Tadhg said with a laugh, "the animal that's riding or the one that's being ridden."

Seeing the familiar mischief in his friend's eyes, Dónal smiled, and for a moment they were two little boys again, grinning at each other like they'd just seen the Queen's knickers. With a last wave, he spurred his horse and rode down the mountainside, knowing there was no point in looking back.

As he left his friends behind and felt the true enormity of what he'd undertaken, Dónal's heart came into his throat. He was alone on the road now and, within just a few hours, he would pass through the boundaries that defined the familiar in his life and into the wider world that lay beyond. He knew his life was changing again, and nothing would be as it had been before. The things he would see and do would add to the cumulative total of who he was and make a different man of him. And when he returned, the people here would be different, too, changed if nothing else by the very fact of his absence.

When he came to the junction with the old boreen that led to Cahernageeha, he stopped, wondering if he should go that way. No, better to remember it as it was, he thought, and besides, the direct way to Riobárd's lay along the main road. So on he rode, not even realizing that he'd come to the first of many forks he'd face along his road, the first of many decisions he'd have to make, the road not taken leading to a destiny forever unfulfilled.

At the bottom of the hill, he came to another fork, the road to the right leading west toward Cahermore, and by another fork, on through Bealbarnish Gap and back around to Allihies. Only the road ahead led him away from home, the road to the east, paradoxically, since his ultimate goal lay in the west. But he didn't hesitate this time, didn't even think about going back, just rode on past the standing stones of Clonglaskan where the young family was buried, turning to them as he passed. How well he remembered that day, the empty eyes of the young man forever burned into his memory. But he didn't stop, just continued on, across the Pulleen River toward Castletownbere and beyond, thinking that Eóghan would be here soon to right their cumulative wrongs. He even held up his head as he rode, thinking proudly of the service he would render Ireland, feeling good that his life had a purpose again.

Soon he came to the turnoff for Dunboy and stopped on the bridge over Dunboy Creek to gaze across the estuary at the Big House, and at the oaks beyond. But then he heard footsteps along the road and turned to find Riobárd Puxley approaching.

"Riobárd!" he called, jumping down from the horse and going to meet him. "Seán said you'd be waiting by the road for me, and God bless him if he wasn't right!"

"He was indeed, Dónal. I've been there for some time now, wondering if you'd forgotten or even changed your mind. Why the late start, if you don't mind me asking?"

"Tadhg and Padge came out to give me a sendoff last night and didn't leave till this morning."

"I see. And you got good and drunk so you'd look and feel your best for the road."

"Something like that. But before I do forget, do you have my things with you?"

"Everything is right here, Dónal," Puxley replied, handing over a small leather purse, "your ticket, a map to Queenstown, the name of the ship, and the date and time of sailing. There's also a letter of introduction to my favorite innkeeper and another to the horse trader, who I'll warn you is a Tinker and not to be taken lightly. As for the traveling money, there's the twenty-five pounds Eóghan sent and another twenty-five from me, a sort of *bon voyage* gift, if you will. Use some of it to get yourself a haircut and new clothes in Queenstown. But be careful with it, Dónal! That's a lot to be carrying around with you, more than most poor people see in a lifetime. Though we Irish aren't naturally given to thievery, the times are desperate, and you can't be too trusting of strangers on the road. Always keep a pound or two loose in your pocket so you won't have to let anyone see the full amount all at once."

"Thanks, Riobárd," Dónal said with a smile, though he felt a little patronized by the lecture. "I'll keep it safe inside my jacket. Did you post my letter to Eóghan and tell him when to expect me?"

"Yes, and I included all your information, so expect him to greet you at dockside. If for some reason he doesn't, there are directions to his house and law office. So then, Dónal, all the details being taken care of, tell me how Sióna is faring."

"Not well," Dónal replied, averting his gaze toward the estuary. "She just won't believe I'm coming back."

"And what if Eóghan won't come with you, Dónal? Will you come back even then?"

Dónal turned to look Puxley in the eyes then. "Yes, I'll come without him if I have to."

Puxley smiled and patted him on the shoulder. "Well, if it's any comfort to you, Dónal, I for one believe you. I've been to America, and I don't think you'll like it there. A bunch of greedy bastards despoiling their patrimony, the Americans are, and I've never known you to be greedy.

"No, I've never envied the rich," Dónal replied, nodding toward the Big House. "All I want in life is a bit of justice."

"Ah, justice is it? That's a rare and precious commodity. Only a fortunate few ever get it, and though they might be poor as Irish church mice, they are yet the wealthiest people on Earth. Is it they whom you envy?"

"No, it's even simpler than that, I'm afraid. I envy those who can sleep through the night without fear."

"Well, now!" Puxley said, appreciating the insight. "Though I've traveled the world over in my day, I've yet to meet anyone so rich or powerful or saintly as to make that claim. When you find him, let me know, so that I may envy him, too!"

"I'll do that, Riobárd. But now, if you don't mind, I'm going to take my leave of you. As you reminded me, it's getting late, and I want to go out to the ruins for a last look, just to be sure I'll remember why I'm doing this."

"Perhaps I'd better come with you then. You're aware that Dunboy is occupied again?"

"Yes, I'd heard young Henry has come back here to live now that he's The Puxley, though I've never yet heard what became of Johnnie."

"Ah well, it's a rather sad story, I'm afraid, and a bit long in the telling. But the short of it is that he had a tragic affair with a girl and died of a broken heart when she spurned him. She was Catholic, you see, and refused him on religious grounds, which is rather ironic, I'd say, given his attitude toward *Irish* Catholics."

"Yes, I'd say so. And what of young Henry? What's his attitude toward us?"

"Well, it's better than Johnnie's, though still not what it should be. But I'm working on him. He's a good man at heart and quite intelligent, so I have high hopes for him. Yet only time will tell, as they say. In any case, he's lord of the manor now and has settled his family into the Big House. So at the very least, Erin has one less absentee landlord to carry on her back. Still, the grounds are strictly forbidden to all save invited guests and those who have business at the house or storage yards. So I'd better come with you, just to be sure you don't find yourself transported to Australia rather than America."

"I appreciate your concern, Riobárd, but I'd rather you didn't. If you don't mind, I'd like to be alone with my ancestors for a bit. But don't worry. I know the back way in and I'll be careful."

"As you wish, my lord O'Sullivan Béara," Puxley replied, smiling and bowing.

"You know, Riobárd, I've always hated it when you called me that. It always seemed so patronizing. But now that I know you're a clansman, I think I rather like it. Indeed, now that I know there's three of us rather than just one, I don't feel so lonely. Sure, I suppose there's actually four, if you count Richard."

"No, I wouldn't go counting Richard if I was you. As much as I've gone out of my way to be Irish, he's gone out of his not to be."

"And why is that do you suppose?"

"I don't know exactly," Puxley replied, averting his gaze. "Richard and I have never been close, even as children, and as his older brother, I've always felt it was my fault, that I've failed him somehow. I suppose that's rather paternalistic, but then it's my nature to look after the weak. And Richard is a weak man, one who has never been able to overcome his baser instincts and do good for his fellow man. I don't know. Perhaps he just resents me for being stronger."

"And what made you that way, do you suppose?"

"Well, the inner strength was always there. But as to what brought it out, well, you already know – Helen of Troy, the love of a woman I can't have."

Hearing Puxley mention his pet name for Órla, Dónal narrowed his eyes. "You don't miss much, do you, Riobárd?"

"Not when it comes to looking after you. How else could I keep my promise to Eóghan?"

Dónal extended his hand to Puxley and looked him hard in the eyes. "I'll see you when I get back, Riobárd."

"Safe home to you, my chieftain. May you indeed find what you seek beyond the waves."

Near the edge of the forest, Dónal tethered his horse and crept forward on foot, stopping well within the shadows. On the lawn below the ruins, he saw a beautiful young woman sitting amid the remains of a picnic, laughing with delight as a man and a little boy frolicked around her. Though he'd never seen them before, from family resemblance Dónal knew the man could only be Henry Puxley, and therefore the woman must be his wife and the boy his son. Wanting a better view, he crept to the tree line and knelt behind an old stump to watch as they took their leisure on the site of his ancestral home.

Of course, his first instinct was anger that Englishmen should have a picnic on this hallowed ground on this date, but it soon gave way to fascination, for he'd had so little contact with the wealthy before, especially in their casual moments. As he watched the woman laughing and clapping, and the little boy squealing with delight as his father threw him into the air, what struck him was not, as he would've suspected, that they were so different from the poor Irish, but that they were so much the same. Indeed, but for their fancy clothes they could've been any young family anywhere in the world, even the one that lay buried at Clonglaskan. How different it made The English seem, seeing them as human beings capable of love and compassion and levity, rather than just some abstract terror that lived in a shadow world and held his people in bondage. Indeed, they were no longer *The English* to him at all.

Then the man set the boy free to run on the grass, knelt beside his wife and kissed her lightly on the lips. "I love you," he said, and she smiled sweetly at him, her love for him apparent.

Dónal blushed and ducked behind the stump, feeling suddenly like a voyeur. He shook his head, wondering that he should have these feelings about the Puxleys, especially on this date and in this place. But then Riobárd was a Puxley, he thought, much more so than an O'Sullivan, and if he could be a good man, then perhaps there was hope for young Henry, too. At least Riobárd thought so.

But then Dónal heard Puxley call for a servant, and peered over the stump to see him helping the woman and boy into a hand carriage while their man loaded their things into its boot. As they wheeled away, Puxley waved and then turned to gaze over the sound. As Dónal watched him standing there with his back turned and completely unaware, he realized he could kill him in that moment and no one would be the wiser till he was well away. Only Riobárd would know, and himself.

'I *should* kill him,' Dónal thought, 'for what his brother did to me, if nothing else. I should kill him and strike a real blow for the Republic!'

But even as he thought it, he knew he wouldn't lift a finger against Puxley. 'I killed Brendan Collins in the service of my country,' he thought bitterly, 'yet I can't kill Henry Puxley, the true enemy of my people. So where is the justice in that?'

Then the moment passed as Puxley turned and walked away. As he disappeared over the rise, Dónal emerged from his lurk and moved in among the ruins. It was already late afternoon and the shadows long, and the old room was cool and dark after the warm sunlight on the lawn. He looked slowly around himself, taking in the walls and ruined staircase and the old window well where he'd sat with his father twelve years before, thinking of the cellar as it had been on that last morning of the siege, with the wounded and dying men stacked on top of each other even as their blood pooled on the floor. He closed his eyes and burned the images into his memory, the better to relay them to Eóghan when he saw him in New York.

But in the midst of it, his stomach growled and he suddenly realized he was hungry, having eaten nothing since supper the day before. "Ah, sure," he muttered to himself. "If the Puxley's can have a picnic here today, then I suppose there's no harm in the rightful owner having a bite, as well!"

After retrieving his potatoes, he sat in the old window well and dug into them as if he hadn't eaten in days. When he'd eaten his fill, he leaned back against the cold stone wall and gazed at the water, watching the waves roll hypnotically toward the shore. In a moment, he began to nod as the fullness in his stomach tugged at his eyelids.

'Maybe I'll just rest my eyes for a few minutes,' he thought, giving in to the feeling. "I won't go to sleep. I'll just rest my eyes . . . "

♔

Dónal woke with a start at the sudden feeling of being pinned against the wall. He'd gone to sleep after all and now they'd caught him trespassing! But no, it was pitch dark and there was no one there. Yet how could that be when he felt hands upon him and his shirt gathered and bunched. Then he heard a voice, deep and resonant though remote and hollow, as if coming from a grave.

'Where is your father?' it demanded. 'Where is he? Where is Dónal Cam?'

Then Dónal understood, and terror took him as the dim shape of a man formed before his staring eyes. He was enormous and dressed in the old way as a warrior, though his armor was rent and torn and his body covered with ghastly wounds. Yet more ghastly still were his eyes, piercing and hard, those of a killer even when he'd been among the living, and God only knew what malevolence they held now.

Then his lips moved and the voice demanded again, 'Where is Dónal Cam?' but Dónal knew the sound was only in his head. When he didn't answer the hands shook him and the voice cried out again, 'Where is Dónal Cam?' so loud that he wanted to stop his ears, but was so terrified he couldn't move his hands. 'Where is Dónal Cam?' and he wanted to jump up and run, but his legs wouldn't obey. 'Where is Dónal Cam?' and Dónal screamed in pain.

"He's not coming, Riocard!"

There was silence then as the man regarded him curiously, almost sadly, his dead eyes even losing some of their malevolence.

"He's not coming, Riocard!" Dónal repeated. "He's *never* coming back for you! He left you here to die!"

The eyes blinked as though in surprise, then opened wide in fury as a high-pitched shriek came into Dónal's head, so loud it felt like a spike being driven through his skull. Then the hands picked him up and shook him in the air before throwing him to the ground. But the ground had disappeared and there was nothing below but the bottomless pit of Hell, and into it Dónal tumbled, down and down and down, a shriek still in his head, though now it was Satan's angels welcoming him to his torment.

⚬⚬⚬

Dónal opened his eyes and blinked against the enveloping darkness, his first thought that he'd fallen all the way to Hell. But then he felt the cool wet grass against his cheek and smelled salt air on the sea breeze. Looking up, he saw stars in the sky and just the tiniest sliver of a moon. There was no voice in his head and no hands were upon him, no ghastly shape hovering over him.

Still, the terror was there, impelling him up from the grass and through the ruins into the forest, terrified that the ghost would suddenly reach out and grab him again, the silence more dreadful than the voice. By the sheerest blind luck he ran into his horse, mounted, and spurred him desperately away, leaving it to the animal to dodge the trees.

Down the path he rode, away from the ruins and past the Big House, in his terror oblivious to the danger of being caught. But there were no lights in the windows, the Puxleys and their servants being long in bed, and he galloped on to the gates, urging the horse to all its speed. Nor did he slow at the main road, still fearing the ghost might be following, hovering just behind, waiting for him to look back before pouncing. So he didn't look, just continued into the night, through Castletownbere and across the stone bridge on its far side, up the hill and past the workhouse, and on till the old horse began to stumble.

Finally then he slowed to a walk, for pity of the horse and fear that he'd trip, bringing them both to grief. His heart was still racing, but the terror was beginning to subside, and he dared a glance over his shoulder. Finding nothing, he sighed with relief. To his left, he heard the trickle of water, and stopped to let the horse drink. Flopping to the ground, he plunged his face into the cold spring, then rolled over to gaze at the stars.

"So the old story is true," he said aloud. "There really is a ghost at Dunboy, and Riocard MagEochagáin still guards the ruins, waiting for a man who'll never return." Then he frowned and bit his lip. "Or was it just a dream?" He didn't know.

He sighed and rubbed his eyes. "This day has been a donkey ride through Hell. I can't imagine anything worse!"

chapter 18

Cousane Gap
County Cork

Dónal dismounted and set his horse free to graze on "God's acre," as the stray grass along the roadside was called. In the field to the left stood the standing stone that had caught his eye as he approached the high gap in the mountains, and he jumped the stone boundary wall and walked toward it. There were many standing stones in his own country, of course, and from his childhood rambles with Ahern he knew their names and folklore, though it had been years since he'd taken any notice of them, familiarity having robbed them of their mystery. Yet precisely because this one stood beyond the pale of his knowledge and experience, it seemed new and mysterious, and he looked it over as if he'd never seen a standing stone before.

"What's your name, and who put you here, and why?" he asked, laying his hands on it. "What secrets of the past do you guard with your silence?"

But the stone gave him no answers, and after a moment he sighed and pulled out his map to see where he was. It showed that he'd reached the Cousane Gap between the Shehy Mountains and Maughanaclea Hills and was about half way to Queenstown already, though it was only Tuesday afternoon. Looking down the mountain along the way he'd come, he realized he'd made good time despite his disastrous start and the fact that he'd yet to push his old horse.

After the roadside stream that first night, he'd ridden on to Adrigole, reaching it just as the cocks were crowing. There he stopped to watch the rising sun light the eastern slopes of Hungry Hill, a new experience for him since he'd never been east of Castletownbere, and just the first of many to come. For after only a day's ride, he was already beyond the pale of the safe and familiar, and from that moment on everything he saw and everyone he met would be new and different, a prospect he found at once daunting and exhilarating. He thought of those left behind then, of Sióna waking to an empty cottage and Tadhg going to work without him. So much had happened already that it seemed like years since he'd seen them last, though it was only the day before. Were they thinking of him, he wondered, and did they miss him as much as he missed them? He hoped not, for the emptiness he felt in that moment was big enough to fill the ocean.

'I can still go back,' he thought, looking back along the road. 'Indeed, I can always go back.' But finding the thought reassuring, he turned and rode on.

At the first public house he came to, Dónal stopped for breakfast, having left his bag of potatoes at Dunboy in his haste to get away. Though the place wasn't open yet, the landlady responded to his insistent knock, whisking the door open and looking him up and down with a jaundiced eye.

"What d'ye want?" she snarled in rude English, glaring at him as if he had magic beans for sale.

"I'd like a breakfast and some tea, if you . . ." Dónal began.

"I don't give charity to no goddamn Tinkers. Now bugger off with ye before I call the palers." Then she slammed the door in his face.

Dónal briefly considered knocking again, but then thought better of it. "If that's the state of the hospitality in this place, then the food can't be any better," he shouted, meaning for her to hear.

Then he led his horse to the next public house, just a few doors down. This time he fished a pound from his pocket and held it up as he knocked. Seeing it, the landlord let him in immediately, and soon he was feasting on a breakfast of eggs and bacon with porridge and fresh-baked bread, and even real tea, not the homemade chamomile that was his staple. Indeed, it was so good that he'd have licked the plate clean if the publican hadn't been watching.

After breakfast he went on to Glengarriff at the east end of Béara, letting his horse go at a leisurely pace so he could take in the beauty of the surrounding countryside. Between the Caha Mountains rising steeply on his left and Bantry Bay spreading toward the Sheep's Head Peninsula on his right, the narrow track of the road ran like a dividing line, winding around the tumbled lowlands and dipping into the occasional stretch of forest. Of the latter, he'd taken particular interest, since, of course, there were no forests on his end of Béara other than the demesne of Dunboy, though he knew that most of the peninsula was wooded in the old days. But the English had cut them all down long ago, shaping the land to their purposes while at the same time denying Irish rebels their preferred haven. The timber they'd mostly hauled away to England to use in building ships or houses, or simply to fuel the furnaces of the Industrial Revolution. So the land was mostly bare now, and it was a wonder that even these small areas had been spared.

At Glengarriff, Dónal stopped and spent a little time exploring the village, his curiosity fueled by the fact that Dónal Cam departed from there on his epic march to Leitrim. Since it would be the last town of any size he would pass through for a while, he ate another meal, too, this time a thick stew of mutton, potatoes and carrots with brown bread and salt butter on the side, and a pint of porter's ale to wash it all down. For flavor, it surpassed even his breakfast, and he devoured it as if it were his last meal.

Afterward, he crossed the old stone bridge over the Barony River and for the first time in his life set foot outside of Béara, riding on to Ballylickey, where a road branched to the left and followed the Owvane River into the mountains of West Cork. Even though the sun was still above the horizon, he decided to stop there for the night, being tired from traveling and not sleeping much the two previous nights. So he led his horse down to the river for a drink and then let him graze before settling down on the bank for the night. He lit a fire of deadwood from the sycamores lining the river and uncorked his jug of whiskey, thinking to have just "a nip or two" to help him off to sleep. When he lay down, the ground was hard and lumpy, and he'd thought of Sióna and their soft bed that now seemed so far away. But he was tired and soon the whiskey and the whispering sycamores lulled him to sleep, and he didn't wake until sunrise.

From there, he stopped only once before reaching Cousane Gap, at a cottage along the road where the man of the house gave him a breakfast of potatoes and buttermilk, refusing his offer of payment in accordance with traditional Irish hospitality. Of course, the food had no flavor to him at all after his two feasts of the day before, and he found himself wishing he'd taken the time to savor them.

While he ate, the man's children huddled by the hearth watching him, three boys and one girl all with curly black hair and blue eyes that sparkled in sharp contrast to their dirty faces. Dónal smiled at the girl, the oldest of them though she wasn't more than ten by the size that was in her.

"What's your name, dear?" he asked.

"Róisín," she replied in a squeaky little voice. "What's yours?"

"I'm Dónal O'Sullivan."

At that, the children's eyes all lit up in recognition. "*You're* Dónal Cam O'Sullivan?" the eldest boy exclaimed. "Our uncle Cathal tells us stories about you and what a great swordsman you are. Will you show us your sword?"

But Dónal just smiled at their innocence. "Oh, no. I'm not the man himself, just a relation."

"Oh," the boy said, disappointed. Dónal even felt a little sad himself, as if he'd let them down by being only who he was.

But then the girl spoke again. "Are you going to stay with us?"

"No, colleen, I'm on my way to Queenstown, and then on to America."

"Is that far away?"

"Yes, it's *very* far, all the way across the Big Water, and it'll take weeks to get there, even on a steamship!"

"Oh. Is that where Heaven is? My Mam's gone to Heaven to be with Jesus and the Saints, and Da said it was *ever* so far away, and we can't visit her till God says it's our turn."

Dónal didn't know what to say, having no clue what they'd been told about Death and not wanting to upset them by saying the wrong thing. But he was saved by their father, who came in from tending his lazy beds.

"Here, now! Give the man some peace to finish his breakfast!" he said, and shooed them outside.

But Dónal had lost his appetite, feeling as though he would be taking food from the children's mouths by eating any more. So he stuck his half-eaten potato in his pocket just to avoid wasting it and took his leave. On the way out he gave the girl a shilling and told her to give it to her father, feeling he owed it to her and her brothers, before hastily riding away. For with no wife to help him, he knew the man would be lucky to keep the four of them alive through the coming winter, and he couldn't bear to look at their beautiful little faces knowing one or more of them would soon be gone.

Riding along the Owvane, Dónal was amazed at the rich country around him, the lush green fields and the broad calm river lined with real trees and not just scrubby osiers, the looming mountains that seemed soft and green with gentle, inviting slopes. Even the wind was just a breeze that played his hair lightly about his face and sang through the treetops. With country like this just a day's ride from Allihies, he wondered why anyone would ever choose to live on the scabby land of Béara, exposed to the ravages of wind and sea. It could only be that, like him, most people had never ventured more than a few miles from their homes, and so didn't know that better alternatives were waiting just down the road.

Now as Dónal stood by the ancient stone gazing into the valley below, he found it difficult to believe that anyone could've starved in the country he'd ridden through. And yet they had, for even it was full of empty cottages, of scarred and tumbled Famine Houses, the Hunger apparently not discriminating between good land and poor. Still, seeing it outside of Béara was something of a revelation to him, even helping him to understand his own Irishness. For as he'd ridden east, he'd begun to see that he was indeed part of that greater Irish nation of which James Stephens had spoken, and that there was a whole country of people beyond Castletownbere who lived and thought and acted and spoke more or less as he did. And whereas before he'd known that he was Irish only in the sense that he wasn't English, he was now coming to understand it in a more essential and positive way. It made him feel good to know that he wasn't so alone, that he was part of something greater than kith and clan. Yet at the same time, his sense of injustice grew, as did his resolve to bring Eóghan home.

So after a brief rest, he mounted his horse and rode on, leaving his home and loved ones ever further behind.

⚭

On Thursday morning, Dónal rode through the lush valley of the River Lee, gazing in naked wonder at the richness around him, at the pastures filled with cattle and sheep and the fields planted with crops of all descriptions, green almost to the point of monotony, having only the sky to frame it and give it scale. Here and there he saw tree-shaded Big Houses, too, whose beauty and splendor made Dunboy seem like a workhouse by comparison, while even the cottages of the poor were well-tended and prosperous-looking, at least in comparison to those of Béara. It made him wonder why anyone would live along the Owvane when there was a place like this in the world, a garden as lush and verdant as Eden itself. It explained why the English had so coveted Ireland, if only to possess the Lee Valley alone, and why the Irish had fought to the point of extinction to keep Her.

Then he remembered Don Phillip's description of the lands around Knockgraffon, and the O'Sullivan's deep and abiding sadness at their loss. "I am Dónal, the bog rat of Béara," he said aloud, his jaw tightening. "Now with meanness and with thrift, I even lack a change of shift!"

With that, he spurred his horse and left his home further behind, both in miles and in his heart.

⟁

As he rode through Cork City, Dónal could only gape in astonishment, the grand scale and frenetic pace of urban life beyond both his experience and imagining. It seemed so foreign, with its endless rows of attached buildings and its bewildering array of streets and bridges all thick with traffic, wheeled, hoofed and footed. Nor were the people the least bit courteous or friendly, pushing and shoving as they bustled about, shouting and cursing in their lilting English that seemed to end every sentence on a rising cadence. But other than yelling at him to get out of the way, they ignored him for the most part, thinking him just another culchie come to seek his fortune in the big city, which would chew him up soon enough and spit him back to the bog whence he'd come. It made him feel lonely and isolated, for all the throng around him, and more than a little fearful. His anxiety was warranted, too, though he didn't know it, for here and there were furtive eyes, taking in his bewilderment and appraising him an easy mark. Not that they thought a ragged spalpeen like him worth the bother, just that his old horse would bring a few shillings at the slaughterhouse. But they let him pass; it was early yet and riper pickings might be had with patience.

As he came to the Grand Parade and turned south, all the church bells of the city began ringing the noon hour, and he stopped to listen. Allihies, of course, had only two churches, Catholic and Protestant, and the Methodist chapel in the Cornish Village, each with only a single bell in its tower. But judging by the music that filled the city and made it beautiful, Cork must have a score of churches at least, and each with an impressive array of bells. He thought of Sióna then, and wished that she were with him to share it. He would have to bring her here one day, he thought, so they could listen to the bells of Cork together.

When it ended, Dónal went on his way, taking the Southern Road and following it out of the city. Soon he was in the country again, its calm and tranquility broken only by the buzzing of flies and the low-ing of cattle. The people were friendly and courteous, going about their labors with a serenity born of the knowledge that God would bring all things in His own time. And though Cork City was large and bewil-dering, at once enticing and forbidding, even it had its boundaries, and outside them things were more or less as he'd always known them to be.

Soon he turned onto the road leading to Passage West, the village from whence he was to cross the Lee to the Great Island, and spurred his old horse to a quick trot. The day was getting away from him and he needed to be in Queenstown by six o'clock if he was to find the horse trader.

❦

From the crowded deck of the river ferry, Dónal watched the docks of Passage West slide away as he sniffed the salt air and listened to the wailing gulls. It felt good to be near the ocean again, for though in all his journey it was no more than a few miles away, he'd had no sense of it while inland, and had begun to miss it. But then again, on Saturday morning he would board a ship and for over three weeks the ocean would be all he'd see. After that, would he ever miss it again? he wondered.

But then the ferry's whistle sounded, indicating their approach to Carrigaloe, and he marveled at how quickly its steam engine had pro-pelled it across the choppy River Lee. When it was berthed and the ramp lowered, the tide of humanity and animals surged forward, and Dónal was on horseback again, heading toward Queenstown.

Soon he rounded a bend and there was the town just ahead, with its prosperous-looking buildings and bustling quays lined with ships. In the enormous harbor beyond were three smaller islands and his eyes went immediately to the one nearest the mouth. Spike Island, it was called, a place infamous for its prison, the holding station for the tens of thousands of Irish who'd suffered the sentence of transportation. Add to them the hundreds of thousands who'd taken the emigrant's

372

road, fleeing hunger and disease and oppression, and the very name of Queenstown had become synonymous with their misery, forever evoking the grief of parting.

As he gazed toward the sea, Dónal thought of them huddling silently on deck, their hearts breaking as Erin slipped inexorably into the sea, their destination exile everlasting. It was for them that he himself would sail, and even more so, that he would return, bringing their salvation with him.

With that thought, he rode into the hubbub of the harbor front, heading for the open market along the quays. He stopped at the first vendor he came to, an old woman sitting beside a cart filled with ratty-looking used clothes, and dismounted to inquire for the horse trader.

"*Dia dhuit, a mháthair,*" he said, forgetting himself.

"'Tis no Irish in these ould ears, son," the old woman said. "So if ye're after makin' yeerself heard, 'tis the English ye'll have to spake!"

"God be with you, mother," Dónal began again, pausing to let her respond, going on when she didn't. "I was wonderin' if you could direct me to Egan Butler."

The woman glared as if he'd said something offensive, before spitting a snuff-blackened glob at his feet. "Ye'll find the Tinker at the foot o' the line, and sure, 'tis still too close for the likes o' me, divil that he is. Ye'll know him by his wares, if the stench of him don't inform ye first. Now get away from me before anybody sees ye. I've troubles enough so."

For a moment, Dónal was taken aback by her rudeness, but then he understood. "If you're thinkin' me a Tinker, too, mother, you're sadly mistaken. I'm just after sellin' my horse."

"Sure, ye are, and I just come in on the last ship meself. Now go on with ye before I call the palers." Then she turned her back and made a show of tidying her cart.

Dónal sighed and moved on. At the end of the row he found a cart laden with metal ware, and though he stopped directly in front of its proprietor, the man didn't look up from his whittling. Nor did Dónal speak to him, finding him a curious sight, dressed all in black from his spit-polished riding boots and stylish though well-worn suit to the buttons on his black shirt. Black, too, were his slicked-back hair and rakish mustache, and even the shadow in his cleft chin. Still he was handsome enough, in that roguish way that appealed to the sort of woman who found danger attractive in a man.

Then the wind changed and Dónal indeed caught his odor, which surprisingly smelled of perfume, perhaps from the oil in his hair.

"I see our Mary Pat's been tellin' tales out of school again, divil that she is," the man said, his voice resonant and clear.

"I'm sorry, what did you say?" Dónal blurted, embarrassed that he'd caught him sniffing.

"What do you want, boyo?"

"I'm lookin' for Egan Butler."

"Wisha, you've found him so. And now that your life's work is done, you can die, lucky fellah that you are."

"Perhaps you misunderstand me, Mr. Butler. My name is Dónal O'Sullivan"

"'Tis grand for you, that, though divil if I remember askin'."

Dónal sighed, trying not to let it rankle, though that seemed Butler's intent. "Riobárd Puxley sent me to you," he said, hoping it would get his attention.

At the drop of the name, Butler slowly raised his head. Seeing him full-face, Dónal understood Riobárd's admonition not to take him lightly, finding a look of self-sufficiency in his coal-black eyes that was neither as simple as confidence nor as complex as arrogance, just that of a man who faced life on its own terms, and won.

"And why would he do such a thing as that? I've no need of a servin' boy, especially one such as yourself, fresh from the bog."

At that Dónal's anger spilled over and he thrust Riobárd's letter in Butler's face. "Here! He sent you this by way of introduction."

"Riobárd knows I can't read, so why would he send me a letter?"

"Do you know his seal, Mr. Butler?" Dónal asked. When the man nodded, he tore it open and began to read aloud:

Riobárd Puxley, Esq.
Oakmount, Castletownbere
Béara, County Cork   16 June, 1861

Dear Egan,

Hoping this letter finds you well, I send my greetings. The young man presenting it is my friend and cousin, Dónal O'Sullivan Béara. On Saturday, 23 June, he will depart Queenstown aboard a steamer bound for America. As he wishes to sell his horse beforehand, I would be obliged if you would buy it. In my estimation, it is worth about four pounds six, though if you disagree, Dónal is open to negotiation. Afterward, if you would be so kind as to direct him to Barry's, I would be most appreciative.

Until next we meet, I am

Your friend,
Riobárd Puxley

P.S. And Egan. Please do not try Dónal's patience by telling him you cannot read.

Dónal glared at Butler then, even angrier than before. But the man just flashed his irritating smile, though behind it he was giving Dónal a second look, knowing Puxley wasn't often wrong about people.

"So you're one of those O'Sullivans, are you?" he asked, deciding to test him further. "Riobárd does like to gab about his descent from Dónal Cam, though bugger if I can figure out why. He was just out for himself and the Divil with the good men of Dunboy."

Dónal took a deep breath and let it out slowly. "Mr. Butler, please. Do you want to buy my horse or not?"

"So you're off to America, are you?" Butler asked, giving him more of it. "Sure, if that isn't gratitude for you! The poor ould woman breaks her back tryin' to support you and then, at the first hint of trouble, you're off to greener pastures! Just like your Dónal Cam, the shoneen!"

"I'm not after stayin' there! I just goin' to get my brother and bring him back!"

"Well, if you do come back, you'll be the first, though divil if I can see why you'd want to, America bein' the land of plenty that it is!"

"Mr. Butler, please. If you're not after buyin' my horse, just tell me and I'll go away. I promise I will."

"Sure, I've no use for him, nag that he is. But since you asked nicely and I owe Riobárd a favor, perhaps I'll consider it, not for his price though, mind you. 'Tis two pounds even I'll give you, and you'll thank me for the generosity that's in it."

"Done, I'll take it so!"

"Ah, young O'Sullivan, but you've so much to learn, don't you?" Butler asked, his English suddenly more polished. "Would you really let me cheat you just because you find me irritating? You'll have to do better than that if you expect to get along in the world. Now I've just taught you an important lesson and, to be sure you understand it, I'll state it plainly: never let a man get under your skin, because once you do, he'll play you like a fiddle. So then. Now that your school day is done, why don't we start over?

"I'm Egan Butler," he said, standing to shake hands, "horse trader *par excellence*. Most people call me Egan, but you can call me Mr. Butler."

"All right, Egan," Dónal replied, grinning with relief. "I'm Dónal O'Sullivan, and I'm after sellin' a horse. Do you want to buy him?"

"Sure, now we're gettin' somewhere, a long time though it's taken," Butler said, dropping back into dialect. "'Tis two pounds I can give you for him, considerin' the age and the miles that're in him."

"What? But why only two pounds when you just said it would be cheatin' me?"

"Why?" Butler asked, seeming genuinely surprised. "Why, you ask? Because I'll be lucky to get four pounds for him myself, and though I'm partial to charity when it comes to advice, I'm not when it comes to horse-tradin', friend, foe or indifferent though you be. 'Tis two pounds and not a penny more!"

"Sure, fine, I'll take it," Dónal sighed, just to get it over with. "Far be it from me to deprive a man of his livin'."

"You'll soon starve, you know, sayin' that to people!" Butler said, amazed that Puxley could be so wrong.

"That may be true for you, Egan, but I've yet to feel the first pang of it."

"'Tis no fault of your own, surely! But I'm done with teachin' you if you won't learn."

"Ah, don't worry for me, Egan. I can take care of myself."

"Worry for you? Son, just give it two shakes after you're gone and I won't remember you were here!"

"Grand so, and 'tis gone I'll be, if you'll just direct me to Barry's."

"'Tis just down the street there. Old John is a decent sort and somethin' of a friend, at least as much as any settled man is to a Traveler. Just tell him I sent you, and he'll have you in clover."

"Grand so," Dónal said, taking his pack from the horse. "You'll take good care of our Odysseus, won't you? He's a lovely fellah, and sure, I'll miss him."

"Like a babe in swaddlin' clothes, I'll treat him, not to worry."

"Good-bye, Odysseus," Dónal said, giving the horse a final rub. "I'll see you in Ithaca."

"Watch your back, young O'Sullivan!" Butler called as he walked away.

⁂

Dónal reached for his pint of porter through the press of men crowding the bar, Barry's being packed with a Friday evening crowd. Having just returned from supper and after-dinner drinks at the Queen's Hotel, he'd stopped in the bar for a pint or two before turning in. Though closing time was still a couple of hours away, he wanted to get to bed early so as to be fresh and alert for the morning.

His stay in Queenstown had been quite eventful since checking in with Barry the night before. He'd found the man cordial and eager to please, especially after Riobárd's letter of introduction. "Sure, any friend of Mr. Puxley's is a friend of mine, good man that he is," Barry had said. "I'll even give you his usual room, the best in the house. 'Tis on the third floor and has a grand view of the harbor."

After depositing his belongings in his room, Dónal took his supper in the bar, where he stayed till closing time, finding the atmosphere warm and congenial. The language of the place was all English, of course, with only the odd bit of Irish tossed in for color. Even so, he was amazed at the diversity of speech, hearing everything from a gentrified drawl to the hard-edged brogue of the mountain and the bog. And there were men to match, too, from dandies to spalpeens and everything between, all sharing the bright conviviality that poured from the taps, the drink being the one thing that made them all equal, it seemed.

Standing alone in the corner, he gazed at the men around him, at the many odysseys brought together in that one place and time by destinies as disparate as their faces. Where had they come from, he wondered, and where would they go from here? Would they make the full circle and arrive safely home again, or would they be waylaid by the hazards of the road, ambushed by the risks they'd taken, the choices they'd made? But he gave it up after awhile, the ale having softened all the hard edges and suffused the room with a friendly glow.

After a sound sleep and hearty breakfast, he went to the barber's for a bath, shave and haircut, before seeking out the haberdasher. Not having time for custom tailoring, he bought ready-made clothes, which with some quick alterations fit him well enough, two shirts, a collar and new shoes. Once changed, he took a good look at himself in the mirror, scarcely recognizing the handsome young gentleman staring back. His mind flashed then on the dirty little boy in Ahern's mirror, and how he'd felt so inferior to the Cornish children. But that was a different place and time, and he smiled, thinking how far he'd come from his windswept hillside. Walking the streets afterward, he was flattered to find polite society greeting him courteously, as if he were one of them. It made him feel like a slave released from bondage, and all because he had a little money in his pocket and wore the clothes of his betters.

For his noon meal he went to the Queen's Hotel, finding it the grandest building he'd ever seen. After a polite greeting at the door from a peeler in the queerest sort of uniform, he was escorted to a table in the dining room by a man in a fine black suit, who actually referred to him as "the gentleman" when directing another man to fill his water glass. His meal was exquisite, too, a large beefsteak with greens and rice, none of which he'd ever had before, rounded out by good wine and fine port. It was the best meal he'd ever eaten by far, and he wondered how he could ever go back to potatoes and goat's milk. But then, maybe he wouldn't have to. Maybe he would move into a town or even Cork City and get a polite situation as a bookkeeper or bank clerk, and though he had no illusions of starting at the top, he was sure he'd be successful in time. After all, he was energetic and intelligent, and never afraid of hard work. Sure, anything was possible, he thought, as he ordered another measure of port.

The afternoon he spent walking around town, slipping into shops and strolling along the quays. He found his ship and checked in with the ticket agent, who assured him that his first-class cabin was indeed reserved and waiting. Then he took a good long look at the ship herself, noting that she was in fine trim for the voyage. Afterward, he strolled through a neighborhood of fine houses fronted by manicured lawns and broad, tree-shaded lanes, and thought how grand it would be to live in one of them. He even pictured himself and Sióna sitting on a shaded verandah, having their tea while their gaggle of red-headed children played in the yard. How lovely she would look in a fine dress with her hair all done up. Sure, it would happen someday, he told himself, taking a nip from his flask.

As the church bells rang four, he headed down to the waterfront on the pretext of offering Butler a drink, though really just to show off his new persona. But finding him gone, he dropped into the nearest pub and drank Butler's pint with his left hand and his own with his right, before strolling back to the Queen's Hotel for supper.

On the way, he passed the old clothing seller and smiled wickedly as she gaped at him. "See, mother? I told you I was no Tinker!"

"Sure, to a blind man, maybe you're not," she called after him, though without the smugness of the day before.

Now as he stood in the crowded bar of Barry's, Dónal smiled at the memories of what had been the most pleasant day of his life, never minding that it had also been the most expensive. To have lived such a day was worth it, even if it was the only one he'd ever have. But he couldn't imagine that, not with the way he felt now. The world was his for the taking, and God help the man who got in his way.

But just then, someone jostled his elbow, causing some of his porter to spill onto his new shoes. He glared and would've said something, but the man was already lost in the crowd. Deciding then that Barry's was too crowded and noisy, especially after the genteel civility of the Queen's Hotel, he quickly finished his porter and left. While he'd enjoyed the press and commotion the night before, tonight was different, because tonight *he* was different, made a new man entirely by the experience of the day.

It wasn't quite dark yet when he emerged, the long summer evening still casting a faint glow. Still, the streets were almost empty, those shuffling between public houses the only ones about. For a moment he considered going back to the Queen's, but then thought better of it. He'd already spent a good portion of his day there and wanted a little variety. So he headed down the front street looking for a quiet place to have a nightcap.

Yet he found none, all the pubs as bursting with activity as Barry's, and was just about to give up and go to bed when he saw a sign above the very last door. "The Sea Dog," it proclaimed and, looking through the window, he could see it was quiet and dark, perhaps even a bit too much, though being so full of himself and the drink, caution was the last thing on his mind.

So he went inside, stopping just beyond the door to let his eyes adjust to the light. What he saw wasn't encouraging, as every eye in the place was turned upon him in dark appraisal. And as their silence grew palpable, a chill ran down his spine, and he thought briefly of leaving. But then the drink spoke to him, telling him he'd been treated as a gentleman everywhere else and, by God, they would do so here, too! And finding it convincing, he strode confidently to the bar, having just the presence of mind to stay near the door.

"God bless all here!" he called out heartily, motioning to the bartender for service. "I'll have a pint and a drop, sir, if you please."

But the bartender didn't move, other than to lean defiantly on the bar. "Show me yeer money, boyo," he said in a drink-hardened voice. "Then p'raps I'll consider it."

Dónal just glared at him, thinking to back him down. But when the man didn't move or even blink, he shrugged and fished in his pockets for coins, finding only a few pence, not enough to pay for what he'd ordered. The rest was tucked away in his jacket and he'd either have to leave or let them see it.

'Maybe I *should* leave,' he thought in a moment of clarity, remembering Riobárd's warning not to flash his money.

But then the man closest to him spoke, his voice so contemptuous that Dónal felt like slapping him. "Yeah, show 'im yeer money, boyo!" he goaded, his thin whiny voice a perfect reflection of his stature and appearance. "Charlie don't give credit, especially to fancied-up little molly-boys that wander in where they're not wanted!"

All reason fled him then and, glaring at the little man, he jerked the notes from the pouch and held them up for the bartender to see.

"Satisfied?" he asked, his voice as low and dangerous as he could make it.

But the man wasn't looking at him anymore, just at the notes as Dónal shoved them back into his pocket. "Sorry, sir, my mistake," he said sarcastically, before turning his back.

But as Dónal was about to put him in his place, the bartender came with his drinks and he turned to pay, counting his change carefully to make sure he wasn't cheated. When he looked up again, the little man was gone.

'I guess I showed him!' he thought.

Downing his whiskey then, he saw that the others were ignoring him now, having seen his like before, the spoiled son of a middling merchant come to rub elbows with *real* men, and so pretend to be one for a while.

When he finished his ale, Dónal briefly considered having another, but then thought better of it. He'd stayed up later than he'd meant to, and would have to sleep fast if he was to be fresh and rested in the morning. So he left the Sea Dog and headed back toward Barry's, whistling a bright tune as he went. Though there was a lingering glow on the horizon, the streets were dark and empty now, and he stopped to gaze at the stars.

"What a grand day," he said. "I can't imagine a better one."

At that moment, a man lurched from a doorway and staggered toward him, just another sot who couldn't hold his drink. But as he was passing, the man stumbled and fell against him, wrapping his arms around him to keep from falling.

"Sure, I'm sorry, sir!" he slurred, his voice oddly quiet.

Annoyed that he might soil his new clothes, Dónal made to push him away, though the man held on tight.

"Just a moment to catch meself, sir, then I'm on me way."

Looking into his eyes then, Dónal was surprised to find him looking not at himself, but at something behind him.

"Unhand me, sir, if you–" he began, but was cut off by a lightning bolt exploding in his head, followed by darkness and a feeling of falling, of melting into a puddle in the street.

"Get his purse, Willie!" he heard a whiny voice saying. "'Tis in his jacket there!"

"*No, not my money!* Please!" Dónal shouted, though his voice was only in his head.

Then the darkness took him, and he knew no more.

chapter 19

Queenstown
County Cork

THEY WERE AFTER HIM AGAIN, *those bad men who pursued him through the dark alleys of his soul, stretching out their hands to grasp him and do God only knew what horrible things to him, so close now that he could feel their malevolence. He tried to run faster, but his legs were as heavy as stone and ached as if they'd been running for a lifetime. But then suddenly he was on a bright street crowded with people who jostled and bumped him as he ran.* Help me! *he begged them,* Please help me! *But they just pointed at him and laughed and, looking down, he saw that he was naked, and tried to cover himself with his hands, though it only made them laugh the harder.* Stop it! *he screamed, covering his ears,* Please, stop it! *He'd heard that laughter before, as a boy at Uncle Séamus's wake when he'd thought he would surely die of humiliation.* Oh, please stop it, please! *he begged, but the laughter drowned him out. And suddenly, he was there again, in the wake house rising up to view the horror in the coffin. Yet it wasn't horrible at all, just a young man with long red hair, so peaceful that he seemed only to be sleeping. But then he saw the streak of white in the forelocks and realized it was himself lying there, and suddenly he was on his back looking up at the little boy he'd once been and feeling his tears as they fell softly onto his face.* Are you going to Heaven? *the little boy asked him.* No, just to America, *he replied.* I'm going to America on a steamship. *But the little boy was gone, and all he could hear was the laughter.*

It was raining when Dónal awoke, the drops falling softly onto his face from a narrow strip of gray sky, all he could see of it for the buildings hovering close on either side. Where he was or how he'd gotten there, he didn't know, much less why he'd decided to sleep outside on such a lumpy mattress. Sitting up to get his bearings, he winced as a spike of pain shot through his head, and gingerly he probed the lump on the back of it. Had he gotten drunk and fallen, he wondered? Yet if so, how had he wound up lying on a pile of rubbish at the end of a blind alley? And since when did Allihies have any blind alleys, anyway? He closed his eyes and tried to think, though it only made his head hurt worse, so thick was it with injury and the drink. But then the church bells rang the hour, and he counted along absently: . . . six, seven, eight, nine. Nine? There were *nine* of them? No, he thought with a frown, that couldn't be right! There should be only eight bells, only eight because . . . because the ship . . . was to sail at . . .

Then Dónal was up and running, out of the alley and down the street toward the waterfront, oblivious to the pounding in his head and the stares of people, past the market place and on to the quays, coming to an abrupt halt when he saw the empty berth where his ship had been. Desperately he searched the harbor for it, thinking in his delirium and frenzy that he could somehow make it come back for him. But there were no steamers either coming or going, nor even a telltale trail of smoke on the horizon.

Realizing that his ship had sailed without him and that his pockets were as empty as a dry well, Dónal's spirits sank into his fancy new shoes. It was the worst thing that could possibly have happened to him, especially since his own foolishness had caused it. Now he was stranded in Queenstown with no ticket and no money, and no way to come by either aside from going home and begging them off Riobárd. But how could he do that? How could he ever face him after this? Indeed, how could he ever face any of them? He'd rather die a thousand deaths than bear a single moment of that humiliation! The only way to redeem himself, it seemed in that moment, was to go on, to find his own way to America, and to bring Eóghan back.

"No, I'll not go back," he said aloud, his jaw tightening with determination. "I'll get my money back and buy myself another ticket! It doesn't have to be first class or even for a steamer. All that matters is that I get to New York!"

But then he sighed and his jaw went slack as he realized that he had no idea where to look for the thieves, or even where to begin. Indeed, they could be anywhere from right under his nose to in his cabin on the steamer. And of course, there was no point in going back to the Sea Dog for information since he had no money to pay for it, and surely those mugs wouldn't rat on their own for anything less. Maybe Barry could help, he thought. At the very least he could collect his old clothes and sell these new ones in the market. That should bring enough to get him off the island and see him though a day or two at least.

With those thoughts Dónal's spirits brightened somewhat, at least enough to put some spring in his step as he turned toward the inn. Yet it quickly evaporated when he saw how people were looking at him and, stopping before a storefront window, he understood the reason. He was a mess from head to toe, his hair matted and his face dirty, while his clothes were soiled and stank of rotting rubbish. No wonder their reactions were so different than on the previous afternoon when he'd been groomed and polished, a young gentleman about town. He'd been one of them then, but now he was different again, and "different" in the sense of "less than." It hurt so badly he felt like crying. But instead he started to run, as fast as he could and without stopping till he got to Barry's.

⚬〰〰〰⚬

From the center of Cork City, Dónal crossed the bridge over the North Channel of the Lee and climbed the steep hill into the squalid slums of Shandon. Following Phillip Barry's directions, he turned right at Church Street and headed toward St. Ann's Cathedral, near which was MacElligott's pub, the place where he expected to find the men who'd robbed him. As it turned out, they were known to the better publicans of Queenstown, being two of the more notorious pickpockets who plied their trade among the travelers passing through the port. Frankie Parris and Willie Walsh were their names, and Barry himself had barred them from his establishment permanently, trying to keep it "free of those of that ilk." His cook was even related to Parris by marriage, and she'd been a font of information, having no love lost for her aunt's scoundrel of a husband. Though they didn't have the brains between them to spell the word "a," she said, they were smart enough not to live where they worked and came down to Queenstown only at odd times, having no desire to land themselves upon Spike Island. Indeed, they'd surely kill to avoid it, she warned, telling him to watch his step if he found them.

Meanwhile, Barry fetched his old clothes for him and was even kind enough to give him a breakfast. When finished, Dónal cleaned himself up and changed into his old traveling clothes, hoping that would make him more difficult to recognize. His new shoes and unworn shirts he wrapped into his bundle, before taking leave of Barry and going to the market.

"So ye're back to yeer ould self again, are ye?" the old woman had cackled. "A tiger can't change his spots, or so 'tis said, and 'tis the same for a man, too. For though he may change his clothes, divil if he can change what's in them."

"That may be true for you, mother," Dónal retorted, "but still I'm no Tinker, just a poor boy who's doomed to a bit of travelin'."

"'Tis one and all the same, so it is. Ye've the look of a Traveler, call yeerself what ye will. Though ye might live to a hundred, sure, ye'll never be a settled man."

"You'd not be tryin' to hex me, now would you, mother? Witchery is still a burnin' offense in some parts, you know."

"I've no need for the black arts when just the naked truth will do. God laid yeer path before ye, and ye'll follow it, willin' or not."

"True, mother, and when I come home from America, I'll tell you the tale of it."

"Son, by the time ye come home, there'll be nothin' left of me but dust!" she retorted, then turned to the business at hand, satisfied at getting in the last word.

From what he was able to haggle from her, Dónal bought himself a berth on the ferry back to Passage West and then walked to Cork City, arriving in the evening tired and hungry. Though he ate nothing, preferring to conserve his money, he rested a while by the river, waiting for darkness.

Now as he approached MacElligott's, he tucked his hair under the floppy hat he'd stolen from an unguarded cottage, pulled it low over his eyes, and stepped warily inside. After a quick glance around, he made his way to the bar, ordered a pint, and then found a spot near the door from which to survey the room. Seeing no sign of Parris, he began to worry that he might have missed him or that he might not come. Nor could he afford to wait long, since his money would only see him through a couple of pints, and he didn't want to look conspicuous without a drink in hand.

Yet even as he did, the door whisked open and there was little Frankie Parris standing not an arm's length away. As he looked toward him, Dónal tensed, though Parris's eyes just passed on, going slowly around the room until falling upon a man with his arm raised. As Parris elbowed his way through the crowd to join him, Dónal looked the other man over carefully, trying to decide if it was Walsh or not from the dim memory of their encounter. Deciding that it probably was, he took another good look at him while draining his pint, then left the pub and ducked into a shadow across the street. They would come out sooner or later, he knew, though he hoped they didn't wait till closing time when the rush of people might make tracking them difficult.

But as the bells of St. Ann's rang the half-hour, Parris came out alone and headed uphill in the direction of the Cathedral. Without waiting to see if Walsh would follow, Dónal slipped from his hiding place and followed stealthily after, gradually making up the distance as they wound through the streets of Shandon. When he was only a few paces behind, Parris passed a narrow alley, and Dónal was on him, slamming him face-first into the side of a building before hurling him headlong into the alley. Before Parris could recover, Dónal had him pinned to the ground with a knee in his gut and the point of a knife against the soft underside of his jaw. Jerking away the hat, he smiled viciously as the man recognized him and his eyes bugged out with fear.

"Oh Jayzis, don't kill me, *please* don't kill me!" Parris pleaded, choking on the blood from his broken nose.

"Now listen to me, you little rat bastard," Dónal snarled, "and listen very carefully. I want my money, and if you don't give it to me right now, this knife will be ticklin' your brain. Do you understand me, Frankie?"

"But I ain't got it!" Parris whined, his eyes desperate with fear. "Willie's got it! Yeah, Willie's got it, and he's gone . . . gone to Blarney . . . won't be back till Monday! I'll get it for ye then, I swear. Just *please* don't kill me!"

Knowing he was lying, Dónal said nothing, just increased the pressure on the knife.

"No, wait!" Parris pleaded, his eyes slipping briefly past Dónal. "I said I'd get it for ye, and I will! 'Tis at me house, just up the street! I'll take ye there now! Just be easy with the knife and ye'll have it so!"

Now Dónal was at a loss, for though he thought the man still lying, there was only so much harder he could push the knife, and for all the ferocity of his threat, he had no intention of actually killing him. Sure, if he couldn't kill Henry Puxley for clan and country, how could he kill this miserable little rat for money? All he could do was take the threat a step further, and gritting his teeth he pushed the blade through Parris's skin.

"*NO!*" Parris shrieked, his eyes slipping past Dónal again. "I said I'd get it and I will! Just wait a minute!"

But seeing his darting eyes, Dónal flung himself to the side just as a shillelagh whistled past and smacked Parris in the chest. Springing to his feet, he lunged under a blow aimed at his head and thrust the knife into the thigh of his assailant, sending him sprawling over Parris. As both shrieked with pain, Dónal picked up the club and stood over them, raising it as if to strike.

"*I want my money,*" he shouted, "*and I want it now!*"

But even as he did, there came the sound of voices from the street behind him. "Here now, what's with all the roolye-boolye?" one demanded, followed by another saying, "Daycent people are tryin' to slape, so they are!"

"Help us, for God's sake! He's after killin' us!" Walsh shouted.

"And robbin' us, too!" Parris seconded. "Help, murther, police!"

"Murther did ye say?" the first man asked and, turning to the street, Dónal saw a crowd of people gathering, one of whom lit the scene with a lantern.

"Jayzis, what have ye done to 'em?" he exclaimed, seeing the bloodied men at Dónal's feet.

"'Tis not what I've done to them that's the rub!" Dónal shouted angrily. "They robbed me and I'm after gettin' my money back!"

"'Tisn't the shape of it from where I'm standin'!" a man retorted.

"Jimmy!" Parris shouted, recognizing him. "'Tis meself, Frankie! Don't ye believe him so! 'Tis himself that's after thievin'!"

"Sure, I can see that, Frankie!" Jimmy replied, and took a step forward. "Come on, boys, let's get him!"

With that the crowd surged forward angrily and, with no other choice, Dónal flung the club at them and fled in panic. Down the dark alley he ran and into the narrow street beyond, turning the first corner he came to and continuing on through the streets of Shandon, the shouts of his pursuers growing gradually fainter and then stopping altogether. Yet on he ran, blindly and wildly, afraid to look back in case they were gaining on him. This time it was no dream. The bad men really were after him, and God only knew what they'd do if they caught him.

But then his tired feet tangled with each other and he went sprawling into the road, and though he was terrified of the pursuit, he had neither the strength nor the will to get up, just lay there waiting for them. Yet nothing came, only a gentle breeze that whispered through the grass.

Dónal raised his head and looked about himself and, finding no houses or buildings, knew he'd run clear out of the city. Pushing himself up then, he greedily sucked in the warm night air and wiped the sweat from his eyes. How far into the country had his madness driven him, he wondered, and in what direction? Only darkness filled the road behind, while in the distance ahead he saw only the light of a single campfire, gleaming red in the black of night. He sighed then, realizing he'd never get his money back now, and that his only choice was to go on, since he couldn't stay where he was and wouldn't go back to Béara.

Rising then, he silently cursed the fate that had brought him to such a pass, shaking his fist at Heaven and wondering why God had abandoned him. Wasn't he the Chosen One, after all, the Messiah of his people? But no, that was just his earthly father's vision, not his Heavenly Father's design. And now all plans had gone awry and all hopes were dashed, leaving him hungry, penniless, lost and alone, just another faceless beggar in the legion of the homeless, his stomach as empty as his prospects. It staggered him to think how far he'd fallen in just twenty-four hours, the best day of his life shading seamlessly into the worst.

"Who am I?" he asked the night. "And why am I here?"

But the darkness gave him no answers.

With a sigh and a heavy heart, Dónal headed for the firelight. Maybe he'd find help there, a supper and a warm place to sleep, or at least some answers. Anything would be more than the nothing he had.

As he approached the light, he saw that it wasn't a campfire, after all, but a large bonfire some distance off the road. It was ringed with the barrel-shaped caravans of Tinkers, and there were many people dancing around it, the sound of their music and laughter coming to him on the breeze along with the smell of roasting meat. Creeping cautiously into a line of picketed horses, he saw that beyond the fire was a long table heaped with loaves of bread and baskets of potatoes and jugs that he hoped were filled with poteen. It was a feast fit for a king, and, indeed, at the center of the table in a high-backed wooden chair sat a man wearing a crown that might have been cut from a tin bucket, his left hand holding a serving fork and his right a carving knife, apparently the emblems of office for a Tinker chieftain. The fire lit his face with a hellish glow and his dark eyes sparkled with the dance of flames, and when he smiled, his teeth gleamed a ghostly white below the rakish mustache slashing across his lip.

It was Egan Butler, of course, and Dónal couldn't have been happier to see him. Yet just as he rose to step into the open, he was seized from behind by strong hands that pinned his arms and propelled him into the light, throwing him to the ground before Butler's chair and holding him there with booted feet on his back. Before he could protest or identify himself, one of his captors spoke in Irish, saying that they'd caught him trying to steal horses.

"I'm no horse thief!" Dónal said in alarm, knowing what Tinkers did to those of that ilk. "Egan, it's me, Dónal O'Sullivan, Riobárd Puxley's friend! I saw your fire from a distance and was just coming to see if I could sleep by it. I was only hiding among the horses to check things out."

"Gerry, Michael! Let him up!" Butler commanded. "I know him and he's no horse-thief, surely, though what he's *really* up to, we'll have to see.

"So it is you, young O'Sullivan," he continued as Dónal rose. "I thought I saw a flash of white in your hair as the lads brought you in. But what brings you out of the darkness like a spirit of the Otherworld? Weren't you supposed to sail for America this very morning?"

"I was indeed, Egan, but I had an unexpected change of plans. It's rather a long one in the telling, and since I don't want to keep you from your festivities, perhaps I'd better save it for morning."

"But that would mean staying the night with us, now wouldn't it? Funny, but I don't recall offering."

"No, I suppose you haven't," Dónal allowed, suddenly unsure of his welcome. "But I'd be happy to pay for it. I don't have much, but you're welcome to it. In the morning, I'll be on my way and trouble you no more."

But Butler just glared at Dónal as if he'd committed a deadly sin. "Just because the settled folk treat us so doesn't mean we're obliged to return the favor, young O'Sullivan! Even so, your story had better be a good one to warrant our hospitality. This is our feast of the Midsummer and another such meal we're not likely to have anytime soon."

Then Butler rose from his seat and addressed his people. "This is Dónal O'Sullivan from the County Cork. He's a settled man, though a friend of mine nonetheless. Bring him a chair and set it next to mine so we can honor him as our guest. Now, since the meat is cooked, let's get on with it before the night gets any older."

As Dónal went to join Butler, four men brought a roasted pig to the table and set it before them. Butler held up his hands for silence as the people gathered around it.

"Let us all be thankful for the bounty we're about to receive," he said, not quite making a prayer of it. "And now, let the feast begin!"

A cheer went up from the crowd as they scrambled for a place in the queue. Butler himself carved the pig, dropping a chunk of meat on each plate thrust before him, though he reserved the first two pieces for himself and Dónal. When finally the carving was done and their own plates heaped with meat, bread and potatoes, he sat down and passed Dónal a jug.

"What should we drink to?" Dónal asked.

"To this meal, and that it not be our last!"

"To this meal, and may it not be our last."

They ate in silence then, both shoveling the food into their mouths as fast as they could, almost as if fearing it would be taken from them if they didn't. As they ate, the music began again and the people went back to their merrymaking, the dancers whirling round the fire in frenzied revelry while the onlookers hooted and clapped their hands, their bellies full but their appetite for bacchanalia only whetted. Then someone threw another log on the fire, raising a shower of sparks into the night like a burnt offering to the gods of darkness and the Underworld. Indeed, it could have been Hell for all Dónal knew, with the fire and the darkness and the chaos, and the dark king beside him presiding over it.

As he turned to Butler, he found the man eyeing him appraisingly, in much the same way he had in Queenstown two days before. "So then, young O'Sullivan, now that you've eaten your fill, tell me how you came to be here instead of on your way to America."

Dónal hesitated before answering, sure that his tale of foolishness would bring him nothing but scorn. "Well, as I said, it's a long one in the telling, but the short of it is that I was beaten and robbed in Queenstown last night and missed my ship this morning. I tracked the thieves to Shandon tonight and ambushed one of them in an alley. But the other came on me from behind, and the noise of the fighting drew a crowd of neighbors. Seeing that I had the upper hand and knowing the thieves, they assumed that I was the one doing the robbing and chased me away. They frightened me so that I ran all the way out of town before stopping. Then, when I saw your fire in the distance, I made for it because I didn't know where I was or what else to do. But I had no idea it was you until I got here, Egan, and I was as surprised to see you as you were me."

"So you got yourself robbed, did you? Somehow that doesn't surprise me. But go on with you. Tell me how it happened."

Dónal looked away from Butler then, not wanting those eyes that had beaten life on its own terms to see how foolish he'd been. "I didn't learn your lesson very well, Egan," he began, and then the whole story poured out, as if he were in the confessional telling of some deadly sin.

"I see," Butler said when he'd finished, his tone as cold as the black end of the moon. "I tried to warn you that innocence is a dangerous thing, didn't I? Yet there's no teaching a man who won't learn, I suppose, and you seem uncommonly stubborn in that regard. But did Riobárd not warn you to be careful with your money?"

"He did indeed, Egan, and sure if I haven't always been at home. But I thought I'd left the wild behind me, and that city folk would be more civilized."

"Ah, my young O'Sullivan, but you've so much to learn. Don't you know that what we call civilization is just a thin veneer over the animal atavism that is human nature? And as for the country being wilder than the city, if anything, it's just the opposite! Compared to the city, life on the land is simple and bucolic: you get up at dawn, eat what's growing in the fields, work all day to grow more of it, then go to bed at dusk. And when the land fails you, you lie down and die, just like all those thousands when the potato failed. But in the city, people have to survive on their wits, struggling against each other in a jungle where only the fittest survive. That's why city people are so resilient, and why culchies like you get chewed up and spit back out to the bog before you even know what hit you. Why, you barely lasted a day before your money was in someone else's pocket and yourself on the road home! It's a wonder you managed to come by it in the first place!"

Seeing the look on Dónal's face, Butler paused and narrowed his eyes. "Or was it even your own money? For the love of God, don't make it worse by telling me it was someone else's!"

"Yes, it was," Dónal admitted, his face sinking into his hands. "My brother sent part of it from America and Riobárd gave me the rest."

"Well, I'll say one thing for you – at least you never fuck anything up halfway! But what are you going to say to Riobárd when you get home? I know he's a forgiving soul, but even he has his limits!"

"I'm not going home. I still mean to go to America. I just have to come up with the fare, that's all."

"That's all, you say? That's *all*? Well, let me tell you something, young O'Sullivan. The cheapest way to New York I know of is to take a coffin ship from Liverpool to Quebec, then walk the rest of the way. But even that will set you back a few pounds, not to mention the cost of getting to Liverpool in the first place! Do you have any idea how hard a pound is to come by these days? Why, you'll be so old by the time you get there that you'll have forgotten why you went! Of course, you could *steal* the money, I suppose, though somehow I don't think you have it in you to be a thief."

Dónal didn't say anything to that, just stared at the fire, not sure if he should be insulted or not. But the man changed the subject before he could decide.

"And tell me something else, if you will," Butler continued, "why is it so important that you bring this brother of yours back here, anyway? Surely it can't be for his own good unless he's a complete idiot. Surely, he's found life better there than it could ever be on this suffering little island!"

"I want him to come home because we need him here."

"Who needs him, and for what?"

"We do. The Irish. He would be a great asset to our cause."

"Oh, I see what you're getting at. By 'our cause,' you mean James Stephens and his lot, don't you?" Seeing Dónal's surprise, he said, "Yes, I know all about him and his secret 'brotherhood.' Riobárd introduced me to him, and even tried to talk me into joining. But I didn't see the point of it."

"You don't see the point of freeing your country from oppression?"

"Not when I'm a free man already. Besides, an Irish parliament isn't going to look any more kindly upon Travelers than the one in London, so why should I risk my life and liberty for it?"

"But, Egan, if we had our own government, we'd be able to develop trade and industry in our country, and there'd be jobs for everyone, even the Travelers. Then you all could come in from the road and settle down."

"*Ha!* Only a fool would believe that settled people would ever accept us among them when they hate and fear us even more than the English. And besides, young O'Sullivan, most of these people are Travelers by choice and not necessity. Sure, some were put on the road by hard times and so had no choice in the beginning, while others were born to it and have never known anything different. But there's something seductive about this way of life, something you have to live in order to understand. It's a free life, and once it gets in your blood, you don't want to be settled anymore. Take me, for instance. I was a settled man right up to the age of twenty-eight, with a house and cattle and land of my own. But then I fell in love with a Tinker girl I met at the horse fair, a black-haired beauty with the body of a goddess and eyes like blue flame. After we married, she tried the settled life for a while, just to please me. But though she loved me with all her heart, my four walls soon became a prison to her soul and my land a yoke around her neck, and I knew that to keep her there would surely kill her. So because I loved her too much to live without her, I forsook the settled life and turned my back on kith and kin to come out on the road with her, and here I've been ever since, even though she died of the fever the very next winter. But the road was already in my blood by then, and I could no more go back to what I'd been before than fly to the moon. I've been a Traveler now for fifteen years and there's not been a man alive who's happier or freer than me. So that's why I don't care whether Parliament sits in London or Dublin, and why I'm not about to risk my life for people who despise me. I've found my own way in life and the Devil with those who can't!"

There was silence between them then, as Dónal pondered Butler's words. "Well, Egan," he said finally, "that's fine for yourself and your Travelers. But us settled folk want to be free, too, you know, and the only way I can see us so is to get rid of the English. That's why I joined with Stephens and took up the Sword of War, and even why I'm going to America. You see, for a long time I thought I was going to be a leader in the fight, but I've since come to see that I'm not the man for it. So that's why I have to bring my brother back, so he can take my place. And believe what you will, Egan, but getting rid of the English is the best thing for all of us, even the Travelers."

"You are a dreamer, aren't you, young O'Sullivan? And just as all men who can't get along in the world, you dream of making it better, and even ennoble your cause by telling yourself it's the best thing for all of us. But tell me, now – How can you know what's good for the rest of us when you've never walked in our shoes? How can you know what's good for Travelers when you've never been one? How can you even know what's good for your own brother? The answer is you can't, because the only feelings you can ever truly know are your own. So if you want to make the world better for yourself, I suppose it's your prerogative to try. But don't patronize me by saying that it'll be good for me, too, because I'm the only one who can judge that!

"So why not just live your own life and stop worrying about everyone else's? After all, *life* is what's important in this world, more so than love or money or honor, or even happiness or freedom! Life is more important even than how you live it, because where there's life, there's hope, and you can always hope to be a better man tomorrow. So guard your life jealously, young O'Sullivan, because at the tail of the day, it's all you really have to call your own."

Leaning in close then, Butler laid a hand on Dónal's shoulder. "And if you want to see how grand life can truly be," he said, his voice suddenly silken and seductive, "then come on the road with me, and let me show you how to be your own man, a *free* man who follows his own dreams and finds happiness in the world as it is. Come with me, Dónal, and I'll set you free!"

Dónal stared at the dark man gazing at him so intently, the fire dancing in his black eyes and suffusing his face with a red hypnotic glow. It all made so much sense to him suddenly, and he longed to surrender, to go with Butler and sever the ties that bound him. He closed his eyes and pictured himself traveling the roads of Ireland, happy and free, his life his own and no one else's. But then he turned a corner, and there was Eóghan, smiling and waving as he approached. *It's good to be home again*, he said, and Dónal thought his heart would burst with happiness.

Dónal started and opened his eyes. Had he gone to sleep and dreamed it, or was it just the drink playing tricks on his mind? He looked at Butler, still with his hand on his shoulder and leaning expectantly toward him. But now the temptation was gone.

"I can't go with you, Egan," he said, his voice soft but resolute. "I have to find my brother, because right now seeing him is more important to me than anything, even life itself."

Butler withdrew his hand and leaned back in his chair. "I see," he said, smiling curiously. "At last we come to the truth of it, and here at the end of all things, I find that you are following your own dreams. Or at least you think you are. And though I may disagree, perhaps I should just practice what I preach and not judge you by what's best for me. Yet you seem to be cursed with an indelible streak of innocence, young O'Sullivan, one that delivers you from temptation only to lead you into the path of evil. But then again, maybe that's what I like about you, that naïve arrogance that says to the world, 'Go ahead and knock me down! I'll just get up for more!'"

"I'm neither as arrogant nor as innocent as you might think, Egan. I killed a man once, a truly innocent man who'd done nothing more to me than take on the peeler's trade so he could feed his family."

"Yet tonight, you didn't kill the men who'd robbed you, men who'd truly done you wrong, men who deserved to die for their trespass against you. Is it because you killed an innocent man that you can't find it in yourself to punish the guilty? Or is it just because you haven't the stomach for it?"

Dónal didn't answer, just slouched in his chair and stared at the fire. He didn't want to think about those things just then. All he wanted was the release that lay in the bottom of Butler's jug. But the man wasn't done with him yet.

"And why aren't you going to do the smart thing and go home to weasel more money out of poor Riobárd? Is it because you have to punish yourself for your own trespasses, or is it just because you can't bear the humiliation of admitting your foolishness?"

Still Dónal didn't answer, though he glared at Butler sidelong, suddenly hating him for his knack of seeing through to the truth.

"I can tell by the look on your face that I've struck a nerve," Butler said. "So I'll leave it for you to think over and hopefully see the light of wisdom."

"I don't need to think it over! I know what I'm doing and why, and like you said, Egan, it's none of your business, anyway!"

"Ah, well, so it isn't. But if that's your final word, then there's nothing else I can do for you, except perhaps to see you on your way. We take the road tomorrow for my own country around Cahir. Come with me that far and you'll be well on your way to Dublin, and to the cheap fares from Liverpool. Call it a courtesy from one traveler to another, if you like but, in any case, come with me. I can teach you a few things about the road that you're in dire need of learning!"

At the mention of Cahir, Dónal's mind flashed on *The Book of O'Sullivan Béara*, and he heard nothing else. "Knockgraffon is near Cahir, isn't it?" he asked, sitting up and turning toward Butler.

"Yes, it is. How do you know about Knockgraffon?"

"It was the ancient seat of the O'Sullivans, from the time when Fiacha Muilleathan was King of Munster until Dónal Mór was driven out by the Normans."

"Ah, yes, I'd forgotten about that. My own ancestors were among those Normans who drove yours out, I'm afraid, and eventually built the great fortress at Cahir. But unlike our cousins, the Earls of Ormond, some of us became more Irish than the Irish themselves, to use the old phrase, especially those of us descended from James Gallda Butler, the one who held the castle for O'Neill when Ireland was yet Irish. But as the younger sons of younger sons became more and more distantly removed from the lordship, we grew to be just as Irish as the rest of the Irish, I'm afraid, impoverished, benighted, and oppressed, carrying the mark of James Gallda's foolishness through all our generations."

"Keep talking like that and I might bring you round to my way of thinking after all," Dónal said, seeing the far-away look in Butler's eyes and hearing the pride of race in his voice.

But Butler just laughed at him, and suddenly he was himself again, just a man and neither saint nor Satan. "No, Dónal, I'm a Traveler to my bones, I'm afraid, a man of the horse and caravan, the campfire and the open road. My heart is given to the beauty that lies around the next bend, and there's no room in it for anything else. But enough of this now! There's fun to be had, and yet here we sit, wasting our time on frivolities when we should be about the serious business of wine, women and song! There'll be time enough for deeper contemplation tomorrow."

He rose then and pulled Dónal up with him. "Come now and drink with me, my royal O'Sullivan friend, a traveling king to the King of the Travelers."

"How did you get to be that, anyway?"

"The same way any man gets to be king, or chieftain or member of Parliament, for that matter. I had enough money to buy it."

Dónal found nothing to say, just stared at Butler with a silly look on his face. After a moment, the man took pity on him and led him to the fireside.

When the musicians finally paused, Dónal asked the piper if he could play a tune, and at a nod from Butler the man assented. Taking a seat, he closed his eyes and began to play the lament he'd composed for his brother, pouring his soul into it so that it filled the night with music, ethereal and beautiful and sad. But as he played, the melody diverged from his masterpiece and seemed to take on a life of its own, as if his body were disconnected from his will and his fingers become the instruments of some unseen force. Yet it seemed somehow natural to him, for what was the point of playing a lament for Eóghan, now that he knew him to be alive and prospering in New York? Rather, it was for all those left behind in Ireland and the hard life they yet lived. And as the beauty of it touched them, the Traveling People fell silent, transfixed, it seemed, by its keening for their individual and collective suffering. So they remained when he'd finished and opened his eyes, the only sounds the crackling of the fire and the soft weeping of a woman.

But Dónal had eyes only for Butler, watching from just beyond the fire, his dark face vivid with its dancing flames, yet aglow now with the warmth of friendship.

"Does that have a name?" the man asked, his voice soft and reverent in the stillness.

"I call it *The Lament for All Things Sad*," Dónal extemporized, knowing even as he said it that he'd never again be able to play it just so.

Butler took off his crown then and actually bowed. "Your pardon for my harsh words to you, my lord O'Sullivan Béara. Now that I've seen your soul, I understand you a little better."

With that the spell was broken, and the people began to move about. Dónal rose and offered the pipes to their owner, but he just shook his head.

"No, you keep them," he said. "I'm not worthy anymore."

chapter 20

Knockgraffon
County Tipperary

IN THE DISTANCE, THE ORANGE FIREBALL of the evening sun made its deliberate way down behind the rounded rumps of the Galty Mountains, its last rays touching the sparse summer clouds with a finger of flame and setting them to smolder in a deepening sky. Closer at hand, the River Suir meandered lazily through the lush plains of South Tipperary, its course a ribbon of glinting silver in the soft evening light. Yet it was only for the land itself that Dónal had eyes, for the sea of green spreading before him like a goddess of fertility, verdant and voluptuous, its broad elegant sweep broken only by gentle undulations sculpted by the loving hand of God. It was the most beautiful thing he'd ever seen, a latter-day Garden of Eden filled with cattle and cultivated fields, cottages trailing turf-smoke from their chimneys, and the ruins of ringforts and tower houses, themselves testament to the richness of the land and the covetous men who'd lorded over it. And well could he understand their avarice, feeling it himself in the burning desire to possess it and hold it to the exclusion of all others.

For it had been O'Sullivan land once, their province and their patrimony, and as he stood within the ancient ringfort of his ancestors and surveyed his majestic heritage, he felt like a prince returning from long exile, as indeed he was. Yet he was a prince in name only and knew it, for their province had been taken from them long ago and their patrimony despoiled by a foreign invader, so that strangers now cultivated the fields and reaped the bounty that God had apportioned to the O'Sullivans. And in that moment, Dónal suddenly hated the man standing next to him, scion of the foreigner who'd stolen his birthright and banished him to a scabby country on the far edge of the world. Indeed, he'd have struck him down in fury had he made but the slightest move. But Egan Butler stood by quietly, as if attending a friend as he mourned the passing of a loved one, understanding only too well the passions this land could stir in a man's heart.

Anyway, the feeling was gone as quickly as it had come. For Dónal was overwhelmed with wonder that anyone could ever have hungered in a place like this, or, indeed, in all of Erin if She had such a breadbasket from which to feed Her children. And all the country he'd passed through since leaving Cork City had been much the same, green and gentle and lush, broken only here and there by soft mountains that could be forgiven the intrusion for their loveliness. Yet even here in Paradise, The Hunger had left its calling card, for the landscape was littered with roofless cottages and pocked with overgrown lazy beds and sullied by the coffinless graves of the famished. In his avarice Man had brought famine to this place that God made Green, and it would be forever scarred by the memory.

Turning back to watch the last of the sunset, he shook his head and sighed. "I've seen so little of the world, and so little of Ireland even. Yet for its very diversity, I think her beauty must be unique among all the nations of the Earth. I've always thought Béara so lovely, you see, so heartbreakingly beautiful in the contrast between green and stone, mountain and meadow, sea and sky. But then I traveled along the Owvane and up through Cousane Gap, and thought it beautiful as well, though it was a different kind of beauty from Béara. Then I saw the Lee Valley and Cork Harbor and East Cork and the Knockmealdowns and Slievenamon, and they were all lovely as well, and as different from each other as they were lovely. So it seems to me that in Ireland a man can be in the midst of the most beautiful country he's ever seen, then go around the corner and be in the midst of the most beautiful country he's ever seen, yet it's completely different from where he just was."

Butler lay a friendly hand on his shoulder and nodded in understanding. "So you begin to understand something of the Traveler's love for the road. Indeed, I doubt there's any among the children of Erin who love Her more than we. For we love Her as a man loves a beautiful woman, desiring Her and wanting to touch Her on every part of Her perfect body. That's why we can't stay in one place very long, because there's always another beautiful part of our lover waiting just around the next bend, one that we've never touched before, or that perhaps we've touched a thousand times and yet each time is just like the first, because it's the *present* time, even though it won't be as good as the *next* time. I've never traveled beyond Ireland myself, but if there's a more beautiful place on this earth, I can't imagine it."

"That's saying a lot for a man like you, Egan. Maybe when I come home I will come out on the road with you for a time, just to see it for myself."

"No man goes on the road only for a time. It gets into your blood too quickly, and before you know it, you're hooked!"

"Maybe. But, tell me, Egan. In all your travels through Ireland, have you ever seen a more beautiful place than this?"

Butler didn't answer directly, just turned and looked over the river valley. "I love this place, too. It tore out my heart to leave. But each place I see is more beautiful than this because it's the next place, even as this place is more beautiful than the last. I love this country, Dónal, all of it, and I'll never get enough of it!"

There was a silence between them then, as they stood side-by-side watching the sunset, each lost in his own thoughts. But when the color began to fade, Butler touched Dónal lightly on the arm and nodded toward the road. "Come on. We'd better go before it gets much darker."

As Butler moved away, Dónal took one last look around just to be sure he hadn't missed anything, then quickly followed. At the road, they mounted their horses and headed north past the ruins of Knockgraffon

Cathedral and on toward the town of Golden, Butler on his black stallion and Dónal again on his old horse, which the man had returned despite his objection that he couldn't pay for it.

"For what little he's worth to me, you may as well have him," Butler had said. "It's only money, after all, and it's not like there'll never be any more of it. Besides, you paid for him the other night with your piping. I've never in my life been touched by music like that, and if I live to a thousand, I doubt if I ever will be again. If you do nothing else in your life but play the pipes, Dónal, your time on this earth will still have been well spent. And we have a need for artists in this world of ours, for they thicken that thin veneer we call civilization."

But Dónal paid him no heed. He'd been too busy pondering the road ahead to think about what he should do with his life. And so he was still as they rode through the twilight together, just the two of them, now that Butler had left his tribe camped on the south side of Cahir on land he still held as a middleman. And though most of it he'd sublet to tenant farmers, he reserved a small plot for his people to camp when he came each summer to settle accounts with his agent. Of course, all his neighbors hated him for bringing them there, and even his younger brothers and relations would no longer speak to him. But he didn't seem to care. He was his own man and complete within himself, at peace with the world around him even if it was not at peace with him.

But for himself, Dónal was glad to leave the caravans behind. Though he'd come to understand the seduction of the road, he also saw the darker side of it, in the hostility and suspicion with which the settled folk viewed the Travelers. *Refuse none from your door, for one may be the Christ*, the old homily went. Yet for the Travelers, another was especially reserved. *I may be poor, but at least I'm better than a Tinker*, it went, and Dónal had seen it applied in every village along the way. Indeed, people would line the road to jeer at them, while children (and even adults) would throw stones and swat stragglers with sticks, and if the Travelers tried to protect themselves the peelers would be summoned to hustle them along, all in an effort to keep them from camping nearby. Of course, there was at least some justification for it, Dónal saw, as the Travelers' reputation for thieving, swindling and panhandling was not completely without basis. Even so, it was hard for him to understand. They were *Irish* after all, and came from all the septs and provinces, so it wasn't as if they were so fundamentally different from their settled cousins. Nor could Butler explain it to him, either, except to say that perhaps the hostility of the settled folk stemmed from their anxiety about the precariousness of their own lives, and their knowledge that they, too, could easily be turned from their homes and set upon the road to wander.

"Anyway," he'd concluded, "the real answer is probably locked so deep in the vaults of time that we'll never know. Travelers have been on the road for time out of mind, maybe even before the Normans came and displaced people from their land, and our numbers have swelled with every calamity that's befallen since. Over the centuries, the hostility and suspicion between us and the settled folk have grown out of all proportion to the true differences between us. But then, I suppose that's true of all the peoples, now isn't it? We're a world of petty tribes, Dónal, and each one fears and despises that which it finds different in the others, even if it's only a matter of whether your house has wheels on it or not."

But whatever the reason, all the hostility vanished when they left the caravans behind, for then they were just two ordinary travelers going about their business, and people treated them with all the warmth and courtesy customary of the Irish. Indeed, they'd spent a pleasant afternoon together, riding through the country and visiting places Butler had known in his youth. He'd even taken Dónal through Cahir and by the great castle from which the town drew its name, *Cathair Dhúin Iascaigh*, Fortress of the Fish Abounding. It was by far the most impressive castle Dónal had ever seen and he could well understand its reputation for impregnability. Indeed, it was the raising of the great castle and subsequent rise in the fortunes of the Cahir Butlers that led to the demise of Knockgraffon as a market town. Now there was nothing left of the latter but crumbling fortifications and the sad ruins of its once-proud cathedral. Even within the ringfort of King Fiacha, the Normans raised a tall motte, which long since had passed into lore as a *sídhe*, a fairy mound, so that even the folk memory of its royal past had slipped away.

He thought it a sad state of affairs, too, not only for himself and the O'Sullivans but for all the Irish, since so much of their history was connected with the place. Indeed, Eóghan Mór himself was said to be buried there, and his son, King Fiacha, and for that reason alone, Dónal thought it should be a national shrine. But of course the English would never allow such a thing, since a shrine to their glorious past might incite the Irish to fight for a brighter future.

As they rode away, Dónal turned for a last look at Knockgraffon, but it was already too dark to see much. Perhaps he would come here to live someday, he thought. Perhaps he would even buy the ringfort and return the line of Fiacha to its ancient seat. It was a more modest ambition surely than his father's dream of reclaiming Béara, but also one he felt more capable of attaining. Anyway, Eóghan could be The O'Sullivan Béara again if he wanted and pursue their patrimony there. But before any of it could happen, he had to get to Eóghan and bring him back, and with that thought and a sigh, Dónal turned back to the long road ahead.

Having decided to go on to Cashel with him, Butler was now leading Dónal to a friend's house where they could get a meal and a bed for the night. They came to it soon after Knockgraffon, and Butler led the way off the road and into the yard.

"This is it," he said, nodding toward the house. "This is where my friend lives. His name is John Fitzgerald and Margaret is his wife, though everyone knows her as 'Peg.' Because my father was his best friend, they've always treated me like visiting royalty, so you can be sure of a warm welcome, too."

As they walked to the door, Dónal gave the place a quick once-over, taking in the fact that it was a prosperous-looking two-story house with a slate roof and plastered walls. Its large windows were cheerfully lit with the glow of candles and the ubiquitous stream of turf smoke rose from the chimneys at either end. Being situated on the north side of the road, he guessed it to have a fine view of the Galtys and the river, which would make for a pleasant setting indeed if the fields about were as lush as he'd seen at Knockgraffon.

Reaching the solid-looking door, Butler gave it a good rap, and was answered by the sound of dogs barking and a man's voice shouting them down. "Whisht, ye mangy monglers, whisht, I say!" he commanded in English, though to no avail. But then his voice came again from just behind the door, shouting over the dogs to know who was there.

"'Tis Egan Butler, John," he said, also in English. "Egan Butler."

But it was no use, and the man called for others to take the dogs away, opening the door only when their commotion receded. In the light of his candle, Dónal saw that he was quite short, though still thickset and strong for the advanced age that was in him. His yellow-gray hair was thin and lank, and his complexion pale and pasty, while his lumpy face was dominated by a nose that might have been called *patrician* had it graced a man less obviously of peasant stock. Indeed, he looked as if he might have sprung from the soil itself and, with his earthy sturdiness and self-satisfied air of middling prosperity, seemed to have been molded by Providence especially to define the term "strong farmer."

Yet when the man saw Butler, his face lit up like dew-dappled flowers on a spring morning. "Egan Butler!" he shouted, his coarse voice booming joyfully into the night as he embraced his visitor. "'Tis yeerself in the flesh, good man that ye are! I thought me ould ears was teasin' me when I heard yeer name! How long has it been now since ye've been with us? Two years, or is it more? And where've ye been keepin' yeerself all that time? But just look at ye, Egan! Why, ye've not changed a bit for all the miles that're in ye, God knows how many they be! Sure, ye're as handsome as ever and still the dark man we lock our women away from, I see. But damn me, if it isn't grand to see ye so! I was wonderin' to Peg just the other day what had become o' ye. Time was when ye was a regular here, even after ye took up the travelin' life. Why I was half afraid ye might've sailed off to Chinie, or even gone for a red Injun in America, such notions as that comin' into me mind. Yet here ye are on me own doorstep, as hale and hardy as ever a man so born. But tell me how ye're keepin', Egan, and where ye've been all this time!"

But before Butler could answer any of his questions, Fitzgerald turned and called for his wife. "Peg! 'Tis Ryan Butler's ould son, our own Egan, come to pay us a visit, good man that he is! Get out here with ye, woman, and give him a proper welcome!"

Turning back to his visitors, he still didn't give Butler a chance to reply. "But who's this solid-lookin' fellah ye've got with ye, Egan? He's not a man o' this parish, now is he? Is he one o' yeer own or just a chance meetin' on the road? But ye're welcome whoever ye are, young fellah, and from whatever tribe ye might come. 'Tis a fact indeed that any friend of Egan Butler is a friend o' me own! But give me his name, Egan, so I can pass it on to Peg and the childer."

For the first time then since he'd opened the door, the man paused for breath, and Butler quickly stepped into the breach, knowing he'd have to make the most of it. "You're no worse for the wear yourself, John, and still faster than a flamin' hare with the chat, I see!"

Fitzgerald laughed at that, a good hearty belly-laugh that brought a smile to Butler's face and Dónal's, too. "Go on with ye, now!" he said, winking sidelong at Dónal. "If ye've no respect for yeer elders, then I'll just leave ye here in the gloamin'."

Before Butler could retort, Fitzgerald turned to Dónal and, grasping his hand in his hard fist, shook it like he meant to shake it off. "Welcome to Lagganstown, me boy, or *Baile an Logáin* as they make it in the ould language," he said, butchering the Gaelic as only a native English speaker could. "I'm John Fitzgerald, and me home is yeer own for as long as ye're pleased to make it so."

"*Go raibh míle maith agaibh*," Dónal thanked him in Irish, just to give him a taste of how the language should sound. Continuing in English, he added, "I'm Dónal O'Sullivan, from Allihies in the County Cork. I look forward to repayin' your hospitality in kind, Mr. Fitzgerald."

"Well, now!" Fitzgerald said, cutting his eyes to Butler and nodding at Dónal. "Here's a lad who could teach ye some manners, Egan, solid man that he is, solid as the Rock of Cashel!

"'Tis a Cork man ye are, is it?" Fitzgerald continued at his manic pace. "And a Gaelic speaker, too? Me own dado had the ould tongue in him, God rest him, but we've had none of it in the family since his time, and himself gone over sixty years now. Sure, I've just used every word of it I have in me, save for the odd bit I've picked up here and there, *sláinte*, meanin' 'good health,' and the words for 'hello' and 'good-bye.' But we've no callin' for it now, just the English, the *Bearla* as ye'd call it in the Gaelic. Still, 'tis a pity, wouldn't ye say, that we can't speak our own language though we call ourselves people o' the Gael? But ye're an O'Sullivan, too, did ye say? We've still the odd one o' yez lurkin' about, though they've mostly gone off to Cork and Kerry now, so 'tis said. But then ye'd know that already, bein' a Kerry man yeerself. Or is it Cork? Sure, 'tis Cork so.

"But tell me now, Egan. How did ye come to be with a Cork man? Have ye been down that way recently, and do ye collect the odd ones as ye go, like a sergeant recruitin' for the Queen? Or did he come to ye here in our own County Tipp? But here, I'm forgettin' me own manners, so it happens when ye come to the age that's in me. Come inside to the fire, and we'll have it all said over a drop and a bite!"

"Peg!" he shouted, turning to lead them inside. "Peg, 'tis our Egan come to pay us a call, did ye not hear me so!"

"I did so, ye ould goat!" a woman's voice replied. "This house was never as big as ye'd have us believe, nevermindin' what the tax man says to the contrary. But just ye give yeer tongue a rest and bring him inside so we can all take the measure of him!"

"'Tis a shame what the world is comin' to in these latter days," Fitzgerald moaned, though with a wink, "when a man's wife will give him no respect in his own house!"

He led the way inside then, past the stairs that rose steeply behind the door and into the room on the left. It was obviously a parlor of sorts, being comfortably furnished with a few chairs and stools arranged about the fireplace. A spinning wheel stood in one corner, and from the look of it, they'd interrupted the woman's evening work. She was waiting for them when they entered, and the first thing Dónal noticed about her was that she was considerably younger than her husband, being about the same age as Butler, and also considerably more attractive, though it would've been hard not to be.

"Egan Butler, 'tis indeed yeerself!" she said, embracing him warmly. "Sure, if ye aren't a sight for sore eyes, handsome divil that ye are! I was beginnin' to wonder if ye hadn't emigrated, so long have ye been absent from us. Why, 'twas the Halloween o' '59, the last time ye was here, sure, when ye brought the turnips for the young ones to make their jack-o'-lanterns. And why so long away with ye, Egan? Was ye indeed across the water? Or was it just a bit o' rest from the ould man's blather ye was after? And for the love o' Mike, man, don't just stand there gapin' at me like I've three heads upon me shoulders. Give me a daycent account o' yeerself!"

As Dónal listened to her speak in the same frenetic manner as her husband, he wondered briefly how the two of them ever managed to communicate. But then Fitzgerald had him by the arm and was introducing his wife before Butler had a chance to reply.

"Sure, Peg, but if ye think our Egan such a fine figger of a man," he exclaimed, "just have a look at this young fellah he's brought with him! 'Tis indeed a shame that our Ellen is such a young one yet, and that our Kate and Mary already have husbands o' their own, else we might be after sproutin' an O'Sullivan branch from the family tree!"

"Sure, if he isn't sharp enough to make a cat turn backwards!" Peg exclaimed, looking Dónal frankly up and down. "What's yeer name, young fellah, and don't be shy like our Egan here!"

"'Tis Dónal O'Sullivan, so he says, no evidence to the contrary presented," Fitzgerald interjected. "He comes from a place called Allihies in the County Cork, more than that, ye'll have to ask yeerself. But sure, if there won't be time enough for that later, it bein' early yet. Let's get the childer off to bed and sit ourselves by the fire."

"John! Phillip! Go and see to their horses," Fitzgerald commanded his two older sons, "and then off to bed with yeerselves. Ellen, go up now and take young Patrick with ye."

Over their objections that they wanted to stay up with "Uncle Egan," Peg shooed the children out, pausing only to introduce them to Dónal. They were all solid and hardy-looking if not particularly handsome, having gotten too much of their father in the mix, it seemed. But it was their youth that surprised Dónal, given the age of their father. Indeed, the phrase *ould goat* took on a new meaning when he learned the youngest was only four. So whatever their difficulties in communication, the two Fitzgeralds had at least managed to procreate.

But Fitzgerald gave him no time to ponder it, drawing them to seats by the fire and spending the next few minutes telling Dónal about his children. In addition to those four, he said, there were five older ones, including two daughters, who were married and living off with their husbands, and three sons, who were all across the water doing seasonal work in England. Thus far, they'd been twice blest, he said, crossing himself, having lost a child neither to the reaper nor the coffin ships. Yet the older boys were all making noise about joining his brothers in America and he didn't know how much longer he could keep them from it, or indeed if he even should. None of them had any real interest in farming, and, of course, there was nothing else for them in Ireland. Yet he didn't think he could bear the heartbreak of watching them take to the emigrant road, never to return. His own five brothers had all gone years before, and he still remembered how the parting had hurt and what it had done to his father. Emigration was such a curse upon them and there'd be no end to it as long as things were the way they were. Yet what could a man do, save to go against his God and have fewer children. But despite the pain of it, he had to admit their going had been a good thing, too, for they'd all found better lives across the water and left the land unburdened for their support. And just as he'd inherited the whole farm from his father and he from his despite the laws to the contrary, so he intended to leave it to only one of his sons, and avoid the trap that so many Irishmen had fallen into of progressively subdividing their holdings until they were too small to support all the people living on them. So if the three older boys didn't want the farm, then maybe in the heel of the hunt, letting them go would be the right thing to do. He had three other sons, after all, and surely one of them would want it. Indeed, his fourth son, young John, seemed to have an interest, and he supposed that when all was said and done it would be him who would carry on the Fitzgerald legacy at Lagganstown. After all, it would be a shame for it to end with himself after four generations on the same land.

"And what o' yeer own family, young man?" he asked Dónal. "Have they been long in the homeplace?"

"You might say so, yes. Before me, they'd lived in the same house for nine generations and at Dunboy Castle for another eight beyond that. And before that, they were just down the road here at Knockgraffon, where they'd lived since Fiacha Muilleathan was King of Munster in the fourth century after Christ."

"Wisha! 'Tis wondersome a man could know so much in these latter days we're in, so muddled have the histories become. Why, I can tell ye no more of us beyond me own dado, though 'tis sprung o' the Earls o' Desmond we was, so he always said. But what o' yeerself now? Do ye know much o' those that come before ye?"

But it was Butler who answered for him. "Sure, John, he does. Indeed, he can trace the line of his O'Sullivan ancestors all the way back to Adam himself. For you see, our Dónal is a real Irish chieftain, bein' a direct descendant of that same King Fiacha that he just mentioned, and of the Lords of Knockgraffon and that branch of the family that later took over in Béara and Bantry. But for our little misunderstandin' with the English, he'd not be in your house at all now, but away safe in his own castle!"

"Go on with yeerself," Fitzgerald said, eyeing Dónal dubiously. "Why, I thought the ould chieftains all died out long ago, them that didn't go off to France with that O'Neill fellah!"

"Sure, if that isn't too far from the truth, more's the pity," Dónal sighed, remembering his feelings at Knockgraffon. "For I'm a chieftain in name only, with neither clan to lead nor province to lord it over. But no, Mr. Fitzgerald, not all of us have died out yet. There's still a few who can trace our ancestry back to the old days when the world was young and the Gael mighty and free. We were lords of power and majesty then, holdin' sway over the fairest, most fertile land this side of Eden. But that was then and this is now, I suppose you'd say, and in this day and time, what are we to anyone but relics of the past, just the long-dispossessed heirs of forgotten petty kingdoms, havin' nothin' but our sterile genealogies to remind us that we were ever anything more? Nothin', I'd have to say, indeed nothin'."

The silence hung heavily among them when he'd finished, Fitzgerald for once seeming to have nothing to say. It was probably a bit above his head anyway, Dónal thought, judging from his round staring eyes. He was just a simple farmer, after all, a man whose interest in the world began and ended at the borders of his fields.

"Do you think we might have that drink now, Mr. Fitzgerald?" he asked, craving release from the melancholy that had gripped him.

"Begorragh so, 'tis just the thing for it."

He made to get up, but just then Peg returned from upstairs and he turned to her with a sly smile. "Ah, Peg-o'-me-heart, the light o' me life," he called merrily. "Before ye sit down, would ye be so kind as to fetch me jug and a rack o' jars?"

"Now, John," Peg admonished, wagging her finger at him, "ye ain't forgettin' what Doctor Carew said about it, are ye?"

"Whisht, woman, don't be givin' out to me when we've company in the house. Why, Egan just revealed his young friend to be a real Irish chieftain, and I'd not have it said that our hospitality didn't take the measure of his nobility. And where's the harm in the occasional drop, divil the age that's in a man? Sure, me own Da, may he rest in peace, took his daily constitutional right up to the day he died, himself nearly eighty and as fortunate we should all be!"

"Sure, but who's to say 'twasn't the drink what killed him so young? But all right, ye ould goat. I can see yeer heart's set on it, no matter the good sense to the contrary. But when the reaper comes a'knockin', just don't say I never warned ye so!"

"Ould goat, indeed! Sure, woman, but I'll never be ould enough for ye to spake to me so, and I never forget a thing, not that ye're after lettin' me! Now run as quick as yeer tongue and fetch me that jug!"

The genuine annoyance in Fitzgerald's voice surprised Dónal, given how he'd made light of her teasing earlier. Yet for all his affability, it seemed that John Fitzgerald took his drink seriously, which raised him a notch in Dónal's estimation.

In a moment, Peg returned carrying a jug and four glasses, which she set on a stool between the men before pouring a generous measure into each. The whiskey glowed an enticing amber in the firelight, and it was all Dónal could do to wait for his host.

But Fitzgerald made no move, just eyed the glasses as though they were full of poison. "Here now, what's that extra one for?"

"Go on with yeerself, man!" she replied, not intimidated by his show of gruffness. "'Tis none but enough in it, and if ye're seein' more, then ye've too much taken already."

"What are ye after here, Peg? 'Tis not for ye, o vanithee, to drink with the guests!"

"What's good for the gander is just as better for the goose, so 'tis said!" She picked up her glass and tossed back her measure like she had hair on her chest. "Now if ye gentlemen will excuse me, I'm off to scare ye up a supper. Ye do have a hunger on ye, don't ye, boys?"

"Sure, Peg, we do," Butler replied eagerly. "We're as hungry as the day we were born!"

"And just as empty-headed, too, so I'll wager," she said with a wink.

"Ye mind yeer tongue, woman," Fitzgerald called after her, "or 'tis the rounds o' the kitchen I'll give ye!" But she was gone, leaving him red-faced and sputtering.

Butler just laughed at him. "Will you never learn, John? On the best day you've ever had, she's still more than a match for you. And sure, what's the point of havin' a woman that isn't?"

"Ah, Egan, if ye don't see to the heart of things, no better man," Fitzgerald acknowledged with a rueful grin. "'Twould be an ould goat indeed who didn't appreciate a one such as herself, young and lovely as she is. Still, there's times when she gets me blood to boilin' so that

414

I think I just might burst with it. A different kind o' man would make her think twice about givin' out to me so!"

"If you were that kind of man, John, she'd never have married you in the first place. But you're not and she did and so here we are, God in His Heaven and all things right with the world. Now if 'tis all the same with you, I'll have that drink before the night gets any oulder!"

"Ah, there I go, begob, forgettin' me manners again," Fitzgerald said, raising his glass. "*Sláinte.*"

"*Sláinte is saol,*" Dónal replied in harmony with Butler before draining his glass. The whiskey was smooth and mellow, parliament and not poteen, and he savored its flavor on his tongue and its warmth in his gut, knowing the world would soon be a friendly place again, all its hard edges softened by the magic of the drink.

"Ah, the Kilbeggan's!" Butler purred, tipping his glass for another. "You can say what you like about him, Dónal, but John Fitzgerald has never been one to scrimp on the essentials, good man that he is."

"Ain't ye the kind one for sayin' so, Egan," Fitzgerald said as he poured another round. "*Slainte!*"

Again they drained their glasses and again Fitzgerald refilled them, though rather than draining his in a single gulp, he sat back in his chair to savor it, eyeing Butler fondly as he did. "Ah, Egan. 'Tis such a pleasure to see ye again after all the time that's in it. 'Twas just the other day I was wonderin' to Peg what had become o' ye and if we'd see ye again on this mortal side o' the veil. Sure, if the roads aren't a caution these days, especially for Tinkers, so I've heard. Still, ye'd know more than meself, seein' as I've never in all me life been beyond the borders of this parish, savin' the odd trip to Cashel or Golden now and again, of which I'm doin' even less than I used to. So I do love to hear the tales that're in it, of the places ye've been, the things ye've seen, the people ye've met. And spakin' o' which, what of our young Dónal here? Ye never did give us an accountin' of him."

"Sure, 'tis simple enough, John," Butler said. "He's on his way to Dublin to catch the Liverpool ferry, and his cousin, a friend of mine, asked me to see him as far as Cashel."

415

"Ah, sure, 'tis work ye're after, ain't it?" Fitzgerald said to Dónal.

"'Tis, in a manner of speakin'," he replied, "but only till I've saved enough for a passage to America. I've a brother that's in the war over there, and I want to bring him home before he gets himself killed."

"Ah, sure, I've heard o' their troubles, though I didn't know 'twas a shootin' war it'd come to already. Me own brother, Phillip, lives in one of them southern states that's broke off to set up their own country, 'Georgia,' I think 'tis called. Sure, give me a minute and I'll show ye his picture."

Fitzgerald went to the cupboard then, leaving his guests to help themselves to another drink.

"Thanks for not telling him the truth," Dónal muttered in Irish.

"You've learned your lesson and there's no point rubbing it in," Butler replied.

"Here it is!" Fitzgerald said, returning with an old daguerreotype. "'Twould be himself and his missus there, their Mary Ellen between, and his youngfellah, Phillip, in the black nanny's arms, his birth bein' the occasion for the letter. 'Twas made . . . let me see now, it says on the back . . . 'Twas made back in '42, and that's eighteen, no begob, *nineteen* years ago. Jayzis, can it be so? Why the youngfellah's a man himself now, goin' on about the same age as our Dónal here, if 'tis no mistake in it! Why, it seems only yesterday that Phillip's letter come, and that the last I ever heard of him. Sure, I wonder if he's even still alive."

Fitzgerald's eyes were far away and his voice barely a whisper as he said the last, his mind having wandered to another place and time. But Dónal was curious about the picture and wanted another look. He'd never seen a Negro before, of course, though he had heard that such people existed, living in the far-away lands of Africa, as dark and mysterious as the jungles they inhabited.

"Can I see that please, Mr. Fitzgerald?" he asked.

"Sure, son," the man replied absently. "Help yeerself."

Dónal grasped it eagerly and turned toward the fire for better light. Yet it wasn't the dark face of the nanny that held his eye, but the fair and delicate face of the young wife as she stood beside her husband, composed and elegant though unsmiling, her beauty radiating a spectrum of loveliness from the sepia tones of the old daguerreotype. She was the most beautiful woman he'd ever seen, her loveliness matching even that of his ancestral home and touching his soul just as it had. Indeed, if Knockgraffon was a latter-day Garden of Eden, he'd surely found its Eve.

"What's her name?" he asked in Irish, the thought slipping out unintended.

"Hm? What's that?" Fitzgerald asked, his mind still wandering the murky roads of the past. "What did ye say?"

But Butler heard, and understood. "Eleanor. Her name is Eleanor," he said, also in Irish. "It's there on the back, if you'd know."

Turning it over, Dónal said it aloud. "Eleanor. My God, even her name is beautiful." Looking at Butler, he found him looking back, a black shadow against the firelight. "How did you know?"

"I've seen it, too," he said, meaning her beauty. "But Dónal. That picture shows her as she was nineteen years ago. She's old enough now to be your mother, if indeed she's still alive, and the years are sure to have left their mark on her, you know."

"Maybe so. But to me, she'll always look just like this."

"Here, now!" Fitzgerald interjected. "What are ye after, goin' on in the Gaelic when ye know I've none of it?"

"Sorry, John, we forgot ourselves," Butler replied. "We were just remarkin' on your brother's handsome wife."

"Sure, if he ain't the man himself," Fitzgerald agreed, "always with more than his share of the luck."

He went on to illustrate with a story of their youth, but Dónal wasn't listening. He was too lost in the beauty of Eleanor to dwell on the homely little man next to her. What would it be like to hold her in his arms, he wondered, and to feel her holding him? What would it be like to kiss her? He knew it would never happen, of course, but he also knew he would never forget her. Never!

After a moment he sighed and laid the daguerreotype on the stool by the jug, feeling suddenly tired and empty. It was late and the drink had worked its magic, releasing him from the tethers that bound him to the waking world. Now he just wanted to lie down by the fire and drift away into welcome oblivion.

But just then, Peg came into the room with a loaded plate in each hand. "I've yeer suppers here, hot and steamy. I hope ye don't mind the eggs and bacon. 'Twas the quickest I could come by, so it was."

With the prospect of hot food to sate his suddenly ravenous hunger, Dónal perked up immediately, though once he'd eaten, his eyelids grew even heavier. Yet the Fitzgeralds were just getting warmed up, it seemed, and stayed there chattering away till the jug was empty and the short hours growing tall, before finally taking their leave and heading for bed.

By that time, Dónal was so exhausted he could barely acknowledge Butler's goodnight before flopping down by the fire and curling himself into a ball. Yet as he lay there with his eyes closed, Eleanor came to him and took him by the hand, lifting him into the sunlight of her smile.

'Will you dance with me?' she asked, her voice as smooth and silvery as the Suir at sunset.

'You're so beautiful,' he said, as they floated in their dancers' embrace. 'So beautiful. So . . . beautiful.'

chapter 21

Cashel
County Tipperary

As he rode northeast toward Dublin, Dónal turned to watch
the Rock of Cashel slipping slowly beneath the horizon behind him,
thinking it odd that it had risen up so abruptly on his approach and
yet seemed to linger as he rode away, almost as if following him, begging him to return and restore its former glory. And glorious it must
have been in its days of ascendancy, standing above the plains of South
Tipperary like an Irish Tower of Babel, its native stone crowned by
magnificent works of the same stone, both testaments to the greater
glory of God. But those days were long past and the majesty of Cashel
but a memory now, its magnificent cathedral standing roofless and
open to the sky, even as the sarcophagus of Cormac, the great Bishop
King who'd consecrated the Rock to God, stood open and empty in
the chapel that bore his name.

He'd walked among the ruins with Butler that morning, thinking of
the days before Cormac when Cashel was the seat of his ancestors, the
Eóghanacht Kings of Munster. As at Knockgraffon, he'd even had a
sense of being a prince returning from exile, though the feeling was
less intensely possessive since the kingship itself was less intensely personal to his ancestors than their green fields around the ringfort of Fiacha.
Then it had passed altogether as they strolled through the burial ground
outside, where he saw the sexton's spade turning over the bones of kings

and princes long dead, their names remembered only in genealogies that no one ever read. What did it matter that he could recite a list of names that connected him directly to them? What difference did it make to anyone, and did anyone even care?

By the time they'd left, his mood was as gray as the stone of Cashel, and he savored the parting drink they shared at the base of the Rock. He was thankful, too, when Butler handed him the jug and said in Irish, "Keep it. You've a longer road ahead of you than I do."

"Now there's a thought for you," Dónal had said gloomily, "considering your road is never-ending."

"I could shorten it for you, if you'd like. I could give you the money for a passage from Dublin, and then you'd be in New York in just a matter of weeks. You could even call it a loan, if it would make you feel better, and pay me back when you return. So what do you say? Will you let me help you?"

Seeing Butler's genuine desire to help, Dónal had been sorely tempted. But after a moment he shook his head. "No, Egan, I can't. I took money from Riobárd and look how that turned out. If I lost yours, too, I don't think I could live with it. Besides, I got myself into this mess and it's up to me to find a way out."

"Well now, as for losing my money, I wouldn't have offered if I thought you would. But I think I understand. It takes a lot for a man to swallow his pride and accept help from another, though doing so isn't a sign of weakness, Dónal, but of strength, of intelligence even. Only a fool freezes to death in the dark when there's a sod to be had for the asking. But all right. Your mind is made up, and I'll not patronize you. I'll just take comfort in the fact that I leave you wiser than I found you, and wish you a fair journey and safe home. Think of me kindly, Dónal my friend, as I will always think of you."

Without waiting for a reply, he'd spurred his horse and ridden away, looking only to the road ahead, the beauty that lay around the next bend. Dónal watched him go till he was out of sight, envious that he always seemed to know where he was going, even when he was going nowhere. Then he'd set his face to the road and ridden away from Cashel of the Kings, leaving it behind just as he'd left everything else, each plodding step taking him further and further into the unknown.

Now as he watched the Rock disappear, he sighed and turned back to the road, spurring his horse to a trot. The day was already half over and he needed to get to Dublin as quickly as possible, since he had only a few pennies in his pockets and the bag of potatoes from Peg to sustain him. What he would find when he got there, he didn't know. But at least Butler had told him at breakfast where to sell his horse and how much he should get for it, and where to find the ferry terminal afterward. He'd also told him that once he was in Liverpool, he should look for help at a Catholic church, since the priest and congregation would likely be Irish.

Fitzgerald had agreed over his mouthful of eggs, saying that according to his sons, Liverpool was hardly less Irish than Dublin now and he'd have no problem finding his own. But he'd also warned him to be careful on the quays, for they were rife with thieving scoundrels who preyed upon the unwary, "the poor ones fleein' the troubles to find a better life for themselves." Dónal had thanked him for the advice, glancing sidelong at Butler, only to find him looking studiously away.

Then Fitzgerald had put down his fork and pulled a small medallion from his pocket, which he'd eyed for a moment before handing it to Dónal. "I've no partin' gift that's fit for a real Irish chieftain, just one for a Tinker, no offense to our Egan, now. 'Tis a St. Christopher's, himself bein' the patron o' travelers, and I thought it might help ye on yeer road. It brought Da home safe after the '98, and it might still have some luck in it."

"Thank you for your generosity, Mr. Fitzgerald, but I'd not feel right about takin' somethin' so precious, especially since it came to you from your father and himself bein' a man of '98."

"Wisha, 'tis no use in it for me with never a night in me life spent away from home. As for The '98, sure, 'twas no luck in it for Da. He lost his ouldfellah to the Redcoats and almost the farm, this close to it he came. So we've no love o' rebellion in this house, nor need to sanctify it with keepsakes. And though it was Da's, still I've the farm from him, and what more could a man want than fifty-five acres o' the best land in all of Ireland? So take it as a token of our friendship and good wishes for a safe home. Go on with ye. Put it round yeer neck and keep it close, and sure, if ould Chris himself won't protect ye."

Later, as Dónal and Butler had ridden away, the old man had shouted after them. "If ever ye chance upon any o' me brothers over there, give 'em a swift kick in the arse for never writin' no more! Safe home to ye!"

Dónal smiled at the memory as he pulled the little medallion from under his shirt. Maybe the rest of his journey would indeed go smoothly now that St. Christopher was watching over him. God only knew but that he could use a bit of luck. After eyeing it for a moment, he kissed it and stuffed it back under his shirt. What would be would be, he knew, but he also knew that in one way or another, he *would* get to America, and then all his troubles would be worth it.

So on he rode, not stopping till well after dark and then only because his old horse was stumbling with fatigue. He camped in a deserted cottage by the roadside that night, lighting a fire in its hearth from a stack of sods left in the shed. And though there was but little over his head, the place felt almost homey as he sat by the fire and ate his supper, with only his jug and the stars to keep him company. But it felt good to be alone again, to be on his own with no one to answer to and no expectations to meet, for though he missed Butler and the fellowship of the Travelers, he'd missed the solace of his solitude even more.

Later, as he lay back looking at the stars, he thought of Sióna and wondered if she was looking at them, too. He'd hardly thought of her at all in the days spent with Butler, and not since that second evening when he'd camped by the Owvane had he really missed her. But even as he tried to picture her, the image of Eleanor chased her away, and he was content to let it. As Butler liked to say, there'd be time for serious contemplation tomorrow. But when the morning came, Dónal had a mind only for the road, mounting his horse before sunup and pushing on through the gentle country of Leinster, the miles flowing under him like a river to the sea. Eóghan was waiting, after all.

It was drizzling the morning Dónal rode into Dublin, and he was wet and cold, his teeth chattering and his mood as gray as the weather. The night before had been miserable, as he was unable to get a fire going in the dampness and hadn't enough poteen left to lull himself to sleep. Through most of it he'd huddled under a tree in his blanket, dozing off only now and again and never for more than a few minutes, his fitful sleep disturbed by dreams of darkness and dread. By the time dawn finally broke, he was more tired than he'd been the night before and the last of his cold potatoes did nothing to revive his spirits. But at least he was in Dublin, having camped on its outskirts by the River Liffey, and with any luck at all he'd be in Liverpool by nightfall, that much closer to the end of his road.

Yet his mind was only on Dublin itself as he followed the Liffey through its center, for the magnificent buildings lining the river and the dozens of shops, pubs and offices they housed. And though his experience in Cork City had prepared him for it, still he was amazed by the sheer size of the place, and yet more so that it felt so crowded and cramped. For despite the rain and the early hour, the streets were so packed with people that his horse seemed to be swimming through a river of humanity as he steered him slowly toward the harbor. Soon it became one big blur of activity to him, the people and carts and carriages all rushing to and fro, while the pitiful voices of the beggars rose above the hellish clamor like those of the Damned:

'Can ye spare somethin' for a poor blind man?'

'Can ye help a poor mother feed her childer?'

'Can ye help an ould one with none to care for her?

'Please sir, can ye help a poor starvin' orphan?'

Nor did the clang and clatter begin to subside till he'd crossed to the north side of the Liffey and passed beyond the Customs House to where the ferry terminal lay. As the assault on his senses eased, Dónal relaxed and sighed with relief. How did people ever survive in that, he wondered, and why would they want to when the peace and quiet of the country was there for the taking? But at least he now understood what Butler had meant about life being so much harder in the city.

Upon reaching the terminal, he dismounted and looked for the horse traders that Butler told him would be there, waiting to buy horses from emigrants like himself who had no further need of them. But finding no prospects, he decided to ask directions of two finely-dressed gentlemen who were coming his way. Yet they passed him by without a glance, taking no more notice of him than if he'd not even been there, much the same as he'd treated the beggars by the Liffey. As he turned to glare after them, one of them pulled something from his pocket, and a piece of paper slipped out with it and fluttered unnoticed to the ground.

Despite their snub, Dónal quickly stooped to retrieve it, the words, 'Sir, I believe you dropped this!' on the tip of his tongue. Yet when he saw it was a five pound note, his mouth snapped shut, for here in one swift stroke of fortune was the answer to all his problems. Indeed, with what he could get for his horse, he would have almost enough money for the ferry and a passage to Canada, and all he had to do was stick it in his pocket and say nothing, and no one would ever be the wiser. But then his conscience prodded him, telling him it wasn't good fortune, but theft, that *he* would know even if no one else did. Yet even as the thought formed in his head, another voice shouted it down. Why should he trouble himself for a couple of stuck-up aristocrats, it said, men who thought even their shite didn't stink? And what was five pounds to them anyway, but pocket change they probably wouldn't even miss? Sure, they were probably landlords who'd squeezed it from the blood of their tenants, so taking a bit back wasn't theft, but justice!

He put the note into his pocket and turned his back on the two gentlemen, silently thanking St. Christopher for taking such good care of him.

Yet even as he turned away, he saw an old man leaning against a nearby wall, a beggar's tin cup in his hand and a knowing look on his weathered face. And as their eyes met, Dónal knew he'd seen it all. Would he report him? he wondered, his spirits suddenly sinking as his face reddened with guilt. Or worse yet, would he demand a share in exchange for silence?

But the old man just nodded, his sly smile revealing toothless gums. "Why the apologetic face, son?" he asked in English. "Ye beat me to it fair and square, youth and vigor be served! Or is it not after me that ye've gone so red and rosy? 'Tisn't guilt that ye're feelin', surely, such highfalutin notions no daycent, self-respectin' thief ever yet harbored!"

"I'm no thief, dado!" Dónal replied, all evidence to the contrary. "I'd not have kept it, savin' that I need it to pay my passage to America."

"Nor meself, God knows, would I ever have kept it, save for me sinful habit o' gettin' hungry every day. But each man to his own vices, no begrudger am I of yeers." Then he grinned again and rattled the few coins in his cup. "Still, if 'tis easin' yeer conscience that ye're after, sharin' a few of them pennies from Heaven will make a good start of it. 'Twould even go a ways toward easin' me own, law-abidin' citizen that I am and not one to turn a blind eye to mischief."

"All right, dado, I get your point. But look here. I've just the one note and no time to go for change. So why don't you take my horse? You can sell him to one of the traders and have money in your fist before the next hour rings. All I ask is that you take him to someone reputable. He's a fine ould fellah, and I'd hate to see him end up at the glue factory."

"Sure, son, I know how ye feel," the man said, snatching the reins from Dónal before he could change his mind. "I'd hate to end up there meself, though 'twould be worse at the workhouse. At least at the glue factory they make quick work o' ye."

"Grand so, then he's yours." Dónal turned to the horse. "Well, it's good-bye again, Odysseus, and this time I'm sure it's the last. Here's a hope for greener pastures."

But the horse said nothing in return, just stood with his head bowed, like a condemned man accepting his fate.

"Take good care of him," Dónal said to the man, before turning away.

"Not to worry, son. I'll see the both of us well-served."

From the old man's tone, Dónal knew he didn't mean it, but it was too late. Besides, he had other things on his mind and couldn't be bothered with the fate of one old horse. The fiver in his pocket wouldn't be enough to pay for the ferry *and* a passage to Canada, so he was back to the problem of finding work in Liverpool and a place to live, while at the same time trying to conserve what money he had. It was indeed a conundrum, one that could only be dealt with when got there, though he'd already begun to regret giving up the horse so easily. But then, no good deed goes unpunished, as Puxley said, and now he'd have to pinch every penny.

It was raining again by the time he boarded and took up station along the after railing, crowding his way in among a press of poor emigrants who gave him space only because he was imposing enough to shoulder them aside. Like him, they were all as wet as the weather, and he wrinkled his nose against their stench, the dank pervasive odor of Irish poverty, knowing he smelled no better himself. It was more than a fortnight since his bath and shave in Queenstown, and he was definitely worse for the wear, his hair being dirty and matted and his chin obscured with stubble, while his clothes looked as if he'd stolen them from a disinterred corpse. Not that anyone took particular notice, given the horde of others who looked just like him. Still he'd gazed longingly on the finely dressed ladies and gentlemen boarding in first class, wishing he could be one of them again, the young gentleman of prospects he'd been for that one glorious afternoon in Queenstown. But it may as well have been a dream for all that remained of it now. At least they were out of sight, safely ensconced in their first class accommodations, and wouldn't be a constant reminder of his lowly condition.

Then the whistle blew, and the crew cast off the lines, and the ferry steamed slowly toward the Irish Sea. As the skyline of Dublin receded,

Dónal thought of all the people and places he'd left behind, indeed everyone and everything that had ever been dear to him. Now even Ireland was slipping away, into the ephemeral realm of memory, that place in the heart where torment and delight walk hand-in-hand. The thought of it brought sudden tears to his eyes, even as the distance increased and the rain came harder, turning the green into shades of mottled gray and his last view of Erin into a blurred vision of melancholy.

This was not the way he'd pictured it, not the image he'd had of himself standing in the sun on the deck of a steamer, bidding *au revoir* to a smiling land that eagerly awaited his return. His tears came as hard as the rain then and he sobbed in his misery, glancing about to see if anyone noticed. But they paid him no heed, just stood silent and gray as stones, no doubt weeping themselves as their own hearts were broken, though he couldn't tell for the rain. They, too, were leaving Erin behind and with Her everything they'd ever known, everyone they'd ever loved, going from uncertainty into uncertainty, a change of scenery their only guarantee, a life less precarious their only hope. They knew they'd never see Her again, of course, never feel Her caress on their bare feet or hear Her voice singing in a clear waterfall, never smell Her sweet aroma in the turf that burned in their own firesides among their own kith and kin. He looked at the mass of people huddled around him and silently cursed Fate for the trick she'd played on them, turning them out of their native land with only this sorry sight by which to remember Her.

Then the ship cleared the end of Howth and the sea turned violent, churning Dónal's stomach into a state to match. Yet he kept his grip on the railing and his eyes glued desperately to the horizon, watching as the coastline came and went with each peak and trough, dreading with each downward plunge that the view would be his last. But when the man next to him vomited over the railing, the sight and smell turned Dónal's own stomach, and the bucking of the ship kept him at it till long after it was empty. When finally he could look up again, there was nothing to be seen but gray water and gray clouds, the horizon fore-shortened by a gray curtain of rain, his last view stolen by the storm.

He was gone now from Erin, sailing into the Diaspora on a wind of misfortune, following the uncounted thousands who'd taken the lonely road before him, the great dispersion of the People of the Gael. Closing his eyes then, he prayed aloud, though softly, so that only God would hear:

> *We played our pipes beneath the oaks,*
> *for there our tyrants required of us song,*
> *and our oppressors mirth, saying,*
> *'Sing us a song of The Holy Ground!'*
>
> *But how shall I sing Her song on a foreign strand?*
> *If I forget thee, O Erin, let my sword arm forget its cunning!*
> *Let my song stick in my throat, if I forget thee,*
> *if I set not Erin above my highest joy!*

chapτer 22

Liverpool, England

As THE FERRY STEAMED UP the River Mersey, Dónal watched the great city of Liverpool appear through the curtain of rain, rising dark and ominous from the river bank like a giant beast waiting to devour him. It wasn't an encouraging sight, especially after what he'd endured on the crossing, with the endless battering of the storm and his own fear and seasickness. The waves had looked like mountains as they loomed over the ship, each threatening to overwhelm her and send her straight to the cold dark bottom. The "Horses of Manannán" the white-caps were called, after the Irish god of the sea, and they charged the ship in endless rows, frothing and stamping, whipped into a frenzy by the skirling wind. Yet by some miracle she rode over them, pitching and rolling, up and down and side-to-side, gliding like a bird on the wind.

By the time they made it across, Dónal had developed a deep and abiding respect for the sea, for her power and majesty, beside which the endeavors of man were as nothing. Indeed, anyone who doubted the existence of God need only experience such a storm at sea to see the error of his ways. He himself had spent most of the crossing praying to Him, in concert with the scores of other poor passengers who crammed the below-decks, clinging to each other in their fear and desperation, and to keep from slipping on each others' vomit. "Please, God," they'd prayed, "just land me safely and I'll be your faithful servant forever," while the list of vices they vowed to abjure would've made a whore blush. Of course, the promises were all forgotten in the rush of relief that came when they finally reached calmer waters. Despite the drizzle, they'd all poured onto the deck for a bit of fresh air and a view of the land, the first-class passengers mingling among their poorer brethren and exchanging a few words, or sharing a bit of hysterical laughter. Like the drink, fear was a great equalizer, too, it seemed.

The ferry was hours late in arriving, and it was after dark before she was safely berthed and the gangway down. As the people began to disembark, Dónal stood by the railing, staring blankly at the dark city before him. It seemed surreal that he'd begun the day in Ireland and was ending it now in England, as if he'd started in Heaven and gone through Hell, only to end up in Purgatory. Up which of the myriad streets did his destiny lie, and how would he know when he got there? The city seemed so big and intimidating, and he despaired of ever finding his way. Of course, he could just give it up and go home again. He had the money, after all, and maybe that's why St. Christopher had given him so much of it, so he could get back to Ireland once he'd seen the error of his ways. But compared with crossing that vile sea again, Liverpool suddenly didn't look so bad. The Irish Sea, they called it, yet for all the familial tenderness Manannán had shown him, the *Saxon* Sea would be a better fit.

With that thought he joined the queue at the gangway and slowly made his way down, his legs wobbly and uncertain. At the front street he stopped again, trying to get his bearings as people slowly filed past, the first-class passengers hopping into waiting carriages or cabs, while those like himself just huddled in the street. After a moment he approached one of the cab drivers and asked directions to the nearest Catholic church. As it turned out, the man was Irish himself and more than willing to help, though Dónal was soon bewildered with the impossible list of twists and turns he rattled off. But before he could ask for clarification, the man picked up a fare and drove away. So after a moment's hesitation, he set off in the general direction described, thinking to get further directions as he went. Yet the streets were dark and empty, ghostly almost in their abandonment, and he was lost before he even knew it, suddenly having no idea where he was or even how to go back the way he'd come. Even the rain had stopped and the only sound was eerie silence, in its way more frightening than the storm, since it seemed to portend worse to follow.

But then he turned a corner and saw a light ahead, spilling into the street through the windows of a pub, and his spirits rose again with the hope it promised. What better place to find Irishmen than in a pub, after all? And sure, if one of them might not offer him a bed for the night and a meal to fill his empty stomach, and maybe even help him find work in the morning. At the least they would see him safely to the steps of a church, though surely not before a pint or two and maybe a drop to welcome him. And wouldn't that hit the spot just now, just the thing to restore his confidence and set his attitude straight. For as dark and lonely as the world was outside, it would be warm and friendly inside that pub, all the hard edges rubbed smooth by the magic of the drink.

So having set himself up for a warm welcome, he was profoundly shocked by the sign posted on the tavern door. **NO DOGS OR IRISH**, it said in bold black letters, and he blinked in disbelief, stunned by its naked bigotry. It made him feel as he had that morning when the gentlemen had passed him as if he weren't there, as he had at the Cornish school when a boy, that he was *different* from those who'd posted the sign, and in his difference *less than* them, as well. It was something he hadn't anticipated, though he realized that he should have, for if the English in Ireland despised the Irish, why would they feel any differently here? Still, the coldness of it froze his heart and made him doubt himself once again. How would he ever find work in such an environment, or save enough to get himself to America? **NO DOGS OR IRISH**! Maybe he should just give up and go home while he still had the money. Maybe all these obstacles were signs that he should be reading, rather than tests of his resolve. Maybe the true test lay in having the courage to admit defeat and face those he'd left behind.

But then Dónal realized this was just what they *wanted* him to feel, that

431

the words were calculated to arouse those exact feelings of inferiority, and thereby defeat him before he'd even begun to fight. "Slavery is in the mind," Ahern had once said to him, and now he could see it was more than just words. A flush of anger swept over him and he stepped to the door, meaning to jerk it open and stride manfully inside. Indeed, they might throw him out again, but it would take more to enslave him than a few paltry words scrawled on a pub door.

But just as he grasped the handle, the door swept open and he found himself blocking the way of several men trying to exit. Seeing that he was unmistakably Irish, the lead man shoved him roughly aside. "Get out o' me way, paddy, and go back to your stinkin' bog of a country while you're at it!"

Even as Dónal clenched his fists, a warning voice spoke inside his head: *Don't do it!* But he couldn't help himself; his ancestors were awake within him and clamoring for vengeance. Anyway, he was so numb with rage that it happened before he knew he'd done it, not even feeling when he struck the man, just hearing a smack of bone on bone and seeing him tumble backward into his friends. There was a silence then as the other men gaped down at him and then up at Dónal, who just stood there blinking, as shocked by what he'd done as they were.

Then the man on the ground shook his head and spit out the blood that was flooding his mouth. "He's knocked out me front teeth, Hugh!" he mumbled, as more blood dribbled onto his chin.

A man knelt down beside him then to have a look. "Oh, Christ, Tom, it's bad!" he exclaimed, then glared up at Dónal. "You're goin' to pay for this, paddy!" he snarled, and sprang at his legs.

But Dónal was too quick for him, and was already running down the street when the man hit the ground. "Get 'im, lads!" he heard him shout, and then the sound of their boots slapping the cobblestones in pursuit. *"Kill the paddy!"* one of them shouted, and as the others took up the cry, he had no doubt they meant it.

But then the leader shouted them down. "No, don't kill 'im. I want 'is balls!"

The words sent a shiver down Dónal's back, and he pumped his weary legs even harder. But he knew it was no use; he was worn out from the crossing and they were fresh, and if he didn't turn and fight, sooner or later they'd catch him and drag him down. Yet how could he stand against so many? What he needed was an equalizer, a weapon to neutralize their advantage. So he scanned the streets as he ran, looking for something, *anything* that would do.

But then he heard the man's voice again, so close to him now that he could almost feel his breath. "I'm right behind you, paddy! You can't get away!"

Dónal was running out of time and knew it, and thinking to gain a few steps, he turned sharply at the next corner, only to find himself facing a high wall at the end of a blind alley. He whirled around to face his pursuers, but found they'd stopped at the entrance to catch their breath. They had him trapped and knew it, and could take their time with him now. Desperately he whirled around in a circle, looking for a way out. But finding none he backed up against the end wall, hoping to use the deeper darkness to his advantage. Quickly he ran his hands over it to see if it was scaleable, but found no footholds in its smooth stone face.

"Give it up, paddy," he heard the man say. "You can't get out and you know it as well as I do! So why not make it easy on yourself? Just give us your balls and we'll let you live. My knife is sharp and you'll hardly even feel it. And just think of the service you'll be doing the world by bringing that many less paddies into it."

Looking toward them, he saw five men silhouetted against the entrance, blocking his way to life and freedom. The leader spoke to the others in a language other than English, and they began to move slowly forward, spreading out across the alley to keep him from dashing past.

Keeping his eyes glued to them, Dónal crouched into a corner, hoping to stay hidden in the shadows as long as possible. At least his flanks would be protected that way and give them less room to maneuver. He took a deep breath and let it out slowly, fighting to control his nerves and pounding heart. His situation was dire, but not yet hopeless. He knew how to fight with his wits, after all, and if he kept his head about him, he might get out of it with all his parts. Then his hand brushed against something on the ground, a rock about the size of a hen's egg, round and smooth. As his hand closed over it, he knew what he would do.

"I'm comin' for you, paddy," he heard the leader say, though now he didn't sound quite so sure of himself. Indeed, they'd halted again about halfway into the alley and were just standing there, and he knew they couldn't see him in the shadows.

"There's no way out, paddy, unless you can climb like a spider!" the man said. But hearing the uncertainty in his voice, Dónal smiled grimly, knowing he had the advantage. They were walking into darkness, into the unknown, and he knew how to use their fear of it against them. All he had to do was be quiet and still, and let their fear feed on itself till he was ready to strike.

"Say good-bye to your balls now, paddy, I'm coming for them!" the man called, and Dónal knew he was trying to goad him into a response. When he got none, he spoke to the others in the foreign language again, and they began to move forward, though slowly, feeling their way in the dark.

Dónal cocked his arm and waited. Just let them come a little closer, he thought, just a little closer. He didn't have to hit the man hard, he just had to hit him. A little closer, come on, just a little more . . . He snapped his arm and heard the rock strike the man squarely, the one on the far side of the alley from him, the one he'd been aiming at.

"Ow!" the man yelped and, startled by his outburst, the others whirled to face him.

But Dónal was already bearing down on the man nearest him, lowering his shoulder to bowl him over, and then on toward the street without slowing. They were after him immediately, of course, but he was safely out of the alley and, with any luck at all, they'd get discouraged and let him go.

At the street he turned a sharp left, but as he did his weary feet went out from under him on the wet cobblestones, and he went down hard on his side and slid to the curb. He rolled over to push himself up, but it was too late — a booted foot smacked into his ribs and sent the breath from him in a rush of pain. Then they were all on him, kicking him and snarling curses that would freeze the dead. He tried to curl up defensively, but it was no use; they just kicked the parts that were exposed.

"Don't kill the bastard, I want 'is balls!" the leader shouted, though the kicks kept coming.

"*Help! Help!*" Dónal managed to shout. "*Please, help me!*"

But then a boot caught him in the head and, as the world went fuzzy before his eyes, he felt a tugging at his trousers. *No, please God, no!* he wanted to scream, but his voice would no longer obey.

Yet just before losing consciousness, he heard the strangest sound, a shrill metallic piping much like the steam whistle at the mines, but smaller, more human in scale.

TWEEEEEE! it came insistently. *TWEEEEEE! TWEEEEEE! TWEEEEEE!*

"Oh Christ, Hugh, it's the peelers!" one of the men shouted, though Dónal didn't hear him.

⟨※⟩

They were after him again, so close now he could feel their breath on his back, stretching out their hands to grasp him and drag him down, down into the dark unknown. His chest pounded and his legs ached. Fear! Pain! Darkness! But then suddenly he was out of the dark alleys and into a sunlit forest, though a forest like none he'd ever seen before, full of strange sights and sounds, puffs of smoke among the trees, cracks of thunder and bolts of lightning whistling overhead. And though he couldn't see them anymore, still he knew they were after him, more dangerous now than ever. 'Help me,' he wanted to scream, 'oh, God, please help me!' But his mouth would make no sounds. Fear, pain, darkness again, terror behind him, his chest pounding and legs aching.

Then a light, a light shining in his eyes, and voices. A face. A woman's face that the light didn't illuminate, eyes and skin as black as a moonless night. The dark spirit had come for him and he couldn't get away! Yet why was she smiling, and why the kindness in her eyes?

"Can you hear me, chile?" *she asked, her voice a lilting song.* "Can you hear me? You're going to be all right. The doctor is here to care for you. Can you tell us your name, or where you live? Do you have any family, anyone we can send for? Can you hear me, chile? Can you hear me?"

Another voice answering. His own, or just an echo in his head? "An tusa sídhe an domhain soir?" (Are you the Dark Spirit of the Otherworld?)

No reply, just a shake of the head and a kindly smile. But the light dimmed and she was gone. 'Wait! Come back! Don't leave me here alone! Please, come back!'

Darkness again, kindness forgotten, fear, pain! They were after him, and he was running, running, running . . .

⧼⧽

There was a light behind his eyelids, the bright light of midday, though he couldn't say how long it had been there or when he'd first noticed it. It was just there. And he was lying in a bed, for there were blankets over him and a pillow under his head, though he couldn't remember lying down in it. But then he felt the dull throb in his head and the cool cloth on his forehead, and thought he understood. He'd been at the drink again and slept late, and Sióna must have put it there, before going outside to avoid his black morning mood. Then he heard a noise, the soft insistent whistle of a kettle, *TWEEEEEE*, and it all came flooding back to him, the storm and Liverpool and the sign on the pub, the peeler's whistle and the words, *Don't kill the bastard, I want his balls!*

With that, Dónal's eyes popped open, and he winced with pain as he moved his hands between his legs, dreading what he would find yet desperate to know. Then he sighed and closed his eyes again.

"Oh, thank God," he whimpered, "they didn't do it after all."

"What did you say, chile?" a woman's voice asked from just beside him, and he jerked in surprise. "I can't understand you. Do you speak English?"

Painfully, he twisted his head to find her, only to recoil in terror, seeing the face in his dream, the dark spirit of the Otherworld.

But she just smiled at him, and his fear melted before the kindness in her eyes. "Don't worry, chile," she said, laying a hand gently on his head. "I won't hurt you."

"No. I know you won't," he replied, wondering that he could be so certain of this strange and exotic creature. With her dark skin and Negroid features surrounded by a halo of kinky white hair, she could've come from another world entirely rather than just from a different part of his own. Yet he knew she hadn't, that her differentness was only skin deep. He saw it in her eyes, in her empathy and compassion, the hallmarks of their shared humanity. They were cut by the same hand from the same cloth, and were equal in the eyes of their Maker.

"No," she repeated, stroking his cheek softly, her hand rough and callused, yet soothing. Indeed, she touched him in the way that a mother does to comfort her child, just as his own mother had done in those long-ago days of his childhood. "You just rest easy and Mother Angela will take good care of you."

"All right," he agreed, closing his eyes again, though he didn't go to sleep. There were questions that needed answering first.

But before he could ask, she spoke again. "Before you go to sleep, chile, I need to know if there's anyone I should send for, anyone who might be wondering where you are."

"No, there's no one. I'd only just gotten off the ferry from Ireland when those men started chasin' me, and was–"

"What? You only just arrived from Ireland last night and already you've gotten yourself into this much trouble? Well now! This city is a rough place, I know, but even so, you made quick work of it!"

"Yes, I suppose I did," he sighed, and then told her the story of the sign on the pub door and the man's words to him, and the rest of it up to his beating in the street.

"Ah, well, I know how you feel about that sign. I've been turned away from many a door in my day, though not for being Irish, mind you. But it sounds like it was a Welsh establishment, and you may not know this, but the Welsh of Liverpool hate the Irish, whom they see as rivals for their jobs. But that's another story for another day. Right now, you need your rest. But before you go back to sleep, just tell me if there's anyone I should send for."

"No, there's no one, no one at all," he repeated, feeling more forlorn and forsaken than ever. "I've no one in Liverpool."

"Well now, I wouldn't go that far. You have me, after all, and I'll care for you till you're well and can see to yourself again."

"But why? Why are you bein' so kind to me when you don't even know my name?"

She just smiled and shrugged. "I used to be a nurse, and before that I was a nanny. So I suppose you could say it's just my calling to care for people. And anyway, I had a boy of my own once, long ago when I was still just a young thing, younger than you, even."

"Where is he now?" Dónal asked, catching the wistfulness in her voice and noting that she spoke of him in the past tense.

"I don't know. He went away to sea and never returned. But that, too, is another story, and as I said, you need your rest."

"Yes. I am tired, and Jayzis, but it hurts to breathe."

"The doctor said you probably have some broken ribs, and you have bruises everywhere. Those men must've been really angry with you to have done so much damage! The Lord knows what they might have done if I hadn't frightened them off with my whistle."

"They were goin' to castrate me," he said quietly, matter-of-factly, though the horror of it brought tears to his eyes.

"Oh my!" she exclaimed, her eyes growing wide in surprise. "Oh my, oh my! Then I didn't arrive a moment too soon, did I? But there, there, chile," she said, wiping the tears from his eyes. "They didn't do anything to you that won't heal, and you're safe with me now. So just close those lovely green eyes of yours and go back to sleep. I'll be right here beside you."

Dónal didn't answer, just closed his eyes and snuggled his cheek against her hand.

"Yes, chile, you sleep now, and Mother Angela will watch after you. There's nothing to fear as long as I'm here."

"My name is Dónal O'Sullivan, just so you'll know."

☙

When Dónal woke again, he was drenched with sweat and shivering uncontrollably, the spasms sending waves of pain through him. He turned to look for Angela, but couldn't see her in the darkness, the fire having burned itself down to embers.

"Angela?" he called through chattering teeth, reaching out with his free hand. "Angela, where are you?"

"I'm right here, Donald-chile," she replied, and he felt her hand on his. "Do you need something?"

"Angela, I'm so cold, and the shiverin' makes me hurt all over! Can you put some more coal on the fire, please?"

But instead of going to the fire, she leaned over him and laid her free hand on his forehead. "Why, chile, you're not cold at all! You're burning up!"

"That's not how it feels to me!"

"No, it wouldn't. But it just means is that your fever is breaking. You're actually getting better, though it may be a while before you feel it. But here, this will help," she said, laying a cool cloth on his forehead. "I'm afraid that's about all I can do for you just now, though. Anyway, the best thing for you is to go back to sleep and forget about it."

"I don't think I can. I'm so cold and it hurts so much!"

"I know it does, chile, I know," she said, her voice soft and soothing. "But maybe a lullaby will help. I'll sing one that I learned from my mother when I was a little girl in Barbados. It came from Ireland, or so she said, from someplace called Drogheda."

Gently she closed his eyes with her rough fingers, cleared her throat and began to sing, stroking his hair as she did. And as he listened, Dónal felt himself relax, felt the shivering ease and the pain ebb. Her voice was so soothing, so warm and sweet and sultry, like the soft sea winds of some tropical island. He loved the sound of it even when she wasn't singing, with it's clear tone and earthy resonance. And though her accent was refined and elegant, of a type that he'd always associated with the gentry, there was something else underlying it, a certain musical lilt, or perhaps the faint suggestion of a brogue. He couldn't say for sure. All he knew was that it comforted him, and he liked it.

Angela looked at him and smiled. He was already asleep, and she hadn't even finished the song. He looked so peaceful lying there, so content, just like her own son when she'd sung him to sleep in those long-lost days of her youth. He was so beautiful, her Hector, a young Adonis, having the best of both her and his white father in him. But then he'd run off to be a sailor and never returned. His shipmates had sold him, she'd always been sure of it, probably in the first slaving port they'd come to, those white men with their shallow morality and base hypocrisy. Even the fact that he was more than half white hadn't saved him, for a single drop of African blood was all it took to make one black, a *nigger*, and as such subject to all the abuse the white man's world was pleased to offer. But no, she couldn't condemn them as a body. They weren't all of them bad. Indeed, she owed her own freedom to a white man, a red-headed Irishman just like the beautiful boy that lay injured in her bed and, however hard her life had been, it would've been harder still had she lived it as a slave.

Angela sighed as the old memories flooded over her, the old bitterness, the old pain, all tattered and tired now after seventy years of wear. Closing her eyes, she said a brief prayer, asking God to forgive her for not appreciating the bounteous gifts she'd been given. But her prayer, too, was tired and tattered, its fabric worn thin by constant usage. She sighed again and opened her eyes. At least for a while she wouldn't be alone.

When Dónal woke again it was morning, though he could see nothing of the sky through the window at the foot of the bed. Taking stock of himself, he was relieved to find that he didn't feel cold anymore and wasn't shivering and, with his fever gone, the pain was reduced to a general ache, which was bearable as long as he didn't breathe too deeply. But of more immediate concern to him was the fact that his bladder was full to bursting, and if he didn't go soon the bed clothes would be drenched with more than just his sweat.

Painfully, he pushed himself up, swung his legs over the edge of the bed and wrapped the sheet around his nakedness. Angela was still asleep, curled up by the bed in a big overstuffed chair and, though he hated to wake her, he knew he needed her.

"Angela," he said, shaking her softly. "Angela, wake up. I need your help."

She was awake instantly and out of the chair, hovering over him in a cloud of concern. "Here now, chile, what are you doing up when the doctor said for you to stay in bed? You just lie back down and let me take care of you. If you need something, I'll get it for you. All you have to do is ask."

"Yes, Angela, I know, and I thank you for it so. But I've got to go to the privy, *now!* So can you please help me to it?"

But she didn't answer, just gave him an odd little smile as she pulled a metal pot from under the bed. "There's no need for that, chile. Just use the chamber pot and call me when you're finished."

Without waiting for his reply, she went out to the hallway and closed the door behind her. And as Dónal stared at the pot in his hands, he had to laugh at himself. "So that's what it's for!" he said, thinking of the one in his room at Barry's. "Sure, if I'm not a culchie then there was never a man so born!"

When finished, he looked himself over for a moment before calling her back in, finding his body just one big bruise. But then, it could've been worse.

While Angela emptied the chamber pot, he walked around the room to stretch his aching legs, then let her coax him back onto the bed even

441

though he didn't feel like resting. But she seemed to want to mother him, to *need* it almost and, for now at least, he had nothing better to do than let her.

"There now, Donald-chile," she said, fluffing his pillow. "Isn't that better?"

"Sure, 'tis grand so, and I thank you again. But Angela, my name isn't Donald. 'Tis *DOE-null.*"

"Oh, I see," she said, repeating it a couple of times, just to get the feel of it on her tongue. "I've never heard it pronounced that way, though I must say I like it better. It sounds more natural, more native, almost exotic in a way. I find the English names so colorless, and then they shorten them for everyday use: Jack and Tom and Will and Bob and Jim and Harry and Dick. But Dónal sounds so singular, so heroic. Does it have a meaning you can translate?"

"Yes, it means 'world-mighty,' and 'tis an old name in my family. Nine of my direct ancestors had it, startin' with Dónal Mór, who died back in 1214."

"You know your family tree all the way back to 1214? Why, that's amazing! It must really give you a sense of history, and of your place in it, to know so much of your ancestors. I know my mother's name, of course, but no one else's, not even my father's."

"You don't know your own father's name?" The thought was as incredible to him as his knowing so much was to her.

"No, I don't. I was born a slave in Barbados, just as my mother before me. But my father was a *Guinea-mon*, a new slave fresh from Africa, and since he didn't speak English he couldn't answer when my mother asked his name."

"Then how did they ever come to be married?"

"Oh, but you are an innocent, aren't you, chile? They were never married; the master mated them together, just as he would his horses or dogs, hoping they'd produce a big strong boy-chile to work his fields. But she had me instead, and the master flogged her for failing him, after raping her, of course. I can still see the scars on her back when I close my eyes, though she died when I was only five. Oh, but she was a such beautiful woman, light-skinned and freckled, with a reddish tint to her hair. She was part white, you see, having gotten it 'in de deep long ago' from an Irishman who'd been sold into slavery by a 'bod mon name Croomwail.' But I don't look anything like her. I'm dark like my father probably was, and the white in me is buried deep down. Not that it matters much, since one drop of Negro blood is all it takes to make one a Negro."

Angela paused then and looked out the window, leaving Dónal to ponder her strange and exotic tale. Of course, he'd heard that Cromwell had sold tens of thousands of Irish Catholics into slavery after his rape of Ireland, but he'd never expected to meet one of their descendants, much less a black one, though it did explain the lilt in her voice.

"Are you still a slave now?" he asked.

"Oh, no, I'm free now, and have been since I first came to England, back in 1805. There is no slavery here and has been none for almost a hundred years."

"But how did you get here in the first place?"

"Well, bless me, chile, you are the one for questions, aren't you? Don't you know that curiosity killed the cat?"

"So I've been told on occasion."

"Well, all right, then, but just be warned of the perils you face."

Then Angela told the story of how she'd come to England, saying that after her mother died, the master sold her to a slaver who took her to South Carolina, where he sold her to a new master in the slave market of Charleston. He owned a large plantation on Hilton Head Island, though he bought her not as a field hand but as a playmate for his young daughter, a sort of living doll with which the girl could amuse herself. And while *plaything* was perhaps a better description, the young missy was kind enough in her own way and rarely abusive, and even let her sleep on the floor in her room and eat scraps from her plate. So compared with the hard life of the field hands, she was down-right pampered, and perhaps even a little spoiled. But eventually the girl outgrew her, of course, and she was put to work in the Big House, toiling from sunup to sundown seven days a week, mopping floors and washing clothes, beating rugs and doing dishes, with Christmas and Easter as her only holidays. Though it was something of a rude awakening for her, still her life as a house-nigger was better than that of a field hand, for at least she didn't have to toil under the lash and the brutal summer sun.

And so her life was until the young missy turned seventeen, when the girl's father decided to take her to Paris to outfit her for her debut, and brought Angela along as their hand servant. But when the ship stopped in Liverpool on the way, she saw her chance to get away and snatched it, bolting from the ship and running as fast as she could. Where she was going or what she would do, she neither knew nor cared, freedom being her only concern. But of course she was spotted, and the master came after her, catching her soon enough and giving her a good thrashing right there in the street. A crowd gathered to watch and she screamed for them to help her, but no one did, and she wept in bitter agony at her failure.

But then a tall red-headed man pushed his way through the crowd and put himself between her and the master. "See here, sir!" he said. "Unhand that lady!"

"Lady, my ass!" the master roared back. "She's just my nigger that run off when I wasn't lookin'! So I'll thank you to mind your own business, sir!"

"No, sir, I'll not do that! This is *England*, sir, and by our laws the very act of setting foot on our soil sets the bondsman free. So I'll not stand idly by while you assault a free woman!"

With that, he took Angela by the hand and made to lead her away. But the master flew at him in a rage and struck him a blow with his fist, which the red-headed man absorbed with barely a flinch. And when the master raised his fist again, her savior was too quick for him, knocking him to the street with one blow. Of course, he got up and charged again, only to be knocked down a second time. After that, the master stayed down, knowing himself to be overmatched.

"You can't do this!" he screamed. "You can't take my property from me! It's theft, and I'll see you in jail for it!"

"Oh, but you are wrong, sir!" the red-headed man replied. "I cannot steal from you that which belongs only to herself!"

Then he led her away without looking back, and she never saw the master again. Of course, she thanked him profusely, but he wouldn't hear it. "Thank me for being a good Samaritan, for simply doing my duty as a Christian? Let me assure you, young lady, that it was my privilege to have served the Lord."

"'Twas an Irishman himself, was he?" Dónal asked when she paused, guessing as much from the way she kept mentioning his red hair.

"Yes, he was Irish by ancestry, though he was born in England and lived here his entire life. His name was William Blake, and he was the grandson of a Galway merchant who'd made a fortune on the Atlantic shipping triangle. And you know what the linchpin of the triangle was, don't you?"

"Slavin'?" Dónal said, making his question sound like an answer.

"Yes, that's right. The way it worked was that English merchants shipped their goods to Africa and traded them for slaves, which were then shipped to the Americas and traded for sugar and cotton and tobacco, which in turn were shipped back to Liverpool and sold by the merchants at enormous profit. The profits, in turn, were used to build modern factories in England, which produced more and better goods for the merchants to trade. Ironically, it wasn't until slaving became less profitable that the English abolition movement arose and spread to the continent. But by then, the Industrial Revolution was in full swing, and England no longer needed the slave trade anyway."

"Sure, if that isn't typical of them, to decide that if somethin' isn't good for themselves, then no one else should have it either!"

"Well, whatever their reason, it was better late than never from my perspective," Angela said, and Dónal wished he could eat his words. "But in any case, by the time Mr. Blake reached manhood, the slave trade was finished in England and the pendulum of opinion had swung the other way. So I think he was more than a little embarrassed that it was the foundation of his fortune, and perhaps that's why he was so eager to help me, as a way of atoning for it. But whatever his

445

reasons, I was thankful for his help and still am to this day, for if he hadn't taken me into his house and cared for me until my baby was born, there's no telling what would have become of me."

"Your baby?" Dónal asked, thinking he'd missed something.

"Yes, my baby. Even though I was barely more than a child myself, the master used me to warm his bed on the long nights at sea, and when I became pregnant, I was more desperate than ever to get away, out of fear that he'd sell me off to Louisiana, or somewhere even worse. But Mr. Blake saved us from such a terrible fate and sheltered me until Hector was born, then hired me to be his own children's nanny. I was still a servant, of course, but at least I was a free servant, working for an honest wage and decent people who treated me with dignity. So I took up his name and lived in the Blake household for almost forty years, my son with me till he went off to sea and never came back. When Mr. Blake died, he even left me a pension so I'd be provided for in my old age, though I got a job as a nurse in the hospital and moved into this room after his wife died a few years later. Of course, his sons offered to take me in, but I said no, that I wanted to make my own way in the world.

"And that's my story up to now, a tale of seventy years stretching from Barbados to South Carolina to Liverpool, and whither hence, only God can say. But now that I've met you, if I do get to Heaven and find Mr. Blake there, I'll be able to tell him that I paid my debt in just the way he told me to."

"I don't understand, Angela. I thought he said there was no need for it."

"He did, indeed. But when I insisted, he told me just to do the same for someone else. So now that I've saved your life, Dónal, or at least your manhood, I'd say that my debt is paid."

"And now that I owe you the debt, Angela, am I to repay it so, too? Is that why you told me your story, so I'd know?"

But Angela just smiled slyly. "You are a very perceptive young man, Dónal O'Sullivan."

"And you are a very complex woman, Angela Blake. Are all Africans like you?"

"I'm not an African, chile, any more than I'm Irish for having one Irish ancestor. My father was an African, true, but I was born in Barbados and have never been to Africa. And even if I went to live there now, just the fact of being a Negro wouldn't make me African, any more than living in Liverpool makes me English. Slaves have no homeland, you see, even the lucky ones who become free, and we bear the stigma of it throughout our lives."

"I know how you feel–" he began, meaning to draw a parallel to his condition in Ireland.

"No, you don't!" Angela interjected and, looking into her eyes, he knew she was right. "You only know how it feels to be oppressed, and though it's bad enough, I agree, slavery is its own special kind of hell."

"I'm sorry. I didn't mean to offend you so."

"I know you didn't, chile. But you have to remember that empathy isn't always the equal of experience."

"No, I suppose it isn't. But still, 'tis better than nothin', isn't it?"

"Yes, I suppose so, at least insofar as it allows us a window onto the feelings of others."

"And if more people took the trouble to look, wouldn't the world be a better place to live?"

"Probably, though getting them to do it is easier said than done. You have to remember, chile, that life is hard. It grinds most people down before they even realize they're caught in its mill, and it's hard to care about the feelings of others when you're just so much chaff in the wind."

"Sure, I do know what you mean by that."

"Yes, I'm sure you've seen your share of it in Ireland. The stories I've heard of what happened there would be unbelievable if I'd not seen the survivors for myself."

"Whatever you've seen or heard, Angela," he said, giving her a hard look in turn, "the reality of it was far, far worse. Hunger is it's own special kind of hell, too, you know."

"And did you go hungry yourself," she asked, undaunted, "or were you merely a witness to it?"

"No, I didn't go hungry," he admitted, sounding almost sorry. "But I did lose my mother to the fever that came with it, dead and buried before I was seven. And then my brother went off to fight in the risin' of '48, and has been exiled in America ever since. Then my father died the very next year, as much from a broken heart as anything. So in one way or another, I lost my whole family as a result of the Hunger, and though I didn't want for food, no one can say I didn't suffer from it! Sure, we all did, every man, woman and child, all of us, famished or not! We're all victims of the Great Hunger!"

Dónal's voice had risen in intensity and by the time he'd finished he was glaring at Angela as if she were the cause of his and his country's accumulated calamities. "I'm sorry, Angela," he said ruefully. "I didn't mean to shout at you so."

"That's all right, chile," she said, taking him by the hands. "It's my fault for letting the old bitterness get the better of me. The Lord knows I've tried to put it behind me. But every once in awhile it creeps up on me, and before I know it, I'm in its clutches again."

"After all you've been through, Angela, I'd say you've a right to be bitter."

"Yes, I suppose so, though I do so want to be rid of it. I want to stop being a victim, and let go of the past so it doesn't weigh on me like an anchor on my soul."

"I know what you mean by that, too. The past weighs heavily upon me, and how I do wish I could forget it."

"Forget, chile? I didn't say *forget*. We can never forget our past. It's always there and part of us, no matter how much we may wish it otherwise. I said I wanted to let it go, to put it behind me so it doesn't drag me down like so many anchors."

"But how? How do you do let go without forgettin'?"

"Why, it's really quite simple, if you think about it," she said, though her sad smile told him it was anything but. "You face it, openly and honestly, and admit that you yourself might be partially responsible for the troubles visited upon you. And then you forgive yourself, as well as those who victimized you, for unless you can do that, you will never be free of the anger and hatred, and the past will haunt you through all your days."

There was a long silence between them then that grew heavy before Dónal finally broke it. "I don't think I could ever forgive the English for the Hunger, or for takin' my brother from me," he said quietly, though really it was of forgiving himself that he was thinking.

"Then you will always be their victim, no matter how hard you fight, and even if you win, if you can't forgive them, you will still be their victim."

And for that, Dónal had no answer.

But before the silence grew heavy again, Angela patted him on the cheek and rose from her seat. "I need to go to the market to fetch something for breakfast. Is there anything in particular you would like?"

"A jug of whiskey would be nice."

chapter 23

Liverpool

IT SEEMED SUCH A LONG TIME since he'd had a look at himself in a mirror, though it was barely a month since he'd stood in the tailor's shop in Queenstown, admiring the handsome young gentleman that other people's money had made of him. But that image was long gone now, worn away by time and distance and the hard life, leaving his reflection tired and tattered, like an old daguerreotype that had passed through too many hands. It showed in his eyes mostly, in the dark circles around them and the wariness in them, in his world-weary expression that spoke of lost hope. Or was it maybe just the drink taken the night before that made him look that way, the cheap Scotch that didn't agree with him and kept him up late? Maybe he was just tired and hung over, and saddened by the parting the day held in store. Or maybe it was the perpetual gray that enveloped the city, the cloying fog of coal smoke that obscured the sunlight by day and the stars by night. Maybe it was a lot of things and not, after all, the cumulative weight of the past bearing down upon him. Maybe he would feel better once he was out of Liverpool and on the road again. Maybe.

"I look old and tired!" Dónal sighed, watching his reflection agree.

But Angela was there to comfort him, just as he knew she would be, just as she'd been throughout his convalescence, waiting on him hand and foot, cooking his meals and filling his jar, absolving his sins by confessing her own. She'd even insisted that he keep her bed while she slept in the armchair, pulled close beside him, of course, in case he might want for anything in the night. Yet for all that she pampered him, she hadn't spoiled him and, just like a good mother should, as soon as he was well and whole again, she'd told him it was time to leave the nest, but not before making sure he had somewhere to go and something to do when he got there.

"No, Dónal-chile, you're not old and tired," she said, taking him by the hand. "You're young and beautiful and you always will be, just like my Hector!"

And though she smiled, Dónal could see the sadness in her eyes. Just like her Hector, he was leaving her and would never return.

"But come on now, chile," she said, tugging him toward the door. "You don't want to miss the ferry, do you?"

"You go on, Mother Angela. I'll be right there."

Seeing her exit, he turned back to the mirror for a last critical look.

"The bog is never far away, is it, ould son?" he asked himself knowing he wouldn't fool anyone.

☙

They stood side-by-side on the pier, watching silently as the passengers filed up the gangway, her arm linked in his, her parasol not quite keeping the rain off their shoulders. Soon he would have to go, too, but for now he was holding back, waiting till the last possible moment before leaving her, allowing them both to squeeze a last bit of sustenance from each other before parting forever. It was a sorry business, this saying good-bye, one he'd come to despise even as he became practiced at it. How did Butler manage it, he wondered, day after day, year after year? . . . *because each time is the present time, though it won't be as good as the next time.* And that was the secret, of course, to relish the future and reject the past, letting the sweetness of *hello* wash away the bitterness of *good-bye.* Could he learn to do it himself? He didn't think so.

Then the whistle blew last call, and he felt Angela squeeze his arm. "You'd better go now, chile."

"I know," he said, not looking at her, afraid of the tears he might find in her eyes. "I'm sorry I have to leave you, Angela."

"I know you are, chile, I know," she said, pulling his eyes up to hers, surprising him with the joy that was in them. "I learned long ago that we can't always have everything we want in life, so I try to be thankful for the things I do get, no matter how small they may be. And I am thankful to have met you, Dónal the world-mighty, thankful for the days we've had together and for the memories I have of them. I'll cherish them for the rest of my life, and when I meet my Maker, I'll thank Him for putting you on His green Earth, for you make it a better place to be."

Tears started in his eyes as he embraced her, wrapping her frail body in his arms and holding her close, thanking God in his turn that she didn't know the truth of him. "You've been a good mother to me, Angela, and I'll never forget you. Never!"

"And you are a good son, Dónal, one that any mother would be proud of," she replied, then released him and stepped back. "But go on now, before it's too late. Go and don't look back. I'm in the past now and you need to look to the future."

"Good-bye, Mother Angela," he said, still hesitating.

"Good-bye, Dónal. Until we meet again, may God hold you in the palm of His hand."

Then she turned and walked away.

He watched her go for just a moment before hurrying up the ramp, the last one to board before the lines were cast and the ferry slipped into the Mersey, heading for Birkenhead on the opposite side. At the rail, he watched as the great city of Liverpool fell away, seeing it now for the first time in the light of day. For though he'd spent almost a fortnight with Angela, he'd ventured outside her room only to go to the privy, proceeding warily even then. Her rooming house was square in the middle of the district known as Welsh Town, after all, and having once escaped the wrath of Welshmen, he wasn't anxious to give them a second chance.

So it was with a certain sense of irony that he turned toward

Birkenhead, since his destination lay in the heart of "enemy" territory, the town of Holyhead in North Wales. For having heard his story and that he needed to earn money for his passage, Angela advised him to leave the city, saying though it was a big place and he might lose himself in it forever, there was no sense tempting fate. Of course, she offered to pay his passage herself, but he wouldn't hear of it, telling her that the debt of kindness he'd run up with her might already be more than he could repay. But she just smiled patiently, like a teacher indulging a favored pupil. "Kindness isn't measured in units, chile, like money doled from a till. Nor has it size nor shape nor color. It either *is*, or it *isn't*, and the amount of its repayment bears no relation to the tender." But he was adamant, and soon she relented, seeing that in earning the money himself he felt he would atone for his sins. She didn't agree, of course, but like a good mother she kept it to herself. It was his life to live and his own conscience to obey.

Yet Angela had paid a call on the eldest son of her late employer, William Blake the Younger, asking if he might have some employment for Dónal in one of his many enterprises. It was he who suggested Holyhead, telling her he owned an interest in the quarrying firm that was engaged in supplying stone for the great breakwater being built across the harbor. He'd been sure that a position might be found for him, especially since men who could speak, read and write English, as well as do sums, were at something of a premium in North Wales. Indeed, the very next day he sent word that a bookkeeper was urgently needed, and that Angela's young friend could start as soon as he got there. Even so, Dónal wasn't enthusiastic, knowing from experience what drudgery bookkeeping could be. But when Angela mentioned the growing number of transatlantic steamers that called at Holyhead, he changed his mind, thinking that if his position didn't work out, he could always sign on with one bound for New York. And maybe he would do that anyway, if the opportunity presented itself.

But for now his only thought was Birkenhead and its railway station, and the trek across North Wales to Holyhead. Taking the St. Christopher's medal from under his shirt, he closed his eyes and said a silent prayer that it go smoothly. He'd had enough troubles already to last a lifetime.

⟨▩⟩

From his seat on the train, Dónal watched as North Wales slid by at the ungodly speed of thirty miles an hour, as he hummed softly to the rhythm of the rails. He was feeling much better now that he was on the road again, the thrilling new experience of train travel having lifted his spirits immeasurably. Indeed, as the train rumbled out of Birkenhead, he'd even stuck his head out the window to get the full feeling of its speed, a wild light shining in his eyes and his long hair streaming behind him like a horse's tail in the wind. Closing his eyes, he gave full voice to his ecstasy, screaming at the top of his lungs like a man having the flesh carded from his limbs. But upon pulling his head back inside, he found a carload of startled passengers, all staring at him as if he'd gone mad. He blushed as red as his hair, of course, and quickly sat down, too embarrassed even to mumble his apologies. The man across the aisle just shook his head in disgust, grunting, "Bloody Irish," before returning to his newspaper, as though it summed up everything one needed to know about the race.

After that, Dónal settled in to watch the scenery, noting with some surprise that Cheshire didn't seem all that different from the Irish midlands, having the same thatched cottages and stone walls, the same tilled fields and grazing livestock, the same verdant lushness born of the same soft weather. Yet for all its similarities, he would never mistake it for the Emerald Isle, its ubiquitous green being subtly different to his discerning eye, less primordial perhaps, less magical, less closely connected to the Otherworld that always seemed so present in Ireland. In his mind, he likened it to the difference between spring and summer, the former promising paths untrodden and pleasures untasted, impulsive and passionate, young and wild and free, while the latter spoke of temperance, discipline and order, its carnality subdued by the fuller wisdom of maturity.

454

But then again, maybe not. Maybe he was just seeing what he wanted to see, his vision colored by his own preconceptions, his abiding prejudice against the Saxon "mainland." He couldn't decide, and it made no difference anyway. He hated the British Empire and always would, no matter what Angela had to say of letting go. For having seen the thriving cities of Liverpool, Birkenhead and Chester, he was now certain of one thing, that the modern world had left Ireland behind, not by choice of the Irish, of course, but of their English landlords. She was England's breadbasket, after all, and to keep Her so, the Irish had to be kept in their place, perpetually relegated to the status of landless peasants, slaves without masters, just so much human machinery to depreciate and scrap. Which, of course, was why they'd never exported their Industrial Revolution to Her shores, for to give the Irish a way to support themselves independently of the land would be to give them a choice in their lives, a choice between serving England and serving themselves. And that much Irish freedom, the British Empire simply couldn't afford.

But then the train crossed into Wales and the land began to change, becoming increasingly tumbled and broken, with hills rising steeply from a narrow coastal plain and marching away southward, dividing the land into myriad natural fortresses wherein petty kingdoms could rise and flourish, where loyalty was local, and unity in the face of outside invasion didn't exist. 'Just like West Cork,' Dónal thought, taking in the ancient homeland of Britain's last true Britons. Indeed, the feeling of it was unmistakably Celtic, with the soft weather blurring the distinctions between green and stone, earth and water and sky, this world and the next, and the living enigma of a heroic age that, though long past, was yet present and elemental. It made him feel at home in a way that he hadn't since leaving Béara, never mind that his beating had come at the hands of Welshmen. In a visceral sort of way, he understood them, could take their place and feel their fury, their lust for battle and vengeance, the sensuous, Celtic impulse of the moment.

And spotting a standing stone atop a nearby hill, he smiled, taking comfort in its atavistic familiarity. Indeed, he could feel a certain kinship with Wales, had a sense of place for it that he didn't in Liverpool or Dublin or even Cork City. Would he like the Welsh people, too? Surely he'd give them an open mind, and anyway, he'd not be among them for long, God willing. After the train and ferry fares, he still had about four pounds left, so in three months, maybe four, he'd be off to New York.

New York!

Good God, what would it be like, he wondered? Would he gain a sense of place for it, or would he remain forever *out of place*, just another culchie blown in from the bog? It didn't matter, he decided. Eóghan would be there, and at Eóghan's side *any* place would feel like home.

Then his thoughts were interrupted as the train came to the outskirts of a town and began to slow. After deciding that it was just another sleepy Welsh fishing village, he was about to close his eyes for a nap, when suddenly an enormous castle came into view. It was a castle like none he'd ever seen before, rising from a knoll of solid rock as if it had grown from it, and so enormous that several castles like *Cathair Dhúin Iascaigh* would easily fit within its massive walls.

"Jayzis, God, what is that?" he mumbled in awe, his face glued to the window and staring as if the great fortress were something from another world.

"Why, it's just a castle, Mick," came a voice from behind him, and turning to the speaker, Dónal found him grinning mischievously. "Have you never seen one before?"

Dónal didn't reply, just gave him a look that would spoil fresh potatoes, before turning back to the window. Who did he think he was to call him "Mick?"

But the man just chuckled, unmoved by Dónal's glare. "Oh, come now, Mick. I was just havin' a bit of fun with you. No offense intended, no harm done. What do you say now? Shall we kiss and make up?"

Dónal looked the man over more closely then, noting that he was big and burly under his finely-tailored suit, his black eyes, hair and beard accentuating his somewhat swarthy complexion. His posture was open and frank, and he had an air of self-assurance about him, the look of a man who wasn't afraid to mix it up when circumstances warranted. Yet his smile was genuine and infectious, and showed that he was indeed just having a bit of fun.

"I'd rather eat shite than kiss your mug, ugly as it is," Dónal replied, smiling in turn.

"Oh, that's rich, Mick!" the man said merrily. "Eat shit, indeed! Though I've often heard it said of you Irish that you misuse the English language to your own advantage, I've yet to hear quite so colorful an example! I'd rather eat shit! I'll have to remember that one!"

"'Twasn't that funny," Dónal said, though he couldn't help chuckling himself.

"Ah, but it was, Mick, it was!" the man said, wiping tears from his eyes. "Ah, me. So this is your first time in Wales, I take it?"

"To be sure, 'tis my first time anywhere outside of Ireland. You may not believe it, but till just a few weeks ago, I'd never traveled more than a few miles from the house I was born in."

"Oh, I believe it, all right. I was much the same in my youth, as indeed were most people I know. I didn't leave my hometown for the first time till I was almost eighteen, and that was just to go to Bangor for the day. But for me, that trip was like openin' a floodgate, and hardly a month has gone by since that hasn't seen me on the road to somewhere."

"And is that where you're headed now? Somewhere?"

"Aye. Somewhere called Holyhead, the place I started from yesterday, the very place I'd never left till the summer of my eighteenth year. It's about as dull and dreary a town as you could possibly imagine, but it's home and there's no place like it, as the sayin' goes."

"'Tis Holyhead I'm bound for myself."

"Oh? Are you to catch the ferry back to Ireland?"

"No, I'm goin' there to work, at least till I can save enough to go on to Amrrica. I've a situation arranged at the quarry, startin' first thing Monday mornin'."

"Well, now, aren't you the industrious one, linin' up your work in advance. And just what situation have you arranged?"

"Bookkeeper," Dónal replied, shrugging with resignation.

"Ah, yes, I heard about young Jenkins gettin' caught with his fingers in the till. He'll be spendin' the next few years as a guest of the Queen, and with nothin' to count but the days till his parole. So you're to take his place, are you? Well, good for you. I know old Edwards will be glad to have you. He's a stone mason by trade, and though he runs a taut ship at the quarry, he can barely count the fingers on one hand. He's fit to be tied with those books and that's the God's honest truth!"

Dónal didn't say anything to that, just stared out the window as he mulled it over. With the quarry manager unable to read the books, what was there to keep him from dipping his own fingers into the till? Of course, he'd have to be better at it than young Jenkins, but then, he wouldn't be lingering after the fact, either. By the time anyone was aware of it, he'd be well on his way to New York, if not already there. So with just a little planning, he could be with Eóghan in a matter of weeks rather than months! The thought of it brought a smile to his face. Yes, things were indeed looking up now that he was on the road again.

But then the man spoke again and brought him back to reality. "Did I say somethin' funny, Mick?"

"What? Oh, no, sorry. My mind just wandered for a moment. And by the way, my name isn't Mick. 'Tis Dónal O'Sullivan, and I'll thank you to call me so."

"Rhys Griffith," the man said, extending his hand over the seat back.

"Pleased to meet you, Rhys," Dónal replied, feeling his hand disappear into the bear paw at the end of Griffith's arm. "Sure, that's some grip you've got there, and 'tis but few I can say that to."

"Me, too," Griffith replied with a wolfish grin.

"To be sure. With that fancy suit you're wearin', I'd have taken you for just another fine jackeen. But with a grip like that, there must've been some honest labor in it."

"You might say so. I started workin' on my father's fishin' boat at the tender age of seven, and had three boats of my own by the time I was fifteen. It wasn't till I was twenty-three that I sold the boats and became a shippin' agent, which is my present line of work, and which gives me the wherewithal to wear this suit. But even so, I'm no rich man, just a hard worker who's had a bit of luck."

"And anyway, you can't polish a turd, now can you?" Dónal quipped, sending Griffith into another round of laughter. But his mind was whirling with the possibilities that having a friend in the shipping business could open up. Maybe he wouldn't have to steal the money after all. Maybe Griffith could get him a cheap fare or help him sign on with a transatlantic steamer. Of course, it was too soon to be asking the man for favors, but he had no doubt he'd be able to work it out of him eventually. Besides, he actually liked the man, so cultivating his friendship would be no burden.

Dónal smiled again, but to himself this time. Yes, things were definitely looking up.

After that, the conversation went this way and that, with Griffith pointing out the sights along the way and giving Dónal a brief history of Holyhead. The town arose around a Roman fortress built to guard the primary trade route to Ireland, he said, and its existence was still closely connected therewith. But now the trade wasn't in commodities so much as in travelers and mail, Holyhead being the western terminus of the London and North Western Railway and serviced by steamers from both Dublin and Kingstown, making it the direct link between the two principal cities of the Empire. In recent years, that trade had been expanded somewhat by the increasing number of transatlantic steamers calling at Holyhead. It was hoped, too, that the completion of the great breakwater would further increase the transatlantic business since it would create a much larger protected harbor. So all things considered, the town was relatively prosperous, given its location at the extremity of North Wales, and was positioned to become even more so in the future. As for Griffith himself, his business could only grow, though he wasn't sure he really wanted it to. Already it kept him from his family more than he would like, and it seemed that his sons would grow up and be gone before he knew it. It was a dilemma without a solution, especially since he was a hard-working man by nature.

After Bangor, Griffith pointed out the Menai Suspension Bridge, the first bridge of its kind in the world, and then the Britannia Tubular Bridge, which the train itself would pass through, with its Egyptian architecture and concrete lions guarding either end of the cast iron tunnels. It was an awesome monument and a great engineering achievement, Dónal had to admit, despite his predilection against the symbols of Empire. Yet when the train plunged inside, its design defects became glaringly apparent, as the noise level increased to a deafening roar and the stench of years of unventilated coal smoke became overpowering, even with the windows closed. But the speed of the train made quick work of it, and in a moment he was back in the light of day, having crossed the Menai Straits to the Isle of Anglesey.

From there, they had a good view of the straits, and Griffith mentioned the battle fought on its shores between the Romans and Druids. *Ynys Môn*, the island had been to the ancient Celts, "Holy Island," so-called because it was the cradle of druidism in the British Isles. But in 60 A.D., the Romans came to stamp out the Druids and put an end to their troublesome rebellions. He would have said more, but at that point Dónal took up the narrative himself.

"The Romans marched from Londinium under the command of Suetonius Paulinus, leavin' a broad swath of death and destruction in their wake," he said, his eyes far away, as though seeing the events he was describing. "But the Britons were waitin' for him at Segontium, arrayed in battle order on the far side of the straits, the Druids in their flowin' robes, dark and forbiddin', the warriors naked, their bodies painted with blue dye and their phalluses erect, the hair of the women streamin' behind them as they ran through the ranks, and all of them howlin' and shriekin' and showerin' the Romans with blood-curdlin' curses and righteous fury. So savage was their display that the vaunted legions of Rome were unnerved and would've fled in terror, but for Suetonius's threat to execute any man who so much as flinched. And when they did charge, many fell under the shower of Celtic spears, their shrieks of agony addin' to the clamor, while others drowned in the swift-flowin' waters, and still others were cut down at the shoreline, the slaughter continuing until the straits were clogged with bodies and blood. But Suetonius was not to be denied, and in the heel of the hunt, it was the Romans who had the victory, overwhelmin' the Celts with their superior tactics, arms and discipline. And when the battle was over, they cut down the sacred groves of Mona and roasted the Druids on their own altars, a sacrilege that was avenged by Boudica at Camulodunum, though her victory was short-lived. And after her defeat at Mancetter, it would be three and a half centuries before Albion became Celtic again, though within another two, it had fallen again, to the Saxons this time."

"Well, now," Griffith said after a respectful pause. "It seems that you know more about our history than I do!"

"No, not really," Dónal said, still gazing at the straits. "I know about the Roman campaigns and Boudica's revolt because I've read the classical accounts of them. But other than that, I don't know much about Wales."

"Well, you're still one up on me, Mick."

"The name's *Dónal.*"

"Whatever," Griffith replied with a smirk, which widened to a grin as the train pulled into a station. "But here's somethin' I'll bet you don't know. We're comin' into the most notable place in all of Wales, the village of *Llanfairpwllgwyngyllgogerchwyrndrobwllllantysiliogogogoch.*"

"The hell you say!" Dónal exclaimed, eyeing him in disbelief. "'Tisn't a name, but a whole bloody dictionary!"

"That's it, all right. *Llanfairpwllgwyngyllgogerchwyrndrobwllllantysilio-gogogoch.* Just look at the sign on the station if you don't believe me."

"Jayzis, God, Rhys, have you no vowels in your alphabet?" Dónal exclaimed when he spotted the name, so long it had to be hyphenated and printed on two lines. "I know our languages are supposed to be related, but damn me if I can make anything of that pile of gibberish!"

"Yes, it is rather a mouthful. It's known locally as 'the Englishman's cure for lockjaw,' but from your reaction, it appears that we'll have to add Irishmen to the list."

"You've the right of it there, boyo! I'll not even try to pronounce it! What does it mean, anyway?"

"In English?"

"No, in Irish. Of course in English, you thick!"

"Well, now, if you're goin' to be rude about it, I just might not tell you. It means, 'The Church of St. Mary in the hollow of white hazel, near the rapid whirlpool of St. Tysilio and a red cave.'"

"Jayzis, I think it's easier to say in Welsh."

"Well, it just so happens that for only a ha'penny you can buy a printed sheet in the station with the name broken down into it's proper syllables and corresponding English pronunciations. So if you really want to learn a little Welsh—"

"Thanks just the same, Rhys. 'Twould take up all my free time, and surely I can waste it in a more fittin' manner!"

"Not in Holyhead. I told you it hasn't much in the way of excitement. Even your own Jonathan Swift once wrote, 'Whoever would wish to live long should live here, for a day is longer than a week, and if the weather be foul, as long as a fortnight.'"

"Ah, sure if it isn't grand that I've so much to look forward to," Dónal said glumly.

꘎

It was already midafternoon when the train crossed from Anglesey to Holy Island and came to a stop in Holyhead. By that time, Dónal and Griffith had cemented their friendship with a pledge to stand each other for pints. But first Griffith needed to check in with his clerk, after which he'd give Dónal a tour of the town and take him out to the quarry, just to get a jump on the work week. Moreover, when he found that Dónal had nowhere to stay, he also offered to put him up in his spare room, which Dónal had gladly accepted, the prospect of shelling out a good portion of his income on rent having been the major stumbling block to his desire for an early sailing. But with that obstacle out of the way, he would be able to leave Holyhead in just a matter of weeks, and without having to steal the money or ask another favor of Griffith. So things had definitely taken a turn for the better, and as he followed Griffith off the train, he fingered the St. Christopher's medal under his shirt, saying a silent prayer of thanks.

Once on the platform, however, he found himself swallowed in the press of people that descended on the train, baggage handlers and porters, hawkers and newsboys and eastbound passengers, the sudden din and chaos reminding him of nothing so much as the streets of Dublin. Could this indeed be Holyhead, the dull, dreary place Griffith had described?

But then he felt Griffith tug at his arm. "Follow me," the man bellowed, as he leaned his barrel chest into the throng. And in just a moment he'd bulled his way through and was outside on the cobbled front street, Dónal following so close behind that he almost tripped on his heels.

"'Tis a bit quieter out here!" Dónal remarked, looking back at the station.

"It'll be much the same in there in a few minutes," Griffith replied. "Once the passengers get settled on the ferry or the train or into a hotel, the whole place goes to sleep again, and only wakes up when another train or steamer arrives. For most travelers, Holyhead is just an appointed hour on the schedule, a place to change from train to ferry, and with the station and terminal right next to each other, very few actually have to set foot in the town. Of those who do, few venture beyond the front street, that bein' where the inns and public houses are. So don't think I was leadin' you down the primrose path, because I wasn't."

"No, I can see that," Dónal agreed, finding the street as quiet and empty as the station was noisy and full. From where he stood, he could see a good bit of the front street and the town climbing the gentle slope behind it, none of it giving the lie to Griffith's description. Indeed, it had a melancholy, almost mournful air to it which the gray weather did nothing to improve and, thinking of Swift's words, he wondered how many days as long as fortnights he would have to endure here.

But then Griffith had him by the arm and was leading him away from the station, pointing out the sights as they went: the harbor, the pier and the customs house; the impressive Railway Hotel where most overnight passengers now stayed, given its proximity to the station and terminal; the Church of St. Cybi within the walls of the old Roman fortress; the Royal Hotel just across the street from the station, in a building it shared with the Eagle and Child. Just beyond the latter, along a street that angled off and led uphill into town, stood the Catholic church, which had just been completed the previous year. It was dedicated to St. Mary Help of Christians, Griffith informed him, and the priest's name was Father Bonaventure, himself an Irishman despite his French-sounding name, as indeed were the majority of his congregants.

"A lot of your fellahs have settled here since the famine, havin' only had money enough to get them this far," Griffith explained, stopping in front of the little Gothic-style church. "The church even has an immigrant aid society to help new arrivals get settled, not that you'll be needin' it, of course. But it would be a good way to meet some of your own, if you've a mind."

"Maybe," Dónal replied automatically, not really listening to Griffith. Rather, he was trying to remember the last time he'd attended Mass, certainly not since the raid on the magazine, but how long before then? And when was the last time he'd taken communion or visited the confessional? Surely it was before he'd taken up residence with Sióna, for even the liberal Father Enright wouldn't bend the rules that far. He remembered how safe and secure he'd felt as a child amid the solemn ritual of the Catholic Church, sitting among the faithful in the crowded pews, knowing that for one hour of each week he had nothing to fear from his fellow man. Maybe if he devoted himself to it, he could feel that way again. Maybe going to Mass and confessing his sins would lighten his load and help him expunge his guilt. 'What the hell', he thought, 'it couldn't hurt.'

But even as he did, a woman carrying a basket of laundry came around the back corner of the Eagle and Child and, catching sight of the two men, stopped to look them over. She was tall for a woman, almost as tall as Dónal himself, and slender, though with plenty of curve to her hips and bust, her immodest clothing clinging to her salient femininity like wet on water. And though her hair was black as midnight, her skin was almost deathly pale, it's perfection only accentuated by the mole above the corner of her mouth. She had eyes the color of envy and her lips were full and red, while her brow glowed with sweat from her labor at the washboard, her cheeks and throat flushed a beguiling pink. Taken as a whole, her appearance was more striking than beautiful, though she was that, too, in a sibylline sort of way. Indeed, the word "sultry" might have been coined especially for her, as she oozed sexuality like a Siren, a latter-day goddess of lust and carnality, the kind of woman that a man would kill to possess and in the act of taking her become himself possessed, like a ship of fools broken on the hard rock of her heart.

And Dónal felt her before he saw her, felt her eyes roaming over him, looking at him the way coarse men look at women, like he was raw meat to a ravenous wolf. Nor did she try to hide it, just met his gaze coolly, frankly, showing him all that she was and daring him to give her his best shot, indeed daring him not to, which would've been harder. He saw it all, too, as clear as the light of day, yet he didn't care. For in that moment, he would've given up everything for her, himself and his immortal soul, anything for the feel of her naked flesh on his, the electric pleasure of being inside her, of fucking her till he died of ecstasy if that's what it took to please her. He felt Griffith tugging at his elbow, trying to pull his eyes away and break the spell, but he couldn't move, couldn't even blink without her consent. He was hers, body and soul. She had only to say the word.

But Griffith was insistent, finally using his bear-like strength to turn him bodily away and drag him up the street. "Come on now, Mick," he said, wrapping an arm around his shoulders to keep him moving. "There's more to see up this way."

465

"Who is she?" Dónal demanded, ignoring Griffith's attempt to distract him, trying to turn for another look. When the man didn't answer immediately, he added, "You may as well tell me, Rhys, because I'll find out one way or another."

"Her name is Rhiannon Morgan. She's a chamber maid at the Royal, the bastard niece of old Mrs. Hibbert, the landlord's wife. But you'll be advised to stay well away from her if you have any regard for yourself as a man. The local women call her 'the Black Death' for their many husbands she's ruined, though not to her face, of course. They're too afraid of her for that, too terrified that she might really be the witch rumor makes of her. In the old days, of course, they'd have just burned her at the stake and been done with it. But in these enlightened times of the nineteenth century, we don't do such things any more, and the women have nothin' to fall back on but ostracism and righteous indignation, neither of which seem to have any effect on her. So they're left to suffer in silence, each prayin' that her own husband won't be next. Not that they have anything to worry about for the time bein', it seems, since she appears to have chosen you as her next victim."

Griffith fell silent then, leaving Dónal to ponder his words as they walked through the town. If they were meant to frighten him, they didn't have their desired effect. After all, what was the worst that could happen – that she would tire of him and move on? He probably wouldn't be around long enough for that, and anyway, he was confident of his ability to keep her interested for the time he would be. And, too, he could play hard to get, could turn the tables and make her come to him. Sure, that's what he'd do, he thought, smiling wickedly to himself. He took a deep breath and let it out slowly, relaxing as he did. It was so much easier to think now that he wasn't locked in the grip of those she-devil eyes, now that he was losing his erection.

Dónal lay on his back, watching as the firelight danced over the rafters, the promised "extra room" turning out to be a separate cottage behind

Griffith's house, the very one in which he'd been born and his father before him and his before him. It was a typical crofter's cottage, similar in design to those in which Dónal had lived in Ireland, the code of Celtic laws that had provided for such things having existed in both countries for a thousand years before the coming of the Saxon. And as was typical of Irish peasants, the Griffiths had held a few acres of land with it from the local squire, most of which they'd sowed in oats while the remainder had been dedicated to their few head of cattle. But their primary income had always come from the sea, from the fishing grounds off Holyhead, which the men of Griffith's family had plied in their small boats for more generations than he cared to know. And still Griffith made his living from the sea, though in a different way and on a far grander scale than they could ever have imagined. For the man now owned not only the few acres his family traditionally held, but fifty more as well, all purchased in cash from the dead squire's estate six years ago. Not only that, but he'd also built himself a new house, a sturdy two-story structure just off the road that led into town. He and his wife, Gwyn, even had their own bedroom upstairs separate from the one shared by the two boys, Owain and Llywelyn. It had taken some getting used to, he'd told Dónal over supper, but eventually they'd grown into it, and now he couldn't remember it being any other way. But though Griffith had come up a long way in the world, he remained genuinely humble about it, sticking to his mantra that he was just a hard-working man who'd had a little luck.

As for location, the Griffith farm couldn't have been better situated for Dónal, as it was less than a mile from Holyhead Mountain, at the southwest foot of which lay the quarry. Griffith had taken him there after showing him the great breakwater itself, which though still only half-completed after sixteen years of work, had already created an enormous area of protected harborage, within which many ships lay at anchor. He'd found the manager, Edward Edwards, in the shack that served as quarry office, and presented Dónal as proudly as if he were his own son. But much to Dónal's chagrin, he'd introduced him as "Mick" O'Sullivan, and the name having stuck over all protests, Mick

O'Sullivan he'd become, even to Griffith's wife and sons. Did they know it was an ethnic slur, he'd wondered, an insult to all Irishmen when applied without invitation by non-Irishmen? Probably not, at least not the Griffiths, though time would only tell of the others.

Yet as in Queenstown, in just the space of an afternoon he'd taken on an entirely new identity, becoming someone completely different, and with just the slightest of cosmetic changes, this time not even reaching skin deep. Once he realized it, he actually liked the idea of being Mick O'Sullivan, since it meant he could be whoever he wanted to these people, that he could shed the chrysalis of his past and emerge a new man. It even gave him a new sense of self-confidence, and he'd followed Griffith up the slope of Holyhead Mountain with his chest out and head held high. But at the summit, he came back to earth when Griffith told him that on a clear day, one could see Ireland from where they stood. Indeed, it was just over there, just across Manannán's Little Water, not so far away, after all.

But still, meeting Griffith had buoyed his spirits and reinforced his impression that coming to Holyhead was indeed a good thing. For after the tramp up the mountain, the man took him home to meet his family, announcing as he burst through the door that he'd brought "Morris from over the mountain," the Welsh euphemism for an unexpected guest. And though Dónal was anxious over his reception, he needn't have been, as Gwyn and the boys took to him as readily as Griffith himself, wrapping him in their familial embrace and making him feel at home. After supper they all sat around the fire together, listening as Griffith told of the great Welsh princes, Llywelyn Mawr and Llywelyn ap Gruffydd, and the last great Welsh rebel, Owain Glyn Dŵr. Though the names and places were different, the stories seemed all too familiar to Dónal, with their recurring theme of a long losing battle against the Saxon foe, of an ancient people, language and culture slipping inexorably into obscurity, soon to be forgotten by an uncaring world.

Later, after they shooed the boys off to bed, Griffith led him by lantern light out to the cottage, where he lit a fire in the hearth and broke out a jug of the local poteen, apologizing for the fact that it was rotgut-raw and that he'd made him wait so long for it. Gwyn didn't hold with the taking of strong spirits in "her" house, he explained, though she'd long ago come to accept her husband's moral weakness on that score. Yet she'd laid the ground rules in no uncertain terms, saying that she would tolerate it only as long as he didn't drink to excess and kept it away from her and the boys, conditions which he'd found acceptable, if inconvenient. But then, many of his fellows were not so blessed, and tipped the jug only at the peril of spending several nights afterward in the shed or under the stars. It was the fault of their Methodist ministers for extolling the virtue of teetotaling, for though the women took to it like ducks to water, he didn't know many men who aspired to be quite so virtuous. But so they had their drop for friendship and one to grow on, and then Griffith took his leave, though he left the jug to keep Dónal company.

Yet none of that was on Dónal's mind now as he lay on his back, watching the light play over the rafters, not even the jug on the floor beside him. Rather, he was wondering what to do about the puddle of semen on his belly, as it was getting thin and threatening to spill over his sides onto the bedding. He'd not thought to bring a rag with him to the bed, as the need to "abuse" himself (as the priests described it) had grown suddenly urgent when he found himself alone with his thoughts of Rhiannon Morgan. In the end, he did nothing, just rolled over onto his stomach, leaving it to the sheet to clean him.

"I'll see to it in the mornin'," he said aloud, hoisting the jug for another drink.

chapter 24

Holyhead, North Wales

IN THE END, DÓNAL HELD OUT FOR SIX DAYS, it being an invitation to drink that led to his downfall, a simple offer of a pint after work from one of his coworkers at the quarry, a fellow Cork man who'd come to Holyhead years before. They would go down to the harbor, he said, to a public house called the Dublin Packet, where Higgins the publican offered a welcome to all homesick Irishmen. Dónal had eagerly accepted, of course, though neither the drink nor the camaraderie of his own had tempted him so much as the chance that she might see him passing and follow after. They were joined by others, and as the group strolled along the front street, Dónal related one of Griffith's stories, that of Sígri, the Irish giant who'd once ruled Holyhead. It was really just a bluff, of course, an attempt at nonchalance, though it didn't keep his heart from beating faster as they neared the Royal Hotel, didn't keep him from being disappointed at not seeing her there, at not feeling her eyes on him or hearing her Siren's call silently beckoning him to his doom. Yet once past, he sighed with relief, suddenly seeing the depth of his folly and resolving not to give in to temptation, to turn her away even if she came to him. Indeed, he wouldn't even stay for a drink, would make some excuse and go back to Griffith's where he would be safe from her, being sure to take the long way around, of course.

But then they came to the row of public houses known locally as the "Five Sisters" for their adjacency to each other, and hearing music and

470

laughter spilling into the street, he followed the others into the Dublin Packet, the lure of Saturday night revelry too strong to be denied. 'What the hell,' he thought, 'a few pints won't hurt anything. I can still go home the long way and she'll be none the wiser.'

Dónal's companions were met with a chorus of raucous halloo's and, before he knew it, they'd melted into the crowd to greet friends and join in the *craic*, leaving him suddenly alone. After a moment of uncertainty, he moved to the bar and ordered a pint and a drop, before settling onto an empty stool near the door. The place did have the feel of home to it, he decided after a look around, with all the Irish faces speaking with brogues, laughing and drinking and chatting up the girls, putting the work week behind them and working on something to feel guilty about come the Sabbath. There was even a quintet of musicians near the fire, hard at work and sweating over a set of jigs while four couples did a set dance in the open space before them. When his drinks came he turned his attention to them, making quick work of the drop but savoring the pint, the former satisfying his need while the latter quenched his thirst, leaving him carefree and relaxed.

But when he signaled the barman for another round, the man's eyes strayed beyond Dónal to something behind him, and he knew from the look on his face and the gathering silence that he'd better look himself. Yet before he could turn around, he felt a slender arm slither over his shoulder and dive under his shirt while another wrapped around his waist, locking him in a grip so tight as to almost constrict his breathing. It was *her*, the Black Death, he knew without question, without needing any more proof than his nipple squeezed between her forefinger and thumb, than her breasts pressed against his back, loose under her garment but tight and firm within her skin, than the smell of her enveloping him in a cloud of sensuality, the sweet, deadly smell of forbidden fruit.

"Are you ready now?" she asked, her hot breath hissing softly in his ear, her resonant voice vibrating in his bones. When he didn't move, she flicked her tongue over his ear and then bit it, just hard enough to make the pain pleasurable. "Come on, Mick, you've kept me waitin' for a week already. Are you ready to show me that you're more than just good looks, that you're a real man and not just another mouse like the rest of these vermin? Are you ready to make me squirm, Mick, are you ready to make me scream? Are you ready to *fuck* me?"

But Dónal couldn't move, couldn't speak, just sat on his stool staring straight ahead, his body as rigid as wood though alive with the sensations of her. The bartender was staring at him, he knew, as were all those around him, as indeed was every single person in the place, even the band and dancers, their silence roaring in his ears just as it had at Uncle Séamus's wake. Only from within himself did any sound come, a small voice calling from deep inside, desperately begging him to save himself and his immortal soul, to tell her to go away and leave him alone, a voice he longed to heed, knowing he'd be lost if he didn't. He even managed to raise his hand, meaning to fend her off, but instead found himself being led to the door, walking as though in a dream, his surroundings as insubstantial as fog. As the door closed behind him, he heard a lone voice break the silence and when the place erupted into laughter, he knew it was directed at him, that he'd humiliated himself and that tomorrow everyone in town would know. But he didn't care, didn't feel anything but her hand on his and the throbbing in his trousers. He was going to give her what she wanted, by God, and the rest of the world could go to Hell.

She led him into a small cottage just behind the Royal Hotel and locked the door behind them. Then before he had a chance to speak or even look around, she was on him, her tongue in his mouth and her hips thrusting against his, ripping his shirt open to pinch his nipples and bite his neck. And Dónal gave it back, gripping her black hair hard in one hand while slipping the other beneath her blouse to rake her back with his fingernails. She shuddered with the pleasure of it, then pushed him back a step to tear his shirt and jacket from his shoulders, before unbuckling his belt and dropping his trousers to the floor.

"Give me your hands," she commanded, picking up his belt.

"What are you—"

"Give me your hands!" she repeated, not waiting for him to comply but grabbing them herself and binding them with the belt.

Without speaking again, she led him to the bed, his trousers still around his ankles and his boots on his feet, pushed him down on his back and secured the belt to the headboard. Dropping her own clothes to the floor, she stepped onto the bed and stood over him, hands on hips and a devilish glow in her eyes, gloating like a warrior over a bested adversary. The sight of her so drove him mad with desire, with her taut body glowing red with the embers of the fire, her breasts high and firm, her nipples small and hard. Seeing his eyes on her crotch, she spread it with her fingers so that he could see the flesh beneath, swollen and glistening, ready to draw him in and close around him like a velvet trap. Bending her knees she lowered herself to his face, squatting above him with her free hand cradled behind his head to guide him home, not that he needed help or encouragement. And as he sucked her into his mouth and locked his tongue on target, she moaned and bucked like a wild horse, coming to a climax in just a few seconds and then again a few seconds later, and again and again till it seemed to him just one long zenith of pleasure. But just when his face was going numb and he felt he could do it no more, she pulled away and slid him inside her, locking his torso between her knees and holding him still for what seemed an eternity, tormenting him with the heat of her while her relentless eyes bored into his. Then finally she began to slide up and down, but slowly, up . . . and down, up . . . and down, until it became a torture, and he struggled and bucked his hips, trying to make her go faster. But she just pulled off and waited for him to calm down, to behave himself, before resuming her deliberate pace, never once moving her eyes from his or even blinking. And when he thought he could take no more and would surely explode inside her, she pulled off again, leaving him gasping and frustrated until she thrust her breasts in his face, her nipples pacifying him as quickly as any baby.

"Bite them!" she commanded, as he sucked and pulled. "Harder! *Harder!* Oh, that's good, that's very good!"

Then she was on him again and slamming her hips into his, her pace as frenetic now as it had been slow before. And when she arched her back and screamed, he let go and screamed with her, not caring that their clamor could be heard all the way to the front street. Afterward, he lay beneath her, gasping for breath, feeling he'd been ravaged, raped, violated, and yet desperately wanting more.

"You're mine, Mick," she murmured in his ear, biting it hard. "Mine and mine alone. Do you hear me?"

"Yes, I hear you," he replied, pliantly, obediently.

The Darkness was all around him, and he found it good.

chapter 25

Holyhead
11 October, 1861

IT WAS ODD THE WAY THEY COWERED before her, Dónal thought as he watched Rhiannon bully the porter, all of them, the cooks, the maids, even the Hibberts themselves, glaring at her back and calling her the Black Death, though not one of them dared say it to her face. Not that it would do them any good, he knew, for when he'd done it, she'd just laughed and thanked him for the compliment. Of course she'd punished him for it, too, tying him to the bed and keeping him hard for over an hour, tormenting him with her hands and her mouth and the things she did to herself, giving him just enough to keep him in a state of sexual frenzy, but always stopping before he could climax. In the end, his erection just melted away of its own accord, his mind and body past the point of exhaustion.

"You just can't take it, can you, Mick?" she sneered. Then she squatted over his face and did herself, just to show her contempt, that she really didn't need him, that she could give herself more pleasure than any man ever could.

"I hate you!" he said, glaring with all the venom he could muster.

"No, you don't," she sighed, as if speaking to a wearisome child. "You hate yourself, and I'm just the mirror that reflects it."

Then she went out and left him tied to the bed, left him alone for hours with nothing to do but wallow in his own self-pity, knowing in his soul that she was right. He could never give her up of his own accord, even though he knew she was destroying him, that he was destroying himself with his lust for her. But he'd become an addict, enslaved to the Darkness that she embodied, needing it and hating it, hating himself for needing it but always wanting more, till it dominated his every waking moment. His body ached for her when she wasn't with him, doing things to him, having him do things to her, deliciously wicked things he'd never imagined could be done. Only sleep brought him any respite, the empty sleep of sexual exhaustion, the drugged sleep of cheap whiskey, the dreamless sleep that left him unrefreshed in the morning, till he almost longed for eternal sleep, so dissolute had his mind and body become. Indeed, Griffith had been appalled at his appearance when he'd come to retrieve him, telling him that he looked like a corpse with his hollow eyes and sunken cheeks. He begged Dónal to come with him, warning that she wore men out faster than shoes, tossing away their empty shells like so much rubbish. But Dónal sent him away, insisting that he was fine and in control of himself, that he could leave her any time he wanted, but that he just wasn't finished with her yet. He knew himself to be lying, of course, that even if he lived to a thousand he'd never be finished with her, would *never* get enough. Even Griffith's offer to pay his passage to America didn't move him, as he no longer cared about Eóghan. He'd given up everything for his addiction: himself, his dreams, his money, his job and even his prospects for one since the whole town was privy to their immorality. He'd snared himself in a trap of his own making, and if he had anything to do with it, he'd never be set free.

But then one evening things changed between them, suddenly and without warning, leaving Dónal stunned and wondering what had happened. She came in late from the Royal, which of itself wasn't unusual, her demonic energy impelling her to work long hours, except that she first went to the market rather than coming straight home for their usual evening tryst. She had a bundle in each arm, too, a parcel of food which she set on the table, and a box, which she set on the bed next to Dónal. Opening it, she laid out a suit of tweeds, two shirts, a collar and a tie, all new and crisp and ready to wear. Terrified that Griffith's warning had proved prophetic, he stared at her wide-eyed, expecting her to tell him to take the clothes and never come back.

But seeing the look on his face, she just laughed. "It's time you started earnin' your keep around here with somethin' other than that big boy of yours," she said, nodding toward his crotch. "The Hibberts need help at the Royal and I told them you'd start in the mornin'. With her caterin' the commissary at the station and him in bed with the gout, there's no one to see after the desk and the dinin' room, so you're the man. Oh, and I told them you're handy with the books, too. That is your trade after all, isn't it, Mick? Bookkeeper?"

But still he just gaped at her, her explanation having explained exactly nothing, the merriment in her laughter leaving him more perplexed than ever. "Go on. Try them on," she said, nodding to the clothes, not waiting for him to comply but dressing him herself. "There now. Aren't you the cat's meow?" she said with an approving smile, standing back to take the full measure of him. "You look almost as good in them as you do out! Of course, you'll need new boots, too, but they'll have to wait till next month, or maybe even Christmas. The Hibberts are tight with their money, you know, that I'm a relation notwithstandin'. But with two wages comin' in, we should manage well enough. Now put your new duds away and I'll cook us some supper."

With that, she turned away, leaving him still gaping, still wondering what she was up to, her behavior so out of character that he'd have thought her a different woman if he didn't know better. She hardly ever said that many words to him all at once, and never had she graced him with a compliment, or a smile that was anything less than a sneer. Then, too, there was a quality about her he'd not seen before, a sort of lightness of being that suggested a transmutation of spirit, almost as if someone had opened the curtains on her soul and let in the light of day. But most disconcerting to him was that she also seemed nervous, as if it were all contrived or perhaps she was hiding something from him.

"Rhiannon, what's this all about?" he finally managed to ask, fearing enlightenment almost more than the dark unknown. "I mean, what's goin' on here?"

But with that she slammed her fist to the table and whirled about, fixing him with her familiar glare. "Why does somethin' have to be goin' on, just because I want you to get off your lazy arse and help put some food on the table? Or is that askin' too much of your highness?"

Then she turned back to the table, leaving Dónal strangely relieved. She hadn't changed after all; she was still the sorceress who'd cast her dark spell on him, the spell he never wanted to be broken. Yet in the next moment, she sighed and turned back to him, gazing at him thoughtfully, as if trying to decide what to say, or perhaps how much to say.

"Look, Mick, there's nothin' goin' on. I'm not tryin' to trick you or anything. It's just that I don't make enough money to support the both of us, so if you want to stay with me, you're goin' to have to earn your keep. And you do want to stay with me, don't you?"

"Yes, I do," he replied, though suddenly not so sure. There was genuine uncertainty in her question, which surprised him and made him wonder if her dark persona was not just a front after all, a mask behind which to hide her vulnerability from an exploitative world.

"Good!" she said, her nervous smile betraying her relief. "I like having you here. You're not like the others. There's more to you than just a hard prick and an empty head."

With that, she turned away from him again, and he let her, being more puzzled than ever, sure that she had some trick hidden up her sleeve. Or maybe this was just another of her games, he thought hopefully, an elaborate lead-in to her telling him what a bad girl she'd been so that he'd bend her over the bed and spank her arse till it was the color of fuchsia, before taking her in the Greek position. She did so like it that way, demanding that he do it harder, *harder*, her own hands busy between her legs, the pain of it only intensifying her pleasure. Just thinking about it excited him and he longed to initiate the game, though that being strictly against the rules, he knew he'd have to wait. Yet even after supper she kept him waiting, instead setting about the task of cleaning the cottage, straightening and dusting and sweeping, with his help rearranging the furniture to make the place "more cozy." And when finally it was done, she stood by the bed and, with her back to him, took off her clothes, folding them over the chair before crawling under the covers.

"Come to bed with me, Mick," she said, holding the covers up for him to slide in beside her. Once he was there, she locked him in a desperate embrace, her arms wrapped around him and her legs entwined with his. "Hold me close, Mick. Hold me like you want to pull me inside you, to make us one person."

He did, of course, just as he'd done everything else she'd ever told him to do, though he felt little enthusiasm for it, being impatient for her to get on with it. But even when she finally let him progress to sex, she wanted it simple and clean, with him on top still holding her close, going slow so she could feel him, all of him, climaxing only once and urging him to come with her, which he did even though he wanted to prolong it. Afterward, he lay on his back with her draped languidly across him, her face snuggled into the crook of his neck, her fingers gently playing through his hair. Then she gave him the shock of his life.

"Do you love me, Mick?" she asked, her voice barely a whisper, though it fairly shouted with fear of rejection.

"Yes, I do," he replied automatically, his eyes suddenly wide and staring. It was a lie, of course, bald-faced and blatant, as love had nothing to do with what he felt for her. He needed her, of course, was addicted to her, and he wanted her, lusted after her, would've done anything for her. But he didn't *love* her, and never would. But surely she knew that. Surely, she would laugh derisively and tell him not to be so gullible, that it was all just a farce and as usual he'd been the fool. That he would've been happy to hear.

But instead, she sighed and kissed him lightly on the cheek. "I love you, too," she murmured, and in that moment he knew she meant it, or at least she *believed* she meant it, that this wasn't just one of her games and that things had really changed, though why, he couldn't begin to fathom. And even after pondering it most of the night, his only conclusion was that she'd finally found a man she wanted to keep and was afraid of burning him out like all the others. Not that he was really convinced, but it was the only thing that made any sense.

In the morning, he was dazed and tired, and not at all happy about being rousted from bed without their usual morning romp. Nor was he happy to be going to work at the Royal, for though he didn't mind doing his bit, he had no desire to be a hotel clerk, especially in this place where everyone knew what they were up to. His apprehension was well-founded, too, his coworkers treating him like a boil on their collective arse, speaking to him only when necessary and making snide remarks behind his back, though within his hearing. Nor was he able to sneak off with her for their usual midday tryst, as he had to keep an eye on the desk while at the same time serving as maitre d' in the dining room. Then Mrs. Hibbert brought him the accounts to go over, and they were such a mess that it took him most of the afternoon to make sense of them. He'd have just done them any which way if he hadn't thought she might notice and report it to Rhiannon, since he was still afraid to alienate her despite his misgivings about the direction their life together was taking.

So by the time his work day ended, Dónal was dazed indeed, feeling like he'd bashed his head against a wall, and trudging to the cottage through wind and rain did nothing to improve his mood. At the door he stopped and said a silent prayer for everything to be back to normal, for her to be waiting for him naked, sprawled on the bed and already at work on herself. But he was disappointed, finding her not only dressed but working at their supper, the table set and candles lit, a scene of such domesticity that it sent a shiver down his back.

"Hello, there," she said, coming to embrace him and buss his cheek. "How was your day? I hope Mrs. Hibbert wasn't too hard on you. But come and sit down. Supper is almost ready and there's tea in the kettle." And there was more in that vein, over supper and by the fire, the small talk of husbands and wives at the end of a workday, common and commonplace, until she ran out of questions to ask him.

"Are you all right, Mick?" she asked when the silence became heavy. "You seem so distant."

"I'm tired, Rhiannon," he replied, his eyes narrow and hard, "and I'm tired of this game. I want to go to bed, and I want you to come with me. I want us to rip each other's clothes off. I want to ravish you, to make you squirm, to make you scream. I want to *fuck* you, and I want us to do it like we just thought it up, like we've always done it before."

There, he thought. It was out and if she wanted to rail at him for breaking the rule against initiating, then so be it. At least things would be back to normal. But when Rhiannon lowered her eyes and blushed, Dónal shook his head in disbelief, wondering if she could really be the same woman he'd spent all this time with, the same woman who'd invited him to fuck her in front of a pub full of people, who'd had sex with God only knew how many men, who'd forgotten more about carnality than he would ever know. How could this be happening, he wondered?

"I'm tired of playin' games, too, Mick," she said, her eyes still down, her voice barely more than a whisper. "I'm tired of bein' the town pariah, the town witch, the town whore. I want you to take me away from here. I don't care where, France, America, China, anywhere, it doesn't matter. I just want to go away with you to someplace where we have no past, where we can live like normal people. And I want to marry you, Mick. I want to have your children. I'll make a good wife to you, and I'll be a good mother. You don't need to worry about that."

She'd finally looked up at him then and smiled, some of the fire coming back into her eyes. "And yes, we'll still have sex like we just invented it. We'll still do all those things that we both so love, those things that we can't get enough of. The only difference will be that the whole town won't be privy to what we're up to. So what do you say, Mick? Are you up to the challenge of taming me?"

"But don't you see, Rhiannon, that I don't want you tamed? Why would I want water when I could have whiskey instead?"

"I . . . I'm sorry, Mick. I–"

"My name is *Dónal,* Dónal O'Sullivan Béara. No one ever called me Mick till I came to Holyhead."

"I'm sorry . . . Dónal, I didn't know."

"No, you didn't, did you? And sure, Rhiannon, if that isn't just my point. You don't know the first thing about me, not my name or where I'm from, or anything of my past, my family, my country. You don't know anything of my dreams. And I know even less about you. All we know of each other is what we've learned in this cottage from fornicatin' mornin', noon and night, and do you think there's really been much in that to suggest we'd be good for each other, or good parents? So how can you say you want to marry me and have my children when you don't even know me?"

"Maybe it's just that I know a good man when I see one," she replied, sounding braver than she looked.

"Really? Then you have better eyes than I do!"

"I see. All right, then. If you want to leave, go ahead. We . . . That is, I will be all right without you. And maybe you're right, anyway. Maybe I'm just a fool for thinkin' I could be anything other than I am. But I'm so tired of it. It's like a cancer eatin' at me from the inside. I wish I could just cut it out and have done with it!"

"I didn't say I wanted to leave you, Rhiannon. I didn't even say that I wouldn't marry you. I'm just sayin' that we don't know each other, and what we do know is no kind of a base to build on. So just slow down and take it one step at a time. All right so?"

Seeing that he wasn't going to leave her after all, she smiled at him slyly then. "Are you going to spank me now, daddy? I've been such a bad little girl, you know."

They played their little game then, going at each other for what seemed like hours. Yet afterward, as Dónal lay on his back with her snuggled against him, he knew it wasn't the same, that something was missing. She wasn't in control anymore, not really, and without that, the whole thing seemed so contrived, so tame, as if they were putting on a show they'd rehearsed a thousand times. And while it left him physically exhausted, he was far from satisfied, and knew that no amount of sex with her would ever satisfy him again. Then, when he finally fell asleep, he dreamed that he was at Dunboy, seeing himself asleep in the old window well and his father trying to prod him awake. *Wake up, Dónal!* his father said. *It's time to go!*

Wake up, it's time to go! The words were still ringing in his ears in the morning, and he knew that it was indeed time for him to wake up and go. He'd been a fool for letting himself get sidetracked like this, for setting aside his pride and everything he ever cared about to answer her Siren's call. What would people think of him if they knew? Indeed, what would his father think?

But as much as he'd wanted to leave that very minute, he knew better, that he had no money and no way of getting any, except through his job at the Royal. He could ask Griffith for help, of course, but that would mean swallowing his pride and admitting he was wrong, which he wasn't prepared to do. But then he remembered the cash in the till, and that, being responsible for the books, he could just help himself to some of it and no one would be the wiser till it was too late. He would have to plan it carefully, of course, so the timing would be just right, and he'd have to be patient and wait for the right opportunity. But then, he wasn't desperate, after all. He had food and shelter and a woman to warm his bed, so there was no need to take any risks.

Yet with each day that passed without an opportunity presenting itself, Dónal grew more anxious to leave, playing out the farce with Rhiannon proving harder than he'd thought. For after their talk, she was obsessed with getting to know him, keeping him by the fire for hours in the evening, asking him questions, telling him about herself, till he was sure the tedium would drive him insane. Even their sex was tame and mundane, for all her assurances to the contrary, just a drink of plain water to a man craving the water of life. It was all so boring, so *normal,* and for the first time he felt truly trapped, stifled, as though deep under water and struggling toward the surface, only to be dragged down by an anchor chained to his leg. He didn't want that sort of life with her; indeed, he didn't want it with any woman now, not even Sióna.

So now as he watched her harrying the porter, he longed to tell the poor man the truth of her, that she was all just bluff and blather, just a big commotion significant of nothing. "Just tell her to bugger off with herself," he longed to say, though he didn't, reminding himself that he still needed her.

But then his thoughts were interrupted by the man standing next to him, the one who'd come in with Griffith just a few moments before and whose bags the poor porter was trying to manage over Rhiannon's invective. "Who is that ball of fire?" he asked in awe, as she disappeared around the corner.

Turning to him, Dónal could tell that it wasn't only her imperious behavior that had impressed him, that he hadn't failed to notice her dark beauty as well. And in spite of himself, he couldn't help but feel a stab of jealousy, sensing that the man knew his way around women, as well as a great many other things.

Griffith had introduced him as James Dunwoody Bulloch, a client of the American firm of Fraser, Trenholm and Company, for whom Griffith served as agent in Holyhead. He was an American himself, fortyish, handsome and well-dressed, a bit taller than Griffith though a bit shorter than Dónal, trim and somewhat slight of build. His piercing blue eyes, bald topknot and heavy facial hair were at first glance reminiscent of James Stephens, though he lacked Stephens's fanatical intensity. Rather, there was an air of quiet competence about him, a certain indefinable quality that was yet palpable. It showed in his intelligent gaze, firm handshake and confident manner, and while Egan Butler might have the look of a man who'd faced life on its own terms and won, James Dunwoody Bulloch knew better than to underestimate his adversary. Adding up the sum of his parts, Dónal reckoned him to be a man that men would follow, a latter-day O'Neill, the kind of man he'd thought himself to be, once.

"Her name is Rhiannon, James," Griffith replied softly, "and she is Mr. O'Sullivan's. . . *paramour*, for lack of a better word."

"Is she indeed?" Bulloch said, turning to Dónal with a wry smile. "Then, sir, you have my envy, as well as my empathy."

"Sure, it could be worse," Dónal said nonchalantly, though inwardly he was having trouble imagining it.

"It could indeed," Bulloch agreed smartly. "She could be your wife."

"God help him!" Griffith exclaimed with a shudder, which made his friend laugh.

Knowing what a close thing it had been, Dónal couldn't help but join him, seeing the dark humor in Bulloch's observation, appreciating the acuity of his insight. And as they shared their laughter with each other, Dónal felt a connection between them, and knew that they could be friends, given the opportunity.

"And you have my congratulations, Mr. Bulloch," he said with a mock bow, "for your ability to walk the razor's edge between humor and insult."

"That's *Captain* Bulloch, if you don't mind, sir. Once a seaman is honored with command, he finds it difficult to give up the title."

"*Captain* Bulloch, then. I thought you might be a sailor."

"Oh? And what made you think so?"

"Because you stand with your feet apart and your knees bent like you expect the floor to roll beneath you, like you're on the deck of a ship."

"You have sharp eyes, Mr. O'Sullivan," Bulloch acknowledged, narrowing his own appraisingly. "I like a man who has his eyes open and his wits about him. Are you yourself a man of the sea?"

"No, sir, I've only been to sea twice, though I've lived within sight of her my entire life. But my cousin is a sailor, the master of his own ships, and my ancestors made their fortune from the sea, though it was from fees levied on fishin' rights and harborage rather than sailin' it themselves. But that was when Ireland was still Irish, before the English took Her from us and destroyed our lordship. Since then, we've been people of the land, firmly anchored to the soil and sundered from the sea that surrounds us."

"Ah, but it's never too late to answer her call, you know. Perhaps someday you'll sail the ocean blue and come to understand the sailor's love for her."

"Perhaps. And perhaps someday you'll visit Erin's Green Isle and come to understand our attachment to Her."

"Perhaps, though if she is more beautiful than my own native Georgia, I find it hard to imagine."

"Here, now!" Griffith interjected. "I don't know why you two are gushin' so over Ireland and Georgia when you're surrounded by the beauty of God's own Wales. But if you're quite finished, perhaps Captain Bulloch would like to freshen up before supper?"

Agreeing that a short respite would do him no harm, Bulloch took his leave of Griffith and Dónal showed him up to his room. Finding everything satisfactory, Bulloch thanked him and even tipped him a shilling. But when Dónal returned to the lobby, he was surprised to find Griffith waiting.

"I need to have a word with you, Mick," he said, and led him into the empty dining room.

Bulloch would be joined later by two men, Griffith explained, another American named Edward Anderson and a German named Henry Holland. They were expecting the imminent arrival of a steamer from Greenock in Scotland, and would be departing as soon as she called in. She was called the *Fingal* and carried a cargo of munitions for the Army of the Confederate States of America, which they intended to run through the naval blockade the United States had thrown around their rebellious southern brethren. Apparently, the Confederates didn't have many factories of their own, and so had to buy much of their war materials in Europe. Bulloch and his companions were all Confederate agents and preferred to keep their presence in town quiet so as to avoid attracting the attention of the United States authorities in Liverpool, who would try to have the *Fingal* impounded if they got wind of her. They would probably succeed, too, he added, since the Queen had declared Britain neutral in the conflict and forbidden her subjects to assist in breaking the blockade. But, of course, if that happened, he wouldn't get his share of the commission, and might even lose his contract with Fraser, Trenholm and Company, which could prove to be lucrative if the war lasted very long.

"Sure, Rhys, what can I do to help?" Dónal asked, anticipating Griffith's request.

"You can keep an eye out for any suspicious-lookin' characters and let Twm or me know if you see any," Griffith replied, referring to his clerk. "Also, you can give Twm a hand with the baggage when the time comes. He'll watch for the ship's arrival and keep his boat ready to ferry them out if the need arises. Other than that, you can make sure they're all comfortable and have everything they need. Since I get a commission on everything that goes through Holyhead, I want them to think of us fondly and come back often."

"And who knows, Mick," he said, as he laid a friendly hand on Dónal's shoulder. "If this goes well, I might even need a partner. Surely you'll be lookin' for somethin' better than this hotel if you mean to stay here, which it appears you do."

"Sure, Rhys, 'twould be grand so," Dónal said, though he had other thoughts entirely. "Just leave it to me and I'll take good care of them. And if I see any knackers lurkin' about, you'll be the first to know."

"That's grand, Mick, and thanks a lot," Griffith said happily, then took his leave.

As he stood in the doorway watching him, Dónal knew that in asking for this favor, Griffith had just given him his ticket out of Holyhead, since now he wouldn't have to feel embarrassed about asking him for the fare. 'One good turn deserves another,' he thought, and closed the door.

⟨҉⟩

Dónal was awakened suddenly by an insistent rapping at the door, and for a moment, he didn't know where he was, as it was still pitch dark outside.

"Who's there?" he called, waking Rhiannon.

"It's Twm Jones, Mr. O'Sullivan. The ship has come in and we need to collect the others from the Royal."

"Just a minute, Twm," Dónal replied, disentangling himself from

Rhiannon and fumbling in the dark for his clothes.

"What does he want?" Rhiannon asked irritably. "Doesn't he know it's the middle of the night?"

"It's nothin', Rhiannon. I just need to help him collect some guests and load their baggage. You go back to sleep. I won't be long."

At the door he found Jones and another man whom he didn't know, both dressed from head to foot in foul weather gear, the stranger carrying a ship's lantern. They were dripping wet from the rain, which had come on a gale on Friday evening, though the wind seemed to be dying.

"Hello, Tŵm," Dónal said. "So the ship has come, then?"

"Yes, Mr. O'Sullivan," Jones affirmed. "She's in the harbor. Mr. Low here came in on her. We need to collect Captain Bulloch and his friends, but the door is locked and we can't get anyone to answer. Do you have a key?"

"No, but Rhiannon does. Just give me a moment to fetch it."

"Please hurry," Low said urgently. "We've had a most unfortunate accident in the harbor. We hit another ship on the way in and sank her. I need to collect Captain Bulloch at once if we are to get away without serious delay."

By his accent, Dónal knew him to be English, and was immediately suspicious. "Is it true, Tŵm?" he asked, taking a close look at Low in the lantern light. "Are you sure it's the right ship and that he came from her?"

"Yes, Mr. O'Sullivan, I am. I was watchin' the harbor all night, just as Rhys told me, and when I heard the crash, I rowed out to have a look. It is the *Fingal*, and I brought Mr. Low directly from her."

"All right, then. Just give me a moment."

"Please hurry," Low implored. "There is no time to lose."

Once Dónal had the key, he quickly led them through the back door and up the stairs to Bulloch's room. He knocked on the door, but didn't wait for a response. Bulloch was sitting upright in the bed when they entered and blinked in the lantern light, obviously disoriented, his eyes going suddenly wide at the sight of Jones and Low in their outlandish dress, as if they were something from a nightmare.

"Captain Bulloch, it's John Low," the man said. "I've come with the *Fingal*. But sir, we had an accident on the way in and a ship has been sunk!"

"What?" Bulloch demanded, his eyes going even wider. "The *Fingal* has been sunk?"

"No, Captain, the *Fingal* is fine," Low said. "She wasn't damaged in the crash. But we struck another ship on the way in and sank her."

"Oh, thank goodness!" Bulloch exclaimed. "For a moment there I thought all was lost. But a ship has been sunk, you say? Perhaps you'd better start at the beginning, Mr. Low."

"Aye, Captain," Low agreed, giving his report even as Bulloch stripped off his night shirt and dressed himself. "As soon as the gale broke last night, we ran for Holyhead at top speed and reached the entrance to the channel about an hour ago. Of course, we entered the harbor at dead slow and with all due caution, but just as we rounded the end of the breakwater we came upon a ship at anchor, and as she had no light up and it being pitch dark, we rammed her at the starboard quarter and sent her to the bottom before a boat could be lowered. Luckily, her crew had their wits about them, and by God's grace, they're all safe. According to her captain, she's an Austrian brig called the *Siccardi* carrying a full load of coal, which is why she went down so fast."

"But the *Fingal* sustained no damage?" Bulloch asked.

"None, sir."

"And the crew?"

"Is all fit and ready to go."

"Good, good. And what is the situation in the harbor?"

"That, Captain, is a bit more dicey, I'm afraid. The crash stirred up quite a commotion, as you might imagine, and the harbor master has been summoned to investigate. As he was already at the dock when Jones and I came in, he'll be aboard the *Fingal* shortly. So if the situation isn't dealt with speedily, Captain, I'm afraid our departure might be seriously delayed."

"Right you are, Mr. Low!" Bulloch said, slipping on his jacket and turning to Dónal. "While we awaken the others, Mr. O'Sullivan, would you please be so kind as to awaken the landlady and ask her to prepare our bill. Also, if you would please round up a cabby to convey us to the harbor, I would much appreciate it."

"Certainly, Captain," Dónal replied, "though, if you don't mind, I'll get the cabby first, then write up the bill myself."

"As you think best, Mr. O'Sullivan."

Dónal hurried downstairs and into the street. Luckily the cabs were already queuing up at the station in anticipation of the morning train, so he didn't have to go far. When he returned, Bulloch was already at the door with his small trunk and Jones was bringing down Anderson's, the man himself following behind. In contrast to them, Holland had brought a huge pile of luggage, most of which he'd left in a corner of the lobby and, while Dónal prepared the bill, Bulloch, Anderson and Jones loaded it.

"What does he have in here, anyway?" Bulloch grunted, as he hefted a large trunk.

"No more items than you or I have in our one bag, rest assured," Anderson replied. "It just takes more tweed to cover the Big Medicine."

The two of them laughed at that, and Dónal joined in, the fat German having made his life hell since the moment he'd checked in. There'd even been an incident a couple of days before when another guest mistakenly took a piece of his luggage, and Holland made such a fuss that Dónal had to cable Kingstown to have it returned by the next ferry. Nor was Holland the least bit appreciative, demanding that Mrs. Hibbert fire him for his laxity with other people's property. It was then that Rhiannon had stepped in, telling Holland in no uncertain terms what she thought of him, leaving him so flabbergasted that he could only sputter, *Mein Gott! Sie ist unmöglich!* Dónal had no idea what he'd said, of course, though whatever it was, Holland didn't know the half of it. But Anderson just shook his head, saying, "You'd better wear your spurs next time you wrestle with a bull, Big Medicine!"

Even as Dónal totaled up the bill, he heard Holland's wheezing breath and the stairs creaking under his weight. "I'm comink, I'm comink!" he was saying to Low, who was doing his best to hurry him along. "Chust giff me a moment, if you please!"

"Good, we're all here," Bulloch said, passing Holland in the foyer on his way to pay the bill.

"Do you want me to come along?" Dónal asked.

"Yes, if you please," Bulloch replied. "We could use your help with the baggage and with the good doctor. And here, this is for you," he said, passing Dónal a pound note, "for all your assistance, and for your trouble in getting Dr. Holland's luggage back."

"Thank you, Captain."

"No, thank *you*, Mr. O'Sullivan. Now, sir, let's shove off."

"Aye, Captain," Dónal replied with a grin.

⊙ͲͲͲ☉

The rain had stopped and the light of dawn was in the sky when they raised the oars and slid up to the *Fingal*, her iron hull looming over them like a black wave. She was a beautiful new steamer, Dónal saw, screw-driven and schooner-rigged, her figurehead a bare-breasted mermaid with fish swirling around her flipper, her name, *Fingal*, proudly adorning her prow. Low had sung her praises as they'd approached, telling Bulloch what a pleasure she was to sail, even in the gale that had dogged them all the way from Greenock. She was actually a passenger ship, he'd continued for the benefit of Holland and Anderson, having been built for the Highland trade in Scotland, though her hold was more than sufficient to accommodate their cargo. She'd seen just enough service to be well broken-in, though not so much as to have worn off all the "shiny and new." And he was equally complimentary of the crew, especially the engineer, though he wasn't so sure of the captain, a Lowland Scot whose name just happened to be Anderson, too. No matter, Bulloch had assured him. With himself, Major Anderson and Low all being former navy men, they'd have no problem.

The ladder being already down at the *Fingal's* bow, Bulloch, Anderson and Low hastened up, leaving Jones and Dónal to get Dr. Holland aboard, no mean feat given his girth and weight. Indeed, it took both of them pushing from below and two men pulling from above to get him up, after which his mountain of luggage seemed like mere child's play. Dónal carried the last piece up himself, telling Jones to wait while he said good-bye to Bulloch.

But once aboard, he found Bulloch surrounded by a group of men, engaged in earnest discussion with a rather officious-looking man whom he took to be the harbor master, while the masts of the *Siccardi* rose from the water beyond like bones from a grave. As Dónal approached, Anderson led a uniformed man away from the group for a private conversation. In a moment, the man nodded and moved away, while Anderson returned to Bulloch's side and whispered something in his ear. Bulloch nodded once and gave Anderson a meaningful look before turning back to the harbor master.

"Gentlemen," he said, "rather than have the customs officers row all the way out here, why don't we come in to the pier to give our statements? Our fires are still up and it will take us only a few minutes to dock the ship. That, I think, would be more commodious for all involved, don't you agree?"

"Why, yes," the harbor master agreed, "that would be most kind of you, Captain Bulloch."

"Good. But as a precaution, I suggest you move your boat away from our bow. Our engines are quite powerful, and I would hate to swamp it in our wake."

Hearing that, Dónal didn't wait for the man's reply. He knew Bulloch had no intention of docking the ship and risking impoundment and, in a moment of sudden clarity, he also knew what he would do.

Hurrying back to the ladder, he leaned over and spoke softly to Jones. "Tŵm, I'm not goin' back with you. Captain Bulloch needs another hand, and I'm himself."

Jones didn't seem surprised, didn't show any emotion at all beyond a twitch of his black mustache. "Rhys said you might do somethin' like this."

Knowing he hadn't fooled anyone, Dónal shrugged and grinned

sheepishly. "Sure, if he isn't the one. But tell him I said good-bye and all the best."

"Will do," Jones replied, and pushed off. "Good luck to you."

"And to yourself, Tŵm," Dónal said, before picking up Holland's case and making his way to the steps that led below.

Once there, he was confronted by a bewildering array of doors lining both sides of the dark passage, and didn't know which might lead to sanctuary and which to discovery. And then he almost jumped out of his skin when a sailor spoke behind him.

"Kinna hilp ye, sar?" the man said in a thick Lowland burr. "Air ye lookin' fer yeer wee cobbin?"

"Yes," Dónal replied, hardly able to understand him. "I'm to share a room with Mr. Low. Can you show me where it is?"

"Aye, sar. That un's yeers thar, th' woon jis' fa'rd o' th' steers."

Without thanking him, Dónal hurried through the door and closed it behind him, sighing with relief. He knew he was safe now, that Low would be occupied on deck until the ship was well out to sea, and then there'd be no turning back. He didn't know exactly where he was going or when he would get there, but at least he was on the road again, and he would work it out from there. After throwing Holland's bag on the bunk, he moved to the porthole, though as it was on the port side he couldn't see much at first, just a few ships lying at anchor and the coast of Anglesey in the distance.

But then he felt the ship shudder as the engines kicked into gear and pushed her slowly forward, through the glass-smooth water behind the breakwater, sweeping her in a tight arc until she was steaming toward the harbor entrance and the open sea beyond. Picturing the astonished faces of the harbor officials and the captain of the *Siccardi*, he chuckled to himself, for surely they knew they'd been duped.

But when the breakwater came into view, Dónal's laughter died, for there on its unfinished end stood a lone figure robed in black, her black hair streaming behind her in the wind, her arms raised in beckoning as the ship slid past. And he was sure she saw him, too, saw his face pressed to the glass, locking her eyes onto his, bidding him return and not leave her there alone. *Come back!* he heard her wail, and though he knew the sound was only in his head, her Siren's call gripped his heart, so that he had wild thoughts of jumping overboard and going to her, even though he couldn't swim. But then she was gone from view and the spell was broken, and he knew himself to be well away from her.

"Good-bye, Rhiannon," he murmured. "Good-bye."

⟨∞⟩

"Why, Mr. O'Sullivan!" John Low demanded. "What are you doing here?"

At the sound of his voice, Dónal sprang upright in the bunk, blinking in the dim light of the cabin. He remembered having lain down, made drowsy by the hypnotic rise and fall of Manannán's white chargers, though he'd only meant to rest his eyes. How long he'd been lying there, he had no idea.

"Hello, Mr. Low," he said, smiling casually. "Were you not aware that I'd be joinin' you?"

"Why, no, I wasn't."

"Sure, I am so. But tell me, where are we? Are we in the Broad Atlantic yet?"

"Almost," Low replied, still eyeing him suspiciously. "We're nearing the end of St. George's Channel and will be in the Celtic Sea within the hour. We've poured on the steam, as Captain Bulloch and Major Anderson are worried that we may yet be pursued."

"I suppose I'd better report to the Captain then. He said to join him once we were out of the channel. Can you take me to him, please?"

Low led the way then, up the stairs and into bright sunlight, the broken storm leaving clear skies and a soft breeze in its wake. Bulloch was outside the wheelhouse talking with Anderson and, seeing them approach, turned to greet them.

"Well, Mr. Low," he said jovially. "I see you've found our stowaway."

"Stowaway, Captain?" Low exclaimed. "But I thought . . . that is, he told me–"

494

"Yes, he's a stowaway, Mr. Low," Bulloch said, turning to Dónal. "I wondered how long you'd stay hidden."

"So you knew I was here, did you, Captain?" Dónal said. "Somehow, that doesn't surprise me."

"Well, it didn't take much to deduce the fact when I saw your Welsh friend leaving without you. But with everything else we had to worry about, one young Irishman more or less didn't seem much of an issue at the time. But so, Mr. O'Sullivan, now that we've found you, the question is, what are we to do with you? Stowing away is a serious crime, you know, and has serious consequences. Or are you something more than you appear, a Yankee spy, perhaps, or even a saboteur?"

"Sure, Captain, I've no idea what a 'Yankee' is, but I assure you I'm neither of the other two. I mean you no harm, nor your ship or its cargo. I just want to go to America, to find my brother in New York, whom I've not seen in many years. I'll be happy to work for my passage, at any task you care to assign me."

"You'll be happy if we don't use you for shark bait, you smart-assed little Mick!" Major Anderson interjected. "I hate to disabuse you of your notion, but the *Fingal* is a cargo ship bound for Bermuda and Nassau, and won't be going anywhere near New York. In fact, it might interest you to know that Captain Bulloch, Mr. Low and myself are citizens of the *Confederate* States of America, which are currently at war with New York and her allies in the North."

"Sure, I'm aware of that, Major Anderson, as well as a few other things that might surprise you. I happen to know, for instance, that this ship is aptly named for the true use to which you mean to put her."

"Indeed, Mr. O'Sullivan," Bulloch said. "And just what might you mean by that cryptic remark?"

"The name *Fingal* means 'fair foreigner' in Irish, Captain," Dónal explained. "It refers to the Vikings who plundered our shores a thousand years ago. And since this ship is *not* an English merchantman bound for Nassau, but a Confederate ship carryin' a military cargo which you intend to run through the blockade, I'd be inclined to call you gentlemen Vikings as well, though of a slightly different sort than those of yore."

"Is that so, Mr. O'Sullivan?" Bulloch said, eyeing Dónal intently. "And tell us, if you would, just how you happened to come by this alleged knowledge."

"Rhys told me," Dónal replied, hoping his candor wouldn't cause the man any trouble. "He asked me to help him watch out for any suspicious-lookin' characters that might be spyin' on you. He only meant to help, Captain Bulloch, and as God is my witness, I've told no one else."

"Oh? And how can we be sure of that?" Anderson demanded. "How do we know you aren't a Pinkerton agent like that man McGuire who tailed me in Liverpool? How do we know you won't blow up the ship once we reach Bermuda, or have the authorities impound us?"

But Dónal ignored him, just held Bulloch's eyes for a measured moment before answering. "Because I'm standin' here lookin' you in the eyes, and I'm tellin' you so, that's how!"

Bulloch held Dónal's eyes for a long moment, too, before nodding, almost as though expecting the answer. "All right, Mr. O'Sullivan. I'll accept that you're not a spy, and are nothing more than you represent yourself to be, a stowaway looking for free passage to America. But that doesn't absolve you of guilt. Stowing away is considered a crime by every seafaring nation on Earth and, more important, from my own point of view, it's against the natural law of the sea. So tell me, if you will, why I shouldn't chain you to your bunk till we reach Savannah, and then hand you over to the authorities."

"Better yet," Anderson interjected, "why not just throw you overboard and be done with it!"

"Because I said I'd work for my passage, and I will!" Dónal replied, still looking at Bulloch. "And as for Major Anderson's suggestion, sure, Captain, the truth of it is that I can't swim."

At that, Bulloch actually smiled and seemed to relax. "Well spoken, Mr. O'Sullivan. As usual, you have your wits about you, and though I don't condone your methods, I do applaud your gumption."

"Well, Edward, what do you think?" he asked, turning to Anderson. "Can this Viking ship of ours use another crewman?"

"Oh, sure, that's just what we need," Anderson replied sourly, "another red-headed Mickie Dago. As if Dixie doesn't have enough already! But as long as he's here, I suppose he might as well earn his keep. Why don't you assign him to the engine room? I'm sure McNair can use another hand."

"Very well, then," Bulloch said. "I'll take you on as a crewman, Mr. O'Sullivan, and your passage to Savannah will be your wages. However, as a strict condition of your employment, and of your continued liberty, you will speak to no one aboard this ship of its true cargo and destination, other than Major Anderson, Mr. Low and myself. Do I make myself clear?"

"Aye, Captain, perfectly so," Dónal replied with a grin.

"Then welcome aboard, Seaman O'Sullivan," Bulloch said, extending his hand.

"Thank you, Captain." Dónal shook Bulloch's hand, and then Low's, Anderson not offering his. "But sir, when you said Savannah, did you mean that that's where we're bound?"

"Yes, indeed!" Bulloch said enthusiastically. "It's my hometown and Major Anderson's, too. Do you know of her then?"

"Sure, in a manner of speakin', I do. A couple of my ancestral relations were killed at the Siege of Savannah while servin' with the French Army, in Dillon's Regiment of the Irish Brigade, to be exact."

"Well, now, that's quite astonishing! Every Savannah schoolboy knows of Colonel Arthur Dillon's regiment, of their valor and the heavy losses they suffered. The battlefield is just on the edge of the city, and it's said that many of those who fell are buried there, though no one knows just where anymore."

"Still, I'd like to go there when we land, just to honor their memory."

"Indeed, I'll take you myself, if time permits. And speaking of time, I'm afraid I've given you all I can spare for the moment. Mr. Low will take you below and get you situated. We'll discuss your assignment later. Until then, you are dismissed, Seaman O'Sullivan."

"Aye, Captain," Dónal replied, then followed Low below.

Dónal found Bulloch at the after railing staring out to sea. "You sent for me, Captain?"

"I thought you might want a last look," he replied, nodding toward the horizon. "You may not see Her again for a while."

Dónal followed his eyes to the northeast, not needing to ask what he meant. They watched in silence until Ireland slipped beneath the horizon, and then Bulloch sighed.

"Is this your first time away from home?" he asked.

"Aye, sir, 'tis," Dónal replied, not bothering to explain that he'd actually been gone since June, that Ireland was his home and not the United Kingdom.

"I remember my first time. I was fifteen and had fulfilled my life's ambition by joining the navy. We lived near the sea and I'd had the smell of saltwater in my nostrils and the wailing of gulls in my ears since before I was born. My mother was dead and my father remarried, and about to move his new wife and family to north Georgia, three hundred miles inland. That being too far from the sea for me, I told him I wouldn't go, that I meant to join the navy and be my own man. I can still remember the look in his eyes, like I'd stuck a knife in his heart. But he didn't try to talk me out of it, just said, 'James, you're my firstborn, my eldest son, the only living memory I have of your dear departed mother. It may be the death of me to let you go, but I can see that your time has come and that you're following the call of your heart. So go with grace and my blessing upon you.' I saw him only a handful of times after that, and he died a few years later. But I thought of his words as I sailed away, standing on the deck watching the land fall away behind me. I thought of everything I was leaving behind, my father, my home, my family, the landsman's settled life. Yet the call of the sea was stronger than any of it, and I've never once regretted it. Now I've joined the cause of the Confederacy, because Georgia is my native land and my allegiance lies with her. But the sea is my home, Mr. O'Sullivan, and my heart lies with her."

Bulloch sighed and turned from the railing. "I'll leave you to it, now. Come and find me when you're finished."

But Dónal didn't answer, his heart being in his throat at Bulloch's words, thinking of everything he'd left behind, wondering if he'd live to regret it. He tried to remember the prayer he said when leaving Dublin, but it wouldn't come to him now, being part of what he'd left behind.

"Keep a light in the window for me," he said finally in Irish, then turned away.

chapter 26

On the Broad Atlantic

FOR AS FAR AS THE EYE COULD SEE there was only sky and water, a
universe empty but for one tiny ship, the endless waves quickly
devouring her foamy arrowhead of a wake as though to erase any mark
of her passing. Dónal had often imagined it as a child, sitting in the
crow's nest as he was now, feeling the power of the sea in the surge of
the ship beneath him, the only sound the wind of her speed. And what
a grand thing that his daydream had become reality without disap-
pointing him, as it had on that terrible day when he'd sailed from
Dublin. But that was another day in another lifetime, and for once in
his life he found himself able to shut it all out and just enjoy the present, to bask in the shimmering peace that surrounded him, the gold-
en light that hovered between sky and water, Heaven and Earth. He
closed his eyes and smiled, feeling the sun on his face and the wind in
his hair, the ephemeral veil that separated this world from the next
sliding gently over him. Only his pipes would've made it better.

"I see you're not going to be sick after all," the man next to him said,
an English crewman named George Freemantle whom Bulloch had
assigned to orient him to the ship.

But Dónal didn't answer, just threw his head back and gave voice to
his ecstasy with the ancient battlecry of his race, shrieking at the top
of his lungs like a boiled potato was being shoved up his arse.

"Good God!" Freemantle exclaimed, startled. "You bloody Irish never do anything halfway, do you?"

Dónal smiled at the man, a bit indulgently, almost as if he pitied him. "You probably won't understand this, George, but we feel that anything worth doin' is worth *over*doin'!"

"You're right. I don't understand. In fact, I'll *never* understand you Irish, not if I live to be a thousand!"

And to that, Dónal said nothing; the man was right and there was just nothing to say.

⚬ᴍᴍᴏ

Dónal fought his way along the narrow corridor toward the stairs, alternately slamming into one wall and then the other as the ship rolled violently beneath him. Bulloch had sent him down to the engine room to assess the situation there, and to ask the engineer if he could increase the speed. What he found was a hellhole of scattered coal and tools, of sweat-soaked firemen cursing and knocking into each other, each shovelful requiring a Herculean effort to move from bin to furnace. Freemantle had told him that the engine room was the worst place to be during a storm, and now that he could see why, he was glad Bulloch hadn't assigned him there. But in the midst of all that chaos, he found the engineer, James McNair, as calm and impassive as ever, thoughtfully smoking his pipe while his men struggled around him, directing their labors with his characteristic economy of speech. And in response to the question of speed, he simply nodded, showing his unequivocal certainty in his blue Highlander eyes.

Now Dónal was anxious to get back to the wheelhouse with his report, knowing Bulloch would be happy to hear it. They were only four days into their journey and already well behind schedule, the ship making only about nine knots even in fair weather, well below the thirteen they'd expected of her given that she was new and equipped with all the latest advances the shipbuilders of the Clyde had to offer. But then she was too heavily laden with cargo to reach her full potential, her outfitters having been overly zealous in their efforts to compensate for

501

the Confederacy's dearth of manufacturing. So it was that Bulloch's brow had darkened when the wind freshened to a gale, knowing he'd have to furl the sails and cut back the throttle, slowing their progress even further.

As for himself, Dónal's stomach had twisted into a knot of fear when the skies darkened and the seas rose, recalling his crossing to Liverpool and not wishing to repeat that horrible experience. But he wasn't sailing with James Dunwoody Bulloch then, wasn't standing at his side as he calmly surveyed the sea, directing the helmsman in a smooth even voice or laying his own steady hands to the wheel when things got especially rough, his face as serene as if he were out for a Sunday row. And seeing the fear in his young novice's eyes, he even took a moment to lay a fatherly hand on his shoulder and give him a few reassuring words.

"This is about as bad as it gets, Mr. O'Sullivan," he said, his eyes steady and sure. "Everything else pales in comparison. If you survive this – and you have my word that you will – for as long as you live, you'll never be daunted by anything again. So buck up and enjoy the worst experience of your life. You'll be a better man for it!"

Dónal's fear melted away then, like snow under a desert sun, knowing the sea wouldn't dare kill him with James Dunwoody Bulloch's word to the contrary. He even began to appreciate the ocean in her fury, though realizing it would be foolish to become too enamored of it. For inasmuch as she was beautiful, she was yet a cold-blooded killer, a ravening beast that would swallow their little ship whole if given the chance, deaf in her hunger to the screams of her victims.

What would that be like, he wondered, to be entombed in the cold darkness of the depths, disappearing so quickly and completely that no one would ever know what had become of him? He looked over at Bulloch then, standing at the wheel with his feet spread and knees bent just as the first time he'd seen him, and wondered if such thoughts ever crossed his mind. Surely so, he thought, for only a fool would be impervious to them, and Bulloch was certainly no fool. Yet it didn't seem to frighten him or deter him from his calling, though surely it must make him face his mortality, and appreciate it.

As though feeling his eyes on him, Bulloch glanced at Dónal and smiled. "Are you all right, Mr. O'Sullivan?"

"Couldn't be better, Captain!"

"Bully, Mr. O'Sullivan!" Bulloch exclaimed, clenching his fist in approval. "Bully!"

Dónal smiled then, both outwardly and in, knowing in his heart that his initial assessment of Bulloch was correct. He did indeed know his way around a great many things, not least of which was the bewildering maze of a man's psyche. It was a talent that stood him in good stead with the crews he commanded, enabling him to make each man feel that he was indispensable, that his individual efforts were vital to the success of the ship and that they were appreciated.

On the second day out from Holyhead, Dónal had accompanied him as he went about the business of getting to know the crew, touring the ship from stem to stern, introducing himself individually to each man on board, cataloguing their names and bits of personal information, smiling and patting them on the back, saying things like, "Keep up the good work, sailor. I'm counting on you." Of course, Dónal knew he had an ulterior motive in it as well, which was to assess their collective ability to run the blockade when the time came and their potential enthusiasm for it, Dónal and the three conspirators still the only men aboard who knew the true nature of their mission. And from the fact that Bulloch elected to take him as his personal aide rather than assigning him to other work, Dónal knew he himself was being evaluated as well, that the man had seen something in him, even in his debauched and dissolute state, and sensed that he had something special in mind if he measured up.

And Dónal hoped with all his heart to measure up, for he knew himself to be in the company of a rare individual and felt honored to have been so chosen, thinking that if the Confederacy had so many such men that she could waste one on an ocean voyage, then she must be a great and powerful nation indeed. If only Ireland had such men, he lamented, men of talent and ability, of wisdom and foresight, men who could inspire their fellows to find the best within them and devote it to their country, and so instill in them the unity of purpose that was so lacking in all their previous attempts to free themselves. And having met Bulloch, he now knew that James Stephens wasn't the man for the job. For while the Wandering Hawk had worked a miracle in raising a revolutionary organization from the ashes of the Great Hunger and the abortive risings of '48 and '49, he'd brought them no closer to freedom than they'd been in 1856 when he earned his romantic epithet.

But so it was that meeting Bulloch had reawakened Dónal to his purpose, which was to find Eóghan and bring him home before he threw away his life in the American war. *Wake up, it's time to go!* his father had told him in the dream, and if he'd added, *Your ship is waiting!* he could hardly have proved more prophetic. Yet there was still a broad ocean to cross and a blockade to run before tackling all the miles between Savannah and New York, not to mention the militarized border that now separated North from South, the crossing of which subjected one to the risk of being shot as a spy if caught. But at least he was on the way and in good spirits again, or would be if this infernal storm would pass so they could set the sails and open the throttle.

So it was speed that was on his mind as he struggled up the stairs and opened the door, only to find the storm more intense than ever. Indeed, it was as dark as dusk outside, though barely past midday, the wind howling like a host of Celts, making mountains of the waves and pushing the rain at them in horizontal sheets, leaving the deck so awash with water that everything that wasn't secured had already been swept overboard. Not wanting to be among them, he hesitated before making his dash to the wheelhouse, carefully timing the waves sweeping over the gunwales and the pitch and roll of the ship.

But just when he was about to put his head down and sprint for it, he saw a man coming toward him, proceeding slowly from handhold to handhold while skirting the wheelhouse on the starboard side. From his tall stature and the sandy beard protruding from his rain hat, he knew him to be Liam Murphy, one of the three other Irishmen on board besides himself, though what he was doing on deck, he couldn't begin to guess.

Dónal waved at Murphy and when he saw that he had his attention, pointed to the door. "I'll hold it for you!" he yelled, though he may as well have saved his breath for all the man could hear.

Yet from his "thumbs up" gesture, Murphy seemed to have understood and, after timing the waves, set off toward Dónal and the door, going as fast as his cumbersome rain gear and uncertain footing would allow. But when he was barely halfway across, the ship lurched unexpectedly, sending him sprawling to the deck, a wave washing him bodily to starboard before he could scramble to his feet.

"*Murph!*" Dónal screamed, fearing he'd been washed overboard. But then the water receded and there he was, still on deck and clinging desperately to the railing. "Murph!" he shouted through cupped hands, trying to make himself heard above the wind. "Murph, don't try to stand up! Just hang on till I get a rope. Hang on, Murph!"

But whether he didn't hear him or ignored the warning in his fear, Murphy pushed himself to his feet and took a step toward Dónal and safety, only to be flipped backwards over the railing when the ship rolled again.

"NO!" Dónal screamed, watching in horror as Murphy rode up on the crest of a wave, frantically waving his hands and struggling in vain toward the ship. Oblivious to the danger to himself, he staggered to the wheelhouse and flung open the door, screaming, "*Man overboard! Man overboard!*"

But Bulloch was already in motion before he'd even repeated himself. "*All stop! All stop!*" he shouted into the voice tube. "*Man overboard, all stop!*" Then he was at the door with Low and Major Anderson huddling close behind. "Where is he?"

"There!" Dónal replied, pointing to starboard and slightly astern.

"I have him!" Bulloch exclaimed. "Get me a rope from that storage bin!"

But just then, the ship rolled violently and the wave that washed over the deck would've taken Bulloch with it but for Dónal clinging desperately to his jacket.

"James, we can't stay here like this!" Anderson exclaimed. "We've got to get underway again or these waves will capsize us! That man's fifty feet away already and he'll be long gone by the time we lower a boat, and besides, what chance would it have in these waters?"

"Who said anything about a boat?" Bulloch demanded, slipping off his jacket and bending down to remove his boots.

"James, you can't be serious!" Anderson cried in horror.

"I am perfectly so, Edward!" Bulloch replied. "Better that we all go down than to let that man die without lifting a finger!"

"James, you can't!" Anderson insisted, grabbing him by the arm. "Or if you insist on this folly, at least send someone else! You're far too valuable to the cause to lose like this!"

"What good is the cause without honor, Edward?" Bulloch demanded, taking the end of the rope from Dónal and tying it around his waist. "And besides, why should I send someone else when I'm the best swimmer aboard?"

Then before Anderson could say anything else, Bulloch sprinted to the railing and dove into the sea.

"James, *no!*" Anderson shouted, running after him. But it was too late; Bulloch was already on his way.

"Here, give him some slack!" Anderson snapped at Dónal, pulling him astern in concert with Bulloch's swimming. "And make sure you don't lose your grip on that rope!"

"Aye, Major Anderson!" Dónal affirmed. "I'm not an eejit, you know!"

But if Anderson heard, he gave no sign of it. "Who's out there, anyway?" he demanded, shielding his eyes to peer through the rain.

"Liam Murphy," Dónal replied.

"An Irishman?" Anderson exclaimed, turning on Dónal with a look of disbelief. "He's risking his life for a *Mick*? Goddamn it, boy, you'd better hope he comes back, or else you'll be joining him out there!"

"Sure, Major, I'll join him out there, and take you with me!"

"Are you threatening me, boy? Why, I'll have you–"

506

"Oh, shite! That's the end of the rope and he doesn't have him yet!"

"*Shit!*" Anderson agreed, and hurried off to get more, leaving Low to watch helplessly with Dónal as Bulloch waved his arms and pointed ahead.

"Oh, God!" Low moaned, leaning dangerously over the rail. "The longer it takes, the further away Murphy will get. Come on, Edward, hurry up!"

But at hearing those words, Dónal knew what he had to do, and was already tying the end around his waist. "Throw it out to me when you get it!" he said, and without waiting for Low to talk him out of it, vaulted over the railing and into the sea.

'*Oh, God, what have I done?*' his mind shrieked as the darkness enveloped him like a tomb, the cold stopping his heart and burning his skin with a pain so intense that only in ripping it from his body could he hope to find relief. But then his head was clear of the water again, and he gasped and flailed his arms, trying desperately to keep himself afloat while the sea tugged at his heavy clothing, threatening to suck him under for good. And feeling the rope go taut about his waist, he knew Bulloch was pulling at him, too, dragging him away from the *Fingal*, away from his only refuge in all this sea of peril. In a panic, he whirled around, only to find her slipping inexorably away, the gap widening even as he watched, his imminent doom now a certainty in his heart. Yet somehow it didn't seem to matter anymore. The cold was gone and with it the fear, leaving only a vague numbness in his soul, a leadenness in his limbs, a fatigue so encompassing that he longed just to close his eyes and go to sleep. And then the *Fingal* was gone and he felt himself floating, not on water but on air, away from all earthly care.

Vaguely, he heard voices shouting at him, insistent and urgent, "Grab the rope, Dónal, grab the rope!" though whether they were living people or just in his own head, he couldn't tell.

"I can't," he protested (or did he just think it?). "I'm too tired!"

"Come on, Dónal, you can do it!" and now it was just one voice speaking to him in Irish, suddenly clear and strong. "Just reach out your hand and take it!"

"Go away and leave me alone. I just want to sleep!"

"Dónal, grab the rope!" the voice insisted, and suddenly there was a face in the blackness before him, Eóghan's face speaking to him. "Grab the rope and let them save you! Otherwise you'll never get to me!"

"Eóghan! Eóghan, I've been looking for you. I've been trying to get to you!"

But Eóghan wasn't there, only the black sky and the rain pelting his face, the frigid sea and voices shouting for him to grab the rope.

"Grab the rope, grab the rope! It's just there to your right!"

Turning his head, he found a life buoy sliding toward him, and with a Herculean effort swung his arm to snare it. Even so, it almost slipped away before he could hug it to his chest, his hands too numb to grasp it. Then he felt a tug on the rope and himself moving through the water, and suddenly there was the *Fingal*, looming above him. Then he was rising through the air and strong hands were pulling him over the railing and onto the deck, where Edward Anderson cut the rope from him and wrapped him in a blanket.

"I thought you said you couldn't swim!" he demanded, as he and Freemantle picked him up and rushed toward the stairs.

"I can't," Dónal mumbled through chattering teeth.

"Then you're either the bravest man I've ever met, or the stupidest! But either way, I salute your Emerald Isle élan, and I ask your pardon for my harsh words to you."

"Apology accepted. But what about Murph and the Captain? Are they all right?"

"Yes, they're fine. They're on deck now and will join you below. You saved your friend's life, you know. If you hadn't jumped in, he'd be lost by now, and maybe James with him, so I'm sure he'll reward you handsomely."

"No, he won't, not Captain Bulloch!"

"Oh? And what makes you so certain?"

"Because he'd have done it for me, and he knows I know it."

chapter 27

In the Coastal Waters of Georgia
The Confederate States of America
13 November, 1861

IT WAS AN EERIE FEELING, watching the thick fog roll off the coastal marshes and advance on the *Fingal,* the land, the night sky and even the surrounding sea disappearing behind a curtain so thick that even the far end of the ship was obscured. Almost, it evoked the feeling of that night long ago when Dónal had found the potatoes rotten and run desperately into the unknown to search for his errant father among the tumbled stones of Guala. But he'd been alone then, a frightened little boy stalked by the monsters of his imaginings, The Hunger and The Fever and The English lurking just beyond the veil of fog, yet so near he could feel their icy breath in his soul. There'd been no one to comfort him then, no James Dunwoody Bulloch to pat him on the back and tell him to buck up, that the fog was actually good because it shielded them from the monsters that stalked them, the Yankees in their dastardly blockade ships.

So there was no terror in this fog, real though the monsters were, just the mundane annoyance of physical discomfort, the chill that cut to the bone and the dampness that soaked his hair, a sleepless night spent in waiting by a young man anxious to get on with it. Indeed, his long-sought objective lay just off the port railing, America, so close that a decent swimmer could be on the strand in a matter of minutes. He'd caught only a brief glimpse of her before the fog rolled in, her dark primeval forest looming against the star-bright horizon. Yet it thrilled him to the core, knowing he was almost there, that in the heel of the hunt and after all was said and done, he'd succeeded in getting himself across the Big Water. Now if only morning would come so they could push on to Savannah!

As he turned away from the railing, Dónal wiped his brow and pushed his dripping hair back from his face. He knew there was no point in staring into the fog anymore, the fact that he was officer of the deck notwithstanding. No one could find them in this soup even if they were looking, and despite the fact that they'd passed within fifty feet of a Yankee blockader on the way in, he was sure they weren't. She was a sailing ship, after all, becalmed in glassy seas and taken by surprise in the depths of night, and with the wind still at dead calm, he had no doubt that she was still just where they left her. Sure, it would be hours before word would spread of the breach, and by that time they'd be safely moored in Savannah, or so Bulloch had said, anyway.

Still, it was a harrowing experience, slipping up on the blockader, knowing her guns could open up at any time, his heart pounding as the alarm went up and her crew scrambled to battle stations, his relief at passing unscathed palpable and enervating. But then the whole voyage had been like that, a series of adventures beginning with the daring departure from Holyhead and continuing right through to the coast of America. First Murphy had been swept overboard in the gale, and then there was the unscheduled stop in the Azores for fresh water, an otherwise straight-forward transaction convoluted by the local health official mistaking them for an African slaver with disease on board. Later, they'd stopped in Bermuda for coal and been subjected to the intrigue of Yankee agents desperate to detain them in port. But with the help of the officers of the CSS *Nashville*, another Confederate ship, Bulloch and company outwitted them. Then, to avoid pursuit, they'd put to sea in the midst of a gale even more severe than the first, knowing even so that the last and most dangerous obstacle, the blockade, was yet to come.

But first Bulloch had to put the proposition to the crew, having waited for security reasons till the last possible moment, till it was necessary to set the final course for Savannah, at which time they would've known anyway. So when the weather cleared on the third morning out from Bermuda, he'd called them together on deck and told them what he meant to do, explaining the dangers to life and liberty they'd face in coming along, assuring them in no uncertain terms that it was their choice to dare it or not, that if the vote was less than unanimous, he'd make for Nassau first and discharge any who were unwilling.

Standing beside him, Dónal had gazed at the crewmen with vicarious pride, knowing they'd guessed it anyway and had already decided, seeing in their eyes the deep and abiding affection they had for their captain. For indeed, he was just that to them, *their* captain, the best man they'd ever served under, the best man they'd ever known. "I'd follow him to Hell," Murphy had said to general agreement, and Dónal knew it to be an understatement.

And despite his humility, Bulloch had seen it, too, and knew that further talk was superfluous. "Will you go?" he'd asked simply, putting aside the rousing oratory he'd prepared.

By way of answer, Freemantle had thrown a fist in the air and shrieked at the top of his lungs, eyeing Dónal slyly as he did his best imitation of a wild Celt. All the others joined in, of course, even Anderson and Low, all stomping their feet and clapping their hands till the deck was aroar with their clamor. But Bulloch just stood quietly among them, his cheeks red and eyes blinking, deeply and profoundly touched by their display of confidence.

"Thank you," he'd said thickly when their noise subsided. "From the bottom of my heart, I thank you."

"No, Captain, thank *you!*" Murphy had retorted, sending them all to cheering again.

After that, they went about the business of turning the *Fingal* into a fighting ship, bringing up cannon from the hold and bolting them to the deck, making powder bags and arming the crew with Enfield rifles. Since many of the men were veterans of the British Navy, it all went smoothly. It helped, too, that the crew were mostly Scots of one description or another (their Lowland burr being more or less the shipboard *lingua franca*) who viewed the prospect of a good fight as an enticement rather than a deterrent. Even so, the last two days had been tense, with every available man standing lookout while the others rotated through the engine room. As it turned out, McNair had divined Bulloch's true purpose even before they reached Bermuda, and had meticulously sorted through the coal to find the cleanest pieces, which he set aside for the final run. So after cleaning the flues, he was able to coax eleven knots from the twin Thompson engines, upping it to twelve when the sea turned to glass earlier in the evening.

And so they'd made it, and now here they were, anchored in seven fathoms and waiting for the morning breeze to blow the fog out to sea so they could steam into the Savannah River. And for all the trials and tribulations of the voyage, Dónal had arrived on the other side a different man from the one who'd sneaked out of Holyhead. Indeed, the experience had proved a catharsis for him, the light of Bulloch's fatherly handling driving back the Darkness and filling him with a new sense of purpose, of optimism and self-worth. For the first time in longer than he cared to remember, he didn't feel the need for the drink, the need to dull the pain of his existence, to blot out the image of Brendan Collins's dead eyes demanding to know *Why?* Nor were his dreams haunted by visions of the banshee or of bad men chasing him, or even of his father's ungentle prompting. His life was full in the presence of James Dunwoody Bulloch, and it made him happy.

Then, too, he himself had come to enjoy a certain celebrity among the crew, who regarded him as a hero for his selfless act on Murphy's behalf, and even looked to him for leadership. Perhaps that as much as anything had restored his faith in himself, especially when Bulloch made him acting ensign and the men who'd been his peers began addressing him as "Mr. O'Sullivan," and doing so of their own volition. It made him realize he wasn't a failure after all, that he could still go back to Ireland and play a significant role in the struggle to come, perhaps not as a soldier *per se*, but then there were, after all, ways to fight without killing people.

And finally there was the broadening experience of the voyage itself, of being part of a crew and working toward a common goal, of being at sea with men of so many different origins, Bulloch and Anderson from America, Freemantle and Low from England, McNair and other Highlanders, Portuguese Antonio and German Dr. Holland, not to mention all the Lowland Scots with their Celtic hearts and Saxon veneer. Bermuda in particular was an eye-opening experience for him, being the first place he'd ever been that was truly different from Ireland. Standing at the rail as they'd coasted into the harbor, he'd been mesmerized by the tropical paradise unfolding before him, by the clear water filled with colorful fish darting among the reefs, by the town of St. George's with its crisp white buildings alternately dazzling the eye with brightness and baffling it with shadow, by the giant sea turtles, shimmering strands, volcanic bluffs and palm trees rattling in the warm tropical breeze. Then there were the people, a majority of whom were of mixed African and American Indian descent, free since the abolition of slavery in 1834 but still strictly segregated, still relegated to the lower rungs of society, even skilled tradesmen like the pilots who guided them in and out of port. They'd had no shore leave for security reasons, of course, so he'd not had a chance to mingle among them, to determine if they were more or less like Angela or if she was unique. Yet many of the crew had been there before and had wild tales to tell of the place, especially of the bordellos full of exotic girls ready to give a man the ride of his life, and of the local poteen, a liquor distilled from palmetto berries and so potent it would melt the iron off the *Fingal's* hull, yet sweeter-tasting than anything this side of God's own shebeen. He'd come away with the impression of Bermuda as an earthly paradise, a place where everyone would want to live, if only they knew they had a choice.

But Bermuda was in the past now as Dónal moved purposefully around the ship's perimeter, checking on the lookouts. His eyes were firmly in the present and his heart set on the future, on finding Eóghan and taking him back to Ireland. He was a new man and anxious for a second chance to prove himself.

Midway along the starboard side, Dónal paused beside Freemantle and laid a friendly hand on his shoulder. "All quiet so, George?" he murmured, more or less rhetorically.

"Aye, Mr. O'Sullivan," the man whispered back, his eyes not straying from the fog. "Quiet as a tomb, it is."

"Aye, 'tis," Dónal agreed, thinking he couldn't have put it better. Indeed, the night was deathly still, the air cold as a corpse, the men a crew of ghosts floating opaquely about the foggy deck, the dripping of dew from the riggings tapping out a soft death march.

"But stay sharp just the same," he added. "I'd hate for us to have come all this way only to get pinched at the doorstep."

"Aye, sir," Freemantle acknowledged, and Dónal turned to move on.

Yet even as he did, the silence was suddenly broken by the shrill crowing of a cock, piercing the cloak of darkness and skipping across the water like a shot, a beacon to follow for any Yankee within hearing distance. It was one of the fowl they'd picked up in Bermuda, forgotten by his keepers in the tenseness of the moment, his instinct telling him it was dawn even though his eyes couldn't see it.

"Goddamn it!" Dónal hissed violently, whirling so quickly that he almost fell on the slippery deck. "Somebody shut it's gob!"

But Freemantle was already at the coop, pulling the offending bird from its roost and quickly wringing its neck. For a moment, they just stood and stared at each other, holding their breath and straining their ears toward the sea, hoping against hope that they hadn't been discovered. Yet just when they were about to sigh with relief, another cock began his morning serenade, this time from the port side, while yet another joined him from starboard.

"Throw them overboard!" Dónal ordered tersely and, with Freemantle's help, hoisted the heavy coop over the rail, while men on the port side did the same.

As they hit the water, all the birds raised a fearful racket, though only for a moment, the ballast stones that kept them from sliding around the deck quickly drawing them to the bottom, leaving only a few feathers floating forlornly on the surface. It was a desperate way to treat dumb animals, surely, but Dónal gave them not a second thought, as he again strained his ears to listen for approaching enemies. But they were lucky, it seemed, and gradually he relaxed, grinning ruefully at Freemantle and shaking his head. How foolish they'd have felt to have been exposed in such a ridiculous manner.

"Mr. O'Sullivan," Dónal heard Low whisper. "Captain Bulloch wants to see you in his cabin. I'm to relieve you."

"Aye, Mr. Low," Dónal acknowledged, thinking to himself, 'I'm sure he does!' At Bulloch's door, he paused and took a deep breath before knocking. Since the deck was his responsibility, he could only hope that the lack of adverse consequences would ameliorate his oversight.

"Come," Bulloch responded, and Dónal found him sitting at his desk, making an entry in the ship's log. "That was quick thinking, Mr. O'Sullivan, throwing them overboard," he said without looking up. "But then that doesn't surprise me, coming from you."

"Thank you, Captain," Dónal replied, surprised that he wasn't being reprimanded, but even more so that Bulloch already knew what had happened. "But then it shouldn't have happened in the first place. I should've remembered that cocks crow at dawn whether it's light or not."

"No, Mr. O'Sullivan, it shouldn't have. But then that was my fault, wasn't it?"

"Sure, I don't see how, Captain. 'Twas me that was officer of the deck, after all. Anyway, you can't think of everything."

"I'm the captain of this ship, Mr. O'Sullivan," Bulloch replied patiently, still pushing the pen furiously across the page. "It's my *job* to think of everything, and I do mean *everything!*"

"Aye, Captain. If you say so."

"I do indeed!" Bulloch said emphatically, closing the logbook with a snap. "But that's not what I called you⏄" But he didn't finish his sentence, a frown crossing his face at the sight of Dónal with his hair slicked back from his forehead.

"Is there a problem, Captain?"

"That brother of yours in New York. He wouldn't happen to be *Eóghan* O'Sullivan, would he?"

"Why yes, he would," Dónal replied, his pulse quickening. "Do you know him, then?"

"Yes, though only in passing, I'm afraid. As I recall, I met him at a dinner party at my sister's house shortly before the war. We both lived in New York at the time, I with my wife and family and she with her husband, a New Yorker named Theodore Roosevelt. Your brother came in the company of a couple of other Irish-Americans, Richard O'Gorman and Thomas Meagher and their wives, though he himself was unescorted. He's quite handsome as I recall, and when one of the ladies asked why he wasn't married, he replied that for him to pick just one wouldn't be fair to the rest. Well! I thought it the most purely arrogant thing to say, but the ladies seemed to take it in stride, as if it made all the sense in the world! But perhaps that's why I didn't make the connection earlier, because you neither look nor act like him."

"Sure, 'tis true for you that we don't look much alike, but we're more alike inside than you might suppose. But is there anything else you can tell me? It's been over thirteen years since I've seen him, so anything would be news to me."

"No, there's nothing of a personal nature, I'm afraid. He left after dinner, and we didn't exchange more than a few words directly. But the conversation was all about the secession crisis in the South, of course, and I remember that he and his friends weighed in rather heavily with their pro-Southern leanings, though I don't think they followed through on them when the war began."

"No, Eóghan and Meagher joined with the Yankees. Sure, they're both officers in an all-Irish regiment, the 69th New York, 'tis called."

"Ah, are they indeed?" Bulloch sighed, seeming suddenly distracted. "Then that makes my task more difficult, doesn't it?"

"I'm sorry, Captain? I'm afraid I don't follow."

"Well, then let me explain it to you, Mr. O'Sullivan," Bulloch said, standing up to face him. "I called you here to ask if you'd be willing to serve with me a little longer. The Confederacy has need of men like you, men of intelligence and ability, of courage and conviction. Indeed, I have need of a man like you, to assist me in Europe with the procurement and outfitting of more ships like this one. You already know how desperately short of materiel we are, and without more of these 'Viking' ships to run the blockade, the war will be lost before we've even begun to fight. So for that reason, I'm prepared to offer you a commission in our navy with the rank of ensign. You'll serve under me, of course, and be based in Liverpool, though your duties may take you far afield from time to time. While I can't offer you anything special in the way of pay, I can promise that the work will be challenging, rewarding and meaningful. So what do you say, Mr. O'Sullivan? Will you help us in our struggle for freedom?"

But Dónal didn't answer, just stared at Bulloch in disbelief, stunned by his offer and flattered that he would think of him so. All he could think of in that moment was how happy he'd been over the last month, of how fulfilling his life was and how he'd finally become the type of man he thought he would be, and all because Bulloch believed in him. And now his mentor, indeed, his surrogate father, was telling him it could continue, that he could go on being happy and fulfilled, that they could go on together if only he would say yes. *Yes!* Of course he would say yes! How could he not when Bulloch had restored so much to him, his self-respect, his dignity, his desire to live? Yes, of course he would join, and yes, he would help in their struggle for freedom! After all, that was a desire he understood only too well. Sure, and when the American war was over, he could even take his freshly-honed revolutionary skills home to Ireland. Maybe Bulloch would even return the favor and come with him! After all, he was a Gael himself, descended from Allan of Moydart, first chieftain of the Clanranald MacDonalds, through his younger son, Dónal Béalach, the one whose daring assault had freed the Lord of the Isles from imprisonment in Tantallon Castle. With blood like that behind him, God only knew what they could accomplish! But even if it didn't work out like that, it wouldn't be the end of the world. His life was looking up again, and things would be good for him in Liverpool. He'd even be able to see Angela and give back some of what she'd so selflessly given him. And of course he'd introduce her to Bulloch, for surely they would get along famously.

Yet even as he thought of Angela, Dónal's eyes slipped past Bulloch to the framed daguerreotype on his desk, the one he took with him wherever he went. It was a family portrait, taken the last time Bulloch had seen his father, showing them all arrayed on the steps of a Big House, his father's home in Roswell, Georgia. Yet it wasn't the Bullochs that attracted Dónal's eyes, but the row of black slaves ranged behind them, their personal retainers, their *house niggers*, the very thing that Angela herself had been in South Carolina.

No, the two of them wouldn't get along famously, he suddenly realized, for Angela was a Negro and Bulloch a proponent of Negro slavery, fighting a war expressly to preserve it as an institution of government, fighting not for freedom but rather to repress it, to keep a segment of his country's population in bondage simply because of the color of their skin. Indeed, the voyage of the *Fingal* was but a mission in that war and, in so faithfully serving the mission, Dónal realized that he himself had served the cause of repression.

'What have I done?' he thought, the recognition of his culpability striking him like a thunderbolt. 'Oh, God, what have I done?'

It went against everything he'd ever believed in, everything he'd ever held sacred. For he knew that freedom wasn't one thing in Ireland and something else in America; it didn't hinge upon the color of a man's skin or the language he spoke, on whether he happened to be born in one place rather than another, or into a particular family or religion. Freedom was an absolute, something that all people had a right to expect, and a right to fight for when it was denied them. So for him to espouse the cause of Irish freedom from English tyranny while abetting the repression of Negroes in America was nothing short of hypocritical. And if there was one thing Dónal couldn't abide, it was a hypocrite.

His eyes shifted back to Bulloch, who was watching him intently, wondering at the emotions that played across his face. But the man Dónal saw wasn't the same one who'd been there a moment before, the fatherly mentor whom he would gladly have followed to the death, but rather just another hypocrite, a man who spoke loftily of freedom while acting to repress it, a serpent who offered the forbidden fruit with poisoned fangs. And indeed, Dónal couldn't help but feel seduced, betrayed, violated, though he had to admit that it had been there for him to see all along if only he had opened his eyes. For hadn't he known the Confederacy to be a slave-mongering nation, and wasn't he on the bridge in Bermuda when Bulloch had treated the Negro pilots as though they were something less than human, calling them *boys* to their faces and *darkies* to their backs? Yes, but he'd ignored it, being too caught up in his own resurrection to take a critical look at what he was involved in, sweeping it into a dark corner of his mind like a dirty little secret that no one would know, so long as *he* didn't tell. But he couldn't ignore it now, for here it was staring him in the face, demanding that he choose between himself and his fellow man, indeed, between evil and good. For in the balance of justice, he knew the Confederate cause to be just that, *evil*, and if the cause was evil, could the men associated with it be anything less?

"No, Captain Bulloch, I can't serve with you any longer," he said, choosing his words carefully. After all, he wasn't on shore yet, and Bulloch could still change his mind about treating him as a stowaway. "Though your offer is tempting, and I'm flattered that you think of me so, I'm afraid I can't accept it. As you pointed out, to do so would mean fightin' against my brother, which is somethin' I could never do. And anyway, Captain, I'm already a soldier sworn to fight for a cause, which is to free my people from English tyranny, and as soon as I find my brother, I'm goin' home to continue the fight."

"I see. Well, I won't pretend I'm not disappointed, though I think I understand. As I said, my sister is married to a Yankee, so I know how it feels to fight against one's own family. But I accept your refusal in the reasoned and considerate spirit in which it was given, and I thank you for your good and loyal service to this ship, and wish you the best of luck in your quest."

"Thank you, Captain Bulloch," Dónal said and turned away, thinking he'd been dismissed.

"Just a moment, if you please. I'm not quite finished with you. Before you go, I'd like to enter your name on the crew list and have you sign it, so that you'll be officially recorded as having participated in this momentous expedition, and so I can pay your wages."

"I don't understand, Captain. I thought my passage was to be my wages."

"Yes, well that was the deal we agreed on, I suppose. But that was then and this is now, isn't it, Mr. O'Sullivan? Come on, son, sign the list. If anyone has earned the right to be paid on this venture, it's certainly you!"

But Dónal hesitated, not really wanting to comply. After all, putting it in writing would be an admission for all the ages that he'd participated in this evil venture. Yet on the other hand, who would ever read it? And anyway, he would need money if he was to make his way north, so why not take Bulloch's?

"All right, Captain, I'll sign," he said, taking the pen.

"Dónal O'Sullivan *Béara*?" Bulloch read aloud, the question in his eyes as much as his voice.

"It's my title, Captain," Dónal replied, squaring his shoulders proudly. "Indeed, I'm *The* O'Sullivan Béara, the chieftain of the O'Sullivans of Béara by right of descent. We were once a great and powerful race, kings and princes, lords of might and majesty. But our lordship vanished with the fall of Dunboy in 1602, and since then we've been relegated like the rest of our people to the lowest rungs of society. Yet we've survived the centuries of oppression and kept our lineage intact, never forgettin' who we once were and who we will someday be again. So that's why I have to go on, Captain Bulloch, to find my brother and continue the fight, so that we might someday restore to our people what is rightfully ours, the land of Ireland."

"What is Dunboy, Mr. O'Sullivan?" Bulloch asked, sensing that it was somehow central to who Dónal was.

"'Twas a castle, the seat of our lordship," Dónal began, and went on to briefly explain the history of the O'Sullivans, the Nine Years War and Kinsale, the siege and what came after. "'Twouldn't rate more than a footnote in a history book, I suppose, but to myself and my kin, Dunboy is hallowed ground."

There was a silence then as Bulloch regarded Dónal reflectively, thinking how young he was to have the past weigh upon him so heavily.

"I see," Bulloch said, wanting to inquire further but thinking better of it. "What are your plans once we're in port, if you don't mind me asking?"

"To go to New York and find my brother."

"That's not much of a plan, young man."

"No, I suppose not, but it's the best I can come up with under the circumstances."

"Perhaps I can help, if you'll let me. To begin with, I would warn you that getting to New York at this particular time might prove more difficult than you think, as well as more than a little dangerous. It's almost nine hundred miles from Savannah, a great distance to travel through unfamiliar territory, especially on what I assume are limited resources. On top of that, the fastest route would take you into the war zone around Richmond and Washington, where the border is heavily patrolled by both armies and those caught trying to cross are some-times shot as spies. Of course, you could go the long way around, but that might take months and end up being no less perilous. So my advice would be to wait a bit, and see how things go. The war is at a critical juncture just now, and there's still much feeling in the North for letting us wayward brothers depart in peace. Who knows but that a couple of more victories in the field might not convince the Union to do just that, rather than fighting a long, costly and bloody war. Indeed, by helping to deliver the cargo in this ship, you yourself have contributed greatly toward bringing those victories about. Not only that, but in running the blockade, we've shown that we have the will and the means to continue the struggle for as long as it takes to achieve our ends. And that, I'm sure, will give the Yankees pause to consider. So since it is still possible that hostilities might come to an early end, I'd hate for you to risk your life and liberty needlessly. The next few months and even weeks will tell us a great deal, and for that reason I urge you to wait."

"Sure, if that isn't grand for you, Captain Bulloch, but my brother is in the Yankee army and may already be at the front. 'Twill do neither of us any good for hostilities to come to an early end if he gets killed in the interim. I need to get to him *now*, so I can get him out of the army and back to Ireland where he's needed, where he belongs!"

"Nor would it do any good for you to get killed trying to get to him. But I see what you mean. Well then, let me propose this: I'm going to Richmond straight away myself, if not today then surely tomorrow. Let me see what I can find out about crossing the border, so you will at least have some information to go on. If it seems practicable, I'll cable you to join me there, or in the alternative send instructions on how best to proceed. If I'm unable to find out anything, or if it seems too dangerous, then we'll discuss what to do when I get back."

"Why don't I just go to Richmond with you? 'Twould be easier, surely."

"Because I'll be busy with other things, Mr. O'Sullivan. Don't forget that my duty to country is my primary concern, not reuniting you with your errant brother."

"Sure, Captain, I didn't mean to look a gift horse in the mouth, and I'm sorry for it so."

"Yes, I'm sure you are. But aside from all that, if you can't cross now, you'll be better off waiting here than in Richmond. My family has a long history in Savannah and I have many contacts. It might interest you to know, too, that Savannah is one of the more heavily Irish cities in our fledgling nation. As many as one in five of her people are Irish-born or born here of Irish parents. The leaders of the Hibernian Society are among her most respected citizens, and I have many friends among them, friends whom I can call upon to help you. As for Richmond, while it's much closer to the border, I have no such contacts there, and since I intend to return the *Fingal* to England as soon as practicable, you would be on your own."

"I can take care of myself!"

"I'm sure you can, and who knows but that Richmond might be the place for you, after all. All I'm suggesting is that you let me scout it out before you make any hasty decisions. All right?"

Dónal eyed Bulloch thoughtfully as he considered his arguments.

While he was eager to finish his journey, the man did have some good points. The trip north was obviously dangerous and difficult, and it made no sense to just go balls to the wall with no information or planning. And as for going to Richmond, while he wasn't convinced that Bulloch was right, it was clear that the man wasn't going to take him, that he felt he was doing him a favor as it was. So he had no choice but to wait, at least for the time being. That being the case, why not let Bulloch do the reconnoitering and then decide what to do? He could always go to Richmond on his own, if that seemed appropriate.

"All right, Captain," he agreed. "I'll do it your way."

"Good. Then since that's decided, let's go topside and see about getting underway. None of us will be going anywhere if we're spotted before Fort Pulaski."

"Not to worry, ould son. Our captain will get us through, good man that he is."

"He'd better, else there'll be hell to pay!"

The morning dawned bright and clear, and the way ahead was open, though the fog still hung not half a mile to the east, shielding them from hostile eyes as they steamed up the coast. Though they were still in-shore with only a few fathoms beneath the keel, Bulloch laid on the steam, hoping to reach the Savannah River and the protecting guns of Fort Pulaski before the fog lifted completely. The men were all at battle stations with their rifles at the ready, straining their eyes in search of hostile vessels.

Yet standing at the port railing, Dónal had eyes only for the land, watching it slip by at twelve knots, America, the Promised Land of the Diaspora Irish. And sure, if it wasn't an eyeful, too, with sparkling white beaches broken by myriad streams and inlets, dark primeval forests dripping with Spanish moss and broad reedy marshes that marched right down to the sea. There were Big Houses, too, where the land had been cleared for planting, as grand and forbidding as any he'd seen in Ireland, surrounded by huge evergreen trees and groomed lawns. Away from them in the fields stood the cabins of the Negroes, who came out to watch as the ship steamed by. He even waved and shouted *halloo* at two boys fishing the breaks but, to his disappointment, they didn't respond. And everywhere he looked there were birds, herons and egrets, gulls in the air, and tiny sandpipers tiptoeing along the beaches, while the majestic nests of osprey adorned the treetops. Indeed, he thought, smiling in the warm sunlight, this was the land of milk and honey if ever God created it.

Soon, the shore gave way and the *Fingal* turned into a broad expanse of water, the Savannah River estuary, the sanctuary they'd been seeking for the past month. On an island off the port bow stood a stolid red-brick fortress, Fort Pulaski, her guns guarding the gateway to Savannah, though not a soul was to be seen on her ramparts. Hearing a cannon shot fired from the starboard bow, he whirled around to find Low sending the colors aloft, though not the Union Jack they'd flown throughout the voyage. Rather, the flag sported a blue St. Andrew's Cross speckled with white stars and stretched across a field of blood red, the Southern Cross, Bulloch had called it, the same flag Dónal had seen on the CSS *Nashville* in Bermuda. An answering shot from behind told him they'd been recognized and, looking back to the fort, he saw the Southern Cross rising there, too, while cheering men streamed to the walls, waving their arms and tossing their hats. The cheer was answered from the *Fingal,* a lone voice lifted in the ancient battle cry and, turning yet again, he found that it was Bulloch himself, screaming like a flaming banshee. Immediately, his crew joined in and the sound of them floated across the water, defiant, triumphant, seductive. The "Rebel Yell," they called it on this side of the Big Water, though it was Celtic settlers who'd brought it here, streaming into the South from all the nations, Wales, Cornwall, Man, and especially Scotland and the North of Ireland, the St. Andrew's Cross on their battle flag chosen in recognition of that connection.

And despite himself, Dónal couldn't help but join in, screaming for joy that he'd made it, that he was safe on the leeward side and nothing more could happen to him now. 'What the hell,' he thought, 'it just feels good!'

In a moment, he felt the ship begin to slow as the engines were throttled back and the wheel turned over to John Makin, a Savannah pilot who'd transferred from the *Nashville* in Bermuda. With the tide ebbing, it was a tight squeeze getting past the two sunken ships that partially blocked the channel, put there to protect the city from seaborne invasion. But Makin got them past, only to strike an oyster bar upon turning back toward mid-channel. Though he immediately ordered the engines reversed, it was no good. They were stuck in the mud and would remain so until the tide rose and floated them off. Even so, Bulloch was no longer worried about attack, the *Fingal* now being safely under the protection of Fort Pulaski's guns. While Anderson went ashore in a boat to cable the city, he stood the men down from battle stations and told them to get some rest. The day being warm and pleasant, many of them stretched out on the deck to sun themselves, while the rest went below to their bunks.

But all that changed when Anderson returned with news that the Yankees had captured Port Royal a few days before, and had a large fleet anchored just a few miles to the north. Though Fort Pulaski could protect them from one or two ships, if the Yankees attacked in force, its defenses would be sorely tested, leaving the *Fingal* a sitting duck. But while Freemantle confirmed the enemy presence from the crow's nest, they didn't appear to be moving toward them. Nevertheless, Bulloch sent Dónal aloft with another spyglass, where he and Freemantle spent the next few hours nervously scanning the horizon.

At about one o'clock, though, a steam whistle announced the arrival of three river tugs sent down to free them, and soon they were steaming toward Savannah. Relieved from his watch, Dónal climbed down to join Bulloch, Anderson and Low on deck. As the *Fingal* rounded a bend, the city came into view, perched on a bluff above the river, and seeing the quays below lined with ships and others anchored in the stream, he wondered if they'd all been trapped there by the blockade, and how the *Fingal* would ever get out again. Then a welcoming shot boomed from the city, and the sound of music and cheering floated across the water to them. He could see that hundreds of people had turned out to welcome them, thronging the quays and even the ships lying alongside, and all in the mood to celebrate. Bulloch ordered an answering shot, and a cheer went up from the crew, who lined the railings for a view.

"They've all turned out to welcome us home!" Bulloch exclaimed, a broad grin splitting his face, while pride shone in his eyes. Glancing at Dónal, he smiled. "Welcome to Georgia, Dónal O'Sullivan Béara. You've come here sooner than I would've expected when we met, though you'll have to wait till the war is over for me to come to Ireland."

"Which war, Captain Bulloch. Yours or mine?"

"Whichever lasts longer, I suppose," Bulloch replied, the smile fading from his face.

"Mine has lasted almost seven centuries, Captain. I pray yours doesn't."

Bulloch had nothing to say to that, and after a moment Dónal turned back to the city. They were quite close now, and he could hear the music above the crowd, a fast march with a happy lilt that the band played over and over. Two of the tugs pulled alongside and guided them gently abreast of the city, where they dropped anchor in the stream. Immediately a boat was lowered and Bulloch, Anderson, Low and Dónal descended into it along with two crewmen to row them in.

As Anderson ascended the ladder at the quay, the noise from above became a deafening roar which continued as the other three followed. At the top, strong hands pulled Dónal onto the quay and the crowd closed in around him, the people shouting and cheering, pushing each other aside to slap him on the back and shake his hand, as if his touch would heal them of all their earthly ills. It was a scene of such joy and chaos as he'd never experienced before, and he could only blink in bewilderment at all the smiling, anonymous faces.

Then Bulloch grabbed him by the arm and pulled him forward. "Stay close to me!" he shouted above the din. "If we get separated I may never find you again!"

Slowly they made their way up the steep access lane to the city above, the music louder now and the crush of people even closer. The entire town was celebrating, it seemed, or at least most of it. For here and there Dónal glimpsed a dark face on the edge of the crowd or peering down from one of the city's great trees. They were neither smiling nor cheering, merely watching the spectacle as it whirled around them. It wasn't about them, after all; they had no part in it, just as they had no part in the nation in which they lived.

But Dónal had no time to contemplate them, as the melody came round again and the people lifted their voices in spontaneous song. Looking more intently at the faces around him, he saw then that some of them were Irish, his own people come here before him, and suddenly he felt an overwhelming desire to join in their song.

'I'm here!' he thought, a broad grin splitting his face. 'I've made it!' At long last he was standing among his own people on the soil of *An tOileán Úr*, The New Island, the homeland of the Irish nation in exile.

Then the melody came round again, and the people sang it again, and again and again, until Dónal got the hang of it and joined in.

And I wish I was in Dixie,
away, away.
In Dixieland I'll take my stand
to live and die in Dixie.

Away, away, away down South in Dixie.
Away, away, away down South in Dixie.

part six

• The Lost Clans of Erin •

chapteR 28

Savannah, Georgia
The Confederate States of America

HE LIKED THE REFLECTION STARING BACK from the plate glass window, his long shaggy hair and month-long growth of beard making him look heroic, or so he thought, a latter-day incarnation of Ireland's legendary past. It was the very image he'd had of himself as a child when playing on the decrepit ramparts of Cahernageeha, pretending he was a great warrior defending his castle. And though he knew it didn't reflect reality, either then or now, he couldn't help smiling at himself. 'You've seen a thing or two since I saw you last,' he thought. 'I wonder what you'll see before I see you next?' But then the smile faded as reality sank in. Indeed, what did lie ahead, rough seas or smooth sailing? There was no way to know but to set his sail and follow the wind.

Suddenly feeling the fact that he hadn't slept in over thirty hours, Dónal sighed and grasped the doorknob, intending to join Bulloch inside the telegraph office. Yet even as he did, another reflection appeared beside him, planting his feet wide apart and thrusting his fists into his hips.

"Ye wouldn't happen to be one o' the lads from the ship, now would ye?" the man demanded and, hearing the Irish in his voice, Dónal perked up immediately.

"I am, to be sure," he replied, turning to find a young man of about his own age, though fully a head shorter and with legs so painfully bowed that even his baggy trousers couldn't hide it.

The little man's blue eyes glinted as he flashed a friendly grin. "And ye're one of our fellahs, too?"

"As ever a man so born!" Dónal replied, liking the look of him. For though he was dressed in laborer's clothing, well-worn and much stained, he sensed an air of confidence about him, which came partially from his assertive stance and his caubeen perched at a cocky slant on his curly black hair, though more so from the way he looked him directly in the eye.

"I'm Dónal O'Sullivan, from Allihies in West Cork," he said, extending his hand.

"*West* Cork, is it now?" the man parroted, shaking Dónal's hand. "And what is there about West Cork that ye'd give it special mention?"

"Ah, nothin', I suppose, except that it's even poorer than *East* Cork, which is sayin' a mouthful for the words that are in it!"

"Sure, if it wasn't much the same for us in *East* Donegal, where 'twas said that, but for the stones, we'd have nothin' to eat at all."

"Donegal, did you say? I've never met an Ulster man before."

"Here, now! Ye've no cause to be insultin' me so! Ulsterman, indeed!"

"Is Donegal not in Ulster, then?" Dónal asked, not catching the playful glint in the man's eyes.

"Ah, me ould son, but ye've so much to learn, now don't ye?" the man replied, shaking his head in mock sadness. "Sure, 'tis in Ulster, but no good Irish Catholic would be caught dead callin' himself an Ulsterman! Only the Proddies call themselves so, and if ye're after chargin' me with such heresy, then we'll have to step into the street!"

"No, no, 'twasn't my meanin' at all!" Dónal assured him, raising his hands in token of peace. "I just meant you were a man from Ulster, nothin' more."

"'Tis more like it then. Sure, I'm a man from Ulster and proud of it, too, bein' as it is the province o' Cú Chullain and the Red Branch, of O'Neill and Red Hugh, not to mention the great and powerful sept of O'Bogan. And 'tis one of them I am, Brian O'Bogan o' Raphoe

South, though most people are just after callin' me 'Bogie.'"

"Bogie, is it? I was wonderin' when you would get round to introducin' yourself."

"All things come to those who wait, boyo, and truer words was never spoken within me hearin'. But here now. All this hootin' and hollerin' has put a mouth on me, and that's even truer still. So what say I stand ye to a jar to applaud yeer exploit, and to welcome ye to the far side o' the pond?"

"'Tis a charmin' offer, surely, Bogie, and far be it from me to turn it down. But I'm still on duty to my captain, and have no money to return the favor."

"'Tis no worry in yeer shortage of coin, Dónal boy. When the lads hear that ye came through the blockade, they'll be queuin' up to stand ye for yeer next one, and me, too, bein' yeer good friend as I am. Just make sure ye've a fine tale in it and neither of us will go thirsty. So why don't ye put it to yeer man and see what he has to say?"

"Sure, why not? 'Tis no harm in the askin'. Wait here and I'll be back before you know I'm gone."

Opening the door just enough to stick his head inside, Dónal found Bulloch deep in conversation with Anderson and Low. "Excuse me, Captain, but will you be needin' me just now? I've just come across a new old friend out here, and he's invited me to his house for tea."

"Sure, go ahead," Bulloch replied distractedly. "Just come back to the ship when you're finished."

"Aye, Captain," Dónal said, and quickly closed the door. "Come on, Bogie. Let's be off with ourselves before he changes his mind!"

With that, O'Bogan led the way through the remnants of the crowd, away from the waterfront and along a broad avenue lined with stately mansions and shaded by the most majestic trees Dónal had ever seen.

"Is it all so grand here, Bogie?" he asked, gazing about in wonder. "I'd heard of the streets bein' paved with gold, surely, and now I'm tempted to believe it!"

"No, son, 'tisn't, and more's the pity. 'Tis just where the jackeens live, the ones with so much money that even their shite smells sweet and flowery. We'll be in Irishtown soon enough, and then ye'll see what the real world is like."

"So none of our fellahs live here, is that what you're sayin'?"

"Ah, sure, 'tis a few, America bein' the land of opportunity that it is, the place where even a Mick can drag himself up from the muck. And some of our fellahs have done quite nicely for themselves, as planters or businessmen, clergy or politicians, old Matt McAllister even gettin' himself elected mayor a while back. Still, the natives call 'em 'lace curtain Irish' just to let 'em know they ain't foolin' anyone, some indication of their mindset, too, it might give ye. Sure, 'tis only for the fact that we're useful to 'em that they tolerate us at all, useful for things like buildin' canals and railroads, workin' the docks and railyards, cuttin' the forests and policin' the city, all the jobs that native whites turn up their noses at, but slaves are too dear to waste upon."

"But why would they turn up their noses at honest labor?" Dónal asked, remembering the workhouse and the millions who'd starved or emigrated because they had no means of supporting themselves. "Are they all so rich that no one has to work?"

"Uch, not by a long shot. 'Tis because they think manual labor to be fit only for slaves, and that any white man who would stoop so low must be too stupid or shiftless to do any better. 'Nigger work,' they call it, and us whites who do it, 'white trash,' not that they'd ever say it to our faces, mind ye."

"Why not? Are they afraid of us or somethin'?"

"Sure, 'tis part of it. After all, we're different from 'em, the childer of a different tribe, and people always fear what they don't understand. But more so, I'd say, 'tis that, in a twisted sort of way, they actually need us, and not just for their dirty work either. Ye see, contrary to what ye might think, not that many people own slaves, and unlike in Ireland, here all white men over the age of twenty-one have the vote, even foreigners once they're made citizens. So the jackeens don't want to push the poor whites too low for fear they might start sympathizin' with the blacks and vote an end to slavery. Not that we'd be likely to

534

do it, mind ye, since we'd be competin' with 'em for jobs then, and might end up worse off than we was in Ireland. Still the jackeens won't risk it. King Cotton won't let 'em."

"King *who?*"

"Not who, son, but what!" O'Bogan replied with a grin. "King Cotton is the cotton plant, the thing that, in one way or another, made all these fine jackeens rich. Either they grow it, or they gin it, or they broker it, or they warehouse it, or they ship it, or they insure it, or they deal in the slaves who work it, or they lend money to people who do those things. Then toss in all the people that work for 'em, and by the time they're all totted up, just about every man jack in Dixie owes his livin' to King Cotton. 'Tis the cornerstone of this whole Confederate nation, and the very reason that it needs slavery, which is to keep the price low enough to compete with countries like India, where so-called 'free' people work for slave wages. 'Tis what brought the Irish here, too, King Cotton, to build the railroads and canals so planters could get their crop to market, their slaves bein' too valuable to waste upon such endeavors. So to make a short story long, that's why the jackeens are considerate of their manners around us, bein' afraid as they are that we might put 'em out o' business."

"So you need them and they need you and everybody needs slavery, except, of course, for the poor slaves themselves," Dónal commented. "And our people support all that, do they? Jayzis, but after seven centuries under the English yoke, you'd think we'd know better!"

"So it may seem to you, Dónal, stranger that ye are. But 'tis only a matter o' self-preservation. I mean, I feel bad for the darkies, surely, but we'd be the ones to suffer if they was all to be freed, and after goin' hungry in Ireland, 'tis not anxious that I am to do it again. Anyway, if I was to speak out against slavery, they'd have me swingin' from a rope before the words was cool, treasonous as they are and bandy-legged Mick that I am."

"Well, I don't know about that. All I know is that it takes moral courage to stand up to wrong when no one else will. A priest taught me that when I was a boy, and I've never forgotten it."

"Sure, if ye want to preach the end o' slavery, then more power to ye. And when they cut ye down from the gallows and lay ye in the grave, I'll say yeer epitaph: 'Here lies Dónal O'Sullivan, victim of his own morality.' But then slavery is nothin' but the will o' God, ye know, or so the Diocese of Savannah would have us believe. Sure, if our own Father O'Neill don't stand up in the pulpit every Sunday and put a blessin' on' Jeff Davis himself, prayin' that he 'smite our enemies with the moral vengeance of the Lord.' All o' which says to me that morality is just a matter o' which side o' the fence ye happen to be standin' on. But anyway, Dónal, if I was you, I'd keep me mouth shut till I knew the way o' things! Trust me, ye'll live a lot longer if ye do!"

"But enough o' that," O'Bogan said, as they crossed a broad sandy avenue and left the genteel district behind. "We've come to my neck o' the woods now, to Oglethorpe Ward as it's called officially, though 'tis better known as 'Irishtown West' for all our fellahs that live here. That's where I work just there, in the freight house o' the Central of Georgia Railroad. That fine buildin' next to it is the terminal, and the roundhouse is just yonder. 'Twas all built by our fellahs, ye know, and sure, if it wasn't for the promise of a job that Da brought us down from New York in the first place."

"You came here from New York?" Dónal asked, his interest redoubled. "Then you must know my brother, Eóghan O'Sullivan."

"Can't say as I do, though we was only there for a few months and meself still a young lad at the time. But then New York is a big place, and I could've spent me whole life there without ever comin' across him."

"I doubt it. He's a big fellah up there, bein' connected with all the chief men as he is. But when was it you were there, exactly?"

"'Twas in the autumn of Black '47 that we come over from Ireland," O'Bogan replied, squinting his eyes as though peering through the mists of time. "Sure, if I don't remember like it was still happenin'. The potato had failed us for three years runnin', and we was hard up against it, seein' no future to us but the workhouse or the famine grave. But then the landlord, bad cess upon him, offered to pay the passage of any that would go, and before I knew what he was after, Da had the ten of us down to Derry and into the hold of a coffin ship, no more luggage to us than the clothes on our backs. 'Twas six weeks o' pure hell, that crossin', us packed in with the others like a cargo o' poverty, nothin' but moldy bread and rancid bacon for our meals, a rusty bucket for our privy. Then the weather turned bad and, soon enough, the place was fouled with shite and puke and piss, just the stench of it enough to make ye give up the ghost. And the fever bein' one of our own, of course, 'twas over thirty gone by the time we made New York, two o' me brothers and a sister among 'em. 'Twas at sea that we buried 'em and without the benefit o' clergy, a thing that stone cold horrified me Mam. I can still see her kneelin' there on the deck, the rain comin' at her sideways, keenin' like the heart was ripped from her chest. Then the fever took me and they thought I was done for, too. But Da said the Lord had taken enough from him, and divil if he'd give him any more. So he nursed me night and day, keepin' me alive just on the strength of his will, and sure if I didn't pull through in the end, sure if I didn't.

"But even when we landed, it got no better for us. A gang o' thieves – Irish themselves, if ye'd know – robbed us o' what little money we had before we was even off the docks. Then the only lodgin's we could find was in a tenement house so afflicted with the rot that even rats wouldn't live in it. Just the one room was all we could afford, even with Mam and Da workin' the skin off their hands and us childer all playin' the street Arab from dawn to dusk, and we was packed in tighter than on the ship, neither window nor grate to comfort us. But the worst of it was watchin' Da skinny away to nothin', himself refusin' to eat till the rest was all fed and so goin' to bed hungry most nights. But when another sister died in the winter, he could bear no more. So he packed us off to Savannah, hearin' there was good work to be had and that the Irish looked after their own. And sure, if the Hibernians didn't find him a situation right away, and one for Mam in one of the fancy houses. The older brothers and sister got work, too, and meself when I was old enough, and though none of us made a fist o' money, 'twas enough to keep us all fed and clothed, and to put a shingle over our heads.

"But even so, I'm all that's left of us now. Both Mam and Da died in the yellow fever o' '54, and me eldest brother was killed at Bull Run on the very first day o' the war, if ye can believe it. Me last sister got married and moved off to Californy, and me last brother is above in Virginia, servin' with Savannah's own Emmet Rifles. Sure, if I wouldn't be with him, too, but for me bandy legs and crooked back, the marks of the fever upon me. Still, after seein' all the fellahs come back with no legs at all, 'tis no misfortune so. Anyway, I've a daycent job and a bit put by, and there's a lass from Wexford town got her eye on me. So for all the troubles that're in it, things could be worse, sure, they could."

O'Bogan fell silent then, and Dónal left it so, though out of awe at the change in his surroundings more so than respect for the man's memories. Indeed, the district they'd come into was as shabby as any he could've imagined, its decaying shacks and tenement houses being as bare of prosperity as they were of paint. Nor was there even a hint of greenery to soften it, the trees having long been sacrificed to the hearth and the stove. Yet there was laundry hanging everywhere he looked, and bunches of women and girls huddled over washtubs, though if they were doing any of it for themselves or their vagabond children, or for the men who lounged idly on porches and stoops, he couldn't tell it from the look of them. Indeed, most of them were as ratty-looking as their neighborhood, a perfect reflection of man in his man-made environment, the word *ghetto* made three-dimensional. It seemed so foreign, and yet at the same time somehow familiar, as if the people were right at home in being out of place. The enigma of it puzzled him, and he stared at the ramshackle buildings all crowded in upon each other and the Irish faces teeming among them, hoping for a moment of clarity that yet eluded him.

"So this is the real world, is it," he said, giving it up, "the place where our fellahs live?"

"Sure, 'tis," O'Bogan affirmed. "Our fellahs and the odd free darkie, plus a few slaves livin' out from their masters. 'Tis the same next door in Yamacraw, itself and Oglethorpe the heart of Irishtown West."

"Irishtown *West*, is it? And what is there about Irishtown West that you'd want to give it special mention?"

"Ah, nothin', I suppose," O'Bogan said with a grin, "just that it's even more disreputable than Irishtown East."

"I thought as much," Dónal said, though he didn't return the grin. "Do you ever miss it, Bogie – home, that is?"

"Uch, sometimes, I suppose, in the evenin' o' the day, for instance, it bein' the time when we used to gather in the end of the house. I can still see it if I close me eyes and wish hard enough, Da smokin' his clay pipe and Mam cardin' her wool, the brothers guessin' at riddles and the sisters pantin' their gossip. I can even feel the cool earthen floor on me feet and the fire scorchin' me arse, and see the darkness closin' in till only our faces are lit. Yet for the life of me, Dónal, I can't smell the turf anymore, them wee slices of Ireland that we sacrificed in the grate. 'Tis none of it here, ye know, no turf to burn. And that's how I know I'm gone from Her, because I can't smell Her anymore.

"'Tis ironic, wouldn't ye say," O'Bogan said, opening his eyes, "that me fondest memory of home should so affirm me sundered state? But bein' that I'm longer here now than I was there, is Ireland really home anymore?"

"Sure, Bogie, 'tis always home," Dónal replied, laying a friendly hand on his shoulder. "And who's to say you won't go back someday?"

"Whatever for?" O'Bogan demanded, and for that Dónal had no answer.

⚬౫ᘒᘗ⚬

It was well after midnight by the time Dónal got back to the *Fingal*, which luckily for him was now berthed at the quays rather than anchored in the stream. He'd spent the intervening hours with O'Bogan, drinking in a back-room pub behind a grocer's shop. "Kavanagh's" it was called after the proprietor, a man whose parents had come from

539

Wexford, though he himself was born in Savannah. And there were others like him, too, men whose faces could be mistaken for nothing but Irish but who hadn't a trace of the brogue in them, having never set foot in their native land. There were even a few sprung from mixed marriages, with one parent of German or Scottish or even English blood. But perhaps most surprising to Dónal was that there were Protestants among them, too, men whose parents or grandparents had lost the connection, owing to the dearth of Catholic churches in the rural South, a transition eased by the fact that once out of Ireland, Catholicism was no longer a matter of nationalism. And yet they all considered themselves Irish, and were accepted as such even by more recent immigrants like O'Bogan.

"God bless all here," O'Bogan called in the traditional manner upon entering, a chorus of voices answering from the bar. The place was already crowded even at that early hour, the arrival of the *Fingal* having brought the work day to a sudden halt as men streamed to the quays to greet her, then crowded into pubs to celebrate her arrival. And O'Bogan was right about the drink, too, for as soon as they heard that Dónal was one of her crewmen, they were falling all over themselves to stand him for one. Of course, they wanted to hear the story of the crossing, as well as all the news from home. "And how is the poor old woman?" they asked, meaning Ireland, even calling Her so in Irish, *an sean-bhean bhocht.* He had to tell it all more than once, of course, as the news went round the neighborhood and more men kept coming in. Indeed, so crowded had Jimmy Kavanagh's place become that by ten o'clock he was out of both porter and whiskey and the party spilled into the street. Most of the men went home then, having their fill of both drink and revelry, leaving the hard-core few, O'Bogan and Dónal among them, to find another venue. They didn't have far to go either, as every Irish grocer had a pub in his back room, and it was only a matter of stumbling down the block to find another. Of course, Dónal had to tell his story again, but it was worth it for the free drinks and warm glow of comradeship. It didn't last long though, for the bartender soon called closing time, and by half-eleven they were on the street again, this time with nowhere to go but home.

But just as they were about to break up and go their separate ways, another group of men rounded a corner and headed toward them, and what followed happened so fast that it was still a blur in Dónal's drink-clouded mind. He remembered an escalating exchange of words, which he wrote off as mere drink-talk until someone shouted, "Get 'em lads," and the two groups charged each other with fists flying. Naturally, he didn't follow suit, being a stranger and having nothing against the men in question. He just watched in bewilderment as the two factions whaled away at each other, splitting the night with their shrieks and curses, and the smack of fists on bone, one of them even raising his clan's battle cry, *O'Donnell abú, O'Donnell abú!* Yet it was then that he experienced the moment of clarity that had so eluded him earlier, realizing that these people seemed so at home in their alien surroundings because they *were* at home, and not in the figurative sense either. Indeed, they hadn't left Ireland behind, they'd brought Her with them, the names, the faces, the speech, the habits, the customs, the folklore, the pubs, the drink, the Catholic Church, the communal ethos, the clan-reminiscent factions, the propensity to violence, even the squalor, poverty and second-class citizenship, all of it! So it was that the Irish of Savannah didn't live *in* Savannah, they lived in the Irishtowns that huddled on either edge of the city, the bits of Erin they'd transplanted to the far side of the Atlantic, a couple of sprawling *clocháns* more Irish than Ireland Herself. And thus the enigma that had puzzled him earlier, how it could be so Irish and yet so far from home, was really no enigma at all.

Yet there was no time to dwell on it, as other sounds came to his ears, the shrill of policemen's whistles and the thump of their charging feet. Without hesitating, he waded into the affray to retrieve O'Bogan, whom he found struggling up after being knocked to the ground.

"Come on, Bogie!" he said, pulling him upright. "The peelers are comin'! The peelers!"

"Cheese it, lads, the coppers!" O'Bogan shouted, and the cry went up among the combatants, "The coppers!" And as quickly as it began, the fight ended, with men scattering in all directions as the blue-coated policemen waded into them, shouting commands in brogue-tinged voices.

"Follow me!" O'Bogan said, leading the way down a side street and through an alley, Dónal fairly pushing him along from behind.

"Is that as fast as you can go?" he prodded, not daring to look over his shoulder for fear of what might be after him.

"I told ye they wouldn't have me in the army and now ye know why!" O'Bogan shot back.

But no one was after them, the police contenting themselves with hauling in the stragglers rather than pursuing the fleet, and soon they slowed to a walk. O'Bogan led the way back to the quays then, taking his leave only upon delivering Dónal safely to the *Fingal.* He staggered up the gangway intending to go straight to bed, only to be told by the watchman that Bulloch wanted to see him right away.

"Jayzis, does the man never sleep?" he lamented, as he made his way below.

Now as he stood outside Bulloch's cabin, straightening his clothes and trying to make himself presentable, he could hear him at his desk and knew that, as usual, he was working deep into the night. But just as he raised his hand to knock, Bulloch summoned him.

"Come in, Mr. O'Sullivan. I've been waiting for you.

"Yes, I've been waiting for you for quite some time now," he continued, as Dónal closed the door behind him. "I gave you leave to have tea, not to spend the entire evening drinking in some back-room saloon. Why, you smell like a distillery, and you look worse. Just what do you mean by taking advantage of my indulgence like that? Have I ever done anything to you, young man, that would give you cause to treat me so?"

All this Bulloch said without pausing in his writing or even glancing up, his voice calm and temperate, his gestures even and contained. Yet his control only magnified his anger, making it palpable and present.

"No, sir, you haven't," Dónal replied softly, suddenly sober and subdued. "And I'm sorry, Captain Bulloch, truly I am."

"Hm," Bulloch grunted, laying down his pen and eyeing him appraisingly. "Yes, I believe you are sorry, though not enough, perhaps, to keep you from doing it again. Drinking to excess is a sign of flawed character in a man, and though you're still young enough to write it off to youthful exuberance, I can see it becoming a habit if you aren't careful. Alcohol is a dangerous thing, you know, and while an ounce might be medicinal, a gallon is a disease unto itself. It feeds the darkness within, that mark of Original Sin we all carry, and the more you feed it the hungrier it gets, until it consumes your soul and buries you in a living grave, deeper and more eternal than those of the dead."

Bulloch rose from his chair then and stood before Dónal, gripping his shoulders and looking him hard in the eyes. "Don't dwell on your inner darkness, and don't feed it with whiskey, lest you squander the gifts you've been given. You have too much to offer the world to waste yourself on malignant introspection, and the world desperately needs what you have to offer. Now I say this as your friend, Dónal, and if you take away nothing else from me, at least take that! Promise me you will! Promise!"

But Dónal couldn't answer. He was too shocked at the clarity of Bulloch's vision, at the ease with which he'd stripped away all his defensive layers and laid bare the shadows that stalked him. No one had ever done it before and it frightened him mightily, to be scrutinized not from the other side of the mirror but from his own. Still, he could say nothing, locked as he was in the righteous intensity of Bulloch's gaze. Yet the man would not be denied.

"Promise!" Bulloch demanded, tightening his grip.

"Aye, sir," Dónal managed finally, willing in that moment to say or do anything to cloak his nakedness. "I promise."

"Good!" Bulloch said, his eyes and grip softening. "Good!" Then he smiled, and patted Dónal on the cheek like an indulgent father. "So tell me. Did you at least have a good time of it?"

"Aye, Captain, I did," Dónal sighed, suddenly exhausted. "I was the toast of Irishtown West."

CRULO

The morning was cold and gray, its heavy blanket of clouds casting a pall over Dónal's spirit even as it did the land, leaving him gloomy and depressed. Of course, the lingering effects of last night's fun didn't help either, though he did his best to hide it from Bulloch, wanting to suffer no more of his scrutiny and disapproval. Nor had he slept well, his dreams being haunted by visions of dark shadows attacking and himself unable to fight back, his defenses impotent. Then Bulloch turned him out at first light to give him a quick tour of Savannah, showing him where his grandfather and great-grandfather had lived and where they were buried before bringing him to the place where they now stood, a field lying between the Central of Georgia terminal and its roundhouse, the place where the decisive battle of the Siege of Savannah was fought in October 1779.

"This is the place I told you about," Bulloch said, his words falling dead on the leaden air. "The besiegers who fell are said to be buried in a mass grave somewhere in this field, though no one really knows exactly where anymore. The British who buried them didn't mark the spot, and the memory seems to have died with that generation."

There was a silence between them then, each being lost in his own thoughts, his own reflections on the killing field this place had once been. Dónal closed his eyes and tried to remember everything he could about his relations who died here, Eóghan and Dónal, two young Wild Geese who'd flown to France seeking freedom, only to be slaughtered in this distant place. How ironic, it seemed, that they'd fought for this ground not knowing it would one day become Irishtown West, a bit of the Ould Sod sprung up on the New Island, and that he'd walked right by it the day before without knowing, without even an inkling of their presence. And how sad that he didn't feel them now, didn't feel connected to this place by the spirits of those who'd come before. Indeed, he felt nothing but emptiness, and the need to fill it with a drink.

After a bit, Bulloch stirred and laid a hand on his shoulder. "I hate to interrupt your meditations," he said, mistaking his closed eyes and bowed head for reverence, "but I have to go now or I'll miss my train."

"That's all right, Captain. I'm ready to go. Sure, if I'm not past ready."

chapter 29

Savannah, Georgia

THE SALOON OF THE SCREVEN HOUSE was a convivial place, spacious and well-lit, and furnished in a style befitting its status as the newest and grandest hotel in Savannah. It was crowded with men, too, smoking and chatting as they partook of its well-stocked bar. After spending the morning and midday in his bunk, sleeping off his head from the night before, Dónal had gone out to get himself a bath and a new suit of clothes, before coming here in search of a drink and the company of his own. It was a place where Irishmen of worth tended to congregate, John Low told him, owing to the fact that its proprietor, James Foley, was one of their own. And hearing the lilt of brogue-tinged voices from the doorway, he knew the man hadn't steered him wrong.

Stepping up to the bar, he ordered his habitual pint of ale and glass of whiskey, then settled into a corner to enjoy them in private. For while he craved the comfort of his own, he wasn't really interested in conversation, especially if it meant recounting his adventures on the *Fingal* again. Last night's notoriety was quite enough, and tonight he just wanted a quiet drink or two to take the edge off before going back to bed.

And as the stuff worked its timeless magic, softening the hard edges and making the world a friendly place, his mind drifted to Eóghan, wondering where he was and what he was doing, hoping he was safe and not at the front. Hopefully, he would be with him soon if Bulloch could find a way (Dónal having decided in that moment of drink-inspired clarity to give him a chance rather than heading north on his own). Christ, but it would be good to see him again, he thought, to look him in the eyes, man-to-man, brother-to-brother, and tell him it was time to come home. And surely he would come, despite Riobárd's opinion to the contrary. Indeed, how could he not with Dónal himself there to convince him? Sure, he would come, and then they would set to the problem at hand, the two of them, side-by-side, leading their people to freedom.

But then reality broke into his reverie, as he realized his glass was empty and stepped up to the bar for another. It would have to be his last, too, he knew, if he was to conserve his seaman's pay against the possibility of having to make his own way north. He'd already spent some of it on new clothes and a shave, feeling the need to make himself look presentable, but he vowed to keep a tight fist on the rest.

After tossing back the whiskey, he was on his way back to the corner with his pint, when a bit of overheard conversation stopped him in his tracks.

"Tipperary, did ye say?" a man asked. "Why, I'm a Tipp man meself, though I'm here almost forty years now. I come from the parish o' Knockgraffon near Cahir."

Turning to the speaker, his mouth dropped upon seeing John Fitzgerald standing there, the man at whose house he and Butler had spent the night. Or at least it was a near copy of him, being about the same age and having the same lank yellow hair and unhandsome face dominated by the same prominent nose, the same shortness of stature, peasant sturdiness, and self-satisfied air of middling prosperity that advertised the strong farmer to all who knew the look. Yet there were differences, too, in his fine dress and polished appearance, surely, though more so in the look of his eyes, which had something about them, a quickness perhaps, a bit of guile that John's lacked. It reminded him of someone else, someone he'd seen but didn't really know, someone . . . And then he had it, the man in the old daguerreotype with the beautiful young wife, John's brother, though his name was beyond him in that

546

moment. Yet surely it was himself standing there and, now that he thought about it, John did say that he lived in Georgia, though whether in Savannah or not, he couldn't recall. But he did recall his wife's name, Eleanor, that latter-day Eve more lovely than the gardenous fields of Knockgraffon, a living embodiment of the word *beauty*. Though he'd not thought of her since Holyhead, or rather since Rhiannon, still her image was burned into his memory, her loveliness in that captured moment still touching him across all the years and miles. And while it was true, as Butler had cautioned, that she was old enough to be his mother now, still he would've given anything to see her, to speak with her and hear her voice, to touch her hand. Nor would it matter what the years had done to her, for to him she'd always be just as lovely as she was then.

With her in mind then, Dónal turned full face toward Fitzgerald and slipped the St. Christopher's medal from around his neck, holding it up in such a way that the man couldn't help but notice. "Do you know this, Mr. Fitzgerald?"

The man excused himself, then moved to Dónal and took the medal in his hand. "Why, 'tis the St. Christopher's me Da got in France," he said, after turning it over and seeing his father's initials etched into the back. "Sure, I'd know it anywhere. But how did ye come by it? Last I knew, me brother, John, still had it in Ireland. Do ye know him then?"

"No, sir, not well," Dónal replied, turning on the charm. "I just met him the once through a mutual friend, Egan Butler, the son of Ryan Butler as you might recall. But I did have the pleasure of his hospitality, and knowin' I was to cross the water, he gave it to me as a partin' gift, and as an introduction to any of his own that I might find over here."

"Did he, indeed? And how do I know that ye didn't just steal it?"

"If that was the case, Mr. Fitzgerald," Dónal replied smoothly, dropping the medal onto the bar, "why would I give it back to you now?"

"Because yeer conscience is troublin' ye, perhaps," Fitzgerald replied, looking him over appraisingly. "But then, ye haven't the look of a thief about ye, not in yeer eyes, anyway. So I'll take ye at yeer word, coincidental as I might find it, and thank ye for restorin' what's not yeer own."

Without waiting for a reply, Fitzgerald dropped the medal into his vest pocket and turned away, giving the impression that their conversation was at an end. But instead, he signaled the bartender for service, ordered two whiskeys and gave one to Dónal.

"Cheers," he toasted, clinking his glass to Dónal's and downing the whiskey in one gulp. Then he nodded to the bartender. "Kelly, if ye please. The same again or somethin' similar.

"So ye're a Tipp man, are ye?" he asked, turning back to Dónal.

"No, sir. Egan and I were on our way to Cashel and stopped at John's for the night. I come from Allihies in the County Cork myself. Dónal O'Sullivan is my name."

"And I'm Phillip Fitzgerald, late o' Tipperary and now o' Clayton County, Georgia," the man said, shaking Dónal's hand.

"Sure, I know all about you. John showed me your family portrait while I was there. 'Tis how I recognized you just now."

"Ah yes, the one with Ellen, Mamie, and young Phillip, 'twould be, the first I ever had taken," Fitzgerald said, his eyes suddenly far away. "'Twas a long time ago, so it was, and many's the change that's in it since."

"Yes, the children must be all grown up by now. As I recall John tellin' it, young Phillip and I are about the same age."

"Ye would be, to be sure," Fitzgerald replied, looking into his empty glass, "had he not died in his infancy."

"Oh Jayzis, I'm sorry, Mr. Fitzgerald, sorry for your troubles and sorrier still for disinterrin' the memories."

"'Tis no fault of yeer own. Ye'd no way of knowin'. Anyway, time has a way o' healin', so 'tis said, though 'tis not as quick about it as the stuff. Kelly, the same again, good man yeerself.

"But tell me of our John. Is he still in the ould homeplace? And what of herself and the childer?"

"They're all grand so, Mr. Fitzgerald," Dónal replied, and went on to recount everything he could remember about them.

"'Tis a grand thing, begob, namin' one o' the lads for me," Fitzgerald said when he'd finished. "Sure, I'd have returned the favor, too, but that only colleens come to us after young Phillip. But isn't John the man himself, havin' such a wee lad and himself pushin' sixty? Why that ould goat! But no, the lad would be older than four by now, would he not? I mean, it must be some time since ye was there, what with the war and the blockade."

"No, sir, 'twas just at the end of June I saw them."

"At the end of June, did ye say? Why that was barely four months ago! How did ye get across the border with all them Yankees squattin' upon it?"

"I didn't," Dónal replied with a grin. "I ran the blockade."

"On that ship that come in yesterday, do ye mean?" Fitzgerald asked, giving him a second once-over. "So 'tis no thief ye are, but a pirate. I'd never have took ye for that either."

"Nor am I one, just a traveler who needed a passage to America, the good captain bein' kind enough to accommodate me. I've a brother in New York that I'm after findin', himself bein' why I've come."

"But why to Savannah? 'Tis no blockade on New York I've heard tell of."

"Ah, sure, Mr. Fitzgerald, if it isn't a long one in the tellin'. But the short of it is that I came to Savannah because that's where the ship was goin', and I figured I could manage the rest from here."

"Did ye now? Ah, the innocence of youth, what I wouldn't give to have it again. Kelly, please! The same again!"

"No, Mr. Fitzgerald, 'tis my turn."

"Here now, put that away! Ye bein' a stranger here, I'd not have it said that my hospitality was lackin'!"

"Sure, but a constant guest is never welcome, so 'tis said. Let me buy you the one, at least, just to keep from feelin' like a moocher."

"All right, then. But just the one, mind ye."

"*Níl aon deoch comh mhaith leis an céad deoch eile,*" Dónal said when the drinks came.

"Sure, and back at ye, whatever 'twas ye said," Fitzgerald said, before draining his glass.

"I said, 'There's no drink like the next one.' I'm sorry, Mr. Fitzgerald.

I forgot you've no Irish in you."

"Not the first word of it, son," the man affirmed, seeming almost proud. "We were never taught the ould language, it bein' dead already and us havin' no use for it, beyond nostalgia. But Da was never a big one for that, mind ye, havin' learned his lesson the hard way in '98. 'Get on with the business of livin' and let the past take care of itself,' he always said, and sure, if I don't preach the same to me own. Indeed, if more had taken his advice, 'twould be fewer of us livin' over here, so there would."

"So our history has nothin' to teach us, is that what you're sayin'?" Dónal asked, not sure he liked the implication.

"History? Come on, son. History is but a prank the livin' pull over on the dead, the one exception, I'll grant ye, bein' Ireland, where 'tis done the other way round. But I ask ye now, is it not high time we stopped bein' prisoners of our history and allowed ourselves some prospect for the future, somethin' beyond makin' the same ould mistakes all over again? And sure, if that isn't the very reason I come here in the first place, to get on with the business of livin' and leave the unlamented past behind. So 'tis not Ireland that concerns me now, but this country, and the only history we have here is what we make ourselves. What a grand thing it is, too, havin' no past to burden ye, nothin' holdin' ye back from the bright future ahead. Ye may not know it now, son, but once ye've had a chance to look around, ye'll see what a fine thing ye done in comin' here. 'Tis a land of opportunity where even the likes of ourselves can rise to the top.

"So drink with me, if ye will, to this new nation we've created, this Confederacy formed in the grand tradition of Washington and Jefferson, a place where freedom and keepin' the black man in his place still mean somethin'."

Suddenly Dónal didn't much care for Phillip Fitzgerald. For in that one brief diatribe, he'd railed against everything Dónal believed in, especially in the way he'd used the concepts in that last phrase as though they weren't mutually exclusive.

"I don't think I can do that, Mr. Fitzgerald," he said, unconsciously squaring his shoulders and drawing himself up. "I'm not so sure I agree with you."

"Ah, sure, son. Ye're entitled to yeer own opinion, so ye are," Fitzgerald said, pulling a huge hunting knife from inside his riding boot and laying it on the bar between them. "But ye know what they say about opinions, don't ye? They're like arseholes – we've all got 'em, but no one's after hearin' 'em. But here, now. Do ye want to fight, or do ye want to drink? Ye can have it either way, ye know."

"Well now, Mr. Fitzgerald," Dónal said, remembering what he was really after, "since the likelihood of either of us changin' the other's mind seems pretty slim, I'd sooner have the drink. Kelly! The same again, if you please!"

⁂

For all the vastness of the country, there wasn't much of it to be seen from a train window, Dónal concluded, the thick forests and flat featureless land of the Georgia coastal plain providing nothing in the way of visual interest. How different it was from his trip across North Wales, where every twist and turn had brought something new to look at. But at least he didn't feel as if he were missing anything while sleeping off his hangover, as the rhythm of the rails, the gray weather, and his full belly tugged at his eyelids with sedative insistence. Indeed, Fitzgerald was already asleep again, his old head lolling on his barrel chest, though the train was barely five minutes gone from the lunch stop. Anyway, there would be time to look out the window later, there still being several hours between themselves and Jonesboro, the stop closest to the man's plantation.

And that was where they were headed, though exactly how it had come to pass, he couldn't remember, the night before being but a blur of whiskey to him. He could barely even remember the coach ride to the railroad station that morning, having still been drunk when he awoke on the settee in the man's hotel room. But somewhere in the midst of their carousing, Fitzgerald had invited him to his home and, of course, he'd accepted, it being his reason for approaching him in the first place. It didn't matter that it was two hundred miles inland and a needless detour from the straight path to Eóghan, or that he might miss Bulloch's summons or run out of money. All that mattered to him was seeing the woman in the daguerreotype, Eleanor, and everything beyond he would deal with later.

⚬᪥᪥᪥⚬

It was well after nightfall by the time the train pulled into Jonesboro, and though they'd left the rain behind at their supper stop in Macon, it was cold and damp out nonetheless, a thick low-lying fog foreshortening Dónal's first view of the town. Not that he cared at that point anyway, being exhausted from the lingering effects of his two-day bender and just anxious to get to a bed. It hadn't helped, either, that Fitzgerald was wide awake after supper and in the mood to chat, plying him with questions about his family and background.

"Just to refresh me memory," he assured him. "We had it all out last night, surely, though 'tis somethin' of a blur to me now. I do remember ye sayin' that ye're a real Irish chieftain, and that ye can trace yeer lineage all the way back to the Lords o' Knockgraffon. Sure, I remember the place well, a great fairy mound set within the remains of an old ringfort. 'Twas the seat o' yeer ancestors, did ye not say? They must've been high and mighty indeed in them times, that bein' some o' the finest land on God's green Earth. Sure, if I wouldn't trade me whole plantation just for John's wee patch of it, 'tis that rich and fertile."

"You don't have to tell me, Mr. Fitzgerald. I've seen it with my own two eyes, remember? And anyway, we still carry its memory in our hearts, even though it's been seven centuries since your ancestors drove out mine."

"Ah, now, lad, yeer not after layin' that ould bit o' guilt on me, are ye? Sure, there might've been some troubles between our folk in the past, but 'twas a long time ago, as ye yeerself pointed out, and we've all changed a bit since then. And if ye doubt my word on it, just remember what the bard had to say:

Not long our air they breathed;
Not long they fed on venison, in Irish water seethed;
Not often had their childer been by Irish mother's nursed,
When from their full and genial hearts an Irish feeling burst!
The English monarchs strove in vain, by law and force and bribe,
To win from Irish thoughts and ways this 'more than Irish' tribe;
For still they clung to fosterage, to Brehon, cloak, and bard;
What king dare say to Geraldine, 'Your Irish wife discard?'

The point bein', son, 'tis a bit late in the day to be speakin' o' my people as anything different from yeer own. We're all just Irish now, no more, no less."

"Sure, Mr. Fitzgerald, you've got me there. But am I right in thinkin' that you yourself might be the bard in question?"

"No, son. I don't write poetry, I just appreciate it, the same as any man o' culture and learnin'. But those are the words of one Thomas Davis, if ye'd know, a newspaper man he was, and himself with a sharp quill on the subject o' rebellion."

"He was indeed, and a man of great influence. But how do you know of him?"

"Ah, sure, son, ye live and ye learn, now don't ye? But if ye'd have the truth of it, then come to Mass with me on Sunday and I'll acquaint ye with our own Father Thomas O'Reilly, himself a poet of no mean distinction and me conduit to the artful words of our native land."

Dónal just smiled at that. "I thought you didn't care about Ireland, Mr. Fitzgerald, yet here you go suggestin' otherwise."

"Ah, sure, if ye don't have me yeer own self. All right then, I do care about Ireland, but only in the way o' nostalgia, the Divil take me father's feelin's to the contrary. But then every man has a soft spot in his heart for the ould homeplace, though it doesn't mean he has to be stuck in the past. Me life and me future are here in this country, and me family's, as well. 'Tis just a memory o' childhood and simpler times, Ireland is to me now."

After that, Fitzgerald had turned the conversation to his wife (whose name, to Dónal's annoyance, he insisted on shortening to "Ellen"), saying that she was Irish, too, though born in America, her people having come from the County Longford. She was a great beauty and a comfort to him in his advancing age, being considerably younger, and a fine mother to their seven daughters, who ranged in age from twenty-one all the way down to four. ('And just who are you to be calling anyone an *ould goat?*' Dónal thought.) As for the girls, he took great pride in seeing them educated as well as possible, even sending them to convent schools in Baltimore and Charleston for their secondary years, except, of course, for the obstinate Annie, who'd refused to go that far from home. But then the war had come and he'd brought his children home where he could protect them, meaning that they were all crammed together under one roof again. He sighed and shook his head then, saying it was surely a punishment for his sins, being the lone man in a house full of women, especially since his brother had passed on. Still, he allowed that things could be worse.

"But what o' yeerself?" he asked Dónal. "Ye've neither family nor missus nor even a sweetheart waitin' at home, as I recall ye tellin' it. 'Tis a sad state of affairs in it, ye bein' the young man o' prospects that ye are. And then there's the burden o' yeer lineage to consider. 'Twould be a sad state of affairs was it to end after so much time. While I've always thought it better for a man to put off marryin' till he's made somethin' of himself in life, I'm not sure a fellah in yeer position has the luxury. 'Tis yeer own business, to be sure, and none o' mine. It's just that such things have been on me mind of late, havin' the two daughters of marryin' age as I do, and more comin' on."

Though Fitzgerald had spoken nonchalantly, Dónal caught the calculating look in his eyes, and understood the man's true motivation in inviting him to his home. It surprised him, too, for on the surface he had so little to offer the daughter of a wealthy planter, newly arrived as he was and possessed of neither property nor money, having only his natural charm, courtliness, good looks and family pedigree by which to recommend himself. But then maybe that was enough for a man with no sons of his own, especially if it would be difficult to find a more suitable match for one or more of his daughters. He remembered John's children then, and how they'd gotten too much of their father in them to ever be considered attractive. Could it be so with Phillip's, too? It was hard for him to imagine, given the remarkable beauty of his wife. But in any case, Dónal didn't encourage it, and though the man let it drop, he was sure he hadn't heard the last of it.

After that the conversation had gone in a different direction, with Fitzgerald commenting on the land they passed through, and where they were going. Georgia, he said, was the largest state east of the Mississippi River, Confederate or Union, now that Virginia was broken in two. It was almost twice the size of Ireland, and had three distinct geographic areas: the coastal plain in the south; the rugged Appalachian Mountains in the north; and in between, a broad plateau of gently rolling land called "the Piedmont," wherein his own plantation lay. But whereas the soil in the coastal plain was dark and rich, that of the Piedmont was mostly Georgia "red clay," which wasn't productive enough to support the large plantations that were common further south. Still, he was able to work the soil to its maximum efficiency by treating it kindly, letting it lie fallow as needed and carefully rotating crops to keep from wearing it out. Obviously, to make such a scheme economically viable required large holdings of land since a significant portion of it might be idle in any given year. But he'd solved that problem over the years by investing wisely, putting off marriage and carefully saving the money he made as a school teacher and then as a merchant so he could buy his land outright and thereby avoid the gombeen man. Then, too, he'd bought "right," taking full advantage of the lower prices available at estate and foreclosure sales so that his money wasn't all tied up in the land, thus enabling him to invest in machinery, draft animals and slaves to work it. Finally, he'd bought selectively, choosing plots for their fertility rather than contiguity, the travel time between them being more than made up in productivity. So it was that he'd become the largest land owner in Clayton County and owned the second most slaves, after his friend and neighbor, Manson Glass.

And, of course, it was King Cotton that Fitzgerald grew on his land, planting other crops only to facilitate his rotation scheme, though he did keep a large vegetable garden adjacent to the house, and enough cattle and poultry to provide for his own family and thirty-five slaves. Sure, if he didn't even grow a few potatoes in the garden, though not the nasty old lumpers he'd had his fill of in Ireland, but good hardy ones that never showed a hint of the curl or the taint. Even so, they didn't eat them everyday, only on Fridays with their fish caught from the nearby Flint River.

It was then that Fitzgerald sighed, and looked out the window into the black of night. "But so it is that I've built up me little empire, and yet have no son to succeed me in it. I'd hoped and prayed that young Della would be himself, as I did with Katie before her and indeed all the others, truth to tell. But no, 'twas not to be, no sons in it for me. Now herself isn't up to it, and after bearin' me so many, I haven't the heart to ask her anyway."

Turning back to Dónal, Fitzgerald gave him a queer sort of look. "I was cursed in it, so I was, by a Cracker woman whose home I bought at foreclosure, itself the one I live in now. 'Twas when I first got into the farmin' business, it happened. I'd bought in two parcels o' land and was tryin' to decide which to build on, when what do you know but the farm in the middle up and fails, and the sheriff is called in to sell it off. What a rare bit o' good fortune 'twould be, I thought to meself, if I could connect me own two bits and get a fine house in the bargain. But then the woman o' the place come beggin' to me for a loan, sayin' they'd nowhere to go if they was put out. 'Not for me own sake, mind ye,' she said, 'but for that o' the childer.' Begob, I thought, if her man isn't the unlucky sort, and he'll go down sooner or later anyway. 'Twas the reason I give for denyin' her, too, though if the truth be known, 'twas nothin' but me own Irish hunger for land. Anyway, I told her no and went to the auction ready to outbid all comers. And so I did, in the heel o' the hunt. But herself was there, too, standin' in the dust beside her man, the childer clingin' to her skirts and bawlin' like their wee hearts was broken. And when she seen the way o' things, she roared at me in a voice like Heavenly vengeance: *Ye've got what ye wanted, ye filthy grabber! 'Tis yeers and ain't nothin' I can do about it. But as God is me witness, Phillip Fitzgerald, ye'll never raise a man child in it!* Then she spit on the ground and stomped her foot to seal it, and away she went, himself and the childer trailin' after.

"And sure, if it wasn't soon after that we lost young Phillip, the poor thing dyin' in his sleep after divil a day o' sickness in all his life. No more lads come to us after, as ye know, just the girls, and all of 'em as healthy as prize pigs. Now don't get me wrong. They've been a great comfort to me over the years, a great source o' pride, too. But still a man wants for a son, now doesn't he, a bit o' manly flesh to stand beside him and carry on the name. Still, it could be worse, I grant ye. The land will stay in the family, after all, which in the heel o' the hunt is what really matters. And though the names o' those who come after won't be Fitzgerald, of me blood they'll be nonetheless.

"But so it is that one o' me girls is goin' to make some man very lucky one o' these days!" he ended pointedly, and Dónal didn't miss it.

Now as he and Fitzgerald followed the liveryman into the stable, the conversation was still on his mind, for the man having invited him to his home as a potential suitor, Dónal knew he'd have to be very careful not to give offense. But then they came to the stall where Fitzgerald's horse waited, and at the sight of him, all other thoughts left his mind. For he was the most beautiful horse Dónal had ever seen, a proud red stallion with a black mane and tail, his coat so sleek that it gleamed even in the dim lantern light, the fire in his eyes reflecting the indomitable spirit within. Upon seeing Fitzgerald, he tossed his head and snorted, pawed with his hoof and pressed against the gate.

"Jayzis, God in Heaven!" Dónal exclaimed upon seeing him. "That is a horse of a horse if ever there was one so born!"

"There, there, me beautiful, me beautiful, me darlin' Mavourneen," Fitzgerald crooned, stroking the horse's muzzle and neck and slipping him a sugar cube. "Be easy with yeerself now. I've come back to ye just as I said I would, just as I always do. We'll have ye out o' there and ready to go in no time, and then we'll show our young Mr. O'Sullivan what a horse of a horse ye really are!"

The horse did indeed calm down then, nuzzling Fitzgerald's cheek as though to kiss him while the man rubbed his neck with both hands, the deep affection between them touching to behold. Indeed, Fitzgerald rose a notch in Dónal's estimation because of it, horses being great judges of character in his experience, and any man who could make one love him that much couldn't be all bad.

"What's his name?" Dónal asked softly, almost reluctant to intrude.

"'Tis Mavourneen, as I said," Fitzgerald replied, as he opened the gate and led him out. "'Me darlin',' it means in the ould language, or so I'm told."

"And so it does," Dónal affirmed, thinking it couldn't have been more fitting. "*Mo mhuirnín*, to be precise. My darlin'."

"Sure, and that's just what he is to me, me darlin' Mavourneen. One of a kind, he is, and when he's gone ye'll not see the likes of him again. He'd rather run than eat and jump a fence than a mare, and he's the best friend I've ever had, two-legged or four. When I come into town of a Saturday and have a few more than is good for me, 'tis him who gets me home before herself calls the curfew, chargin' across the fields like a streak o' greased lightnin', while divil so much as joggin' me in the saddle. I could never have sold him away for the Cause like they asked; 'twould've broken me heart like sellin' one o' me childer. Anyway, they'd have sent him back soon enough, for he'll let no man ride him but me!"

Fitzgerald went about the business of saddling him then, crooning all the while and stroking him at every opportunity. Meanwhile, the liveryman saddled another horse for Dónal and, when all was ready, they headed out of town and into the country, moving through the fog like ghosts.

As they clopped along, Dónal shivered and drew his jacket close. He hadn't bought a topcoat, thinking the two warm and sunny days before to be typical of the weather he'd encounter. Indeed, he'd always heard it got warmer the further south one went and, according to the *Fingal's* maps, Georgia was many degrees of latitude south of Ireland. Yet it was just as cold and damp here as on Béara, if not more so, and though he was prepared for many surprises in the New World, this wasn't one of them.

"Is it always this cold?" he asked through chattering teeth.

"No, son," Fitzgerald replied. "Sometimes it's even colder! And if this winter is typical, we'll have ourselves a good snow or two before 'tis over."

"'Tis grand to know I've so much to look forward to."

"Ah, now, son, 'tis only the bad news I've given ye. The good news is that spring comes early, and sure, if it isn't a sight to behold. Did ye ever hear tell o' the dogwood tree? It erupts in a burst o' white flowers the like o' which ye've never seen, like snow in the woods, 'tis that thick with 'em around here. After seein' it, ye'll have an altogether different opinion o' the place, so ye will."

"I'm sure I would if I was still here. But I mean to be back in Ireland by then, God willin'."

"Arragh, I was forgettin' meself, though why ye're so set on it is beyond me. Ye've no stake in the country, after all, havin' no family or land o' yeer own. Anyway, the future is here, on this side of the water. So why not take my advice and forget about Ireland?"

"Ah, sure, Mr. Fitzgerald, if that isn't another long one in the tellin'. But the short of it is that my brother and I have a job to do. More than that, I can't tell you, except that it's tied up with Ireland's status as a colony."

"Ah, I see the way of it now. Ye're one o' them Fenian fellahs, ain't ye, the ones that go paradin' around Atlanta like they was the second comin' o' Brian Boru? Why, if them is the fellahs that're to set Ireland free, yeer gran'childer will never see it!"

"Who knows but that you're right. Still, I have to go back so my brother will come, he's just that sorely needed."

"All right, son, I'll not be the one to push it on ye so," Fitzgerald conceded, seeming annoyed. "But just ye consider what ye might be passin' up here before makin' such a rash decision!"

After that, they rode in silence, until the outline of a house suddenly loomed up before them. "Here we are," Fitzgerald said, as he led Dónal around back. "This is me place. 'Rural Home,' I call it, though 'twas never a good reason in it, really. I just like the sound of it so.

"Ye can hitch yeer ould one here," Fitzgerald said, as he dismounted and looped his reins over a hitching post. "I'll get Ol' Jess to see after 'em. Just give me a moment to scare him up."

After doing as directed, Dónal turned to the house for a better look. He was surprised at how small it was, having assumed that the largest plantation in the county would have a grand house to match. But it was scarcely larger than the old Fitzgerald homeplace at Lagganstown, to which it bore an uncanny resemblance, now that he considered it. Was it just coincidence, he wondered, or had the man chosen it for just that reason? Yet how so if the acquisition was indeed spurred by nothing more than his grabber's lust for land? Perhaps there was more to the story than he'd told, or more than he knew himself even. But in any case, Dónal could divine no more of it just then. All he knew for certain was that it seemed awfully small for such a large plantation, especially considering that a family of nine lived in it. No wonder the old man was so anxious to marry off his daughters.

Hearing Fitzgerald approach, he turned to find him coming out of the fog with a lantern in hand. "Ah, there ye are," he said, speaking not to Dónal, but to someone behind him.

Turning around, Dónal almost jumped out of his skin. There was a man standing not three feet away, though he'd heard not a whisper of his approach. He was old and bent, with kinky hair and beard growing in a white circle around his midnight face, while his grizzled features, stooped shoulders and gnarled hands bore testimony to the hard life he'd lived. And as he calmly gazed upon his master, awaiting his bidding with the patience of resignation, his eyes spoke of many years gone behind, of a lifetime of much sorrow and little joy. Yet there was strength in them, too, and even a hint of pride, the kind that comes from having endured the worst that life has to offer and yet having survived, even keeping a bit of human dignity in the process. Though set on African features, it was a look familiar to Dónal, one he'd seen occasionally in Ireland on the faces of miners and laborers, small farmers and fishermen, those men at the bottom whom life had yet failed to grind under its heel.

But if Phillip Fitzgerald saw it, he gave no indication. "Ol' Jess," he said in a tone of casual command, "see to the horses and then go straighten up the guesthouse. Fill the wood box and light a fire, and be sure to put extra blankets on the bed. Our Mr. O'Sullivan will be with us for a while and we want to be sure of his comfort."

"Yassuh, Mauzuh Fitz," Ol' Jess replied, his voice resonant and surprisingly clear. "Do dat be's all, suh?"

"Sure, 'tis," Fitzgerald replied dismissively. "Ye can go back to bed after."

"Yassuh. G'night, Mauzuh Fitz. An' you, too, suh."

"Goodnight to you, as well," Dónal replied, though the man had already turned away.

Fitzgerald watched him disappear into the fog, shaking his head. "Sure, if he isn't gettin' uppity in his old age."

"Why do you call him that, 'Ol' Jess,' I mean?"

"Buggered if I know. I bought him with the farm and 'tis the name he come with. Anyway, what difference does it make? He's just a darkie."

"He's a human being, for Christ's sake!"

"Sure, if ye say so. But come on. Let's get out o' the cold before we catch our death of it. There's a drink and a fire waitin' inside."

Though under other circumstances Dónal would've argued the point, he allowed it to pass, remembering that the reason he'd come here was now separated from him only by the thin walls of the house. Would she be waiting up for her husband, he wondered, as he followed him up the steps? Would he indeed get to see her tonight or would he have to wait till morning, each hour between an eternity in Purgatory? She was there in his mind's eye as they passed through the door into a narrow hallway, her beauty transcending the years and miles to be as fresh and new as when the old daguerreotype was first taken. And as they came to the parlor, he felt his heartbeat quicken at the sight of a woman standing by the fire, only to be disappointed upon realizing it wasn't her. Rather, it was a young woman about his own age, one of

Fitzgerald's daughters from the look of her, having his same blue eyes, short stature and blond hair, though she was also decidedly more attractive. Seeing that she was dressed only in a long robe over her night things, Dónal stopped short, not wanting to intrude on her modesty. Yet she paid him no heed, just rushed into her father's open arms.

"Papa!" she exclaimed dramatically. "Oh, Papa, I'm just ever so glad you're home!"

"Ah, now, if it isn't me darlin' dear, me precious Annie waitin' up for me so!" Fitzgerald said, bussing her cheek. "And how are ye, a storeen? Did ye miss me?"

"Oh yes, Papa, just ever so much!" she replied without a trace of Irish in her voice, another child of the Diaspora who'd never set foot on her native soil. "Why, I cried myself to sleep every night wishin' you'd hurry up and come on home! It seemed like you were gone for just ever so long!"

"'Twas only four days, girl, not the four years yeer whingin' would make of it!" Fitzgerald admonished, though his smile left no doubt that it was music to his ears.

"Well, it seemed like years to me, Papa, and then Mama wouldn't let me wait up for you," she whined, her lip quivering at being so mistreated. "But I just couldn't go to sleep without seein' you. I just couldn't! So I came downstairs when I heard you outside, just to tell you how happy I am that you're back. Did you miss me, too, Papa?"

"Why, no, I didn't, not one little bit."

"Oh, now, Papa, don't you tease me like that! You know I just go to pieces when you do!"

"Annie, me dear, me darlin' Annie," Fitzgerald lilted, cradling her face lovingly in his hands. "'Twill be the day Gabriel blows his horn, the day ye go to pieces over anything! Now I thank ye for yeer fond welcome, princess, but I know that sour face ye put on when ye're short of sleep. So get yeerself up to bed so we'll have none of it tomorrow."

"Yes, Papa," Annie replied, dropping her eyes coyly. But then without raising her head, she gave her father a queer sort of sideways look, one that set alarm bells ringing in Dónal's head. "But, Papa. Didn't you bring me anything from Savannah?"

"Why, Anne Elizabeth, and here I was after thinkin' ye'd never ask! I did bring ye a wee somethin' as a matter o' fact."

"Oh, Papa, I knew you would!" Annie exclaimed, clapping her hands and smiling gleefully, though the look in her eyes reminded Dónal of nothing so much as a hungry fox. "What is it? Let me see!"

"Let's see now, where did I put it?" Fitzgerald replied, patting his pockets as though he couldn't remember, until she was fairly hopping with impatience. "Ah, 'tis here!"

Slowly then, he pulled the old St. Christopher's from his pocket and dangled it before her. And though it glinted in the firelight, the gleam went out of her eyes.

"Why, Papa, whatever is that old thing?" she asked disdainfully, as though he'd offered her a wooden penny.

"Why, 'tis an heirloom of our family, Annie, the Fitzgeralds of Lagganstown in the County Tipperary. Sure, 'tis the very St. Christopher's me father brought back from France after The '98. See his initials carved into the back, 'J F' for James Fitzgerald? 'Twas almost forty years since I'd seen it meself, it comin' to me just yesterday in Savannah. But here now. Why the sour puss? Don't ye like it?"

"Why, of course I like it, Papa. I like all the presents you bring me. But it's just that . . . well, it's just that I thought maybe this time you'd bring me that string of pearls you promised me, so I could wear them to the Christmas ball in Atlanta. You know how much it means to me!" She lowered her eyes then, and her lip quivered as if she would cry. "You gave Mamie pearls for her birthday this year, and you know my birthday is just before the ball! Now Mamie will get to wear hers and I won't have any. It's not fair, Papa, it's just not fair!"

Placing his fingertips under her chin, Fitzgerald brought her face up so he could look her in the eyes, which were indeed glistening with tears. "Now look here, Annie. 'Tis no callin' for it. I've made it perfectly clear there'll be no pearls till yeer twenty-first birthday – which as ye well know is how old Mamie is – or until ye marry, whichever comes first. So ye'd no call to get yeer hopes up like that, seein' that ye haven't a serious suitor and are eighteen this year. And please, Annie, don't be jealous of our poor Mamie. Let her have her moment in the sun. Yeer day will come, so it will. So dry up them tears now and be thankful for what yeer given. 'Tis but nothin' I brought yeer sisters, after all."

At that, the look in Annie's eyes changed from petulant to wolfish as she took the medal from his hand. "Oh, Papa, thank you," she said, throwing her arms around him again. "Thank you so much for thinkin' of me. You just don't know how much it means to me!"

"Ah, sure, Annie, I think I do. Indeed, I know exactly what it means to ye. Ye're the child o' me heart, so ye are, and I know ye as well as I do me own self."

But Annie wasn't listening anymore, just eyeing the medal in her hands. "Is it silver, Papa?" she asked, trying to sound nonchalant, though not quite making it in Dónal's ears.

"'Tis indeed, though 'tis not worth terribly much, given the lack o' size that's in it."

"Oh, I see," Annie said, the petulance in her voice again before she could stifle it. "But however did you find it in Savannah after leavin' it behind those many years ago?"

"This fine young lad that's with me brought it. Me brother in Ireland give it to him, the one that still lives in the ould homeplace. And 'tis that what makes it so special, don't ye see, the connection to our family, to our roots that go back hundreds o' years in Ireland and even beyond, all the way to Italy and the Dukes o' Tuscany. So 'tis in the proud heritage it represents and not in money that its worth is to be found, a heritage ye should be proud of yeerself, and prouder still to pass on to yeer childer. For who knows, Annie, but that someday one of 'em might grow up to be famous, a great planter perhaps, a doctor or a bard, even President of the Confederacy, anything bein' possible in America. And though his name won't be Fitzgerald, 'tis one of our own he'll be, begob, and he'll have this to remind him of it!"

But Annie wasn't listening to him, her attention now on Dónal, taking in his rumpled clothes, uncombed hair and shadow of stubble, her cold, imperious look leaving no doubt that she wasn't favorably impressed. Yet he gave as good as he got, matching her unblinking stare with one of his own. She didn't scare him, not after Rhiannon, though he'd seen enough to know that wariness was warranted in dealing with her.

"'Twould appear that I'm forgettin' me manners again," Fitzgerald said, turning to Dónal. "Mr. Dónal O'Sullivan, please allow me to present me daughter, Miss Anne Elizabeth Fitzgerald."

"How do you do, Miss Fitzgerald," Dónal said, echoing the man's formality as he came forward and extended his hand.

But she just looked at it as if it were something disgusting. "A gentleman never takes a lady's hand unless she offers it first!" she said, her intended disdain coming off as hollow rote.

'The next time I see a lady, I'll remember that,' Dónal wanted to say, though he stifled the impulse. "Your pardon, Miss Fitzgerald, but you have me at a disadvantage. I'm a stranger in your country and unfamiliar with its customs. Please understand that I mean no offense, and bear with me while I learn."

"Well, that's awfully gallant of you, I'm sure," Annie replied, trying to sound lofty and superior. "But you're the one who has the advantage, sir. After all, I'm hardly dressed for receivin' guests, and a true gentleman would never have presented himself to me under such circumstances."

'And a true lady would've blushed and run at the first sight of me,' Dónal was about to say. But he was cut off by Fitzgerald, as it seemed that even he had had enough of her for the time being.

"Enough now, Annie!" he scolded. "Ye're bein' uncivil to our guest, and I'd not have him think our hospitality lackin'. I'll have ye know that Mr. O'Sullivan is a real Irish chieftain, and that he ran the blockade on a ship loaded with guns for our lads in the field. So ye should be treatin' him as an honored guest, instead o' fillin' his ear with highfalutin chat!"

"Oh, Papa," Annie chided playfully, trying to turn the thrust of his annoyance, "you sound just so positively *Irish* when you talk like that!"

"Sure, I am positively Irish," Fitzgerald retorted with a little heat in his voice, "and ye, too, despite yeer birth in exile! So ye just remember that, missy, or I'll give that wee trinket to Mamie instead. Now bid Mr. O'Sullivan a proper goodnight and be off with yeerself."

Though the threat was empty and they all knew it, it had its desired effect. "Yes, Papa. Whatever you say, Papa," she said, smiling sweetly. "But there's really no need to be cross about it."

Turning to Dónal, she extended her hand and did him a little curtsy. "A pleasant good evenin' to you, Mr. O'Sullivan," she said, gracing him with a smile as sweet as salt.

"And to you, Miss Fitzgerald," he replied, bowing slightly. "You'll excuse me for not shakin' your hand, but as a wise man once told me, *seachain lámh an alpaire, mar ní chneasta a bhíonn sé riamh.*"

"Why, sir, whatever did you say to me?" she asked, blinking in surprise.

"Beware the graspin' hand, for 'tis never gracious," he replied with a wolfish grin. "'Tis an old sayin' we have in Ireland, and I used our native tongue so you'd know what bein' Irish *really* sounds like!"

"Well, I *never!*" Annie exclaimed, so taken off guard that she actually blushed. But then her eyes narrowed dangerously, and she gathered herself like a coiling snake, though her father stepped between them before she could strike.

"Sure, 'tis a rare piece o' wisdom, Annie," he said, "one that ye'd be well advised to remember. But 'tis past time ye were asleep and dreamin'. So give us a kiss, and then off to bed with ye."

"But Papa—"

"No buts about it, girl! Give us the kiss and then off!"

"All right, Papa." She sighed and kissed him lightly on the cheek before turning away. But at the doorway, she paused. "I'll see you in the mornin', Mr. O'Sullivan," she said, just to let him know she wasn't giving in so easily.

"'Tis a pleasure to which I look forward, Miss Fitzgerald," he replied brightly, just to let her know she didn't scare him.

"Oh, no, sir. The pleasure will be mine!" And then she was gone, her footsteps on the creaky stairs all the warmth she left behind.

"Ah, sure, if that girl isn't too much sometimes for even me," Fitzgerald sighed, shaking his head. "And aren't ye the one, makin' her blush so? 'Tis a rare feat ye accomplished, though there'll be hell to pay, or I'm a darkie."

"She's just a young one so," Dónal said, and shrugged. "She'll forget it by mornin'."

"Son, that girl never forgets anything, especially a slight! Not to say she didn't have it comin', but she'll go to the Divil before she takes it lyin' down. Sure, my Annie's a caution, so she is, and though I love her dearly, she's sure to make some poor fellah very unhappy one of these days. Very unhappy indeed!"

Though he said nothing, Dónal couldn't have agreed more. He was just glad it wasn't himself going in harm's way, for given a chance, that young Lilith would suck a man dry and dance on his bones.

"Ah, well," Fitzgerald sighed. "She will do as she will and there's naught to be done about it now. So make yeerself at home while I pour us a drink."

With that, he turned to the sideboard that stood along the central wall and busied himself with a decanter and glasses. As he did, Dónal took the opportunity to glance around the room, noting that while the size and shape of the house might resemble the one in Lagganstown, the similarity ended there. For excepting the hearth and chimney, this house was constructed entirely of wood, and was elegantly appointed with expensive-looking furnishings, which though neither showy nor conspicuous in style, were definitely of the highest quality. Also, there was an extensive library of books housed in matching bookcases along the back wall, so many that some were stacked on their tops as well. Scattered about on the end tables and mantle were various knick-knacks and *objets d'art*, a crystal decanter and glasses, a china bowl, a grandfather clock, the types of things that finish a room and give it personality.

Yet of everything in the room, it was the portrait above the mantle that held his attention, her eyes gazing into his own as though they were blind to all else. She was older than in the daguerreotype, surely, though the years had only enhanced her beauty, adding wisdom and empathy to her goddess-perfect features. However did such an angel end up with an ould goat for a husband and that devil-child for a daughter? he wondered.

"I'm a lucky man, so I am," Fitzgerald said, as if hearing his thoughts.

"Indeed so, Mr. Fitzgerald," Dónal acknowledged softly, "for surely she is beauty itself."

"Careful now, son," Fitzgerald admonished gently. "A jealous man would take umbrage to such a frank appraisal of his wife. But no, I'm not the one for it. For as lovely as she is to look upon, her heart is lovelier still, and I know it beats only for me, ould and ugly as I am. So admire her as much as ye want. I can respect the good sense that's in it."

Seeing the love in the old man's eyes as he gazed upon the portrait, Dónal was suddenly ashamed of himself, for his covetous feelings surely, though more so for thinking they could ever be returned. 'What in God's name am I doing here?' he wondered.

"I'm sorry, Mr. Fitzgerald," he said. "I meant no disrespect."

"I know ye didn't, son," the man replied, handing Dónal a full glass. "But here now. Let's have our drop and be off to bed ourselves. The mornin' comes early around here, and we've already a head start on it. Cheers!"

"*Sláinte*," Dónal replied, and drained his glass. "Sure, if that isn't itself in the flesh. 'Tis the native stuff, is it?"

"No, son, 'tis Tennessee parliament whiskey, the best the South has to offer," Fitzgerald replied, refilling their glasses from the crystal decanter. "The local poteen is known as 'white lightnin'.' Ye'll know it for the bite that's in it, like the Earl o' Hell's lash, so it is."

"Then I look forward to a good beatin'," Dónal said with a grin. "*Sláinte!*"

"I'd be careful what I wished for if I was ye. Cheers."

"Ah, yes," Fitzgerald continued after draining his glass. "I'd offer ye more, but that herself doesn't hold with havin' drink taken in the house, except on formal occasions, as which I'm not sure this would qualify. Anyway, I've had me fill o' the day that's in it. So come along and I'll show ye to yeer cottage. Ol' Jess should have it ready by now."

Fitzgerald led the way then, and Dónal shivered as the damp night air bit through his clothes. But the cottage being close by, he was inside again soon enough.

"Here we are," Fitzgerald said as he closed the door. "I think ye'll find it accommodatin' enough. 'Twas the house o' me late brother, Michael, God rest him."

Dónal saw that the place was indeed homey enough, being sturdy, dry and warm, especially with a wood fire roaring in the small grate. And while the furnishings weren't up to the quality of those in the house, they were certainly more than adequate, especially the big bed with its heavy quilts and feather pillow. There were even oil lamps on the table and nightstand, and a mirror and razor for shaving, so he could at least make himself presentable when he met *her* in the morning. Indeed, it would do quite nicely, he decided, for surely he'd had worse.

"Since it looks to be in order, I'll leave it with ye," Fitzgerald said. "Breakfast is at seven sharp. Don't be a slug-a-bed or ye'll miss it!"

"Goodnight, Mr. Fitzgerald, and thank you for your hospitality."

"'Tis a pleasure, son. And sure, if it isn't good to have another man about the place again. Goodnight to ye now."

Dónal closed the door and went to warm himself by the fire. But just as he was about to settle in, there came a knock at the door.

"Come in, Mr. Fitzgerald," he said. "I'm still decent."

Yet it wasn't Fitzgerald who entered, but Ol' Jess. "Oh, hello, Ol' Jess," he said, rising to greet him. "I'm glad you came back. Now I can thank you for settin' the place up for me, and introduce myself properly. My name is Dónal O'Sullivan, and 'tis my pleasure to meet you."

But Ol' Jess made no move to take his outstretched hand, didn't even look at it, just glared at Dónal with all the contempt one human being could muster for another. "I's not 'lowed to touch de white folks . . . *suh!*" he said proudly, as if it were beneath his dignity anyway. "It ain't fittin'!"

And though Dónal was taken aback by his hostility, he instinctively understood what he'd done to cause it. He'd reminded Ol' Jess of his

569

relative position in life, that he was a black man, a member of an 'inferior' race, a slave, and even though he'd meant just the opposite, in so doing he'd insulted the human dignity the man had struggled so hard to maintain.

"I'm sorry, Ol' Jess," he said, with all the sincerity he could muster. "I didn't know. I'm new here and don't know the way of things yet. But please believe me that I meant you no offense."

"Yassuh," Ol' Jess replied simply, though whether it meant his apology was accepted, Dónal couldn't tell. At least the look in his eyes softened, and the contempt was gone. Still, he knew that an unbridgeable chasm lay between them, that protest as he might that he wasn't one of *those* white men, there was just too much water under Ol' Jess's bridge for him to ever trust Donal.

For a long moment neither of them spoke, until Dónal realized the man was waiting to be spoken to before speaking himself, that he was following the rules of the society he lived in, rules Dónal better learn himself and quickly if he wished to avoid another embarrassing *faux pas*.

"Was there somethin' you wanted to ask me, Ol' Jess?" he asked.

"Yassuh, dere is, if'n dass all right wit' you."

"Sure, I don't mind. Ask me anything you want."

"Yassuh. Well suh, I's just wonderin' if'n you's gwine be de new oberseer?"

"I'm sorry, what did you say?" Dónal asked, unable to cut through the accent and dialect.

"I said, is you gwine be de new oberseer?" Ol' Jess repeated, speaking more slowly. "You know, de new boss man."

"Oh, I see," Dónal replied, though he had no idea what an *oberseer* was. "No, I'm not. I'm just here for a visit, that's all."

"Yassuh."

"Is there anything else?" Dónal asked after a moment.

"Nawsuh, dass it."

"Well, if that's it, then I'll say goodnight to you now," Dónal said, understanding that the man was waiting to be dismissed. "I'm sure you're as anxious to get to bed as I am."

"Yassuh. G'night, suh."

When he was gone, Dónal stared at the door for a long moment, before sighing and shaking his head.

"What kind of a world are these people living in?" he said in Irish.

chapter 30

Rural Home Plantation
Clayton County, Georgia

OH GOD, WHAT HAVE I DONE? *he shrieked, as the darkness enveloped him and the cold stopped his heart, burning his skin with the Fire of Damnation.* Oh, God, if you'll just let me go back and change it! *he wailed as he sank into the abyss, the weight of his sins leaden upon his soul, the pain a dagger in his heart. But it was too late and he knew it; there was no going back and no forgiveness of sins, no deliverance from the Darkness within. And deeper it pulled him, and deeper, the well of his despair bottomless and insatiable, a hunger devouring him from within. But just when all hope left him, he heard a voice in the void, sweet and seductive.* Come to me! *it sang, ever so softly.* Come, and let me ease your pain! *And turning toward it he saw a beckoning hand, fair and feminine, a slender lifeline in this sea of ruin.* Yes, oh, yes, oh, God yes! *he cried, reaching out to it.* Take it away, oh, please, take it away! *And there she was before him, her angelic beauty a beacon in the Darkness, her smile a promise of warmth, relief, redemption.* I love you! *he wept, his tears a fountain of fealty.* I know you do, *she sang, pulling him deeper, deeper, ever deeper.* I know you do . . .

⌒⫘⫘⫘⊙

"Mistuh O'Sullibun?" a voice called softly. "Mistuh O'Sullibun? Is you awake, Mistuh O'Sullibun?"

Blinking his eyes, Dónal saw a face hovering above him in the dim light of morning, reddish-haired and green-eyed, though with African features and brown skin, the curious mix finished by a patch of reddish freckles splattered across his broad nose.

"*Cé tusa?*" he asked, forgetting himself in his drowsiness.

"I's sorry, suh, but I don't know none dat Jew-man talk."

"I'm sorry myself. I forgot where I was for a moment. I just asked who you are."

"Yassuh, I sees it now," the man said, flashing an infectious smile. "I's Yellah Joe, is who I is."

"*Yellow* Joe, is it now? And why do they call you that?"

"On account'a I bein' a high yellah an' all, de which of it be's dat I got light skin, if'n you don't already know what it mean. Jawdan's de name what my Mammy done give me, just like de ribber in de Bible. 'Course now, don't nobody be callin' me dat no mo' since she done died, 'cept fo' de Mizzy Fitz, dat is."

"I see," Dónal said, taking note of the fact that the man was just slightly older than himself and extraordinarily tall, having a few inches on Padge even. "Well, my name is Dónal O'Sullivan, and I'd offer to shake your hand, but that it seems to be against the rules around here."

"Yassuh, dass right, leastways 'tween de white folks an' de colored folks, dough I do shakes de hands of de other colored fellahs when-some-ever I meets 'em. And sho', if'n dat don't happen a lot now dat Mauzuh Fitz done made me de carriage driber. 'Course, everybody done already know who I is on account'a I bein' de tallest fellah in de whole county, colored or white."

"Sure, I can see how that could be," Dónal said, wondering why he always attracted the chatty ones. "How tall are you, anyway? Do you know?"

"Yassuh, I sho' do. I's siss feets an' nine inches tall, an' I know's I is 'cause dey done measure me once 'pon a time when de fair come to town an' all de farmers brung in dey prize animals for judgin', and den dey done 'cide while dey's at it dey gwine give a prize for de biggest nigra, too. An' sho', if'n Mauzuh Fitz don't be so happy over winnin' dat prize dat he don't give me de table scraps fo' my supper!"

"Well, you're sure the tallest man I've ever met. I've a friend back in Ireland who comes close, but you've a couple of inches on even him, I'd say. And speakin' of Ireland, you wouldn't happen to be part Irish yourself, now would you?"

"Nawsuh, leastways not dat I be knowin' nothin' 'bout," Yellah Joe replied, seeming puzzled.

"Sure, I suppose not," Dónal said, fearing he'd made another *faux pas*. "With your red hair, I just thought you might be, which is why I asked."

"Wellsuh, now I is a half-breed, if'n dass what you mean. My Daddy was a Scotchman, name o' MacIntosh or some such, dough it don't make no diff'rence none, seein's how I can't use no last name noways. He be's de oberseer on de farm where I's born at, an' dass where I done got my talls from an' my red hair, too, was from him. 'Course now, I don't 'member much else 'bout 'im, bein's I's just a littl'un when de mauzuh done sol' me off'n dat farm. Dat was after my Mammy done died, an' he didn't had no use fo' no li'l yard chirrens what didn't had no Mammies."

"How old were you when that happened?"

"Wellsuh, I don't rightly know, bein's I ain't never learned to count none. But ol' Benjie now, he 'speck I's two maybe t'ree when dat happ'm. He reckon I's 'bout twenty-fo' now, twenty-fi' mebbe, goin' on how many summers I can 'member. But shoot, knowin' how many years ol' you is don't matter none if'n you can't count de nex' 'uns noways. An' dass what I keep tellin' 'im, too, dat it don't make no diff'rence to a slave none, bein' dat one year be's de same as de nex', an' it de same as de nex'n after dat, till one day you's done dead an' gone an' don't nobody even 'member you's been here."

Suddenly realizing that his words might give offense to his master, a worried look came over Yellah Joe's face. "I's sorry fo' sayin' dat, Mistuh O'Sullibun. I didn't mean nothin' by it. De Mauzuh Fitz be takin' real good care of us an' I ain't got no cause to be fussin' 'bout it none. It's just dat you be's real easy to talk to fo' a white man, an' I done fo'got my place fo' a minute. So you ain't gwine tell 'im, now is you?"

"No, of course not. What you say to me will stay just between us, and I give you my word on it so. And anyway, I didn't think you were complainin'. I just thought you were tellin' the truth."

"Yassuh, dass what I's doin', all right. But sometimes de troof ain't what a colored man ought'a be tellin', if'n he know what's good fo' 'im, 'specially when he be talkin' to a white man."

"Really? And here I've always heard that honesty is the best policy."

"Yassuh, I 'speck it is fo' y'all white folks." Then a mischievous grin crossed Yellah Joe's face. "But if'n you don't mind me sayin' so, Mistuh O'Sullibun, it sho' seem like you got a lot to learn 'bout some things."

"So people keep tellin' me, Yellah Joe. Or would you rather I call you Jordan?"

"Nawsuh, I don't reckon so. Like I said, de Mizzy Fitz be's de only one what call me dat, an' if'n you won't tell nobody I said so, I kind'a likes it dat way."

"Oh, and why is that? Don't you like the name?"

"Yassuh, I likes it fine. It's just dat I likes it even mo' dat she be's de only one what calls me it."

"Oh, I see. You like it that it's her special name for you, is that what you're sayin'? Are you fond of her then?"

"Yassuh, we's all be likin' de Mizzy Fitz, 'cause of de way she be lookin' after us so good. She be's finer'n ah-ree angel, she do. Course, you already know's dat, now don't you, Mistuh O'Sullibun?"

"I've heard it said on occasion, to be sure, though I've yet to meet her in person. I only just arrived from Ireland on Wednesday, and I just met Mr. Fitzgerald for the first time on Thursday night. But I'll meet her at breakfast, and then–"

"Oh, lawdy, lawd, lawd!" Yellah Joe interjected, slapping a hand to his forehead. "Here we been talkin' all dis time an' I done fo'got dat Mauzuh Fitz done sent me out here to get you up fo' breakfast. He gwine be madder den ah-ree rattlesnake if'n you be's late!"

"Not to worry, Yellah Joe. I'll tell him it was my fault. But if you could get me some hot water for shavin' while I dress, that would speed things up a bit."

"Yassuh, I do dat fo' you, an' I be quick 'bout it, too! Oh, an' yo' clothes be hangin' dere in de chest. Mauzah Fitz done had Bessie May give 'em a good pressin' fo' you while you's sleepin'. Do dere be's anythin' else you be needin' 'sides de water?"

"No, Yellah Joe, that's it. And thanks for everything."

"Yassuh," Yellah Joe said, ducking his head at the door. "I be back right now in a minute."

Dónal stared after him for a moment, shaking his head in wonder. What a breath of fresh air he was after the reticence of Ol' Jess, a smiling giant with not a mean bone in his body, so good-natured that the insults life so abundantly heaped upon him seemed to slide off like rain from a duck's arse. And yet he was so shackled by the rules of this twisted society that he wasn't free even to tell the simple truth. It was shocking to contemplate, and deplorable, and incredibly sad.

"What kind of a world are these people living in?" he again wondered aloud.

⊙παιϘ

Dónal shivered as the cold air hit him, freezing the hairs in his nose and his breath into a cloud, even as the frost-covered ground crunched underfoot. But it wasn't the cold that was on his mind just then, or even the clear blue sky with its promise of warmth to come. Rather, he was busy taking in his surroundings, finding the land open to the horizon in every direction, the trees having been cleared for farms and pasturage, leaving only a druid's circle of oaks around the house as a reminder of the forest that had once been. Turning in a slow circle, he saw that just beyond his own cabin stood a jumbled cluster of smaller ones, the dwellings of the slaves judging by the many Negroes in view, set so close together as to almost touch, a sort of wood-frame version of the ubiquitous Irish *clochán*. Indeed, it brought to mind old Cahernageeha and the cottages in its lee, huddling together for mutual protection, a peasant's ringfort against a darkening world. Not that it would do them any good, any more than the *clochán* had done his neighbors. For, like the Irish, the Africans had been conquered by a people more cunning and culturally mature, suffering centuries of subjugation and exploitation as a result. Indeed, the parallel was so obvious and compelling, that Dónal wondered how any Irishman could ever condemn a fellow human being to such a dehumanizing existence. And yet as he turned around, the reality of it was right there, Phillip Fitzgerald standing in the back doorway of his Big House, surveying his domain with the proud eye of the conqueror. And sure if the house didn't deserve to be classified as such, though it was but a poor relation to the Big House of Dunboy, for it dominated its surroundings with the same air of military occupation, as though besieged by the hostility of the bondsmen living in its shadow. It even looked a bit like a tower house, standing tall and angular, its unpainted clapboard siding weathered to a stone gray, its draped windows turned defensively inward.

'Can you not see what you're doing?' Dónal's mind shouted at Fitzgerald. 'Are you indeed so blind?' But he kept the thought to himself as he hurried up the steps.

"I'm sorry if I'm late, Mr. Fitzgerald," he said aloud. "I hope I didn't keep you waitin' so."

"Not to worry, son, ye're right on time," the man replied brightly. "I sent Yellah Joe out early, knowin' him for his gift o' gab as I do. Sure, if that darkie wouldn't talk the ears off a corpse. But here now, turn around with ye. I've somethin' to show ye."

Doing as asked, Dónal saw what had put the gleam in the man's eyes and the thrill in his voice, the land of Clayton County spread out before him like a feast for the gods. It was a profound sight, he had to admit, one that touched him in much the same way as Knockgraffon had, though the feelings were entirely impersonal. Indeed, with the morning sunlight flashing on the Flint River as it meandered through the rolling country below, it even looked a bit like South Tipperary, erasing any further doubt about Fitzgerald choosing this place for its resemblance to his Irish home. It wasn't identical, surely, having no mountains like the Galtys to foreshorten the view, no Celtic knot of stone walls, no crumbling fortresses and no thatched cottages trailing their ubiquitous streams of turf smoke. And, of course, the soil was Georgia red rather than peat black. Yet it was close enough that forty years of separation and twenty of familiarity must surely have eroded those differences from Fitzgerald's memory.

"There it is," the man said softly, "me pride and me joy, the verdant fields of Rural Home. And ain't ye after seein' it at the right time o' day, when the soft mornin' light turns it all misty and golden, like the landscape of a dream."

At those words, Dónal turned his eyes from the land to the old man next to him. It was true as he'd said that he was no poet, and yet he was possessed of such profound appreciation for beauty in all its forms. So how was it possible that he could propagate something as brutally ugly as the slave *clochán*, which was also part of the vista before him? But then he remembered something Seán Ahern had said long ago, on a rainy afternoon spent by the fire discussing Homer's classics. The reason Odysseus was so believable as a character, he'd said, was that Homer had made him so completely human, imbuing him with all the contradictions that real people are composed of, so that he came off as neither completely good nor completely evil, just as an average man doing his best to survive in a cold hard world.

As comprehension dawned on him then, Dónal blinked his eyes in unwanted revelation. For if it was true that human beings were just one big tangle of contradiction, how could he expect Phillip Fitzgerald to be any different? Indeed, how could he expect *himself* to be any different? It was something that hadn't occurred to him before, that maybe he was holding himself up to an impossible standard, trying to be Achilles, when Odysseus was the best any man could ever hope for. And yet . . . and yet, where did one draw the line? For surely it was possible to be more good than evil, but once the compromise was made, what was there to keep a man from tumbling into the pit of Darkness?

As he thought about it, his eyes strayed back to the slave *clochán*, to the men and women there who had no choice in life beyond their master's dictates, who weren't even free to tell the truth. Comparing the life they lived with his own made him feel foolish for even thinking such thoughts. No, wrong was wrong, he decided then, and it was better to aspire to a higher standard, even if it couldn't always be met. But then, how was one to reconcile failure, since doing so would in itself be a compromise? And how did one live with the guilt?

"See, son?" Fitzgerald said, interpreting his silence for awe. "This is what's possible in America, even for an Irish Catholic, and 'tis itself the reason our future is here."

Though there was great pride in his voice as he trumpeted his accomplishments, in that moment Dónal saw in him only a strong farmer self-made into minor gentry by exploiting other men. And though Fitzgerald would surely have argued the point, he was really no different in that regard from the Anglo-Ascendancy in Ireland, men who lorded over stolen land and exploited the natives to their own advantage. Indeed, had he accumulated such holdings there, he'd likely be the last to even live on it. His children, or at best his grandchildren, would be off to Dublin or London to live the good life and recite the myths of their glorious past. *Yes,* they would say, *we're descended from the Earls of Desmond, don't you know, and of course all our men were educated at Trinity. And since grandfather actually grew up in France, why, we're not really Irish at all.* Indeed, who knew that it wouldn't happen here?

"Sure, Mr. Fitzgerald, that may be true enough for you," he said, "and yet you choose to live in a place that looks remarkably like the home you left behind. Now why is that, do you suppose? Is it merely nostalgia, as you say, or is it because deep down inside you'd really rather be there than here?"

Fitzgerald didn't answer for a long moment, just stared up at Dónal with a curious look on his face. "Does it really matter? 'Tis a cold hard fact that I'm here and that I'm never goin' back. So in the heel o' the hunt, does it really matter?"

"No, I suppose not, practically speakin'. But just don't patronize me any more by tryin' to deny your feelin's for Ireland! They're as much a part of you as your father and mother, somethin' you can no more escape than you can walk on water, and I can see them in everything about you."

"Ye don't miss much, do ye, son?" Fitzgerald asked, his eyes narrowing appraisingly.

"No sir, I don't," Dónal replied, perhaps a little too readily.

"No, I'd say not." Then Fitzgerald smiled, and took Dónal affectionately by the arm. "Come inside now, and meet herself and the young ones."

Following his host into the house then, Dónal saw that his womenfolk were waiting for them in the dining room, all dressed in their Sunday best and lined up as though to receive an honored guest.

"Ah, here they are so," Fitzgerald said brightly. "Ladies, allow me to present the honorable Mr. Dónal O'Sullivan, late o' the County Cork in the Kingdom of Ireland, himself bein' chieftain o' the Clan of O'Sullivan Béara and hereditary Lord o' Béara and Bantry, on top o' which he's also a hero o' the Confederacy, havin' served as an officer aboard the CSS *Fingal*, the ship that ran the blockade while I was in Savannah. Mr. O'Sullivan, please allow me to present me daughters, whose names I'll get to presently, and me wife, Mrs. Eleanor Avaline McGhan Fitzgerald."

"Welcome to Rural Home, Mr. O'Sullivan," Eleanor said, extending her hand. "It is a pleasure to make your acquaintance after all the nice things my husband has said about you. Please make yourself at home and stay with us as long as you'd like."

Taking her hand, Dónal bowed formally, his heart racing at her touch and his mind in a whirl. She was everything his imagination had made of her and more, for he couldn't have imagined her voice like liquid silver or the silken touch of her hand, the luminosity of her pale Irish skin or the halo of her golden hair, shimmering in the light of the window behind her. And though the blush of youth was indeed long gone, she was the more beautiful for the dignity and poise brought by maturity. Looking deeply into her eyes of Irish blue, he searched for a sign that she found him beautiful, too. But what he found instead surprised him and moved him to pity, for though she'd buried it deep within, out of sight of the casual observer, Dónal yet saw the abiding sadness that was in her. Indeed, it was a look he'd seen before, in the eyes of his own mother, that of a woman whose heart had been broken slowly, one unfulfilled dream at a time. It touched the romantic in him and, just as with Sióna, made him want to wrap her in his arms and shield her from whatever it was that made her sad, fighting to the death if that's what it took to make her happy.

"No, Mrs. Fitzgerald," he said, straining to keep his voice steady, "the pleasure is mine, and the honor, too. For though your beauty out-shines even the ability of Oisín to describe, 'tis yet transcended by that of your heart."

His words brought a blush to her cheeks and a look of surprise to her eyes, even as her daughters tittered behind her. "Why, Mr. O'Sullivan," she said, laying a hand over her heart, "I do think you mean to flatter me."

"No, ma'am," Dónal assured her, bowing his head. "'Tis no flattery in the truth."

"Well, now, I don't quite know what to say," she remarked, the silvery tones of her soft Southern accent a symphony in his ears, "except that of all the things my husband said about you, he never once mentioned your silver tongue. But I do thank you for your chivalrous compliment and ask your forgiveness for my unseemly bashfulness. It's just that we're not accustomed to such courtly European manners here in our little backwoods community."

"I'm afraid it's I who must ask for pardon, Mrs. Fitzgerald. I fear I've been too forward in my speech when only good intentions were in my heart."

"There is no need," she replied, gracing him with a gentle sad smile. "Though I may not know much of the world beyond my own little corner of it, I do know a gentleman when I see one."

"Ma'am," he said humbly, dropping his eyes, and forcing himself to release her hand.

Tearing himself away from her then, he knelt on one knee, so as to be face to face with the smaller children. "And you must be young Izzie," he said to the smallest, a bundle of freckles and strawberry curls, who blushed and hid her face in her mother's skirts.

"And 'tis our Katie, the next one," Fitzgerald said, taking up the roll.

"*Dia dhuit, a Chaitlín*," Dónal said, taking her small hand in his. "'Tis Irish, if you'd know, and it means, 'God be with you, Katie.' 'Tis how we say 'hello' in Ireland."

"You have *awfully* pretty eyes," she replied, speaking her mind as only children can, before giggling and hiding her face in her hands.

"Why, thank you, Katie. You're awfully pretty yourself."

Next came Dellie, who at nine was a bit bolder than her younger sisters. "How do you do, Mr. O'Sullivan," she said, doing him a little curtsy.

Then came twelve-year-old Sadie, who was by far the prettiest, having inherited her mother's beauty undiluted by her father's lack of it. "Welcome to Rural Home, Mr. O'Sullivan," she said, her voice lilting with the same silvery tones as her mother's.

"*Go raibh míle maith agat, bean uí Ghearailt, as ucht d'fháilte chaoi,*" Dónal replied, bowing slightly at the waist. "A thousand thanks for your gracious welcome, Miss Fitzgerald."

The girl smiled at him, in a coy sort of way that told him his impression on her, at least, was favorable. 'Give that one a few years and she'll break every heart in the county,' he thought, returning her smile before moving on.

Next came Agnes, who at fifteen had already blossomed into a young woman. She wasn't as pretty as Sadie, but she had sparkling eyes and the look of wit about her. "Will you teach me to speak Irish, Mr. O'Sullivan?" she asked after their introduction.

"'Twould be a pleasure, Miss Fitzgerald, though I'll warn you 'tis not an easy language for native English speakers to learn."

"That's all right, I'm not afraid of a challenge," she assured him, her eyes dancing with mischief. "After all, I live in the same house with Annie!"

"Shut up, you!" Annie hissed, elbowing her and glaring at her snickering sisters.

"Mind your manners now, girls!" Eleanor admonished, bringing a chorus of, "Yes, Mama," from the offenders. Still, Agnes favored him with a wink and a grin, before he turned to Annie.

"Miss Fitzgerald," he said simply, bowing his head.

"Mr. O'Sullivan," she sighed, her look of studied boredom leaving no doubt as to what she thought of the whole production. Yet he noticed she was wearing the St. Christopher's prominently outside her blouse, as though it were suddenly her most prized possession. How she must've lorded it over her sisters, he thought, that their father had chosen her to have the family heirloom. No wonder for Agnes's gibe.

Finally then, Dónal came to Mary Ellen, the eldest daughter and presumably the reason he'd been invited here. At twenty-one, she was fully a woman and in her prime for marriage, though upon seeing her, he understood why her father might be willing to stretch a bit in finding her a match. Unfortunately, she'd gotten very little of her mother's beauty, being plain and somewhat mousy in appearance, which she didn't help with her dowdy dress and hairstyle. Yet she wasn't downright ugly, and surely there were plenty of men who could do worse, especially considering what her father had to offer in the way of a dowry. But then her field of choice didn't necessarily include all those men, being artificially constricted by her elevated social status and the fact that she was a Catholic in a Protestant country, and with most of the eligible men away at war anyway, her options for a "suitable" match were probably quite limited. So all things considered, it no longer seemed so odd that her father had lit upon him as a possibility, especially since he thought him a "young man of prospects."

"And this is our Mary Ellen," Fitzgerald said, his intentions betrayed by the inflection of his voice, "though we're after callin' her 'Mamie' amongst ourselves."

'Even her nickname is dowdy,' Dónal thought, as he took her outstretched hand. "How do you do, Miss Fitzgerald," he said, bowing informally as he had with the other girls.

"Mr. O'Sullivan," she replied softly, giving his hand but a brief squeeze before pulling hers back and dropping her eyes.

There was a moment of silence then, as Dónal waited for her to say something else or at least to look at him. But she did neither, just stood there looking at the floor, until he felt compelled to say something, *anything*, to relieve the awkwardness. Her discomfiture was so painful to behold that he felt sorry for her, especially since every eye in the place was fixed critically upon her, silently impelling her toward a good impression.

"'Tis very nice to meet you, Miss Fitzgerald," he said finally, and then struggled for something else. But what could he say, really, being caught between the rock of having to treat her neutrally so as not to lead her on, and the hard place of not hurting her feelings or offending his hosts? Not that she gave him any openings for either.

But it was Fitzgerald who came to the rescue, having the good sense not to push it all at once. "Well, now that we've the pleasantries out o' the way," he said brightly, rubbing his hands together, "let's get to the business at hand."

Taking Dónal by the elbow, he led him to the seat just to the right of his own at the head of the table. When they were all at their places, Eleanor at the far end and the girls alternating sides in descending order of age, Fitzgerald bowed his head and offered up the grace.

"Bless us, oh Lord," he intoned, "for these our gifts which we are about to receive from Thy bounty through Christ our Lord. Amen."

"Amen," they all chorused, and joined him in crossing themselves before taking their seats.

As soon as they were settled, two slave women came forward and began to serve them, setting out bowls of biscuits and butter, pouring glasses of fresh milk, and scooping scrambled eggs and fat bacon onto their plates, along with something that might've been porridge but for the whiteness of it. Feeling his stomach gnaw at him insistently, Dónal selected a spoon from the dizzying array of silverware by his plate and scooped up a bite of eggs. But hearing Fitzgerald clear his throat pointedly, he looked up to find him nodding at the other end of the table. Looking that way, he found all the girls staring at him while Eleanor regarded him with a curious sort of expression, something between pained and apologetic.

"If you don't mind, Mr. O'Sullivan," she said almost hesitantly, "we like to wait until everyone is served before beginning."

Noting her upright posture and the fact that her elbows weren't on the table, he put down his spoon and straightened himself in his chair. "Please accept my apology, Mrs. Fitzgerald, and you young ladies, as well. I've only recently come ashore from a month at sea, and my manners seem to be a bit tarnished from the salt air."

But before she could respond, Annie interjected from across the table, speaking to Sadie in a stage whisper as if continuing a conversation from before. "See? I told you he was just bog-Irish!"

"Why, Annie, what a perfectly horrid thing to say," Eleanor scolded. "Mr. O'Sullivan is our guest and I'd not have him think we're no better than white trash ourselves. Now you apologize to him right this very instant."

"Oh, Mama, now there's really no reason to be cross about it. I mean, what proof do we have that this man is all the things he says he is? And so what if he is, anyway? All those titles don't mean anything in America, and they surely don't make him a man of means or substance. Why he looks like a common Tinker, if you ask me, and he certainly has the manners of one. And after all, we all know the only reason Papa brought him here is because Mamie can't get any decent suitors on her own."

At the word "Tinker," a dead silence fell over the room, with even the slave women stopping in their tracks. Apparently, even these children of the Diaspora knew of the ill repute attached to Travelers. Yet, far from being insulted as Annie had intended, Dónal could've kissed her in that moment for taking him off the hook with Mamie, since neither of them could reasonably be expected to take the other seriously after that.

"Anne Elizabeth, that is quite enough," Eleanor said, keeping her voice even and calm. "No one asked for your opinion, young lady, and you have certainly done us no credit in offering it. Now you will apologize to Mr. O'Sullivan as I asked, and to your sister as well, or you will go to your room and stay there until you see fit to change your mind."

Knowing what he did of Annie, Dónal fully expected her to put up a fight, and indeed, she glanced at her father to see if he would come to her aid. But finding him pointedly ignoring her, having learned from harsh experience not to let her trap him in the middle, she decided to try another tack.

"Well now!" she said dramatically. "I really don't see why I should be punished for simply tellin' the truth. After all, that's what you and Papa have always taught me to do."

"You're not being punished for telling the truth, dear," Eleanor replied patiently. "You're being punished for your disturbing lack of tact and for your abiding insensitivity to the feelings of others. But then, whether you will be punished at all is really up to you, now isn't it? All you have to do is apologize as I asked, and all will be forgiven."

But Annie made no reply, just stared at her mother without a hint of contrition. "I see," Eleanor said after a moment. "Since you apparently lack both the decency and the courage to atone for your transgressions, then you will go to your room and stay there until you care to change your mind. Do I make myself clear, young lady?"

"Yes, Mama," Annie sighed, as though suddenly bored. Then she rose from her seat and sauntered from the room, her defiant footsteps on the stairs leaving no doubt as to her feelings. But it really was an amazing little display, Dónal reflected, for in the same breath, she'd drawn even with him and stolen the limelight from her sister, all while making a martyr of herself, at least in her own eyes.

"Ye think that's such a good idea, do ye, woman?" Fitzgerald asked when she was gone. "The last time she stayed up there for a week, and 'twas far harder on us than ever it was on her. And in the heel o' the hunt she gave us no satisfaction anyway."

"It was harder on you perhaps, husband," Eleanor retorted calmly, "and the reason she gave us no satisfaction is that you gave in to her! But yes, I do think it's a good idea. In fact, I think it's a grand idea. Someday that girl is going to have to learn some manners, and now is not too soon to start."

"What she really needs is a good *spanking*," Mamie opined heatedly, surprising everyone.

"'Twould be easier to give a bobcat a bath," Fitzgerald grunted, and turned to his breakfast, wisely giving up the field. For though Annie was his favorite, the one who would inherit the family totem and be chieftain after him, he had to sleep in the same bed with his wife, and no sensible man ever closed his eyes on an angry woman.

"Please accept our apology for our daughter's behavior, Mr. O'Sullivan," Eleanor said, "and for us airing our dirty laundry in your presence. I assure you that neither will happen again."

"No apologies are necessary, ma'am," Dónal replied, rising from his seat and bowing. "Sure, if there isn't some truth in the girl's words, myself bein' but the descendant of great lords, after all, and not actually one in my own right. Anyway, her sour mood is partially my fault, us gettin' off on the wrong foot last night as we did. But I'm willin' to let bygones be bygones, and I'm sure Annie will be, too, once we've a chance to talk about it."

"Don't count on it," Agnes countered.

The chuckle died in Dónal's throat when he saw that she was deadly serious, making him wonder for the first time if he should be truly afraid of the little hellion. But then, what could she do to him in the short time he'd be there, especially since it looked as if she'd be sequestered in her room? He shrugged it off and applied himself to the daunting task of figuring out which piece of silverware to use on what, which he accomplished by discrete observation. When finished, he felt someone at his elbow and looked up to find one of the slave women there.

"Would you like some tea, suh?" she asked, her voice a squeaky monotone.

"Yes, please," he replied, smiling politely. "And thank you."

"Yassuh," she said, pouring his tea and turning to Fitzgerald without returning his smile or even looking him in the eye.

Turning back to his meal, Dónal found the girls eyeing him curiously again, and he wondered what he'd done this time. To his surprise, it was young Katie who enlightened him.

"You don't have to say 'please' or 'thank you' to them," she said, as though repeating rote. "It's their place to serve us."

"'Tis right ye are, Katie dear," Fitzgerald seconded. "But ye have to remember that Mr. O'Sullivan is new here, and doesn't yet know all the rules of our peculiar institution."

"But don't you have slaves in Ireland, Mr. O'Sullivan?" Dellie asked, seeming astonished at the prospect.

"No, we don't," he replied, equally astonished that she should ask. Hadn't her father taught her anything of their native land? "We Irish are ourselves slaves in Ireland, slaves without masters."

"But white people can't be slaves," she countered. "Only darkies."

"Oh Dellie, dear," Eleanor interjected, "how many times must I tell you not to use that word when speaking of our servants? It is vulgar and suggests a lack of breeding, and I'll not have it in my house. You must always remember that they are not our equals, and for that reason we have certain obligations towards them, among which are to exercise benevolence and restraint in their treatment and to show the proper respect for their sensibilities. That's why using that word is inappropriate, especially in their presence. Do you understand, dear?"

"Yes, Mama. I'm sorry."

"That's all right, dear. Just please remember not to do it again."

"Yes, Mama, I won't."

Dónal stared at Eleanor in disbelief, wondering how she could presume to lecture her daughter on respecting their servants' sensibilities, while at the same time talking about them as if they weren't even there. How did she think that made them feel? And though she obviously meant well, at least as judged from within her societal context, how could she reconcile respecting their sensibilities with keeping them in bondage? Why couldn't she see the logical (or illogical) conclusion of her own argument? It just didn't make any sense!

Glancing at the two women, he found them busy making themselves look busy, self-consciously trying to pretend that none of what was happening concerned them. And yet he knew they'd heard and that their feelings were no different than his would've been in their place.

Studying them for the first time, he saw them to be mother and daughter, having the same thin and wiry build, the same Caucasian nose, angular face, and medium complexion that suggested an admixture of white somewhere in their background. It made him wonder if, like Yellah Joe and Angela's Hector, they, too, were the children of an overseer, or even of the master. Indeed, were they sprung of Fitzgerald himself? There was nothing obvious about them to suggest as much, but then he couldn't be sure they weren't, either. The only thing that would lead him away from such a conclusion was Yellah Joe's statement about how well "the Mizzy Fitz" looked after them. Surely such a woman would have no truck with a philandering husband, especially as it concerned forcing himself upon his slaves. But then, how would she ever know?

'Christ, is there just no end to it?' he wondered.

෨෩

"Sure, if he ain't in one of 'is uppity moods again," Fitzgerald remarked on Ol' Jess, as he and Dónal watched him walk away after bringing the horses from the barn, "and meself with no recourse but to put up with it since herself won't let me whip him, nor any of 'em for that matter, shirk in the fields though they might. And with no threat o' the lash to keep 'em in line, I sometimes find meself wonderin' who's the slave and who's the master around here."

"Well, if you'd have my thoughts on it," Dónal said, "I think you're both enslaved to each other, but only they know it."

"I don't know that I'd go that far now, though 'tis fair to say that we are dependent upon each other for our livelihoods. But ye know, this war is goin' to change all that, one way or t'other. Sure, if the Yankees win, they'll put the kibosh on it straight away, and there'll be the end of it. And even if we win, we'll have to get rid of it sooner or later. The pressure from the international community will be too great, especially from England and France, and we're too dependent on 'em for trade to ignore it."

"Then why not get a leg up on it and free your slaves now? 'Twould put you that much ahead when it came to it."

"Well now, 'tis far easier said than done, even if I was of a mind to, which I'm not. First off, there's none to replace 'em, what with the war, and assumin' that white men would be disposed to the work, which they wouldn't. Then ye have to consider what people would think, which, as much as I hate to admit, is a mighty argument in these parts. Ye have to remember, son, that this country has gone to war to preserve its way o' life, somethin' that most of its people think was ordained by God Himself, and 'tis not considered very patriotic to question God just now. Then, too, Irish Catholics are in the minority here, and 'tis more than a few who think we're just as sinister and deviant as the darkies and ought to be kept down with 'em. So 'twould be a desperate thing to attempt, even 'twere it all to work out in the heel o' the hunt.

"And yet and still, the most compellin' reason not to free 'em is that it wouldn't be in their best interest either. I mean, where would they go? What would they do? Who would take care of 'em? They can't take care o' themselves, ye know, not after a lifetime o' bein' looked after, especially in a country where they're seen as nothin' but two-legged draft animals with a bit o' pidgin in their gobs. So for right now at least, I think it's best for all of us to just watch and wait and let things play out as they will."

"But if you're sure to free them someday, why not educate them against the eventuality, so they'll be prepared for it when the time comes?"

"'Tis against the law first of all, son, and I'll not be riskin' me own freedom for the sake of any man, be he white, black, purple or puce. Sure, but I've me own family to see to, somethin' I can't very well do from a jail cell, now can I? And anyway, it might be years or even decades before an end comes o' slavery, and do ye think educated people who are capable o' takin' care o' themselves would be inclined to wait for it? Not on yeer life, they wouldn't, and then I'd have an insurrection on me hands, not to mention the law and the weight o' public opinion comin' down on me. So thank ye just the same, but I'll cross that bridge when I come to it."

"Sure, 'tis grand for you, Mr. Fitzgerald, bein' the white man that you are. Yet of all your neat little reasons for keepin' your slaves, you never touched upon their facility, or lack of it, for learnin'. And why is that, do you suppose? Could it be that, deep down inside, you know they're not quite as inferior as you would have everyone believe? Could it be, rather, that you keep them enslaved simply because it's in your own best interest? Is that the truth of it, Mr. Fitzgerald, that you keep them enslaved simply because you want to?"

"Jayzis, why are ye after harpin' on me so? I didn't make the rules! But since ye're hell-bent on havin' the truth of it, then yes, 'tis itself, more or less. Sure, I'd even go so far as to say that the only reason they're inferior is because we've made 'em so, and 'tis only because we keep 'em down that they stay that way. But then, 'tis just the way o' the world, so it is. The strong rule and the weak suffer, and I keep slaves so me family won't be among the sufferin' poor like we was in Ireland. Now don't get me wrong, son. I don't go out o' me way to make me darkies suffer. Indeed, I take great pains to ensure they're properly fed and clothed and housed, that they have doctorin' for their ailments and the free darkie preacher every Sunday, all o' which makes 'em better off than we ever were in Ireland, 'free' men though we were called back there. But then again, how free can a man really be when his each wakin' moment is just a struggle to survive to the next? And which is worse anyway, to suffer in freedom or to have a bit o' security in slavery?"

"But that isn't the point, Mr. Fitzgerald, and you know it! Slavery isn't a matter of the body; it's a matter of the mind and the spirit, and to have them caged is the worst thing a human being can suffer! And with your own experience of it in Ireland to draw on, you should know better! Indeed, of all people, the Irish should know better!"

"'Tis yeer opinion that, boyo, and though ye're entitled to it fair enough, I'd just bid ye remember me own opinion on the subject of opinions, if ye'd know what I think of it! But ye could opine for the length and breadth o' the mornin' and still not change me mind. I've heard all the arguments before, and still the crux o' the matter is that I'll hold slaves for as long as it's in me family's best interest, and not a moment less. And sure, if Himself in Heaven won't punish me if I'm wrong, but I'll risk even that for the sake o' me childer!"

Dónal opened his mouth to retort, but at the sight of Fitzgerald with his feet spread wide and his hands planted aggressively on his hips, glaring up at him with blood in his eyes, he thought better of it. There was no point in arguing anymore, and he knew it. The little man was as stubborn as he was ugly, stubborn as only a stiff-necked Irishman could be, and he'd have a better chance of catching fish piss than changing his mind. Anyway, it wasn't his war to fight, no matter the depth of his feelings. His war was at home in Ireland, and the sooner he got to Eóghan, the sooner he could get back to it.

"Well, Mr. Fitzgerald," he said, "while I don't agree with your principles, at least I can say you're no hypocrite."

"No, indeed!" Fitzgerald replied proudly, mistaking it for a compliment. "No man has ever had cause to indict me so. I speak me mind openly and frankly, and I speak the truth."

'The truth, indeed!' Dónal thought. 'The truth is whatever you people want it to be. I've had enough of the truth for one day.'

⟲∭⟳

The town of Jonesboro wasn't much to look at, Dónal decided, just a clutch of brick and clapboard buildings fronting the railroad and main street, along with a couple of churches and a small residential district that quickly gave way to countryside. He supposed it to be more or less typical of Southern villages in that regard, an assumption he would find to be more or less accurate. Having come in with Fitzgerald to return the rented horse to the livery, he'd taken the opportunity to look around while the man was about it. Spurring the gray filly his host had lent him toward the end of town, he came to the railroad station, where a northbound train was boarding amidst a small but bustling crowd of people.

'I should be on that train,' he thought. 'I've no business here and no good reason to stay. Sure, I could just tie up the horse and be gone before anyone was the wiser.'

But he knew the thought was wasted. The touch of Eleanor's hand was yet too imminent, the sound of her voice in his ears too compelling. It was a fool's dream, surely, and he was a fool for dreaming it, but he wasn't ready to wake up just yet. For once gone, he knew he'd never see her again, and he wanted more than just one morning's memories to take with him.

Hearing the conductor call "All aboard," his eyes were drawn to a knot of people on the platform, in the midst of whom stood a handsome young man in a gray uniform, probably an officer from the look of him. As Dónal watched, the man scooped up the little boy at his feet and drew him into a joint embrace with the young woman at his side, the three of them holding each other as if they would never do so again. Releasing them, the man turned to an older couple and bowed to each in turn, before tearing himself away and heading for the train. Hearing the weeping of the women and the little boy calling, "Daddy, Daddy, Daddy!" Dónal's heart went out to them, having witnessed many such scenes of pathos in Ireland, homeland of the American Wake. And given the vagaries of war and the likelihood of finality, he knew it to be an apt analogy.

But just as the man set foot on the stairs, an elderly Negro called to him and shuffled forward with a wicker basket in his gnarled hands. "You fo'got yo' dinnuh, Mistuh John," he said, handing it over.

"Why thank you, Thomas," the young soldier said, eyeing the old man fondly. "And I also forgot to say good-bye to you, didn't I?"

"Yassuh, you sho' did. But dass all right. I know you got yo' mind on de baby and Miss Becky and dem ol' folks o' her'n. But don't you worry none. I be lookin' after 'em fo' you. You just hurry up an' get dis war bidness took care of, 'cause I know dey's gwine miss you sump'm terrible!"

"And what about you, Thomas? Aren't you goin' to miss me, too?"

"Yassuh, you knows I is. I knows it ain't fittin' for me to say dis,

Mistuh John, but if'n I'd ever had me a boy-chile, I'd a'wanted him to grow up to be just like you is."

The young man's smile faded then, and there was a catch in his voice as he spoke. "Thomas, I think that's just about the nicest thing anyone ever said to me."

Then he drew his old friend into his embrace, and the two of them stood so for a long moment, sharing their affection in casual indifference to the shocked stares of strangers. Hearing the conductor call again, the old man stepped away to let his young master board the train, off to fight the people who were trying to break his bonds of servitude.

"Take care o' yo'self, Mistuh John. Don't you let dem Yankees git de best of you now, you hear?"

Then he shuffled back to the waiting relations, knowing that whatever the outcome of the fight, nothing would ever break the bond of love between himself and Mistuh John.

But Dónal could only shake his head as the train left the station and the platform slowly cleared. There was just so much about this country and its people that he found baffling, and he doubted he'd ever understand it all. Yet for the first time, he had an inkling of how the English must feel about Ireland and the Irish, and why they'd struggled so to make them conform to their own familiar ways. But his empathy brought no sympathy, either for them or the slave-mongering Confederates. They were both wrong, and both had to be stopped.

Then Fitzgerald rode up and led the way out of town, taking "the scenic route" as he called it, to exercise the horses and give Dónal a look at the countryside. As for the topography, there was nothing much of interest, Dónal decided, just gently rolling terrain as far as the eye could see. But what surprised him was how thickly forested it still was in places, with deep woods of mixed evergreen and deciduous, the remnants of the great forest that had existed before the white man came and shaped the land to his own design. Indeed, even Fitzgerald could remember it, in the days of his youth when Georgia was still the frontier and tribes of Indians lived just over the horizon. A great wonder and delight the forest had been to him after the bare plains of Tipperary, and he admitted a certain regret for its passing, recalling trees so big that two men couldn't reach around them, their canopy so thick that perpetual twilight reigned beneath. But then he'd no one to blame but himself, he conceded, having done his part to clear the land of both trees and Indians. And all things considered, the land was better for it anyway, he asserted, being now settled and productive and civilized, bearing the fruit of man's labor even as God intended.

Yet Dónal saw an abiding sadness in it, too, in the many Negroes working the fields and mending fences, cutting trees and digging ditches, doing all the mindless, repetitive, backbreaking tasks that sooner or later break the spirit and erode humanity. The *Fir Bolg Dubh*, he came to think of them in analogy to Erin and Her downtrodden poor, the Black Men of the Bags, and he wondered just how much of this Confederate nation was built upon their moil and suffering. Most of it probably, he decided; indeed, most of it. So while the land was certainly settled and productive, "civilized" was not a descriptive he'd have chosen. *But that's the way of the world, son. The strong rule and the weak suffer.* Glancing at Fitzgerald then, Dónal wondered if Egan Butler the Tinker would agree with him, or Angela Blake the former slave, or for that matter, Seán Ahern, the slave without a master. He shook his head and silently chided himself for not getting on the train.

❦

The sun was low on the horizon by the time they turned for home, the soft afternoon light made even softer by the drink they'd taken, the sadness of the land concealed behind its ephemeral veil. They'd spent the afternoon drinking at the home of a horse breeder named Jack Elliott whose ancestors had come from the County Fermanagh in the last century, filtering down the Appalachians along the frontier once known as the "Irish Line" for all the Ulster Protestants who'd settled it. Known in later years as the "Scotch-Irish," they'd become a hard-bitten breed of backwoodsmen, Indian fighters and pioneers, producing some of early America's most celebrated heroes in men such as Davy Crockett,

595

Jim Bowie and Sam Houston, not to mention Presidents Jackson, Taylor and Buchanan. Using experience gained in Ulster in stealing land from the natives, they'd expanded the American frontier at the expense of the Indians, taking their Presbyterian ethic of self-reliance with them. "God helps those who help themselves" was their credo, and it soon became axiomatic that while they faithfully kept the Commandments, they kept everything else they could get their hands on, too.

As for Elliott himself, once the Indians were cleared from the Piedmont, he'd brought his young family out of the mountains in search of decent pasturage for his herd, which had grown quite large before the war. Indeed, Fitzgerald's own Mavourneen was foaled by one of Elliott's mares, though his sire was the stallion of a Tinker chieftain, one of the ten tribes who wandered through Georgia, Alabama and the Carolinas trading horses and doing metal work, the traditional occupations of Irish Travelers (which, of course, explained how the Fitzgerald children knew of them). But most of Elliott's herd was gone for the war effort now, along with his four sons, all of whom had joined the Clayton Dragoons, a cavalry regiment raised from the local men.

But it wasn't for talk of Ireland or horses or the war that they'd visited, but for whiskey, Elliott in true Scotch-Irish fashion keeping a still on his property. And sure, if it wasn't rotgut of the highest order, just as Fitzgerald had warned, with a bite like the Earl of Hell's lash and eminently deserving of its local agnomen of "white lightnin'." But since Fitzgerald had promised his wife he'd stay out of the taverns, a visit to Elliott's shebeen was their only option, however finely the hair was being split.

After drinking as much as they dared and procuring a couple of bottles "for later," they mounted their horses and returned to the road, trotting along for a bit until Fitzgerald stopped for a look at his watch.

"'Tis a late one that's in it, to be sure," he said, giving Dónal a sideways grin, "and only the shortcut will get us home in time. Ye will try to keep up, now won't ye?"

"Don't worry for me, dado," Dónal shot back. "Just see that you don't get us lost!"

But Fitzgerald was away before he'd finished, thundering across the fields like a bishop after his bottle, his coattails snapping in the wind of his speed. And Dónal was right behind him, too, so close initially that he had to squint against the storm of dust and debris kicked up by the flying hooves of Mavourneen, though gradually the distance between them widened, the little filly being no match for the great stallion. Still, she ran better than any horse in his experience, the thrill of it greater even than his ride in the crow's nest, for he felt her power directly, body to body, sinew to sinew. And on they galloped and on, the rich old peasant and the penniless young nobleman, dashing across fields, taking ditches and fences in stride, dodging through stands of trees without slowing. When they passed within spitting distance of a colonnaded Big House, the sound of its cheering denizens sent Dónal's flesh to tingling, even as he answered with his ancient battlecry, *Lamh foisteanach abú*. But his excitement quickly faded when the filly clipped a boundary fence, sending the top rail crashing to the ground. He knew she was tiring and couldn't keep up the pace, game though she might be. So when they crested a rise and he saw the river below, he slowed her to a quick trot, knowing there was no sense killing them both in a race they couldn't win.

Ahead, the gap widened as Mavourneen ran on, smooth and tireless as a locomotive, the man on his back hardly moving for all the activity beneath. At the river, Fitzgerald reined him in and led him onto a shoal for a drink.

"That was one hell of a ride, so it was!" Dónal exclaimed as he rode up.

"'Twas indeed, son," Fitzgerald agreed, "and I thank ye for makin' it sportin'. Himself usually leaves 'em at the gate, but ye was with me all the way."

"Sure, I'd nothin' much to do with it. 'Twas herself doin' all the work."

"Ah, but she was just the legs of it so, and though yeer modesty speaks well for ye, 'twas yeerself that was the brains in it. Only a fine piece o' horsemanship could give Mavourneen a run like that."

"Ah, well, if you say so."

"I do, and I'm much appreciative. A good steeplechase is one o' the pleasures o' life, if ye ask me, and with the Elliott boys gone, there's been none to give me a run for it of late."

"The pleasure was all mine, Mr. Fitzgerald. Sure, we'll have to do it again sometime."

"Aye, we will indeed. But just ye mind yeer tongue around herself now. She thinks me too old for the hazard that's in it, and she'll have me hide tacked to the wall if she hears of it."

"Your secret's safe with me, dado. I'll not breathe a word!"

"Good man, yeerself!" Fitzgerald said, as he uncorked a bottle and passed it to Dónal. "And mind yeer tongue about these, too. Just keep 'em safe in yeer cabin, and we can have a drop whenever we like."

After sharing a drink, Fitzgerald led the way toward Rural Home, skirting the river before crossing on a covered bridge, and then heading gently uphill. The sunset flashed on the windows as they approached, setting them aglow with the color of flame, even as it did the Flint River in the distance. Gazing over the land then, Dónal saw again the similarity to Fitzgerald's Irish home, a likeness that in all this country seemed to exist in only this one place. But while he could well understand why the man had chosen to live here, was it really worth the price he'd paid for it? Dónal hoped not.

⌾

The fire was warm and bright, snapping and crackling with the sap of fat pine and hickory, its light bathing their faces with a convivial glow as they basked in familial warmth. They were all there, of course, even Annie, gathered in the parlor for their evening prayers, Fitzgerald in his overstuffed chair with Izzie and Katie on his lap, Eleanor and the older girls on the sofa, rosaries in hand, Sadie and Dellie on chairs by the fire. It was a scene that would've stirred the heart of many an Irish exile, a living memory of the time before the Diaspora, when they'd still been in their own homes by their own firesides, among their own kith and kin. Indeed, but for the missing smell of turf, it could've been any family in any cottage in Ireland, at any time in the last thousand years.

And they'd made Dónal part of it, too, drawing him into their circle to share in their most intimate family moments, their daily communion with God. And though the words he recited had lost all meaning for him, they yet inspired a feeling of contentment within him, of being one with the world and one with God, and one with the golden-haired angel who sat across from him, unaware of his feelings for her.

Feeling his eyes upon her, Eleanor smiled at him, gently, sadly, and he smiled back, thinking he wanted the moment never to end.

CRULO

The night sky was clear and bright, and Dónal's mind was as far away as the stars as he stepped onto the porch of his cottage, his thoughts on Eleanor and her sad, gentle smile. So when a voice spoke from the darkness, he started and whirled about.

"What's that?" he demanded, peering into the night. "Who's there?"

A man stepped into the pool of light spilling from the window, standing at right angles so that only his left side was illuminated. He was as dark as the night itself and built like a stone wall, as tall as Dónal and with massive shoulders and a bull neck, and arms that looked as though they could crush stone in the crook of an elbow. Even his bald head was round and muscular-looking, and it rippled as he pursed his brow. Yet the look in his eyes was harder still as he gazed boldly at the white man before him, unbowed and unblinking.

"I said, the Master was correct, you know," he repeated softly, almost patronizingly, his voice low and melodious and with perfect enunciation, not the pidgin of the other slaves, a language half-learned from halfhearted instruction.

"Correct about what?" Dónal asked when the man didn't explain himself.

"About us being inferior only because you've made us that way," he replied, flashing a brief mirthless smile, before falling silent again.

"I see. Tell me, where did you learn to speak like that?"

"Like a white man, do you mean? Why, in a white man's school, of course. Where else?"

"Oh? I thought slaves weren't allowed in school."

"And you are correct. But then, I wasn't a slave when I went to school."

"I don't understand. Do you mean to say you were born free and then became a slave?"

"You are a quick study, I see."

"But how? I thought the foreign slave trade was abolished here decades ago."

"Yes, it was, and ironically it was the very act of abolition that ensured my enslavement, since it created an artificial shortage of slaves even as the rise of King Cotton increased the demand for them, thereby sending their value through the roof."

"Yes, go on," Dónal coaxed when the man didn't continue.

"It's a basic economic concept, but if you would have me spell it out, I was born of free parents in Philadelphia, the City of Brotherly Love, as it's called. Yet one of those loving brothers, a black man like me, kidnapped me at the age of twelve and sold me to a Maryland slave trader. It was a rather common practice at the time, given the large sums of money involved, and I've come across other victims of it here and there. And before you ask, I did protest my free birth to that first master. But what reason had he to take the word a young buck nigger, especially when he'd just paid top dollar for him? In any case, he had a ready cure for my 'delusion,' as he called it. Remind me to show you the scars sometime."

The man fell silent again, and Dónal eyed him curiously, not really sure what was happening between them. "Why are you tellin' me this?" he asked finally.

"I'm not sure if I know myself, really. But when I heard you speaking with the Master this morning, you sounded like a man possessed of the courage of his convictions, and I suppose I just wanted to see if it's true."

"I'm not sure I understand."

"Knowledge is power, my young Achilles, and secrets are a burden only the strongest can bear. Are you strong enough to bear mine?"

"Sure, I'll give you my word on it, and my hand," Dónal replied, answering the challenge with one of his own.

"Oh no, paddy," the man countered, the rage within him bubbling suddenly to the surface. "It'll take more than the word of a white man to win my trust."

"How then?"

But the man didn't answer, just smirked and shook his head, and made to turn away.

"Wait!" Dónal said. "You didn't tell me your name."

"Benjamin Franklin Campbell, at your service," the man replied, bowing slightly at the waist.

"Dónal O'Sullivan Béara, at yours," he said, returning the courtesy, though he knew it had been meant as sarcasm.

With that the man turned on his heel and disappeared into the night, but not before allowing Dónal to see the "R" branded into his right cheek, the special punishment reserved for runaways.

chapter 31

Rural Home Plantation
Christmas Day, 1861

IT WAS THE SILENCE MORE THAN ANYTHING that drew him to the door, the lack of hubbub that usually marked the mornings at Rural Home, as the slaves prepared for their long workday. Yet it was the snow that held him there, the majestic flakes floating gently down, so thick as to blur the horizon between Heaven and Earth, each adding imperceptibly though inexorably to the virgin mantle already covering the land. It blanketed the roof of the Big House and frosted its windows; it clothed the naked limbs of the oaks and lent a semblance of cheer even to the brutish slave cabins, softening the rough edges of the world and leaving it a warm and friendly place, intimate and benign. And this show of Nature was just for him it seemed, there being no one else in sight, nor even any faces at the windows. Just himself alone, just as it had always been.

Dónal closed the door when the chill became oppressive and set about reviving the fire. He was almost six weeks at Rural Home now, far longer than he'd intended to stay, though it hardly seemed any time at all. For the days had been pleasant and full, as the Fitzgeralds drew him into the bosom of their family and made him feel a part of it, while at night he had the stuff of Jack Elliott's shebeen to keep him company, along with the occasional drop from Fitzgerald's decanter. Much of the time he'd spent in the old man's company, riding about the countryside when the weather permitted, visiting his friends and relations, helping him with business or personal matters, or just racing across the fields in a reprise of their first steeplechase, the outcome always being the same, of course. Then, too, there was bookkeeping to be done, Fitzgerald performing the service for local planters and merchants who either couldn't do it for themselves or wouldn't, Dónal's facility for the task impressing host and clients alike. And from that work and the few hours he spent each week tutoring the girls on Ireland and Her history, he was able to earn a bit of money, the man insisting on paying him even though he was already providing room and board. That it went straight into Elliott's pocket, Fitzgerald didn't mind, as it afforded him a way to evade his wife's rule against drinking in the house on nonsocial occasions. Indeed, it might have been his design for all Dónal could tell, though he didn't hold it against him. For with all the time they'd spent together, he'd come to a deeper understanding of the man, even finding a bit of affection for him, knowing in return that when Fitzgerald called him "son" now, it was more than just an epithet.

And all of that despite the fact that nothing had developed between himself and Mamie, she being no more interested in him than he was in her, thankfully. As for the other girls, Annie hated him, of course, and all the more since she'd had to apologize to him when threatened with staying home from the Christmas ball. With Agnes, he'd struck up a friendship based on their shared intellectual curiosity, while the three younger ones regarded him as a sort of oversized playmate, a role he filled willingly enough, having never had any little siblings of his own. But Sadie, on the other hand, was a different story, as she'd had a crush on him since their first meeting and took every opportunity to further it, flirting with him shamelessly, hanging on his every word, his every glance. Not that he wasn't flattered by it, such was her beauty, but she was too young for him, and he knew he'd leave long before she wasn't. Anyway, he had an infatuation of his own.

For in all that he did, his thoughts and focus were ever on Eleanor, reliving the moments they'd spent together, anticipating the next, plotting ways to make it last. It was so difficult to find any time with her, between her husband dominating his days and her own duties in the household, not to mention the many children tugging at her skirt tails. Yet one afternoon he'd had her to himself, when he'd driven her to the home of a neighbor who'd lost a son in the war. He'd done his best to make the most of it, of course, telling her about himself and asking her probing questions, doing his best to let her get to know him, to subtly impress upon her that he was worthy of her affection, on whatever level she was willing to give it. It seemed so natural, too, as he found her easy to talk to and a sympathetic listener, like Sióna had been in the happy time before the Wandering Hawk lit upon them. Indeed, it had unburdened his soul, talking with her so, and his affection for her soared to a new level, and then again when they reached their destination.

For it was but a mean shanty of a place, no better than those of the Fitzgerald's slaves, the poor woman whose home it was having neither husband nor relations nor even friends for comfort and support, only the one son now lost in the rich man's war, a son conceived out of wedlock, if rumor was to be believed, which explained her isolated state. At first she was loathe to let them enter, protesting that she and her home weren't fit to receive such people of quality. Indeed, Eleanor's friends even tacitly agreed with her, refusing to come along on the grounds that it wasn't "fittin'" for them to associate with white trash. Yet Eleanor had persisted, gently, tenderly, until the woman relented, though she seemed ill at ease at first, having nothing to offer in the way of refreshment or even decent chairs for them to sit upon. But it didn't last, as Eleanor's empathy and kindly manner eased her heart, to the point that she was able to pour out her grief in a torrent of tears, Eleanor holding her close and stroking her hair, comforting her as only a mother who'd lost a son could. When they finally took their leave, the woman knelt before Eleanor and kissed her hand, saying, "If you ain't a angel, Mizz Fitzgerald, then I don't know what one is." And Dónal could but agree with her.

They'd been silent on the way home, Eleanor lost in grieving for the poor woman while Dónal had no words to express the many emotions he felt, love, respect, admiration, awe, unworthiness. Yet he'd desperately wanted to talk to her, and to hold her in his arms, to have her hold him and tell him everything would be all right, just as she'd done for the woman in the cabin. What a release it would be to pour out his grief to her, to confess his sins and obtain her absolution. But then, what would she think of him if he did? How could she ever come to have feelings for him if she knew who he really was?

Only when they'd pulled to a stop at the Big House did she turn to him, taking his hand in hers and holding his gaze, the look in her eyes telling him the smile on her lips was for him alone.

"Thank you, Mr. O'Sullivan," she said, her voice as soft as the light of dawn, yet slicing his heart like a silver blade.

"Call me Dónal," he replied, hesitating before adding, "Eleanor."

"Dónal," she said, and with a squeeze of his hand was gone.

Thinking of that exchange now, Dónal moved to the armoire and sniffed at the evening clothes Fitzgerald had bought him to see if he could detect her scent. It was just on Saturday night that they'd danced together at the Christmas ball in Atlanta, Dónal mortified at his own clumsiness yet thrilling at the chance to hold her in his arms, however briefly, however chastely. *You're so beautiful*, he'd wanted to tell her as they floated in their dancers' embrace. *So beautiful.* But, of course, he hadn't. Indeed, they'd hardly spoken to each other, just whirled about the room with the other waltzing couples, though she'd smiled at him before returning to her husband's side. And now there was no trace of her on his jacket, having been buried beneath all those other young ladies who'd come after, as he'd found himself the beau of the ball with so few young men around. *Did you meet the Fitzgeralds' handsome young friend?* the buzz had gone. *Yes, he's an Irish nobleman, they say, The O'Somethin' of Somethin' or Other. Well, he can lord it over me just any ol' time he wants to!* But he'd paid them no heed. His heart was elsewhere, given to a married woman old enough to be his mother.

Catching his reflection in the mirror, he shook his head disapprovingly. "God help you, boyo," he said. "God help you."

"We're in here, son," Dónal heard Fitzgerald call as he closed the door and stamped the snow from his feet.

Following his voice into the parlor, he found the family dressed in their Sunday best and gathered round the hearth as though for evening prayers, the women with their rosaries and the Bible on Fitzgerald's lap. Yet it was something else that stopped him short and held his eye, the shapely young pine he and Yellah Joe had cut down the day before and brought inside, now transformed into a Christmas Tree by strings of beads and bows of red ribbon, the many-rayed tin star adorning its top and gaily wrapped packages at its foot. He'd never had one himself, of course, there being no trees suitable for it on Béara, and the beauty of it touched him deeply, a fitting tribute to this season of peace and harmony. Taking it all in, he thought it perhaps the homiest scene he'd ever seen, with the ice-crusted windows and the fire crackling in the hearth, the tree warming the room with the magic of Christmas while the family basked in the glow of God's love. And he was going to be part of it, too.

"Merry Christmas, son," Fitzgerald said warmly, rising from his chair to welcome him into the fold. "Come in and help us celebrate. We've been waitin' for ye."

"And a Merry Christmas to you," Dónal replied, his spirit high within him, "and to you, too, Mrs. Fitzgerald, and to all you Misses Fitzgerald. A finer day for it, you couldn't have asked for!"

"'Tis true indeed," Fitzgerald agreed, leading him to a chair by the fire. "'Tis nothin' like a bit o' snow to put the icin' on the cake, now is there? And now that we're all here, let's get on with it so!"

Taking his seat, Fitzgerald opened his Bible and adjusted his spectacles. "The Gospel Accordin' to St. Matthew," he intoned, and began to read.

As Dónal sat among them then, listening to a story he'd heard countless times, a visitation of faith came upon him, and the words became suddenly real, a living event rather than just symbols on a sterile page. Indeed, he could see the Magi as if they were standing before him, could smell the animals in the manger and hear the murmurings of the newborn Baby cradled in Its Mother's arms. Perhaps it was the ambience of the room and the embrace of the family, or perhaps it was something deeper, more primal. Yet in that moment, he knew the gospel to be more than mythology, for he could feel its innate, undeniable holiness, as though witnessing the blessed event himself.

"May I see that, please?" he asked when Fitzgerald finished. Taking it in his trembling hands, Dónal began to read the story again, though in Irish this time, the words leaping from the page as if printed in his native tongue.

They were all eyeing him thoughtfully when he'd finished, even the incredulous Annie for the moment seeming subdued and contemplative. For though the language was unintelligible, they'd understood in their hearts, the words sparking a recognition in them, some ancient folk memory perhaps that transcended space and time to evoke the Irishness of their souls.

"Was that the Gaelic?" Eleanor asked softly, looking at him as though they were the only two present. "I had no idea it was such a beautiful language."

"Sure, 'tis beautiful indeed," Dónal agreed, eyeing her intently, "beautiful and sad, just like the people who speak it and the land we live in. 'Tis our heritage and our patrimony, its every word an embodiment of millennia of collective memories, all distilled on the tongues of druids and aged through generations of bards and priests, warriors, lords and peasants. I've never understood how anyone could live in Ireland and not be able to speak our language. They always seemed so cut off to me, so excommunicated from The Land and all She has to tell of Herself. For to look at a standing stone and call it a "standing stone" expresses nothin' of its majesty and mystery, its ancient holiness and present beauty. Yet the single Irish word, *gallán*, captures it all in just its two syllables. But you can't know that, you can't really *know* Erin unless you can speak to Her in Her own language. I don't know if it makes any sense to you, Mrs. Fitzgerald, though your blood is as

Irish as mine. I don't know if you can truly understand it, having never walked the Holy Ground."

"Well, I don't know about Ellen and the girls," Fitzgerald interjected, "but I can tell ye for meself that I'm sorry now for never havin' any o' the ould language when I lived there. Hearin' ye speak of it so gives me a new understandin' of its connection to the land, and if I'm anything in this world, 'tis a man o' the land."

Dónal said nothing in reply, just eyed the old man respectfully. He'd heard, and understood.

But it was Annie who broke the spell, of course, stifling a stage yawn. "My, how you Irish men do go on! Here y'all are wastin' time on talk when there's presents just screamin' to be opened."

"Ah, sure, but that's me darlin' Annie!" Fitzgerald exclaimed, bolting upright and slapping his knee. "Always the one for havin' first things first, and right ye are, begob. Sadie, 'tis yeer turn to pass out the presents, I believe. Youngest first and one at a time, girl, ye know the drill! Here we go now!"

The room came suddenly alive then as Sadie sprang to the tree, quickly selected a package, and brought it to Izzie, who was fairly hopping with impatience. Though it was almost as big as herself, she made quick work of the wrapping, squealing with delight when she saw the new doll inside. At her father's prompting, she held it up and showed it around, eliciting a chorus of *oohs* and *aahs* from her mother and sisters. Then it was Katie's turn, and Dellie's, the pattern being repeated through all the girls and their parents, Fitzgerald receiving a new pipe of mother-of-pearl and mahogany while giving his wife an emerald pendant on a gold chain.

And Dónal watched it all happily, joining with them as they made over their presents and gloried in the spirit of the season. But once Fitzgerald finished showing his pipe, he figured the gift-giving was done, and that suited him just fine. It was enough that they'd included him, and anyway he was suddenly ravenous for the breakfast waiting in the dining room.

But to his surprise, Sadie scooped another package from under the tree and brought it to him. "Here, Dónal," she said softly, becoming suddenly coy. "This is for you. I hope you like it."

"Sure, I don't know what to say," he said, feeling his heart in his throat. "Just to have been included was present enough for me. I'm just sorry that I don't have anything for all of you."

"We know that, Mr. O'Sullivan," Eleanor replied gently, and he looked up to find her smiling at him. "And that's all the more reason for us to have gotten you something."

"Thank you," he said humbly, thinking the smile she gave to him alone was all the gift he'd ever need.

"Well, go on with ye, son, open it so!" Fitzgerald prodded, seeming more anxious than Dónal to find out what it held.

Carefully untying the bow and opening the paper, Dónal saw a beautifully polished wooden box, inside of which lay a shiny tin whistle, the very instrument Seán Ahern apprenticed him on before teaching him the pipes.

"How did you know?" he asked of Eleanor, though she just nodded at Sadie.

"How?" he asked, his eyes boring into Sadie's. "How did you know I could play?"

"I . . . I didn't," she replied hesitantly, finding his sudden intensity disconcerting. "But you whistle a lot, and sometimes you hum when you're thinking. So I just thought that since you seemed to like music you might want something to play it on."

"Yes, you're right," he said, his face relaxing into a smile. "I love music, and I've missed playin' it somethin' fierce, though I didn't realize it till just this very moment."

Looking down at the little instrument then, it suddenly seemed so long since he'd made his music, as if it were the experience of a different lifetime, a thing unknown to him rather than the constant companion it had always been. Picking it up, he hefted it in his hands and felt the cool metal against his skin, set his fingers to the holes and touched it to his lips. It seemed so light and simple after the pipes, primordial almost, mysterious and magical in the way music was to him when he'd first learned to play. His hands trembled with anticipation as he ran through the scales, the notes dancing in his ears and setting his soul afire. Closing his eyes, he took a deep breath and dove in, playing the last tune he'd learned before taking up the pipes, a slow air called *Dóchas*, Irish for "Hope," a fitting reintroduction to the whistle, he thought.

He played self-consciously at first, fearing his long hiatus would show in mistakes. But by the second time through the melody he knew it wouldn't, that making music came as naturally to him as breathing, and if he didn't play for a thousand years it would still come back to him. And with that, he launched into a quick march called "Silken Thomas" after an Earl of Kildare, his fingers flying over the holes as Fitzgerald let out a whoop and they all clapped their hands in rhythm. And then Dónal was up and marching around the room, a latter-day pied piper leading the exiled children of Erin on a flight of fancy, a capering parade to nowhere.

"*Crom abú! Crom abú!*" Fitzgerald shouted as his clan fell in behind him. "On the Fitzgeralds, *Crom abú!*"

ᏳᎻᏯ

The snow was still falling as Dónal accompanied Fitzgerald and Eleanor to the cabin shared by Campbell and Yellah Joe, the last on their round of Christmas visitations, an experience he'd found bittersweet at best. For though he approved of their effort to brighten up Christmas for their servants, he couldn't help but contrast the circumstances in which master and slave observed it. There was no joy of the season in the squalid cabins, no Christmas tree or exchange of presents, no reading of the Gospels, only the welcome respite of a day off from work. For though the white man's God promised them salvation in the next life, He gave His dark-skinned children little to be thankful for in this one.

"'Tis the last of them, begob," Fitzgerald muttered as they came to the door. "Let's be quick about it, shall we? Sure, if I'm not colder than a frog on a mountain!"

"Well, if it's too cold for you to spend a few minutes in the cabins," Eleanor said, "imagine what it must be like to live in them."

"Ah, woman, don't start with me now. Ye know I take good care o' me darkies, better than any master around. Sure, but didn't I just give them all new clothes and boots and an extra measure of wood against the chill that's in it?"

"Be that as it may, husband, I'll not have you being rude to our servants. They serve us faithfully and well, and the very least you can do is take the time to wish them a proper Merry Christmas."

"All right, all right," he muttered, giving it up. Taking a deep breath, he swept into the cabin without bothering to knock (even their privacy being his property, it seemed), calling out a hearty "Merry Christmas" as he did.

"Yassuh, Mauzuh Fitz," Yellah Joe replied pleasantly, rising to greet them. "Merry Chris'mas to ya'll, too! Ya'll come on in an' set down by de fire. Ol' Bessie May done give me a pot o' coffee fo' you, an' it won't take me but two shakes to po' it up."

"Why, thank you, Jordan," Eleanor said, taking a chair by the fire, "and you, too, Benjamin. That was awfully thoughtful of you. It is right cold outside."

"Yassum, I know dass right," Yellah Joe said as he poured two cups of coffee and handed them over. "I's sorry I ain't got nothin' fo' you, Mistuh O'Sullibun, but I knows you don't like coffee none."

"Don't worry for me, Yellah Joe. I'm grand so," Dónal lied, it being chilly in the cabin despite the fire burning in the mean little grate. Even Campbell wore a flannel shirt, a broad concession for a man who seldom wore long sleeves, his long hours in the smithy keeping him uncomfortably warm most of the time.

But Dónal could see there was more bothering him than just the cold, as he stood listlessly to the side, gazing pensively out the window. 'Another year gone and I'm still a slave,' his attitude seemed to say, 'another year of my life wasted.' He wished there was something he could say or do to ease his melancholy. But there was nothing, and by now he knew better than to try.

"We've brought your Christmas presents," Dónal heard Eleanor say, and turned to find a grin splitting Yellah Joe's freckled face.

"Yassum, I knows you is," he said, "'cause I done seen dat ol' bag Mistuh O'Sullibun be's a'carryin'. Yas-suh-ree, I just loves gettin' my Christmas presents."

"Good," Eleanor said with an indulgent smile. "Then why don't you sit down on the bed and we'll give them to you. Benjamin, would you please sit down, too, so we can all celebrate together?"

Campbell hesitated for a moment, and, feeling the tension in him, Dónal wondered if he might refuse. But then he turned and sat down on his own bed opposite Yellah Joe. "Yassum, Mizzy Fitz. I's just lookin' at de snow. I ain't seen dat much of it since I's a chile," and only Dónal heard what he left unsaid: *in Philadelphia.*

"Yes, it has been a long time since we've had this much," Eleanor agreed. "But isn't it nice that we have a white Christmas this year?"

Though Campbell didn't reply, Dónal could see what he was thinking: '*You* have a white Christmas *every* year.' But Eleanor was too busy with the gifts to notice.

"Perhaps Mr. Fitzgerald would like to go first," she said, following the same routine as in the other cabins, the same as every other year, it seemed.

"Sure, why not," the man replied, taking the large bundles Dónal pulled from the bag and handing one to each, their new clothes for the coming year. "Here ye go, lads, one for the each of yez. Hopefully, the stuff will fit better than last year. Ye two are hard to provide for, given the size that's in yez."

But while Yellah Joe gleefully tore into his package and made a fuss over the contents, Campbell merely poked through his enough to keep from giving offense, before setting it aside and muttering his thanks. Seeing the anguish behind his blank face, Dónal's heart went out to him, thinking how depressing it must be to have done a year's labor hard enough to be considered special punishment in any prison, and have as his only reward one set of new clothes and another year of the same to look forward to. It reminded him of his father and the miners of Allihies, men who toiled their days away in sunless drudgery and had only indebtedness to the Company to show for it. Was one really less a slave than the other? Or did it even matter what they were called, for as Fitzgerald himself had said, how free can a man really be when his each waking moment is just a struggle to survive to the next? No, they were equally oppressed and equally in need of liberation.

But he had no time to ponder it just then, as Eleanor was asking him for the remaining packages, her own special presents to the two men. "Let's see now," she said, taking the first. "This one is for you, Jordan. Merry Christmas."

"Oh, Lawdy, Lawd, Lawd, Mizzy Fitz!" Yellah Joe exclaimed, ripping through the paper to find a broad-brimmed straw hat. "Mm, mm, mm! Dat sho' is a fine lookin' hat! Sho', if'n it don't be just like de one you wears when you's workin' in yo' flower garden."

"Why yes, Jordan, it is. I know how the sun torments you in the summer, and I thought this might help a bit. I have the same problem, you know."

"Yassum, I know dass right, an' I sho' do 'preciate you thinkin' 'bout me dat a'ways!"

"You're welcome, Jordan," Eleanor acknowledged with a benevolent smile. "It's the very least I could do."

Then she turned to Campbell. "Now let's see, Benjamin," she said, taking the package from Dónal. "Since only one is left, it must be for you. Merry Christmas."

Mumbling his thanks, Campbell dutifully unwrapped the package, though his eyes went wide in shock at seeing what was inside. "How did you know?" he asked in a subdued voice, in his shock forgetting to affect the slave dialect. "How did you know I could read?"

"What?" Fitzgerald demanded in surprise, having turned away to warm his hands at the fire. "What did ye say?"

Yet he may as well have not been there for all the notice Campbell took of him, his dark eyes boring into Eleanor's, searching for her motives and intentions. Then thinking he understood, his eyes shifted to Dónal, suddenly full of anger.

"No, Benjamin, Mister O'Sullivan didn't tell me," Eleanor said, "though I'm not surprised that he knows. House Mary told me, though I assure you it was not her intention to betray you. You see, one day last summer I caught her leaving the house with a book, and being rather puzzled by that, I asked what she intended to do with it. When she told me, I told her to be more careful next time. So you see, Benjamin, a white woman can be trusted with a secret, too."

"A secret indeed, woman!" Fitzgerald interjected angrily. "Just what do ye think ye're after? Need I remind ye o' the consequences that come o' teachin' a colored man to read?"

"I didn't teach this man to read, husband, and neither did you. So we have nothing to fear from the law in this matter. All I have done is give him a Bible, so that he may spread the Gospel among his people, even as you and Mr. O'Sullivan did among yours. And while that is certainly no crime, I might have even saved you the expense of hiring the free Negro preacher on Sundays, if Benjamin agrees."

"Ah, woman, as fine as that may be, ye might've asked me before ye did it. 'Tis my place to make such decisions and not yeers, after all."

"Be that as it may, husband, this is hardly the time or place to discuss it."

Turning back to Campbell, she laid her hand on the book. "And that is my condition upon this gift, Benjamin, that you use it to spread the word of God among your people. Do you agree?"

"Yes, Mrs. Fitzgerald, I agree," Campbell replied.

"But mind that ye don't go teachin' any of 'em to read, now!" Fitzgerald added, shaking his finger in the man's face. "For if I find that ye have, ye'll be up to yeer arse in a Louisiana rice paddy before ye can say the words. Do ye hear me, boyo?"

"Nawsuh, Mauzuh Fitz, I sho' won't be doin' dat," Campbell replied with a look so angelic that Dónal had to stifle a grin, guessing that even Ol' Jess would be reading by the next Christmas.

"Ye'd just better not!" Then Fitzgerald rose and nodded toward the door. "Come along, Mrs. Fitzgerald. We don't want to overstay our welcome, now do we?"

Without waiting for an answer, he stormed through the door, leaving it open behind him.

"Thank you for the coffee, Jordan," Eleanor said, and then turned to Campbell. "Spread the Word, Benjamin. Spread the Word."

"Yes ma'am. Merry Christmas, Mrs. Fitzgerald."

"Merry Christmas to you, Benjamin, and to you, Jordan. Good day."

With that, she followed her husband through the door, and Dónal closed it behind her. "Well, what do you think of that?" he asked.

"What do I think?" Campbell asked. "I think that if I live to be a thousand, I'll *never* understand the white man, that's what I think!"

"Well," Dónal said, grinning sheepishly, "if it makes you feel any better, even other white men don't understand the Irish."

"Now that I can understand," Campbell replied, smiling back in spite of himself.

Knowing there was nothing else to say, Dónal turned to go, but finding the snow still falling, he paused in the doorway to watch.

"Did it snow like this in Philadelphia?" he asked, feeling Campbell beside him.

"Yes, and I used to love it, too, especially when my father took me sledding in the park."

"Maybe you'll go back there someday, and take your own children sledding in the park."

But Campbell just gave him an 'Are you daft?' look that would've done Tadhg Ahern proud. "Sure, Paddy, and Jayzis is after comin' back, too, they say," he said in an exaggerated brogue. "But I ain't waitin' up nights."

chapter 32

Rural Home Plantation

THE EVENING WAS STILL AND WARM, and the crickets just beginning their serenade as Dónal sat down on his porch to watch the sunset. Spring had come to the American South, bringing with it gracious days and comfortable nights, the land bursting with new life as flowers bloomed and trees budded, while dogwoods graced the forests with a profusion of cross-shaped blossoms, as beautiful as Fitzgerald had promised. It was a different kind of spring than Dónal was accustomed to, more sumptuous, more luxuriant, more starkly contrasting with the season just ended, more of everything that spring was supposed to be and, with its coming, he'd begun to understand why Southerners had such a passion for the South.

Of course, it had its dark side, too, in the sudden thunderstorms that scourged the land and spawned the occasional tornado, like the one that had passed within a few miles of Rural Home, leaving a swath of death and destruction in its wake. Then, too, the coming of spring was dreaded by the slaves, as it marked the beginning of long days in the fields, sweltering under a sun that would grow only more intense as spring advanced into summer. Already he could see what it did to them, to Yellah Joe as he stepped and fetched, and Campbell as he hammered away in the smithy, and to Peter and Gracie and House Mary and Yard Mary and Nat and Sally and Scipio and Caesar and Bessie May, and all the others whom he'd come to know as human beings and not just two-legged capital. Yet he'd also accepted that a force stronger than he would be required to bring slavery down, such as the Yankee army perhaps, or the irresistible impulse of greed. It would happen sooner with the former, certainly, though the latter would do it just as surely, since the economics of the "peculiar institution" were already slipping in that direction.

So Dónal didn't worry about it, though he did his best to be respectful of the slaves' humanity. Indeed, he was too busy enjoying the lap of luxury into which he'd fallen, with its three good meals a day, plenty of whiskey, enough work to keep him pleasantly stimulated, and a family who'd adopted him as one of their own. Indeed, he'd grown complacent in his creature comfort, finding the life of a country squireen rather more to his liking than that of a dispossessed, disinherited, disenfranchised peasant clinging precariously to a windswept hillside. And far from being as different as he'd thought initially, Southern culture actually had many similarities to that of Ireland, from the heavy Celtic settlement in the early days, certainly, though reinforced by continuing immigration right up to the start of the war. So many of the people he'd met had proudly informed him of their own Celtic connections, to Scotland, Wales and Protestant Ulster, mainly, though one old fellow had sought to minimize the distinction by saying that all *Selts* were basically the same when you got right down to it. "Sure, if that isn't true for you, Dado," Dónal had gibed, "though only a Sassenach would pronounce *Kelts* so." Yet he'd agreed with the man's sentiment.

As for other cultural similarities, there was the Southern mania for hospitality to begin with, which was observed at all levels of society and in all its forms and expressions, as strictly as if Brehon censure threatened the malfeasant. Then there was their preoccupation with religion, which was predominantly Protestant in its expression, of course, though Catholicism and even Judaism were tolerated among the middle and upper classes, so long as the practitioners were otherwise upstanding citizens (*and* so long as there weren't too many of them). Indeed, as the only Irish Catholic immigrant of any standing in the county, Fitzgerald was more a novelty than anything else, the fact that he'd been twice elected to the statehouse evidence that this trinity of handicaps wasn't held against him.

Then, too, there was the Southern affection for whiskey, which came directly from the Irish and Scots, of course, being the people who'd invented the stuff after all. And though the taking of "strong spirits" was considered taboo under their particular interpretation of Protestant morality (which in this instance extended even into the Fitzgerald household), the code tended to be rather more elastic in its practice than in its preaching. Indeed, there'd been a decanter on the sideboard or a jug by the hearth in just about every home he'd visited, Southerners favoring whiskey over both ale and wine, the former being disdained as a drink for the "lower classes" (even among the lower classes), while the latter was considered pretentious, even effeminate, though he'd yet to see a good Southern man turn down either when whiskey was lacking.

And as was the case in Ireland, the drink seemed to be a leveling factor among Southern men of different social standings and backgrounds, the public house being the one place where Crackers could rub elbows with wealthy planters and address them familiarly, conditions which applied in no other setting or at any other time. Indeed, the drink was the only leveling factor, it seemed, there being a massive unwritten code by which people were judged and classified and categorized within the Southern caste system. Everyone had their place, he found, including himself, and to accord a person more or less respect than warranted was considered a critical breach of etiquette. So Dónal had to learn the place of each person he encountered, and whether his position was higher or lower than his own, so he could give or receive the proper deference. In this, he was coached by Fitzgerald, who gave him subtle hints about a man's status, things like, "John here owns almost as many slaves as I do," meaning John was a wealthy planter and so a man of substance, or "James has a few acres in cotton along the Flint," meaning James was a small farmer and of not much accounting. Only the lowest class of whites was easily categorized, as they were the ones who deigned to work with their hands, and naturally a white man who worked like a nigger couldn't be accounted much better than one. Of course, most of these laboring whites were also immigrants, which in turn meant they were usually Irish, people accustomed to the bottom rung of the social ladder and who accepted manual labor without qualms, especially since recent bad experience taught them that in idleness lay the surest road to ruin.

But then again, monetary wealth was not the only factor to consider, since even poorer whites could be deemed substantial if they had a "good reputation" and/or came from a "good family" (meaning one with a good reputation), while conversely, even the wealthiest could be held of no account if they lacked either or both. So it was that reputations were guarded fiercely and jealously, because, just as in Gaelic Ireland, they were one of the prime determinants of standing in society. All of which, of course, dovetailed neatly into the Southern compulsion to "act right," since failure to do so would tarnish one's reputation and denigrate one's social standing, as well as bring ill repute upon one's family. And of all social evils, bringing a "bad name" upon one's family was considered the greatest, since it adhered to all family members and could take generations to absolve. Then, too, on a practical level, it made "suitable" marriages harder to come by, which in the long run could be detrimental to the family's fiscal health, thereby loosening one of the cornerstones of its reputation.

All of this, in turn, helped explain the Southern propensity for violence since, in defending his honor, a man was actually defending his wealth, both literally and figuratively. But then violence was a way of life in Gaelic Ireland, too, and for much the same reason, reputation being one of two determinants of wealth. The other, of course, was cattle, which, being portable and easily stolen, also had to be guarded fiercely and jealously, thus contributing to the development of the clan as a paramilitary unit. In fact, cattle raiding was considered an honorable pursuit in the Gaelic world, given that a man could increase both his physical and reputational wealth thereby. Similarly, a Southerner could enhance his standing among his fellows by being a good boxer or handy with a gun, and sure if Fitzgerald himself wasn't esteemed for his ability as a wrestler and for his acumen with the Bowie knife that lurked in his boot. And as in Ireland, too, violence and the drink were often boon companions in the American South, the barroom donnybrook being as much a part of Southern culture as Irish. Indeed, Dónal had already witnessed a few brawls in the taverns of Jonesboro and Atlanta, especially on St. Patrick's Day, when there'd been more non-Irish celebrating than Irish, it being a convenient excuse for *everyone* to get drunk, it seemed.

Another Celtic feature of Southern culture was the preoccupation among men with their leisure time, which, like their Irish brethren, they frittered away on drinking, smoking, hunting, fishing, horses, card-playing, animal-baiting, cock-fighting, or just in good conversation. "No race on earth is as adept at doing nothing as are the Irish!" Dónal had once heard Richard Puxley snarl in frustration. Yet it seemed that in Southern men the Irish had met their match, as many of them seemed to have nothing but leisure pursuits to occupy their time. Of course, slavery was at the root of it, for both rich and poor alike, the former having slaves to work for them while the latter disdained manual labor as "nigger work." As for supporting themselves, poorer men tended to do so through such "honorable" occupations as cattle herding, whiskey distilling, and horse breeding, which left ample free time to supplement the family cauldron through hunting, fishing, or, in time-honored Irish fashion, rustling from the neighbors. To the extent that farming was practiced among the poor, it was largely relegated to women, and among Southern men, "woman's work" ranked only slightly higher on the occupational scale than nigger work. But one leisure pursuit that was solely the province of the rich, and one that they *never* talked about, was the bedding of female slaves, though the large number of light-skinned Negroes spoke volumes as to its prevalence. And of all the hypocrisies inherent in black slavery, Dónal found that one the most heinous, that female members of the "inferior" race were yet good enough to service the baser instincts of their white masters.

Of course, few if any of these leisure pursuits extended to Southern women, for they did *not* drink, as it wasn't considered "ladylike," nor did they smoke, ride, hunt, fish, fight, or have sex with the male slaves. Among wealthy women especially, life had little to offer in the way of meaningful pursuits, as they were not allowed any sort of work beyond management of the household, which, though it often was as big a job as managing a business, was still woman's work after all. And yet they exercised enormous influence over Southern society, being as it seemed to Dónal the guardians of cultural orthodoxy. For many of these women had little else to do but ride around in their carriages visiting others of their ilk, to sit in parlors sipping tea and gossiping about their friends and neighbors and acquaintances, as well as people they didn't even know. Indeed, it seemed that they'd taken up the mantle of the Gaelic bards, being the keepers of the sharp tongue and biting wit, holding the druidic power to destroy a person's reputation with a bit of satirical hearsay or scandalous innuendo. And as with every caste system, that of the South trickled down from the top, binding the poor whites to follow in the footsteps of their betters if they aspired to ever be like them. And *that* was the social glue that bound slavery in place, he found, that so many poor whites aspired to someday owning slaves, which in turn explained why they'd gone to war in such great numbers to defend an institution in which they otherwise had no stake.

As for the rich men who'd gone to war even though it was legal to pay a substitute to fight for them, it often seemed to be their women-folk who propelled them as much as any sense of duty. For under the Southern code of chivalry, failing to serve was deemed dishonorable and would bring disrepute upon the family, something no self-respecting Southern woman would allow. In that regard, they reminded Dónal of the Celtic women who'd attacked their own warriors after they'd given up the field to the Romans, slaughtering even their husbands, sons and brothers rather than letting them live in ignominy. And like them, Southern women were willful and proud, and though they supposedly held a subservient position in a patriarchal society, it was they who held sway over their families and households, the core element of

Southern society, and it was they who guided their men in thought and deed, firmly but subtly, so that often they weren't even aware of it.

In light of all that, Dónal had begun to have a better understanding of Annie, though she seemed an extreme example of the species. Perhaps it was because she was both Southern and Irish, and so cursed with a double dose of those attributes which, for good or ill, so marked both cultures. Or perhaps it was just because she was a spoiled brat and would've been as she was no matter what. He didn't know and didn't care, so long as she left him alone, which for the most part she did, treating him as if he were beneath her notice. And that suited him just fine. For having attained the exalted status of "the O'Something of Something or Other," he didn't need her validation.

But aside from finding himself on familiar ground culturally, there was the burgeoning Irish population of Atlanta to reinforce his feelings of home, especially on Sundays, when he found himself safely ensconced within the friendly confines of Irish Catholicism, surrounded by a congregation that spoke with a collective brogue in response to Father O'Reilly's Cavan lilt. Indeed, in some ways he felt his Irishness more keenly in the Church of the Immaculate Conception than ever he had at home, where he'd known himself to be Irish only in the negative sense, in that he wasn't English. But finding immigrants here from all the four provinces and many more born in America of Irish parents, he knew himself to be part of a greater Irish nation that would soon encompass the entire globe, if it didn't already.

And then there was the St. Patrick's Day celebration in Atlanta, when after morning Mass and a day filled with parades, orations, toasts and general carousing, he'd attended the evening banquet with Fitzgerald, sitting beside him at the head table and even being introduced as one of the dignitaries, a status assured by his standing as a real Irish chieftain. Though it seemed ironic that being The O'Sullivan Béara meant more in America than ever it had at home, he'd also begun to understand what might have happened to Eóghan in New York, how the good life had dulled his sense of urgency toward Ireland, especially since going back meant returning to a life of servitude, both to his country and to its English masters. Sure, if Dónal didn't feel it himself, in that going forward in his quest meant that he, too, would eventually have to go back, a thing he found himself in no hurry to face. Anyway, he rationalized, the border was closed to him now that he'd lost his connection with Bulloch, and with the war heating up, it looked to stay that way for the foreseeable future.

On top of all that, of course, was his hopeless infatuation with a woman twice his age, a married mother of seven, all borne of a man whom he regarded kindly. She gave him no encouragement in it, of course, beyond the occasional coy smile or the odd times he'd glance at her and catch her glancing away. Though he convinced himself it meant nothing, that she would never betray her husband even if she wanted to, still, he could love her from a distance, could fantasize about holding her in his arms, about being her protector, her shield against whatever it was that made her sad. For she deserved to be happy if anyone on this Earth did, and it seemed to him that in making her so, he would find redemption from his sins and thus from his inner pain and suffering. Though deep inside, he knew it would never happen, he also knew that if he left it would *definitely* never happen.

So in the heel of the hunt, Dónal did nothing, and the more nothing he did, the more his inertia gained momentum, until leaving Rural Home became just a delusion, something he would think about tomorrow, a day of reckoning that conveniently never came.

Thinking of Eleanor even now, Dónal's eyes strayed to the upstairs window behind which she lay in bed. It was curtained and dark, of course, the light long extinguished, as indeed was the rest of the house except for the parlor, where Fitzgerald sat reading by the fire. He pictured her lying there asleep, her luxurious hair spilling across the pillow, the bed warm with the heat of her body, her breast rising and falling with each soft breath she took. How he ached to go up there and lie down beside her, to hold her as she slept, to kiss her softly on the forehead, a simple gesture to convey his love, admiration, worship and desire to make her happy.

After a bit, Dónal sighed and rose to go inside. The darkness was complete now, both outside and in, and it was time for a drink to drive it away. Sure, if it wasn't past time.

Yet even as he did, he heard someone tapping softly on a slave cabin door, followed by the sound of it opening and closing, and then more tapping on other doors. Peering into the moonless night, he could just make out the slaves gathering into a knot in the yard and then trooping silently toward the barn. Wondering what they were up to, he followed at a discreet distance, giving the barn a wide berth and coming up on its back side where the entrance to the hayloft lay. Someone had lit a lantern inside, and peering through a knothole he could see that the grouping was all men and that they were engaged in some sort of discussion, though he couldn't make out the words. His curiosity getting the better of him, he quickly scaled the ladder and slipped in through the loft door. Peering over the edge, he found Ol' Jess and Campbell angrily facing each other, while the others stood round them in a contemplative circle.

"I don't care what you say, Benjie," the old man said emphatically, "now ain't de time fo' us to be runnin' off! Dem Yankees is gwine win dis war sooner or later, an' den we's all gwine be free. But we gots to wait fo' it to happ'm, can't you see dat? An' shoot, Benjie, even if'n we was to run off now, de white folks'd just catch us and bring us on back, and you knows better'n anybody what dey do to runaways. Even de Mizzy Fitz can't save us from dat sorrow."

"Yeah, I knows all dat, ol' man," Campbell allowed, "but I don't care no mo'! Dis bein' a slave is gwine be de death o' me, just as sho' as yo' ass is black, an' if'n I's gwine die anyway, it may as well be tryin' to free myself. So I ain't waitin' fo' no damn Yankees what don't care no mo' 'bout us dan de mauzuhs do. I's gwine *now*, and I's gwine 'lone if'n none o' you slaves be's man enough to come with me!"

"Don't you call me dat, niggah!" Ol' Jess roared, waving a gnarled finger in Campbell's face. "Don't you *ever* call me dat! Just 'cause I's smart 'nough not to run off now don't make me no less a man den you is!"

"Get yo' hand outta my face, ol' man," Campbell said, twisting Ol'

Jess's arm painfully. "You ain't no man. You's just Mauzuh Fitz's ol' black Paddy. Dass all you's ever been, an' dass all you's ever gwine be!"

"Let 'im go, Benjie," Yellah Joe said, stepping between them. "He don't mean nothin' 'gin you. He just don't wanna see us get hurt when dey ain't no chance o' gettin' away."

"Aw, fuck you, Yellah Joe! You just as much a slave as he is!"

"Yeah, dass right, Benjie. I's a slave, all right! I's born a slave an' I's prob'ly gwine die one, too! But dat don't mean I like it none! Dat don't mean dat I like steppin' an' fetchin', an' sayin' 'yassuh' an' 'nawsuh' an' playin' de fool fo' every smart-ass Cracker I sees just 'cause he gots two white parents an' I only gots one! An' it don't mean I like bein' bought an' sol', neither, an' it sho' don't mean I like havin' ol' Mauzuh Fitz p'rade me up'n down like I's some kinda prize mule! Nawsuh-ree, Benjie, I don't like it one bit. But dat don't mean I's gwine be stupid 'bout it, neither! Ol' Jess he's right 'bout dis. De time ain't come fo' us to run off yet, an' you knows it just well's I do!"

"Yeah, dass right, Yellah Joe. I knows it, but I just don't care no mo'. You hear me? I just don't care! Dis life ain't worth livin' if'n I gots to be a slave, so I's gwine even if'n it do kill me! An' ain't nobody gwine stop me, neither, not you, not Mauzuh Fitz, an' not even dat paddy what's up dere in de loft spyin' down 'pon us!"

At those words, all the men's faces turned upward in fear. "Shoo', dass Mistuh O'Sullibun up dere!" one of them exclaimed. "We's in fo' it now!" moaned another. "He gwine tell on us fo' sho'!"

"Well, lookee what de cat done drug in," Campbell jeered, as Dónal shinnied down the ladder and stood before him. "If'n it ain't ol' Mauzuh Fitz's white niggah!" Then he dropped his pretense at the slave dialect. "Well, Mr. O'Sullivan. It would appear that once again you have the opportunity to prove the courage of your convictions."

"Sure, Mr. Campbell, if it doesn't at that," Dónal replied. "But then you already know I won't say anything, now don't you?"

"Sure, Paddy, I know you won't turn Judas on us, though not because it's the right thing to do, mind you. You'll do it because you think it ennobling, because you think that in helping the downtrodden you raise yourself above the savages and into the ranks of the civilized. Well, you know what, ould son? There's no such thing as civilization in my experience of the world. We're all animals together here, you, me, blacks, whites, all of us. It's the one way in which we're truly equal, and no amount of self-serving liberality will change it!"

"Sure, that may be true for you, Mr. Campbell, but you're dead wrong if you think that's my motivation. I'll do it because I've been in your shoes, so I have, and I know what it feels like to hunger after freedom. You forget that we Irish are just as much under the yoke in our country as you are here. For seven hundred years the English have ground us under their heel, so much that we're in danger of disappearin' as a people. Sure, if they didn't already starve a million of us to death, and send that many more packin' for foreign strands. So don't think I need any motivation more than that, because I, too, know what it feels like to be a slave!"

"A slave! *A slave?* You think you know what it's like to be a slave? Well, let me tell you something, young Mr. O'Sullivan, you don't know shit! Just because the English treat you like a slave doesn't mean you *are* one, because you were certainly free enough to leave Ireland and go to a place where you aren't treated like a slave, a place where you can be your own man and make your own way in life. And that's a freedom we don't have! We can't go anywhere else to find a better life, because our masters keep us here at the point of a gun! And that's why you can never really know how we feel, no matter how bad you think your life was in Ireland! So please, paddy, don't insult our intelligence by pretending to be one of us! You're a white man in a white man's world, and you will never, *ever* know what it feels like to be black!"

Faced with such a compelling truth, Dónal could only dissemble. "Be that as it may, I still agree with Ol' Jess. 'Twould be suicide to run away just now. But sure, 'tis your own business and none of mine."

Without waiting for a reply, Dónal turned and left the barn. As he reached his porch, he heard a murmur of voices behind him and knew the men were heading back to their cabins. Without looking back, he went inside, sat down at his table and poured himself a good measure of Jack Elliott's whiskey. But just as he was about to knock it back, Campbell opened the door and stepped inside. For a long moment he didn't say anything, just eyed Dónal thoughtfully. Then he sighed and looked down at the floor.

"They voted not to go," he said softly. "It was unanimous."

"Did they now?" Dónal grunted, before tossing back his whiskey and pouring himself another. "'Twas wise of them so."

"Yes, I suppose." Then Campbell raised his eyes to Dónal. "Will you help me?"

Dónal sighed and looked at his glass. "Sure, I'll help you," he said, letting his eyes stray back to Campbell. "But you'll never make it."

"It doesn't matter," the man replied, his expression as blank as stone. He hesitated for a moment then, as if struggling with the words that came next. "Thank you," he said finally, and was gone, leaving the door open behind him.

"Don't mention it," Dónal said, raising his glass to the darkness.

⌘

The wind has a voice tonight, *someone said, and he cocked his head and put a hand to his ear, trying to catch the sound of it over the lashing rain and pounding thunder.* It sounds so mournful and sad, like it's keening for poor Eóghan.

And then he remembered where he was and what he was doing, keeping the death watch at his father's bedside. But no, he saw, as the mist rolled back and things came into focus. There was no bed, just a coffin on a table, like the one in which Uncle Séamus had slept, though he knew he wasn't in Uncle Séamus's cottage. Nor was he a child for that matter, but a grown man able to stand on his own two feet and look down into the coffin, down on the handsome young man with the piercing blue eyes and streak of white in his jet black hair.

Eóghan, is that you? *he asked, for he could see that he wasn't dead at all, but merely resting.*

But the man didn't answer, just cocked his own head. Do you hear it? *he asked.* She's come for me!

And then there was no mistaking it, the wail of keening, coming louder and stronger, until he thought his ears would surely burst with it. Looking up then, he saw her there, hanging from her cross, her dead eyes open and boring into his own, her dead mouth wailing for the suffering of the living.

She's come for me, *the young man said.* Send for the priest, she's come for me.

⌇⌇⌇

Dónal awoke with a start, the sound of keening still ringing in his ears, though it was distant now and muted, coming from somewhere beyond the walls of his cottage. 'Oh, God, she's come for me!' he thought in horror, his heart racing, sudden beads of sweat springing from his brow. 'It's my turn to go, and she's come for me!' Rising from his bed, he padded softly to the door, trembling with mortal terror at what lay beyond, yet unable to resist her call. As if in a dream, he opened it, gasping in horror when he saw her there, floating across the yard like a waking nightmare, luminous and spectral in the moonlight.

"Oh, Jesus, God!" he moaned in Irish, shrinking from the door. "Oh, Jesus, deliver me!"

At the sound of him, she stopped and turned his way. "Mr. O'Sullivan? Is that you?" she called softly, her voice silvery and ephemeral, not that of a waking nightmare, but of a living angel.

"Yes, Eleanor, it's me," he replied hastily, relieved, though at the same time mortally embarrassed. "Just a moment if you please. I'm not decent."

"Jayzis fookin' Christ," he muttered as he slipped into the shadows to put on his clothes. "If I'm not a fool, then there was never a one so born!"

"Are you all right?" she asked when he emerged, speaking softly so as not to awaken anyone. "Did I startle you?"

"Yes, I'm all right," he lied, his heart still pounding, though now at the sight of her standing before him, clad only in a long white robe over her nightclothes, her luxurious golden hair spilling loose about her shoulders. "And no, you didn't startle me. I heard a noise outside – it woke me, actually – and I just opened the door to see what it was."

"Ah, so you heard the vixen, too, then. I went and chased her away so she wouldn't draw the males."

"Sure, I suppose that's what it was," Dónal agreed, looking into the night lest she see what was in his eyes. "Did she wake you, too, then?"

"Oh, no, Dónal, it wasn't her, just my own foolish dreams, I'm afraid. They're so silly, really, but how can one help what one dreams?"

"You can't, and sure, if God doesn't know I've tried."

"Do you have bad dreams, too?" she asked, laying a hand on his arm to turn him toward her. "Now what could a nice young man like you possibly have to dream about that could be so bad?"

"Oh, lots of things," he replied, moving closer, so close that he could feel the warmth of her and smell her night scent. "Things you don't want to hear about. Horrible things, ghosts and monsters and bad people chasin' me, people I can't get away from no matter how I try, people who want to hurt me, and even worse, people who will never, *ever*, leave me alone."

A tear started in her eye then as she saw the pain that was in him, and that it welled up from the depths of his soul. "Oh, you poor man," she said, laying a hand lightly on his cheek. "You poor, haunted young soul. Whatever could have happened to you to cause such everlasting pain?"

Taking her hand, he kissed her palm lightly and cupped it to his cheek. "'Tis nothin', Eleanor," he said, taking her other hand and gazing deeply into her eyes. "At least, nothin' I can't live with. But tell me. What could possibly trouble the dreams of an angel like you? What wakes you from your sleep and sends you into the night seekin' solace from the Darkness? Tell me, Eleanor, and I'll protect you from it. Tell me, and I'll drive away your sadness."

She smiled at his gallantry, though it faded under the intensity of his gaze. "It's dark," she said, turning her eyes inward upon the panoply of her dreams. "I'm standing at my window and it's dark outside, though I know it isn't the darkness of night, but of a pall over the land like a cloud of smoke. And there's a red glow on the horizon, too, though it isn't the sunset because it's coming from the north, from Atlanta, and it's fire that I see. Suddenly, I hear noises in the yard, and looking down I see an army of men, hundreds of them, all running away to the south, their faces twisted in fear at what's pursuing them. And it frightens me, too, for I can see the enemy advancing over the horizon, coming on in row upon row until their blood red coats blot out the land. 'It's the British Army,' I think, 'and they're coming for my land! I've got to run! I've got to get away!' But it's too late! There are hands at my throat and I can't breathe! 'I can't breathe!' I want to shout. 'I can't breathe, I can't breathe, I can't breathe . . .'

"I can't breathe," she said, focusing on Dónal again. "And that's why I wake up, because I can't breathe. Oh, Dónal, it's just so horrible!"

As the pain overwhelmed her, she covered her face with her hands and sobbed out her abiding sadness, the sound of it a sword thrust to Dónal's heart. Without thought for the consequences, he wrapped his arms around her, cradling her head against his chest as he stroked her hair and rocked her gently from side to side.

"Whisht, Eleanor, 'tis but a dream," he said in his most comforting tone, his heart rising within him at the chance to be her protector. "There's no British comin' to take away your land. It's just an old folk memory left over from Ireland, nothin' more."

"No, Dónal, you don't understand. It's not a dream at all; it's my punishment!"

"Your punishment? What could you have ever done to deserve it?"

"It's my punishment for failing to appreciate my husband and all he has done to provide for me, for us."

"I still don't understand. You've lost me entirely now."

"It's my punishment for being selfish, for wishing that that very thing would happen, that we would indeed lose this miserable land, and for praying to God to let it happen! I never wanted to live out here

630

in the country, so far from civilized people and civilized life. I'm an educated woman, and I want to associate with people of my own ilk, people of learning and culture, people who appreciate art and music and literature and ideas. It seems so little to ask, really, since we wouldn't have to sell the farm or move further away than Atlanta, if Phillip would only hire an overseer to manage things for him. After all, with the train and telegraph service, just ever so many people are doing it that way now. But no, he says, overseers are a waste of money, and so I'm doomed to spend my days as mistress of a wretched little African village, populated by people of such withering ignorance that the very sight of them makes my skin crawl. And oh, how I do hate them for it, even though I know it's not their fault because we've forced it upon them. Why, I even hate them that they go on living year after year, for without them cotton wouldn't be king and my husband would be in another business, and I wouldn't have to live out here in this godforsaken wilderness. And so I'm being punished for that selfishness, too, it seems, for failing to love them as I would love myself, and for my lack of repentance for the crime I've committed against them. Oh, God in Heaven, forgive me for failing You so!"

With that, she buried her face against his chest and gave herself over to sorrow, her body heaving with the pain that was in her. "There, now, don't cry," Dónal crooned, holding her tight against him, sure of his ability to make the pain go away. "'Tis not as bad as all that."

"Oh, but it is, Dónal, it is! I'm the most horrible person I know, because I'm aware of all my failures and yet lack the grace to do anything about them."

But for all that she sought to denigrate herself, it only made her grow in Dónal's eyes. "Eleanor Fitzgerald," he said, softly kissing the top of her head, "you are the kindest, gentlest, most loving and caring woman I have ever known, and I would give my life to make you see it, too."

She raised her face to him then, but rather than pulling back to look at her, he kissed her on the forehead, while at the same time sliding his hand along the side of her face to lift her lips to his. It wasn't something he'd intended to do, really; it just happened, a consequence of all his pent-up desire for her, though it felt as natural as if God had ordained it and all the forces of Nature were bringing it to fruition. And feeling her body quiver against him, her lips conforming to his, he knew that she wanted it, too.

But then her hands were suddenly between them, pushing him hard away.

"*Mister O'Sullivan!*" she exclaimed, backing away from him, her eyes filled with shock and moral indignation. "Sir, I do think you mean to take advantage!"

"No, Mrs. Fitzgerald, no!" he exclaimed in horror, his inner voice screaming at him, *You fool, you fool, you stupid bloody fool!* "You misunderstand me! I meant nothin' of the sort. I only wanted to comfort you in your distress!"

"And just how did you propose to do that by kissing me?" she demanded, her voice as cold as a serpent's eyes.

"I . . . I didn't mean to . . . that is, I only wanted . . . I'm sorry, Mrs. Fitzgerald, I didn't mean anything untoward, truly I didn't. All I meant to do was comfort you, because . . . because you're such an incredible, beautiful woman and I just couldn't bear to see you in such pain. If I made a mistake in my method, then I'm sorry for it, to be sure! But you've got to believe me when I say that I would never, ever presume to take advantage of your friendship so! I swear it, Mrs. Fitzgerald, on my dead mother's grave, I do swear it!"

"Don't swear, young man, it's a mortal sin!" Eleanor retorted, and though her voice was softer, it now had the tone of an angry mother in it, as if to reinforce their relative positions.

"Yes, ma'am. I'll not swear it, but 'tis true all the same. You have my utmost respect, and I honor your friendship above all worldly possessions, and I assure you that I would never purposely do or say or even think anything that would in any way be hurtful or offensive to you. Can you not believe me? Can you not forgive my mistake, one I made only because I care so deeply for you?"

She hesitated then before answering, gazing deeply into his eyes to search out the truth in them, the moments passing like years as he awaited her judgment. "Yes, I believe you," she sighed at last. "I believe you didn't mean anything, and that you wouldn't do anything to hurt or offend me. And I forgive you. But it's just that you surprised me so!"

"Yes, ma'am, I know I did, and I'm sorry for it."

"Yes, I know that. And anyway, I'm the one to blame. I lost control of my emotions, something a true lady never does, especially in her *nightgown*, of all things!"

"No, ma'am, 'tis no fault of your own. 'Tis no one's fault, really, just a misunderstandin'."

"Yes, I suppose so. But Mr. O'Sullivan, lest you should misunderstand my feelings for my husband, let me say plainly that while he certainly isn't perfect, I have no room in my heart for any man but him."

"I never thought any different, Mrs. Fitzgerald."

"Good," she said with a Christian smile, one that cut to his heart for the lies he'd made her believe, though more so for its being so impersonal. "Then I'll bid you good night, and pleasant dreams."

"And yourself, Mrs. Fitzgerald," he replied, though she'd already turned away.

Watching her go was like falling back into a dream, as she floated across the yard, luminous and spectral in the moonlight. Indeed, it was a nightmare of a night, one that he knew would haunt him for the rest of his days.

Turning away, he went straight to the bottle by his bed. "Ah, Jayzis," he mumbled, finding it only about half full, "but that's not going to be *nearly* enough."

chapter 33

Rural Home Plantation

THE AFTERNOON WAS STILL AND STIFLING, the heat radiating from the ground in visible waves while the humidity was so thick as to blur the horizon and turn the cloudless sky almost white, the combination sapping a man's strength in less time than it took to think it. Yet it was the swarming gnats and darting flies that bedeviled Dónal more as he trudged through the cornfields with Yellah Joe, drawn as they were to the salt of his sweat and the blood of his many mosquito bites, which despite all warnings to the contrary, he couldn't help but scratch. What a contrast summer was to the genteel Southern spring, the days becoming hellish as May melted into June, and he and the Fitzgeralds were suffering frightfully from it, their moonbeam complexions and North European constitutions affording them no protection whatsoever. It was hard on the slaves, too, of course, with their long workdays, though he was surprised how well they bore it, going stoically about their labor, day after day, year after year, until Death finally brought the freedom for which they so yearned. They were amazing people in many ways, these Black Men of the Bags, and he respected them mightily for their ability to endure such hardship and yet keep alive their hope for a better future. They were like the Irish in that, and if it was true that strength came through adversity, then both peoples would have no shortage of it when it came their turn to join the ranks of the free.

And if everything went according to Dónal's plan, he would see that one man among them would do just that. For the night encounter with Eleanor had galvanized his resolve, making him see that not only was he wasting his time, but that he'd overstayed his welcome in the process. Not that she was doing anything directly to make him feel that way, as she treated him cordially and respectfully, if somewhat distantly. Yet it made him face up to what he'd known in his heart all along, that his business lay elsewhere and it was high time he got on with it. So, taking the opportunity to kill two birds with one stone, he'd spoken to Campbell about his promise to help him escape, and the two of them had devised a scheme to that purpose. They would depart on the coming Sunday while the Fitzgeralds were in Atlanta for Mass, Dónal leaving a note that he'd heard from Bulloch in Savannah and decided on the spur of the moment to pay him a visit, taking Campbell along for assistance and company. Though of course his cheek at commandeering their servant would raise eyebrows among the Fitzgeralds, he was sure it would be several days before they became suspicious that anything else was afoot. By that time they would be well away, having made their way north to Richmond by train, while posing as a young gentleman traveling with his manservant to visit relations. From there, things became rather fuzzy, as they had no way to plan for crossing the border until they got there and did some reconnoitering. But at least Dónal had money set aside for bribes and assistance, and with prudence and a bit of luck, they'd part company in Washington and go their separate ways toward reuniting with family, Campbell in his native Philadelphia and himself among the 69th New York Regiment.

It was an audacious plan, Dónal knew, and surely fraught with peril. Yet he didn't allow himself to think about it, lest it daunt him into a relapse of inertia, something he'd vowed to avoid at all costs. Still, he couldn't help feeling guilty about Yellah Joe, that he would be taking away his best friend without warning, and even more so for leaving him behind. But the border crossing would be hazardous enough with just the two of them, and a third man, especially a conspicuously large, red-headed Negro, might make it all but impossible.

Hearing Yellah Joe grunt behind him, Dónal glanced over his shoulder to find him shifting his bundle of fishing gear from one broad shoulder to the other, while changing hands with his heavy bucket of worms. "Look at you, all dressed up like a Tinker's donkey!" Dónal had gibed when the man came to get him for their weekly fishing excursion, though remembering that night in the barn when he'd declared his repugnance at being treated like a prize mule, he'd regretted the words immediately. *But dat don't mean I like it none!* Yellah Joe had said of his status as human chattel, so surely he would find the animal metaphor offensive. But he'd just grinned good-naturedly, taking the jest in friendly fashion, just as Dónal had intended it. Indeed, leaving Yellah Joe behind would be one of the hardest things he'd ever done.

"Are you sure I can't help you with any of that?" Dónal asked, mainly to assuage his own conscience, knowing the reply would again be negative.

"Nawsuh, I's got it," Yellah Joe replied. "It ain't dat heavy. 'Sides, Mauzuh Fitz won't like it none if'n he catch me lettin' you do de work."

"Ah, don't worry for him. Bogan Mask stopped by the house for dinner today, and if he's true to form, they'll still be at it when supper rolls around."

"Yassuh, I knows what you mean 'bout dat. Dat Rev'rend Mask be's a caution, all right. *Rouse ye, rouse ye, fo' de Kingdom of de Lawd is nigh!*" Yellah Joe chanted, in imitation of the circuit-riding preacher's favored, though well-worn, mantra. "I wonder how many time he done already said dat dis mornin'."

"Enough to make the ould man crazy with it, to be sure, though he'll give as good as he gets. After all the years ould Bogie's spent tryin' to convert him to Calvinism, you'd think by now he'd have cottoned to the fact that it can't be done. And he should know better anyway, bein' that himself is Donegal Irish on his mother's side."

"Wellsuh, I don't know nothin' 'bout dat, but I think de Mauzuh kinda like havin' somebody to fuss with now an' again, de which of it bein' why he let de Rev'rend come roun' in de first place."

"Sure, if you don't have the right of it there. He can be an ornery little runt when the mood strikes him so."

"Yassuh, if'n you says so. *Rouse ye, rouse ye, fo' de Kingdom of de Lawd is nigh!* What you reckon dat mean, anyway, Mistuh O'Sullibun?"

"Well, Yellah Joe, it could mean a lot of things. For instance, it could mean that the end of the world is comin' soon and we'd all better get ready for Judgment Day. But that doesn't seem likely in my way of thinkin', that it will all end in one big bang with all of us facin' Himself together. What I take it to mean is that life is tenuous, meanin' that none of us knows whether we'll be alive from one minute to the next, and so we'd better be prepared to face our judgment whenever it comes. Do you follow me so?"

"Yassuh, I reckon so. You means dat since nobody knows when dey gwine die, we's all better be good all de time, case it happen when we ain't 'speckin' it none. Dat right, Mistuh O'Sullibun?"

"To be sure, more or less."

"So de which of it is den, dat I gots to be good all de time an' 'bey all de Mauzuh's rules an' work hard even if'n I don't feels like it, 'cause de Lawd done made me a nigra slave, an' if'n I wants to get to Heb'm, I gots to be a good'un. Leastways, dass what de white preachers be tellin' us when-some-ever dey comes 'round. You think dass right, too, Mistuh O'Sullibun?"

Hearing the words, Dónal knew he should've seen it coming. "No, Yellah Joe, I don't . . . " he began, turning his head to look into his friend's eyes, though seeing them round with fear cut him off.

"Look out!" Yellah Joe screamed, though Dónal knew it was too late, feeling his foot among the coils and then the whiplash of its strike, so swift that he didn't know he'd been bitten until finding it clinging to his inner thigh.

"Jayzis, God in Heaven!" Dónal exclaimed softly, not so much in shock at the bite as at the sheer, unutterable monstrosity of the thing. It was a rattlesnake, that much he knew from the dead ones the men brought in from the fields, though one of such enormity that it had to

637

be the father and mother of them all. And looking into its small, alien eyes, he saw that it was looking back at him, watching his own eyes even as its venom flowed into his veins, waiting for the inexorable hand of Death to draw them closed and render him fit for consumption, a fresh piece of meat to be leisurely devoured. In that moment, it seemed that the rest of the world had fallen away, leaving just the two of them locked in their deadly embrace, hunter and hunted, predator and prey. It seemed surreal to him, as if happening to someone else, and he could only watch in fascination as Yellah Joe yanked it away and killed it with one swift motion, a twist and a jerk and a pop of breaking spine, his huge hands barely encompassing its body. And still his mind wouldn't accept the reality of it, even as his eyes strayed from the still-writhing monster to the twin points of blood staining his pants, to Yellah Joe gaping in horror. Sure, it was just a dream, a nightmare, a phantasm, and the horror would be gone when he awoke, leaving only a vague sense of uneasiness in its wake.

But then the pain hit him, striking with the impact of a locomotive, buckling his legs and knocking him hard to the ground. It was real all right, he knew then; he'd been bitten by a snake and surely his death was only a matter of moments away. Feeling the pain spread through his leg, he screamed in torment, tearing at his pants as though to save himself by ripping his leg from his body, a thought that indeed sprang into his panic-stricken mind. But it was already too late, he knew, feeling the venom coursing through his veins even as his leg went numb, faster and faster as fear pushed his heart-rate higher, his animal instinct for survival paradoxically speeding him toward oblivion.

Then Yellah Joe whisked him up and ran toward the house, screaming for help at the top of his lungs. "Hurry, Yellah Joe!" Dónal urged, closing his eyes and clinging to both his friend and life with all his might. "Oh, God, please hurry!"

But even as Yellah Joe bounced him along, he felt his body begin to relax and his heart-rate slow, the images in his mind going dark from the outside in, until there was only a tiny pinpoint of light in the center, like that at the end of a long tunnel. 'This is it,' he thought. 'I'm dying.'

As he neared the end of the tunnel, the light grew ever wider, until the Darkness was gone and he found himself standing on the shoulder of a mountain, in the midst of a green land bathed in golden light. And She was there to meet him, young and alive now, unscathed by Earthly predations and Otherworldly only in Her beauty, Her smiling green eyes telling him he had nothing to fear.

Come and walk with me for a bit, She said, taking him by the hand.

Am I dead? he asked, feeling only relief now that it was over.

Oh, no, you're not dead. But then there's really no such thing as Death, you know, just a change from one reality to another, like crossing this mountain from one valley to the next.

And with that, they came to the mountain's edge, and gazing across a verdant valley he saw a stone fortress in the distance, much like old Cahernageeha, though as it would have been when it, too, was young and strong, the citadel of lords mighty and proud.

Am I in Heaven? he asked, but She just laughed, the music of it a singing waterfall.

Then where am I?

You're where your heart is, where you've always been.

Ireland?

But she didn't reply, just turned him gently away. Come, it's time to go back now.

But I thought you were taking me home!

No, you have to find your own way home, She said, Her smile enigmatic now.

And with that, they were back in his cabin at Rural Home, looking down at his body stretched upon the bed, racked and feverish.

I don't want to go back, he pleaded. Please don't make me!

It isn't up to me, She said softly, letting go of his hand. But don't worry. We'll meet again.

Will I find Eóghan? At least tell me that!

But She was gone, even as the Darkness closed around him.

There was an angel hovering over him when he awoke, blue-eyed and golden-haired, and for a moment he thought he was still dreaming, seeing Eleanor as she'd been in her youth. But then he realized it wasn't her at all, but Sadie, and that tears streamed down her cheeks as she clasped his hands in hers.

"You're awake!" she whispered hoarsely. "Oh, thank God, you're finally awake!"

And with that, she buried her face on his chest and let loose her anguish, built up over days of watching anxiously at his bedside.

"Here, now, what's all this?" he asked weakly. "Surely, you didn't think I was goin' to sleep forever, did you?"

"Yes, but I did! I thought you'd died and left me! Your heart stopped beating, and you stopped breathing for so long that Papa even sent for the undertaker. Oh, Dónal, I just couldn't bear to lose you! I just couldn't!"

"Ah, sure, girl, 'tis all right now. You're not goin' to lose me. 'Twill take more than a little shnake to do me in."

"Oh, but it wasn't little at all!" she protested, rising up to look at him. "It was a great big horrible snake with fangs like butcher knives! Why, Papa said it could've killed an elephant even, and as for little Izzie, well, it would've just scared her to death! And when I saw your leg already all black and swollen when Yellah Joe brought you in, I was sure the doctor would have to cut it off! And then he said you were going to die. And then . . . and then you stopped breathing, and . . . oh, I just can't bear to think of it!

"But you're awake now, and you aren't going to die, and your leg will heal up just fine, and . . . and I'm not going to lose you after all. Am I, Dónal?"

"No, Sadie girl, I'm not goin' anywhere," he assured her, though catching her look and tone, he finally began to see what she meant by it.

But even so, he was taken completely by surprise when she bent down and kissed him on the lips. And though it was a little girl's kiss, close-mouthed and innocent, still he felt the passion behind it.

"Oh, Dónal, I do love you so," she whispered, snuggling her cheek to his, her breath hot on his ear. "And you love me, too, don't you?"

And now he was wide-eyed and staring, wondering how he was going to get out of it without leaving her completely devastated. He'd known all along that she had a crush on him, though try as she might to get him to encourage it, he'd done nothing of the sort.

But then a pointed *Ahem!* from the door sent her flying from him.

"Mama!" she exclaimed, red-faced and mortified. "Mama, I didn't know you . . . I mean, I didn't do . . . that is, I–"

"Yes, Sadie dear, I know," Eleanor said, her words benign but not her voice. "But come now, don't you think we should let Mr. O'Sullivan get some rest?"

"Yes, Mama," the girl replied contritely, and was gone before the words were cool.

But for a long moment, Eleanor just stood in the doorway, eyeing Dónal with the most purposefully blank look he'd ever seen.

"You know I did nothin' to encourage that, don't you?" he said, wondering at the same time what emotion she was concealing: hate, anger, jealousy? "Sure, I'd just awakened, and it all happened before I could stop it."

"Oh, yes, I know. And you are innocent in it, I'd say. Yet it happened all the same, just as a few other things have just 'happened' in your time with us. And speaking of that, Mr. O'Sullivan, just out of curiosity, do you know how much longer you plan to be with us?"

"No, ma'am, I don't," Dónal lied, not wanting to jeopardize his plans with Campbell. "But I assure you that nothin' like it will ever happen again."

"Oh, yes, I'm quite sure of that," she said, and was gone.

⸙

Dónal rode slowly along the road, letting the mare choose her own pace, his head drooping with exhaustion. It was only the second day since he'd awakened, and he was still weak from lost nourishment and the lingering effects of rattlesnake venom, with only the urgency of his errand driving him from bed. For hearing the doctor say he was going to die, Campbell had run away in a fit of despair, with Yellah Joe following soon after in hopes of bringing him back. Or at least that was what Ol' Jess reported, saying Yellah Joe feared mightily for his friend's life, since runaways were tracked with vicious dogs handled by equally vicious men who liked nothing better than to make examples of their prisoners. "Dey's de worse white men de Good Lawd done ever put on dis here earth," he'd said, "'sides de oberseers, dat is." So Dónal dragged himself from bed and set out to find his friends before they could come to grief, spending the entire day at it before turning toward home.

But as he rode through a wood, the crack of a whip brought him upright in the saddle. Peering through the trees to the right, he could just make out the shapes of men and horses in a small clearing, in the center of which stood Yellah Joe tied to a flogging stake. Spurring his horse without thought for the consequences, he charged headlong through the trees screaming at the top of his lungs, his green eyes blazing and red hair flying wildly behind. Thinking the Devil himself was upon them, the men scattered before his fury even as their horses and dogs stampeded into the woods. But Dónal had eyes only for the man with the whip, and he bore down on him and bowled him over before he could reach the safety of the trees. Wheeling sharply, he turned back to Yellah Joe.

"Dat you, Mistuh O'Sullibun?" Yellah Joe mumbled, his pummeled face and welted and bloody back a testament to the barbarity of the master race.

"To be sure, Yellah Joe," Dónal replied gently, as he cut his bonds. "I've come to take you home. Can you stand long enough to get on the horse?"

"Yassuh, I sho' can. It gwine take mo'n a whuppin' from a li'l ol' white boy to knock me down! But you's gwine have to show me de way. My eyes be's swole all de way shut."

"She's just here beside you, Yellah Joe. Give me your foot and I'll help you up."

Yet even as Yellah Joe swung into the saddle, Dónal heard an angry voice behind him. "Just what the hell do you think yer doin', Paddy?" it demanded, as a hand grabbed him by the shoulder and made to spin him around.

But Dónal was too quick for him, having his knife at the man's throat before he even saw it, while in the same motion jerking his revolver from its holster. "What I'm doin' is returnin' Mr. Fitzgerald's property to him before you can do any further damage. You've no problem with that, do you, boyo?"

"That nigger's a runaway, an' Mr. Fitzgerald hired me to bring 'im back!"

"And so you have. I'll take him from here and you can bugger off back to whatever hole 'twas you crawled out of!"

"Goddamn it, boy, I'm a officer of the law an' you're interferin' with my sworn duty. Mr. Fitzgerald wants me to bring back both them runaways, an' the sooner I find out where the other 'un's at, the sooner I can do it. But that ain't gonna happen 'less that nigger there tells me, and he ain't gonna tell me 'less I beat it out of 'im. So if you know what's good for you, just back off and let me take care of this."

But Dónal didn't bother to answer, just kneed the man in the groin and turned away. "Come on, Yellah Joe. We're goin' home!"

"Goddamn it, Billy, don't just stand there gapin'," the man grunted. "Shoot that sum'bitch!"

"Say what?" the man addressed retorted. "Shit, Horace, you crazy?"

"No, I ain't crazy, goddamn it! Shoot 'im!"

"Uhn-uh, Horace, no way! Havin' some fun with a runaway nigger's one thing, but there ain't no way I'm gonna shoot a white man, just 'cause he done got the drop on you! 'Sides, I know ol' Donald there from Elliott's place, an' he ain't a bad sort, even if he is a Mick."

"Billy, you shit for brains, he's interferin' with the law!"

"No, he ain't, Horace. He's just interferin' with you collectin' the bounty on two niggers, 'stead o' just one! An' anyway, that boy wasn't

643

gon' tell us nothin' no matter what we done to 'im. So let's just give 'im to Donald, an' us go have a drink. You'll still get paid for bringin' 'im in."

"Goddamn you, Billy Hayes, that ain't the point, an' you know it! That man's defyin' my authority, an' you're lettin' 'im get away with it!"

"Ah, fuck you, Horace Turner, an' your precious authority, too! Come on, boys, let's go."

"You ain't gonna get away with this, Paddy!" Turner said, glaring at Dónal.

"I already have!" Dónal replied, then turned his back and led the horse away.

⌾〰〰〰⌾

They were all silent as Dónal led the horse into the yard, the slaves gathered in a knot behind Ol' Jess and the Fitzgeralds clustered on the steps, black and white equal in their horror at the sight of Yellah Joe. And silent they remained as Nat and Caesar helped him into his cabin, Ol' Jess and his people keeping a vigil by the door while Eleanor and Bessie May tended his wounds. Indeed, the only sound came from Dónal, as he hid his face against his horse and wept, overcome not with grief and exhaustion so much as embarrassment that his skin was white, that he belonged to a tribe capable of such willful and wanton cruelty.

"'Tis as bad as that, is it?" Fitzgerald asked softly, laying a hand on his shoulder.

"That bad and maybe worse if I hadn't put a stop to it!" Dónal replied bitterly, his eyes narrow and hard. "Sure, they might have killed him, so much *fun* were they havin'!"

"Ah, me. 'Tis a shame and a misfortune, Yellah Joe bein' the gentle soul that he is. Yet and still, the fault is but his own. He knew the beatin' that was in it, from me as surely as them, since not even herself can save a runaway from his appointed leather."

"But he didn't run away, don't you see? He was just after bringin'

644

Benjie back, which you'd have known if you'd listened to Ol' Jess!"

"I can't help the reason that was in it. He knows he's not allowed off this farm without me permission, no ifs, ands or buts about it! I mean, where would we be if they all fucked off and left just anytime they pleased? 'Twould be chaos, it would, and as bad for them as us!"

"Yes, freedom does have a certain element of chaos in it, I suppose. But how can you know it's bad for them if you've never let them try it?"

"Now look here, son. I know there's been a shock in it, but that darkie only got his due."

"That 'darkie' is my *friend*, and I'll thank you to remember it so!"

"Sure, if that isn't liberal of ye, fine jackeen that ye are. But the laws that govern the races in this country don't allow for it, and as long as ye're a guest in me house, I'll thank ye to remember *that* so!"

"To hell with your laws and races! My race is the *human* race, and I credit no others!"

"Be that as it may, the rest of the world does, and I find it hard to believe that ye're right and all the rest of us wrong. Now I've nothin' more to say on the subject. So I suggest ye go to yeer cabin and get some rest. Sure, ye'll see it all different after a drop and a sleep."

"No, I won't," Dónal replied, then turned his back and stalked away.

⟨※⟩

In the morning, Dónal's first thought upon rising was for Yellah Joe, and he limped across the yard to his cabin, stopping outside the door to see if he was awake. But seeing his eyes closed, he was just about to turn away when the man called out to him.

"Dat you out dere, Mistuh O'Sullibun?"

"'Tis indeed, Yellah Joe," Dónal replied, and went inside. "How did you know it was me?"

"Oh, I can always tell it's you by de way you walks."

"Oh, and how is that?"

"All quiet and sof'-like, like you's tryin' to sneak up on sump'm maybe. I ain't never know'd a white man walk dat way befo'. Most of 'em makes lotsa noise, like dey's big an' pow'ful, an' ain't scared o' nothin' an' nobody. Reckon it must'a been a spell since a ol' wolf done jump out 'hind a tree an' gobble one y'all up. But den you come 'long and walks like you's tryin' not to touch de groun'. Now why you do dat fo'?"

"Ah, Yellah Joe. 'Tis a story with neither end nor beginnin'. You'd just have to live my life to understand it. But I suppose the short of it is that it's my father's fault."

"Oh. Well, I don't know nothin' 'bout dat, seein's I ain't never had no daddy befo'. What's it like anyway, Mistuh O'Sullibun, havin' a daddy, dat is?"

Dónal didn't answer right away, for the moment finding himself daunted by the enormity of the question. Yet as he thought about it, images of his father ran through his mind, of the angry man he'd so often been, of the way he'd humiliated him at Uncle Séamus's wake, and of that fateful day at Dunboy that had set him on the long road to where he was. Surely he couldn't tell Yellah Joe those things. But then he remembered that glorious day when his father took him into town for new clothes, and the pride he'd felt when he patted him on the back and said, *Good man, Dónal.* Was there ever a better day than that? If so, he couldn't remember it.

"Well, Yellah Joe, it seems to me that the best way to answer is to ask you a question yourself, and that is, what's the best thing that's ever happened to you, or that you could ever imagine happenin' to you?"

"Shoo', dass easy. Bein' free."

"Well, that's what it's like then."

"Wellsuh, seein's I ain't never gwine have no daddy myself, I reckon I's just gwine have to have me some chirrens of my own one dese days, so's I can make dem feel dat a'way. Course now, I ain't gwine do it 'less I's free. Nawsuh, I can't bring no babies into dis world if'n dey's gwine have to be slaves, 'cause I do know what dat feel like."

In the face of such magnanimity, Dónal felt small indeed. "You're a good man, Yellah Joe, and I'm proud to be your friend."

"Beggin' yo' pardon, Mistuh O'Sullibun, but we ain't friends. Only free mens can be friends with one 'nother."

Though the words stung, Dónal knew they weren't meant to. "Well, if you were free, Yellah Joe, would we be friends?"

"Yassuh, I reckon so. Yassuh, if'n I's free, we be friends."

"Good," Dónal said, and rose from his chair. "I'll take that for now. See you later."

Once outside, Dónal stopped to wipe his eyes. After that conversation, he knew he couldn't leave Rural Home without taking Yellah Joe with him. He might have to wait a bit longer, but what were a few days in the grand scheme of things? Maybe he'd even take him to Ireland, if he wanted to go, the man being half a Gael, after all.

Going to the chicken coop then, he grabbed the first hen he could reach, deftly wrung its neck and headed toward the kitchen.

"Bessie May," he said, tossing it on the cutting board, "I want you to fry this up for Yellah Joe!"

"Lawsy, do de Mauzuh know you done kilt dat bird?" Bessie May demanded, eyeing him suspiciously. "Dem chickens be just fo' de white folks!"

Laying his hands on the little woman's shoulders then, Dónal gave her his most winning smile. "Ah, Bessie May, me darlin' dear, but what himself doesn't know won't hurt him, now will it?"

It took a moment for his meaning to sink in, but when it did, a sly grin spread across her face. "Nawsuh, I reckon not."

"Good," he said, winking conspiratorially before turning away.

"White folks!" she muttered when he was out of earshot.

chapter 34

Rural Home Plantation

THE THUNDERSTORM PASSED as quickly as it had come, its brief but violent downpour serving only to worsen the already stifling humidity as it raised a veil of steam from the sun-broiled earth. And humidity was one thing Dónal had learned to hate about the American South, even in his brief experience, for it made him sweat constantly and profusely, to the point that he never felt clean no matter how often he bathed. Indeed, he already felt sticky though he was barely ten minutes out of a cool tub, the mere exertion of getting dressed and walking across the yard enough to raise a glow on his skin. Nor did it help that he was wearing his evening clothes, which were not exactly conducive to comfort anyway, being of heavier fabric and somewhat constrictive in their cut. But at least there would be good whiskey in it, he thought, since Eleanor's ban would surely be lifted for the guest that waited in the parlor, the Fitzgeralds wanting desperately to make a good impression on him.

For Mamie had finally gotten herself a suitor, one whom she and her parents found equally to their liking, and for most of the day Rural Home had been abuzz with activity in preparation for his visit. His name was John Stephens, and Dónal knew him to speak to, their paths having crossed on many Sundays at Mass. He was a fellow Irishman, native to Offaly (or King's County, as the English made it), though he was already long enough in America to have chosen sides in the war, as evidenced by his commission in the Confederate Army. As for the rest of him, he was a bit older than Mamie, being in his late twenties, blond, blue-eyed, and handsome enough in a Leinsterman's sort of way, especially in his crisp captain's uniform, though not so much as to make her look bad by comparison. On the contrary, she seemed to reach her full flowering when in his presence, her inward happiness that a mature, serious man had finally shown an interest in her perhaps adding the glow to her cheek and the smile to her eyes.

Yet for all that he was happy for Mamie, Dónal found it difficult to believe that Stephens was interested in her for herself alone. Indeed, he'd seen him turn more than a few heads among the marriageable young ladies of the congregation, an Irish Catholic army officer being a rare enough commodity that surely he could have his pick among them (especially since he was a rear-echelon man assigned to the Quartermaster's Corps, and thus unlikely to leave his bride a widow). So there had to be something else that turned his head toward Mamie, something like the twenty-five hundred acres that her aged father had only daughters to leave to, perhaps, and the opportunity to place himself first in line by marrying the eldest. And Stephens did seem to have an acquisitive look in his eyes, perhaps being as Fitzgerald himself had phrased it, "as hungry for land as any Mick with a speck of it under his fingernails is sure to be." But then, people got married for worse reasons, Dónal rationalized, and who was he to judge, after all? Anyway, since it was neither his business nor his concern, he would just content himself with being a spectator and enjoy the evening for what it had to offer, food, drink and the camaraderie of his own.

"Ah, there ye are, me boy," Fitzgerald called as Dónal entered the parlor. "Come in and say hello to our guests."

"*Guests?*" Dónal asked, questioning the plurality, though he could see for himself that Stephens had brought someone with him. He was another army captain, judging from his uniform and insignia, though the similarity between them ended there. For the other man was tall and striking, a bit younger than Stephens and, like Dónal, long and lean of build, with fine aristocratic features whose masculinity was defined by the look in his sea-gray eyes. And whereas the uniform made the man in Stephens's case, his friend would've cut a dashing figure even in beggar's rags.

'Sure, Johnnie, if you don't have a lot to learn,' Dónal thought as he sized him up, 'bringin' a man like that along when you go courtin'.'

"Aye, Captain Stephens was kind enough to bring a friend," Fitzgerald said, "and a mighty honor it is for us to have him in our home. But let me introduce ye proper before I get ahead o' meself.

"Our Captain Stephens, ye know, o' course. And now allow me to present Captain John Mitchel, Jr., late o' Newry in the County Down, and presently o' Charleston in the great state o' South Carolina. Captain Mitchel, I give ye Dónal, The O'Sullivan Béara, hereditary Count o' Berehaven and Lord o' Béara and Bantry. And let me say to the three o' yez, what a great pleasure it is to have ye here, young lions of Ireland that ye are and with so much of Her bound up between ye."

"'Tis a pleasure to meet you, Captain," Dónal said, shaking Mitchel's hand and returning his appraising gaze, "especially if I'm correct in assumin' that you're the son of himself."

"I am indeed, sir," Mitchel nodded, his American speech having only the memory of Ulster in it. "And I don't need to ask, for Mr. Fitzgerald has already confirmed that you're the brother of Eóghan O'Sullivan, a friend of my father's from the old days in Ireland."

"I am, to be sure," Dónal affirmed, his interest in Mitchel suddenly redoubled. "Do you know Eóghan yourself, and can you give me any news of him? I've not seen him since '48, and anything you can tell would be appreciated."

"Yes, I know him, though not well, I'm afraid. I was only fifteen when we met, back in '53 after my father escaped from Van Dieman's Land. We moved to Tennessee not long after, so it's been some years since I've seen him myself. Yet I do remember him telling us about his family over supper once, that there was no one left to him but a brother who was still at home in Ireland. But when I asked why he didn't bring you to America, he said that Ireland needed you more than he did. It seemed an odd thing to me at the time, which is probably why I remember it, yet not as odd as finding you here on a Georgia plantation. Just how did that come to pass, if you don't mind me asking?"

"Ah, sure, if it's not a long one in the tellin'. But the short of it is that I didn't mean to be here at all, but above with Eóghan. I just took a wrong turn along the way."

"Yes, I would say so. But how did you get through the blockade? Or have you been here since before the war started?"

"Oh, no, I just arrived in November. I came on a blockade runner called the *Fingal,* if you'd know."

"You came on the *Fingal?* We heard of her in Charleston, of course, though the newspaper accounts were rather sketchy. I'd dearly love to hear the full story, if you've a mind to tell it."

"Oh, he does, to be sure," Fitzgerald interjected. "But let's put it by for later, shall we? We've a jug o' Tennessee's finest courtesy of Captain Stephens, and while 'tis true that itself gets better with age, the same cannot be said o' me, *ochón.* So let's take the measure of it before I get any older, and before herself comes down to put the kibosh on it."

Fitzgerald led them to the sideboard then and poured their drinks. "Here's to it, lads," he said, raising his glass, "the Confederacy as she is, and Ireland as She ought to be – free and independent."

"Hear, hear," Stephens agreed, knocking back his measure with the others, before offering a second toast to their host, then a third to Mitchel and a fourth to Dónal.

"And let's not forget our patron in this lovely stuff," Fitzgerald added somewhat thickly, "Captain Stephens himself!"

"To Captain Stephens!" they all chorused, with Fitzgerald adding, "May his days be long and me gran'childer many."

At that, Stephens choked on his whiskey, coughing so hard that Mitchel had to thump him on the back. "Was there a bone in that one, John?" he asked, sending them into a fit of laughter.

But before Stephens could retort, a pointed *Ahem!* brought their attention to the front of the room, where Eleanor stood with Mamie, giving both the depleted bottle and her husband a raised eyebrow.

"Well!" she said. "I see that we've arrived just in time."

"And so ye have, me dears," Fitzgerald said without missing a beat. "Come here now and grace us with yeer charm and beauty."

And indeed they were lovely, Dónal thought as he watched Fitzgerald draw them into the room and present them to each of the young men in turn, even Mamie, arrayed as she was in her most flattering dress, her pearls glimmering at her neck while her face glowed with the prospect of romance. By contrast, her mother was dressed almost as though for a funeral, her hair pulled into a severe bun and with not a hint of jewelry or adornment to her, a deliberate and obvious attempt to downplay her own appearance in relation to her daughter's. Yet it had just the opposite effect in Dónal's eyes, seeing through as he did to the beauty in her heart. 'You shine like a star of Heaven,' he thought, 'and nothing you do will ever change it.' But she held no attraction for him anymore, the encounter under the stars having seen to that. Indeed, he intended to be off the very next Sunday, leaving her behind without a second thought.

As Fitzgerald finished the introductions, he turned to his wife with something of a puzzled look. "And where's our darlin' Annie? Surely 'twas no mistakin' she was to dine with us, too?"

"No, there was no mistake," Eleanor replied with a pointed look. "She just isn't feeling quite herself this evening and prefers to remain upstairs. Of course, she sends her apologies to our guests, and her good wishes for a commodious evening."

"'Tis a pity, begob, for she'll miss a rare time of it," Fitzgerald said, understanding that his daughter was in one of her moods and had been told to stay upstairs by her mother. "Ah, well, 'tis nothin' for it but to go on. So let us proceed to the table, and dispense with the hunger that's upon us. Captain Stephens, if ye would be so kind as to escort our Mary Ellen?"

"Of course," Stephens replied with a bow. "'Twould be an honor and a pleasure."

"Why, Captain Stephens," Mamie drawled, fluttering her eyelashes ever so slightly, "how you do flatter me."

"Not at all, Miss Fitzgerald. 'Tis naught but the truth in it."

Seeing her face light up like a crystal chandelier then, Dónal couldn't help but feel happy for her. A good man was just what she needed to bring her out of herself and, assuming this one wasn't just after her father's land, he definitely had the potential. And how grand that she could enjoy her moment in the sun without competition from her overbearing sister, for if anything could spoil it for her, it was surely Annie.

Taking Stephens by the arm, Mamie led the way into the dining room, and the others followed. Once they were all settled at the table and the grace had been said and the service begun by Bessie May and House Mary, Fitzgerald turned the conversation to Stephens, asking questions about his background and family, and other types of things that fathers generally want to know about their daughters' suitors. While he was doing so, Mamie said nothing, though she watched her beau with shining eyes, glorying in the smiles he flashed her way while barely noticing her soup.

Having taken the measure of Stephens and not wanting to make him uncomfortable, Fitzgerald then turned to Mitchel, asking if he would be staying long in Atlanta.

"No, sir, unfortunately not," Mitchel replied. "As a matter of fact, I completed my assignment yesterday and stayed over only at John's request, as he wanted me to second him this evening. And in that regard, I must say that I was loathe to come without an invitation, my affection for John notwithstanding, and I do hope my presence is not an imposition."

"Of course not, me boy!" Fitzgerald exclaimed. "Our door is always open to Irishmen of any ilk and standin', especially those who've taken up the cause of our adopted homeland. 'Tis a great admirer of yeer father that I am, and not so much for his service to Ireland, mind ye, as for his devotion to the South and our way o' life. Sure, if I didn't read his newspaper – *The Southern Citizen*, was it not? – from cover to cover and back again, so fine were his words and so eloquent his defense of our peculiar institution. And how good it does me heart to see the apple fall close the tree, a fine son like yeerself every man should have."

At that, Dónal's eyes shot to Mitchel, shocked to hear that his father, a man who'd given up his own freedom in serving the cause of Irish liberty, accused of pro-slavery sentiments. Surely he would deny it. Yet to his dismay, Mitchel just bowed his head.

"You honor me, sir," he said, "and I am humbled to be mentioned in the same breath and tone as my father, for whom I also harbor the greatest respect and admiration. I'm sure he would be gratified to know that his efforts are appreciated."

"Indeed they are, me boy, and by none so much as his fellow Irish Confederates. To be sure, there are those o' the Nativist persuasion who think we're no better than . . . well, ye know than what, and his words have gone a long way toward showin' 'em the arse end of it, excuse me French. But what will go even further is the service o' men like yeerselves, for no greater loyalty can a man show his country than his willingness to die for it."

"Again you honor me, sir, though I must confess that my service to the Confederacy is no greater than duty demands, and is indeed less than that given by many another."

"Ah, Jack, now don't be puttin' on the poor mouth," Stephens interjected. "Tell them about Fort Sumter!"

"Oh, well, there's not much to say of it, really," Mitchel said, blushing.

"Not much indeed! Why, 'twas your own 1st South Carolina Artillery that fired the first shots of the war, and if that's not much to say, then I'm a Tinker!"

"Is that true, Captain Mitchel?" Mamie asked admiringly. "How terribly exciting that must have been, to stand on the cusp of history like that."

"Yes, Miss Fitzgerald," Mitchel allowed, "I suppose it was. But to tell you the truth, my duty since has really been quite tedious. I'd much rather be at the front with my brother, James, who is Captain of the Montgomery Guards, a fine company of Irishmen serving with the 1st Virginia Infantry."

"Why, that's very commendable of you, Captain, I'm sure," Eleanor said. "But surely you must realize that they also serve who only stand

and wait. I'm sure our generals know what they're doing, and I'm equally sure that your patience will be rewarded with our ultimate victory, tedious though your part in it might prove."

"Yes, ma'am, you're probably right," Mitchel said reflectively. Then, as her true intent sank in and he remembered why he was there, his eyes went narrow and shifted to Mamie. "Indeed you *are* right, right as rain! We all serve the cause to the extent of our gifts and opportunities, and honor is not to be found in the form of service, but in service itself. And while it falls upon some to stand at the front, there are many more who shoulder a heavier burden, that of keeping them fed and armed and supplied. I don't know if you've ever heard it said that an army marches on its belly, but I can assure you that it's quite true, and without the contributions of men like John here, men who abjure personal glory in pursuit of the higher goal, we'd have lost the war before it even began. So if anyone can claim to be a hero of the Confederacy, it is surely him!"

Watching it all unfold, Dónal was impressed with the subtlety and precision with which the Fitzgeralds had directed it, like a good team of solicitors establishing their case, leaving nothing for Mamie to do but weigh in with a favorable judgment. And she did not disappoint.

"Oh, yes, we are quite aware of Captain Stephens's contribution to the war effort," she said with a smile. "After all, we have the example of Mr. O'Sullivan and his adventure on the *Fingal* to teach us that wars are fought in many ways, and that heroism wears many guises. So I must tell you, Captain Stephens, how very much I admire your dedication and your commitment to duty, for you have the courage to remain at your post while other men, who are often lesser men, succumb to the lure of personal glory. But I say let them have the limelight, for a true hero needs it not."

"Miss Fitzgerald," Stephens said humbly, "'tis beyond my ability to say just how deeply your words have touched me. But if ever I feel my contribution to be lackin', I shall remember them, and you, the charmin' and intelligent, and dare I say, beautiful lady who spoke them."

"Thank you, Captain Stephens," Mamie replied, her cheeks flushing appropriately scarlet, though her eyes held steady on his. "With gentlemen like you leading us, our victory is assured."

To that, Stephens made no reply, just nodded his head and returned her smile. And glancing around the table, Dónal saw the Fitzgeralds smiling, too, at each other and in triumph, assured that Stephens was as good as hooked and needed only to be reeled in. Yet even as they stood on the pinnacle of parental happiness, there came the sound of footsteps on the stairs and the rustle of feminine fabrics, and somehow Dónal knew it was all in vain.

When she swept into the room, he didn't bother to turn around, not wanting to give her the pleasure. But when he saw the visitors' eyes go wide and heard her mother exclaim, "Why, Anne Elizabeth, whatever do you have on?" he couldn't help himself.

Rising from his seat with the other men, he found her standing in the doorway, her eyes sweeping the room with regal ascendancy, her studied posture suggesting that it was her domain and they were all her subjects. And for all his accumulated disdain, Dónal had to admit that she did look stunning, dressed as she was in her ball gown, a gay and brightly-colored garment that highlighted her ample bosom and slim waistline. But more daring still was the emerald pendant that dipped into her décolletage, her mother's present from the previous Christmas, which from the look on Eleanor's face, she wore without permission. Indeed, she'd made herself as beautiful as she was capable of being, though Dónal knew it was only skin deep. For everything about her was calculated to outshine her sister, and in so doing she revealed the true ugliness of her heart, at least for those with eyes to see it.

"Oh, I am sorry, Mama," Annie lied blithely. "I thought you said we'd be dressin' formally this evenin'. Why, silly ol' me. I must've misunderstood what you meant by 'formal.'" Then she batted her eyelashes at the visitors, and said, "You gentlemen will just have to excuse me while I go back upstairs and change."

"'Tis no need in it, Miss Fitzgerald!" Stephens exclaimed. "You're perfectly fine as ye are!"

"Yes, Miss Fitzgerald," Mitchel seconded, his tone less enthusiastic. "Don't trouble yourself on our account."

"Well, I do declare," Annie said, "if that isn't just ever so chivalrous! Why, the very idea that those dirty Yankees think they could beat us when we have such fine gentlemen as you in our officer corps! I thank you, Captain Stephens, and you, Captain . . . Mitchel, is it not?"

"Yes, indeed, Miss Fitzgerald," he said, bowing slightly. "Captain John Mitchel, Jr., at your service."

"Anne Elizabeth Fitzgerald at yours, Captain," she replied with a smile and curtsy. "Well then, since it seems to be all the same to everybody, I think I'll just stay as I am."

At that, Eleanor shot a furious glance at her husband, who just shook his head and nodded toward the guests, the gesture telling her not to make a scene of it. So having gotten away with her grand entrance (whatever hell there might be to pay for it later), Annie turned to the table.

"Oh, I see there's no place for me," she said in a aggrieved tone, her lip quivering slightly. "Whatever shall I do?"

"Here, Miss Fitzgerald, take my place," Stephens volunteered.

"Oh, Captain, I just couldn't, what with you bein' company and all," she said. "Why, it just wouldn't be fittin'."

"Yes, Captain, stay where you are," Eleanor said. "We'll set a place here next to me."

"Oh, Mama, if you don't mind, I'd rather sit between Mamie and Mr. O'Sullivan," Annie countered, taking advantage of the situation to place herself centrally across from the guests. "That way, I can see everybody better."

Without waiting for approval, she turned on Dónal with the phoniest smile he'd ever seen. "Mr. O'Sullivan, would you be a dear and fetch me a chair?"

"Sure, Annie, why not?" he replied with deliberate familiarity, before taking a chair from the wall and placing it behind her. But seeing her bend more deeply at the waist than necessary, shamelessly drawing the two captains' eyes to her bosom, he pushed it hard against her so that she plopped down more quickly and with rather less grace than she might have preferred.

"Sorry about that, Annie," he said lightly, ignoring her glare. "It slipped."

"Oh, that's quite all right," she lied, quickly regaining her composure. "These little things do happen."

Turning back to the guests, Annie let her eyes linger on Mitchel, brazenly taking the measure of him behind a fetching smile. "It was so awfully gracious of you gentlemen to come to see us tonight. We do get lonely out here, bein' so far from Atlanta and all. But tell me, Captain Mitchel, how is it that we've not met before? Are you not stationed in Atlanta?"

"No, Miss Fitzgerald, unfortunately not," he replied. "My posting is in Charleston, at Fort Sumter to be precise."

"Oh, how simply marvelous for you. Why, I've always thought Charleston such a lovely place, and so full of Southern charm and grace. I should dearly like to live there myself someday. And what of your wife, Captain? Is she fortunate enough to be there with you?"

"Actually, Miss Fitzgerald, I'm not married, though I am promised to Miss Claudine Rhett, one of Charleston's loveliest belles."

"Is that so, Captain?" Annie said, her interest in Mitchel suddenly gone. "How very nice for you."

"Thank you, Miss Fitzgerald. I shall pass along your good wishes."

"Yes, do. And Captain Stephens, I know you have no wife in Atlanta."

"To be sure, Miss Fitzgerald," he acknowledged, "and a misfortune it is, though one I soon hope to remedy."

"Indeed, Captain. How very fortunate for the ladies of Atlanta."

"Sure, Miss Fitzgerald, if I didn't know better, I'd say you were after flatterin' me!"

"Oh, no, Captain, it can't be flattery if it's the truth!"

"Sure, I suppose not," Stephens allowed, grinning like a schoolboy.

"No, of course not. And I'm sure you'll have the pick of the litter when you get around to it. Why, I'll bet the ladies just positively swoon over that lovely Irish accent of yours. Of course, I've always harbored a strong fascination for Ireland myself. Why, I'd just dearly love to visit there someday, so I can see all those places Papa keeps goin' on about. Do you think I'd find it agreeable?"

"You would to be sure, Miss Fitzgerald. Ireland is like . . . like . . . well, 'tis like no other place on earth, so it is! 'Tis magical and beautiful, and . . . and green, Miss Fitzgerald, like you've never imagined green could be! And there's a feelin' of history there, too, a feelin' of belongin' that we don't have here, of bein' rooted to the land like we were born of it."

"My, how simply marvelous you make it sound," Annie said, leaning forward as though intent on his words, though really the better to display her cleavage. "It must be a special place altogether. But you know, Captain, there's somethin' I've been wonderin' about, and perhaps you wouldn't mind explainin' it to me."

"To be sure, Miss Fitzgerald. You've but to ask."

"Well, now I don't mean to give any offense, Captain, but it's your name, 'Stephens,' that is. It just doesn't sound all that terribly Irish to me. In fact, Papa's good friend, Alexander Stephens, whom you, of course, know is our gallant vice-president, told us that his people were all Protestants from over in England somewhere. So how is it that Stephens can be both English Protestant and Irish Catholic at the same time?"

"Sure, 'tis simple enough in the tellin'. Our name was originally *Fitz*Stephen and so Norman in its origins, just like your own. And like your ancestors, we took up Irish ways and customs and kept to our Roman faith, becomin' in the end more Irish than the Irish themselves, even though our name became shorter and more English-soundin'. But that sort of thing isn't unusual in Ireland, is it, Jack?"

"No, not at all," Mitchel affirmed. "A great many names have changed and become anglicized over the years, as English supplanted Gaelic and new people came into Ireland and made it their home. Even my own forebears came originally from Scotland, though who's to say we're not Irish just because of our name and Protestant faith. But surely, of all the Irishmen now living, few can boast a more ancient or regal lineage than Mr. O'Sullivan. Why, he's descended through an unbroken line of kings and chieftains all the way back to the very beginning of Irish history!"

"Or so he would have us believe, anyway," Annie smirked, "though we have yet to see any proof of it."

"Oh, I assure you, it's quite true, Miss Fitzgerald," Mitchel countered. "I know because I once heard his brother recite his ancestry all the way back to Adam himself."

"Is that so, Captain? Well, I certainly have never been witness to any such of a thing as that, and even if I was, it wouldn't prove anything. Why, just any ol' body can spout off a list of names."

"If you'd seen Eóghan do it, if you'd seen the look in his eyes, then you'd know the truth of it."

"Well, I didn't, and whatever your impression might've been, Captain Mitchel, I'll just have to reserve my own judgment till I do."

"Perhaps you won't have to. Perhaps Mr. O'Sullivan himself will enlighten you."

At that, Dónal felt all their eyes turn to him expectantly, though he just twirled his wine glass, studiously ignoring them. Annie had put him in a sour mood, and he didn't feel like humoring her, or the rest of them, for that matter. They weren't his own, Irish though they might be. Indeed, they were just like the English in Ireland, a nobility self-imagined, their ascendancy built upon the suffering of others, a band of hypocrites proclaiming liberty as their creed while only avarice lurked in their hearts. And in that moment, he hated them for it, all of them, even Eleanor.

But then he heard a voice in his head, speaking from the past: *No, you hate yourself, and I'm just the mirror that reflects it!* Was it true? he wondered, his eyes blinking in revelation. Was his hatred merely a reflection of what he found within himself? Then his eyes fell upon Bessie May, standing silent in the corner with House Mary, like two sticks of furniture stored for the moment out of the way, objects to be used or ignored according to their owners' caprice. And as his gaze met hers, he remembered the evening he'd brought Yellah Joe home, and how she and Ol' Jess had come to his cottage to thank him. "You's a good man, Mistuh O'Sullibun," she'd said, "even if'n you is white." She was waiting for him, too, he saw, waiting for him to put these people in their place, for however mortal his sins, he was still better than them in her eyes.

And with that he began to recite, slowly and deliberately, his relentless eyes on her at first, and then roving the table to fall on each of them in turn. "I am Dónal, the son of Eóghan, the son of Diarmuid, the son of Dónal, the son of Phillip, the son of Eóghan . . . " and so on, back through the one hundred thirty-one generations to Adam, his eyes coming to rest on Annie as he finished.

"We were great lords once," he said, "though 'twas so long ago that even the stones of Dunboy have forgotten us. But our day will come again, and we'll rise from the dust of history to reclaim our own, and then no Irishman will ever be held in bondage again."

There was a silence then, as the men nodded their heads thoughtfully, eyeing Dónal with a mixture of awe and respect. Yet he could see that they didn't get it, didn't understand how it applied to them, didn't feel the contempt in which he held them. And then Annie broke the spell.

"My, how you Irishmen do go on about the past," she said with a stage yawn. "You know, Papa always says that a man who forgets history is doomed to repeat it, but I think that if you Irishmen don't forget the past, you'll be doomed to live in it forever!"

The silence that followed then was deep and profound, as they all gaped at her, though she just batted her eyes and smiled, as if she'd made some unmemorable remark about the weather.

Then Stephens suddenly rapped his knuckles on the table, so hard and loud that Eleanor jumped. "Sure, if the girl doesn't have the right of it so! Here we are keenin' over poor ould Erin when we should all be thankful we're gone and well away. After all, we left because there was no future for us there, and we should rejoice in the future we've made for ourselves here! So let's have a toast to the Confederacy! May her future be as bright as Ireland's is bleak!"

"To the Confederacy!" they all echoed, except for Dónal, who just glared at Stephens.

"What's the matter, Mr. O'Sullivan?" the man asked, "Will you not join us?"

"No, Captain Stephens, I think not," Dónal replied icily. "For while you might've given up on Ireland, I still mean to return and do what I can to free Her."

"But why, Mr. O'Sullivan? Why waste yourself on a fool's dream? Why not stay here and fight the good fight? We will win, you know, and then our Confederacy will be as free as Ireland has never been, and probably never will be!"

"Free?" Dónal said, gesturing angrily toward the slave women. "How can you call it free when one race is in bondage and the other is bound to the very institution of bondage? No one is free here, and if you can't see it, it's because you're a damned-fool hypocrite! This thing you've created isn't a nation, it's an *abomination*, and if God is indeed just, you'll surely feel His wrath for it!"

Then Dónal rose from his chair and leaned threateningly toward Stephens. "And one more thing, Johnnie-boy, just so we understand each other. You'll not insult Ireland again in my presence, not if you want to live long enough to die for your precious Confederacy.

"Now, if you'll all excuse me," he said before the red-faced Stephens could muster a retort, "I'm not feelin' quite myself this evenin'."

And with that he walked away, though unable to resist a parting shot, he paused at the doorway. "And Annie, the next time you want to wear your mother's jewelry, you might do her the courtesy of askin' first!"

☙☙☙

"Ah, there you are," Mitchel said, finding Dónal on the stoop of his cabin, nursing a jug of Elliott's finest. "I was afraid you might've gone to bed already."

"Ah, no," Dónal said. "I'm not quite that drunk yet. So the party's over, is it?"

662

"For most of us, yes, though John and the old man are still chewing the fat. You should've stayed. It got pretty lively in there for a bit."

"I'm sure it did. Did you happen keep a count of how many times my name was taken in vain?"

"I lost track at a million six," Mitchel replied with a grin, though it quickly faded. "John took it pretty hard, you know. It was all we could do to keep him from charging out here after you, especially with that girl egging him on. Tell me, is she always like that?"

"Oh, no, she's usually worse. She was just on her best behavior tonight, tryin' to impress you army fellahs, as she was. But we've never seen eye-to-eye, the two of us, so 'tis no surprise in it for me."

"Yes, well, I don't think you'll have to worry about John. But I'm afraid you might've overstayed your welcome here. The old man didn't mince words telling us what he thought of your behavior, especially after all he's done for you, as he put it."

"Sure, he's always been pretty forgivin' before. Is your boy as dear to him as that?"

"Oh, I don't think it's John so much as what you might've done to his reputation for hospitality."

"Ah, sure, reputation and hospitality, the bane of Irishmen and Southerners alike, it seems. Well, I'm sorry for the trouble that's in it, truly I am. But at least he kept the good Captain away from me."

"Actually, it wasn't him so much as his missus."

"Eleanor? What did she do?"

"She told John you don't care about honor and wouldn't fight fair, that you have a darkness in your heart, and if provoked you would surely kill him. Now please don't take offense. Those were her words, not mine. Still, it's a strong accusation. Do you know why she might have made it?"

"Sure, more or less, and she's right about me not fightin' fair. But I wouldn't kill the little sparrow-fart, not for any reason, and I would hurt him only bad enough to keep him from gettin' up for more."

Dónal paused and sighed. "So they're all against me now, are they? Ah, well. 'Tis high time I was leavin' anyway. God forgive my foolish-

663

ness, but how I rue every minute I've spent here now."

"Well, at least you won't leave any long faces behind, especially John's, now that he seems to be joining the family."

"So he and Mamie got together after all, did they?"

"Oh, no. He's not after her anymore. He and that Annie hit it off like they were two sides of the same wooden nickel, and he didn't say so much as boo to Mary Ellen after you left. I feel bad for her, too, having her hopes dashed like that, and by her own sister, no less."

"Divil if she's not used to it. Our Annie's a rare thuckeen, all right, graspin', ungracious and spoiled as tainted poreens. If your Johnnie can't see it, then he deserves what he gets, the eejit!"

"But that's what I don't understand. John isn't stupid at all, nor would I have taken him to be so easily flattered. But then, the same woman can affect different men differently, and maybe it was just the brazenness with which she went after him."

"Actually, Jack, she was after you at first, prize bull that you are." Then a thought occurred to Dónal, and he narrowed his eyes. "You're not spoken for at all, now, are you?"

"Oh, yes I am, though I would've told her so even if it was a lie. I've seen a thing or two in my day, clinging to my Da's coattails as he bounced us around the world, at least enough to know trouble when it slaps me in the face, and sure, if that woman isn't the word itself."

"'Tis puttin' it mildly, to be sure! But you know, Jack ould son, I've had enough of Annie Fitzgerald for one night. The only trouble I'm after just now is in the bottom of this jug. Will you join me in it, or does the takin' of holy water go against your Protestant morality?"

"Bite your tongue, man!" Mitchel said as he grabbed the bottle. "And what shall we drink to? John and Annie and their eternal happiness?"

"No, not to them. Let's drink to Erin, and that I may see Her again soon."

"To Erin then. May we *all* see Her again soon." Then he took a swig and shuddered as it burned his gullet. "For fuck's sake, Dónal! What are you after, trying poison me?"

"Sure, I thought you'd find it familiar, bein' the product of an

Ulsterman, as it is."

"Ah, yes, nothing but the finest," Mitchel said, though he couldn't keep from wincing as he took another drink. "But here, now. Don't let me have all the fun."

"Don't worry for me, Jack ould son. There's plenty more where that came from."

"Good man, yourself, Dónal!"

After that, they drank in silence for a while, enjoying the cool of the evening and the comfort of each other's company. Soon the bottle was empty, and as Dónal set it aside, Mitchel cleared his throat.

"Do you mind if I ask you something, Dónal?" he said.

"Sure, Jack, why not. We're all friends here."

"What you said at dinner about slavery. Did you really mean it?"

"Yes, Jack, I did, every last word of it."

Mitchel paused, seeming hesitant to speak further. "Well," he said finally, "just don't be surprised if Eóghan doesn't agree with you. Before the war, his sympathies were all with the South. In fact, it came as quite a blow to us when he and his friends decided to throw in with the Yankees. If they'd joined with us they could've brought an army of thousands with them, and that alone might've persuaded the Union not to fight."

"Sure, Jack, I know all about Eóghan, and if he thinks slavery is a good thing, well, I'm just sorry for what America has done to him. But it doesn't change anything. All I care about is takin' him home, and the rest I'll deal with later."

"All right, Dónal. I'll say no more, except that it may not be so easy for him to just up and leave the army, even if he wants to."

"I'll cross that bridge when I come to it, Jack. But I'm too tired and drunk to think about it just now. So let's have no more talk of Eóghan or slavery, or even poor ould sufferin' Erin. Just tell me somethin' nice, Jack. Tell me somethin' happy. I'm three thousand miles from home, and my jug is empty."

"Well, I can think of one thing," Mitchel said, grinning as he pulled a flask from his pocket. "My jug is full."

"You're a lovely fellah, Jack Mitchel, Orange though your blood may be."

"Why, Mr. O'Sullivan, how you do flatter me!"

"Not at all, sir. 'Tis naught but the truth in it."

chapter 35

Rural Home Plantation

THEY WERE AFTER HIM AGAIN, *those bad men that pursued him through the dark alleys of his soul, stretching out their hands to grasp him and do God only knew what horrible things to him, so close now that he could feel their breath on his back, their malevolence in his heart. He tried to run faster, but his legs were as heavy as stone and ached like they'd been running for a lifetime. Closer they came, and closer, as his legs became heavier and heavier, until he could run no more and collapsed to the ground.* Help me! *he yelled,* Oh, please God, help me! *But it was too late. They were upon him . . .*

They were upon him, and Dónal was fighting back even before he was fully awake, the knee in his back telling him that it wasn't a dream this time, that the bad men really were upon him.

"Get off me!" he yelled, struggling desperately to free himself, though the cold steel at his wrists told him it was already too late. "Help! Phillip, help!"

But even as he cried out, a gag slipped between his teeth and jerked cruelly tight, while rough hands manacled his feet and drew taut the rope between them and his wrists, so that he lay hog-tied and helpless, mute and in shock, unable to move anything but his head. And only

667

then did they stand back from him, to catch their breath and admire their handiwork, which had been completed with a speed and precision that could come only from having done it before.

"Shit, are we good or what?" one of them said.

"Yeah, we're good all right," another agreed. "But come on, now. They said to do it quiet-like, so let's git 'im outta here 'fore anybody wakes up."

At those words, Dónal's heart froze in his chest, knowing that if "they" were the Fitzgeralds, there was no hope for him. But why? Why would the old man give him up like this? Sure he was mad at him after Stephens's visit, but why throw him to the wolves when he could simply ask him to leave? It didn't make any sense.

But then the men were on him again, carrying him outside to dump him roughly into the bed of a wagon. And as they drove away, he caught a glimpse of *her* watching at the window, her face illuminated so that he would see, and know who had brought him down.

⌒⊃⊂⌒

The sun was high in the sky by the time the wagon ground to a halt. And though Dónal was numb and sore from the jarring ride, his physical discomfort was nothing compared to his fear. For though his captors had talked freely among themselves, they'd given no hint as to his fate, leaving his imagination to run wild with speculation. Were they going to kill him? Or did they have something worse in mind? Sure, they could do anything they wanted and no one would ever be the wiser. But he would know in a moment, surely, for the men were down from the wagon seat and standing over him.

"Well, lookee here," someone said, and Dónal jerked his head around to find Horace Turner approaching. "Seems like ol' Paddy ain't so tough after all. Shit, he done pissed hisself, he's so scared. Boy, Ol' Judge Paisley ain't gon' like you stinkin' up his courtroom."

"Yeah, I bet he gives 'im six months just for that," one of the kidnappers observed.

"You got that right," Turner agreed. "An' I bet he gits six more for bein' Irish, an' six more for bein' Cath'lic , an' another six just for bein' red-headed. An' that's on top o' all the time he's gon' git for bein' a nigger-lover."

"Yeah, he's in a world o' shit, all right," the other man said.

"I heard that," Turner said. "Let's git on with it now, boys. We still got a way's to go 'fore we're done with 'im. Y'all git 'im outta the wagon while I go scare up the judge."

As Turner walked away, his cronies pulled Dónal from the wagon and stood him upright. "All right, boy," one of them said. "It's time to go meet the Devil."

With that, they grabbed him by the arms and dragged him into a cabin, scraping his shins roughly over the stoop and jerking him to a stand inside. Before him stood a broad table, on the far side of which sat a large man, eyeing him with a look that spoke of self-anointed superiority. For a long moment, the room was silent, as Turner and his cronies waited obediently for the man to speak, subdued it seemed by his brooding presence.

"Is this the man for whom I issued the warrant, Mr. Turner?" he asked finally, his speech a curious mixture of Piedmont drawl and clipped enunciation.

"Yassir, Judge, he's the one," Turner replied.

"One Donald Sullivan?"

"Yassir."

"All right then, let us begin," the man said, rapping a gavel. "Hear ye, hear ye, this court is now in session, the honorable John Bull Paisley presiding. Mr. Turner, the warrant if you please."

"Yassir, Judge, it's right here," Turner said, tossing a folded piece of paper onto the table. But when Paisley shot him a withering glance, he dutifully unfolded it and laid it out before him.

"Donald Sullivan," Paisley intoned, looking over the paper, "you stand accused of multiple crimes, to wit, aiding and abetting runaway slaves, assaulting a duly-deputized officer of the law and interfering with the performance of his sworn duty, and failure to present yourself for induction into the armed forces of the Confederate States of America. What say you, sir, to these charges?"

But finding Dónal still gagged, Paisley sighed condescendingly. "Mr. Turner, if you please. This is a court of law, not the Spanish Inquisition."

"Yassir, Judge," Turner said as he untied the knot. "Sorry 'bout that."

"Now then, sir," Paisley said, ignoring Turner to repeat his question. "What say you?"

"Well, first of all, Judge," Dónal said, "my name is Dónal O'Sullivan, not Donald Sullivan, and secondly, I'm not guilty of anything but keepin' this gobshite and his cronies from killin' a slave that belongs to my friend, Mr. Phillip Fitzgerald!"

"Oh, yes, I'm well-acquainted with Phillip Fitzgerald. I lost my seat in the state house to him a few years back. So you're a friend of his, are you? That's very interesting. And are you Irish, too, Mr. Sullivan?"

"It's *O*-Sullivan, goddamn it, and yes, I'm Irish," Dónal shot back, his look defiant but his heart sinking.

"And judging from your profanity, you are a papist, too, no doubt."

Seeing the way things were going, Dónal didn't answer, just glared at the man with all the venom he could muster.

"I see," Paisley continued. "And you are how old?"

"Twenty-one."

"And you have lived in Georgia how long?"

"I've been here about six months, but—"

"And you have never heard of the Conscription Act, I take it?"

"Yes, I've heard of it, but it doesn't apply to me! I'm not a citizen of this country. I'm only visiting with the Fitzgeralds until I can make my way north to reunite with my brother, after which I intend to go home. Sure, I was goin' to leave tomorrow!"

"Mr. Sullivan, please," Paisley said, sighing sarcastically. "I don't ride around on a donkey, you know!"

"But it's the truth, I tell you! And anyway, if I was to fight in this war, 'twould be against slavery and not for it!"

"Ah, so you are an abolitionist, then, and ergo a Yankee sympathizer. Tell me, Mr. Sullivan, have you been sent here purposely to subvert the laws of this nation and seduce its citizens with your seditious rhetoric? Are you, in fact, a spy, Mr. Sullivan?"

"No, I'm no spy, any more than this place is a nation. 'Tis but a home for the bewildered where the inmates have taken charge."

"Yes, well, be that as it may," Paisley said with a thin cold smile, "as long as we are in charge, you will have to obey our rules, now won't you? And our rules explicitly prohibit the aiding and abetting of runaway slaves."

"But I didn't do that, damn you! All I did was keep Turner from—"

"Killing a slave that belongs to Mr. Fitzgerald. Yes, I heard you the first time. But you see, Mr. Sullivan, it isn't quite that simple."

"What're you talkin' about? Of course it is."

"Mr. Turner," Paisley said, without taking his eyes from Dónal, "is it not true that you were in the process of questioning the said runaway as to the whereabouts of his accomplice, himself also a runaway slave, when Mr. Sullivan assaulted you and forcibly removed him from your custody?"

"Yeah, that's right, Judge," Turner replied. "He—"

"You need not elaborate, Mr. Turner," Paisley said, raising a cautionary hand. "A simple 'yes sir' or 'no sir' will do."

"Yassir, Judge."

"And speaking as one who is experienced in the tracking and apprehension of runaway slaves, is it your opinion, Mr. Turner, that had you been allowed to continue your interrogation, you would have obtained the information you sought?"

"Do you mean, would he a'tol' me where the other nigger was at?"

"Yes, Mr. Turner," Paisley sighed.

"Yassir, Judge, he'd a'tol' me all right."

"But as a result of Mr. Sullivan's interference, you were, in fact, unable to complete your interrogation, is that not true, as well, Mr. Turner?"

"Yassir."

"Which left you unable to apprehend said accomplice."

"Yassir."

"And to the best of your knowledge, has the said accomplice been apprehended since?"

"Nawsir, he ain't," Turner replied, the grin on his face showing that he finally understood where Paisley was leading.

"Thank you, Mr. Turner," Paisley said, taking his eyes off Dónal long enough to reread the paper in front of him.

"Well, I think I've heard about enough here," he said, regarding Dónal thoughtfully. "Donald Sullivan, I find you guilty as charged on the first two counts of the indictment, and sentence you to one year at hard labor. But, whereas the third count is beyond my jurisdiction, after completing your sentence, you are to be remanded to the Provost General of the Army of the Confederate States of America for prosecution for the crime of evading conscription. Now, there being no further business to attend to, this court is adjourned!"

Paisley rapped his gavel in punctuation and made to stand.

"You can't fookin' do that!" Dónal shouted. "You can't convict me without a proper trial, on the word of one sadistic Cracker whose only interest in this thing is money! You can't!"

"Whether I can do it or not, Mr. Sullivan, is a moot point now that it's done, wouldn't you say?" Paisley countered calmly.

"Jayzis, this is worse than a home for the bewildered! 'Tis a mad fookin' nightmare with no awakenin'! 'Tis a—"

But even as he railed against them, his captors forced the gag back into his mouth, and he had to watch in silence as Turner slipped a wad of bills into Paisley's hand, for "court costs" as the latter phrased it, part of Dónal's own money stolen from his cottage.

"Here is your verdict and order of punishment," Paisley said, handing Turner a piece of paper, that it was prepared in advance proof in Dónal's eyes of their collusion. "You know what to do with it."

"Thanks, Judge," Turner said. "Pleasure doin' bidness with you."

"As always. To whom do you intend to sell him?"

"Oh, I thought I'd try Alvie Miller first, on account o' he usually pays the best."

"Oh?" Paisley said with a raised eyebrow. "But I thought Miller only drove Negroes."

"Yassir, that's right. But I just thought that since our boy here loves niggers so much, he might as well see what it's like to be one hisself."

Taken off guard, it seemed, Paisley actually chuckled. "Why, that's very good, Mr. Turner, very good indeed. I didn't know you had it in you."

"Thanks, Judge," Turner said with a smile of his own, though it evaporated when he turned on Dónal. "All right, boys, let's git on with it."

The men grabbed Dónal then and dragged him back outside. Turner followed, though Paisley stopped him at the door.

"Oh, and Mr. Turner," he said, "why don't you give him twenty good ones, just to teach him some manners."

"Yassir, Judge," Turner replied, rubbing his hands gleefully. "It'll be my pleasure!"

⟨∽⟩

The wagon ride seemed interminable in the heat of the midday sun, and Dónal's body was one big lump of pain by the time it was over. Still, the fear was worse, though he was fairly sure they weren't going to kill him now, and too, the shock of it still lingered, of how far he'd fallen and who had been responsible. *Why did you come here,* a voice in his head demanded, *and why did you stay so long? How could you have been so foolish? How could you have been so naïve?*

And intermingled with those feelings was his fury at being convicted by a kangaroo court without any reasonable opportunity to defend himself. It was just like in Ireland, where countless thousands had been convicted of crimes without even understanding the charges against them, simply because they didn't speak English. And why had Turner bothered to begin with, he wondered? Why not just sell him to the slave driver and be done with it? Perhaps it was to humiliate him and destroy his will to resist by showing him how utterly defenseless an individual was when confronted with the power of the state. Or perhaps they felt some punctilious compulsion to put the façade of legality on it, even as they had done with the institution of slavery, and so convince

673

themselves that the sanction of human law justified it. Oppression was the law and the law made it legal, and it was not to be questioned by the oppressed. It was enough to drive him to despair, and he struggled to maintain his equanimity, knowing that he needed to keep his wits about him if he was to deal with his present circumstances.

As the wagon pulled to a stop, Dónal twisted his head to find that they had come to a railroad, alongside of which stretched a line of toiling Negroes, all shackled to a chain that tied them together at the ankle. Watching over them were a couple of white drivers on horseback, with whom Turner and his cronies exchanged greetings before hailing their leader.

"Hey, Alvie!" Turner called, and Dónal heard the hoof beats of the man's approach.

"Well, lookee here, if it ain't ol' Horace Turner," the man said in greeting. "Hey there, Hollis, Wallace. How you boys gettin' along?" Then he caught sight of Dónal in the wagon bed. "Well now, what y'all got there? Y'all bringin' in a bounty or somethin'?"

"Done already brung 'im in," Turner replied. "He's a ol' nigger-lovin' Mick we caught up aroun' Jonesberry this mornin'. Ol' Judge Paisley done give 'im a year's hard labor for helpin' runaways, an' I figgered you'd get the best out of 'im."

"Well now, Horace, I don' know 'bout that. I ain't got nothin' but niggers here, an' I'd have to think twice 'bout stickin' a white man in with 'em. Hell, I ain't never seen it done before, an' I'm thinkin' people might not take too kindly to it."

"You ain't gotta worry 'bout that none. Anybody wants to put up a fuss, you just tell 'em what he done an' show 'em this here paper from the judge, an' that'll shut 'em up. Hell, nobody likes a nigger-lover, 'specially if he's a red-headed sum-bitch Irish Cath'lic. Everybody'll see he's just gettin' what he's got comin'."

"I don't know, Horace. I ain't so sure 'bout that."

"Now lookee here, Alvie. That sum-bitch done just about the worst thing a white man can do, an' even ol' Judge Paisley said there ain't no more fittin' punishment for it. An' 'sides that, Alvie, you owe me a favor, an' I'm fixin' to call it in on you."

"Shit, Horace. If I didn't know better, I'd say you got somethin' personal agin' that boy."

"You got that right. He come between me an' a bounty an' then tried to make a fool out o' me in front o' my posse. An' that's why layin' 'im off on just any ol' gang won't do a'tall. I want 'im took as low as a white man can be took, an' can't nobody do that better'n you. An' like I done said, Alvie, you owe me, an' I'm callin' you on it. So you gon' take 'im, or am I gon' hafta put out the word that Alvie Miller don't pay off 'is debts?"

"Now, Horace, there ain't no need to git ornery about it." Miller moved closer and dropped his voice so the slaves wouldn't hear. "I just wanna be sure we doin' the right thing here, is all. I mean, what're them niggers gon' think if we put a white man in with 'em, after we been tellin' 'em all their lives how we's better'n them? They gon' git the notion we's full o' shit, that's what's gon' happen. An' goddamn, if this bunch ain't hard 'nough to drive without 'em gettin' uppity, too."

"Alvie, it don't make a shit what them animals think! They all gon' die on your chain gang anyway, an' 'sides, if they got time to think it's just 'cause you ain't drivin' 'em hard 'nough. So you just stop your belly-achin' an' git used to it. This boy's your'n whether you like it or not."

"All right, Horace, all right. But just so you know, this squares us up an' I don't owe you shit no more. So don't come 'round here with nothin' like this again. You hear me?"

"Yeah, I hear you."

"All right, then. Y'all git 'im down so's I can git a look at 'im."

"Y'all heard the man," Turner said. "Git 'im on down."

At that, Turner's men dragged Dónal roughly from the wagon and stood him in front of Miller. "Stand up straight, boy, so the man can see what you made of!" Turner said, pulling his head up by the hair.

With his hands and feet shackled and the gag still in his mouth, Dónal could only glare, though Miller took no notice as he walked around him, poking and prodding, and looking him up and down like a buyer at a cattle auction.

"Uhm, uhm, uhm, Horace," Miller said, shaking his head. "Just what you 'speck me do with his sissy li'l ass? He looks like a goddamn girl with all 'at hair, an' his hands is soft as titties. Hell, I bet he ain't never worked a decent day in his whole life. An' he's Arrish, you say? You know them Paddies don't last long in the sun."

"He'll do just fine, Alvie, once we put the fear o' God in 'im. 'Sides, you know them Arrish take to railroad work like pigs to shit. So don't even think about jewin' me down on the price, 'cause I ain't havin' it!"

"The hell you say, Horace. You know well's I do that times is hard, what with this war draggin' on like it is. Money's tight, son, an' a dollar won't buy what it used to. 'Sides, I only git 'im for a year, 'cordin' to this here paper, an' not for life like them there niggers. So you'll take what I give you an' be thankful you're gettin' it."

There was more like that as the men dickered back and forth before finally reaching an agreement. And as it proceeded, Dónal could feel the eyes of the chain gang upon him, even as they continued to work, the selling of a white man into servitude a new thing in their experience. *You'll never know what it feels like to be black*, Campbell had told him. Maybe not, but he was beginning to understand what it really meant to be a slave.

Once the bargain was struck, some striped convict clothes were brought from the supply wagon, and Turner held his revolver to Dónal's temple while the other two unshackled his legs and put the pants on him. But when one of them picked up the shirt, Turner waved him off.

"Not yet," he said, grinning viciously. "We gotta break 'im in first."

"I's hopin' you's 'gon say that," Miller said. "Come on, paddy. It's time to take your medicine."

With that they dragged Dónal to a nearby telegraph pole and, with Turner's revolver again at his head, shackled him to it, stretching his hands up over a spike, before removing the gag and ripping his undershirt from his back. Then they walked away, leaving him to dangle like meat on a hook, all alone and helpless as the day he was born.

For a long moment, all was silent as Dónal cringed against the pole, the sweat running into his eyes as his mind raced with fear. *No, please God, no!* he wanted to shout, to plead with them, though he knew it would do no good, that it was what they wanted him to do and what they were waiting for. And having seen the marks on Yellah Joe's back and knowing how the lash had tormented him, body and soul, he longed, even *ached,* to comply. Yet he also knew that Yellah Joe had survived it, that he'd had the moral and physical strength to withstand the pain so that his friend would be spared, that he would have kept his mouth shut even unto death. Where did a man find that kind of strength, the kind his father had shown in carrying Seán Ahern from the mines? He didn't know, was too blinded by panic to see that it came from within. So in his moment of final desperation, Dónal did what all people who lack faith in themselves do: he closed his eyes and began to pray.

"Hail Mary, full of grace, The Lord is with Thee," he mumbled. "Blessed art Thou amongst women, and blessed is the fruit of Thy womb, Jesus. Holy Mary, Mother of God, pray for us sinners, now and at the hour of our death."

"Hail Mary, full of grace, The Lord is with Thee," he repeated, his voice growing louder with his fear.

And again, "Hail Mary, full of grace," so loud now that he didn't hear it coming, wasn't aware until the lash bit into him and his body exploded with pain, arching his back and constricting every muscle, every nerve, every fiber of his being, the burst of air from his lungs aborting the scream that welled up within. For what seemed an eternity he hung there, quivering in agony as he awaited the inevitable, the *whoosh-whoosh-whack* of leather slicing the air, the lightning bolt of pain as it struck. Nor did it disappoint, coming fast and furious, until the pain was all there was and he shrieked out his torment to Heaven and Hell and all Creation, his soul for sale to any and all who would deliver him. And then, as suddenly as it had begun, it was over, the scream dying on his lips as the last echoes of thunder faded from his mind.

When it seemed they wouldn't hit him again, his body went limp and slumped against the pole, the physical pain already ebbing though the torment of his soul was just beginning. *Oh, God, my God, why have you abandoned me?* he demanded silently, knowing that if they'd dragged him into the town square and gang-raped him, his degradation could not have been deeper. Yet in his heart he knew the answer: he was being punished for his smugness in thinking he knew what pain was, that he'd lived the hard life and so had earned the right to feel sorry for himself. But all that had come before was just an essay in the craft of suffering, for now he understood how privileged he'd been, and how he'd failed to appreciate it.

And as they took him down from his cross and led him to his destiny, he felt their eyes upon him, the Black Men of the Bags, and knew that they'd seen and heard it all, bearing silent and indelible witness to his final and everlasting humiliation. He was truly their equal now, he knew, having learned by experience what their lives were really like.

"What you gon' do with 'im now?" Turner asked, as they put the shackle on his ankle.

"I'm gon' put 'im to work an' git my money's worth," Miller replied. "Shit, what else would I do with 'im?"

"Nothin', I reckon. I just wanna make sure you ain't gon' be soft on 'im."

"You ain't gotta worry 'bout that, Horace. I ain't gon' give 'im no slack. I'll stick 'im in next to that big ol' scar-faced buck there. He's the meanest sum-bitch nigger I done ever seen, an' I know he'll keep 'im in line!"

"Ain't that right, boy?" Miller yelled at the man in question.

"Fuck you," the man replied and, following the sound of his voice, Dónal found Campbell looking down at him, his menacing posture belying the sadness in his eyes.

"Yeah," Turner said with a malicious grin. "He'll do just fine."

⟨⟨⟨✴⟩⟩⟩

Though the night was warm and pleasant, Dónal shivered uncontrollably as he lay on the ground, facedown and shirtless, while Campbell did what he could to doctor his ravaged back. "I'm so fookin' cold," he moaned through chattering teeth, the pain of it almost recalling the lashing itself.

"Actually, you're burning up with fever," the man corrected. "But don't worry— it'll pass soon enough."

"And how the fuck would you know?"

"You forget I've been through it myself. Indeed, we all have, many times. And probably, we'll all go through it many times more before we die. It's just the nature of our circumstance."

"Sure, 'tis grand to know I've so much to look forward to."

"I'm just trying to prepare you for it, that's all. Forewarned is fore-armed, so they say."

"Sure, but *they* aren't here right now, are they? And *they* don't give a good goddamn whether we live or die, now do they?"

"No, they don't. It's just ourselves alone, and the sooner you get used to it, the better off you'll be. But don't feel too sorry for yourself. After all, you only have to endure a year of it."

For a long moment, Dónal didn't say anything, thinking it may as well be eternity for all the difference it made. But then he put himself in Campbell's place and understood that from his perspective, a year was no time at all.

"You're right," he said finally, "and I'm sorry for my whingin'."

"That's all right. I've experienced this, too, you know, being free and then suddenly jerked into slavery. I remember that first night vividly, and I know just how you feel."

"Yes, and now I can truly say that I know how you feel, too."

"That's right, you do." Campbell paused, before adding, "I'm sorry this happened to you. You don't deserve it. You're a good man, even if you are white, and if I can do anything to help you, I will."

"No, Benjie, I'm not a good man. I just pretend to be one so people will like me. You just don't know me."

"Maybe not. But I do know what you did for Yellah Joe, and that's enough for me."

"Oh? How do you know that?"

"I was there when they caught him and I saw you rescue him. The dogs had run us to ground in a thicket, and before I could stop him, he gave himself up. He was going back anyway, he said, so there was no sense in both of us getting caught. So I stayed where I was and watched the whole thing, watched without lifting a finger as they tortured him and threatened to kill him if he didn't tell where I was. And he would've died before giving me away, he's that good a friend. So I figure I owe you."

"No, you don't. 'Tis a life worth savin', his."

"Oh, but I do. It's my penance for not having the courage to do it myself."

"'Twas nothin' you could've done but go down with him. So don't go blamin' yourself for livin' to fight another day. You were only doin' what he wanted, after all."

"But that's not the point, and you know it. He was my friend, the only one I've ever had, and yet I wasn't willing to die for him. So what kind of friend does that make me?"

"Ah, sure, Benjie. All I know is that he wanted you to be free and 'twas more important to him than his own life. So what kind of friend would you be to throw that back in his face? A pretty piss-poor one, I'd say. I mean, sometimes friendship isn't in what you're willin' to do for someone, but in havin' the grace and the good sense to accept what he does for you."

"Ah, I see. So does that mean that if I'm able to help you, you'll have the grace and the good sense to accept it?"

"What're you sayin'?" Dónal asked, raising himself to find Campbell eyeing him intensely.

"I'm saying, Mr. O'Sullivan, that you've done what I asked. You've shown me the courage of your convictions, and if your offer of friendship is still open, I'd be honored to accept it."

In spite of everything, Dónal couldn't help but smile at that. "Call me Dónal," he said, extending his hand.

"Call me 'friend,'" Campbell replied, shaking it.

The heat was unmerciful in that long Georgia summer, as the sun blistered Dónal's face and parched his withered body, until only salt leached from his pores and all he could think about was his next drink of water. He was worn down from it, too, mentally and physically, as the days became a blur and his troubled sleep brought no respite, just a long nightmare without awakening, a Hell on Earth more terrible than anything the Otherworld could threaten. How he envied the black men for their ability to endure it, for their hardiness bred of long generations of slavery, a trait with which their shortsighted white masters would surely have to reckon someday.

And of all of them, these men of the chain gang were surely the toughest, being incorrigibles for the most part, repeat runaways or prone to violence, or men who simply couldn't be made to work by any other means. For that reason, Miller had picked them up cheaply, their former owners just being content that someone would pay to take the problem off their hands. The rest were like Campbell, runaways who'd been captured by unscrupulous bounty hunters and "fenced" to even more unscrupulous drivers like Miller for more than the bounty offered by their rightful owners. Nor did they run much risk of being caught at it, since unlike the planter or farmer, their workplace was transitory and their workforce mobile, and anyway, all blacks looked alike to whites. Of course, it was the war that made it all practicable, slaves being too valuable to waste on such work under normal circumstances. But with the railroads being vital to the war effort and white labor mostly gone for cannon fodder, men like Miller were flourishing.

So it was that he'd driven the gang from place to place, working them from sunup till sundown seven days a week, until they'd come to the railyard of some generic Georgia town whose name Dónal hadn't bothered to learn. Not that it mattered anyway, any more than the day of the week or a flying fuck at the moon. Indeed, he didn't care about anything anymore, having lost all hope of deliverance despite Campbell's best efforts to shore him up. All that mattered was getting through the day without incurring the lash, to keep himself moving enough to make it look like he was working. So on he toiled, ignoring the trains that came and went, as he did the passersby with their stares of curiosity or remarks on his condition.

But then he heard a voice call out, an Irish voice calling him by name, its faintly familiar tones making him wonder if it came from inside his own head. "Dónal? Dónal O'Sullivan? Is it yeerself, man?"

Following it across the yard toward a train around which Confederate soldiers were milling, he saw a man waving his hand. "Dónal, it's me, Denny! Denny Driscoll from Eyeries!"

And then he had him, Denis Driscoll, a relation of his mother's who'd once lived on Coulagh Bay. He hadn't seen him since his American Wake in '56, when he'd played the pipes and Driscoll had wept at the sound, knowing it to be his last night by his own fireside among his own kith and kin. Yet Dónal would know him anywhere, from his prematurely white hair and the whip scar on his cheek, the result of a childhood lashing at the hands of the landlord.

Without thought for the consequences, Dónal hailed him back. "Denny, help me!" he shouted in Irish. "I'm a prisoner against my will!"

But even as Driscoll started toward him, Miller put his horse between them and brandished his whip. "You there, paddy! Get your ass back to work, 'fore I dose you with cowhide!"

"Denny, help me before he kills me!" Dónal persisted, knowing that this might be his only chance at deliverance.

Having given his warning, Miller swung his whip, though Campbell jumped between them and took the blow, not even flinching as the leather cut into his chest.

"Get outta my way, nigger!" Miller growled, as he swung again. But Campbell just raised an arm, so that the whip wrapped itself around it, allowing him to wrest it from Miller's grasp.

"Goddamn it, boy, you gimme that back right now, else I'm gon' beat the black off'a you!"

"Fuck you, Miller!" Campbell retorted, holding his ground. "I'll take no more orders from you!"

At that, Miller's eyes narrowed like a snake readying to strike. "Fuck me?" he shrieked as he drew his revolver. "Fuck me? No, nigger, fuck you!"

And with that he shot Campbell square in the chest.

"*NO!*" Dónal yelled, as his friend fell. Kneeling beside him, he cradled his head in his arms. "Benjie! Speak to me, Benjie! Don't die, Benjie! Oh, please God, don't let him die!"

But Campbell just smiled peacefully. "No, Dónal, it's all right," he said through the blood trickling from his mouth. "I'm finally free." Then the light faded from his eyes, and he suffered no more.

"No!" Dónal said quietly, as tears welled in his eyes. Then he shrieked in anguish, and rose to face Miller. "You murdered him, you white-trash son of a bitch! He was a better man than you've ever thought about bein', and you shot him down like a dog, just because you could!"

"Yeah, that's right, paddy," Miller said with a vicious smile. "An' now I'm gonna shoot you, too. Just 'cause I can."

But even as Miller leveled his gun, there came the sound of weapons being cocked, and looking beyond, Dónal saw Driscoll at the head of a band of soldiers, Irish to the man, and all with their guns trained on his tormentor.

"I can't speak for yeerself," Driscoll said pointedly, "but if 'twas me, I'd be thinkin' long and hard about pullin' that trigger, so I would."

"Now, lookee here, son," Miller said, and cautiously holstered the revolver. "This ain't none o' y'all's bidness. That feller there's a convict an' I got the papers to prove it. So why don't y'all just git an' leave 'im to me? I wouldn't wanna have to call the coppers on you or nothin'."

"Ah, sure, we're after goin' back to the train, all right, but not without me cousin there. So just be the fine fellah that ye are and hand over the key, and we'll be gone before ye know it."

"I ain't gon' do no such of a thing. I done told you I got the papers on 'im, an' you'll take 'im over my dead body!"

"Sure, if ye insist," Driscoll said, raising his rifle.

"You threatenin' me, boy?"

"Sure, but ye're not the swiftest hound in the hunt, now are ye?" Driscoll said, taking careful aim at Miller's head. "Let me spell it out for ye so. At the count o' five, either the key or yeer brains will be lyin' on the ground in front o' me. So, here we go. One . . . two . . . three . . . four . . ."

"All right, all right!" Miller shouted, flinging the key to the ground. "Here! Take 'im! But mark my words, paddy, you ain't heard the last o' this!"

"Oh, I think I have," Driscoll said, as he picked up the key and unlocked the shackle. "Come on, Dónal, let's go."

But Dónal wasn't ready just yet. "Give me the key," he said and, taking it, he unlocked Campbell's shackle. Then he gently closed the man's eyes and folded his arms on his chest.

"Good-bye, my friend," he said. "Safe home to you."

pαʀᴄ sᴇvᴇn

• Johnny, We Hardly Knew Ye •

chapter 36

Fredericksburg, Virginia
12 December, 1862

Tired as Dónal was, there was just no sleep to be had in the sunken road, the ground being too hard and damp, and the stone wall biting too deeply into his scarred back, while the cold exacerbated the ache in his barely-mended shoulder. Then, too, there was the buzz of activity around him, the narrow space being crowded with men, some eating supper or chatting by the fire, while others cleaned their muskets or played cards, or did one of the myriad other things that soldiers do to kill their empty time without boring it to death. But for all that, it was a simple gust of wind that made him give it up entirely.

'Jayzis Henry Christ,' he thought, burrowing deeper into his scavenged greatcoat. 'How can it be so blisteringly hot and so bone-chillin' cold all in the same place? If God knows what the Yankees want with this Southern Confederacy, I sure as hell don't!'

Opening his eyes then, Dónal gazed at the men who'd saved his life, the Irishmen of the Lochrane Guards. How different they looked now than when they'd liberated him, seeming more like refugees from the workhouse than soldiers, their months of living in the elements leaving them grimy and rank, their clothes tattered and stained and bearing little semblance to the standard-issue uniforms they'd once sported. Indeed, they now wore whatever they could scavenge, whether from clotheslines or the bodies of the dead, Yankee or Rebel, it didn't matter, so long as it covered their nakedness. Nor was their condition any different than the rest of Lee's army, excepting the higher-ranking officers who were mostly wealthy enough to keep themselves decently outfitted. Yet for all their ragged appearance, they were still a force to be reckoned with, having beaten Pope soundly at Second Bull Run before mounting an invasion of Maryland, where at Sharpsburg they'd fought a force of twice their numbers to a standstill.

And Dónal had been with them, too, having enlisted in the Confederate Army, the last thing in the world he would ever have imagined himself doing, and of all twists of fate perhaps the most ironic. For after liberating him, the Lochrane men had brought him with them on the train to Richmond, feeding and doctoring him, dressing him in a spare uniform and making sure he had all the whiskey he cared to drink. Of course, they'd wanted to know his story, and he'd told them enough to satisfy their curiosity, relating a carefully-edited version designed to play on their sympathy. But only in Driscoll, his blood relation, did he confide his true purpose.

"Sure, I remember him well," Driscoll had said of Eóghan. "A great man for the cause, he was, and after me to join with 'em, too, which I'd have surely done but for the farm and me aged Mam. 'Twas a mighty sorrow to me when I heard he was dead, for I thought him a man among men if ever 'twas a one so born. But now ye say he's alive after all, and taken up with the Yankees to boot? 'Tis an earful and no mistakin', that."

"'Twas somethin' of a shock to me, too," Dónal allowed.

"Ah, to be sure. And now ye're after findin' him, are ye? 'Twon't be easy with the border the way it is. Do ye have a scheme for it so?"

"No, not really. I'm just hopin' somethin' will turn up in Richmond, though I've no money to help me along the way, nor even to feed myself in the meantime."

"'Twill be a hindrance to ye, that. Yet and still, I've a solution that might kill both birds with just the one stone. Why don't ye join up with us? We're headin' to the front with Lee, so I've heard it said, and no closer to the Yankees can ye get than that. Sure, ye can slip across the lines just anytime ye like. So what do ye say, Dónal? Will ye join us?"

"'Twouldn't be my first choice, Denny. But then, what others do I have, really?"

"Sure, 'tis grand so! Just leave it to me. I'll take care of everything."

So it was that Dónal became a Rebel soldier, a private in the Lochrane Guards, or as they were officially known, Company F of the Phillips Georgia Legion, one of four infantry regiments that made up Drayton's Brigade. Their *nom de guerre* they'd taken from their sponsor, Judge Osborn Augustus Lochrane, who was, ironically, a friend of Phillip Fitzgerald and with whom he and Dónal had shared the dais on St. Patrick's Day. Mustered from the Irish population of Macon, Georgia, they'd trained at Big Shanty and spent the early part of the war encamped near Hardeeville, South Carolina, seeing little action beyond a couple of minor skirmishes. Even so, they'd already lost a fifth of their men by the time they reached Richmond, being down from an initial strength of more than eighty to just sixty-six. Even their captain, Jackson Barnes, had resigned due to old age and disability, leaving First Lieutenant Pat McGovern in command. At Richmond, their brigade was assigned to Jones's Division of Longstreet's Corps, which, along with Jackson's Corps and Stuart's Cavalry, made up Lee's Army of Northern Virginia.

All this Dónal learned on the train ride and in camp near Richmond, where the brigade waited to join Lee, mostly from Driscoll and his friend, Dick Gillespie, though First Sergeant Richard O'Neill was also a font of information. Around campfires and on the march, he became acquainted with his fellows and learned that they represented all the four provinces of Ireland, including a few Cork men, though there were no other O'Sullivans and only Driscoll hailed from Béara. Many of them were brothers, too, including the Deignans, Furlongs, Walshes, Doyles, Duggans, Dowds, and four each of the McGoverns and Caughlins. And aside from the Lochrane men, there was at least a sprinkling of Irish in just about every company in Lee's army, many of which were predominantly or even wholly Irish, such as the Emmet Rifles of the 1st Georgia Regiment (in which Brian

O'Bogan's brother served before being killed in the Seven Days' Battles), the Montgomery Guards of the 1st Virginia (of which Jack Mitchel's brother, James, was captain), the Irish Volunteers of the 27th South Carolina, and the Jasper Grays of the 16th Mississippi. Perhaps the most notorious were the Emerald Guards of the 8th Alabama, who'd mustered-in wearing green uniforms and carried a flag that displayed George Washington backed by the Southern Cross on one side, while on the other it showed a golden harp on a green field encircled with shamrocks and the legends *Erin go bragh* (Ireland forever) and *Faugh a ballagh* (clear the way). Yet it was Louisiana, with its great port city of New Orleans, that boasted more Irish soldiers than any other Confederate state. Indeed, Hay's and Starke's Brigades were so heavily Irish that to stand in their midst and shout, "Hey, Pat and Mike," would bring a deafening response. So all told, there were thousands of Irishmen serving under Lee (among whom he was persistently rumored to be an Irish O'Lee), so that no matter where he went in camp, Dónal could hear the lilt of his native land and speak with men who'd walked the Holy Ground.

And in the army, the Irish had found a certain degree of acceptance, where they were recognized for their élan and fighting spirit, a notoriety that contrasted curiously with their civilian reputation for endemic violence. Even so, there were no Irish generals, either native or American-born, and only a handful had attained the rank of colonel or regimental command, a condition generally ascribed to Southern prejudice against foreigners and Irish Catholics in particular. Of those of higher rank, the most familiar to the Lochrane men was Colonel Robert McMillan of the 24th Georgia, a Presbyterian from the County Antrim who now made his home in Clarkesville. He was a lawyer and planter in civilian life with no previous military experience, though he did bring something of a martial heritage to the job, being the grand-nephew of Richard Montgomery, the Dublin-born American general who'd fallen at the Siege of Quebec during the American Revolution. Two of McMillan's sons were also serving under him, a major named Robert Emmet, and a captain who went by Garnett but whose given name was understood to be Henry Gratton. (A third son, James, who took his middle name from John Philpot Curran, had died young.) But while McMillan spoke proudly of his Irish origins, he wasn't entirely trusted by the Lochrane men, especially those from Ulster, who viewed him as just another Orange aristocrat. Indeed, it was Pat McGovern, a Cavan man, who summed up their feelings.

"Ah, sure," McGovern had said, "they're after makin' a fuss over the Ould Sod now and again. But ye'll notice, now won't ye, Dónal, that the lads are all named for famous Protestants. I mean, I've never yet heard of him namin' any of 'em for Hugh O'Neill, for instance, or Michael Dwyer or Dan O'Connell. So I'd take it all with a grain o' salt if I was ye."

The same was not true, however, of James Mitchel, who was held in the highest regard by Irishmen throughout the army, Ulster Protestant though he was. But then his father's sacrifice for Ireland was legendary, as was his defense of slavery, which they understood reflected well on all of them. And like his older brother, James had memories of Eóghan from his time in New York, Dónal found. As they talked about it, he even confided his purpose to Mitchel, who promised to help if he could, though he warned Dónal to keep his intentions to himself as much as possible. Indeed, he could find himself in the stockade if he wasn't careful, he said, if not worse. Then, too, there were the Fenians to consider, who though they might occasionally communicate across the lines, had a vested interest in policing the loyalty of their fellow Irishmen, hoping as they did that their respective governments would reward their patriotism after the war by helping with an invasion of Ireland. And Mitchel also had other information for him, telling him that the 69th New York was now part of a Yankee Irish Brigade under the command of none other than Meagher himself, who'd now attained the rank of brigadier. Moreover, they were part of McClellan's army of the Potomac, which Lee's army had recently faced in Virginia and would undoubtedly face again soon. So at least Dónal knew that Eóghan wasn't far away, though how he would get to him, he'd yet to divine.

So it was that Dónal steered clear of the Fenians, even though he was one of them and had hoped for their help. Yet, he couldn't resist telling them what he really thought when they came around to recruit among the Lochrane men, that if they really wanted to fight for Erin, they should just get on with it and not waste their time on the American war, especially since it meant fighting against fellow Irishmen. Of course, they roundly denounced his ideas, and even Driscoll chided him, saying, "Ye'd better hope there's no informers about, else ye find yeerself in front of a court-martial. They shoot absconders in this army, so they do, and 'twould go hard on the rest of us if the natives think we're after puttin' Ireland first. So I'd keep me gob shut, if I was ye, the better to live happily ever after!"

But if there'd been any informers listening, Dónal's words had yet to come back to haunt him. And anyway, the army was on the move the next morning, beginning a series of maneuvers that soon culminated in a second showdown at Manassas, Dónal's anticipation growing as the two forces moved closer together. Yet as soon as they arrived in the theater, he saw how naive he'd been to think he could just slip across the lines during a pitched battle. For in all the chaos and confusion, the best a man could do was to keep his head down and not get separated from his unit, since in their fear and frenzy, men tended to shoot first and ask questions later, and a lone man wandering the field ran the risk of becoming everyone's target.

Luckily for Dónal though, Longstreet (known affectionately as "Old Pete" for his deliberate nature) arrived a day late and held his division in reserve until the afternoon of the third day, sparing them from most of the heavy fighting. Moreover, owing to the ineptitude of their commander, General Thomas Fenwick Drayton, Dónal's brigade straggled well behind the others. Though a West Point man, Drayton wasn't a career army officer and owed his commission more to his friendship with Academy classmate Jefferson Davis than to any martial ability. He paid no heed to discipline, training or organization, a laxity which filtered down the ranks and seriously undermined the brigade's morale and combat readiness. Of course, he was called all sorts of derogatory names behind his back, even by his colonels, though the Lochrane men coined their own special epithet for him—"the Ould Eejit."

Once they caught up though, the Lochrane men had a good view of the action from their position astride the Manassas Gap Railroad at the far right of Longstreet's line. And what Dónal witnessed that afternoon shocked and horrified him beyond his ability to describe. For the new rifled muskets, which were accurate up to a hundred yards and could kill even at three hundred, had drastically changed the dimensions of the battlefield. Yet tactics having yet to catch up with the new technology, the generals were still following the old strategy of massing for decisive frontal assaults, the tight knots of humanity presenting targets that even a blind man could hit.

So despite the dearth of close-in fighting, the slaughter was horrific on those open fields of Manassas, and they were blanketed with the stricken by the end of the day. But worse even than the sight of it was the wailing of the wounded at night, as they begged for water or food or their mothers, or for someone to just come and put them out of their misery. And it was through this inferno that Dónal wended his way, sneaking away from his company and past the pickets to join those who were gathering up the wounded, though his purpose was not theirs. But it was slow going, the carnage sickening him beyond all despair, and he heaved till nothing was left to throw up but his own guts. For the air was sickly-sweet with the smell of blood and the ground sodden with gore, and men lay where they'd fallen, twisted and hideous, some missing heads or arms or legs, some with their entrails littering the ground, many of them still alive and suffering as they waited for deliverance. *Help me!* they moaned, the sound imprinting itself indelibly into his soul. *Help me! Kill me! Oh, please God, make it stop!* So palpable did the sound become, and so ponderous the horror, that he stopped in his tracks, disoriented and unable to go on.

And as the tears streamed from his eyes, all he could think of was how he'd loved to play at war as a child, how he'd dreamed of fighting for Ireland's freedom. Yet never could he have imagined the reality of war on this scale, even after killing Brendan Collins, or understood its true cost to humanity. And how ironic that war and the exploits of warriors were so often described as "glorious," when surely only a fool or a ghoul could find any glory in this. A vision came to him then, of the green fields of Knockgraffon strewn with the bodies of the slaughtered. Would freedom won at such a price be worth it? Indeed, would anyone be left to enjoy it?

"Jayzis fookin' Christ!" he exclaimed, cursing his tragic innocence. "How could I have been so naïve?"

But then a voice called to him from the darkness, an Irish voice. "Ye wouldn't have a drop for dyin' man, would ye?"

"I would, to be sure," Dónal said thickly, wiping his tears to search for the speaker. "I've the poteen, though 'tis not the best, I'll warn you."

"'Twill do, whatever it is. I'm in no way of bein' picky."

"Where are you?" Dónal asked, unable to find him among all the bodies.

"Just here in front of ye, himself with his hand in the air and the hole in his gut."

Dónal spotted him then, lying with his legs splayed before him and his head propped on a dead man. Kneeling beside him, he offered his flask, though the man just shook his head.

"Would you mind raisin' me up?" he asked. "I can't move anything below me arms. There's a good man."

Dónal lifted the man gently and cradled him in his arms, shuddering violently at the feel of blood and the gaping hole in his back. "Can you hold the jug?" he managed to ask.

"Sure, that much I can manage," the man replied, taking the flask and drinking from it. "Oh, 'tis grand so, and bless ye for comin' in time. They've none of itself in Heaven, ye know, or so Father Matthew would have us believe. But I figger if I have it on me lips when I pass through the gate, 'twill be with me for all eternity."

"Sure, 'twill indeed. So go on with you. Drink up."

"I don't mind if I do," the man said, and took another drink. "There, 'tis enough so. I've the measure of it now. Anyway, 'tis probably just pourin' out the holes that're in me, and I'd not be the one to waste it."

"All right then," Dónal said, and made to ease him back down.

"No, don't, please!" the man exclaimed, grabbing at him. "Just hold me. 'Twon't be long now."

"All right. I'm here, and I'll stay as long as you want."

"Thank you for it," the man said, laying his head against Dónal's chest. "Ye're a good man yeerself, though I don't know yeer name."

"'Tis Dónal. Dónal O'Sullivan, from Allihies in West Cork."

"'Tis John I am meself, ramblin' John O'Casey from Lough Melvin in the County Fermanagh."

"'Tis grand to know you, John."

"To be sure, Dónal, and I thank Himself for bringin' ye to me, no better man. But as grand as ye've been already, I'm after askin' for more. I've a card in me pocket with me name and me mother's address in New York. Would ye mind pinnin' it to me shirt so they can let her know what's become o' me?"

"New York, did you say? You aren't with the Irish Brigade, are you?"

"One of Meagher's own, do ye mean? No, and why do ye ask?"

"My brother's with them, and I'm after findin' him."

"Ah, well, 'twon't be here that ye'll find him, I'm afraid. Meagher is with McClellan, and himself over in Maryland somewhere, last I heard."

"So what am I doin' here then?" Dónal asked rhetorically.

"Sure, Dónal, who am I to tell ye, if ye don't know yeerself? Anyway, 'tis the tail o' the day for me now, and I'd have a bit o' rest. So sing me a lullaby, if ye will, a good Irish one, and let me go to sleep to the sound o' yeer sweet liltin' voice."

By the time Dónal had finished, O'Casey was gone from him. "Safe home to you, Johnny-boy," he said through tears, laying him gently down and wrapping his arms about the flask.

Then he rose and gazed about himself, disoriented and unsure of where he'd come from, much less where he wanted to go. Finally his feet started of their own accord, or so it seemed, leading him blindly through the carnage toward what he thought were the Union lines, only learning of his mistake when challenged by Confederate pickets. He turned then, and gazed dully back across the field, as though weighing whether to have another go at it. But there was no choice to be made; it was just too much to stomach. So he stumbled back to his own company and flopped to the ground without acknowledging Driscoll's greeting, eventually falling into a troubled and restless sleep.

The next day was spent mostly in waiting, as the battle raged on the far side of the line while Longstreet hesitated to attack. But then late in the afternoon, Old Pete finally gave the order, and his men rolled up the Union lines and drove them from the field. Again, Drayton's Brigade straggled, and so suffered the fewest casualties of any brigade in the battle, a distinction that brought them only derision from their fellows. Yet even so, three of the Lochrane men were wounded, Mike McGovern, Denis Drew, and Joe Mitchell, who later died of his wounds. As for Dónal himself, he lagged behind even the stragglers, finding a hole to hide in and not coming out until the fighting was well over. It wasn't his war and he'd no intention of either killing or dying. Indeed, he hadn't even loaded his musket. All he wanted was to get to Eóghan.

Yet after Manassas, he was confused about where to go, having no notion of where he was, much less Eóghan, nor even any idea of what to do about it. Moreover, he now saw that joining the army wasn't such a good idea after all, as he ran the additional risk of being shot as a deserter if caught trying to slip away. But then his mind was made up for him by none other than Lee himself, who, being anxious to capitalize on his victory, decided upon an invasion of the Union and set his sights on Maryland, a slave state where widespread Southern sympathy could only work to his advantage. And that being the direction Dónal wanted to go, anyway, at least according to John O'Casey, he let events carry him along.

The march across country was grueling in the intense summer heat, with little rest and only such rations as they could forage, even the whiskey running short with none to buy and no time to make any. Yet Dónal's spirits had risen at the news that they were indeed nearing

McClellan's army, which was wheeling down from the north to cut off their advance, and he hoped for a respite before battle was joined in which to sneak across the lines.

But those hopes were dashed when, on the afternoon of September 14, they heard the sound of gunfire from the hills beyond Boonsborough, where the Yankees were trying to push through Daniel H. Hill's Division into the valley beyond. And then to his horror, Dónal had found himself in the thick of it, when around three o'clock, Drayton's and Anderson's Brigades were sent to Turner's Gap on South Mountain to reinforce Hill's left flank. As his regiment filtered out along the wooded ridge, he found it easy to slip to the rear, snuggling in behind an outcropping of rock from which he could see what was going on without exposing himself to danger.

Nor had he long to wait, either, as the Yankees soon came streaming up the hill, their blue shapes flitting in and out of the trees till it seemed the forest was alive with them. Closer they came, and closer, his fear rising as puffs of white smoke heralded their fire and bullets smacked against trees and ricocheted off rocks. *I'm hit!'* someone screamed, and he saw Willy Carroll fall to the ground holding his left thigh, a patch of red spreading across his trousers. And still the Confederates held their fire, waiting . . . waiting . . . until the order came from Drayton, and every musket discharged simultaneously, shattering the forest with a deafening roar and halting the Yankee advance. They raised the Rebel Yell then, exulting in their moment of victory, only to let out a collective groan when the Yankees regrouped and continued their relentless way up the hill. Frantically, they reloaded, fired, reloaded, and fired again, suffering more and more casualties as the blue tide surged closer and closer.

And then a curious thing happened, something that Dónal struggled ever after to describe. The Rebel line just melted away, like snow under a summer sun, the men suddenly abandoning their positions as if by silent agreement and tumbling headlong down the hill, some even dropping their weapons in their panic to get away. And Dónal found himself running after them, his heart pounding in his chest as bullets

697

buzzed around him like a swarm of angry bees, the terror behind impelling him ever faster. Glancing over his shoulder, he caught a glimpse of blue-coated men pouring over the ridge, before catching his foot on a tree root and crashing hard into an old stump. The impact stunned him, and his legs were wobbly when he rose, though he struggled on as best he could, till coming to a sudden stop at the sight of a wounded Rebel resting against a tree.

It was John Duggan, a Cork man and his own second lieutenant, and he smiled sadly as Dónal gazed upon him. "Get on with yeerself, man. 'Tis gut-shot, I am, and nothin' to be done for it."

Yet his voice galvanized Dónal into action, and he stooped to lift him. "No, John, I'm taking you with me!"

"Don't be a fool, man!" Duggan exclaimed as Dónal slung him over his shoulders. "I'm done for! Leave me here!"

"We'll let the surgeons decide that."

"They can't amputate yeer belly, ye thick!"

But Dónal didn't answer, just continued on, though he'd taken only a few steps when a Yankee stepped into his path and ordered him to halt.

"I told ye so, ye eejit!" Duggan exclaimed. "Now put me down and let me die in peace."

But Dónal was too busy sizing up his captor to respond, noting his clear blue eyes, pale skin and curly black hair. And in the heat of the moment, he did something that he would later regret, though he could never remember making the decision.

"*Dia dhuit*," he said, greeting the young man in his native tongue, praying he'd understand.

"*Dia is Mhuire dhuit*," the boy replied automatically, as if greeting a neighbor out for a Sunday walk. Then he just stared at Dónal with a silly look on his face.

"Where are you from?" Dónal asked, still speaking in Irish.

"Killala in the County Mayo," the boy replied, his musket dropping as he did.

"I'm a Cork man, myself, as is my friend here. He's got a bullet in his gut and sorely needs a doctor. So I don't mean to be rude, but I'm going to take my leave of you now and head on down the hill. Safe home to you."

With that, Dónal moved to step away, only to feel the boy's musket in his ribs.

"Look, son," Dónal said in a patient tone. "I'm going on whether you want me to or not. If you feel like you have to shoot me for it, well, I'll not hold it against you. But I'd hate for you to have it on your conscience, shooting an Irishman in the back, that is."

Then he brushed the musket aside and continued on his way, holding his breath until hearing the words, "*Slán abhaile*," from behind.

"*Slán leat*," he replied, quickening his pace.

After that, he made it back to the Confederate lines without further incident, his legs burning with fatigue by the time he reached the surgeon's tents. Laying Duggan on one of the makeshift tables, he fell to the ground in exhaustion, not bothering to rise when the surgeon came to do his examination.

"How far'd you carry him?" the man asked after a moment.

But Dónal didn't answer, just pointed to the mountain in the near distance.

"Well, you shouldn't a'bothered. He's dead, and even if he wasn't when you picked him up, you should'a known I can't fix a gut wound. I ain't God, you know!"

Then he turned his back and walked away, leaving Dónal to stare in disbelief.

In camp later that evening, the Lochrane men gathered to take stock of themselves. Aside from Duggan, there were six missing and unaccounted for, including Willy Carroll, Paddy Geary, Richie Deignan, Billy Fahey, Dick Furlong and Pat McGovern. And what was almost worse, they learned that only their brigade had turned and run while the rest of the line held firm. Of course, there was even more scorn and abuse from their fellows, leaving their mood collectively foul and bringing hard words for Drayton.

"Sure, if he won't get us all killed before he's done with it, the Ould

Eejit!" Paddy Furlong exclaimed bitterly.

"No, he'll not get us killed," Sergeant O'Neill countered. "He'll just embarrass us to death."

"Well, somethin' ought to be done about it!" Con McGinley said. "I mean, can't Lee see what's goin' on here?"

"Sure, he does," O'Neill said, "but his mind is on bigger things just now."

"Well then, maybe we should do it ourselves," McGinley suggested. "I'm not after dyin' if I can help it, especially if it means gettin' shot in the back!"

"Be careful with that kind of talk now, Con," O'Neill cautioned. "'Tis naught but trouble in it."

"Still, 'tis a thing to consider," John Kelly mused. "Sure, if I wouldn't do it meself but for herself and the childer to think of!"

"Well, here's a fiver for 'em on Dick's behalf!" Furlong said, throwing the money at Kelly's feet. "'Tis the fault o' the Ould Eejit's that he's missin', and I'd not have it happen to the rest of us!"

"And here's five for Pat, and five more for Mike!" Denis McGovern seconded.

"And five for John, too!" Duggan's brother, Neill, added.

And before Kelly could say no, there was a pile of money in front of him and an even bigger pile of expectations. But he just sat there with a sick look on his face, obviously wondering how he was going to get out of it. Then Dónal stepped in.

"Put your money back in your pockets, you thicks!" he said. "John's not going to do it and you all know it!"

"And just what do ye care?" Paddy Deignan snapped angrily. "'Tisn't yeer brother that's dead or wounded, or rottin' in some Yankee prison. The Ould Eejit cost us seven good men today and three more at Bull Run, and we've nothin' to show for them but the scorn of our fellahs. So I say we get rid of him!"

"'Tis right ye are, Paddy," McGinley seconded to a general murmur of approval, "and the sooner, the better!"

For a long moment, Dónal said nothing, just stood over the money with his arms crossed until they settled into an expectant silence.

"You know, Paddy," he began coldly, "'twas me that carried poor John down off that mountain today, and 'tis me who's soaked in his blood, and me that had to tell poor Neill the news. So if you think I don't care, then you've got another thought comin'.'"

Deignan dropped his eyes, then, though Dónal was far from finished with him.

"And another thing, Paddy. If you think our fellahs scorn us now, what do you think they'll say if we kill our own general? They'll say we're a bunch of back-stabbin' traitors, that's what, nothin' but bog-trottin' Paddies who can't be trusted with guns because we'll just get drunk and shoot each other with them! And 'twill be all of us that they'll court-martial, you know, not just poor John here, or have you never heard the word 'conspiracy' before? Nor will it end just with us, for they'll be sayin' the same of every Irishman in this army and every Irish man, woman and child in this whole country, North and South. *See?* they'll say. *I told you they were no good.* And if that happens, Paddy, if we bring ill repute upon our own, then you'll find out what scorn really is, because our people will scorn us worst of all, so they will. So if that's what you want, then I'll not be the one to stand in your way. After all, I really don't care one way or the other, now do I?"

And with that he walked away, leaving them to sort it out for themselves.

In the morning, Jones's Division moved across Antietam Creek to Sharpsburg, taking up defensive positions just outside the town on a ridge above the creek. From there, they had a good view of the Yankee positions on the far side, and Dónal wondered where in all that mass of humanity Eóghan could be. Again, he hoped for a lull that would allow him to slip across the lines, but it just wasn't to be. For as soon as they came within range, the Yankee batteries opened up on them, keeping up a more or less constant barrage for the next two days. Then on the evening of the 16th, a skirmish broke out on Lee's far left, which, though brief, was fierce and hard-fought, a harbinger of what the morning would bring, it seemed. The night that followed was especially dark with a steady drizzle of rain, and sensing it was his last chance, Dónal slipped down the hill to where Robert Toombs' Brigade defended the Rohrbach Bridge to see if he could get across. But there were just too many men watching it, too many guns trained upon it for him to risk it. So he returned to his company to wait out the night.

"Why didn't I just let that fellah capture me on the mountain?" he chided himself. "Why did I have to play the hero? Why didn't I just listen to John and leave him there?" But, of course, there were no answers to those questions, or at least none that he would let himself hear. His instinct to be like his father had gone completely wrong, and he knew it.

But his night of consternation was a short one, as the Yankee assault began at 5 A.M. and continued unabated through the foggy and overcast morning. Thankfully for Dónal, most of the early action was concentrated on Lee's left and center, in the Cornfield, the East Woods, the West Woods, the Bloody Lane and other areas that would afterward become synonymous with the word "slaughter." What action there was on the Confederate right was concentrated on the Rohrbach Bridge where the Yankees tried to force a crossing. But Toombs's inspired and determined defense denied them, leaving the men atop the ridge with little to do but watch and wait.

And as the morning passed away, Dónal paced restlessly back and forth, watching as clouds of gun smoke marked each new arena of combat, fearing that Eóghan might be in one of them. 'God, please keep him safe,' he prayed silently, over and over, alternately hoping and dreading that he was among those trying to force the bridge.

Then in the early afternoon, Toombs's position became untenable and his men came streaming back up the hill, taking up defensive positions on the far right of the line. In the lull that followed, the Yankees crossed the bridge en masse and formed up below, while the Confederates reinforced their defenses and consolidated their positions. During that time, Drayton moved his men forward to a stone wall, behind which they awaited the inevitable.

At about 3:30 it came, as the Yankees surged up the hill, pausing only to re-form in a depression before raising a cheer and charging the

Confederate line, oblivious to the hail of death that rained down upon them. As he watched them come, Dónal could smell his own fear in the sweat that poured from him, hating that he could only wait for them to come and get him and nothing to do about it but pray. Would he be so afraid if he was truly motivated to fight, he wondered, or was he just a coward?

It was a question without answer, and one he had no time to ponder, as the Yankees were suddenly upon them, leaping the stone wall and fighting hand-to-hand with the defenders, Dónal cringing against the wall as men screamed and cursed and fought and fell, John Kelly with a bayonet in his ribs and Con McGinley with a bullet through his forehead. 'At least he wasn't shot in the back,' he thought absurdly, gazing into McGinley's dead staring eyes. But the affray was as short as it was desperate, as the Confederate defense melted away and the Yankees pursued them into town, leaving Dónal alone with the carnage. How quickly it had happened, his mind registered without forming the thought, how thin the veil between life and death and how instantaneous the transition, how irrevocable the finality.

But then the sound of running feet invaded his senses, as more blue-uniformed men leapt the wall and dodged through the fallen, rushing to reinforce their comrades. And as he watched them run, something sparked in his mind and he remembered his purpose.

"I surrender!" he yelled, standing and throwing his arms into the air. "Don't shoot me, I surrender!"

"All right, Reb," one of the Yankees said, "we won't shoot you. Just be still and keep those hands in the air. Willingham, you take him to the rear with the others."

"Yes sir, Lieutenant," the designated guard had said, coming forward and nudging Dónal in the ribs with his musket. "Come on, Reb, let's go."

"Do you know of the 69th New York?" Dónal asked without preamble, as he stepped over the wall.

"Sure, it's part of the Irish Brigade. Why do you ask?"

"Because my brother is one of their officers, Lieutenant Eóghan

O'Sullivan. Do you know of him, by chance?"

"Lieutenant *Colonel* O'Sullivan, you mean. And hell yes, I know of him! Shit, everybody does since he won the Medal of Honor at Malvern Hill! But if you're his brother, then why are you fightin' for the Rebs?"

"Sure, if it isn't a long one in the tellin', but the short of it is that I never meant to be. I just got stuck in the South and it was my only way out. But now that I'm captured, I want to join up with him. Will you take me to him?"

"Well now, I can't do that just all on my own. I'll have to take you to the detention camp first, and let them . . ."

But even as Willingham spoke, Dónal found himself flying through the air and landing heavily on his shoulder. And as he lay there, fading in and out of consciousness, a chorus of bells ringing loudly in his ears, the tide of battle turned again and the Yankees came streaming back from the town, passing over him in a wave of panic as they raced for the bridge. Seeing them go, he knew somewhere in the far reaches of his mind that there was something he wanted from them, that he should hail them and ask for it, though he couldn't for the life of him remember what it was. But then they were gone anyway, and other men came running after. Two of them picked him up and bore him away, taking him to a place of such horror that it could be none other than Hell itself. And was that Satan standing over him? He'd seen the face before and knew he didn't like it, though whether it was from life or just the Hell of his own dreams, he didn't know.

"So you're back, are you?" the face said, leaning closer. "And Jesus, would you look at all that blood! If that's all yours, boy, I don't think there's much I can do for you."

"'Twas another fellah with him, I think," another voice said, one that Dónal knew he should recognize but didn't, "a Yankee judgin' from the scraps o' blue, that bein' about all that was left of him."

"Yeah, you're probably right," the Satan-face agreed. "My guess is that he took the brunt of it and shielded your friend here, which would explain both the blood and why he's still alive."

There was a lapse in the conversation then, during which Dónal's clothes were cut from him and rough purposeful hands scanned his body, though he couldn't feel any of it. Then the Satan-face was back, feeling his neck and looking deeply into his eyes.

"Will he make it, Doc?"

"Yeah, I think so," the Satan-face replied. "He's cut up pretty bad with shrapnel, but it looks worse than it is. His left shoulder's broken, and he's in shock and might even be deaf, though I won't know that till later."

'No, I'm not deaf; I can hear the bells ringing,' Dónal's mind assured him, though having thought it, he couldn't remember why.

"At least he ain't gut-shot like that fellah he brung down off the mountain," the Satan-face continued. "But don't plan on seein' him for a while. He'll be six months in the hospital if he's a day."

After that, the Satan-face went away and another took its place, a kindly, smiling face that Dónal knew he should recognize, but couldn't place. "Did ye hear that, Dónal? They're goin' to fix ye up good as new and give ye a nice long rest in the hospital. So don't worry about a thing. Dick and me will see that they take good care o' ye."

And then he was alone, not knowing where he was or how he'd gotten there, only that there was great pain and suffering around him, though the awareness was fleeting, and new each time it came to him. In between, he was in a world of his own, neither dreaming nor waking, conscious nor unconscious, living nor dead, but somewhere between them all, above and beyond, some undefined state of being in which he walked roads unknown and unremembered, the Nirvana of mystics, the transcendence of the faithful, each step a birth and a death all its own. But all good things must come to an end, and gradually his mind began to clear, and he knew he was at the field hospital and wounded, though how it happened and how he'd gotten there, he couldn't recall. And with awareness came pain, a generalized ache at first, that soon intensified until it was all his consciousness, a black hole absorbing the light of life and giving back only suffering. Yet even worse was the fear, for he could hear the screams of the unanesthetized patients as the surgeons cut and sewed them like garments, and knew that lay in store for him, too.

Then they came for him, laying him on a stretcher and taking him to one of the surgeries, an open-air abattoir fenced off by sheets hung from ropes stretched between trees. It was lit by the red light of dim lanterns and flickering, noxious torches, while doors ripped from nearby houses and set on sawhorses served for tables, and men who'd long ago given up empathy for the sake of their own sanity served as surgeons. What color his door-table had once been he had no idea, for it was blood red by the time they laid him upon it, being at the same time slippery and sticky in the way that only blood can be. The surgeons, too, were in the same state, soaked in it up to their elbows, while their aprons hung heavy with gore.

And as he turned his head to one side, his eyes lit upon a pile of arms and legs in the corner, raised like a pyramid to the gods of slaughter and carnage, making him realize that his suffering had only just begun.

"Let's git after his arms and legs first," he heard someone say, "and then do the rest."

"Oh, God, no!" he whimpered. "Please don't off cut them off! Let me die, but just please don't cut them off!"

"Relax, son, we ain't gonna cut nothin' off'a you," the surgeon said. "We just gonna get that shrapnel out and then fix your shoulder. Once everything heals, you'll be good as new, 'cept for the scars. But from the looks of your back, you're used to that already. How'd you come by 'em, anyway?"

"The English did it to me in Ireland."

"Yeah, I've heard other fellahs say that, too."

And then they started on him, working methodically from his legs up, the surgeon digging out pieces of metal with fingers and pliers while his assistants closed the wounds with stitches, the pain of it excruciating and electric, his raw and exposed nerves making him jerk and twitch, till he no longer had any choice in the matter and shrieked out his torment into the night. When it was over they cleaned him off, applied bandages and set his arm in a sling, before wrapping him in blankets and laying him on the floor of a nearby house, a makeshift hospital filled with a legion of the wounded. In the morning he was evacuated along with the others, a long line of wagons taking them to hospitals in the rear, in Dónal's case all the way to Richmond, where he remained for almost three months before discharging himself against the advice of his caretakers.

During his convalescence, he learned much about the great Battle of Sharpsburg, where almost 23,000 men were lost, either dead, wounded or missing. In particular, he heard that it was A. P. Hill's Division that turned the tide on the Confederate right, arriving from Harper's Ferry at precisely the right place and at the last possible moment to save it from collapsing and taking the entire Confederacy down with it. 'Of all the rotten Irish luck!' he swore to himself, knowing that otherwise he'd be reunited with Eóghan now, if his brother was indeed still alive. For Dónal had also heard of the Bloody Lane and the Irish Brigade's decimation at the hands of men commanded by an Alabama general, named, ironically enough, Robert Emmet Rodes. Meagher himself had his horse shot from under him, it was said, though there were persistent rumors that he'd simply fallen off in a drunken stupor. Of course, the Confederate Irish vilified them as mere bigotry, for though he was an enemy of their adopted country, the great Meagher of the Sword was still a hero to them.

For Dónal, his time in the hospital was one of deep depression, as his days were spent with brooding on his many months on the road, on his own bad decisions that had led to so many wrong turns and dead ends, while his nights were restless and fitful, as unspeakable things stalked his dreams. Nor had it helped being surrounded by the wounded, so many of whom were hideously maimed or mutilated, though even worse were the scores of syphilitics, with their constant mad raving and withered, scabrous bodies. So by the time news came that Lee was facing the Army of the Potomac again, he was desperate to get away, and pulled himself from his bed to have another go at it, feeble as he was.

"Sure, if ye aren't one of the lucky ones so," an old Irish nurse said to him as he left. "Ye get to walk out of here and with all yeer parts on ye, to boot."

"Ah, well, mother," Dónal said darkly, "good things happen to you when you're good lookin'!"

"Sure, if they don't," she agreed with a knowing smile. "Safe home to ye, me pretty."

"And to you," he replied, though she'd already turned away. And with that, he'd left the hospital and made for the train station, stopping at a saloon along the way to make sure he'd look and feel his best for the trip.

So it was that he'd come back to the Lochrane Guards just the evening before, getting an especially warm welcome from Driscoll and Gillespie, who were surprised to see him back so soon. They had a bit of news to tell him, too, as there'd been some significant changes in the ranks during his absence. First of all, Pat McGovern and Richard Deignan had been returned to them in a November prisoner exchange, and been subsequently promoted to captain and first lieutenant, respectively. At the same time, Michael Walsh had been raised from second lieutenant to first, and John Moore from sergeant to second lieutenant, giving the company a full compliment of officers, though it now had only three sergeants and one corporal. Even so, they were sufficient for the forty men now left in the ranks, the combination of casualties, captures, desertions, discharges and illnesses having whittled them down to less than half their initial strength. Nor were they untypical of Lee's army, which had been so decimated that he could scarcely field half his nominal strength anymore.

Secondly, and more important, the Ould Eejit had finally been relieved and his brigade broken up, with the Phillips Legion now being part of an all-Georgia brigade consisting of the 16th and 18th Georgia, Robert McMillan's 24th, and the Cobb Legion, named for the brother of their new brigade commander, General Thomas R. R. Cobb. At first, news of the transfer had been well-received by the Lochrane men, as they'd reckoned anybody an improvement over

Drayton. Yet they'd quickly cooled to the distant and aristocratic Cobb – a tee-totaling, Know-Nothing of a martinet who turned out to be yet another political appointee – especially once they learned of his anti-immigrant (and thus, anti-*Irish*) stance at the Confederacy's constitutional convention, sentiments that extended even to McMillan, who was himself a Protestant aristocrat. And if Cobb felt that way about McMillan, they reasoned, what could Catholic peasants like themselves ever expect from him? It galled them, to say the least, and their resentment of Cobb ran deep, especially since they were showing their loyalty to the Confederacy by fighting for it.

So the changes had brought no improvement in morale, and the men were in a collective funk as they huddled in the sunken road. But though Dónal felt bad for them, it wasn't his problem. He was just waiting for darkness to fall, so he could slip away and head up the Rappahannock River to outlying farms, where he hoped to steal a boat and row himself across, before making his way back to the Yankee camp on the far side. It wasn't much of a plan, he realized, but it was better than waiting here to be caught up in another battle, which, from the troop movements of the day, seemed imminent. In any case, doing something was better than doing nothing, and he'd figure it out on the fly if he had to.

But in that moment as he sat with his back to the wall, Dónal's mind was on something more basic, the smell of frying bacon and the rumble in his empty stomach.

"Hey, Dick," he called, meaning Gillespie, who was cooking over a nearby fire with Driscoll. "You wouldn't have enough for me, too, would you?"

"Uch, sure, Dónal, help yeerself," Gillespie replied in his Ulster burr. "'Tis plenty for all."

"And a drop, too, perhaps?"

"Sure, that too, so long as ye go easy on it. Ye're mighty thin in the skin, if ye'd have my take on it, and this stuff is itself and no mistakin'."

"No matter. 'Twill still be sweet on my lips all the same."

"Uch, to be sure. Just remember that I warned ye so."

"Sure, mother, I'll keep it in mind."

After that, he was mostly silent as he shared his meal with his two friends, his eyes straying to the town of Fredericksburg in the near distance and the low hills rising on the other side of the river. How peaceful and serene it seemed in the evening light, making it hard to believe that an army would soon issue from it, intent upon bringing death and destruction to all who stood in its way. Yet surely they wouldn't come this way, he thought, across a half-mile of open muddy plain toward 2,000 muskets entrenched in a sunken road and behind a stone wall, while at least as many more manned the heights above, along with plenty of artillery. No, surely the Yankees wouldn't be so foolish, for how could anything possibly live through such a firestorm?

But then, who was to say what Americans would or wouldn't do in this terrible war of theirs, for he'd yet to see them spare any humanity upon each other. And how blind they were to what it was doing to them, as they foolishly squandered the shining dream that was once America, and how arrogant their belief that God was on *their* side, when surely He was on the side neither of slavery nor of wholesale slaughter to end it. He only hoped Eóghan was still alive and that he could get him out of it before it was too late.

It was deep dusk by the time Dónal finished his meal and washed it down with a last swig of whiskey, and he was just about to slip away when all the men around him went suddenly silent. "Jayzis, 'tis himself in the flesh!" someone murmured and, hearing the sound of approaching footsteps, he could only assume that it was Lee, since no one else commanded that sort of awe.

But then a voice rang out in the gloaming, an Irish voice deep and resonant, that of an orator.

"Do I have the privilege of addressing Dónal O'Sullivan Béara?" it asked.

Turning to face the speaker, Dónal knew him immediately, though he'd never seen him before, for his likeness was unmistakably etched on the faces of the two young men flanking him, his sons James and

Willy, though not quite to the same degree as their older brother, Jack.

"To be sure, Mr. Mitchel, himself in the flesh," Dónal replied, and rose to shake the man's hand.

"Then I am pleased and honored to meet you, sir," John Mitchel said, bowing deeply.

"As I am to meet you, Mr. Mitchel, though 'tis the last place I'd have expected it to happen. What brings you here, sir, if you don't mind me askin'?"

"Why, I've come to visit my sons, of course, just as any father might. And to get news of Jack, whom I hear you've recently seen."

"So I have, though I didn't spend much time with him, really. But I can say that he's well and happy, if a bit bored with his posting, perhaps. Still he has a lady friend in Charleston, where he's thinkin' of settlin' when the war is over, though he did express a certain nostalgia for the old days in Ireland. He'd like to go back for a visit someday, and hopes that you might go with him."

"Yes, well, that depends upon the wishes of our fair Queen, doesn't it. But time will tell, I suppose."

"Sure, 'twill indeed, and may we all live so long."

"May we, indeed. And I'll not ask what brings you here, since James has told me already."

"Yes, and what of my Eóghan, Mr. Mitchel? Have you seen him, or heard tell of him? Is he alive and with those Yankees over there?"

"Yes, he's alive and, from what I hear, doing quite well for himself. He's a lieutenant colonel now and Meagher's adjutant, and they're singing songs about his exploits in the pubs of New York. He'll be a general before all is said and done, which comes as no surprise, of course, since he succeeds at everything he attempts.

"But I would like to know more of you, young O'Sullivan," Mitchel said, pointedly changing the subject, it seemed to Dónal, "and of your adventures since leaving Ireland. According to James, you've had quite an odyssey."

"I don't know that I'd go that far with it, Mr. Mitchel."

"Nonsense, my boy. Every life is an odyssey, a voyage of discovery

711

and adventure, and though few of us enjoy the celebrity of Odysseus, our stories are no less significant for it. So come with me now and tell me yours. The boys and I are going to stroll out to that house in the field there to get a closer look at Fredericksburg. Join us, and we can chat as we walk."

Though he desperately wanted to get away, there was something odd about the way the Mitchels were looking at him, indeed, as if trying not to look odd. And why the pretense of "strolling" through no-man's-land to look at a distant village in the dark, when the whole world knew that Mitchel could barely see two feet in front of him? They were up to something, Dónal decided, and he'd better go along to find out what.

"Sure, Mr. Mitchel, I'll go, though I can't stay long, mind you."

"That's fine. If we're too long, you can always come back without us."

But it was only a few minutes walk to their destination, and they were still exchanging pleasantries when the large brick house loomed in front of them.

"Here we are already, it seems," Mitchel said, "and I've yet to hear the first thing about your adventures. Ah, well, some other time perhaps. Should we go inside, James, do you think?"

"Sure, Da, why not. My lads have the duty, and I'm sure they'll appreciate a visit from you."

With that, James led them through the back door and down the central hallway to the front parlor, which was dimly lit and empty, but for a single man on the far side. And though he was shrouded in shadow, Dónal knew him instantly, would've known him anywhere in the world, even without hearing his voice or seeing the streak of white in his coal-black hair.

"Hello, Dónalín," the man said, voicing the greeting Dónal had so longed to hear. "'Tis a long way from Cahernageeha."

But for all that Dónal had fantasized about this moment and the joy and happiness he would feel, now that it was here, he could barely choke back the sob that welled up from his soul. As though hearing the call of his heart across all the years and miles, Eóghan opened his arms to him, and just as he had as a little boy, Dónal lay his head on his big brother's shoulder and, for that moment at least, let go the Darkness that haunted him.

"You know, the older I get, the less patience I have for the duplicity and hypocrisy of politics," Mitchel said, eyeing them approvingly. "Yet and still, it is good to have friends in high places."

"Thanks, John," Eóghan said, acknowledging his old friend. "I owe you for this."

"No, you don't, Eóghan. Safe home to you."

And with nothing more, Mitchel followed his sons from the room and closed the door.

And there the brothers stood, locked in their embrace, the love flowing freely between them, the years falling away as they renewed their bond.

"I've missed you so, Eóghan, I can't even tell you," Dónal said, when the lump in his throat let him speak.

"I've missed you, too," Eóghan said. "Sure, I've missed you growing up. What happened to that little boy I left standing by the roadside?"

"A lot happened to him, Eóghan, more than you want to know, really."

Looking into his green eyes then, Eóghan found them filled with the same sadness and intensity as the last time he'd seen them. "Still the same old Dónalín, I see. Still too serious for your own good."

"Some things never change, I suppose."

With that, they stood back and eyed each other, taking in the changes the years had wrought. But while Eóghan had much to note, he looked much the same to Dónal, having aged hardly at all, it seemed, only the look in his eyes being subtly different, having now a hint of wariness, perhaps, and a touch of cunning, just enough to erase the frank innocence of youth.

"'Tis good to see you, Dónal. Sure, if I hadn't given up hope, after the ship landed without you and Riobárd could give no news. What happened?"

713

"'Twas a long road with many turnin's. Let's just say I came as I could and leave it at that."

"All right, then. I'll not ask for more, though I can see there's melancholy in it. But tell me one thing, at least. How did you end up in the Rebel army?"

"'Twas not what I intended, Eóghan, believe me. Not in a million years would I have chosen to fight for slavery. But for the time and where I was, it seemed the thing to do. And since I got through to you in the end, I suppose it was."

"Yes, so it would seem, though with just a bit of bad luck, we could've found ourselves shooting at each other, you and me!"

"Sure, you might've shot at me, Eóghan, but not I at you. 'Tisn't my war, this, and I've no intention of either killin' or dyin' in it. All I wanted was to get to you.

"And now that I have, what I've come to say is that it's not yours, either. You've no stake in it, beyond trainin' as a soldier, and now that you've done that, why risk yourself further? The Americans can get along without you. Sure, what's one Paddy less or more to them when there's boatloads arrivin' every day? But Ireland can't get along without you. We need you, Eóghan. We need you to lead us. You are our messiah and we desperately need you to save us. So won't you please come home and save us, Eóghan? Won't you please?"

"Dónal, I can't do that. I can't just up and leave what I've started here. You're wrong if you think this isn't my war and that I've no stake in it. It is and I do, as does every Irish man, woman and child in America. This war we're fighting has nothing to do with secession or state's rights or slavery, but with acceptance, *our* acceptance as good and loyal Americans and our right to live here as equal and enfranchised citizens, and it's on these battlefields of Maryland and Virginia that we're winning it, regardless of the side we've chosen or even the outcome. So don't you see that I'm already serving Ireland, or at least the part of Her that's now in America, the millions of Irish people who can never, *ever* go home again, even when She is free? So no, Dónal, I can't leave now. I have to stay and finish what I've started. But I promise you I'll come home as soon as it's over and bring an army of trained Irish soldiers with me."

"Eóghan, have you walked through all this with your eyes closed?" Dónal demanded, his eyes suddenly cold and hard. "Have you not seen the slaughter that's in it, or have you closed your mind to its reality? Do you not see that it's goin' to go on and on for years and years, until one side finally annihilates the other? And at the tail of the day, do you really think anyone will want to go back to Ireland and start it all over again? Sure, they'll be sick to death of it and you'll be lucky to muster even a company! So don't tell me you're comin' home at the head of an army, because I know you're not! And don't tell me they can't do without you here, because we both know they can! But we can't, Eóghan, the Irish can't! You're the one, the only one, and 'tis no one else to take your place."

Then his eyes softened and he laid his hands lovingly on his brother's shoulders. "So come home with me, Eóghan, now, before it's too late. Just give it up and come home. I'm beggin' you, as your brother and with all my heart, to please come home. You know in your heart it's the right thing to do."

For a long moment, Eóghan hesitated, and, seeing the turmoil in his eyes, Dónal begged him silently, intensely. But then he sighed and shook his head, and Dónal knew he'd lost, even as their father had.

"I can't, Dónal, I just can't. It just wouldn't be honorable."

"Still the same old Eóghan, I see," Dónal sighed, shaking his head sadly. "Still after bein' Achilles when just bein' yourself would do. But all right. I can't say I understand, but neither can I honestly say that I'm surprised. So if you won't come with me, then I'll just have to stay here with you."

"What?" Eóghan exclaimed, a smile spreading across his face. "What did you say?"

"You heard me, you thick," Dónal replied, shaking his brother. "I'm stayin' with you. Sure, if I didn't spend too many years missin' you to ever be parted again. So if you're after stayin', then I will, too."

"Sure, 'tis grand so, Dónal! With you at my side there'll be none to

715

stop us! On the O'Sullivans, *lamh foisteneach abú!*"

"If you say so. But let's get on with ourselves! The night's not gettin' any younger, you know."

But even as he said it, Willy Mitchel flung open the door in a panic. "General Cobb is comin'! You've got to go, *now!*"

Hearing his approach, Dónal looked wildly for another way out. But Eóghan was already at the window, throwing back the drapes and raising the sash.

"This way, Dónal!" he exclaimed, and was gone.

But it was too late. Dónal had just made it to the window, when a voice stopped him. "Get away from that window, soldier! Don't you know there's Yankee sharpshooters out there?"

And though it broke his heart, Dónal knew he had no choice, for to follow Eóghan now might get them both killed. Better to let him go unmolested and return to his original plan of crossing the river. Still he hesitated, for after all this time and all the way he'd come, to be parted again so soon was almost unbearable.

"Private, I'm giving you a direct order!" the voice persisted, coming closer. "Get away from that window, and I mean *now!*"

"Yes, General," Dónal said, using every last bit of his will to close the sash and draw the drapes. "I was just after a bit of fresh air."

❦

Crouching in the sunken road, Dónal gazed through the haze of gun smoke, trying to see if another assault was forming in the town. Surely not, he thought, given the grievous losses they'd already suffered, the field being so thick with blue-coated bodies that a man could walk across it without touching the ground, and not one of them within a hundred yards of the sunken road. Surely the strength of their position was evident now, and the generals wouldn't be so callous or stupid as to send more men into the death trap that was Marye's Heights. But then, he'd been equally sure that they wouldn't try it to begin with, so who knew what they might do in order to save face. At least there'd been no green flags among them so far, and he prayed there would be none, that if Eóghan was in the battle to at least let him be somewhere else and not here in the slaughter.

But then a bullet whizzed by his ear, and he ducked behind the wall, reminding himself that he was still in a battle and not invulnerable, a fact borne out by the casualties his company had suffered, with Neill Duggan, John Flanagan, Patrick Furlong, Pat Keating and Paddy McGuire all being wounded, while both their regimental and brigade commanders, Colonel Cook and General Cobb himself, had been killed, leaving McMillan in overall command.

And as he huddled with his back to the retaining wall, Dónal cursed himself again for getting caught up in the moment rather than leaving with Eóghan immediately. For afterward, he'd been unable to get away, as Cobb had kept everyone in the house trying to get an explanation of why Mitchel's men were there instead of his own. And by the time he'd finally let them go, a heavy snow had been falling which continued until almost dawn, only to be replaced by a thick layer of fog. So even the elements were against him, it seemed, as if Fate weren't enemy enough. If only night would come, and let him slip away and across the river. Just let there be darkness and he'd be with Eóghan again.

But then he heard a sound from the field that made his blood run cold, a distant high-pitched shrieking more like a Rebel Yell than a typical Yankee huzzah.

"Oh, good Christ, it's Meagher!" Gillespie exclaimed beside him, though Dónal knew it without being told.

And as though in a trance, he stood and gazed over the field, oblivious to the bullets whizzing around him. There they were, advancing at the double-quick and screaming their battlecries, a solitary flag floating in the wind before them, dipping as the bearer fell and rising as another took it up, never letting its sacred Green touch the ground. From the hill above, the artillery rained down upon them, punching gaping holes in their line, a dozen men falling with each concussion. Yet on they came, gaining momentum and rallying their fellows to rise and join them, their faces collectively turned aside as though braving a hailstorm, never slowing their pace, terrible and magnificent to see, the Irish Brigade, the Men of the Gael advancing on the field of war.

A cheer went up from the heights at their valor and the men in the road joined in, though not the Irishmen of the Lochrane Guards. They stood entranced, their muskets at their sides and their hearts in their throats, watching as their countrymen advanced to the slaughter. They'd known it was possible, of course, though never had they believed it would actually happen, leaving them no better prepared than if they'd never thought of it.

Yet only for Dónal was the nightmare complete, for he knew Eóghan was out there, lying on the field already perhaps, armless, legless, eviscerated, dead. Or perhaps it had yet to happen and the next instant would bring it, or the next, and Dónal died a thousand deaths with each man that fell.

Then suddenly a voice broke into his nightmare, Robert McMillan's Ulster burr. "Come on, lads, load up those muskets! I know those are Meagher's men out there, but we've got to show our comrades what good and loyal Confederates we are! So come on, Lochrane Guards, load up and get ready!"

At that, Dónal's trance was broken and he sprang into action.

"No boys, no, don't listen to him!" he screamed. "'Tis our own fellahs out there, our own Irish brethren with whom we should be united and not shootin' down like dogs! This isn't our war and the Irish Brigade is not our enemy! So don't listen to him! He's just another Proddie aristocrat after usin' us for his own gain!"

Then McMillan was upon him, red-faced and glaring. "Hold your tongue, private, or I'll have you arrested!

"Listen to me, lads!" he shouted to the others. "The whole Confederacy is watching us here, and what we do will affect all our people, every man, woman and child, from this day forward! So don't let them down, lads! Show them our loyalty. Show them we're Confederate soldiers and that to us those men are just another bunch of Yankees! If we do, they'll accept us as their own forever after! I promise you, they will!"

"No, don't listen to him!" Dónal countered. "He's not one of us! He's just an English stooge and what he says doesn't matter!"

"Sergeant, arrest that man and take him to the rear!" McMillan ordered.

"Don't listen to him!" Dónal continued, as hands were laid upon him. "Please!"

"Sergeant, *now!*" McMillan roared.

But it was Pat McGovern who decided it. "Come on, lads, load 'em up. We're Confederate soldiers, now, and for better or worse, that's where our loyalty lies. Sure, we all dream of goin' home someday, but that's all it is, just a dream that'll never come true. This is our country now, and we've got to show that we belong.

"And besides," he added bitterly, "we wouldn't want to deprive this Orangeman of his moment in the sun."

Though McMillan glared, he said nothing, for McGovern's words broke the spell and the Lochrane men took up their positions, silently and somberly, turning their muskets on the advancing blue line.

"No, boys, don't do it. No!" Dónal shouted, struggling with his guards.

But no one turned to him, not even Driscoll or Gillespie. The die was cast and Ireland had lost.

"READY!" came the order down the line.

"*NO!*" Dónal shouted, now struggling desperately. "*NO! EÓGHAN! EÓGHAN!*"

Then a pistol butt crashed into his head and he crumpled to the ground, hearing but one last thing before all went dark:

"FIRE!"

⊙⟶⟶⟶⟶⟵⟵⟵⊙

All was dark when Dónal awoke and, feeling shackles upon his ankles, for a moment he thought he was back on the chain gang. But then the painful lump on his head brought back the events of the day, and he knew himself to be the prisoner of another evil.

"Will we never learn?" he sighed, remembering the order to fire, and knowing that Irishmen had murdered Irishmen.

"You awake in there?" a voice asked from beyond his cell door.

"To be sure," Dónal replied. "Where am I?"

"In the basement of Brompton," the man informed him, meaning the big house atop Marye's Heights where Lee had his headquarters. "They brung you in this afternoon. I hear they gonna court-martial you tomorrow. Wha'd you do, anyway?"

"'Tis a long one in the tellin'."

"Well, I ain't got nothin' but time, son, an' for tonight at least, neither do you."

But Dónal was having none of it. "Who won the battle? Did the Yankees ever get to the wall?"

"Not even close. We really clobbered 'em! So if you're a Yankee lover like I hear tell, you had a pretty bad day of it!"

"Sure, if you only knew the half of it."

☙ ⁘ ❧

It was in the grand parlor of the mansion that they'd set up the court, and Dónal stood in the center of the room before a long table. Behind it sat his trinity of judges, Lee in the center wearing the loneliness of command like a shroud, Longstreet on his left, deliberate and rumi-native, and Jackson on his right, zealous and intense, slightly detached from reality in the way that religious fanatics always are. Beside Dónal stood the man who'd been appointed to defend him, some staff officer whose name he'd not bothered to catch, while further to the right stood the prosecutor.

Thus far, the proceedings had been brisk and smooth, with the prosecutor taking less than an hour to present his case. Indeed, he'd called only two witnesses, McMillan himself and one of the Fenians who'd come to recruit back in August. It was cut and dried, really, and he'd not even bothered to pay attention, knowing it all to be true and that he had no defense. And anyway, if they wanted to make an example of him, there was nothing he could do to stop them.

The time having come for the defense to present its case, Lee called upon Dónal's counsel to do so. "The accused does not wish to call any witnesses, General," the man said, glancing sidelong at Dónal, "only to make a statement in his own behalf."

"Is that true, Private O'Sullivan?" Lee asked, turning his steady blue eyes on Dónal.

"'Tis," Dónal replied, standing with his arms crossed defiantly and looking down his nose at Lee.

"All right then. Proceed."

"I didn't want to fire at the Yankees because my brother was among them," Dónal said, looking only at Lee.

There was a silence then, as Lee waited for him to say more, seeming surprised when he didn't. "Is that all you have to say, Private?"

"One would think it enough, General, for men of compassion, that is."

"Well, Private O'Sullivan, one can certainly understand your not wishing to fire at your own brother, and if you had explained this to Colonel McMillan, I'm sure he would have excused you. After all, he is a man of compassion, and since he is also Irish, I'm sure he would have understood your conflict. However, what I don't understand is why you tried to incite the rest of your company to join you, especially at such a crucial juncture of the battle, or why you on a previous occasion exhorted the Irishmen of this army to desert. Those sound like the actions of a spy to me, or at least a provocateur. So what have you to say on those points?"

"Only that all Irishmen are brothers, General, and that we should be united in the struggle against our ancient oppressor rather than killin' each other for your benefit."

"I'm afraid your defense does you no credit, Private, as neither we nor the Yankees are at war with England."

"And neither does your slave-mongerin' credit you, General Lee, nor this insane asylum of a country you've made up for yourselves!"

"Yes, well, be that as it may, my slave-mongering is not on trial here.

But you are, Private O'Sullivan, and you face some very serious consequences if found guilty. So if you have anything of substance to say in your defense, I suggest you say it now."

"No, I've nothin' else."

"Then that being the case, I declare this court to be in recess while we consider our verdict," Lee said, and made to push back from the table.

"Now, General Lee," Jackson interjected, "I don't think there's anything much to consider here. The facts speak for themselves and the defendant offers no defense. So I'm sure I speak for the court when I say that we should find him guilty and shoot him at dawn!"

Lee eyed Jackson for a moment before nodding his head and turning to Longstreet. "General?"

"Well, now," Longstreet replied in his deliberate manner. "I am inclined to agree with General Jackson in his assessment of the facts and guilt of the defendant. However, I should not be so hasty as to condemn this young man to death without an appropriate period of deliberation. After all, we have many things to consider here, not the least of which is the impact of our actions upon the Irishmen of this army, most of whom have shown themselves to be brave and loyal Confederates. I personally would be more inclined to exhibit the compassion with which we have been challenged, and return a lesser sentence of, say, five years at hard labor. That will certainly send the message that divided loyalties will not be tolerated, while at the same time showin' that in our humanity, we understand a man's reluctance to fire upon his own brother."

Nodding at Longstreet's words, Lee turned back to Jackson. "General, I would be inclined to agree with General Longstreet's proposal, though I would also like to hear your reasons for thinking the death sentence appropriate in this case."

"General, what is required here is not an expression of our compassion or our humanity," Jackson said firmly, the flame in his fanatical eyes showing why he was known as Ol' Blue Light, for the way they came alive when men were dying around him. "Rather, what is required is a demonstration of our absolute determination to defeat this godless scourge of Yankeedom and free our fair Southland of its oppression and tyranny! Therefore, we need to send a clear and emphatic message to all foreigners that if they wish to be citizens of our great Confederacy, then they must give themselves to her heart and soul, forsaking all loyalty to the lands of their birth and even to members of their families who might seek to assail her! And that, simply put, is why I believe the death sentence is warranted in this case, and why I urge you to put aside any feelings of mercy you might find in your heart and deliver it!"

"General Jackson makes a strong case, Private O'Sullivan," Lee said. "Are you sure you have nothing else to say before we pass judgment upon you?"

"Just this, General," Dónal replied. "I've done hard labor before, and I'd rather be shot than do it again."

Lee blinked in surprise, and for a moment seemed at a loss for words. "In that case, Private O'Sullivan, this court finds you guilty as charged and sentences you to death by firing squad, sentence to be delivered at dawn tomorrow. May God have mercy upon your soul."

◠◡◠◡◠

"So I'm to be shot at dawn," Dónal said to his empty cell. "Isn't that dramatic! Ah, well, at least I'll go out with a bang."

Then he sighed and rolled off his cot, his attempt at black humor not having its desired affect. He shuffled to the door and knocked to get his guard's attention. "Any chance of a drop for the pain that's in it?"

"Sure, I'll see what I can do when my relief comes," the man replied. "Think you can last till then?"

"Do I have a fookin' choice?" Dónal muttered. Aloud, he said, "Thanks, I'd appreciate anything you can do."

Going back to his cot, he closed his eyes and let his mind wander, thinking of home and the people he'd left behind, of the road he'd traveled and all its twists and turns, of all he'd been through trying to get to Eóghan, only to have lost him again as soon as he found him. How many things he would do differently if only he could, how different he would make his destiny. But then, maybe not. Maybe destiny was absolute and came to the same end no matter the turns one made along the way. Ah, well, at least the Mitchels would let Eóghan know what had happened to him, and maybe the news would even change his mind about going home. Maybe when all was said and done, that would be his service to Ireland, to be shot at dawn so Eóghan would finally see the error of his ways and go home. Sure, that had to be it, he told himself, and he would even write him a letter just to make sure.

But as he rolled off his cot to ask the guard for writing supplies, he heard the keys jiggle in the lock, and then Willy Mitchel spilled into the room with the guard close behind.

"What are you—" Dónal began, though Mitchel cut him off.

"Come on, we don't have much time!" he said, unlocking Dónal's shackles and pulling him up from the cot.

"But what about himself there?" Dónal demanded, meaning the guard.

"Don't worry, he's one of us," Mitchel replied.

"My mother's from Wicklow Town," the man said by way of explanation, "and my father's father came from Coleraine."

"No, no." Dónal countered, one step ahead of them. "I mean, won't you get in trouble for this?"

"He would if he stayed behind," Mitchel replied with a grin. "So that's why he's goin' with you."

At Dónal's quizzical look, the man just shrugged. "My brother's on the other side, too."

"The 1st Virginia has provost duty," Mitchel said when Dónal turned the same look on him, "and when he heard they were goin' to shoot you, he volunteered, and James arranged it."

"Thanks," Dónal said to the guard.

"Don't mention it," the man said, shrugging again.

Then they were moving through the bowels of the basement and into the kitchen with its back door to freedom. And there Mitchel left them for a moment, going up the steps to reconnoiter.

"It's all clear," he said softly when he returned. "These steps lead outside so we don't have to go through the house. We'll go as a group and if anyone stops us, let me do the talkin'. Ready? Let's go!"

And with that, they were up the steps and away. But despite the danger, what they saw in the night sky brought them to a sudden halt.

"Good God a'mighty, what's that?" the erstwhile guard hissed.

"'Tis the Northern Lights," Dónal replied. "I'd no idea you could see them this far south."

"I never have before," Mitchel commented.

"It looks like God himself is celebratin' our victory," the guard said.

"Or somethin' worse," Dónal said, feeling a sudden chill. "Come on with yez now. There'll be time enough for it later."

Mitchel led them quickly down the hill then, stopping in the sunken road by the small clapboard house where Cobb had fallen the day before.

"Here," he said, pulling two bundles of Yankee clothing from under it and handing one to each. "Put these on when you get out to the brick house where you met Eóghan. There's no pickets out, so you don't have to worry about bein' challenged, at least on our side."

"What about those men in the road there?" Dónal asked, hearing the low murmur of their conversation.

"That's James and our own fellahs of the Montgomery Guards," Mitchel replied. "But don't worry. If anyone sees you, they'll just think you're goin' out to scavenge. The dead Yankees are still out there and it's been goin' on since dark. But get on with you, now! And safe home."

"And to you, too," Dónal replied. "And tell James I said thanks."

"He already knows," Mitchel said, and turned away.

"Ready?" Dónal asked his companion. "Then let's go."

And with that they headed into the night, crossing the field toward Fredericksburg, finding it clear and open for the first fifty yards or so. But then they came across something shining eerily white, the body of a Yankee soldier, all twisted and grotesque as he lay in a pool of frozen blood, his death throes forever graven into his Irish features by the rigor of death and the frigid weather. The scavengers had stripped him bare, of course, taking even his underwear in their desperate need, leaving him as he'd come into the world, naked and alone. And there were more beyond him, in ones and twos at first, and then in piles of three and four deep, and all in the same ransacked, desecrated state as the first. Not that Dónal dared to look at them, the fear of seeing Eóghan's face keeping his eyes forward and high, though nothing could drive the image of it from his mind.

At the house they changed into their Yankee clothes and headed on, soon crossing the mill stream that bisected the field, and picked up their pace, being through the worst of the carnage now. At the edge of town, they encountered a few men huddled around a small fire, ostensibly on sentry duty though they were more concerned with keeping themselves warm, it seemed, and didn't even give them a second look.

"This is where I leave you," Dónal said to his companion. "Thanks for everything, and good luck to you."

"Yeah, you too," the man replied, holding back to let him go on alone.

As he walked into town, Dónal saw that it was largely deserted, but for small groups of men here and there, huddling around fires and passing canteens. Stopping at the first to ask for Meagher's headquarters, he was shocked to learn that he was throwing a party in the town hall.

"Sure, you're after pullin' my leg, aren't you?" Dónal asked, incredulous that anyone could find anything to celebrate after the horrors he'd just witnessed.

"No, Captain, it's the God's honest truth," the man replied, addressing him by the insignia on his jacket. "Apparently, some highfalutin politicians came down from New York with new regimental flags, and he's puttin' on the dog for 'em. It's a good thing they didn't get here a couple of days ago, or he'd already be needin' new ones."

After getting directions, Dónal thanked the man and hurried on, his feeling of disbelief growing as he neared the lighted hall and heard raucous voices raised in laughter amid the clink of glasses. It seemed surreal to him, as he stood in the doorway and gaped at the tables piled with food and drink and waited upon by Negroes in white jackets, so

726

incongruous to the barbarity of the battlefield, so disrespectful of the men who lay upon it, unburied and unhallowed. Even the four green flags standing behind the dignitaries at the far end, three new and one rent and tattered, did nothing to lessen his amazement.

But then a voice brought him back to reality, that of a Yankee sergeant speaking with a brogue. "Can I help ye, Captain?"

"To be sure," Dónal replied, scanning the dais expectantly. "'Tis Lieutenant Colonel Eóghan O'Sullivan I'm after. Is he here?"

"Do ye mind if I ask what ye want him for?" the man asked, after hesitating a moment.

"I'm his brother," Dónal replied, the hair on the back of his neck rising at the look that came into the man's eyes.

"I see. Would ye mind waitin' here for a moment?"

Without waiting for an answer, he went to the head table and spoke to the man seated at its center, whose eyes shot to Dónal. Dismissing the sergeant, the man rose and spoke to two others, who rose in turn and followed him to the door.

"Are you Dónal?" the man asked gravely, his accent that of an English gentleman. "I'm Tom Meagher. Eóghan spoke of you often."

But Dónal didn't take his extended hand. "Eóghan's dead, isn't he?" he asked, his voice flat and final.

"I'm afraid so. He was killed leading the 69th against Marye's Heights. A bullet came from behind the wall and severed an artery in his leg, and he bled to death before anything could be done for him. It seemed so insignificant, just a flesh wound from the look of it. Indeed, a half-inch one way or the other and he'd still be with us. His men carried him back, risking their own lives, such was their love for him. We have him lying in state at the Catholic chapel down the street. Would you like to go there?"

But seeing that Dónal couldn't reply, Meagher took him gently by the elbow and led him through the streets of Fredericksburg on the longest walk he'd ever taken, each step a thousand miles, each second a lifetime, each heartbeat a thousand deaths, though it was indeed only a short distance.

The casket lay open before the altar, and the four of them stopped beside it, Meagher and his fellows bowing their heads respectfully. Yet for a long moment, Dónal just stared straight ahead, as if not looking would make it not so. But finally he sighed and lowered his eyes, and there was Eóghan, sleeping peacefully in his box of Death.

"All the men loved him," Meagher said. "I loved him. He was a great friend and a great son of Erin, and I shall miss him terribly."

But though he knew the man was trying to help, Dónal had no room in his heart for other people's grief just then, or for their compassion. "Would you mind leavin' me alone with him for a bit?" he said, making it more a command than a request.

"Sure, Dónal, we'll go now. But when you're finished here, come and find me. I know you were stuck with the Rebels against your will, and you're free to go wherever you want now. But there's a spot for you on my staff, if you want it. I could use a good man like you."

Turning to Meagher then, Dónal took a good look at him for the first time, his eyes narrow and appraising. "Were you in the battle, General Meagher? Did you lead your troops into the field?"

"Er, no, I didn't," Meagher replied, his eyes wavering under Dónal's scrutiny. "I have a rather painful ulcer of the knee which kept me from taking the field on foot. So after addressing the men and sending them forward, I had to go back into town for my horse, and by the time I found it, they'd already been repulsed and were coming back."

But all Dónal could think of were the rumors about Sharpsburg. "Thank you for the offer, General. I'll think about it."

"Good man. Come, gentlemen. Let's give The O'Sullivan Béara some privacy."

Once they were gone, Dónal stayed only a few minutes himself. There was nothing for him to do, really, nothing to say, nothing to feel. And indeed he felt nothing, beyond an abiding sense of emptiness, his spirit drained away by the hard life and loneliness, and the pervasiveness of Death. He'd tarried along the road and now, by a matter of hours, he was too late. Eóghan was dead and Dónal had no one to blame for it but himself.

"Oh, God, my God, where will I find forgiveness?" he said aloud.

But as he was turning to leave, his eyes lit upon the crucifix behind the altar, and for a moment he thought it was Her hanging there, red-haired and beguiling, butchered and defiled. But no. It was only Jesus.

Outside, Dónal walked as in a trance, his feet finding their own way to the Yankee pontoon bridge and across the river, men screaming at him to get down as Confederate shells exploded all around. But he knew they wouldn't get him, that though the whole world might die around him, he was yet damned to live. Life long and lonely would be the punishment for his sins. On the far side, he found a campfire and lay down beside it, falling immediately into the empty sleep of moral oblivion.

In the morning, he wrapped a bloody rag around his head and hopped onto the back of a hospital wagon, slipping away at the first town and grabbing himself a change of clothes from an unguarded line. Walking through the town, he saw a young red-haired man looking at him from a shop window, and stopped to look back. But finding him haggard and disheveled, his hollow eyes a perfect window into his empty soul, he went on his way. He didn't know that sad stranger, didn't want to make his acquaintance.

In the burial ground outside of town, he climbed a low hill and stood looking to the east. Should he go back? he wondered briefly, though he knew the question was empty, that there was no choice to be made. Ireland wasn't home anymore, and there was nothing left of the man he'd once been, and how could he ever escape the knowledge of it there? At least here he had the road and the drink and two continents in which to lose himself, and those who loved him would never have to know how miserably he'd failed them.

"How could I have been so naïve?" he asked the tombstones.

But the Dead gave him no answer.

He sighed and ran his hands through his hair. "I need a drink," he said, and turned his face to the road.

The Darkness was upon him, and he could stave it off no longer.

part eight

• Ithaca •

chapⱦeʀ 37

Cahernageeha
Béara Peninsula, Irish Free State
17 June, 1923

Young Timothy Ahern brought his lorry to an abrupt halt and hurried to help the elderly passenger from his seat. Once out, the old man leaned on him for a moment to steady himself before pushing on. He'd come a long way to get to this place, by railroad from San Francisco to New York, and thence by steamer across the Broad Atlantic, and the trip had taken its toll. But even that paled in comparison to the ride up the hillside just now, the old boreen having never been fit for more than carts and many years having gone since it was used for even that, and the potholes and stones had thrown him about mercilessly. Straightening himself and letting go of Tim, he took a deep breath and gazed about uncertainly, shading his eyes from the bright summer sun while trying to reorient himself to these once familiar surroundings, indeed, to see them again with the eyes of youth. For this place had been his home once, long ago in that other lifetime when he'd been young, and he'd carried his memories of it through many years and miles and to many distant places. But now that he was here, actually standing on the Holy Ground, his memories suddenly deserted him and his mind was as blank as the clear sky above, as if his youth were but a dream that vanished upon awakening.

Yet one thing at least had not changed – the wind still blew as it had then, sweeping up from the sea and across the bare hillside like an army of conquest. And from it the place had taken its name, *Cathair na Gaoithe,* "Fortress of the Wind," though he'd always thought *Cathair in aghaidh na Gaoithe,* "Fortress *against* the Wind," more appropriate, as it had surely been just that to all who'd ever sheltered within its walls. He listened as it rustled the grass and whistled through the rocks and, closing his eyes, tried to hear it singing again through the branches of the great yew tree. But it was no use; the present was too strong, and there was nothing left to him of those younger days.

Opening his eyes, he looked to where the great tree had once stood, where it would be standing still if not for the malicious deed of an arrogant young man. It was gone, of course, and no trace of it remained, beyond a slight depression in the grass where the stump had been. But the ruined cottage was still there, though the years had been no kinder to it than to him, leaving it weathered and worn, the wreck of what had once been a home even as he was the wreck of what had once been a young boy, scarred with the mark of the battering ram as he was with the mark of the fang, the lash and shrapnel. The front wall was tumbled to the ground and much of the back, so that only the three gables marked it for the home it had been. And while the *clochán* of neighboring cottages was almost completely gone now, having been used over the years as a convenient quarry for building stone, his old home seemed not to have been touched, the local people perhaps not realizing it to be separate from the ringfort and leaving it alone in deference to the custom of respecting the monuments of the ancients.

After a moment, he moved away from the lorry and carefully picked his way through the jumble of stones and into the midst of the cottage. Closing his eyes he tried to picture his family there, all sitting by the hearth together, laughing and happy, Eóghan, his mother and father, himself. And though it had never happened in real life, he knew it could have. Sure, there could've been love in this house and all their lives saved, if only his father could've given up the rage that drove him in pursuit of his terrible quest, the Holy Grail that generations of O'Sullivans had sought after and never found. But all that came to him was the man as he'd been on that fateful day at Dunboy, broken in body and spirit, finding his salvation in passing the burden on to his son, a boy too young and frightened to know better than to accept it. If only he'd said, "No, Da, I don't want to do it." But he was just a little boy then and desperate for his father's love and approval. How could he have known the man had neither to give?

Dónal O'Sullivan opened his eyes and gazed at the devastation around him. How ironic, he thought, that anyone could ever mistake this godforsaken hovel for anything ancient or sacred. Yet, he had to admit that it was indeed a monument of sorts, a monument to the tragedy of lives that might have been, of lives corrupted by the domination of an inadequate man.

He's not sleeping, you little thick, he's dead!

In all of Dónal's years, *ochón*, how many times had he heard the laughter? How many times had he found himself back in that place, his heart pounding and his fists clenched and shaking, the pain as fresh and new as if it were still happening? How many times had he hidden himself away from it in sex and the drink, knowing he would be the worse for it later but unable to deny his addiction to the few hours' release they brought? And how much more pain would there be, how much more Darkness before Death brought him to the Light?

And that, of course, was why he'd stayed away so long, because to come back would mean having to face those questions, to stop running and stand with his back to the wall, to look squarely into the eyes of the ghosts that haunted him, and find a way to forgive his father, and himself.

"But how can I ever forgive all that," he asked the stones, "and where will I find healing if I don't?"

But the Fortress of the Wind gave him no answer.

Dónal sighed and turned away. There was just one place left to look.

ᏬᎢᎢᏝᎧ

Standing at the top of the sea cliff near the ruins of Dunboy, Dónal gazed absently at his shadow writ large on the rippling water below.

735

Young Tim had driven him down from Cahernageeha, through the rusting gates that now stood permanently open and into the once-forbidden sanctuary of the conquerors. The forest was cool and dark as they drove through, and he felt the urge to go no further, to just sit down in the comfort of the shade and let the sleep of Eternity put an end to his suffering. But he didn't; there were things that needed to be done yet, things that only he could do. So they drove on, crossing a clearing in which cows grazed and cresting a slight rise to find the Big House, still sitting on its little knoll where English cannon had once stood. Yet even it was different now, Henry Puxley having doubled its size with an addition that had never been completed, as his young wife had died in 1867, and he'd left Ireland brokenhearted, never to return. But more so, the change was due to the events of 1921, when revolution had swept over the land and the Irish Republican Army had put it to the torch, the old grievances against the Puxleys still fresh, though they'd had no real presence there for over fifty years. The ruins were still blackened in places, and it was sad and gray, yet as much a symbol as ever, though of vengeance now rather than mastery.

But Dónal didn't stop at the Big House either, just continued on to the old ruins, finding them the same as the last time he'd seen them, exactly sixty-two years before. Even the sun played obligingly among the stones, casting the shadows as they'd been then, it being about the same time of day. He walked through the doorway past the gallery staircase and into the roofless cellar, standing by the window where he'd sat with his father and Seán and Tadhg, and where sleep had stolen over him on that last afternoon long ago. But the familiarity hadn't cheered him, for it was a killing field, a place still haunted by the restless spirits of men sacrificed to military necessity, knowing even with their dying breaths that they'd been abandoned.

As he moved to the cliff, the sound of water slapping at rocks sparked his memory, and he thought of the first time he'd seen the Pacific Ocean. He'd taken off his shoes and walked into the cool wet sand at the water's edge, and thought how far away he was from Béara, half a world in space and a lifetime in his heart. Yet even there, he couldn't escape the shadow of Dunboy.

And so he'd traveled on, going south through Mexico first and on into South America, crisscrossing the continent for years before heading north again to give *El Norte* its turn. He even headed toward Georgia once, though he got no further than New Orleans before finding the so-called New South to be just as backward, bigoted and Bible-bound as the Old South had been. Nor was its white population in the least bit repentant of the two and a half centuries they'd held their black brethren enthralled, a crime so vast and deep that it could only accurately be described as perpetrated against humanity itself. Indeed, the Southern Cross still flew defiantly in many places, and discrimination was the order of the day, while Lee, Jackson and Davis were worshipped as cultural icons, men who'd "fought for what they believed in," a polite veneer suggesting that their beliefs were somehow honorable. As for the slaves themselves, they were mired in the serfdom of sharecropping, tied to the land just as surely as they'd been before, though now they were like the Irish, slaves without masters, free in name only. So as it had been before, Southern culture was still an impenetrable enigma to him, often brutal though sometimes elegant, strangling itself in a tangle of superficiality, complex and yet ultimately empty.

And having quickly gotten his fill of it, he traveled on.

But though loneliness was his constant companion, he seldom wanted for female company, finding willing women wherever he went. For he remained handsome even into his great age, and could still be charming when it suited his purpose. And when neither was sufficient, he had a sad tale to tell of himself that made women want to take him in and protect him from a hurtful world, especially when they saw the scars. But never did he find any love in it, just a salve for his broken heart, a sanctuary as temporary as his ubiquitous whiskey. So when their love became burdensome, one by one he left them behind, and traveled on.

Then in the 1880's, at the height of the copper boom, he rode into Butte, Montana, going straight to the offices of the "Copper King," the great Marcus Daly of the County Cavan, where he hoped to find a job as a bookkeeper and salt away some money before hitting the road again. But as he dismounted, he heard someone shout his name and turned to find a red-headed giant barreling down upon him, his crushing embrace reminding him of the time as boys when Padge had tried to do it for real.

"Dónal O'Sullivan!" Padge shouted, hugging him tighter. "Sure, I never thought I'd see ye alive again!"

"And you won't if you don't put me down, you big galoot!" Dónal wheezed back. But he couldn't resist Padge's infectious joy, grinning broadly and shaking his massive hand. "'Tis grand to see you, Padge, grand so!" And noting the expensive (and expansive) cut of his clothes and the solid gold watch chain at his vest, he added, "And sure, if you aren't a fine sight of it, too, all fat and happy like Mrs. Murphy's pig! What've you been up to that's made you such a dandy? Did you marry rich or somethin'?"

"I did, to be sure, though I made me own fortune first, I'll have ye know."

"What, as a miner?"

"No, as a mine *owner*," Padge replied proudly, though he struggled to contain his laughter as he continued. "Why, I'm a fookin' baron of industry, if ye can believe it. Sure, I even named me youngfellah J. L. P. O'Sullivan. And ye know what the J. L. P. stands for, Dónal, now don't ye?"

"Oh, fook no, Padge! You didn't name the poor bugger for John Lavallin Puxley, surely!"

"No, ye're right, I didn't. It just stands for John Lawrence Patrick, the first bit bein' me wife's father's name and the last me own! And though I never liked the sound of it, really, 'twas worth it just to see the look on yeer face. 'Twould've stopped a seven-day clock cold in the mornin'!"

But then Padge went suddenly serious on him. "Have ye been home, Dónal, or had any news of it since ye left?"

"No, Padge, I haven't, beyond hearin' that the mines were closed."

"Sure, 'tis true enough. Indeed, most of the fellahs are here in Butte now and a few even work for me, Con O'Shea and Mike Murphy just to name a couple. And before ye ask, Dónal, yes, I take better care of 'em than the Company back home, better than those rotten hoors ever thought about on the most charitable day they ever had. So does Marcus Daly and the other Irish fellahs, because we've all been on the other side of it and know the feelin'.

"But no, Dónal, 'tisn't what I meant at all. There's somethin' important, *really* important, that ye should know, somethin' . . . somethin' that I'm not after tellin' ye out here in the street. And would ye look at the time now. Sure, if I'm not late for a meetin' with Marcus himself, and let me tell ye, the Copper King gets royally agitated when he's kept waitin'. But that saloon there across the street belongs to a friend of mine, a Cork man himself named Mickey Tynte. So why don't ye go there and wait for me, and I'll come as soon as ever I'm able. 'Twon't be two shakes, I promise ye."

"Sure, Padge, if you say so."

"Good man, yeerself. Just tell Mickey ye're a friend of mine from Allihies, and he'll take care of ye."

Then Padge slapped Dónal on the shoulder so hard he almost fell. "Jayzis, if it ain't The O'Sullivan Béara come back to life right before me eyes! Just wait'll the lads hear it! They'll all be after seein' ye!"

But Dónal didn't go to the saloon across the street, just mounted his horse and rode away, going on for days without stopping in a town again. Whatever news Padge had to tell, he didn't want to hear it, or to see forgotten faces or hear of the life he'd left behind. For there was no going home for him, not yet at any rate, and so he traveled on.

But by 1910 he'd grown too old to live the Traveler's life anymore. He had arthritis and could no longer sit a horse for any length of time, and traveling by rail wasn't really *traveling* in the Irish sense of the word. So he settled into an old soldier's home in San Francisco to endure whatever time was left to him. He'd lived so long now, for so many years past hope or happiness, and he was ready for night to draw down around him and relieve him of his burden. But Death wasn't kind, and after a year or so he took to writing poetry to relieve the monotony. It wasn't something he meant to do, really. It just came to him one day, when a glimpse in the mirror took him back to Ahern's cottage and his first brush with self-consciousness. Where had this old man come from, he wondered, and what had become of that little boy? Then the words just came to him and he hurried to write them down.

I looked at him, and then quickly away, finding him repulsive, and yet, somehow compelling.

Looking again, I saw an expressionless face that had once been handsome, and could be again, if he could but smile. But I knew he hadn't smiled in years. Not really.

Looking into his eyes, I thought, 'Jayzis, you'd better shut them before you bleed to death!' for they were bloodshot and bleary, and burdened with the baggage of hard living. If it's true that the eyes are the windows of the soul, then I was looking through broken panes into eternal Darkness.

His breath stank of the morning after, of the water of life that had doused the flame of his spirit, a jar of rotgut where the precious soul of a little boy had once been. What happened, little boy? What happened to make the man in you surrender?

I pitied him, and even shed a tear for him, though I made no effort to comfort him, gave nothing of myself to relieve his suffering. After all, it was his own fault for not fighting back, for not saying no.

I turned away when his tragedy became tiresome, and silently thanked God that he wasn't me. No, I could never be like that. I could never be like that man in the mirror.

He called it *Reflection*, of course, and after that, writing became for him what music had been in his youth, a sanctuary into which he could pour his heart and turn the pain into images of beauty, tragic, heartbreaking beauty.

Later, when he compiled a body of work, the home's administrator read some of it and passed it on to his brother in Chicago, who just happened to be in the publishing business. And the man was so impressed that he took a train all the way to California to see Dónal about publishing it. At first he said no, wanting nothing to do with the idea. But then he thought, 'Oh, what the hell?' and let the man proceed. Though unorthodox for the time, the resulting volume was well-received and, with the two that followed, had brought him enough income to buy a small cottage in Sausalito, the first house he'd ever owned. Yet never did he think of it as his *home*. "I'm going to my house," he would say of it, never, "I'm going home."

But it was the third volume, published in 1919 and entitled, *Of the Mountain and the Bog,* that had brought him back to this lonely little place at the far edge of the world. For just at the beginning of March, a letter had come to him through his publisher with the return address, "John Ahern, Bantry," and, opening it with shaking hands, he found it to be from Tadhg's eldest son. He'd read the book, he explained, as had his brothers and sisters, and they were wondering if the author was the same man who'd been fostered by their late grandparents, Seán and Órla. "If so," the letter went on, "'we'd be greatly pleased if you would contact us at your earliest convenience, as we would very much like to know the man whom our father always spoke of as the best friend he'd ever had. (Indeed, his dying words were, 'If only I could see Dónal again.') But more important, we have some of your belongings that our father kept after his parents passed away, and insisted that we keep, too, as he was sure you would come back to claim them someday. Also, there are some important things that you should know which can only be properly related in person. So it would give us great pleasure, Mr. O'Sullivan, if you would come back to Béara, as we would all dearly love to meet you. Sincerely, John Ahern, for my brothers and sisters, Dónal, Michael, Patrick, Mary and Margaret."

Of course, the tears were flowing by the time he finished, all the pain of all the years coming down on him like the burden of Atlas. Yet it wasn't for himself that he was crying, but for those he'd left behind, for the pain he'd caused them, and the way their lives had been diminished by his absence.

"Ah, well," he said to himself at length. "I suppose there's yet time to make things right before I die." Then he sat down and wrote his response. "I am himself," it said simply, "and I will come."

So it was that he sailed back across the Broad Atlantic, coming into Cobh (née Queenstown) on the deck of a great ocean liner, his heart pounding in his chest at the sight of the green land smiling in the sun, cheerfully welcoming him home. But he didn't tarry in that place where his plans had gone so awry, going straight to the station and taking the first train to Bantry.

They were all there to meet him, of course, John Ahern and his brothers and sisters, their twenty-two children and forty-three grandchildren, all the descendants of his friend and brother, Tadhg Ahern. They looked at him curiously for a moment, until John, who was most like his father in looks, stepped forward and politely introduced himself and his brothers and sisters. And after a few pleasantries (all delivered in English), he got down to business.

"You'll want to go to the bank straight away, no doubt," he said. "We've kept your money in trust for you all these years, and the papers to transfer it are ready, though you'll have to go in and sign them personally."

"My money?" Dónal asked, blinking in bewilderment. "And what money would that be?"

"Why, the money from the business, of course. Da always insisted that half of it was yours since you put up the investment to start it, and that you'd surely come back for it someday. Were you not aware of the arrangement?"

"The business?" Dónal asked softly, though he'd understood.

"Sure, the business, Ahern and O'Sullivan, Ltd. We've built half the new buildings in West Cork over the last fifty years, and there's over a hundred thousand pounds waiting for you, what with the gombeen, and such."

At that, Dónal was stunned to silence. A hundred thousand pounds, just sitting in a bank in Bantry! After all those countless nights he'd slept on the cold hard ground, sometimes going without food or even whiskey, the very idea was so incomprehensible that he could only laugh. *A hundred thousand pounds!*

But John Ahern didn't laugh. "Dunboy is up for sale, you know. The IRA torched the Big House in '21, and what remains is to be sold at auction. You could buy it with the money and build yourself a new castle. Why, you could even be The O'Sullivan Béara again, if you'd a mind. We know of the old quest, you see. Da passed it on to us so it wouldn't be forgotten. Maybe this is your chance to fulfill it."

As Dónal eyed the man, something of the old steel returned to his green eyes. "Now why would I be after such a thing as that, Johnnie? I'm eighty-two years old and have no one to pass it on to after I'm gone. Sure, I could be The *Last* O'Sullivan Béara for a couple of years, scatterin' about like an ould culchie who's done well at the fair. But if 'tis all the same to you, I think I'll pass."

But Ahern didn't answer, just turned to his family, who, as though on cue, parted in the middle, leaving a young woman standing alone with a little boy. That she wasn't one of the Aherns, Dónal could see right away, from her wild black hair and big dark eyes, and the fact that she was more slender than the stocky descendants of Tadhg, being beautiful in much the same way as Síona had been. But it was the boy who held his eyes, huddling close to his mother and holding her hand. He was no more than seven by the look of him, and had fine aristocratic features and a long lean build. And though he had his mother's dark hair, his young eyes were green, the color of the new green of Spring, just like the old ones that gazed back at him so intently.

"'Tis your great-grandson, he is," Ahern explained, though Dónal knew it already. "His name is Dónal after you, just as his father and grandfather before him. So you see, there is someone to pass it on to after all."

"So Sióna was with child when I left her," Dónal said softly.

"No, she never had any children that we know of. Your son was born in Wales and brought to Allihies by a man named Rhys Griffith. His mother had died in childbirth, and Griffith hoped to find you here. But you weren't, and so Da took the boy in fosterage and raised him as his own, though 'twas never any secret made of who his real father was. Then, when he was eighteen, Da gave him the heirlooms and took him to Dunboy and told him the whole story. 'Twas on the 17th of June, 1880, and soon after, the boy sailed off to America to find you. He spent three years there traveling all around, going first to the big Irish cities and then anywhere else we'd settled in numbers. But though he occasionally ran into people who said they might've seen you, he never found you or even come across a warm trail. So finally he gave it up and came back here. After that, he went to work with Da and stayed at it till 1890, when he died in a construction accident. But he left behind a son to carry on the legacy, though he died young, too, I'm afraid, killed at the GPO during the Easter Rebellion. But that lovely wee lass there was with child herself, and the boy was born not long after. And since then, I've had them in my house, rearing the lad in fosterage just as I did his Da, just as my own Da did his."

"Just as Séan did me," Dónal added pensively. "And what became of Sióna then?"

"We don't know for sure. Soon after Griffith came, Da went out to check on her and found the cottage empty. She was gone, and 'twas nothing ever heard of her again."

Dónal said nothing to that, just closed his eyes to hold back the tears and stifle the guilt.

"Your son and grandson have been added to the book," Ahern continued, "and I've brought their photographs to show you. Though you can't tell it from the pictures, of course, they both had your green eyes just like himself there. And I've also brought you these."

He bent down then and picked up a yellowed linen bag and a battered leather case. Dónal just nodded silently without taking them, knowing what they held, but in that moment having eyes only for the boy.

Now as he stood atop the sea cliff holding the bag in one hand and the case in the other, he turned and looked down at the little boy looking up at him, green eyes wide and questioning, so different, and yet so much like the little boy who'd come here seventy-four years before. 'I could buy this old place and pass it on to you,' he thought. 'I could make you The O'Sullivan Béara, just as my father did me.'

But the pain of that memory was too much for him, and his mind screamed, '*No!*'

"No!" he agreed aloud. "Just let it end with me! I'd have us be the Men of the Bags no longer!"

And swinging his arm then, Dónal sent the bag sailing through the air and into the water, the small splash it made surprising him greatly, considering all the dead weight it held.

"Why did you do that, Gran'da?" the boy asked.

"That, Dónaleen, is a long sad story, as long and sad as the story of our race."

"But I like stories, Gran'da. Won't you please tell me?"

"No, Dónaleen, I'll not tell you that one. Not now and not ever!" Then he held out the leather case. "But I will give you a present. You like presents, too, don't you?"

The little boy's green eyes lit up at that, and for a moment Dónal felt as if he were looking into a mirror, seeing himself as he'd once been. "Oh, yes, Gran'da! I do like them so!"

Laying the case on the ground, Dónal watched as the boy gleefully opened it, and then looked up in puzzlement at what it held. "What is it, Gran'da?"

"'Tis my old set of pipes. *Uilleann* pipes, they're called, and they make the sweetest music the world has ever heard! Magical music, it is, music that makes your heart sing and your spirit dance, music that tells the story of our race, the People of the Gael. And that, Dónaleen, is the best way to hear it told! If you'll come to live with me, I'll teach you to play them, and then you can tell the story yourself, in your own way and from your own heart."

Then Dónal paused and frowned, as if not liking what he'd just said. "That is, I'll teach you to play the pipes, if you *want* me to. For your life is yours to live as you please, and I'll lay no burden upon you as my father did upon me. So will you come? I'll buy us a house in Bantry where you and your mother and I can all live together, and I'll teach you to play the pipes, or anything else you care to learn. And I'll love you, Dónaleen, with all my heart and soul, just as your father would have. So will you come? Please?"

The boy didn't answer, just looked at his mother with the question in his eyes. But she didn't speak, just nodded to let him know the decision was his. As he looked back at his great-grandfather, he could feel his old eyes boring into him, as if trying to open a window onto the future.

"Will you come?" Dónal asked again, holding out his hand just as Eóghan had done so many years before. "Please?"

The boy puckered his eyebrows, and for a long moment just stared at the bony old hand. Then slowly he reached out and grasped it, ever so lightly, though he smiled when his young eyes met the old ones watching him so intently. And though his heart was in his throat and tears burned his eyes, in that moment, Dónal was happier than he'd ever been, that one precious smile telling him his life wasn't a waste after all, and that he would indeed find healing.

"Can we go now, Gran'da? The wind is cold here, and this place is ever so sad."

"Sure, Dónaleen, we can go now. We're finished with Dunboy. Forever!"

Dónal led the way then as they walked back through the ruins, a Trinity of pilgrims leaving the Holy Ground behind. But at the top of the rise, he turned back again. There was still one thing left to do.

"Riocard MagEochagáin!" he called in Irish to the one who still kept watch, waiting for a chieftain who would never return. "Riocard MagEochagáin, your duty is done! I am Dónal son of Eóghan son of Diarmuid, last chieftain of the Clan Dónal Cam, and I release you from your charge. Go in peace and let Dunboy trouble you no more!"

A sudden gust of wind sent a sigh through the oaks, and for a moment it seemed that a shadow passed over the sun, like a giant bird heading out to sea. But as quick as the thought, it was gone, leaving nothing but the grass and the stones, the sunlight dancing on the water, and the eternal Green of Ireland.

And as he turned his back on Dunboy, Dónal reflected on the long and twisted path that had led him to his destiny, of his youth squandered on other people's dreams and his lifetime lost in the wilderness, living beyond the pale of love and earthly communion. He'd been a Tinker damned to travel, but his traveling days were done, his journey over, his odyssey come full circle. For he'd finally found his way home, and for whatever time remained to him, he would be a father to that precious little boy with eyes the color of the new green of Spring.